DUMBARTON

●

Dumbarton
(Stewart)

The
Lennox

Duchal
(Campbell)

■

RENFREW

●

King's
Inch
(Ross)

■

Skelmorlie
(Montgomerie)

■

Craigends
(Cunninghame)

■

PAISLEY

●

★

Renfrew

Stanely
(Maxwell)

■

Glengarnock
(Cunninghame)

■

Ellestoun
(Sempill)

■

Glanderstoun
(Stewart)

■

Southannan
(Sempill)

■

Kilbirnie
(Crawfurd)

■

Cunninghame

Hunthall
(Dunlop)

■

Ardrossan
(Montgomerie)

■

KILWINNING

● ★

Kilmaurs
(Cunninghame)

■

Eglintoun
(Montgomerie)

■

Kyle

Seagate (Montgomerie)

■

KILMARNOCK

●

IRVINE

●

The Firth of
Clyde, c. 1489

- - ⌐ Political Boundary

● BURGH

■ Castle or Fortified Residence

★ Major Abbey or Religious
    Foundation

THE GRYPHON AT BAY
Copyright © 2017 by Louise Turner

Cover photograph © Louise Turner
Cover design © Hadley Rille Books
Edited by Alex Shine and Megan Lucas

ISBN 978-0-9971188-5-8

Ebook edition alao available

Published in the United States of America and the United Kingdom by

Hadley Rille Books
Eric T. Reynolds, Publisher
Olathe, Kansas 66062 USA
www.hrbpress.com

In February 1508, Cuthbert Cunninghame, Earl of Glencairn and 3rd Lord Kilmaurs, asked to be exempt from the jurisdiction of Hugh, Earl of Eglinton, 3rd Lord Montgomerie, on the grounds that 'the sade Lord Eglinton had slane his fadir.' The incident took place at some time between July and November, 1489, but the context of Kilmaurs' death remains unknown to this day.

This novel is inspired by these events.

'Yet it cannot be called prowess to kill fellow-citizens, to betray friends, to be treacherous, pitiless, irreligious. These ways can win a prince power, but not glory.'

From 'The Prince' by Niccolo Machiavelli

Cast of Characters

<u>The King's Men in the Westland</u>

<u>The Montgomeries of Eglintoun</u>
Hugh, 3rd Lord Montgomerie, Bailie of Cunninghame, Justiciar of Arran and the West
Helen Campbell, his wife, (daughter of Earl Colin of Argyll, sister of Archibald
Campbell, Master of Argyll)
John Montgomerie, eldest son and heir to Lord Hugh
Bessie Montgomerie, daughter of Lord Hugh
James Montgomerie of Bowhouse, younger brother of Lord Hugh
Robert Montgomerie, younger brother of Lord Hugh
John Montgomerie of Hessilhead, cousin of Lord Hugh

<u>The Sempills of Ellestoun</u>
Sir John Sempill of Ellestoun, Sheriff of Renfrew
Margaret Colville, his wife
Katherine, Mariota and Alison – her maids
Elizabeth Ross, widowed mother of Sir John
William Haislet, manservant to Sir John
Mary White of Bar, betrothed to William Haislet
John Haislet, William's son
John Alexson, son of Mary White
Jamie Colville, Margaret's half-brother

<u>The Campbells of Argyll</u>
Colin Campbell, Earl of Argyll, father-in-law to Hugh, 3rd Lord Montgomerie
Archibald Campbell, Master of Argyll

<u>The Cunninghames of Kilmaurs</u>
Robert Cunninghame, 2nd Lord Kilmaurs
Christian Lindsay, his wife
Cuthbert, Master of Kilmaurs (later 3rd Lord Kilmaurs), his eldest son
Archie Cunninghame, younger son of Robert, 2nd Lord Kilmaurs
Guido Cunninghame, younger son of Robert, 2nd Lord Kilmaurs
Margaret Hepburn, mother of Robert, 2nd Lord Kilmaurs, widow of Alexander
Cunninghame, 1st Earl of Glencairn, 1st Lord Kilmaurs and sister to Patrick Hepburn,
1st Earl of Bothwell
Sir William Cunninghame of Craigends, Coroner of Renfrew and Constable of Irvine,
younger brother of Robert, 2nd Lord Kilmaurs
Andrew Cunninghame, Sir William's eldest son

The Crawfurds of Kilbirnie
Sir Malcolm Crawfurd of Kilbirnie
Marjorie Barclay, his wife
Robert Crawfurd, Master of Kilbirnie, Sir Malcolm's eldest son and heir
Marion Sempill, his wife, sister of Sir John Sempill of Ellestoun
Andrew Crawfurd, younger brother of Robert Crawfurd

Other Local Lairds
Archibald Boyd of Neristoun
Marion Boyd, his niece
Sir Adam Mure of Caldwell
Constantine Dunlop of Hunthall
Maxwell of Stanely
Whiteford of that Ilk
Sir John Ross of Hawkhead

Rebels Fighting Against King James IV and his Government

The Stewarts of Darnley
John Stewart, Earl of Lennox
Matthew Stewart, Lord Darnley, his eldest son and heir
Margaret Montgomerie, Countess of Lennox, aunt to Hugh, 3rd Lord Montgomerie
Alexander Stewart, younger son of John Stewart, Earl of Lennox
Sir William Stewart of Glanderstoun, illegitimate son of John Stewart, Earl of Lennox
Elizabeth Sempill, wife of Sir William Stewart, older sister of John Sempill of Ellestoun

The Lyles of Duchal
Robert, 1st Lord Lyle
Margaret Houston, his wife

The Douglases of Angus (The 'Red Douglases')
Archibald 'Bell the Cat' Douglas, Earl of Angus
Elizabeth Boyd, his wife, aunt of James, Lord Boyd (murdered by Hugh, 3rd Lord
Montgomerie in 1485)
George, Master of Douglas, eldest son of Archibald Douglas, Earl of Angus
Gavin Douglas, younger son of Archibald Douglas, Earl of Angus
Marjory Douglas, daughter of Archibald Douglas, Earl of Angus

Personages at the Court of King James IV
Patrick Hepburn, Earl of Bothwell, Master of the King's Household
Adam Hepburn, Master of Bothwell

Senior Churchmen
William Elphinstone, Bishop of Aberdeen
Robert Blacader, Bishop of Glasgow

To Eric Reynolds, publisher and editor *extraordinaire*. Without your enthusiasm and support, all this would never have been possible...

Chapter 1

The Earl of Angus smiled, grateful that his voyage was nearly over. From his vantage point in the prow, he could see London's jostling sprawl all around. Lights shimmered like jewels on the coal-black waters of the Thames; the reflected glow from countless candles and braziers, nestling behind the open windows of buildings which lined the shore and the broad expanse of London Bridge beyond.

Water lapped soft against the harbour wall and the slap of oars ceased; moments later, the ship's hull bumped against the jetty. Men's shouts echoed in the night, Scots and Englishmen working together with unusual accord to secure the vessel.

Slouching against the rail, Angus watched the proceedings carefully. He'd stayed in his quarters throughout most of the journey, only venturing up on deck when the clear sharp smell of the sea gave way to the river-stink of human waste and rotting foodstuffs.

Some men might have grown impatient at the delay, but Angus had learned long ago that patience brought its own rewards. He tapped his fingers lightly against the timber, saying nothing.

A seaman looked up. "All's ready, Your Grace."

Stifling a yawn, Angus stirred. The moon was climbing high already. It must have been approaching ten of the clock or so on a balmy August evening.

With a few swift steps he'd put the voyage behind him and was back upon dry land. A road led from the jetty, wharves pressing close on either side: there in the gloom he saw horses waiting. Eight in all, saddled as if in readiness. Half-a-dozen lightly-armoured men accompanied them. One stepped forward, the sudden movement making Angus grip his dagger, alert for danger.

"Greetings, my lord." The soldier's voice marked him out as an Englishman. "I seek a man who was expected to disembark this night. A nobleman, with your qualities and stature. The Scots call him 'Bell the Cat'."

Reassured, Angus relaxed his hold on the weapon. "I am indeed that man. Archibald Douglas, Earl of Angus, is my name." He paused, suddenly wary. "Might I ask who sent you?"

"I bring greetings from Sir John Ross of Montgrennan. He sends horses, and armed men for your protection. He asks also that you accept his hospitality for the night."

"That's a most gracious offer." Angus grasped the reins of the nearest horse. "Where might we find Sir John Ross at this hour?"

"He has lodgings close to the Palace of Westminster."

"And is His Grace King Henry residing there at present?"

"His Grace is expecting you. He'll speak with you on the morrow."

"I look forward to receiving his counsel," Angus replied. "Now let's be on our way. We mustn't inconvenience Sir John any further."

"Ah, Angus!" Ross of Montgrennan rose to greet him. He was an imposing figure, tall, graced with a knight's robust build. And blessed with fine features that Adonis himself might have been proud of: fair-haired and square-jawed, with bright blue eyes. "It's splendid to see you again." He gripped Angus' hand, briefly. "Welcome to our little home from home."

"You're looking well, John." Angus studied his surroundings intently. Montgrennan's 'little home from home' would have put many a Scots noble's place to shame. Fine Flemish hangings adorned the walls, books were stacked on every table, with gold plate piled high upon the buffet. He noted, too, that Montgrennan wasn't alone. Slouched in a big oak chair by the empty fireplace was another Scots nobleman, John Ramsay, erstwhile Earl of Bothwell.

Angus nodded in half-hearted acknowledgement. Their paths had crossed already, seven years before. In a different place, a different time...

Seven men had died that day, hanged at Angus' command. Close allies of King James III, every one. And Ramsay... Youngest of them all, aged just eighteen years. He'd been spared because of his youth, and because the king's pleas to spare his life had been so heartfelt, so vehement.

If Ramsay harboured any resentment for what had happened back then, he gave no sign. He merely yawned and stretched, as if in the presence of a trusted friend. "Exile has its drawbacks," he said. "But at least we're granted some comforts." He was a thin quick young man, with a thick thatch of black hair beneath his bonnet, darting dark eyes and a ruddy complexion.

"We earn our keep, of course," Montgrennan added. "We keep His Grace informed regarding the situation in the north. And offer our counsel, as and when required."

Angus smiled. "Since King Henry is blessed with such counsellors, I can't think why he wishes to speak to me."

"Fresh opinions are always welcome." Montgrennan steered Angus to a vacant chair. "Besides, you must be better informed than we."

"I'm not so sure," Angus said. "From what's transpired, I'd be inclined to think otherwise."

Ramsay leaned forward. "Can we assume then that you didn't complete your pilgrimage as planned?" He winced, faintly. "I'm sorry, if you curtailed your journey on our account."

"It's not the first time that affairs of the soul have been waylaid by more earthly matters." Angus nodded to Montgrennan. "And thank you, for informing me so promptly."

"What are friends for?" Montgrennan paused by the buffet. "I can arrange for food to be brought, if you'd like. You must be famished after your journey. In the meantime, perhaps you'd take some wine?"

"Thank you."

"The timing of your ill-fated pilgrimage was curious," Ramsay said.

Please return or renew book
by last date shown above.

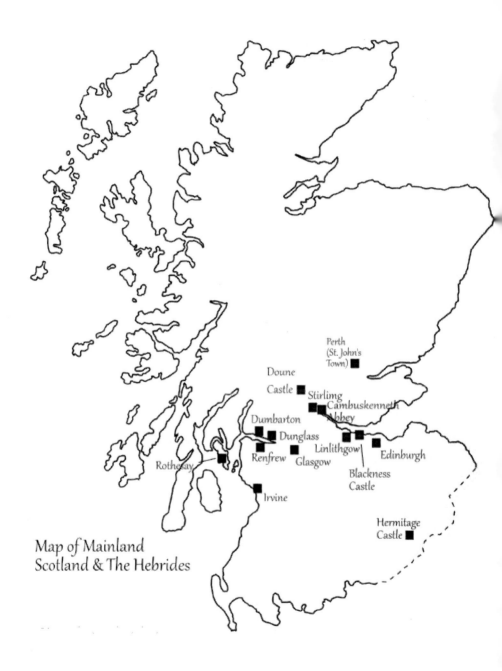

Perth
(St. John's
Town) ■

Doune
Castle ■

Stirling ■
Cambuskenneth
Abbey ■

Dumbarton
Dunglass ■
Renfrew ■ Glasgow ■

Linlithgow ■
Blackness
Castle

Edinburgh ■

Rothesay ■

Irvine ■

Hermitage
Castle ■

Map of Mainland
Scotland & The Hebrides

"I heard that trouble was brewing," Angus replied. "I thought it wise to leave until the situation resolved itself."

"And now Patrick Hepburn's taken advantage of your absence." Montgrennan passed Angus a goblet, then settled into an empty chair, flicking his gown aside as he sat down. "I'm sorry to hear about the March Wardenships."

"My head remains securely on my shoulders. For that, I'm grateful."

Montgrennan chuckled. "Indeed. But what next, Angus? They may use this Lennox business to imprison you. You're on good terms with King Henry. That doesn't bode well at present."

"I might say the same of you."

"Ah, yes," Montgrennan agreed. "Are we not the vile and evil counsellors, who sought to promote the in-bringing of Inglismen, for the detriment of the realm?" He shook his head. "Our friends in the north are prone to exaggeration."

"You'll be in no great hurry to return."

"Life at the English court has much to recommend it," Ramsay said. "The Scots can be so... uncivilised. Their speech is uncouth, their manners despicable." He smiled. "If the choice were mine, I'd be loath to leave this place."

Montgrennan stirred. "But young James needs guidance," he said. "Balanced guidance." He sipped some wine. "Besides, I've no desire to let other men prosper at my expense. I'll reclaim what's mine, just as soon as I can."

"That time might soon be upon us." Ramsay sprang to his feet. He grasped a parchment lying on a nearby table and thrust it into Angus' hand.

Montgrennan flicked a lazy hand in its direction. "Your thoughts, if you please."

Angus ran his gaze across the bold black script. "It's from your nephew, is it not?" He frowned. "Sempill of Ellestoun wasn't a *sir* last time I heard his name."

There was a snort from Montgrennan. "If they think I'll take the word of this half-wit as surety, they can think again."

"You should be proud of him. He seems to be following nicely in your footsteps."

"A pawn," said Montgrennan, "whose actions are guided by greater men." He lazed back comfortably in his chair. "I wonder why they're making such efforts to win my favour. Perhaps their grip is failing." A sly smile crossed his lips. "It strikes me, Angus, that together we could hold Scotia's fate in our hands. We could help one another. And help young James, too."

Angus gnawed upon his finger, saying nothing. The irony amused him. That he could be sitting here plotting with Montgrennan and Ramsay, who'd both done their best to shore up James the Third's government as it rotted and crumbled round his ears. Montgrennan, the Lord Advocate, had fled to England with his tail between his legs after the last fatal battle that claimed the life of James himself.

And Ramsay... He'd been absent from the field that night. Mustering English support, some said. Though too late for James, whose son had seized the throne after his death.

Angus stayed quiet a little longer, just so Montgrennan and Ramsay wouldn't think he was too eager. "The Earl of Douglas is growing old," he said. "There remains the problem of his inheritance."

"Who better to advise you on this matter than myself?" Montgrennan replied. "The intricate details of our laws are indeed my speciality. But all that can be addressed in the future, I'm sure. For the moment... What are your plans?"

"I'll ride north. And find out how this business with Lennox is progressing."

Chapter 2

The Island of Bute, August 1489

The boat's keel grated on the shingle shore, the vessel slewing to one side as it juddered to a halt. One of the men-at-arms, born of farming stock in the hills of Cunninghame, cursed and crossed himself.

But Hugh Montgomerie had no fear of boats. And no fear of the sea, either. While his men still gathered their wits, he wasted no time in disembarking. Winding his gown over one arm to keep it clear of the water, he put a hand to the gunwhale and heaved his long lean frame over the side. It was a drop of three feet or more: his sword belt battered against his legs and he sank deep into the gravel, but kept his footing regardless.

It was an undignified arrival for a King's Officer. By the time he stood upon dry land he was soaked to the knees, his shoes waterlogged, the rest of him splashed from head to toe. The handful of retainers who'd accompanied him eyed him anxiously and followed at a careful distance.

But for once Hugh was in good spirits. It had been a pleasant journey, across a short stretch of sea that was smooth as glass and strewn by sparkling shards of sunlight. Solan geese escorted them, gliding past on stiff white, black-tipped wings. Sometimes they soared high and plunged like stones into the depths, dagger-like bills poised to spear the unfortunate fish below.

Now the birds had the ocean to themselves once more. The vessel that had carried them from Skelmorlie lay stranded on the shore like a beached whale, and there it would stay until this business was behind them.

Taking a last lingering look at the still blue waters and the green hills of the mainland beyond, Hugh turned with a sigh, casting impatient eyes on his destination. Rothesay Castle was an antiquated, ill-fashioned stronghold, compact and squat within its moat, drum towers crowded close to repel attackers. From here it looked impregnable; but he knew the old stories, about how it had once been taken by the Norsemen, who hacked with their axes at the soft walls until the masonry gave way.

Now its role as staunch defender of the Westland had been all but eclipsed. To King and Court, who spent most of their lives in the east, Rothesay was a backwater, a place of little consequence.

A ramshackle castletoun huddled close about its walls, a cluttered mass of thatched cottages with fields and gardens attached. Chickens patrolled ranks of cabbages and kale, dogs dozed on thresholds. Already the locals were gathering: as he strode up the beach, Hugh nodded to them briefly.

These lands were his now, gifted by the King just months before. He'd have wished for better circumstances when meeting his new tenants – his shoes squelched with every step and despite his efforts, water dripped from the hem of his gown – but

13

his lieges seemed respectful enough. Still, he supposed it didn't really matter what they thought, as long as they paid their taxes and tithes on time.

Up at the castle, a group of horsemen were departing, providing some manner of a welcoming party at least. Soon the steward cantered up. "My lord!" he puffed. "I heard news of your arrival." Dismounting, he thrust the reins into Hugh's hands. "Thank you so very much for coming."

"I presume it's a matter of great importance." Hugh climbed into the saddle. "It must be, if you've had a man scouring the Westland looking for me. I hope it justifies the effort on both our parts. I'm a busy man, with much to occupy my time."

"It's all *her* fault, Lord Hugh. She demanded to speak with the Keeper of the Castle. She's been here a week now, making our lives a misery."

"She's a Stewart. What exactly did you expect?" Hugh paused. "Now what were the King's instructions regarding young Master Lindsay?"

"He said the boy was to be thrown into a deep dark place where he couldn't even see his own feet and left there for at least a year. The men who brought him did exactly what was asked and left soon after. *She* arrived the following day, and since then... My God, Lord Hugh. You wouldn't believe what I've had to contend with."

"I'm sure I'll soon find out," Hugh replied. "Keep her distracted until I'm ready. I'll summon her in due course."

The room was blissfully quiet. Hugh slouched in his chair, goblet of wine in hand, and closed his eyes, grateful for the respite. He'd ridden hard, from his kinsman's place at Hessilhead in Cunninghame, to his lands at Skelmorlie. He'd found a man there who could sail him out to Rothesay, without delay, and all for a haranguing harpy of a mother, a woman only too eager to stir up trouble on her son's behalf.

He didn't welcome this excitement: less than a fortnight ago, he'd been attending the siege at Duchal Castle. Now, just when he thought he'd put affairs of state behind him for a little while, he found himself waylaid again.

And at a time when he had other pressing matters to concern him...

There was a smart rap upon his door. "Lady Agnes Stewart, my lord."

He took a last mouthful of wine to fortify himself. "Send her in."

The door opened. The venerable Lady Agnes looked slight and insubstantial, a bent old dowager who walked with a stick. Her gown was drab dark blue and utterly lacking in finery, save for a gem-studded cross about her neck. Her matching hood was faintly askew, revealing steel grey hair beneath. She gave the impression of a tired yet dignified old soul, until one looked at her face, and saw the fierce scowl, the hard stern features.

"Lady Agnes," Hugh said, pleasantly. "How may I assist you?"

"So you've arrived then?" She confronted him from across the table. "Have you heard what they did to my boy? They threw him in the pit, with no food, no water. He'd be dead by now, if I hadn't come here to take care of him. The way this self-styled King of yours behaves... It's a disgrace to all the Scots Kings, and to the Stewarts in particular. To treat his lieges like this-"

"Obviously your son did something wrong," Hugh cut in. "Why else would he be incarcerated?"

14

"-Thieves and murderers, the lot of you!" She waved her stick at him, undaunted. "And in this nest of rogues, you're the worst by far-"

Hugh studied her, scowling. If she'd been a man, she'd have hung for all those slanders and accusations. But she was shielded by her sex, and from the shrewd glitter in her eyes, she knew it, too. "Lady Agnes, you malign me," he said through gritted teeth.

"Then prove it." Her tone was triumphant. "If you're truly an honourable man, then help my boy."

He sat up with arms folded, lips pursed in measured disapproval. "He offended the King."

She gave a martyred sigh, and flung a bulging cloth pouch down before him. It clinked as it came to rest upon the board. "Twenty five pounds, Lord Hugh. I expect my son to receive treatment commensurate with that sum." She held his gaze, undaunted.

Hugh reached for the bag. It felt reassuringly heavy: when he opened it, he saw coins gleaming within, gold and silver lyons and unicorns. "I'll have him moved to better quarters."

"You're so very kind." Bowing her head, she made a great show of pulling a handkerchief out from her sleeve and dabbing at her eyes. "Perhaps you're not the tyrant men say you are."

"A tyrant, Lady Agnes? Heaven Forbid." Hugh stirred. "Now let's unearth Master Patrick. Before his confinement drives him mad."

The prison was bad enough, a dank airless chamber with just a tiny window to light it. The pit was worse. As soon as the hatch was lifted, the stench wafted out, damp stone and stale air tainted with urine, filth and vomit. It was enough to turn even Hugh's stomach. He coughed, as discreetly as possible, and somehow stifled the urge to sneeze. Not that Lady Agnes would have noticed; she was too busy weeping and wringing her hands in a contrived effort to prick his conscience.

Hugh cast her a despairing look, then leaned over the hole and peered into the blackness below. "Master Patrick? Move aside. The ladder's coming down. When you're ready, I want you to join me."

A few moments passed, then they heard a shuffling sound. Soon a dishevelled head appeared, a young brown-haired man who sported a ragged beard. His face was deathly pale and drawn and he stank to high heaven, clothes stained and crusted with dirt and excrement.

Patrick Lindsay seemed like a man in a swoon, dazed, disoriented. "I thought I died," he whispered. "I thought I saw the Holy Virgin, but then I knew I'd been condemned to Purgatory." He blinked as he became accustomed to the light. His gaze lit on Hugh, and his eyes widened. "Oh my God. He wants me dead."

"I'm your gaolor. Not your hangman." Hugh glared at Agnes Stewart. "Give him a bath. And fetch him a change of clothes. I don't want to breathe the same air until he's cleaned up."

"How long was I imprisoned?" Patrick Lindsay spoke through a mouthful of food. He still seemed pale and sickly, but at least now he looked presentable, dressed in a fresh set of clothes that befitted a gentleman, with his hair combed and his face freshly shaven. "It seems like forever."

"You were in there a week, by all accounts. You'd be there still, if the messenger hadn't found me."

"-God, the chill's settled deep into my bones. Like an ague..." The young man shuddered, casting wary glances about him. "I don't think much of the baker," he added. "I thought I'd break my teeth."

"At least you were granted bread. That's more than most men can expect in such circumstances." Hugh studied him carefully. "This is a remarkable affair. Whatever did you do to provoke the King's displeasure?"

Lindsay shovelled another handful of roast mutton into his mouth and chewed it a while before gulping down some more wine. "My brother was called before a council to account for his actions last June. I defended him." He wiped his napkin against his mouth. "The King thought I put Lord David's case rather too eloquently."

Hugh chuckled, softly. "That's an unusual crime, I must say."

"It's an outrage. My brother did nothing wrong. He fought for his King, as we all did that day. Though why I bother to voice dissent in your presence, I don't know. The King's mastiff in the Westlands, that's what you are." He looked Hugh in the eye, accusing. "What's to become of me?"

Hugh studied him carefully, recalling recent dealings he'd had with another young man cast in this same mould. Eloquent, self-righteous, burning with injured indignation in the face of adversities both real and imagined... "You'll be detained here, at the King's pleasure," he told young Master Lindsay. "But arrangements have been made that will ensure you enjoy more favourable conditions than those you've endured so far." He paused, letting his words sink in. "But I expect something in return," he added, tone hard, uncompromising. "Your co-operation, and assurances that you won't try and slip your bonds."

"Why does it matter? Am I considered a threat to the King?"

"There's revolt and rebellion throughout the land. Can you blame the King if he wishes to see his enemies confined securely? Especially those renowned for their skills with rhetoric."

Lindsay shrugged, ill-humoured and petulant.

"Now you'll forgive me, I hope, if I don't linger too long in your company." Hugh leaned across the table and replenished the young man's wine. "I've important business to attend to." He raised his goblet. "To peace and prosperity," he said. "Let's hope that in a year or two, we can all sit back and watch our families flourish."

"As long as it's not at the expense of others," muttered Lindsay, darkly. But he lifted his own cup and took a healthy draught regardless.

Chapter 3

The Place of Eglintoun

"She's like her father," Old Janet commented. "I said that right from the start."

Helen Campbell smiled gently down upon the babe that squirmed in her arms, all soft plump body and pink flailing limbs. Young Marion Montgomerie was freshly-bathed, newly-dried and hungry. The howling hadn't started yet, but Helen was sure it wouldn't be too long in coming. Setting Marion down upon the pale lace shawl in her lap, she deftly wrapped the child within its folds. "I know," she soothed. "It's hateful to be bound in all that swaddling. But you'll be glad some day. When you grow up straight and tall and young men clamour for your hand."

It had been a straightforward birth. The babe had slipped out before an hour had passed. But Helen was exhausted nonetheless. A week had gone by now, and still she only stirred to wash and visit the privy. She'd never known such lethargy before; she wondered if it was old age catching up with her at last. At twenty-six years, she wasn't getting any younger.

But when she saw that tiny scrap of life cradled in her arms, her trials were forgotten. She'd see the eyes gazing up at her, hear the gurgling laughter as the child smiled in response to her voice, and each time a glow of warm delight would wake inside her, spreading out until it seemed to fill her very soul.

Pushing some stray fronds of dark brown hair away from her face, Helen slipped her kirtle down from her shoulder. She lifted out her breast and pulled the infant close. Marion settled, locking tiny lips about the nipple, balling her fists and drifting into silence.

Helen hummed softly, but Marion was oblivious to all but the milk. As the babe pulled with all her might at her breast, Helen felt a sense of wholeness, of unity.

What Hugh would say if ever he found out she was suckling her own child was debatable. But he was still away and for the time being she could do as she pleased. The men had returned from their summer campaign a week ago, but as yet there'd been no word from Hugh.

It was always this way, whenever she delivered a child. It was as if he went out of his way to avoid her as the lying-in reached its conclusion. Perhaps he thought his presence would somehow jeopardise the birth. Or perhaps – and she considered this more likely – he just didn't want to endure the commotion.

Horses clattered into the yard, she heard men shouting. She paid no heed: there was always bustle at Eglintoun, armed retainers being marshalled or provisions being delivered.

Old Janet peered out through the open window. "The master's home," she said.

Helen smiled, concealing her relief. "Then we'd best welcome him, hadn't we?"

*   *   *

17

Young Bessie led the way, dragging her father by the hand like an unruly hound straining at the leash. At thirteen she was almost a woman, but at moments like this she still seemed innocent, child-like. "She's so beautiful," she was saying. "Wait until you see her..."

Helen's flock of maids curtsied as one, but Hugh didn't even acknowledge them. He looked tired, shoulders faintly slumped, face dark with a day's growth of beard and black hair bedraggled. He brightened briefly when he saw Helen. "We can afford a wetnurse."

"Hello, wife," said Helen. "How good it is to see you. I'm so glad that you're well, and that the child is safe."

Bessie scurried to Helen's side. "I told Father how I sat through the birth," she said. "And how I held your hand and helped the midwife."

"She was a great comfort to me," Helen told Hugh.

He shrugged.

Old Janet curtsied before him. "Shall I take your cloak, my lord?"

Hugh absently unpinned the garment, then thrust it into the old woman's arms. He gazed at Helen, earnest, beseeching. "I'm sorry I missed the birth."

"That's what you always say."

"I'd have come back sooner, if I could."

"It's alright, Hugh. I understand."

"What'll men say," he added, "when they hear that the Lady of Eglintoun nurses her own child..." He cast a baleful glance towards the maids.

"Come on now." Old Janet ushered the girls away. "There's much to do." She beckoned to Bessie. "You too, child. Give your poor father some peace."

Once the crowd had dispersed, Hugh flung his bonnet aside with a sigh then sat down on the edge of the bed.

"Is it such an evil deed, for a mother to nurse her own child?" Helen asked.

"No..." He rose and gently kissed her forehead. "I'm sorry. A good husband would have slain a thousand men to be at his wife's side."

"Oh, hush! There's no need for that." She coaxed the babe away from her breast. "Here's our daughter," she said. "Be careful with her."

Hugh took the babe without a word. He looked reproachfully at Helen's exposed breast; she sighed and tucked it back inside her kirtle.

When he pushed aside the shawl, Marion responded, stretching out her hands. Hugh extended a finger towards her and she gripped him, tightly. He smiled, the smile he always gave when his latest child was presented before him.

This time it lingered. "Has she been given a name?"

"Her name is Marion. As we agreed."

"She's a treasure," he said. "A gem of a child." He hoisted Marion up and kissed her brow.

"Now give her back," Helen said. "Before the milk goes through her. If she empties her bowels all over you, we'll never hear the end of it."

Hugh carefully placed Marion back in his wife's arms. "She takes after you," he said. "Sweet-tempered, and beautiful to behold." He leaned close and kissed Helen on the cheek. "I'm proud of you."

"So how was your business?"

The Gryphon at Bay

He resumed his perch on the edge of the bed beside her. "Cruikston was taken. Duchal was taken. But Dumbarton stands firm. Which is no surprise. Your father's been given the unenviable task of starving them out."

Helen winced. With the Earl of Lennox still entrenched in Dumbarton castle and her brother Archie Campbell married to his eldest daughter, it made Earl Colin of Argyll's task all the more difficult. "That'll please him no end."

"I suspect his heart won't entirely be in the task."

"So what will the King do?"

"That's no longer my problem." He sounded faintly smug. "Though Archie can't really complain. He's already profited greatly. He's been granted Lord Lyle's lands, for as long as the forfeiture is upheld. The repair of Duchal Castle will cost a significant sum, but the King's agreed to pay the masons, so it won't drain Archie's coffers too much."

"So the bombards were deployed?"

"It was the only way," Hugh told her. "Lady Lyle was very determined."

"She must have been. To have endured such a thing."

"The guns were magnificent. You should have seen the smoke and fire billowing out. And the sound! It echoed back off the hills..."

"Did many die?"

"They were a canny foe. They hid deep in their cellars and in the end all walked out unharmed. Though they were rather dusty... And the King was merciful. He let them live."

"He's a good man. A very good man."

"Your brother sends his love, and hopes you fare well in the birth. And Sir John Sempill asked me to convey his good wishes."

"That's splendid! He's won his knighthood."

"I thought the news would cheer you."

"And what of his wife? Did the news cheer her?"

Slipping an arm about her shoulders, he settled close. "When I last saw them, my love, they were transformed. The way they looked at one another over dinner... Why, the air prickled with lust. I thought they'd tear the clothes from one another and take each other there, upon the board..."

"Please, Hugh! I'm in no fit state to laugh like this."

"What of my lands?"

"All's well. The Cunninghames have been very quiet. There's been no raiding."

Hugh sat back, arms folded, the ghost of a glower on his face. "Biding their time, probably."

"And Mattie. Have you any news of him?"

"I spoke with Mattie. He's well. Or as well as can be expected, considering his situation..."

Dumbarton Castle

A spider lurked high in the arch over the window. It had been there four days now: craning his neck, Matthew Stewart could just catch sight of it, crouching patient by its crevice as if it, too, weathered a siege...

Louise Turner

Matthew slumped back against the wall with a sigh. He was bored beyond belief. And frustrated, too. His hand itched to hold a sword again, he was sick and tired of being caged in this lofty prison.

"My poor old place," Lady Lyle said, from where she was sitting by the empty fireplace, bent over her sewing. "You should've seen the mess they left it in. They knocked a big hole through the wall of my chamber. Why, the birds'll be nesting there by springtime." She shook her head. "And all my precious things. All gone."

"I know," Matthew's mother, Margaret Montgomerie, Countess of Lennox, agreed without even looking up from her needlework. "It's a dreadful shame."

Matthew picked irritably at a loose thread on the cushioned seat beneath him. Sometimes he envied the womenfolk, who found comfort in their mundane tasks. Sitting still for hours on end just wasn't in his nature: if he loitered too long, all his hopes and fears crowded up close like hellhounds and he had to move in order to escape them.

Rising to his feet with a sigh, he muttered his excuses to the ladies, then headed out to stretch his legs.

Matthew strolled along the battlements, relishing the solitude. Far below, the waters of the Clyde stretched calm and enticing, dotted with a few tiny ships.

Over the last few months, his life had settled into a routine that had by now become second nature. He'd rise early from a troubled sleep and pace the wallwalk, halting on the seaward side to look in vain for English ships.

Then he'd move on, pausing again on the landward side. He'd count the ever-growing cluster of tents and pavilions that made up the King's host, springing up like toadstools on an autumn morn near the town of Dumbarton.

And once this ritual was complete he'd retreat to the chapel. He'd pray to God for strength and succour. But God never sent arms or men to relieve the stranded garrison. He didn't even grant Matthew peace of mind.

They were running short of fodder. And short of the luxuries that a man became accustomed to: fresh meat, salt, spices. But they were hardly starving. Every week or so under cover of darkness, a ship would slip into the boat naust at the base of the rock, bringing bread and wheat and barrels of ale.

When he'd finished his patrol, he returned to the hall. Though he'd stalked out in disgust, despairing of the women's trivial talk, he knew deep inside that he needed the comfort of their presence. It reminded him that there was a world beyond these walls, a world that someday they might all return to.

In his absence, the ladies had been joined by others. Robert, Lord Lyle had settled there, along with Matthew's younger brother Alex. Lord Robert had taken the boy under his wing, making sure he worked hard at his fighting skills, doing his best to raise the youth's spirits. Right now they were confronting each other across the table, frowning over a chessboard: grizzled knight and untried youth, channelling their concentration into games of strategy and deception.

"A shrewd move, perhaps," Lord Robert said. "But only time will tell if it proves to be a sound one."

The Gryphon at Bay

Matthew glanced round, mildly interested. He sat back down in his regular space by the window, allowing himself a sympathetic smile as he heard the clack of ivory hitting wood.

"Ah!" Alex dropped his head in his hands. "My queen is lost..."

"Don't whine, Alex." Margaret Montgomerie countered swiftly. "You're far too old for that."

The door opened, a servant ventured inside. "My lady, you have a visitor."

The countess looked up, perplexed. "Here?" She exchanged a bewildered glance with Matthew. "We're not expecting anyone."

"It's Elizabeth Sempill."

"Goodness!" For a moment, the countess's composure wavered. "Show her in!"

When his gude-sister Elizabeth entered the hall, Matthew hardly recognised her: she'd replaced her usual velvet with a plain grey gown of wool and a white starched hood. She was an imposing woman: tall, rather haughty in demeanour. She must have been thirty-three years of age by Matthew's reckoning, but she didn't look it. She seemed ageless, with clear bright skin and glorious grey-blue eyes.

She curtsied. "Countess Margaret."

"We'll have no such formalities, Elizabeth," Setting down her needlework, the countess rose to her feet. She grasped the younger woman's arms and kissed her on both cheeks. "It's a delight to see you!"

"And a surprise," Matthew added. "I thought the Archangel Michael more likely to grace our place."

"Mattie!" his mother snapped.

"I understand why I'm not welcome," Elizabeth countered swiftly. "But I can scarcely be blamed for your circumstances."

"Don't listen to Mattie," the countess said. "He's weary of this. We all are. How did you pass the gates?"

"They think I'm a midwife," Elizabeth replied. "I've brought gifts." She drew a leather bag out from beneath her cloak. "Salt. Two pounds of it. And a flask of *aqua vita.*"

"Oh, how very thoughtful. Thank you!" The countess grasped the bag, smiling. "We'd love you to stay, but..."

Elizabeth waved her hand in haughty dismissal. "I've lodgings in the town."

Matthew laughed inwardly, satisfied by her response. Elizabeth's name and lineage might have been a source of contention, but there was no denying that she was a bold woman, and resourceful, too.

As a youth he'd often lain awake in his bed for hours, lovestruck and miserable, wondering why a woman of her quality had been granted to his bastard brother William, and not himself. But at long last he was cured. These days when he looked upon her, he was reminded of her brother, John Sempill of Ellestoun. The straw-headed, angel-faced wretch whose defiance had caused all this trouble in the first place.

Matthew yawned and stretched out his legs. "Your timing was impeccable," he said. "We were talking about your kinsman: he's *Sir* John Sempill now. And Sheriff of Renfrew, besides..."

"Oh?" Her reply was noncommittal.

"He's thrown poor Lady Lyle out of her place," Matthew added. "And seized all her belongings."

"I'd heard," she said. She paused, face troubled. "Have you any news of my husband?"

"He rode north with Father. He was well enough last time I saw him."

"Ah." She seemed wistful.

"Until they return, we're beleaguered," Lord Robert said.

"You must keep good heart," Elizabeth said, firmly. "The path that brought you here's of little consequence. What matters now is that you're on the side of righteousness."

"What news from Renfrew?"

"All's quiet. They haven't troubled the lesser households."

"Not yet, at any rate," Matthew said. "They may change their minds. One of these days, your brother might come calling,"

"Then I'll beat him with a skillet, and chase him from my place," she retorted. "He's profited enough from this."

"That's no way to talk about your brother."

"Forgive me, please, if I can't spare a kind word for him. I was supposed to receive the final portion of my dower on my father's death. There's still no sign of it."

"Perhaps you should try grovelling. He'd like that, I'm sure."

"I'll be dead before that day dawns."

"Ah, such sweet words," said Matthew. "You're more Stewart than Sempill, there's no denying it."

"I thought Sir John was very gracious," Lady Lyle spoke out.

"He took your books," Matthew reminded her.

"Not all of them. And he didn't take my jewels."

"Daft woman," muttered Lord Robert. Lifting his head, he regarded young Alex serenely. "Checkmate," he said.

Chapter 4

The Place of Duchal

Late in the morning, all that could be heard was the *tap-tap-tap* of hammers. The sound reverberated around Duchal's empty courtyard and shattered turrets, punctuated only by the rumble of the crane and the occasional barked instruction from the masons.

It had taken two bombards less than a week to reduce the Place of Duchal to this miserable state. It would, Sir John Sempill suspected, take considerably longer to restore it.

Slowly but surely, life was returning. Now the masons were established, bread had to be baked, and ale brewed. The fermtoun's residents had seized on the opportunity, supplying the masons with everything they needed. Better still, it looked as if the forthcoming harvest would be a good one.

"We've salvaged what we can." The master-mason gestured to the pile of squared stone blocks at their feet. "But we're well short of what's needed."

"Then arrange for a consignment to be delivered, and we'll cover the costs as required." John plucked a fragment from the heap and studied it intently, admiring the chamfered edge, the neat finish. "It's excellent workmanship."

"It's a crying shame to see it treated this way. A hundred years it stood firm..."

"If it was still standing firm, your services wouldn't be required," John retorted. "But I'm curious about one thing. How did you know to come here? I thought it would be weeks before we found masons."

"We were working on the Lord Kilmaurs' place at Kerrielaw. There's been difficulties all along. Consignments of stone impounded and the like... Then just last week one of Montgomerie's people rode by. He offered us a tidy sum if we abandoned Kilmaurs' place and moved on to Duchal." The master-mason pulled an unenthusiastic face. "The consequences of staying didn't bear thinking about."

"No," said John. "I'm sure they didn't."

Once his horse was readied, John left for home. Slouching in the saddle, he let the reins slide through his fingers. His black horse stretched out its neck and strode onwards at a long, loose-limbed walk, relaxed and comfortable.

It was a pleasant day for travelling, a light breeze easing the summer heat. Finches and linnets darted alongside, the calls of yellowhammers ringing out from nearby fields. With the sun beating bright from above, John was glad of his bonnet.

For once, his thoughts were cheerful. For the first time since he'd succeeded his father as Laird of Ellestoun and Sheriff of Renfrew, he had no fears, no worries. But with his first child on the way there was no room for complacency. He'd been a helpless onlooker when his sister Marion had miscarried the previous winter: the last thing he wanted was to sit back and do nothing while his young wife Margaret weathered her pregnancy alone.

So it was with Margaret's welfare foremost in his mind that he changed course, heading west past Knox's lands of Ranfurly, then turning south towards Pennald and the parish of Kilbarchan.

The smell of pottage and freshly baked bread greeted him as he stepped inside the cottage. The light was poor, besides the doorway, the low walls were pierced only by two small windows on the leeward side. One tallow candle burned upon the table and there was a fire in the centre of the room.

A woman stood there. She leaned close to stir the cauldron that hung over the flames, singing softly to herself. Her gown of beige wool was bright and clean, her hair concealed beneath a stiff white hood.

He doffed his bonnet. "Mistress Mary?"

She started. "Bless my soul!" Still clutching the spoon, she turned to face him. "I never thought I'd see the day..."

Glancing round, he found evidence of new-found prosperity. Two beds stood at the far end of the cottage, while a long wooden kist, robust but plainly fashioned, was set against the wall nearby. "You've used my gift wisely."

She smiled, but didn't catch his eye. "We're very comfortable now. Thank you." Setting the spoon aside, she smoothed out her skirts.

He sighed and clutched his bonnet in his grip. "May I sit down?"

She gestured to a stool.

Pushing his gown aside, he settled. "I wondered if you'd spare a few moments." He paused. "I won't keep you long."

She shrugged and dragged another stool alongside.

"Did William speak with you?"

She relaxed at last. "He did."

"What did you say?"

"He has a way with him. How could I refuse?" A smile crept across her face. "We'll be married as soon as the church permits it."

"Good." He sat tall, hands clasped before him. "Have you decided what's best? I know you'd be loath to come and stay at my place, but... He's indispensable."

"His daughter keeps some fields at Kenmure. William thought we might exchange the tacks. He said he'd talk with Master Semple."

"I'll speak with Alan myself, and make sure that everything is agreed to your satisfaction."

She studied him a moment, frowning. "John," she said at last. "Why did you come? I thought it was behind us..."

"It is."

"Ah." Her hand fluttered nervously at her throat.

"Was my company so intolerable?"

"Our lives have moved on."

"I know that," he said. "And yes, there's no need for me to meddle in your business. Forgive me, if it's caused annoyance. It's not the reason I called. It's my wife. She's missed two courses."

"What age is the lady?"

"She'll be seventeen years next May."

The Gryphon at Bay

"And her hips?"

"Narrower than some, I think."

She considered his words a while, head tilted. Looking at her now, she was just as he remembered her, careworn, faintly weary of the world.

He leaned close. "I'll do whatever's needed. I won't lie with her, if that's what's required to keep them both safe."

She threw back her head and laughed. There was warmth in her features, he no longer felt he was confronting a stranger. "Oh Johnny!" she said, clutching his arm tight. "Don't listen to those old fools in the church. If it's a loving bond between man and wife, no harm'll come of it."

"When should she keep to her bed?"

"I've seen poor women drop their babes in the fields then carry on working as though nothing's amiss. Meanwhile rich ladies suffer because they've been confined to their bed for months on end. Your wife should be the judge of what she can and can't do. Let the lady walk or ride a horse for as long as she's willing and able. She's the one who must endure the birth."

"Thank you." He fumbled in his purse and pressed some coins into her palm. "You've put my mind at rest."

Mary placed her hand on his. "Congratulations, Sir John. I'm delighted for you both. I'll pray God grants you a son, for that'll ease the burden on you." She rose to her feet. "All else is forgiven and forgotten? If you don't mind my asking, that is. No harm's meant, Johnny. I care for you, that's all."

"And I appreciate that, thank you." He frowned, faintly. "We've both worked hard to make amends. But..." He twisted his bonnet tighter, studying his feet. "I don't like to burden her with worries, not when life at Ellestoun's still new to her."

She studied him intently. "Sooner or later, you'll have to trust her. I know it's hard, John, but you can't curl up like an urchin when things go wrong and expect her to love you, spines and all." She looked him up and down. "You're looking well, mind."

"So are you." John stood alongside. "When's the wedding?"

"The bans will be read this Sunday coming. If that's acceptable."

"Of course."

"William's a good man. And very kind."

"And he's won the heart of a good woman. I couldn't have wished for better. For either of you." Grasping her hands, he held them tight. "Goodbye, Mary. We'll speak at the wedding, I hope. That is, if I'm invited."

Chapter 5

The Place of Kilmaurs

Fluttering above the looming bulk of the tower-house, the banner of the Cunninghames seemed insubstantial, a tiny shred of white silk sailing bravely in the breeze. Pausing briefly at the gates, Lady Christian Lindsay cast it one last wistful glance, then turned and strode briskly out beyond the barmkin.

"Come on!" Guido Cunninghame paused ahead, his slim boyish face glowing with excitement. "If you're not quick, you'll miss him."

"Give your poor mother some peace!" Christian replied. "I'm not so young and nimble as yourself." Lifting her skirts slightly, she stepped off the pebble-strewn track and onto the rough ground beyond.

The summer sun was warm on her face, the close-cropped grass unusually dry beneath her shoes. Guido's slight figure darted ahead, leading her towards the level area that lay just outside the castle walls. Every few strides he'd glance back, anxious and impatient.

She quickened her pace. She was joining a small but select audience: her husband Rob was there, along with her son Archie and her gude-mother, Lady Margaret Hepburn, Dowager to the late Alexander Cunninghame, 1st Earl of Glencairn.

They'd gathered to watch a single horseman, who steered his roan through a succession of circles and turns. Her eldest son Cuthbert, heir to the Cunninghame lands and titles.

Or what was left of them...

Christian still remembered the days when this unhappy stretch of shattered turf had been a garden, filled with flowers and herbs and fruit trees. Then one summer night their enemies had burned the trees and hacked down the flowers.

They hadn't bothered to replant it.

She missed the garden. And those days which were no more than a bitter memory, days of peace, prosperity.

She grimaced as she picked her way over to where Rob and the Dowager were waiting. The route was even more filthy than she'd anticipated, the ground of the makeshift tiltyard churned by the passing of horses.

Just one patch of grass survived around the base of the stout timber post supporting the quintain. A swivelling cross-arm was attached near the top; one end held a heavy sack of sand, while the other had a wooden shield nailed to it. There was a piece of cloth attached, quartered squares of red and blue.

Montgomerie's colours. Even here, at the heart of their lands, his presence stalked them.

Cuthbert sat secure in the saddle, a slim boy of sixteen years, very fair to behold, with flowing black hair and ruddy cheeks. His horse rolled along at a smooth canter, head pulled low, tail swishing with every stride.

The Gryphon at Bay

Watching her firstborn, Christian realised with a jolt that all those years spent learning to tilt and wield a sword were at last bearing fruit. Her little boy was fast becoming a man.

The thought made her proud and fearful all at once. It only seemed like yesterday she'd birthed him.

Folding her arms tight across her body, Christian strode across the hoof-pocked ground to join Rob and the Dowager.

The Dowager didn't even glance in her direction. A grim-faced woman in her fifties, she always dressed in sombre hues of brown and dark blue. She kept her gaze fixed unerringly on Cuthbert, as if watching him progress in the knightly arts was the only thing she cared for in this world.

Rob nodded, vague acknowledgement. "Thank you for joining us."

Taking her place at his shoulder, Christian shrugged, non-committal. She cast her husband a weary glance, noting the face that had grown so familiar through the years. A face that, although friendly and comfortable, wasn't particularly handsome. The passing seasons were taking their toll: the streaks of grey in his black hair and his neatly clipped beard were growing ever more pronounced, a sign that his worries were preying ever heavily upon his soul.

"Alright!" Rob called. "Let's begin." He kicked at the grass and grimaced slightly. "I can't tarry long. Will had important business in Kilmarnock today. I'd best go and meet him on the road."

"What manner of business?" Christian asked, but Rob didn't reply.

Spinning his mount around, Cuthbert approached at a canter. The sharp snorts of his horse pierced the silence, its relentless hooves shaking the ground.

Horse and rider halted just feet away. "Lady Margaret," Cuthbert acknowledged the Dowager. "And the Lady of Kilmaurs herself." He extended his hand towards Christian. There was a flourish in his gesture, the subdued extravagance of a knight or a king's champion. "Your favour, my lady."

Christian pulled a lace handkerchief from her sleeve and placed it in his palm.

He bowed his head and smiled, careful and courteous, then wheeled his horse around and was gone.

At the far side of the tiltyard, Guido took his place with the other boys: his older brother Archie and his cousin Andrew Cunninghame, Master of Craigends. Andrew clutched a sheaf of wooden lances; pulling one loose, he held it ready as Cuthbert cantered towards him.

Christian bit her lip, fighting the urge to weep. She wished she could protect her son, coddle him by her side forever. But Cuthbert cared nothing for his mother's concerns. He was eager to throw himself headlong into the world, with all its suffering and woe.

Checking his horse slightly, Cuthbert snatched the lance from Andrew's grasp. "Watch me!" His tone was commanding. He circled his horse tight on its hocks then held the reins firm so it skipped on the spot. Only then did he spur it forwards, whooping loud as it erupted into a gallop.

Bracing himself against the cantle of his saddle, Cuthbert lowered his lance. It whacked the wooden shield and the cross-arm swung about, the hefty bag of sand coming to rest where he'd been just moments before.

His young kinsmen cheered, and the Dowager smiled, tightly. "He's doing well."

Rob didn't answer. In the early years of their marriage, he'd been a kind attentive husband; Christian loved him still, in a weary, regretful kind of way, though he'd changed over the years, grown more distant and aloof. She couldn't even remember when she'd last shared his bed. Each night he'd sleep alone, with a draught of *aqua vita* to console him.

There was another roar of approval as Cuthbert returned for his second pass, hit the shield again then sped onwards.

"Two strikes!" Andrew Cunninghame called.

Cuthbert turned again. "Let's make that three."

This time when lance hit shield, the shaft snapped. Christian gasped, suddenly anxious. But Cuthbert remained safe in the saddle. He retrieved another lance and soon he was pressing his horse back into its rolling canter.

"Well done," Rob said. "Three strikes counts as a victory in any man's book." Without another word, he turned and trudged back towards the castle walls. "Saddle my horse!" he called to the waiting servants. "I must be gone."

Cuthbert rode up close with his lance gripped tight. There was a strange feral gleam in his eyes and a smile on his face, and this time as he rode away the angle was different,

The lance pierced the sack and Cuthbert grimaced, twisting it deep. "There!" he called. "Straight through the heart!"

Sand poured from the slit like blood from an open wound. Christian stared, sickened by the thought, but the Dowager remained impassive.

"You've mastered the joust now, Cuthbert," she said. "Your grandsire would be proud of you." She cast a baleful glance towards Rob's departing back. "If only he were here to witness your progress."

The Place of Ellestoun

Sunlight poured into the ladies' chamber, spilling across the dark timber floor. It was approaching the end of a long, hot afternoon; the air would have been stifling, had it not been for the fresh breeze that blew in from the fields, carrying the faint mingled scents of kye, horses, and woodsmoke.

Margaret Colville rested on the cushioned seat by the open window, her maids gathered close about her. Katherine, the eldest, sat perched by her side, distaff in hand, feigning maturity while Mariota and Alison giggled and chattered about inconsequential things.

Margaret smiled, only half-listening. "Hush," she said. "I can scarcely hear myself think. Why should William play to us, when we don't even appreciate his skills?" She nodded towards the man who sat patiently nearby, a lute balanced in his lap. "Let's have something a little less brisk."

"The tale of a lady who sits forlorn by her window." Katherine cast Margaret a sly glance. "Waiting in vain for her bold knight to return."

Margaret pretended to ignore her, lifting another shirt into her lap. There'd been a dearth of mending in the first few months of her marriage; being a proud man her husband hadn't stooped to ask for her help in keeping his wardrobe in order.

The Gryphon at Bay

Now Margaret was trying hard to restore his clothing to an acceptable standard, the basket at her feet piled high with shirts, hose and the occasional doublet, all battered and worn from hard use. She enjoyed the challenge of making something appear as good as new. And even the dullest of chores was made pleasurable with the help of laughter and music.

"Well, Lady Margaret, what would you care for?" William Haislet asked.

Lady Margaret... She liked that. It made her feel important. "Sing to us of love," she said. "Of the beauty and anguish that it brings."

Catching her eye, William smiled and nodded. He was old enough to be her father, solid in build, sedate in manner, with a thick mane of frosted brown hair that reached his shoulders. She'd dismissed him at first as just another servant. It was only later she'd learned that he was perhaps the most precious of the treasures concealed in her new household, a lutenist, and an exceptionally fine one at that.

He had other roles as well, arguably more important ones. As John's manservant, William should have accompanied his master on his expedition to Duchal. But when Margaret asked if William might stay behind, John had relented.

Soon she was listening entranced as William's voice rang out, rich and deep. He sang of love and loss, and a knight's despair, because he was riding to war, and away from his lady's side. *All's well with the world,* she thought, smoothing out the shirt in her lap. The cuffs were frayed, the collar, too. *He'll be home soon, and tonight you'll have him all to yourself...*

William's voice faded, the song was over.

Margaret frowned, thoughtfully. "I wonder where he is."

"You mustn't worry about him," William said. "He can take care of himself."

He was right, she supposed. Turning the shirt over, she found that one of the seams had gone under the oxter. A haphazard line of black thread showed where someone had made a ham-fisted attempt at repairing it. "A word of advice, William," she remarked. "If you must mend John's clothes, then at least use thread of the same colour."

He laughed, wry amusement. "Ah," he said. "Now that wasn't my doing, I must confess. I've a much neater hand than that. Sir John, however..."

"-Cannot count needlecraft amongst his skills," Margaret said. "Well, that comes as no surprise." She broke off with a smile, then added, "William, I've noticed little things about your manner just recently. A certain spring in your step. A tendency to break into song at the slightest urging. I'm curious, to say the least..."

He studied his lute intently, running his fingers along the curved wooden edge with the delicacy of a lover. "The master's in better spirits these days."

"And that's all it is?"

William blushed, faintly. "Not exactly, Lady Margaret." He paused. "I'm to be wed."

"That's splendid news! So who is the lucky lady? Do we know her?"

"A widow. Of good heart and gracious manner."

"Does Sir John know of this?"

"I confided in him," William said. "And sought his advice in the matter."

She sighed, feigning sorrow. "What will we do, William? When you're wed, you won't have much opportunity to keep us entertained."

"Ask the master," said William.

"John?" Margaret frowned. "He sings?"

"Like an angel," said William. "And he's very proficient with the lute, too. He'll deny it, of course. But if you ask nicely, and his mood's right, I'm sure he'll oblige you."

"Well, fancy that..." She drew a sharp breath, hearing a horse approach, entering the cobbled yard at a trot. Her heart was beating fast already, she'd have stood to catch a glimpse of him, if it hadn't been for the girls, who gazed intently in her direction, poised to utter some witty comment at her expense. For once, she thought, she'd deprive them of any further opportunity to tease her.

William lifted his lute once more, and soon its mellow tones drifted through the room.

Straining her ears, Margaret heard footsteps at last, a quick quiet tread with a faint clink of spurs. There was a light rap upon her door, and John breezed in, breathless from the climb.

"Katherine," Margaret said. "Go to the kitchens and ask the servants to take a tub of hot water to the master's chamber."

Katherine rose to her feet. She curtsied briefly before John, who frowned slightly, and glanced aside.

Margaret pretended not to notice. Old insults and injuries had left their mark; she feared it would be a long while yet before her husband managed to spare Katherine anything more than brief, polite acknowledgement. "Welcome home," she said, turning her face away, discreet invitation.

Leaning over, he delivered her a swift chaste peck on the cheek.

"Sit down." She patted the cushion alongside.

His frown deepened. "I'm filthy."

"Come on." She tugged his hand, and he sat without a word.

Margaret turned back to her sewing, revelling in his presence. When he sat this close, she marvelled at how big and imposing he was. His feet, clad in simple square-toed shoes, dwarfed her own, his shoulders looming over hers.

"William was telling me his glad tidings," she said, noting the bright grey-blue depths of his eyes, and the long proud line of his nose, faintly crooked after the incident at the wappenschaw, but handsome nonetheless.

"Ah, yes." He stared ahead, oblivious to her scrutiny. His deep gold hair hung unkempt over his shoulder, faded and pale from the sun in places. She itched to take a comb to it.

"You knew?" she asked.

He gave a vague smile. "I suspected."

"Do you know the lady?"

He hissed through his teeth, faint unease. "Yes."

Margaret frowned, puzzled. "We should hold the feast here," she suggested, and when he didn't answer, she added, "It's the least we could do. For William."

"We'll see."

There was something about his manner. Slight awkwardness, even a little embarrassment. It concerned her a little, but she shrugged it aside. He was always like that when the girls were around.

The Gryphon at Bay

She laid a hand upon his thigh. He seemed content, so she let it rest there. "I thought you'd be home sooner."

"I was delayed," he said. "I'm sorry." He looked at her just briefly, but his gaze didn't quite meet hers.

She didn't press him. He'd talk later, when they were alone. About his business at Duchal, and how the crops were faring. And all would be well between them. Tugging on his arm, she leaned close and whispered in his ear, "Let's go to your chamber. You'll feel much better when you've bathed."

Chapter 6

The Place of Kilmaurs

"It's been a terrible year," the Dowager said.

Christian didn't reply. Bathed in the warmth of the afternoon sun, she was in no mood for melancholy. She concentrated instead upon her sewing, where in her lap the Holy Virgin's face was taking form. She'd been working on this tapestry for ten years now and it wasn't even halfway finished, but it provided a welcome respite from the drudgery of darning and mending.

"You should've been a countess, Christian. And my boy Robert an earl." The Dowager stabbed the needle deep, her face set and hard. "My husband was never a traitor. He was loyal to the end, God rest his soul..."

Snapping the silk thread between her fingers, Christian weathered the Dowager's tirade in silence.

"-Perhaps the King was right to forfeit the title," the Dowager continued. "Robert's not worthy of an earldom. He can't even avenge his poor father's death. Montgomerie should be cold in his tomb by now. Not making our lives a misery-"

Hearing hooves approach outside, Christian set her sewing down. "Excuse me."

The Dowager shrugged, and turned back to her needlework without another word.

Christian swept away, leaving the hall and hurrying down the spiral stair. Pushing open the door, she stepped out to see a dozen horses being walked in the yard, coats sleek with sweat, flanks steaming.

She spotted Rob at last, loitering near the stables with Cuthbert: Rob's younger brother Sir William Cunninghame of Craigends was there, too, as rough in his manner as Rob was careful and restrained. Both men pored over a parchment, while Archie and Guido crowded close.

Rob looked up. He was smiling for once. And it wasn't tight and uncomfortable, pinned on for her benefit. It was a broad glorious smile that made the years fall away from him. "It's a great day, my love," he said. "A momentous time for the Cunninghames."

William kissed the document and brandished it high. "God bless Tom Spark of Bartonholm!"

"All it took was a purse of gold coins. Pressed into his palm at the right moment." Rob wrapped an arm round Cuthbert's shoulders and hugged his son tight. "We've outflanked the enemy, for once."

"So next time that arse Montgomerie tries to chase me out of Cunninghame on account of my 'trespassing', there'll be trouble," Will said. "I've as much right to be here as him."

She felt suddenly cold. "What're you talking about?"

Will thrust the parchment into Cuthbert's grasp. He seized Christian's arms and birled her round, so fast she gasped for breath. "Oh, sweet Christian," he chortled.

"Most noble lady of Kilmaurs..." He took her hand and kissed it. "I'm the Constable of Irvine. It's my duty to keep the King's peace throughout the Marymass Fair."

"*He'll* be there. There's bound to be trouble."

"It's in the Lord Montgomerie's best interests to maintain order." Rob's tone was patient, as if he addressed a child. "He failed at the Bailie Courts and yes, perhaps we had a hand in that. This time any rioting won't be on our account. It'll be his own rabble that brings him down."

"Won't King James be pleased!" Will laughed. "When he finally learns that Montgomerie's lost his grip on Cunninghame."

"I wish you wouldn't provoke him," Christian said.

"It's different now," Rob replied. "He's chained and muzzled."

"Some wine, I think." Will slapped Cuthbert on the back. "To celebrate. And we must tell your grandmother the good news." He steered the boy away.

Christian didn't stir. "Rob..."

"Yes, my love."

She couldn't bring herself to look at him. "Please reconsider."

"Chrissie, please..." Gripping her shoulders, he leaned his forehead against hers. "We must seize every advantage. If not for ourselves, then for Cuthbert. When my time's done, I want my heir to have something to thank me for."

"Your mother's full of spleen. Don't pay any heed..."

"Perhaps she's right. I'm not by nature a warrior: that's Will's calling." He paused. "But there's other ways of winning wars. Take Sempill of Ellestoun... He was in a sorry state last year. Now look at him. In all that time, he scarcely struck a blow. It's like a game of chess. One move at a time, sometimes gaining, sometimes losing..."

"Those are sound words, Rob." She broke off, then added in a low voice, "Even so... The strain will be enormous. Montgomerie already holds the high ground. For you to win it back, you must strive twice as hard."

"It's a worthy fight. It must be done, for Cuthbert's sake." He squeezed her hands, gently. "All will be well," he told her. "Dame Fortune's smiling upon us at last. I can feel it in my bones."

The Place of Ellestoun

Margaret burrowed in the kist for a fresh doublet, adding it to the pile of clothes alongside. Closing the lid, she sat back on her heels, pausing to revel in the warmth of the sun on her face. There was no need to hurry: John still lazed in a big wooden tub before the fireplace.

Margaret stood, casting an appreciative glance around the place she now called home, taking in a laird's chamber that though comfortable, was not overly opulent. The room was spacious and well-lit, with windows piercing three walls and a substantial fireplace in the fourth. Elegant tapestries hung from the timber-panelled walls, hunting scenes mostly, with one depicting Adam and Eve standing amidst Eden's bounty.

Picking up the fresh clothes, she carried them to the bed and laid them down there, uneven floorboards creaking with every footfall.

She leaned her cheek against the carved oak bedpost, where the dark red curtains hung, heavy and slightly faded. "Everything's ready."

"Thank you very much. I'll be out in a moment." Breathing deep, John pulled his head beneath the water one last time then re-emerged, pushing his wet hair back from his face.

John lay along the cushioned window seat beside her, a sheet wrapped loosely around his body. His eyes were closed, he seemed half-asleep.

Holding his head in her lap, Margaret carefully combed out his tangled hair. A feeling of warmth, of overwhelming contentment, drifted through her. *He's back now,* she thought. *And here he'll stay, God willing...*

He reached for her hand. "I visited a midwife."

"What did she say?" she asked, voice guarded.

"That you should keep your strength for as long as possible." He settled himself more comfortably. "Can you ride a horse?"

"I had a pony once. I hunted with my brothers. Then one day I had a fall. From then on, they wouldn't let me near a horse."

"If I found you a sedate and placid horse, would you try again?"

"On one condition," she said. "If you teach me, you must also instruct my girls."

"I'm sure that can be arranged." His tone was unenthusiastic.

Catching his reluctance, she thought it best to change the subject. "I'm so pleased for William."

"Yes..."

"He should celebrate his nuptials here."

"I'll consider it."

"He's a loyal servant. Surely-"

"Margaret." John opened his eyes, but he wasn't looking at her. "There are difficulties."

"What kind of difficulties?"

"I know the woman. Intimately." He sat up. "The servants know who she is. I don't want any embarrassment for you. Or for either of them."

"Oh." She blinked, taken aback. "Does William know?"

"Of course he knows."

"Then he's doing this for you?"

"No. He's marrying her because he loves her. And because she loves him." He was still scowling, feet planted square before him, shoulders hunched.

"You're not seeing her now, are you?"

"Of course not."

"So where's the harm in celebrating the marriage here? Will it hurt you to see her given away?"

He drew a sharp breath and glanced at her in quick reproach. "Don't hold her in poor esteem because of what happened. The situation was dire over the winter. She did what she did to help her children, not for any gentle feelings towards me-"

"John-"

"-I'm sorry for any distress it caused. And for the disgrace it's brought her. I was lonely and afraid. My judgment was unsound..."

"John..." She clutched his arm. "It's alright. Let's put it behind us..."

34

He didn't reply, his muscles taut. Margaret slipped her arm around his back, pulling him close, rubbing his shoulders gently until the tension ebbed from him. "We should be happy," she said. "Lie down. Calm yourself."

He shrugged and settled once more.

"What am I to do with you? You take offence at the slightest thing..."

He didn't answer.

"You mustn't try so hard to be beyond reproach." Margaret leaned down and kissed his head. "I forgave your transgressions. And you said you'd forgiven mine."

"Yes, I know."

"Then what's troubling you?"

"I fear for you. You shrug all this aside as if it's nothing..."

She laid a finger against his lips, silencing him. "I'm doing what's required of me. I attend mass each morning. And I shall do exactly what the midwife tells me. You must trust in God, John. He's been so generous just recently. Why should He fail us now?"

Chapter 7

It wasn't the best weather for travelling: sharp showers lashed the land, blowing in quick from the south-east. Between these bouts of rain, the ground steamed beneath warm sunshine. The sinking sun painted the hills a brilliant glowing gold: in the north and east, the clouds looked leaden.

Travelling onwards at a leisurely pace, the Earl of Angus took in a landscape that was familiar, comforting. His path through Liddesdale took him past tumbling waters which danced and sparkled in the sunlight; he smiled as he noted the foolhardy antics of a dipper bouncing from stone to stone, seemingly oblivious to the churning torrent that surrounded it.

It felt good to return to the marchlands, so inextricably linked with the Douglas name and traditions. He was heading for the Place of Hermitage, a Douglas stronghold that sat within a quiet valley in the eastern marches. Once it had been the isolated refuge of a holy man. Now after long years of Douglas rule, it was instead a place of evil rumour and fear.

Sir James the Good; Archibald the Grim; James the Gross... A succession of Black Douglases, notorious for their exploits. Each had dwelt there, before the stronghold passed to the Red Douglas line in the time of Angus' great-grandsire.

Now the Black Douglases had all but faded from memory. James, 9th Earl of Douglas, was the last of their line, an old infirm man who languished as a prisoner in the King's keeping.

At last Angus glimpsed the blank harled keep shining pale against the yellow-gold and green of the hills. A stern, forbidding place, no windows pierced its lower walls: Hermitage had been built with defence foremost in mind.

Even now its mere mention could fill men with dread. Angus knew all the dark tales from its past; as he approached, he recalled how a hundred years earlier, his ancestor Sir William Douglas waylaid Alexander Ramsay, the Sheriff of Liddesdale. Wounded in the skirmish, Ramsay was abandoned in the prison pit to die.

It was said that when nights were calm, Ramsay's pleas for mercy could still be heard. And yes, there'd been times when Angus thought he'd heard a man's cries seep from the depths of the thick stone walls. Though being more practically minded, he was more inclined to attribute these sounds to the living. There were always men held captive at Hermitage; common reivers, mostly, imprisoned then hanged for acts of theft and pillage.

Leaving his horse in the courtyard, Angus climbed the narrow wooden stair which led into the castle. News of his arrival had already reached the household: servants bowed as he crossed the timber walkway and stepped beneath the double set of portcullis to the warmth of the tower within.

"My lord," the steward greeted him. "Lady Elizabeth bids you welcome. She will join you shortly – she has not yet finished dressing."

The Gryphon at Bay

"I'll be in my chamber." He paused at the stair which led up to the kitchen-tower. "Did Bonnie have her pups?"

"Six in all, Your Grace," the steward replied. "Two dogs, four bitches."

"What age?"

"Nine weeks now. Their coats are bright silver. All bar one, that bears a black mark upon its muzzle."

"Hounds fit for a king?"

The steward smiled. "Most certainly, Your Grace."

Angus shed boots and cloak, poured himself a measure of wine then sank down in his chair with a sigh.

It had been a long, tiring journey. He'd sailed to York, then after that he'd resorted to the roads. He'd spoken with the Bishop of Durham, before having brief audiences with Lord Dacre and the Earl of Northumberland. These meetings had been cautious affairs, neither party wanting to appear eager to court the other. But his English counterparts knew as well as he did that to successfully impose the law throughout the Marches, some co-operation was required.

Now these tiresome negotiations were behind him, Angus could relax in conditions that though comfortable, were rather basic. It was such a long difficult route to Hermitage that only the absolute necessities were brought here: mattresses and bedding, a few soft furnishings. The walls looked forlorn, with just one tapestry to break the monotony of the dark oak panelling: a poor dog-eared thing, chewed by moths and wrinkled with age.

"Archie?" Knuckles rapped lightly on his door, heralding the arrival of his wife, Elizabeth Boyd. She was a tiny woman, quick, bright-eyed and brisk. Five years his senior, on first impression she seemed weak, frivolous, but Angus knew her better than that. She could be an absolute harridan, when she deemed it necessary. But she was the kind of harridan that any sharp-witted nobleman welcomed for a wife, infinitely more useful than a soft-breasted child-bride. He'd never thought her beautiful, but he valued her counsel. She was devoted to him and his success at court, and no man could wish for more than that.

He rose to his feet as she entered. Taking her hand, he delivered her a delicate kiss on the cheek. "Lovely to see you, my dear."

His greeting was tolerated, nothing more. "You received my message?" she demanded. "About that devil Patrick Hepburn? And the March Wardenships?"

"I received a message. But not from you."

She frowned. "Then whom?"

"Ross of Montgrennan. I met with him in London."

"Archie..."

"He was most supportive."

She shook her head, lips pursed. "A dangerous bedfellow, Archie..."

Angus smirked. "In more ways than one, if rumours are right..."

"What did he say?"

"My instincts tell me that he's been in correspondence with Lennox all along. But the King has recently approached him, offering to negotiate."

"He'll assist the man who grants him more."

"I reckon he'll back the King. Lennox left us because he was sick of snatching the scraps from Patrick Hepburn's table. He won't want to share power with Montgrennan. He hates the man."

"And you, if I remember right, don't think much of him either."

He handed her his goblet. "Montgrennan has sound wits and a flawless intellect. It would be far better to count him as an ally than as an enemy."

She took a careful sip. "What will you do?"

"I'll do what I've always done," Angus replied. "Watch and wait." He stretched with a sigh. "I hear that Bonnie's dropped a fine litter."

Elizabeth laughed, softly. "You show more interest in your horses and your hounds than you do your children."

"My children are at an age where they can take care of themselves." He reclaimed his wine and swallowed a long draught. "Bonnie's a fine beast," he said. "If her pups are half as worthy, then I'm sure that they, too, will have a part to play in our future success. I'll visit the kennels once I've rested a while, and see how they're progressing."

The Place of Kilmaurs

It was the greatest force the Cunninghames had mustered for a year or more. Fifty-five men gathered in the yard, clad in padded brigandines, armed with spears and swords. The stink of horse hung heavy in the air, the barmkin echoing with men's voices and the occasional rattle of hooves.

Sir William Cunninghame of Craigends cast his gaze across the company, one last check to make sure that all was well. His heart beat quick with anticipation: this time he knew there was no room for error. They had to perform at their best: strong, disciplined, and above all, fearless.

Sensing his mood, his steed could no longer contain its excitement. It pulled at its bit and side-stepped, eager to be off.

Craigends jerked the reins. "Stand at peace, damn you!"

Across the yard Rob sat relaxed upon his horse. From the looks of him, he might have been embarking on a carefree jaunt to Kilmarnock. The Lord Kilmaurs didn't much care for war, but when he rode out with his men, there was a quiet dignity about him that won respect and loyalty.

Cuthbert and Guido waited nearby: Cuthbert grinned with eager expectation, while Guido seemed cautious, subdued.

Catching Rob's eye, Craigends raised his hand. "Alright!" he bellowed. "Let's be gone!"

"Follow me, men." Rob led the way, flanked by his sons, and slowly the troop of men-at-arms filed through the narrow gates set within the barmkin wall. The sound of hooves grew louder, until it was a steady thunder against the cobbles.

Craigends felt his heart lighten. A glorious blaze of joy and confidence filled his soul. He'd almost forgotten what it was like to have the black clouds lift like this, to glimpse the sun...

"Come on now!" he urged the stragglers. "You're like a gaggle of women, with all this fussing and fretting. Move yourselves."

They stirred into a ragged trot.

"Will!" Christian hurried from the door of the tower-house. "Can you wait a moment? Please..."

His horse sprang into a half-rear. He fought to hold it back. "Ho there, Chrissie," he said through clenched teeth. "How may I be of service?"

Standing beside his horse's shoulder, she looked very small and slight. She was lovely still, with a dainty oval face, delicate lips and haunting hazel eyes. But the last year had aged her: there were creases in her brow he hadn't noticed before. "Why didn't he say goodbye?"

"We're not riding to war," he told her. "This is a show of strength, that's all."

"Keep them safe," she whispered. "All of them."

Craigends reached for her hand and gripped it tight. "Cuthbert's in safe hands. Andy knows to look out for his cousin."

Christian smiled. "God speed, Will."

He nodded. "Amen to that." Tightening his reins, he closed his heels against his mount's sides. It sprang away at a canter, ears pricked, eyes fixed on the tails of the departing horses.

The Marymass Fair, Irvine Burgh, August 1489

Standing at the mercat cross in Irvine, Hugh Montgomerie could smell nothing but the scent of fish, pungent in the air.

He wrinkled his nose in distaste. He was quite partial to fish. It graced his table most days. But after just one day in Irvine's bounds, he doubted he could stomach it for a week or more.

Still, a westerly breeze was preferable. If the wind chased through the town itself, the smell could be unbearable. Rotting flesh from the tanning pits and shambles, manure from the middens and backlands.

Pulling his gown up higher onto his shoulders, Hugh scuffed an irritable foot against the cobbles. At this particular moment, he hated towns, and everything to do with them.

He was stationed at the mercat cross with his younger brother Robert in attendance. The provost and several burgesses were there, too, along with half-a-dozen Montgomerie men-at-arms who leaned upon their spears and talked amongst themselves.

Rows of ramshackle stalls and luckenbooths now occupied the market place and Main Street. A queue of prospective traders stretched back from the cross, produce piled high on carts and barrows. Once their goods were assessed, and the required fees and duties paid, the stallholders would leave to set out their wares in their allotted places. They'd be subject to further visits from the Constable throughout the day, to ensure that their prices were correct and that all was well.

Hugh watched carefully as another bundle was set down, its bindings opened. Packed tightly within was a mass of hides and pelts: ox and lamb, mostly, with a few striped cat-skins thrown in for good measure. The burgesses counted through the items, making the necessary calculations for duty, then several ox-hides and a cat-pelt were removed.

He rocked back and forth on his heels, pleasantly satisfied. A chalder of grain here. A crate of chickens there. It all added up. And when the Marymass Fair was done, the spoils would be distributed. A share would go to the poor folk, the rest divided up between the burgh officials: the Provost, the Constable, the elected members of the burgh council, and of course, himself.

Robert fidgeted and coughed slightly.

"What's the matter with you?" Hugh snapped. "Don't tell me you *want* a riot?"

Of all his brothers, Robert was most like him: tall and slender, clean-shaven. "Of course not," he replied. "It's just *too* quiet."

Hugh grunted a noncommittal response.

"My lord?" A young man came sidling through the crowd. One of his people, wearing a brigandine, and sporting a rusty sallet on his head. "The Laird of Hessilhead requests your presence at the Kirkgate. There's a disturbance..."

"Tell the Constable to deal with it."

"That's the problem, my lord. There's been no sign of Tom Spark of Bartonholm. Now Sir William Cunninghame of Craigends has shown up claiming that *he's* the constable..."

"There." Robert's tone was smug. "What did I tell you?"

Hugh scowled. His mood had been pleasant until now. The air was warm, it wasn't raining. The streets were reasonably clean, and the wailing of the circling gulls hadn't been too intrusive.

Now their mewing cries set his teeth on edge.

Hugh glared at a nearby trader, as if he were to blame for everything. The unfortunate man blanched and dropped his box of cabbages, which rolled everywhere.

Robert crouched to pick them up. So did some of the burgesses. The trader apologised profusely, his face crimson.

Hugh kicked a stray cabbage aside. He was half-a-mile from the Kirkgate. In the time it would take him to get there, anything could happen...

He grasped his brother's gown and hauled him upright. "Stop grovelling, for God's sake and look after things here. I'll be back once I find out what's happening."

Cradling an armful of cabbages, Robert nodded wordlessly.

It was like fighting against an incoming tide. There were people everywhere, and livestock, too. Hugh pushed and snarled and cuffed the heads that lingered in his path, but progress was still painfully slow.

"Mind yer backs!" a voice bellowed.

The crowds parted, a line of horses approached. Skinny knock-kneed brutes destined for market.

Hugh held his ground. "Are they broken?"

Their handler beamed with pride. "Oh yes, sir." His face fell as Hugh seized the nearest horse. "That'll be fifteen pennies–"

"The brute will be returned." Grasping a handful of mane, Hugh sprang onto the creature's back. It was a poor stunted thing: his feet were at its knees and there was just a rope halter to guide it.

The Gryphon at Bay

It laid its ears back and swished its tail, so he growled in his throat and even then it didn't stir. He lashed the beast's shoulder with the rope: it sat on its haunches, then lurched forwards.

Everyone sprang aside, anxious to avoid the hooves.

He made steady progress, past the houses that jostled along the south end of Main Street. At last he glimpsed the tower of the Church of Saint Mary the Virgin, rearing high above the thatched roofs.

Eventually he reached the Kirkgate, where the harled walls of the church reared to his right nearby. He found a score of Montgomerie retainers clustered there beyond the kirkyard, some mounted, most on foot.

Hugh's brother James sat upon his horse by the gate. "There you are," he said.

"Better late than never." Hugh glanced beyond the gateway. His cousin, John Montgomerie of Hessilhead, stood alone there, a thickset bearded man in plate armour. Like Leonidas he held the pass, confronting a mass of armed men.

He counted at least two score gathered there, beneath a banner that bore the sable shake-fork of the Cunninghames. At their fore sat Sir William Cunninghame of Craigends: a seasoned knight approaching forty, strong, and irritatingly robust.

Craigends waved. "Good day, Lord Hugh! You're looking well, sir!"

Craigends' brother Robert, the Lord Kilmaurs, sat sullen and self-righteous nearby, with a gaggle of younger boys alongside. Hugh recognised Craigend's lad Andrew amongst them, along with Robert's heir Cuthbert, who sat smirking on his horse as if the whole affair were a colossal joke.

Hugh nodded to Kilmaurs. "Good day, Lord Robert." He tried to sound civil, at least. "I hear Sir William now calls himself the Constable?"

"Aye," Craigends said. "Just as you call yourself Bailie of Cunninghame. And Justiciar of Arran and Bute." He gestured towards Hugh's horse. "That's a mighty steed," he said. "What happened to the last one? Did you beat the poor beast to death in a fit of rage?"

Cuthbert sniggered.

Hugh cast the boy a disdainful look. "Last I heard, Tom Spark of Bartonholm was our constable," he said. "No one told me otherwise." He dismounted, then wandered out beyond the gate. Halting at his kinsman's side, he rested his hand lightly on his sword hilt.

Craigends watched him carefully. "Thomas is getting on in years," he said. "And after all the trouble at the Bailie courts..."

"-Caused by yourselves, if I remember right-"

"-He thought it wise to pass the task on to a younger, fitter man."

"He chose *you?*"

"Cunninghame or Montgomerie, it's all the same to him," Craigends said. "I made him a most generous offer."

"With a knife at his throat, most like."

"Come now, Lord Hugh," Craigends replied. "We don't all stoop to your methods."

"You have proof?"

"Of course." Craigends pulled a rolled parchment from the depths of his gown.

Louise Turner

Hugh opened it and scanned its contents without a word. "Alright." He beckoned to his men. "Let them pass."

Chapter 8

Irvine Burgh

The boards were laid out in the tolbooth, the provost and burgesses sitting ready. Already the hall was crowded with townsfolk, all dressed in their finest clothes: tradesmen, guidwives, merchants. They talked quietly amongst themselves, casting anxious glances at the armed Cunninghame retainers who stood lined up along the walls.

The church bell struck eight.

The provost sat with hands clasped and eyes downcast. The notary fiddled with his quill.

No one spoke.

Craigends sighed. There was still no sign of Hugh Montgomerie. He'd taken yesterday's tidings remarkably well; he'd kept a tight rein on his kinsmen and men-at-arms and there hadn't been a whisper of trouble all night. Now, though, he was making up for it.

It was just typical, Craigends thought, that Montgomerie would try and obstruct the Constable's court. But then – he reminded himself - that was in keeping with his nature. Awkward and wilful, like a petulant child.

The door banged open and in strode Lord Hugh. "I'm sorry I'm late."

His words were more challenge than apology. The crowds shrank to let him pass, half the faces glowing with relief, the other half biting their lips and looking away. A small army of Montgomeries followed, spurs ringing loud, boots thumping against the timber floor. Lord Hugh's brothers were present, his cousins, too, along with another dozen men-at-arms besides.

A ripple of unease passed through the assembled townspeople, and Craigends felt the hairs on the back of his neck prickle. He feigned levity nonetheless. "Good of you to join us, Lord Hugh."

Montgomerie breezed into place beside him. "I was unavoidably delayed."

"Figs are good," Craigends said, half under his breath. "They'll keep you nice and regular."

Montgomerie's eyes narrowed, but he said nothing. Lord Hugh's friends might have called him graceful and imperious in bearing, like a mighty hawk or eagle, bright-eyed and fierce.

But Craigends considered such comparisons fanciful. In his eyes, Lord Hugh was more like a papingo; he dressed in brightly coloured silks and velvets and gleamed with gold.

Glancing in Montgomerie's direction, he hoped for some sign that Lord Hugh felt the passage of years as much as anyone. Perhaps the lank black mane was receding slightly at the temples. But there were no flecks of grey. And his teeth were still bone white and irritatingly free from blemish.

43

Craigends nodded to the provost. "Now the Lord Montgomerie is with us," he said, pleasantly, "we can begin. Can the first defendent step forward?"

Hugh glowered at the board and sat tight in his chair, arms folded, as Craigends counted through the heap of pennies one last time, infuriatingly slow.

A smirk of triumph flickered across the Constable's lips as he scooped the coins into his palm and poured them into a leather bag. "Now who's next?"

"Mistress Janet Montgomery!" The call went out.

Baffled by the summons, the guidwife in question looked up. She was standing amongst a group of older burgesses, modestly dressed in a plain brown gown and crisp white hood. "My lord Constable?" she asked, frowning.

"You're fined six pennies for the adulteration of foodstuffs."

"But I didnae-"

"Be silent!" Craigends commanded. "It's alleged that the flour you sold yesterday was less than pure. It contained sawdust."

"That's a lie!" Mistress Montgomery responded, cheeks flushed with fury.

"The flour was examined, the allegations found to be correct." Craigends spoke loud to be heard over the mutterings of the Montgomerie contingent. "You'll pay six pennies now, or your fine will be doubled." He nodded. "Next!"

Two sturdy Cunninghame retainers grasped the old woman and jostled her forward to the table. Her gaze met Hugh's, her eyes were bright, desperate. "I didnae do it. I swear by Almighty God-"

"Do you have the money?" Craigends cut in.

Hugh breathed deep, trying to maintain his composure, his dignity. These days, his temper was improving. Five years ago, he'd have stormed out in a rage and declared the entire proceedings a mockery of Justice.

He wasn't alone in his displeasure. Many amongst the crowd were restless, looking about them, seeking reassurance from friends and kinsmen. They were just as hamstrung as he was: for every scowl of displeasure, someone else was smiling with grim satisfaction.

Mistress Montgomery delved deep in her purse. "Take it!" she snarled and tossed the coins down.

Avoiding her gaze, Hugh picked at a snag in the board cloth, bristling with silent rage. It was all so obvious. Alongside the usual charges of theft and breach of the peace, there'd been a number of cases like this. The accuser was always a Cunningham, or someone known to be sympathetic to the Cunninghames. The defendent, a Montgomery. Or married to a Montgomery. Or in the service of a Montgomery. The fines were hefty, all protests of innocence dismissed or ignored.

"A pox upon your justice!" Mistress Montgomery spat, as the Cunninghame retainers jostled her away.

"I'll pretend I didn't hear that!" Craigends retorted. "Can I have the next defendent?" He checked his ledger, briefly. "Master Andrew Montgomery!"

Another elderly burgess shuffled forward, face sullen. "Master Montgomery," Craigends continued. "You are hereby accused of selling underweight loaves. You were passing off as tuppenny loaves what transpired to be penny loaves. And the flour used to bake this bread was too coarse. You claimed your loaves to be symnel, when they were quite clearly wastel..."

Hugh shifted slightly. His head ached with frustration, he seethed inside. He desperately wanted to sigh, or drum his fingers against the board, but he couldn't, not with the eyes of so many Cunninghames upon him. This was the Constable's court, though in this instance, it was debatable whether the Constable of Irvine was really carrying out his duties in a just, unbiased manner.

It would have been easy to call his kinsmen to arms and demand redress. His retainers were waiting for his summons; he could see expectation in every scowling face and clenched fist. But that way he'd be playing right into Craigends' hands. The Cunninghames wanted a riot, so for a second time that year it would look as if the Montgomeries were incapable of keeping order in the burgh.

Hugh was determined to prevent that. Even if it meant having to witness the distress of his kinsmen and tenants at such close quarters.

The church bells rang ten of the clock and Hugh wilted inside. They weren't even two hours into the proceedings.

The Place of Ellestoun

Studying him from her vantage point on the lochside, Margaret was trying hard not to laugh. "You look ridiculous!" she told him.

"Don't make so much noise!" John retorted. "You'll scare the fish away." Net in one hand, lightweight fishing spear in the other, he waded further out into the reeds that flanked the lochside. Velvet-soft silt settled around his toes, the water chill against his legs.

"It's not decent!" she persisted. "What if someone sees you?"

He'd shed hose and doublet for this task, replacing his silk shirt with a linen one which reached halfway to his knees and was knotted between his legs for the sake of decorum. "The men dress this way in the North. All summer through."

She pulled an unenthusiastic face. "How horrible. With those great big hairy legs..."

He looked up. "And the hairy faces, too."

"Savages."

John smiled, and shook his head. Despite her feigned irritation, it was clear she was enjoying this expedition. She rarely ventured out beyond the gardens, so when he'd offered her the opportunity to wander by the lochside, she'd leapt at it. She'd brought a blanket and spread it out over the close-cropped grass and she was sitting there now with an open book in her lap and a basket alongside half-filled with fish. Confident that they wouldn't be disturbed, she'd slipped off her shoes and pulled up her skirts slightly, exposing her feet to the sun.

The child wasn't due for another six months or so, and as yet he could see no obvious change in her. Her rich brown hair was tucked beneath a velvet hood, her dark blue gown cut low across her chest, the flesh above obscured beneath a thin white partlet which reached almost to her neck.

She glanced up, frowning. "Don't stare like that, John. It makes me nervous."

He shrugged and turned away.

"I do hope no-one's watching," she persisted. "You're the laird. You're supposed to set an example to the rest of us."

"Everyone's far too busy to care." And it was true. Harvest was underway, distant figures toiling in the fields at the far shore.

"If God had wanted you to catch fish with your bare hands, He'd have given you claws. Like an otter."

"Oh, give us peace!" He broke off, catching the flicker of movement in the shallows. Like a hunting heron, he froze, not daring to move or even breathe. Watching and waiting, poised to strike.

There was a flurry in the silt and he plunged the spear down. He'd caught the fish; it thrashed in its distress, pinned and helpless.

Once he'd briskly netted it, he lifted it from the water. "You shouldn't be so uncharitable," he told her, wading forth with his prize cradled close to his chest. "I've brought you five trout, and a pike."

"You wrecked havoc on one with a spear."

"It was a long hard struggle."

"With a trout?"

"You wouldn't understand." The fish was gasping its last; he paused to club it with his dagger then dumped its corpse in the waiting basket.

"If that was all we had to eat tonight, we'd starve." Margaret edged away as he sank down beside her.

John laughed and untied his shirt. "Let's hope the cooks are more appreciative of my efforts." He looked about him, trying to catch sight of his hounds. "Caesar! Pompey!" he called.

Alert to his voice, they came running. They'd been prowling in the reedbeds further down the shore: they slumped down nearby, legs and bellies caked with mud.

"Don't come any closer!" Margaret scolded. "I won't have your muddy paws all over me."

John leaned close. "Are you talking to them, or to me?"

She giggled and pushed him roughly away.

He turned aside, rubbing his legs dry then pulling on his hose. He was just lacing them closed when the hounds leapt up, baying loudly. He looked up, concerned, realised then that a man was approaching Ellestoun from the Beith road.

Even from this distance, John could see that he was wearing brigandine and helmet. He was armed with a sword, too. He led a lean bay horse, which limped as it moved.

Margaret sprang to her feet, suddenly agitated. "John, look!"

"I shouldn't worry," John said. "One man doesn't make an army. He probably needs to find a farrier for his horse."

"No, it's not that..." She trailed off, squinting through the sunlight with a hand over her eyes, then turned to John, frowning. "It's Jamie!" she gasped. "What's he doing here? Do you think he's brought bad news from Ochiltree?"

John shrugged. "Your guess is as good as mine."

"Get dressed, John!" Margaret urged him. "Please hurry!"

The Gryphon at Bay

"I'm trying!" John recognised him now, Jamie Colville, Margaret's bastard half-brother. Hauling off the sodden shirt, he gave his body a cursory wipe with the blanket. "Go and speak with him," he said. "I won't be long."

They were already deep in conversation by the time John arrived. James Colville nodded in curt greeting, a big broad man, bearded and scowling, and John's senior by several years. "Horse is lame," he muttered. "Clipped a stone a half-mile back."

John cast a careful eye over the horse, noting its lathered coat, the wild gleam in its eye. Small wonder it had missed its footing: it looked as if it had galloped all the way from Kyle. Jamie, too, looked unsettled, glancing here and there as if he half-expected pursuit.

"We'll take him back to the place and see what can be done for him," John said. "You'll join us for dinner?"

"Aye, that'd be appreciated." Jamie fidgeted a little, then blurted out, "A roof over my head'd be appreciated, too, Sir John." He hesitated, eyes downcast. "I'm a fighting man," he said through gritted teeth. "I can earn my keep."

"We'll talk about this later," John said, doing his best to act as if nothing were amiss. "Let's go inside, shall we? I have a precious cargo to deliver to the cooks..."

With the entire household gathered for dinner, the hall at Ellestoun was packed. Men and women sat crammed around the lower tables, while the family took their places on the dais, accompanied by their senior household staff.

Jamie Colville sat with John, sharing his trencher and cup. Even so, he seemed ill at ease, gobbling down food as if he hadn't eaten in a month or more.

Margaret wondered more than ever what had driven her half-brother away from home, but Jamie was not forthcoming, and John didn't seem inclined to press him.

Eventually Jamie slumped back in his chair, scowling at his trencher as if its presence disgusted him. "Ochiltree's in a right sorry state these days," he muttered. "Davey says he'll do anything to get William's marriage declared invalid." He paused to take a sip of wine.

John glanced up, interested. "Does he have any legal grounds for this?"

"None has been forthcoming as yet. I suspect the only evidence he thinks he needs is force of arms. He says he doesn't recognise William's child as the rightful heir of Ochiltree." He broke off, scowling. "If the dispute escalates, we'll all be expected to take sides."

"And you'd rather not get involved," John said.

"I'm a bastard. Whatever happens, I get nothing."

Margaret stared at her trencher, remembering the last few months she'd spent at Ochiltree. When she'd been carried away from her childhood home, she'd ached inside with despair. Now, though, she was relieved to be away from the battered little tower-house that nestled deep in the hills of Kyle.

Katherine nudged her. "Can I have some sauce?"

Margaret pushed the small bowl closer. As lady of the house she'd invariably dine with John, but today she was granted Katherine as a dining partner. Which meant she had to snatch the choice scraps whenever she had the chance.

"Still not wed, Kate?" Jamie asked Katherine. "I'd have thought some man would have claimed your hand by now."

Katherine blushed, and stared at the board.

"If they're not quick about it," Jamie muttered in brisk aside to John, "I might take her myself. She's flourishing here." He cast an appreciative eye over all Margaret's maids, lined up with their mistress along the distaff side of the table. "They all are."

"The women manage their own affairs," John said. "Speak to Margaret about these things. Though I'm sure she'd be reluctant to lose her."

"They're better off here." Jamie took another massive draught of wine, and the scowl crept back. "- Away from that damned Kennedy witch who rules our place with a grip of steel. Father was delighted when he brought a Kennedy into the family. God rest his soul, John, he never guessed the trouble she'd cause. If anyone so much as speaks a word against her, she'll go on and on about how the family suffered in my grandsire's day, and how they deserved everything they got."

"And what exactly is the story?" John asked, wiping his fingers on the napkin draped over his shoulder. "I know the 9th Earl of Douglas murdered your grandsire, but I've never been told the circumstances..."

Margaret swallowed, remembering fearful stories that had left her shivering in her bed at night. "My mother told me that the Douglases laid siege to Ochiltree," she said. "When my grandsire surrendered, they hacked off his head while the women looked on. Then they burned the place."

There was silence.

John glanced at her briefly. "Your grandsire was very bold. To have challenged the Black Douglases..."

"The animal who killed him still lives," Jamie muttered.

"Earl James?" John replied. "A broken man, so I've heard. He's been incarcerated five years now. The last in a long line of objectionable men."

"Surely those days are over," Margaret said. "It's been twenty years or more since the Earls of Douglas had their stranglehold over the lesser families."

"Perhaps," Jamie replied. He too was making good use of his napkin. Which surprised her, for her half-brother had always been just as inclined to use his clothes. "But if we want to keep the Douglases in check, then we must be strong and vigilant. That, Sir John, is why you need armed retainers."

"It's a matter I've already given some thought," John said. "If a man's to succeed, then his best course is to seek the support of a stronger, more powerful lord. In these parts, it would have to be the Montgomeries. Or the Cunninghames. Or failing either of them, the Stewarts." He grimaced. "I'd rather face a traitor's death than grovel to the Stewarts."

"What about Lord Hugh?" Margaret asked. "I thought he was your friend."

"Hugh's an acquaintance, nothing more. I'd be much more comfortable if I could protect myself without his help."

"An independent household in the Westland," Jamie said. "Answerable neither to the Montgomeries, or the Cunninghames."

"Determined to uphold the peace, instead of perpetuating old feuds," John added. "That's what I hope to achieve, if God permits."

"Amen to that," Jamie said.

The Gryphon at Bay

Margaret sighed as Katherine snatched the last scrap of meat from their trencher. "We could have some more lamb," she suggested. "John, I don't suppose-"

"Certainly."

He passed her the platter and she smiled.

Six months ago, she would never have thought she could be content with a man like John. She'd wanted to marry a knight renowned for his prowess in battle, a man like Hugh, Lord Montgomerie.

She laid a hand upon her belly, pleasantly satisfied. These days she often thanked God for her good fortune. Over the last few months, she'd come to realise that a circumspect man made a much better husband and a much better father for his children, too.

Chapter 9

Irvine Burgh

Daylight had almost faded, but the shutters remained open in the diminutive hall of the Cunninghames' townhouse; partly to air the place, partly to hold back the darkness. Already the candles had been lit, in this dour and gloomy room where the plaster walls carried the faded remnants of paintings that had first been put there in his grandsire's time.

Craigends wasn't a man for sentimentality. He cast his austere surroundings a baleful look and heaved himself into his chair without a second glance. "Worth it?" he asked, of no-one in particular. "Of course it was worth it." He grasped the mug of ale and gulped some down. "I'd have paid Tom Spark of Bartonholm twice that sum if he'd asked it."

"The look on Lord Hugh's face was priceless," Cuthbert said.

"Better than bear-baiting," Craigends agreed.

"Least there's room to work now the board's been cleared." Rob lifted two leather bags onto the table. Money spilled out: pennies mostly, but with a few groats and half-groats amongst them. "At this rate, we'll soon recoup our expenses."

"Ah, but don't forget," Craigends said. "Making money's not our prime motive."

Rob smiled at that. He settled on the bench, Guido alongside. "Now," he said. "Let's see what we've got." He sifted through the coins. "Look for the groats, Guido. That would help me greatly."

Cuthbert slumped down next to his father. Rattling his fingers against the timber, he sighed loudly.

Rob flashed his son an irritated look.

Craigends fought the urge to smile. At that tender age, he'd have found confinement equally frustrating. "Ah," he said, lifting a hand to his ear. "What beautiful silence."

"We could burn the mill." Cuthbert sat up, suddenly alert. "That'd put an even bigger dint in his coffers."

"Don't be daft, boy," Rob muttered.

"You shouldn't be so hard on the lad," Craigends said. "It's good to see there's fire in his belly."

Rob didn't reply. His attention was back on the coins; he stacked the pennies into little piles, neat and precise.

Cuthbert watched him a few moments longer, then wandered to the window and sat down there, scuffing his heel idly against the floor. "The night's still young. And we're cooped up like this..."

"Cuthbert, I've every faith in you-" Rob began.

"-What's there to fear? Lord Hugh's men are all garrisoned..."

"Perhaps..."

The Gryphon at Bay

"I'll go to the nearest tavern. I'll drink some ale, play a few games of dice. There's no harm in that, surely." Cuthbert scowled at his feet. "If I'm caged here all night, I'll go mad."

"You could try helping me," Rob suggested.

"There's more to life than counting money," Cuthbert retorted.

Rob stared at his son, thoughtful, apprehensive.

"Loosen his leash, Rob." Craigends caught Cuthbert's eye, the youth gazed at him, hopeful. "There's one of our men on every corner. The lad'll be quite safe. And Andy will go with him, won't you?"

Young Andrew had been playing a card game at the far end of the board. Keeping out of trouble, as was his wont. He looked up and smiled. "Of course, Father."

"Just make sure you keep away from the Seagate," Rob warned.

"I'm not a fool," Cuthbert retorted. "Besides... I carry a sword. And I can use it."

"That's just what Lord Boyd said," Rob replied. "Look what happened to him."

Seagate Castle, Irvine

Hugh knelt before the *prie-dieu*, rosary gripped tight in his hand. He flicked furiously through the beads, murmuring words of devotion to God and the Virgin, over and over again.

He'd retreated to his chamber after dinner, staying there throughout the rest of the day. The sun had gone down long before: outside his walls, the bustling of the town was fading for another night.

Despite all his efforts, an image still haunted him, seared into his thoughts with fearful clarity. A pleasing picture, of Sir William Cunninghame of Craigends, Robert Lord Kilmaurs and Cuthbert, Master of Kilmaurs. All hanging neatly by their necks from the gateway at the Kirkgate.

And all quite dead.

It was idle fancy, nothing more. *More's the pity*, he reflected, bitterly, then checked himself, for the Church was quite clear in its teachings. They said the line between thought and action was blurred, that to even entertain thoughts of murder was just a small step from carrying out the deed itself.

If that was the case, then Hugh was guilty of committing the most dreadful sins on a daily basis.

It wasn't as if he didn't acknowledge his frailties. He'd spent a small fortune on pardons and indulgences through the years. And he'd tried very hard to curb his blazing temper. His confessor had once suggested– very politely – that an over-abundance of fiery humours might be to blame. That if the Lord Montgomerie was bled once in a while, then perhaps his temperament would cool.

But Hugh wasn't prepared to let a single drop of blood escape his veins voluntarily. Not when far too many men out there were lining up to shed it for him.

* * *

Eventually he abandoned his devotions and retreated to his chair. Where he sank down with a sigh, a cup of wine held loose in his hand.

The silence was oppressive.

Louise Turner

At times like this, the past returned to haunt him. Six years it had been. Six years, since the young Lord Boyd had died at his hands. Just fifteen years of age, a youth who should have grown to manhood, taken a wife and raised an heir.

He should never have come back...

Boyd's father had been exiled for treason years before by James the Third. But after his death, the boy returned to Scotland. It was rumoured he'd meant to start a rebellion, though perhaps he'd merely hoped to restore his family's fortunes. But he wasn't welcome. Far from it. King and counsellors considered him at least an embarrassment, at most a vile threat.

Boyd's dangerous, Montgrennan had said. *He's in league with Albany. We must remove him, if our King's to remain secure upon his throne.* He'd gazed at Hugh in that unsettling way of his: eyes bright startling blue, teeth pale and perfect. *You want to be granted the Bailie's office? Then why not prove you could exercise his duties? Bring us Boyd, so he may account for his presence here. His Kilmarnock lands are still forfeit: if you serve us well, we may be able to grant them to you.*

Montgrennan had paused and smiled. A dazzling smile, brilliant, plausible. *But bear in mind, Hugh, that it would serve us greatly if Boyd never reaches Edinburgh alive...*

Hugh had been younger then, more naive. When he set out in pursuit of Boyd, he'd meant to capture the boy, to bring him back to Edinburgh for trial. That way others' hands would be stained with the young man's blood.

But Boyd wouldn't yield. He'd swaggered up, sword raised. *I'm not afraid of you, Montgomerie. Let's settle our differences, man to man.*

Perhaps it was Boyd's reckless determination that goaded him. Perhaps it was something else. Hugh couldn't remember now. What he did recall, all too clearly, was the look of blank surprise and horror on the youth's face, when Hugh's sword sliced through his vitals...

Screwing his eyes shut, Hugh rubbed his forehead. The headache was still there. There was no escaping it. He took another gulp of wine, reminded himself that tomorrow, all this madness would be over. He'd return to Eglintoun, where Helen would be waiting...

He smiled, conjuring her face, her voice, in his thoughts. But his concentration was broken. By a strident voice, shouting loud outside his window.

His eyes opened, he was instantly alert.

It was long past curfew. In theory, all drunken revellers should have been bundled off to their beds long ago. The Cunninghames, obviously, were being lax in their duties.

He could barely make out any words through the thick castle walls. He paid no heed and was about to retire when a stone rattled against the shutters. It was quickly followed by another. And another.

Hugh made straight for the window, but didn't open it. He knew better than to present a clear target to the enemy. Putting his ear to the wood, he listened carefully.

"You're a knave, Montgomerie! A lying, treacherous dog. I swear, in Holy Mary's name, that I'll kill you."

Taking a sharp hissing breath, Hugh paused briefly to grasp his gown and retrieve his sword belt, then headed for the door.

The Gryphon at Bay

Across the yard, the gates banged loudly and quivered.

"I'll have your head, you murderous rogue!" a youth called out from beyond.

Hugh's pace quickened, he climbed quickly up onto the wall-walk. Two of his men were on watch there: one he knew very well indeed, a battered old veteran who'd served the family twenty years or more. The other was a fresh-faced lad who smiled uncertainly as Hugh approached.

The older man had a crossbow at his shoulder and was poised ready to shoot. "My lord," he acknowledged. "We were about to summon you."

There was another loud thud at the gate.

Hugh peered over the parapet, down into the gloomy street beyond. Two boys loitered there, one prowling in the shadows, the other less bashful. He hurled himself at the gate, kicking it, beating it with his fists. "Fiend!" he yelled. "Assassin!"

"Well, well," Hugh said. "Young Master Cuthbert's come wassailing."

"Had too much wine, I expect," his retainer commented.

Hugh gripped his shoulder briefly. "It's alright, James," he said. "I'll deal with them."

The other youth ventured out of the shadows at last. It was Andrew Cunninghame, Craigends' boy. Casting Hugh a fearful look, he hurried to his kinsman's side. "Come on!" he urged, trying to haul Cuthbert back. "We must go."

"No!" Cuthbert shook him loose. "This is my town. I'll wander where I like. If I want to piss at Lord Hugh's gate, then who's going to stop me?"

"Pissing at my gate will achieve nothing," Hugh spoke out. "But if that's how you want to be remembered by your grandchildren, then by all means do so."

Cuthbert glanced up, scowling.

"Master Cuthbert." Hugh's tone was cordial. "To what do I owe this pleasure?"

"You murdered my grandsire." Cuthbert pointed an accusing finger towards him. "I want to challenge you. To a judicial duel. A *outrance*."

Hugh leaned against the parapet, arms folded. "Really?"

"I want to avenge the death of the Earl of Glencairn."

Andrew moved in to steady his cousin. "I'm sorry, Lord Hugh," he said. "We were in the tavern."

"Methinks you've failed in your duties, Master Cunninghame," Hugh said. "Aren't you supposed to protect your kinsman? Instead, you've brought him to the lion's den."

"We'll be gone now, my lord." Andrew's voice shook. "Come *on*, Cuthbert."

"I want justice. I'll have it, by God!" Shaking him loose, Cuthbert drew his sword. "Come and face me, you coward!"

"You heard him," Hugh said. "The boy wants justice." He beckoned to the men below. "Open the gates."

Venturing out into the street, Hugh halted at a careful distance. "I'm here, as you requested. State your grievances."

Cuthbert roared and lunged at him, sword raised.

Hugh side-stepped, watched impassive as Cuthbert lurched past and slammed, gasping, into the unyielding bulk of the castle walls. He breathed deep, calm. It had been a frustrating day. Now, at its end, he was in command of the situation.

He watched Cuthbert carefully, using every movement, every gesture to assess his foe's prowess. At the same time, he kept an eye on the Master of Craigends, wary in case he suddenly had to fight on two fronts.

Cuthbert propped himself up against the stonework, steadying himself. His face was flushed, he seemed dazed, unfocused.

Hugh stalked back and forth. He tossed his gown to the ground and drew his sword. "Come on, he said. "I haven't got all night."

The boy's eyes followed him. Then suddenly he stirred, sword sweeping a wide arc before him. "I'm not afraid of you, Montgomerie."

"I know that." Hugh neatly evaded the blow.

"I'm more than a match-"

This time, the words died in his throat as Hugh engaged him, deflecting the blows, pushing so close the cross-guards locked and grated.

Cuthbert pushed back, grunting with the effort. Hugh smiled grimly: it was all about poise, control...

Twisting his sword free, Hugh stepped back.

Cuthbert stumbled, and swore loudly.

Hugh rested his sword point-down and leaned lightly on the hilt. "My heir puts up a better fight," he said. "He's only seven."

There was laughter above. Hugh glanced up: half-a-dozen Montgomerie retainers were on the wall-walk, watching.

Cuthbert saw them, too. His face burned bright with rage, he uttered a howl of fury, then charged.

Hugh swept up his sword, countering Cuthbert's attack with ease. Had it been any other man, in any other circumstances, he'd have been less forgiving. But Cuthbert's moves were clumsy, stilted.

The pressure on his sword wavered. At that moment, Hugh flicked his blade aside and stepped back.

Cuthbert's sword clattered to the ground. Thrown off-balance, the youth teetered.

Hugh moved in close. Heaving his shoulder under the boy's oxter, he entwined his leg round his opponent's and pulled it out from under him.

Cuthbert fell onto his back, winded. He moaned softly and struggled to rise, but couldn't: Hugh was pressing a foot against his chest, holding him down.

Lowering his sword, Hugh rested the tip against the young man's throat. "Don't pick fights with your betters."

Cuthbert gulped for breath. "You're going to slay me, aren't you?"

Andrew Cunninghame wailed and drew his blade.

"Keep back!" Hugh glared at him. "Or I *will* kill him." He gazed down on Cuthbert: though the youth's dark eyes were wide with panic, he still managed to maintain his composure, his dignity. "Boyd fought like a man," Hugh told him. "And he died like a man." He stepped back and sheathed his sword. "I don't slaughter boys. Get a few more years beneath your belt, and perhaps we'll meet again to settle this business. Until then-" Leaning over, he hauled Cuthbert to his knees, "-keep nursing at your mother's breast. Listen to her wisdom, and perhaps you'll live to see manhood. Now come on, whelp. Let's get you back to your den."

The Gryphon at Bay

There was a fearful pounding at the door. Craigends had been dozing; he awoke with a start. "What in God's name-"

"Hush." Rob stared at the door, watchful, wary. He'd been playing chess with young Guido, but now he rose to his feet and reached for his sword belt.

Men spoke in raised voices downstairs. Craigends shook his head, wondering if he'd been mistaken. He could've sworn he'd heard Montgomerie...

Footsteps thudded up the stairs.

The door flew open, and there was Lord Hugh. His turnout wasn't quite as impeccable as it had been earlier in the day: he'd shed his gown and his doublet was askew. His face was slightly flushed and he had a gleam in his eye, the look of a man heady from the fight. In one hand he held an unsheathed knife; the other hauled Cuthbert by the gown as if he were an unruly pup being dragged by the scruff.

Andy followed, slump-shouldered and sheepish.

Craigends stood, speechless with horror.

Montgomerie scowled back. "What the Devil's wrong with you?" he demanded. "Did you think I'd bring you back a corpse?" He pushed Cuthbert towards Rob. "He came prowling round my place, singing carols at my door. He begged me to slay him, but I explained to him that it was neither the time, nor the place."

No-one spoke.

Slipping his dagger back in its scabbard, Montgomerie nodded to them. "Goodnight, gentlemen. I brought you this gift in good faith. I trust you'll do the honourable thing and grant me safe conduct to the Seagate?"

He turned and hurried out.

Rob sighed, and strode to the window. Thrusting open the shutter, he called into the street, "Grant the Lord Montgomerie safe passage!"

Cuthbert leaned his elbows on the board, glowering. His face was scuffed down one cheek, his clothes askew. Apart from that, he was unharmed. "He mocked me. Talked down to me as if I was a child."

Craigends poured Cuthbert some ale, then refilled his own cup. He retreated to his chair and settled there. "Be thankful he was so patient with you. If you'd tried this nonsense five years ago, he'd have cut off your head and lobbed it through the window."

"You were told to steer clear of the Seagate," Rob snapped. "The day you learn to take advice is the day we all sleep soundly in our beds."

"Hauled me through the streets he did," Cuthbert muttered. "Laid his stinking hands on me..."

Rob raised his brows. "If that's the worst sin he commits against you, then you're damned lucky."

Cuthbert's scowl deepened. "Why didn't you slay him when he came barging in here?"

"Because he had the grace and decency to escort you home."

"Does one flash of goodness make up for a decade of evil deeds?"

"That's enough!" Rob countered. "Bite your tongue and learn to curb your anger. Work hard to improve your swordsmanship. And for Heaven's sake don't take him on unless you're in full command of your senses. Then maybe, God willing, the day will dawn when he finds himself on his knees pleading for your mercy."

Cuthbert brightened. "Now that's a pleasing thought."

"Isn't it just?" Craigends stretched out his legs, and took a deep, consoling draught of ale.

It had been a strange sort of day. He was thankful it was almost over.

*   *   *

They watched from every wynd and corner. Armed Cunninghame retainers, leaning on spears or sharpening swords against the quoins...

Feigning nonchalance, Hugh gripped his sword-hilt and kept his eyes forward. The assembled Cunninghames scowled as if he were the Devil incarnate, but let him pass unmolested.

Rob Cunninghame had kept his word: he was a decent man, even if his kin were rogues.

Hooves echoed through the streets ahead and Hugh lengthened his stride, suddenly reassured.

A whole host of Montgomeries approached. They rode three abreast down Main Street, a deliberate display of strength. At the fore rode Hugh's cousin, John Montgomerie of Hessilhead, clutching the reins of Hugh's grey warhorse.

"Don't look so worried." Hugh grasped the reins and sprang into the saddle. "There's still some honour left in this world."

Hessilhead shook his head. "I find that hard to believe." He spat on the ground. "You should've felled the boy."

"Nonsense."

"It'll come back to haunt you."

"Perhaps." They'd reached the market square; Hugh raised his hand, and his men halted. "Follow me," he called, turning his horse around. "Our work's done for the night." His retainers parted to let him pass and he threaded his way through, taking his place in the van with Hessilhead at his side.

As he headed back for the Seagate, Hugh felt a certain warmth and satisfaction inside. For once, he'd curbed his base instincts and acted with dignity and restraint. And under trying circumstances, too.

The Blessed Virgin would be proud of him.

Chapter 10

The Place of Ellestoun

Outside the tower-house, Margaret and her girls stood lined up by the door like young birds on a branch, bright-eyed and chattering.

John hurried past them, heading to where old Henry the groom was waiting outside the stables.

Half a dozen horses loitered there, ready for inspection. They were small, lightweight animals, quite unlike the heavy sumpters and the coursers that he was more familiar with.

But a horse was a horse regardless. What he sought was an animal of sound limb and amicable temperament – whether he'd find it here was, however, a different matter.

"I've brought some very pretty horses, Sir John." The horse-trader peered out at John from beneath a grubby blue hood. "To go with some very pretty ladies." He leered in the girls' direction.

John frowned, annoyed on their behalf. "It could be the prettiest horse in the world," he retorted. "If it's lame, it's no good to anyone."

The other man threw back his head and laughed, exposing broken, discoloured teeth. "You're a hard man to please. But I'm sure we'll find you something."

John didn't reply. Hooking his fingers in his belt, he waited while the first horse was trotted past. He watched carefully, noting how it stumbled slightly when it was turned around.

Henry hissed under his breath.

"I saw it," John muttered.

When the horse was brought up close, John crouched alongside, tucking the folds of his gown over his arm to keep the hem from trailing in the dirt. He ran his hand lightly down the beast's legs, feeling bumps and scars beneath the coarse black hair.

He shook his head.

The next one trotted sound. But its back sagged with age. When he opened its mouth, he saw the worn stumps of its teeth. "Too old," he said.

The horse-trader shrugged, visibly disappointed.

Margaret and the maids watched enrapt as all this business unfolded. He tried to ignore them, to shrug aside their collective scrutiny.

Though they'd lived under his roof five months now, they were as unfamiliar as they'd ever been. He'd learned long ago that Katherine – tall, willow-thin and flat-breasted – was Margaret's loyal commander, while Mariota and Alison were mere followers. Alison, at fourteen years, was the youngest: plump, giggly and a little ungainly. While Mariota was a shadow of a girl, quiet and subservient.

John reached out to stroke the horse's neck. Its head moved, quick as a serpent, teeth snapping shut about his sleeve. He swore and slapped its nose. "Back, you devil!" He turned to Henry, grimacing. "Absolutely not."

"Are you alright?" Margaret called.

Irritated by her concern, he tugged his gown higher, feigning indifference.

Just one more horse remained. A lean, honey-coloured mare. It was quite amenable to his touch, even-tempered, with bright, curious eyes.

Satisfied, John took the reins and a handful of mane, then leapt up onto the mare's back. He took the creature out beyond the walls, checking its paces. It seemed obedient enough: it moved off when asked, and was just as easy to stop, with a pleasant ambling gait.

Margaret watched from the wall-walk: on his return, she joined him in the yard.

"Henry seems happy enough," John said, dismounting. "What do you think?"

"She's a very pretty colour," Margaret said. She smiled at the horse-trader. "What's her name?"

"Eh?" The horse-trader looked blankly at John.

"That's up to you," John told her. "I'll take the beast," he said. "Providing the price is acceptable."

"She's very sweet-tempered. You don't often get a horse like that..."

"How much?"

"For you, Sir John, twenty-six silver pennies-"

"I could buy a perfectly good courser for that."

"But the lady's taken with her," the horse-trader persisted. "Twenty, then."

"Eighteen."

The little man winced. "You drive a hard bargain, Sir John." He spat in his palm and extended his hand. "Done."

       *   *   *

The Place of Eglintoun

"A pox upon Tom Spark of Bartonholm." Hugh slumped in his chair, scowling. He pulled off one boot and tossed it carelessly aside. The other was soon sent sliding across the floor after it.

"Whatever has he done to provoke such malice?" Helen picked up the boots and set them neatly down by the kist at the far wall.

Hugh's staghounds settled serenely at his feet, oblivious to his ill-temper. Their tails swept gaps in the sweet rushes strewn across the floor, revealing the wooden floorboards beneath.

"He sold the Constable's title to Craigends..." Hugh's scowl deepened. "And Craigends, of course, is enjoying his new powers to the full. He made a mockery of me."

Helen poured a measure of wine, saying nothing.

"He made a mockery of the King's justice, too." Hugh shook his head. "I grew to like Tom Spark over the years. He was steady, and reliable. I can see now, though, that the man's as twisted as the rest. The viper! Saying one thing to my face and plotting behind my back-"

Perching upon the arm of the chair beside him, Helen pressed the goblet into his hand.

"-I should pay Tom Spark a visit." Hugh scarcely even paused to draw breath. "Slay his kye and burn his barns, then see what he has to say..."

"And what, pray, will that achieve?"

58

He looked at her, blinking. "Nothing, I suppose."

She smoothed the fur-trimmed collar of his gown with her fingers. "Then why do you even entertain the idea?"

He laughed. "Oh, Helen. Without you, the world would be a fearful place..." The scowl returned. "I should have foreseen this. I should have approached him first. Before those wretched Cunninghames outflanked me. I could have doubled any offer they made-"

"Perhaps their offer was not negotiable." She pushed the folds of his gown aside, seeking out the laces that fastened his doublet.

Hugh was oblivious. "-Wretched vermin. And Cuthbert. That whining runt of a boy... God, the world would breathe a sigh of relief if someone dealt with him, once and for all."

"I hope you won't take it on yourself to perform that service. If he's that skilled at upsetting his fellow men, then I daresay someone else will carry out the task before long." Undeterred by his indifference, she slipped her arm around his neck. Leaning close, she kissed his cheek. "Rest easy, my love," she whispered, "and forget your troubles for a while. You're home now. With me. Let's enjoy our time together, while we can." She slid into his lap and settled comfortably there.

He didn't resist as she worked her hand down behind her hips, exploring his loins with a practised touch. He was interested already, all thoughts of the Cunninghames forgotten.

"I see you're better now," he said.

"I took to my horse this afternoon and rode out with the children. But there's one thing lacking in my life. It's been three months or more since you last shared my bed. I'm cold at night. And so very lonely..."

He squeezed her tight and kissed her lips. "Then you'll be neither cold nor lonely tonight. Nor for the foreseeable future, if I can possibly help it."

Dumbarton Castle

Deep in the shadowy gloom of the stables, half-a-dozen horses stirred and whickered hopefully as Matthew and Alex Stewart approached. Matthew paused alongside a tall black gelding: breaking a piece of bread, he rested the crust in his palm. "There now," he said. "It's not much, I know. But every little helps."

The horse gobbled it, eagerly.

"Poor Ajax," Matthew said softly. "He hates confinement as much as any of us." He ran his hand down the jet-black neck, feeling the crest beneath his fingers.

Ajax was wasting away. The gelding's muscles felt soft, weak: ribs and backbone jutted out beneath a once-silken coat, the harsh groove of a poverty line ran down its hindquarters. Its elbows and knees were scarred from lying against bare stone, the timber struts of the manger scored with toothmarks. Bored and hungry, Ajax was tearing its prison apart.

"When do you think Father will return?" Alex asked.

"I'm beginning to think we shouldn't be so reliant on him."

"What do you mean?"

"Harvest's fast approaching. The encampment round the town is shrinking."

"They're leaving?"

"The Northmen would throw themselves before the enemy if their chieftains demanded it, but even they accept that their wives and children must have food to keep them through the winter. Slowly but surely, they'll slip away like ghosts in the night..."

"And then what?"

"The King will summon more men to replace them. Before that host can muster, we must act. We must ensure that the King's task is made as hard as possible, with winter approaching..."

Alex frowned. "The town..."

"The lords won't want to wallow in the mud," Matthew agreed. "They'll want pleasant, comfortable lodgings for themselves and their men. We must deny them their comforts..."

A smile crept across the youth's face. "It's a bold plan, Mattie."

"It's unfortunate that Elizabeth remains here. I don't want her caught up in the melee."

"Someone should warn her..." Alex broke off, frowning. "They'd let me through, surely? I could say I'm the stable boy, that we urgently need the advice of the midwife for one of the womenfolk..."

"Just so long as you're cautious. And don't bring attention to yourself."

Alex grinned. "To serve as a spy... That would be a worthy quest."

"Elizabeth will have news to share, I'm sure. About the strength of the host, and whether the bombards have arrived yet." Grasping his brother's shoulders, Matthew shook him, gently. "But for God's sake, don't tell Mother. She'd flay us both."

"By God's truth, my lips are sealed." He looked at Matthew, eyes shining. "There's just one condition."

"And what's that, pray?"

"When you ride on the town, I want to ride with you."

Matthew slipped an arm about his brother's shoulders and hugged him tight. "This is a man's quest that you're embarking upon, Alex. When you return, you'll be a man in all our eyes. Of course you'll ride with me."

Alex nodded, satisfied. He paused a while, reaching out to stroke Ajax's solid flank. "Mattie," he whispered. "Will King James hang us?"

"Don't talk of such things." Matthew stared deep into the horse's dark eye, comforted by its trust, its honesty. "Of course he won't."

Chapter 11

The Place of Ellestoun

"Hurry up!" Margaret paused at the foot of the spiral stair. "Let's not keep him waiting!" She lingered impatiently while the girls caught up, then stepped out into the yard.

The mare was harnessed and ready, John holding its reins loosely in one hand. Her husband looked so tall and elegant, she thought, with his black bonnet perched upon his head and his gown draped about his shoulders.

Katherine curtsied, blushing. "We're sorry about our attire, Sir John. Lady Margaret said we shouldn't ruin our good gowns."

"I hadn't noticed anything amiss." He had that distant look again. "Are we all ready?"

"Oh, yes," came the chorus.

"Then we'll head out to the orchard, and find some level ground."

He led the way, while they all scurried to keep up, hiding their apprehension behind a mask of excitement.

Once they reached the grassy swathes beyond the gardens, he stopped. "Who's first?"

Mariota and Alison blushed and whispered, while Katherine looked uncomfortable.

Determined to lead by example, Margaret stepped forward. The mare seemed immeasurably high, she couldn't even see over its withers. "How do I get up?"

"I'll help you," John said. "But I need someone to hold her."

"Katherine," Margaret said.

Katherine blanched. "Will she bite?"

"No," said John. "But I might, if you let her move off." Passing the reins to Katherine, he stepped close and grasped Margaret firmly about the thighs, hoisting her up into the saddle.

Margaret gasped, taken aback. He'd caught her skirts, exposing more flesh than she'd liked. But at last she was perched on the horse's back, clinging tight to the mane as she gathered her wits.

"Sit tall," John said, setting her foot carefully in place upon the footrest. "As if you're the Empress of the World."

*   *   *

The Place of Kilmaurs

The door of the laird's chamber loomed ahead, dark and solid. Undeterred, Christian lifted the latch and strode inside.

Rob sat at the table, rental rolls and counting board before him. "God, I'm weary of this business." He sighed and rubbed his eyes, blinking. "Rebuilding Kerrielaw's already cost twice as much as I'd anticipated." Leaning back in his chair, he slapped his hand against the board. "Montgomerie's sent three gangs of masons fleeing: the latest ones want a dozen men for protection and twenty shillings paid in advance."

"Where's Cuthbert?" Christian demanded.

"He's a man now. You mustn't coddle him." He moved a few jettons across the counting board and winced.

"But to let him travel abroad without a father's guidance. Don't you care if something happens to him?"

"Oh, Chrissie..." Casting one last despairing look towards the rolls, Rob pushed back his chair and hurried to her side. He took her hands and held them, gently. "He's travelling to Kilmarnock. With Andrew and Guido."

"Guido! But Guido's still a child."

"He's almost fifteen. It's time he left his mother's care." He smiled that faintly pitying smile of his. "They'll play dice, get drunk and brawl. The way boys have since time immemorial. They've kinsmen there. They'll be looked after."

She leaned against him, unable to speak, filled with sudden inexplicable dread.

"Oh, my love," he said. "What's wrong?"

"I fear for him. He's so bold, and reckless. I have dreams, Rob. Dreams that he's slain. Dreams that *you're* slain. It seems so real. I wake up, weeping, with those hateful scenes fresh in my mind, and I wonder if it's all a portent..."

"I'm so sorry." He cradled her face in his hands. "You're too sweet, too trusting for these lands. I should never have brought you here..."

"I just wish Fortune could treat us kindly..."

"You mustn't worry," he said. "The boys promised they wouldn't stray far. But with the weather so fair, who can blame them for wandering? It's the way of young men, that they want to test their mettle. I was the same, when I was their age."

"Did a monster stalk the land? When you were a boy?"

"They aren't fools, Chrissie. They'll keep well within the bounds."

She opened her mouth to speak, but no words came. She glanced aside, unwilling for him to witness her fear.

"What's wrong, Chrissie?" he asked, softly.

She couldn't reply. *I don't trust him. Not any more. He lies to me. I know he lies to me. My own son...*

The Place of Eglintoun

"So where is he?" Hessilhead strode into Hugh's chamber with all the blustering swagger of its rightful owner. Tossing his cloak aside, he heaved himself down into a vacant chair: James and Robert Montgomerie followed, sitting down together at the foot of the bed.

Helen paused to retrieve Hessilhead's cloak. "He won't be much longer. The Master of Montgomerie doesn't want to be wearied with logic and rhetoric. He's running circles round his tutor and Hugh decided to intervene."

Hessilhead chuckled. "A boy after my own heart." He leaned back in his seat. "You're looking well, Helen. But I hear you dropped a daughter this time."

The Gryphon at Bay

She folded the cloak and laid it down upon the bed, then poured a measure of claret from a flagon on one of the kists. "Hugh has no complaints." She handed him a goblet.

"Here's to the latest member of the brood." Hessilhead lifted it with a flourish. "Hugh's a fine judge of breeding stock. Whether it's horses or women."

Helen smiled, slightly. Satisfied that Hugh's guests were comfortable, she sat down by the window.

Before long, Hugh joined them. "Good morning!" He swept over to his chair, dogs in close attendance. "I won't bore you with particulars. You know why you're here."

"We're right glad to see you," Hessilhead grumbled. "It makes a refreshing change..."

"Last year was an exception," Hugh retorted. "This harvest's a different matter. We're all here, with significant forces at our disposal."

There were satisfied mutterings from his kinsmen.

"I'll plan our strategy in advance," Hugh continued. "Bear in mind, though, that last year Kilmaurs' men-" He paused, catching each eye in turn, "-or what was left of them after the rout at Stirling-" He had to wait while the chuckles subsided, "-were scattered across the realm. Now, unfortunately, they're organised. Robert?"

Robert Montgomerie shrugged. "I don't anticipate any problems."

"You should keep a close watch on Hessilhead and Giffen," Hessilhead cut in. "They suffered endlessly last autumn. Ardrossan, too."

"And there were some minor instances of thieving on the bounds of Eglintoun and around Stanecastle," Hugh agreed. "This year, we'll make sure there's a strong presence. We'll ride the bounds on a regular basis, and nip any unrest in the bud."

"What about Skelmorlie?" James Montgomerie asked.

"With my visits to Glengarnock still fresh in men's minds they'll be reluctant to take up arms. Sir Humphry Cuninghame's too old to be much of a threat. All he wants now is to die peacefully in his bed. But I agree: we shouldn't be complacent."

"It's your presence that makes most of an impression," Hessilhead reminded him.

"I know. So once I'm content that I've done what's required here, I'll take a small force and ride north to Skelmorlie. That way, my tenants there won't feel unduly neglected."

The Place of Ellestoun

Katherine wriggled out of her gown. "I stink of that horse."

"Put your dirty clothes in the basket." Margaret sat up on her bed, savouring the scent of her newly-scrubbed skin. With the air so warm, she was content to sit in just her kirtle. "There's no need to send everything to the laundry-women just yet. Best we keep these aside and use them again."

Katherine cast Alison a sly glance. "He didn't offer me a ribbon for my hair."

Alison blushed. "Don't tease me."

"You weren't scared at all," Margaret added. "You just wanted him to help you down." She grasped a comb and tugged it through her damp dark brown hair, one vigorous stroke after another. "Was it a pleasure? To bury your face against his manly chest?"

"I- I don't know," Alison's face turned a brighter shade of crimson.

"When he picked me up, I thought my heart would burst," Mariota said.

Margaret smiled. "Consider it just punishment for all those times you've mocked me."

"Alison will dream of him tonight," Katherine said.

"So will you," Mariota countered. "Don't deny it."

"And I shall have him," Margaret declared, triumphant.

"Or rather, he'll have you," said Mariota. "He has such lovely hands..."

"You never thanked him," Margaret mentioned, then waved her comb towards Katherine. "Once you've dressed, go downstairs and call on him. Tell him I want to speak with him."

Katherine blanched. "But it's late," she argued. "What if he's retired for the night?"

"It's still light outside," Margaret replied. "He'll be reading. Go on. He'll appreciate the visit."

John sat by the window, legs stretched out along the cushioned seat. His Book of Hours rested in his lap, but his thoughts were straying beyond his devotions. He gazed out at the the world beyond his walls: the smooth blue waters of the loch and the fields of ripening corn.

Not for the first time, he bowed his head and thanked God for his good fortune.

His hounds were lounging on the floor alongside, basking in the evening sun. When footsteps thudded lightly against the timber floor above and peals of muffled girlish laughter rang out, they sat up, tails wagging.

John reached down and scratched Pompey's chin. "They're just girls," he told the hound. "Young and flighty, full of nonsense. Why, I daresay they're just as fearful of me as I ever was of them-"

He broke off as a knock sounded upon his door. "Sir John?" a girl's voice called.

"Yes, Katherine?"

"My lady was asking for you..."

He stifled a yawn. He was too tired to weather the girls' collective vigour, but the rebuttal had to be delivered tactfully... "Ask her to join me later," he said. "I'm... I'm not dressed." Which was almost true, for he'd already shed gown and doublet for the night.

Katherine's footsteps dwindled.

No sooner had he resumed his reading than the door opened and in they all came, with Margaret at the fore. Like a flock of nymphs or maenads, with their hair flowing loose and their gowns gaping at the back.

Caesar and Pompey ran to greet them, and Margaret leaned over to rub Caesar's ears. "You sent William away for the night," she said, with a hint of reproach. "There's no one to entertain us."

"I'm not much company," he said. "But please make yourselves at home. There's gaming boards in the kist."

The Gryphon at Bay

He remained aloof while the girls seized command of his chamber, ransacking the kist and arguing over the chessboard. It was as if the years had slipped away and he was a boy again, sitting by the window reading while his sisters squabbled amongst themselves.

"You will play tables," Margaret instructed, sternly. "And you'll play it quietly. You'll disturb the master with all this noise."

Alison and Mariota settled on the floor and Pompey went over to inspect the proceedings, lying on the board and disrupting the game. Margaret and Katherine, meanwhile, sat with their needlework, trying hard to look mature and respectable.

"You were very gracious, to give so much of your time," Margaret said.

"Not at all," said John.

"Alison would like to apologise for her foolishness..."

Alison glanced up. "I'm sorry!"

"Perhaps she'd be happier with a smaller horse?" Margaret continued.

"Nonsense," said John. "She just needs practice."

"We all need practice," Margaret said. "I want to be riding out with you before a month's out."

"Then we'll go out tomorrow," said John. "And the day after that. Until you're all confident."

Chapter 12

The Palace of Linlithgow

The Lion Rampant flapped from one of the corner turrets, proof that James and his court were in residence. Reassured, Angus allowed himself a brief smile as he spurred his horse on towards the gatehouse.

The task ahead wasn't an easy one. In the early days of James's reign, he'd been highly favoured. As the young King's tutor, he'd been responsible for ensuring that James received an education befitting his status and guidance on all matters moral and intellectual.

But since those heady days his star had faded. He'd been eclipsed by the Hepburns and Homes who'd insinuated their way into James's inner circle.

Those same Hepburns and Homes who even now would try their best to bar him from the young king's company...

He was spotted, his arrival duly reported to those who mattered. By the time he rode into the busy courtyard, he found the welcoming committee ready and waiting.

Patrick Hepburn, Earl of Bothwell stepped forward and smiled in greeting. "Ah, Angus! What a pleasant surprise." But a smile from Hepburn could never be enough to put a man's mind at ease: he had a proud, cruel face, with piercing eyes and a distant air about him.

Angus masked the thoughts of malice, conjuring instead a reflection of Hepburn's smile. Just to show that he wouldn't be intimidated... "I'd have come sooner," he said. "Alas, I was delayed."

"Did you reach Amiens? And pay your dues to God and the Saints?"

"Unfortunately not," Angus replied, smoothly. "News of some urgency reached me. I was forced to turn back."

Hepburn's expression didn't waver. "You're referring to the March Wardenships. I'm sorry, if you were inconvenienced. But with trouble at home, it was vital we kept a strict hold on the Marches."

At least he'd tried to make an excuse, Angus thought, sourly. "No matter," he said. "I wondered if I might speak with the King." And when Hepburn didn't reply, he added, "He's expecting me, you know. I had strict instructions that I was to report to him on my return." That was a lie, but it wasn't beyond the bounds of possibility.

"Very well," Hepburn replied. "This evening, after vespers. He'll speak with you then."

When the time was deemed appropriate, he was taken to a small reception room, deep in the heart of the palace.

James awaited him there, rising from his chair as Angus entered. He carried the trappings of kingship with ease, and yet... He was still the bright-eyed enthusiastic lad that Angus remembered, grace and poise tempered faintly with the awkwardness of youth.

"Your Grace." Angus dropped to one knee.

"Let's not stand on ceremony, my friend." James helped him to his feet. "It's so very good to see you. You've been sorely missed." He clasped his shoulder. "You'll stay and drink a cup of wine?"

"I'd be delighted."

It was only now, at such close quarters, that Angus could fully appreciate the change in him. James had grown at least another inch over the past few months. He'd filled out, too, around the shoulders and body. A soft growth of beard covered his chin, a boy's beard, perhaps, but James was obviously determined to leave it in place, a reminder to the Patrick Hepburns of this world that he was well on the way to manhood.

"Look at this." James ushered Angus towards a stretch of wall between two tall glazed windows. A pristine tapestry hung in pride of place there: it depicted a unicorn, a dazzling white beast, with the details of mane, tail and beard picked out in silver threads. The creature stood with one foreleg raised, proud and glorious against a forest floor carpeted with flowers. "Isn't it magnificent? I had it sent over from Brugges."

"A fine item," said Angus. "An object of taste and discernment."

"Grace and valour in equal measure. Purity of thought, and strength of purpose..." James turned to Angus. "These are the qualities I would possess as a king, and as a man."

"They're qualities you possess in abundance already," said Angus. He looked James up and down. "You're looking well."

"I am well. Very well..." James broke off. "But how are you?" And how was Amiens?"

"I never reached Amiens."

James's face fell. "Because of the Wardenships? I'm sorry. It wasn't my doing."

"I know that." Angus glanced aside. "I've brought a gift, Your Grace. A pitiful trifle, I fear. But something you might appreciate nonetheless." He clapped his hands and in traipsed a servant, bearing a wooden box, its slatted sides painted with images of stags, hares and hounds.

"This is very gracious of you." James placed the box down on a nearby table. There was a rustling noise inside, a pale muzzle emerged from one of the slats. A smile spread across James's face. "Oh, Angus, what is this?" Opening the lid, he snatched the nearest pup by the scruff and lifted it high. Two more puppies poked cautious heads out of their prison, blinking in the candlelight.

"Two dogs, one bitch," Angus said. "They'll make worthy additions to your pack. Their parents were bred in the Marches, where they've hunted all their lives." He rummaged within the folds of his gown and produced a rolled-up parchment. "I've brought details of their bloodlines."

Clasping the pup close, James grinned in undisguised delight. "They'll have pride of place amongst my hounds. And some day we'll ride with them together." He set the pup back in its box and briefly studied its litter-mates. Then he gently shut the lid, and beckoned to the servants. "Remove them to the kennels, and instruct the huntsmen that they're to be given the best of care." Turning to Angus, he seized his hands. "Are you with us long?"

"For three days, Your Grace. Then, alas, I must be gone."

"You'll hawk with me tomorrow. We can talk then."

The Lands of Auchenharvie

From dawn to dusk, the farmers worked with feverish haste, armed with reaping hooks and bills. The womenfolk followed on behind, tying the cut corn into stooks.

While the poor folk laboured, their lord had duties of his own. For over a week now, Hugh had left Eglintoun at dawn, arrayed in full plate armour, riding at the forefront of an armed band of men.

It was an exhausting task, to make this progress through his lands. But Hugh was determined to nip any trouble firmly in the bud.

Whenever he passed, work stopped. His tenants doffed their bonnets and called out words of encouragement. He crossed their fields with care, skirting their crops and taking great pains not to startle the livestock.

But as soon as he ventured beyond the bounds, his manner changed.

Tightening his reins, Hugh sat deep in the saddle, urging his grey warhorse onwards. The field of bere barley seemed to shimmer in the morning sunlight, a mass of whiskered heads nodding in the light breeze.

When Zephyr strode hock-deep through the growing crop, it was as if the horse was wading through a golden sea, leaving a crumpled mass of torn stalks and crushed grain in its wake.

Zephyr's mighty hooves were merely the first injury. The insult soon followed: a score of mounted men-at-arms riding five abreast, liveried in Hugh's red-and-blue colours.

Only one or two brave men stayed to watch the destruction. They leaned upon their bills, faces grey with despair. For six months or more, they'd sweated and toiled to safeguard this treasure, chasing off pigeons and plucking weeds from every rig.

If Hugh hadn't been personally present, there'd have been insults hurled. Maybe one or two stones, too. But his reputation was enough to stifle all thoughts of resistance.

Hugh spared the luckless peasants no more than a casual glance and gave their troubled circumstances little thought.

All that mattered was that the world was quiet, and the harvest was progressing.

The Palace of Linlithgow

The hawk fluttered and flapped on the falconer's wrist: a female goshawk, with soft barred plumage and a cruel hooked beak. When the hood was pulled off, her brilliant yellow eyes blinked fierce in the sunlight.

"Release her!" James ordered.

And she was gone, dwindling to a speck above the gently rolling hills beyond the loch.

The Gryphon at Bay

A line of boys headed down to the lochside, stout sticks in their hands. They progressed along the shore, beating the reeds and shouting.

Ducks flapped from cover, quacking in alarm. The air was thick with them. Then in their midst a dark shape plummeted down. There was a flurry of feathers, a martyred cry from a stricken duck, then hawk and prey came to rest amongst the reeds.

The falconer moved in to remove the quarry.

James glanced warily about him, checking that all the Homes and Hepburns who formed his council were out of earshot. "How was London?"

"Busy," Angus replied. "And offensive to the nose."

James laughed, softly. "And my noble cousin, King Henry. You passed on my goodwill?"

"Of course."

"He spoke nothing of offering assistance. A few ships, perhaps?"

"He showered Your Grace with compliments and platitudes. But I could detect no real evidence of support."

"Ah..." James clapped his hands, and gestured to the hawking party. "That's very good. Let's move on."

"Your Grace," Angus spoke out.

James cast him a querying glance.

"My kinsman, Earl James," Angus continued. "Rumour has it his health is failing. I'd like to visit him, if I may." He paused. "I hope you'll forgive my presumption. It is but a charitable act, for a man nearing the end of his life who lacks the consolation of his kinsmen."

"A charitable act?" James retorted, half-smiling. "I doubt that, Earl Archibald."

"I understand there may be concerns," Angus continued. "That's why I thought it important to warn you of my intent. My actions may be misconstrued..."

"Your actions will certainly be misconstrued. But Angus..." James dropped his voice to a whisper. "You and I have always been friends. And I hope this friendship will continue. Certain factions amongst my government dislike you. And they've been making moves against you." He sighed, wearily. "I've never had any reason to doubt you," he said. "Visit the Earl. With my blessing. But don't expect me to protect you when others find out your business, and seek to twist it to their own ends."

Chapter 13

The Lands of Kilbirnie, Cunninghame

John led the way as the small cavalcade of riders approached the Place of Kilbirnie. He kept the pace slow for the sake of Margaret and Katherine, for both young women were still far from confident with handling their horses.

They'd kept to the road throughout their journey, respecting those men and women who still plodded through the fields cutting the last of the corn. The frenzy of the past week or so had abated: stooks were drying in the sun, the harvest celebrations already underway in the cottages and fermtouns.

John nodded to a group of curious farmers as he passed: it had been three years or so since he'd last visited Kilbirnie. The Crawfurds' place was just as he remembered it, yard meticulously swept, thatch on the outbuildings fresh and neat.

They'd already heard news of his arrival: Sir Malcolm Crawfurd was waiting outside the tower-house, Lady Marjorie Barclay alongside.

"Hello, John. What a delight it is to see you!" The old laird stepped forward and took John's reins. Though his hair had faded from jet-black to silver, his features seemed unchanging: his face was comfortably worn and pleasant, his beard neatly trimmed. "What brings you out this way?"

"I'm taking Margaret to Largs and Southannan," John explained. "I hope it won't inconvenience you if we stay here tonight? There's five of us in all."

"Of course not," Lady Marjorie replied. "You know you're always welcome here." She nodded to the door of the tower-house. "Marion will be pleased to see you," she said, "She'll join us shortly."

Sure enough, the door was opening, and there was his sister, an elegant figure in wine red gown and gabled hood. She waved in greeting, a broad smile on her face. "John!"

He raised his hand in response, then dismounted, relinquishing his horse into the care of a groom. "Where's Robert?"

"He's out hunting," Malcolm replied. "He should be home by nightfall."

*　　　*　　　*

The Place of Eglintoun

Restive in the cold morning air, the gathered horses tossed their heads and whinnied.

Zephyr stood amongst them: Helen saw the big grey waiting there and headed over to join it. Pausing alongside, she ran her hand down its dappled neck. "Hush now," she said. "He won't keep you much longer." The horse's ears flicked at the sound of her voice, the dark eye watching her intently. Clutching its head close, she lightly kissed its face. "Take good care of him, Zephyr," she whispered. "And speed him home to me..."

The Gryphon at Bay

Hugh strode out from the armoury, surrounded by servants and men-at-arms. He was encased in plate armour, a battered old set crafted in his father's time. The steel was discoloured in places and dented in others, but it served its purpose.

It wasn't often that Helen witnessed him in full array. He seemed remote somehow, unfamiliar. When he moved, his gait seemed clumsy. But he was impressive nonetheless. He towered over his men, a solid mass of steel and flesh, puissant, invulnerable.

Hearing the clatter of armour, Zephyr tensed. Helen stepped back just in time; the grey horse pawed the ground and let out an ear-splitting neigh that resounded through the courtyard.

Hugh raised his hand. "Ho there, Zephyr!" he called. "I can hear you, loud and clear."

His men laughed, relaxed, good-humoured.

Helen patted Zephyr's shoulder one last time, then wandered over to where Hugh was talking with his retainers. She loitered a short distance away, confident that Hugh would seek her out in his own time to say goodbye. She'd grown used to such partings over the years. She had faith in Hugh, and his prowess as a knight. But she still felt a gnawing ache inside as she watched the preparations for his departure.

With his gauntlets already in place, Hugh paused briefly so his manservant could tie the quilted cap beneath his chin. Another servant placed the mail coif upon his head, and then his helmet was secured.

"Let's be off," Hugh said. While his men headed for the horses, he left them so he could walk with her. "I'll ride to Skelmorlie. Expect me back in four days."

She nodded.

He grasped her hands, gently. He smelled strange, his familiar scent masked by vinegar, grease and stale sweat from his arming doublet. "I've left two-dozen men at your disposal. You may use them as required."

"I'll ask the Virgin and the Saints to keep you from harm."

"I'd appreciate that." He glanced towards Zephyr, restless, impatient. His men waited there, talking quietly amongst themselves.

"Keep safe now. And hurry home."

"Goodbye, my love." He leaned close and kissed her lips. "I'll be back before you know it."

The Place of Kilbirnie

The hills crowded close, gloomy and forbidding. Margaret shivered at the sight of them: these lands seemed like a Godforsaken wilderness, where no man could prosper. It comforted her to see the walls of Kilbirnie Place standing solid and strong nearby, a last bastion that kept the wild country at bay.

In the lea of the Crawfurds' place, the apple trees clustered close to the walls as if huddled for protection from the winter winds, their gnarled trunks rising crooked from the mossy grass. The branches were heavy with fruit, leaves rustling in a stiff breeze from the west.

It felt like a lifetime ago that Margaret had last walked with Marion in the orchard at Ellestoun. She remembered it clearly; the buds yet to open, the warmth of summer far away.

With the unpleasant memories of her wedding night still fresh in her thoughts, she'd been hostile towards her new family. And frightened, too, of what the future held for her.

"It's like a bad dream now," she told Marion. "A fearful nightmare, best forgotten."

Marion hitched the basket more comfortably under her arm. "Have you spoken to John about this?"

"He doesn't like to talk about it."

"No, I daresay he doesn't." Her tone was brisk, dismissive.

"You blame him for what happened, don't you?"

"My brother's very dear to me." She paused, flexed her fingers about the edges of the basket, her vexation clear. "But... How could any sister condone their brother for how they behaved that night? It angers me, that you think yourself responsible."

"It was difficult at first," she whispered. "For both of us. I treated him very harshly, Marion. I made it clear that I despised him. As a husband, and as a man."

"His conduct wasn't exactly beyond reproach."

"You were right, though. You told me he was sorry, and that he would try hard to make amends."

Setting down the basket, Marion took Margaret's hands in hers. "It's over," she said, gently. "Don't punish yourself for what can't be changed."

"But when he was wounded, he took a draught and it nearly killed him." The words came pouring out, she couldn't have stopped them. "I asked him later why he did it, and he said it was because I wanted it..." She stifled a sob. "What hurts most is that I don't think he cared whether he lived or died, because I'd made him so unhappy."

Marion slipped a consoling arm about her shoulders. "He didn't die, did he? And if he was moved to do anything so stupid, then you should be reassured, because it must truly mean he loves you."

Margaret gulped loudly, fighting back tears. "I'm so sorry."

"Life's always uncertain when you're carrying a child. All your worries increase a thousandfold. But it'll pass." Marion rummaged in her sleeve for a handkerchief. "Poor John. He was always so confident that he would never succumb to Love's lure. Now he makes Robert's efforts seem quite paltry in comparison." She picked up her basket once more. "I know John suffered greatly last year. We were all very worried about him. But when you arrived yesterday, I knew his trials were over. When he told us his glad tidings, there was such pride and joy in his face. It was glorious to behold."

Margaret smiled at that. It comforted her, to hear Marion say such things. It gave her hope for the future, too, for even now there were times when she looked at John and couldn't fathom what he was thinking. Marion, by contrast, could read her brother's subtle ways with ease. Margaret envied her in that respect, though she supposed it wasn't surprising. Marion had known John twenty years now, while she'd lived with him for just five short months.

The Gryphon at Bay

Plucking an apple from the nearest bough, Marion studied it briefly, then set it in her basket. "So you're heading for Southannan tomorrow? I went there once, when I was very young. It's smaller than Ellestoun. Not very comfortable."

"John says his father never liked the place. That's it's been neglected for ten years or more."

"You're very lucky." Marion reached for another apple. "Sir Malcolm and Lady Marjorie wouldn't dream of letting me travel so far when I'm carrying a child."

"John told me of your troubles. I'm sorry."

"It's God's will," Marion replied. "I hope and pray that some day I can bear them a son. Sir Malcolm was very patient, allowing poor Robert to wait so long for my hand." She patted her belly, absently. "I've been carrying the child four months now. And so far, all's well. But I have such fearful memories of the last time..."

Margaret studied the ground, unsure how to respond.

"Tell me," Marion said. "Is it true that John remains friends with Lord Hugh?"

"Lord Hugh has helped us greatly over the last few months. He's always welcome at our place. Though John is careful not to rely too much upon him." She glanced at Marion, suddenly wary. "Why do you ask?"

Marion shook her head. "I never thought my brother would put his own success before our household's dignity and honour."

"Whatever do you mean?"

"Lord Hugh killed our father."

Margaret drew a sharp breath. Something was stirring in her thoughts, dim recollection of a conversation with Jamie. A long time ago, before she was married.

Since then she'd never given the matter much thought. But hearing it now from Marion's lips seemed shocking. Because it didn't make sense that someone as devoted to justice as John would set aside such an injury lightly.

"I'm surprised John didn't tell you."

"He doesn't talk much of these times."

"Lord Hugh is very charming and pleasant to those he favours. But he's done evil things, and he's hated in these parts. It would be of immense benefit to John if you could wean him away from Lord Hugh and back to those who genuinely have his best interests at heart."

"He's my husband, Marion. I can't tell him what to do."

"There are subtle ways to influence a man."

"But I could never change his nature. John's loyal to Lord Hugh, just as he's loyal to me. And rightly so, for Lord Hugh has been very generous just recently."

"Not because of any finer feelings towards John, you can be sure. Montgomerie's a poisonous man. He burns, he plunders, without a care for the poor folk whose lives he destroys." She turned to Margaret, her pale face flushed with anger. "The Cunninghames are right to defy his jurisdiction. He's a tyrant without a shred of mercy in his soul. And yet the King rewards him for his cruelty..." She shrugged and glanced aside. "If there was any justice in the world, he'd be made to account for his crimes."

"He will eventually," Margaret replied with cheerful confidence. "I'm sure John would argue that until that day dawns, we must all just learn to live with him."

The Place of Kilmaurs

Within the great hall the mood was buoyant. A fire roared in the hearth, warming the heart as well as the flesh. Candles had been lit to cheer the place, their yellow-orange flames flickering in every corner.

"Ah, that was a worthy fight!" Craigends slumped down by the window, goblet of wine in hand. Now the heady rush of battle had worn off, the aches were setting in: nothing serious, just the familiar twinges of muscles and tendons well used. He grinned at Rob. "It's good to get home."

"Aye," Rob agreed. "You're right there." Wiping his nose with the back of his hand, he swore as he saw blood there. "Damn. It's started up again."

Craigends chuckled. "Be more careful next time."

Twenty of their men were there with them, sweating – and in many cases, bleeding – after the fray. One man had a fearsome wound in his shoulder: the Dowager was with him, treating the injury with practised hands. Christian moved amongst the others, her maids in attendance. The women bore flasks of *aqua vita* and fresh linen, while the servants handed out ale and wine.

"Least we didn't have the boys to worry about." Rob dropped his voice to a whisper, keeping a careful eye on Christian to make sure she was out of earshot. "As skirmishes go, it was a little fraught for my liking. I'd prefer my heir to hone his skills on something a little less difficult."

"He must learn some time."

Rob winced. "I know." He sat back, stifling a yawn. "Later in the year, we'll blood him. Once the worst of the fighting's over. It was a fine idea, Will, to send him off to Craigends. Perhaps a young maid'll catch his eye..."

"I think he's got different quarry in mind. He was hoping to visit Sir Humphry at Glengarnock. The hunting's good in the hills round there. And young Andy knows the place like the back of his hand."

"Just so long as they don't try their hand at poaching..."

Craigends laughed. "That all depends whose land they're poaching from-" He broke off as Christian approached.

She saw Rob's bloody nose and frowned.

Rob smiled. "It's nothing."

"Horse tossed its head at the wrong moment," Craigends said. "Caught Rob square in the face."

"A silly accident." Rob reached out his hand. "Give me a cloth, Chrissie, and attend to those who need it more."

She passed him a wad of linen.

"Least that's one of Hessilhead's brutes who won't be riding to war again," Craigends said. "He'll be lucky even to walk."

"What of Lord Hugh?" Christian asked.

"No sign of him." Craigends gulped down another mouthful of ale. "He's been seen round Eglintoun and Stanecastle. And that, I presume, is where he'll be staying."

"So we'll keep harrying Hessilhead, for the time being at least," Rob said. "If that draws him away from home, we'll raid Eglintoun. He can't be everywhere at once."

Christian fixed those haunting dark eyes on them, and said nothing. She paused to wipe a graze on Craigends's forehead, then she was gone.

The Gryphon at Bay

*   *   *

What had become of the world, Christian thought, when she could shrug aside mens' suffering and gaze on torn flesh with such dispassionate eyes? Remaining sternly oblivious to all the curses and moans as she sought to mend wounds and heal hurts.

Like Rob, she could find consolation in the knowledge that they'd fared well. With Rob and Will satisfied by the way events had played out, she, too, was obliged to feel satisfied.

But a little part of her, buried deep inside, didn't count victory by strength of numbers. In the eyes of that secret self she harboured, one man risking death was too many.

And yet this was the world her sons had been born to. The world which Cuthbert was eager to embrace...

The Dowager returned to the hall. She'd had the injured man removed to more comfortable quarters. "I stitched the wound," she said softly. "But the blow struck very deep. If the rot sets in, his fate is sealed. But we'll do what we can."

Christian nodded. "I'll visit his wife tomorrow."

"Tell her that she's welcome at the place," the Dowager said. "And that if the worst should happen, she'll be provided for."

"Has Cuthbert returned?" Christian asked.

"I haven't seen him. Rob'll know where he is. Go and ask him."

But it was an hour before she was free to spend any time with Rob. She found him sitting by the window, legs sprawled before him, arming doublet hanging open and shirt damp with sweat.

"You should wash, and change your clothes," Christian rebuked gently.

"I'll do that, my love. Just as soon as I recover my strength."

"Can I fetch you some food?"

"Some cold mutton," Will said. "And some bread."

"Where's Cuthbert?"

Rob glanced up, sharply.

Will smiled. "Don't fret, Christian. He's gone to Craigends. With Andrew and Guido. They'll be safe enough there."

"But it's beyond the bounds of Cunninghame. He's trespassing!"

"If they run into the Sheriff, Andy will make up a reasonable excuse."

"The Sheriff's a lackey of Lord Hugh's..."

"That's putting it a bit strong," Will retorted.

"The boys are safe there," Rob spoke out, firmly. "They can do what boys do, and come home when they want to. Now please, Chrissie. Fetch us some food, and let's have no more of this nonsense."

Chapter 14

They left Kilbirnie early in the morning, climbing ever upwards until it seemed to Margaret that they'd reached the top of the world. Their horses followed a narrow track that wound its course amongst huge intimidating hills that rose high on either side, scrub-clad and desolate.

On a wet day, it would have seemed brutal and barren. But when the sun shone so brightly and the gowans and thistles still painted colourful swathes amongst the copses of hawthorn and rowan, Margaret could marvel at it and savour every moment.

John rode ahead on his big black horse. His dogs darted like ghosts alongside; every so often they'd bolt from the path and he'd have to call them back. They'd spotted several deer already, but only in the distance, shifting shapes amongst the vegetation.

Margaret stayed close to John, with Katherine alongside. William followed, leading a fully laden sumpter horse. While at the rear came Jamie, keeping a watchful eye on the party.

"Jamie has been very attentive towards you," Margaret remarked to Katherine.

"I hoped you hadn't noticed."

"He's looking for a wife. And now he's in John's service, it would make sense for him to wed you."

"I suppose so..." Katherine's tone was grudging.

Margaret studied her carefully. "Whatever's the matter?"

"I don't know what I'd say, if he asked for my hand. It would be very kind of him, but... I'd like him better if he bathed more."

"He's better than he was."

"That's not saying much."

Margaret fought the urge to smile. She fixed her eyes on John, who sat relaxed upon his horse, hair gleaming deep gold in the sunlight, bonnet sitting in jaunty disarray upon his head. Her heart fluttered at the thought of him, she wished she could be heading back to Ellestoun, to the familiar comfort of his chamber... "I once thought that all that mattered in a husband was that he was a man of power and influence." She paused, then added in a low voice, "These days I'm convinced his most important quality is cleanliness."

Katherine giggled.

"I shall speak discreet words with Jamie, and see if I can make him mend his ways. Perhaps he'll be more inclined to do so if he knows a woman's heart is at stake."

Margaret gripped the mare's mane tightly as it made its cautious way down the hillside. She kept sliding forward in the saddle, the pommel digging deep into her thigh.

The path they followed was steep and rocky: far below, cottages and farms seemed absurdly small. Even the sight of them made her feel dizzy with fear.

The Gryphon at Bay

Ahead, John's horse sat back on its haunches as it negotiated the tricky terrain. Katherine gasped and Margaret looked round, anxious. But her maid still sat safe in the saddle, though her jaw was set firm with terror and her hands, like Margaret's, were entwined within the mane.

When the ground at last levelled out ahead, John halted. He leaned on his pommel, watching as they completed the descent. "You should sit back more," he advised. "And keep a tighter hold of your reins. Your poor horse will stumble if you're not careful."

"Must you be so critical?" Margaret asked. "That was terrifying..."

He shrugged and turned away. "It would've been even more terrifying if you'd fallen."

With the difficult part of their journey completed, Margaret could look around her. A tall tower-house stood a half-mile distant. And staring past John, she could see the sea.

She'd only ever set eyes on it once before, when she'd first travelled to Ellestoun as John's wife. She'd been desperately unhappy then, and the ocean that day had reflected her mood, grey and restless. Now it shone like glass, a sparkling sheet that stretched out into the distance.

"Is that your place?" Katherine asked John, gesturing towards the distant tower-house.

"That's the Boyles' place of Kelburne," John replied. "We're on their lands now, so we mustn't stray. Southannan's a few miles to the south. But since the weather's fair, I think we should pay a visit to Largs, and make sure that all's well there."

Everywhere they looked, men, women and children plied the fields, piling bound stooks high onto ox-carts, sometimes carrying them on their backs. They were singing as they worked, savouring the warmth of late summer.

As their visitors rode past, they left their tasks and approached, the men carrying their bonnets before them. John soon abandoned his horse and moved amongst them. He talked with the men, carefully examining the ears of wheat, bere and oats presented before him.

While the women lingered nearby, staring at Margaret and Katherine, whispering amongst themselves.

Margaret shivered, and pulled her cloak tighter.

Sensing her disquiet, William halted his horse alongside.

"Can you see what they want?" Margaret asked him.

Dismounting, he approached them. They conversed briefly, then he turned to Margaret with a smile. "They mean no harm, Lady Margaret. They know Sir John well enough. They were curious about you."

She glanced towards John, who was deep in conversation with his tenants and quite oblivious. If this was to be her first progress through his lands, then she supposed she should follow his example. "Come closer," she encouraged the women. "Let me talk to you."

They crowded around her, women of all ages, many with children gripping their skirts. They admired Margaret's fine gown, and promised her that she'd be blessed with many strong sons. A small girl came forward, clutching a posy of meadow flowers, which she thrust towards Margaret.

"Thank you very much," she said, and plucked them graciously from the child's grasp.

*   *   *

He hadn't meant to linger so long here, but his tenants wanted to talk, to share their hopes and concerns for the coming winter.

John felt obliged to hear them out. They'd all suffered much through the previous year. Most had been burned from their homes, their livestock stolen or slaughtered. Injuries that John could not repay in kind, for they'd been carried out in the king's name.

He cast an anxious glance towards Margaret, fearing she'd be sitting idle on her horse, irritated by the delay. Instead, she'd taken it upon herself to speak with the womenfolk, weathering their curiosity with cheerful patience.

In the first few months of their marriage, he'd wondered if she'd ever be willing to work alongside him as a wife was meant to. Watching her now, it was as if those unhappy days had never even happened.

Once the novelty of their presence wore off, everyone went back to their tasks, leaving the two of them alone there. Jamie and William had already set off down the road with Katherine, their pace excruciatingly slow because of the sumpter horse.

John was ready to follow, but Margaret loitered a little longer, gazing out to sea. "I love the ocean," she said. "It's vast, and majestic. This is a wonderful place to hold lands. Why didn't your ancestors build their place here?"

"They had Southannan, I suppose. And with the Norsemen a constant threat, a place perched right on the coast seemed precarious."

They halted close to the shore, and sat there in silence a while. Margaret watched the waves lap against the beach, fascinated by their rhythm, soft, monotonous. The ground beneath was rippled with the lines of rigs, clearly visible now the crops were shorn to stubble.

"So many islands," Margaret said. "Which one's that?"

"Cumbrae," John said. "It belongs to the Montgomeries."

"And these are the Largs lands?"

"That's right. They once belonged to John Balliol. My ancestors found favour with King Robert the First. They were granted Largs when Balliol was disgraced-" He broke off, fearing she was bored, but when he caught her eye she seemed content. Whatever her true thoughts, she had the grace to look interested, at least. "Come on," he said. "Let's find the others."

They rode south along the broad swathe of land that stretched from the shore to the looming hills they'd crossed not long before. There was a church nearby, a cluster of cottages scattered in its vicinity. And elsewhere, more enigmatic monuments from another time: vast heaps of stone, and a tall pillar of roughly-hewn rock that overlooked the sea.

Drawing close to the stone pillar, Margaret reined in her horse. "What's this?"

"A battle was fought here, two hundred years ago. When the Norsemen invaded these shores, the Scots defeated them, wounding their King. The fallen are buried in the mounds that stand near the church, while that stone marks the site where King Haco was struck down."

A smile spread across her lips, her face lit with wonder and excitement. "How marvellous!"

"The men of Norway retreated north," John told her. "And there they've stayed ever since, thank God. No doubt some day their descendants will come marauding once again. That's why the men of the Westland can't afford to fight amongst themselves. They lose sight of their real enemies." He gathered up his reins. "Now we'd best be on our way, if we're to reach Southannan by evening."

"Are we going near the big grave?" Margaret asked.

"We can pass it if you like," he replied. "Why?"

She studied the posy of flowers, still clutched tight in her hand. "I'd like to lay some flowers there,"

"Then let's visit their resting place and pay our respects," John agreed. "They were valiant men, who paid a heavy price to keep the Norsemen from our shores."

Chapter 15

The Sempill place at Southannan was a modest tower-house nestling within its barmkin wall. It was another hour before they reached it, riding at last through the scattering of cottages that lay nearby, clustered around a small stone-built chapel.

Compared to Ellestoun, the tower-house was indeed small. It reminded Margaret of her old home at Ochiltree; a forlorn-looking place roofed with pale stone slabs, walls badly in need of harling.

Inside the yard, some daub-and-wattle outbuildings jostled against the barmkin wall; there were stables, and a hall with shuttered windows. Chickens clucked and strutted across the cobbles, a sleepy dog stretched and yawned.

"Sir John!" A man came running from the range. Aged fifty years or so, he was short in stature and rather stout. He halted, puffing from the exertion, his agitated gaze darting around each of his visitors in turn. "I am so, so sorry. I didn't know you were heading this way. And with ladies, too..." His face crumpled. "Nothing's ready."

John dismounted. "That's alright, Ninian. We don't expect to be treated like royalty."

"The rooms aren't aired, and the linen's still packed."

"We'll take what we're given," John replied. "And be grateful, too."

The laird's chamber smelled damp, musty. The bed stood forlorn, bereft of curtains and mattress, the timber floor thick with dust.

Margaret ran her finger along the carved wooden bedpost. More dust had gathered there; when she raised her hand, she found her fingertips rimed with grey. "How long has it been since the family stayed here?"

John shrugged. "Ten years or so. My father thought Southannan lay at the edge of the world." He rubbed his hands together and shivered. "Our poor old place. It's been neglected, hasn't it?"

"I can't think why. It must be comforting, to lie in your bed at night and hear the sea..."

"I've always thought so." Crouching by the fireplace, John peered up the empty chimney. "Least there's no birds nesting. We'll set a fire in each chamber, and let it burn for a couple of days to air the place properly. Tomorrow I'll check the roof, and see what else needs to be done before the winter." He straightened, and wandered over to join her. "This afternoon we'll hang the linen and clean our bedchamber. That way we might be granted a room to ourselves." Wrapping his arms about her, he pulled her close.

She settled against him with a sigh.

He didn't speak. There was something melancholy about his silence. "John," she said. "What's troubling you?"

"It's been a year since I inherited these lands," he said. "In all that time, I haven't visited them once. They must think me heartless."

80

The Gryphon at Bay

"Did they suffer through the winter?"

"Most were burned from their homes. They trudged to Ellestoun, over those cruel hills, lashed by the wind and rain. They took what beasts they had, while their children stumbled on behind." He broke off, scowling. "I'd hang Matthew Stewart if I could," he added, "for what he did to those poor souls."

There was an edge to his voice. A ghost of the anger she'd witnessed at first hand in the past. But when she squirmed round and looked into his face, she found nothing untoward there.

He caught her anxious glance and smiled. "Come on," he said. "There's much to do. Floors to be swept and fires laid."

"That's what servants are for."

"Honest labour's good for a man," John retorted. "It brings him closer to God. But you, my love-" He kissed her gently on the forehead. "-are exempt. Because of your condition."

Crouched upon a grassy bluff overlooking the sea, the tower of Skelmorlie was a grim, weathered old place, with stained harling and moss streaking the pale slabs of its roof. Small windows pierced its solid walls, built to keep out the wild winds that blew in from the sea as much as the arrows of attackers. Behind it to the east towered the bleak inhospitable hills. Hugh took one last look in their direction and shivered. He had no desire to venture into that miserable country on the morrow.

But for the moment at least he could relax. The waft of roasting meat drifted from the kitchen; he breathed deep, relishing the scent. He'd be dining on venison, most likely. If these lands were good for nothing else, at least they produced fine deer for the board.

As a young man he'd often hunted here. Now, though, he wasn't granted the luxury of such pleasures, subjugated instead to the ceaseless demands of politics and administration.

He glowered at the thought.

His unfortunate servants read his mood wrongly. They stood stiff and proper, visibly cowed by his presence. Numbering just ten in all, there were a venerable steward and his wife, two aging cooks and two younger women who did the laundry and helped out about the place. Along with two old armed retainers, a groom and a kitchen boy. As Hugh passed by, they bowed or curtsied, eyes fixed upon the ground.

The steward stepped forward. "Your chamber's prepared, my lord. And there's hot water ready, if you want to refresh yourself after the journey. Dinner will be served in a few hours, but if you'd like bread and meat brought to your room, we can certainly oblige..."

"I'll wait. A man should make an effort to curb his appetites." He nodded to the groom. "Take good care of my horse. He's worth more than the rest of these nags put together."

Once he'd shed his armour, he washed away the dirt and sweat of the day and changed into more civilised attire.

Hugh flung himself down along the bed with a groan. Just one more day and he'd be heading home again, his labours complete.

Staring at the dark timber joists above, he yawned. He was weary. Weary to the core. He wondered if this was the way his life would always be, one endless patrol of his bounds after another.

He rubbed his eyes and sighed. He wasn't used to harbouring such melancholy thoughts. It wasn't in his nature. A sign that age was creeping up on him, perhaps...

Hugh laughed at the thought, and sprang to his feet. Wine had been left ready, in a flagon that stood on the kist by the bed. He poured some into a cup then wandered to the window.

Slouching against the ledge, he stared out at the vast expanse of sea beyond. The greater and lesser Cumbraes dominated his view, islands that had had been with his family for generations.

He'd added to them just recently, gaining custody of the Royal lands in nearby Arran and Bute. With all these isles to his name, he supposed he should invest in a ship or two...

Taking a swig of wine, he pulled a disgruntled face. It was too thin and rather sour to taste. It was somehow ironic: he owned almost every piece of land as far as the eye could see, but he wasn't granted anything as simple as a palatable cup of wine. At least the steward of Eglintoun made sure that the cellars were always stocked with the best claret...

Don't fret, he told himself. *You'll soon be back there...*

With that pleasing thought, the melancholy was gone. He was reassured by the course his life had taken over the past eighteen months or so. He was Bailie of Cunninghame, Justiciar of Arran and the West, and a Privy Councillor. And all because one king had fallen and another more worthy risen to take his place.

He should have been satisfied with his lot. But it still wasn't enough. Perhaps, whatever successes he achieved, it would never be.

The Place of Southannan

The fires were lit, the boards set out in the hall. The men unpacked the linen and the mattresses and laid them out to air, while Margaret and Katherine headed upstairs to clean the laird's chamber.

As Katherine swept the floor, Margaret wiped the dust from the kists and the bed. It was satisfying to watch the place take shape. Hard work, yes, but what made it enjoyable was that Margaret knew she didn't *have* to be doing any of it.

"I'll sleep well tonight," she told Katherine.

"We'll be lucky if we actually have a place to sleep at all," came Katherine's gloomy response.

Men's voices on the stair heralded John's arrival, Jamie close behind.

"Good God Almighty!" John said. "A man can't breathe for the dust."

"Missed something, Kate." Jamie grabbed a handful of cobwebs that hung from the fireplace. "Here." He lunged at Katherine, and smeared them over her breast: she shrieked and lashed out with her broom. But he side-stepped, laughing, and Katherine's blow went wide. She struck John instead, delivering him a hefty whack on the buttocks.

Katherine's face drained of colour. and Margaret drew a sharp breath, expecting a stinging rebuke.

"I'm sorry," Katherine whispered, close to tears,
John winced and rubbed his hip. "Whatever did I do to merit that?"
"I didn't mean- I aimed for Jamie, and..."
John shrugged and smiled. "I'm sure I'll survive." He doffed his bonnet and bowed, an extravagant, courtly gesture out of place in a man still dressed for travelling. "Ladies, I've been asked to tell you that we'll be dining soon. Perhaps you'll want to change your gowns..."
"We can't," Margaret retorted. "Not while there's men marauding in our chamber. If you'll kindly leave us in peace, perhaps we'll make it to the board in good time."

The table groaned with food. Two chickens and a goose had been slain for the occasion, and there were copious amounts of fish, freshly caught. There were oysters, too. John swallowed them down without hesitation, but Margaret found the texture so unpleasant that she nearly brought her first one straight back up again.
"Oysters must be an acquired taste," she told Ninian's wife, "I was raised far from the sea, and they hardly ever appeared on our board."
"I'm sorry there's no fresh meat," Mistress Janet replied. "Most of the young beasts have already gone to market. We could slaughter an ox, I suppose, but we'd have to hang it a week."
Margaret glanced towards John, hoping he'd offer to hunt, but he was deep in conversation with Ninian.
"-I don't know what's afoot," his steward was saying. "I saw Lord Hugh come riding past a few days ago. Armed for war and mounted on that muckle grey horse of his with three men-at-arms following on behind. Dour-looking souls, they were. The kind of men you'd best not look at the wrong way..."
"Did you ask what was amiss?" John asked.
"He was in no mood to stop and pass the time of day."
"It's probably nothing," John said. "He likes to make his presence known. If he hasn't been summoned to Edinburgh for court business, then he's probably got nothing better to do with his time."

The only available bed lay in a little room in the attic of the guest range. It was regularly used by Ninian and his wife, but Mistress Janet insisted that the lady of the house needed rest. *You've Sir John's bairn inside you,* she argued. *You should both be looked after...*
And that was the end of it.
Margaret was too excited to sleep. She could hear the sea, and smell the fresh sea air. Katherine pressed against her: they'd shed their gowns so they'd be more comfortable, but their kirtles couldn't keep out the chill with just a thin linen sheet and two blankets of fustian to cover them.
"Oh, Katherine..." Margaret giggled. "That was a priceless moment. When you aimed for Jamie and caught John square on the backside."
Katherine moaned. "I don't want to think of it."
"He took it very gracefully." Margaret rolled onto her back. "It's very quiet, isn't it?"

"Like the grave. There's not a soul out there."

"I wish John was here. What if someone stole in and plundered the place?" She broke off, heart pounding. She could've sworn she'd heard quiet footsteps on the stair.

Katherine clutched her, tightly. "Did you hear that?"

The door creaked open. "It's me," John said. He was carrying a candle, its light casting a restless orange glow about his head and shoulders. "Is everything alright?"

"No," Margaret said. "It's very dark, and still."

"Do you want me to stay here with you?"

"Please." She watched as he set the candle down in the fireplace. "There's room next to me."

"I'll lie down by the fire."

"But I'm cold."

"And what about Katherine?"

"She won't mind," said Margaret. "Please, John. Just for a little while."

He came over to the bed. Pulling his gown tightly about him, he lay down next to her.

"Please get in. Keep me warm."

Muttering some half-hearted misgivings, he shed gown and doublet then slipped in next to her.

Wrapping her arms round his waist, Margaret burrowed closer. She could feel the heat of his body through his clothes. He smelled stale and sweaty, for he hadn't thought to wash. But she didn't mind. She was happy to have his familiar scent filling her nostrils, warm, faintly spicy... At her back, Katherine rolled over and moved away slightly, indicating her displeasure.

Margaret didn't care. Lying between the two of them, her chilled flesh was thawing out at last. She felt safe, secure, overwhelmed with drowsy contentment.

"In a day or so the tower will be aired," he said.

He seemed distant, detached, like a brother or cousin would be. "I wish the food was better," she said. "We should've brought some spices. Perhaps some red meat would help?"

"I'll hunt tomorrow."

"Not that I'm complaining," she said, then added, "Thank you. For taking me on this adventure."

He laughed softly. "The first of many, I hope." Rolling away, he settled more comfortably. "Now go to sleep. It's been a long day."

Chapter 16

The Lands of Skelmorlie

"That's the baggage on its way," Hugh told his retainers. "We'll tour the bounds one final time. Just to err on the side of caution."

"No harm in that, my lord," James agreed. With his scarred face and missing ear, he looked a disreputable soul. But he was proving an invaluable source of wisdom to young Colin and Davy, who were riding out with their lord for the first time.

They climbed up into the hills, horses picking their careful way along the stony track with heads held low. Cottages were frequent sights at first: squat, daub-and-wattle structures with heavy thatched roofs to keep the wind and rain at bay. Out in the stackyards, the hay ricks were piled high with fodder, ready for the winter.

Everyone came out to watch. Men removed their hoods and women curtsied low, while children peered from windows and doors. Most were too timid to approach, though some trotted alongside. They gasped in awe when they saw Hugh, with his armour and his sword and his magnificent horse.

He smiled and nodded as he passed, stopping occasionally to ask if all was well. They seemed content, so he continued on his way.

Eventually they left the last of the cottages behind them. Even here poor folk scratched a living amongst the thin soils and vast stretches of bog, living in isolated hovels, taking sheep and cattle reared on the lower ground and grazing them in the high pastures during the summer months. They made a reasonable sum from that, but for much of the year times were hard.

Yet they never gave up. They kept on striving to support themselves and their families, though sometimes it seemed as if God Himself conspired against them.

Hugh reined in his horse, savouring the view. He could see right across the Firth of Clyde, past Arran and the other islands to Kintyre and beyond. The wind whipped against the coarse grass, rustling through stunted bushes of whin, rowan and hawthorn.

He breathed deep, enjoying the fresh clean air, untainted by the stink of middens or manure spreads. "Ah," he sighed. "If only the whole world could be like this. Peaceful, content with its lot..."

James grinned. "Amen to that, my lord."

"God is so very gracious," Hugh continued. "I'll call by the abbey on the road home, and light a candle in recognition of His Goodness."

"You mean to turn back now?"

"We'll be at Eglintoun in time for supper." Hugh stood in his stirrups, searching the hills one last time. Settling back into the saddle, he stared with interest at an isolated plume of smoke in the distance.

It seemed out of place somehow, unexpected...

He gestured to James. "How far, d'you reckon?"

The other man shrugged. "A mile or so. Maybe more."

"That takes us right to the limits of my lands." Hugh leaned upon his pommel, frowning. "It won't do us any harm to investigate further." He tightened the reins. "Come along, men. Make haste."

The fire had done its work. All that remained of the cottage were its gable ends, and some neighbouring stretches of wall. The roof was no more than a pile of charred thatch and timbers. And wedged beneath that, a corpse, burned almost beyond all recognition.

Hugh dismounted. Carrion birds loitered nearby: a brace of corbies and a buzzard. They perched upon the wallhead, watching and waiting.

As Hugh approached, they flapped reluctantly away. "The Devil's messengers." He crossed himself. "God rot them."

Wandering around the wrecked farmstead, he could inspect the damage more closely. There'd been two small buildings, both now destroyed. A trampled quagmire beside one showed it had been a barn: the livestock had been stolen, leaving a clear trail that led off into the distance.

Hugh smiled, grimly. The thieves thought they'd get away undetected. Instead, they'd have the Lord Montgomerie himself hunting them down.

He flexed his fingers, turned and retraced his steps. The anger glowed like an ember, deep inside.

As he passed the ruins of the cottage, he glimpsed a pale flash from the corner of his eye. It was a woman. She cowered in a corner, wearing no more than a kirtle. When he clambered close, she shrieked and shrank against the wall. Her long golden hair was tangled and matted with blood, her garment torn, exposing shoulders and breasts. A child clung to her knee, a girl of seven or eight, naked and trembling.

The woman clutched the child close and moaned.

Hugh dropped to a crouch. "It's alright." He could feel the heat from the burned thatch through the soles of his shoes. "I won't harm you."

But she didn't move. She buried her face in the child's hair, her shoulders heaving with sobs. While the little girl howled and bawled fit to wake the dead.

"My lord?" James called.

"Stay there!" He glanced heavenwards, inwardly berating himself, for he'd spoken more sharply than intended. Reaching out his hand, he urged, "Come on now. You can't sit here all day. You'll die of cold." He paused to let the words sink in, then straightened. "I'm coming closer." Taking one cautious step after another, he added, "Pass me the child, and I'll take you to safety."

They huddled there unmoving.

Grasping the child's arm, Hugh hauled her away. The mother wailed, the girl screamed even louder, struggling in his grasp. "Be still!" he told her. "Let me help your mother."

The child gripped his neck, snuffling quietly. He kept one arm wrapped around her while he leaned down and helped the woman to stand. He had to carry her so she wouldn't burn her bare feet against the smouldering remains of the roof. Once he'd set her down again, she hobbled painfully at his side, eyes fixed on the ground. She was shaking, whether from cold or fear he couldn't tell.

The Gryphon at Bay

His men sat still upon their horses, faces solemn. Even old James – who'd witnessed many brutal sights in his time and committed a few barbarous acts of his own – looked shaken.

Hugh set the child down. "Colin!" he called. "You'll go with them. Take off your brigandine, so she can be granted some dignity."

The young man nodded and slipped off his padded leather jerkin. He rode up to Hugh, passed the garment down to him and waited while Hugh draped the brigandine gently about the woman's shoulders.

Hugh laid a mail-clad hand against her battered cheek. "Colin will take you to Skelmorlie. There's women there who can see to your hurts. Did they slay your husband?"

She glanced away and swallowed.

"They'll be repaid in full for their crimes." Hugh glanced at the child, who clung to her mother, shivering. Crouching next to her, he took a careful hold of her chin, and coaxed her head around. Her eyes were wide with terror, her face smudged with dirt and soot, with clean trails marking the path of her tears. "Don't be afraid," he said, softly. "You'll be riding with Colin. He'll look after you and make sure you find somewhere warm and safe to stay tonight. Hold on..." He lifted her high so Colin could grasp her in his arms, then once she was secure, he hoisted the woman up behind the saddle. "Don't let go, for God's sake."

The horse moved off.

Hugh watched in silence. The glowing ember he'd been nursing was gone, the anger running through his veins like liquid fire. He took one deep breath after another, feeling his pulse beat faster...

Seizing Zephyr's reins, he sprang into the saddle. "Come on!" he called to his men. "We're hunting!"

"My lord," James ventured.

"Yes?" Hugh's gaze was fixed on the trampled swathe of grass before them.

"Don't take this wrong, my lord, but... There's just the three of us, and we're in the most Godforsaken country."

"They're reivers. That's all. They'll be protected by Kilmaurs' hand, but I don't see his direct involvement. He wouldn't stoop to rape. Nor would any of his kinsmen."

James didn't reply.

"A mob came here. They were savage, yes, but undisciplined. We'll be more than a match for them."

"Yes, my lord." For once, James did not sound entirely convinced.

"We must mete out justice. Swiftly, and without mercy."

"Granted, my lord. But..."

Hugh hauled Zephyr to a halt. He scowled at them both. "Are you with me?"

"Yes," James spoke out, voice resolute. "We're with you."

The trail led on through the hills, heading east and veering slightly to the south. They followed it for hours. They passed the marchstones that marked the edge of Hugh's lands, and still the hoofprints went on and on.

Hugh wasn't sure whose lands he was crossing. He didn't think he was on Cunninghame's Glengarnock estate; he was too far west for that. These hills may have belonged to the Crawfurds, or perhaps more likely, the Sempills.

He didn't much care. He was enforcing the King's laws; it didn't matter whether his presence was welcome or not. Young John Sempill would be sympathetic, while the Crawfurds wouldn't dare question him.

"Look!" James pointed to a nearby hillside.

"I see them." Three horsemen, just sitting there, watching.

"They're quality steeds," James remarked.

"Yes, they are." Hugh turned his horse. "Come on. Let's talk to them."

The horsemen rode off when the Montgomeries changed course to intercept them. They kept their pace slow, until Hugh gave the order to trot. Then they, too, picked up their speed.

"I've seen a roan like that before," Hugh commented. "Master Cuthbert's steed."

"Do you think he was responsible for this?"

"I doubt it, though he may have played some part in rousing the rabble." Hugh raised his hand. "Hello!" he called. "I'd like a word, Master Cunninghame."

The young men stopped and turned to face them: Cuthbert, Andrew and Guido Cunninghame, all ashen-faced and nervous.

Hugh signalled for his retainers to walk. "Now there's some guilty men," he said. "But what they're guilty of, I'm not sure..." He spurred Zephyr onwards, moving slightly ahead. "Wait there!"

"Lord Hugh," Cuthbert Cunninghame spoke out. "To what do I owe this pleasure?"

"Are these your lands?" And when the youth didn't answer, he pressed home the attack. "Hadn't you best head back to Glengarnock, where your safety's assured?"

"You're equally guilty of trespass, my lord."

"I'm the King's Officer. I travel where I please."

Cuthbert exchanged sullen glances with his kinsmen. "What do you want?"

"One of my tenants was slain last night. His wife was raped, his cottage razed."

"Our people suffer such indignities on a daily basis," Cuthbert countered. "If you want sympathy, seek it elsewhere."

Hugh's voice hardened. "You misunderstand me. I want to know what you're doing here. Riding through these hills, watching every move I make, when the ashes of that farmstead are scarcely cold."

"Rot in hell, Montgomerie." Cuthbert steered his horse away.

"Halt!" Hugh urged Zephyr after him.

"Keep back!" Cuthbert unsheathed his sword. "I'll protect myself if necessary."

Hugh pulled his horse to a standstill and drew his sword in readiness. "An explanation, Master Cunninghame!"

"You heard him!" Guido spoke out. His voice was shaking, his face white. He held a lightweight hunting crossbow, levelled and pointing at Hugh with a bolt in place. "I'll shoot."

"Don't be such a fool!" Hugh snarled.

"My lord?" James came cantering up, sword held ready.

The Gryphon at Bay

Guido jerked round. There was a snap, the bolt whizzed past Hugh's ear.

It struck James with such force that he was knocked back in the saddle. He cried out, teetering there with one hand clutching his breast. Then slowly, without a sound, he fell.

The three boys scattered at a canter, and Davy moved to follow.

"No!" Hugh called. "Stay here." He slid from Zephyr's back. "Fuck," he muttered. "Hell and Damnation." He trudged over to where James lay prone upon the ground.

James groaned. "Ah, Christ..."

Hugh knelt alongside. He beckoned to young Davy. "Come here. Help me."

Davy dismounted and crouched close. He looked pale, uncomfortable, a man not yet used to dealing with the dead and the dying.

James moaned, softly. The bolt stuck out from his chest, piercing brigandine and flesh beneath. Blood seeped through the leather, a vivid crimson stain.

"Hold still." Hugh unbuckled his gauntlet with his teeth and let it drop. "Let's take a look at you."

James drew a shuddering breath. His face was moist with sweat, his eyes half-closed. "You'll see to my affairs?" He clutched Hugh's hand.

Hugh closed his fingers tight. "Nonsense," he retorted. "You'll be alright."

James laughed, weakly. The breath rattled in his chest.

Drawing his knife, Hugh sliced through the clothing. It was as he'd thought: the bolt had lodged to the right of the breastbone, down from the shoulder. The lung was pierced, leaving James with two or three hours to live, at most.

Hugh swallowed. "Davy will ride back and fetch help," he said. "I'll stay with you."

"Pull it out," James whispered. "It'll make the end quicker."

"I can't do that. I'm sorry." Shifting slightly, he lifted James up and laid his head against his thigh. "Rest easy now," he said. "Davy will be back before you know it."

He loosened the sallet and slipped it from the dying man's head. He stroked the sweat-soaked hair, muttering what words of consolation he could.

"Pray for me, Lord Hugh..."

"Yes." His voice shook slightly. "Of course I will."

The moments dragged their feet, the sun sinking lower. Still Hugh waited there: James drifted into a swoon, the faint wheezing in his chest proof enough that his soul hadn't fled just yet.

Davy patrolled the nearby hillsides, keeping watch. *A good lad,* Hugh told himself. *Knows exactly what's required...*

An hour passed, maybe longer, before Davy returned. "Is it done?"

"Almost." Hugh laid the body down, and clambered to his feet. "Well done, Davy. You did a good job of minding my back."

"I'll fetch his horse."

They stood there together, until they were sure the last breath had passed. Hugh crouched down and gently pressed the eyelids shut. "Let's get him home," he said.

Hugh stepped back to regard their handiwork. The dead man was slumped sideways across the saddle, bound to the stirrups by wrists and ankles. "It's an undignified way to travel," he told Davy. "But I won't have those savages picking his corpse clean and leaving it for the corbies." He nodded to the younger man. "Take him back to Skelmorlie. Once's he's prepared, remove him to the church at Largs. Tell them I'll pay whatever sum's required."

"What about you, my lord?"

"I have business to settle."

Davy's gaze met his, just briefly. "But... I mean... Don't you think it might be..." His voice trailed away.

It wasn't like Davy to talk back to his betters; when Hugh searched the young man's face he saw genuine concern there.

Hugh smiled, reassuring. "Look at me," he said. "I'm in full array. I could take on thirty men and walk away unscathed."

Davy glanced aside and swallowed. "I fear treachery."

"They're simple folk, these reivers. They seize what they can from the weak, and flee from those who'd injure them." He gripped Davy's shoulder. "Have faith. Let me deal with this my own way."

Chapter 17

The cattle were confined in a tumbledown bothy, a dozen scrawny creatures with matted coats that hung like dirty thatch over their eyes. They jostled close and called softly in the gloom.

It had taken him an hour or more to track them down. Already the light was fading, sun sinking low over the hills.

Hugh cast a careful glance about him, searching for any sign of life.

The place was deserted.

It was unsettling. He'd assumed the path that led him to the kye would also lead him to the reivers.

Zephyr blew through flared nostrils, fitful, impatient.

Dismounting, Hugh approached the bothy with sword drawn, wary in case his foe still lurked there.

But when he peered into the shadows, all he saw was the knock-kneed limbs of the cattle. The ground beneath their hooves was poached and pocked, the dung piled high and stinking.

He sighed, and sheathed his sword.

There was a ramshackle gate in the wall, nothing more than a few rotten timbers lashed together. Drawing his knife, he hacked at the rope which secured them.

Zephyr squealed, loudly.

Hugh turned to see a man in coarse drab clothing grappling with the horse's reins. Startled by the rough handling, Zephyr plunged and lashed out.

Hugh strode towards him, knife in hand. "Take your hands off my horse!"

The man dropped the reins and fled.

"Stinking peasant." Hugh stamped off in pursuit. "I'll gut you for that."

The figure darted out of sight, and Hugh paused, suddenly wary.

Too late. The ground was alive with men. They'd lain in wait, using the undulating land to conceal themselves. A score or more, clad in humble farmers' clothing: woollen cloaks and hoods, leather jerkins. Armed with wooden cudgels, pitchforks and bills, their grimy faces were hard, determined.

They charged, brandishing their weapons, screaming loud in hatred and defiance.

Rage swelled within him. Dropping his knife, he pulled his visor down and drew his sword. He chanced a glance over his shoulder, saw the ruined bothy standing just thirty yards distant. He needed its solid walls for protection, for the backs of his thighs weren't enclosed by armour.

Just beyond the reach of his blade, they halted.

Hugh swallowed. He licked his lips, trying to convince himself that his mouth wasn't dry with fear, his heart wasn't beating faster... *There's nothing to be afraid of,* he reminded himself. *They're men of no substance. Noisy and undisciplined...*

He stood tall, unbowed. Made it obvious he was eying each in turn, an indication that he wasn't averse to gralloching any one of them, if they dared come too close.

Little by little, he edged his way towards the bothy. He held the guard position, though it was wearing on the arms. If they took a step closer, he'd snarl and brandish his sword.

They backed away, each time. But they were slowly closing the trap. Tightening the circle, keeping him well away from the bothy, and comparative safety.

Miles from home, Hugh thought. *With twenty men or more hanging round like corbies about a corpse.*

A wise man would be pissing himself...

He sighed and flexed his fingers, one hand after the other. The grip of the hilt felt comfortable in his grasp.

Stones rattled off his cuirass. Hugh cursed beneath his breath, seeing precious little through the visor. Shapes moved, just beyond the field of his vision. But most of the time they waited, patient as wolves.

Sweat trickled down the small of his back. He shifted his grip, wincing. He couldn't hold this stance for ever. Sooner or later he'd tire. He wondered if they knew that.

A figure lunged close. He sprang forward to intercept them, bringing his sword down. Then he gasped, as something smashed against his head. The steel resounded about his ears: he blinked, dazed by the force of it.

He shook his head, staggered forward a few steps. Another blow struck him, so hard his helmet swivelled. His neck jolted, sending a sharp pain shooting through his spine.

And suddenly, they were on him. Screaming out their rage, battering him with cudgels and the hafts of their pitchforks.

Hugh fell to his knees. He struggled to rise, but couldn't. His right leg was restrained by something, a billhook, perhaps. Its curved blade dug deep, just behind his knee.

They were taunting him, but he couldn't make out any words. Hands gripped his arms, someone tried to seize his sword but he'd locked his fists tight and he wouldn't let go. Fury burned afresh inside him, he gulped down one deep breath after another, summoning all his strength.

A blade ripped down his right thigh, inside his leg where the *cuisse* didn't protect him. Not deep enough to cripple him, just enough to make him bleed. The straps that secured his armour were severed: it flapped loose, exposing more flesh beneath.

Fuelled with new determination, Hugh ripped himself free. Pulling himself up to his full height, he roared out defiance. Vision blurred and head spinning, he forged forward, slashing, chopping, hacking. His blade met tissue and bone and men dropped like flies.

His limbs were trembling. Blood seeped from his wounded leg. He shook his head and blinked, trying to clear his sight.

But at least he was standing amongst carnage. He smiled grimly at the thought, then his leg went from under him. He fell to his knees, too spent to defend himself.

They wrested the sword from his grasp, then hacked and pulled at his armour, slicing through the straps as if butchering a beast, sometimes cutting flesh in their haste.

Gritting his teeth Hugh weathered the onslaught in silence. They hauled off his arming doublet, his shoes. He was stripped to shirt and hose, lost in a sea of jostling, baying men. They punched and kicked and beat him with their cudgels until he lay slumped in the mud, unmoving.

He was dragged to his knees. He wasn't aware of any pain, just a strange, light-headed detachment. His arms were seized and wrenched behind his back, his wrists bound roughly together.

Someone shook him. "Here he is! The Devil of Eglintoun." A harsh laugh rang out. "Shall we show him what we do with devils?"

Hands tore at his shirt, ripping the fabric. A knife sliced through the laces that fastened his hose. They mocked him and tore at his flesh and spat upon him, because the demon that haunted their nightmares was but a man like any other.

Breathing deep, he let his thoughts turn to the Passion. To the suffering of Christ, the scourging, the crown of thorns and the long march to Calvary.

He understood it now. With perfect clarity. *Agnes Dei, qui tollis peccata mundi, miserere nobis...*

Fingers tightened in his hair, his head was hauled back. "Do you know why we're doing this?"

Hugh frowned, and his vision settled. He saw the face of his tormentor, features ravaged by hardship and despair, twisted with rage.

"Our wives and children withered and died, because of you." The voice rose in intensity. "You're not a man, Montgomerie. You're a beast. And you'll die like a beast."

He met the fury with silence. He looked into the man's eyes, serene, remorseless.

"Bleed him like a pig," someone called.

No one moved.

"What's the matter with you all?" Another man stepped close, knife drawn. He dragged the blade across Hugh's belly, from below the ribs to just above the groin. "See? He bleeds. Like the rest of us."

The mob jeered louder, and three men pressed close, bolder than the rest. They pushed him, roughly, pawing at the wound and pinching his flesh so he'd yelp. But it only made him more determined to stay silent.

He smelled the stink of ale on their breath. Concentrating his thoughts, he took in every detail of their features, engraving every observation into his memory in the hope that some day he'd have retribution.

The man who'd cut him tugged at his hose. His privy parts spilled out, a fist closed about them, crushing so hard Hugh nearly swooned.

He squeezed his eyes shut. *Don't cry out.* A low, hissing moan escaped his lips.

"Shall we geld the beast before we slay him? Is that not a just act? For all the children he stole from us?"

"Enough!" Cuthbert Cunninghame's voice rang out. "Leave him be!" He shouldered his way through the mob, flanked by Andrew and Guido. "It's not your place to butcher him. Take the kye and go."

No-one stirred.

Undeterred, Cuthbert took his place at Hugh's side. "You heard me."

Without a word, they retreated.

Hugh swallowed. The blood was pooling at his loins, the air chill against his exposed flesh. He started to shiver, and hated himself for it. "Master Cuthbert." His voice was hoarse, barely audible.

Cuthbert crouched before him. "They've left you in a sorry state, Lord Hugh." Grasping Hugh's chin, he forced his head up. "All you've ever done is spread hatred and resentment in men's hearts. These black birds are coming home to roost tonight." He touched the wound that crossed Hugh's belly, raised his hand and inspected the blood on his fingers. "With my kinsmen's deaths to avenge, I've every right to claim the killing stroke."

Gripping Hugh's shirt with one hand, he straightened and stepped back, out of sight. A dagger grated in its scabbard, its tip settling sharp at the nape of Hugh's neck.

"Will you beg me for mercy, Lord Hugh? Before I put you out of our collective misery?"

"Wait!" Andrew Cunninghame gasped. "You mustn't do this. It's dishonourable!"

"It's worse than that!" Guido broke in, voice shaking. "It's cold-blooded murder!"

Hugh took a deep breath, steadying himself. "Don't listen to them," he said. "Kill me."

"Ah, so you're begging me to end your suffering?"

"No." His voice came out firm, determined. The fear was gone. After enduring all this pain and humiliation, he knew now that his soul was prepared. "It's not like that. It's not like that at all..."

"For God's sake, cousin!" Andrew Cunninghame called. "Don't stoop to this!"

"Don't listen to him," Hugh spoke out. "Slay me. While you have the chance."

Cuthbert's breath hissed in his throat, the grip on the dagger wavered.

"You can't do it, can you?" Hugh challenged. "You can't slaughter a man kneeling helpless at your feet."

"Hold your tongue!"

"Come on! Kill me! At least I know my soul will be safe in God's keeping." He wrenched his head up, met Cuthbert's gaze and held it. "Would you have such confidence, Master Cuthbert, if our situations were reversed?"

"I told you to be silent!" Cuthbert slapped Hugh across the head, so hard he gasped. "Serpent!"

"Do the honourable thing," Andrew muttered. "Leave him be. We're miles from nowhere. He's lost his horse. And he's bleeding like a butchered ox. How is he ever going to find his way back home?"

"You know that's the right thing to do," Guido added. "Please, Cuthbert..."

"And deprive Lord Hugh of a martyr's death..." Cuthbert shook his head. "Oh, my poor Lord Hugh..." The young man's fingers teased through his hair. "That's what you wanted, isn't it? To die honourably, like a knight. Instead, you'll rot on a hillside. The great Butcher of the Westland, stripped of all his finery and pecked clean by the corbies... A fitting end, I think." He leaned over and cut Hugh's bonds. "There," he said. "I'll be gracious, and grant you this much. You won't die in comfort, but at least you're not a captive."

"This is an accursed place," Andrew complained. "Let's be gone."

Cuthbert sheathed his dagger. "Dame Fortune is capricious. Taking such a mighty man and casting him down to the depths..." He retrieved his horse and climbed into the saddle. "Relish the earth's embrace," he said. "It's the last thing you'll ever know." He paused. "Unless of course my tenants return for you," he added. "Then you'll face a sorry fate, won't you?"

Chapter 18

The Place of Eglintoun

Dinner came and went, and Hugh still hadn't returned. The baggage arrived, which meant he was on his way, but as the day wore on, there was still no sign of him.

Helen thought nothing of it at first. Plenty of things might have detained him: a grievance between tenants, a chance meeting on the road with one of the local lairds.

But as afternoon turned into evening, black doubts crept into her mind. He'd been delayed before, but he'd always sent word. An apology. An explanation. Some indication that he was safe and well.

Helen perched against the parapet to watch the sunset, looking out upon the road that led towards Ardrossan and Kilwinning. She peered into the gloaming, seeking the shape of a grey horse.

The sun was sinking, a burning red orb in the west. For once Helen found herself unmoved by its beauty. A cold, empty feeling of dread stole through her, tendrils tightening around her heart.

Footsteps scuffed soft against the steps. "Surely he should have been home by now," Bessie said.

Helen bowed her head, unable to speak.

"Mama..." Bessie laid a consoling hand on hers.

"Stay with me a while."

Bessie leaned against the wall beside her. "Do you think something's happened?" Her smooth young brow was creased with concern, her grey eyes, so like her father's, bright with agitation.

"He's a good husband. He doesn't neglect his wife. He doesn't forget."

Bessie stifled a sob.

Helen glanced down, concerned, seeing tears running down the girl's face. Slipping an arm about her shoulders, Helen hugged her tight. "We must have faith in your father. He's a bold man. A mighty man. Let's not weep for him just yet."

     *   *   *

He couldn't move at first.

He'd suffered enough through the years to have an inkling of what was wrong. He'd fractured some ribs, that much was certain. And while he didn't think the blow to his crown had cracked his skull, the searing pain in his head and his blurred vision worried him. His backbone was intact, for his arms and legs, though desperately weak, still functioned.

It was a long while before he tried to stand. Transforming good intentions into reality was, however, more difficult. His legs buckled each time: he'd curse and rest awhile, then try again.

What he wanted, more than anything, was to lie down and suffer undisturbed. But that was a luxury he could ill afford. Cuthbert was right: the rabble might return, and though he'd been resigned to death when it seemed inevitable, the truth was that he didn't want to die.

She's waiting, Hugh told himself. *Don't leave her there, ignorant of the truth...*

Picturing her face gave him the strength he needed. He lurched upright. His bollocks ached, he tasted blood. His stomach heaved and he was sick, spitting out skeins of red-tinged bile. Wiping his sleeve across his mouth, he saw the cloth smeared with crimson and winced.

Nothing serious, he told himself. *Just a short walk home. That's all...*

Fragments of his armour littered the muddied ground. There was no sign of his arming doublet, and his shoes were gone, too. But his sword was there, jammed point-down into the earth. He'd have taken it with him, but his fingers were too stiff and sore to grip the hilt. Besides, he doubted he had the strength to even lift it.

As for Zephyr...

There was no sign of the beast. With luck the horse had fled. Its path would surely lead it to Eglintoun, where eventually his predicament would be understood.

Until then he was forced to rely on his strength and wits to get home.

He glanced one last time at his beleaguered sword. The last dregs of sunlight made the metal gleam and glow like a wayside cross, placed to guide a weary pilgrim on his way.

Hugh gritted his teeth and set off. His route was straightforward enough. He would head west, towards the setting sun. Its rim could still be seen, a burning crescent disappearing behind the hills.

If he followed that course, he'd at least reach the coast. Finding Skelmorlie would be quite easy after that. The breeze was coming from the west, which meant he'd still be able to find his way once night fell.

But he knew his chances of success were small. One leg was dragging, every sinew burned with the effort. The air was growing cool already, the grass slippery with dew. He had to dig his toes deep to keep from sliding.

He hobbled along as best he could, though every step brought torment and he was shivering with cold. He thought once more of the Passion, of the suffering Christ had endured for the sake of all Mankind.

Holy Mary, full of grace. He gripped the simple crucifix he wore about his neck. *I place flesh and soul in Your care. Don't let this ordeal be in vain. By some miracle let me live, so I can learn from this and become a better man...*

When the sun rose the following morning, he was in a bleak, windswept valley. He'd been getting slower as the night wore on, sometimes having to drag his right leg with both hands to make it move. He wondered just how far he'd travelled. He suspected it wasn't more than a mile.

His thoughts were drifting, he was growing steadily weaker, more light-headed. Every few steps he'd gasp as he crushed his toes against stones or trod on something sharp. He was glad of the jolt it brought him, for it forced him to his senses, if only briefly.

He needed rest. A ruined cottage stood nearby, but it was too obvious a hiding place: if he perished that day, he wanted to make sure that Cuthbert Cunninghame was led a merry dance before he found the corpse.

Hugh ground his teeth and limped resolutely on. Glancing about him, he eventually spotted a tiny hollow by the river, screened by rocks and bushes.

Retreating beneath the overhanging growth of rushes and grass, he clutched his knees close, shivering, but could find no solace in sleep. He thought of Helen and the children, and at least picturing their faces brought some comfort.

Though the thought that he might never see them again made him want to weep.

The Place of Southannan

"He was there when the mists cleared." The farmer leaned against his bill, his gaze fixed firmly upon the horse that grazed by the shore. "Thought it best to tell you, Sir John, rather than try and catch the beast."

"You did the right thing," John said. "Thank you."

The horse in question was chillingly familiar, a big dappled grey stallion, with a strong neck and powerful quarters. To see it loitering there in full harness was unexpected, out of place...

John approached carefully, bucket in hand. "Come on, Zephyr," he coaxed, shaking it so the oats rustled inside.

Lifting its head, the horse regarded him calmly. Its nostrils flared, then it resumed its grazing. Its saddle sat crooked on its back, broken reins trailed at its feet. Zephyr was bleeding, too, scraped on its knees and along its belly.

Murmuring soothing words, John stepped up close and seized the reins. "There now," he said, running a careful hand down its neck. "You're in safe hands now. But where's your master, Zephyr? What's happened to him?"

Margaret watched from the neighbouring stall as John set to work with a pitchfork, laying a deep bed of straw for the new arrival.

Peering over the hurdle partition with chin resting on folded arms, she studied Zephyr closely, a faint frown on her face. "That's Lord Hugh's horse, isn't it?"

"Yes, it is." With the stable prepared, he pulled off the bridle, easing the grass-encrusted bit from the stallion's mouth. When he lifted the saddle, he winced, for its flesh was chafed and raw about the withers.

Margaret sighed and fidgeted, her unease palpable. "Why would he abandon his horse?"

"Not from choice, I'm sure." He scratched the horse's head while it lipped at his clothes, eager for food. "If I don't catch Jamie, then tell him to bathe the beast's wounds. And make sure he's fed and watered."

"Perhaps he bolted?"

"Seems unlikely," John ran his fingers through the long mane. "I'd best ride to Skelmorlie, and see what's amiss."

Their horses waited, eyes half-closed and ears drooping. Rolled-up blankets were tied behind each saddle: they'd come in useful, John thought, if they were forced to spend a night or two on the hills.

"Did you pack food?" he asked William.

"Enough to keep us a few days."

"How about some linen, and a flask of *aqua vita?*" He caught William's eye. "Just in case there's trouble."

William gave a tight little smile. "It's done."

His hounds lay slumped across the cobbles, savouring the warmth of the sun on their flanks. When John whistled to them, they sat tall, expectant.

"Keep the gates barred at night," John said.

Margaret glanced warily about her. "Whatever for?"

"No one must see that horse. If anyone asks after it, deny all knowledge. Say it's your husband's business. Anything."

She masked her fear with annoyance. "Perhaps you should have left it where it was."

"Hugh would want him cared for properly." He looked at William, who stared back, straight-faced and sombre. "We'll return once we have news of him. Hopefully, we'll be back this evening. If not, don't be anxious."

"Please don't get embroiled in his problems!" Margaret blurted out.

He hugged her close. "I'll be back before you know it."

"With Lord Hugh, no doubt." Her voice shook. "You should have words with him, John. It's not right that you should be chasing around after him like this. At the very least, you should charge him a fee for stabling his nag."

Chapter 19

The Place of Skelmorlie

"State your business!" The challenge came from a grim-faced man-at-arms. He peered over the parapet of the barmkin wall, brandishing a loaded crossbow.

John tried not to act as if anything were amiss. "I seek the Lord Montgomerie. Is he here?"

"He left for Eglintoun yesterday." Another Montgomerie retainer swaggered out from the gateway, a scowl on his face. "You'd best seek him there."

"I found his horse this morning."

"What makes you think it was his horse?"

John exchanged a weary glance with William. "A dappled grey stallion, of Spanish blood? There's only one man in these parts keeps a horse like that..."

The young retainer swallowed, his unease clear. "Come this way."

He was escorted to a sparsely-furnished hall, where the steward awaited him, a slight man with bright silver hair, thin-faced and wary. "Sir John Sempill," he said. "This is a pleasure. I'm sure Lord Hugh would be delighted to hear you've asked after-"

"Be honest with me," John cut in. "If he's in danger, I must know. And if I can help, tell me what's required."

"What harm can it do?" the young Montgomerie retainer spoke out.

"Davy, please!" The steward tossed his companion an agitated look. "Let's not break his Lordship's trust."

The young man met John's gaze. "We set out to tour the bounds yesterday morning," he said. "A farm had been burned. A man was killed there, his livestock stolen. We found his wife." He swallowed. "She'd been violated."

"And Lord Hugh?"

"Something happened in the hills. We lost a man. I brought the body back, and my lord proceeded alone." He broke off, visibly agitated. "He- He told me to go. He said he thought the thieves were men of little consequence."

"Enough!" the steward snapped, then turned to John. "Your concern is appreciated, Sir John." His tone was sharp with dismissal. "But there's no need for you to help us. Rest assured that we'll send word to Eglintoun without delay."

"Raise the alarm if you like," John retorted. "It won't be any use if he's already dead. Grant me some men, so we can at least try and find him."

"Sir John." The steward sighed, faint exasperation. "We can't let a stranger handle our affairs, however worthy his intent."

"He's a friend, for God's sake!" John snapped. "I won't stand by and do nothing!"

With the steward studiously avoiding his gaze, John turned in desperation to the young retainer. "If you can do nothing else, then at least take me to where it happened."

The Gryphon at Bay

*   *   *

They spotted the birds first. Crows, buzzards, kites, hanging low in the sky.

John spurred his horse into a canter, making straight for the spot. For all his faults, he thought, Hugh surely didn't merit an end like this...

He found the birds circling over a ruined bothy with a trampled patch of muddied grass nearby. The place was like a shambles, ground stained with blood. Lying discarded amongst the gore was a dismantled set of armour and a sword, sticking upright in the ground.

"That's his blade, isn't it?" William said, quietly.

John didn't answer. For Hugh to have abandoned his sword was unthinkable. "Let's hope he wrecked havoc on his foes before they overwhelmed him," he said at last.

"Do you think they took him captive?"

"I hope not," John cast a wary glance towards their companions, who sat glum upon their horses, locked in melancholy silence. Leaning close to William, he dropped his voice so the Montgomeries couldn't hear him. "I doubt they'd treat him kindly, if this is anything to go by."

He dismounted with a sigh. Pacing the battleground, he searched for any hints of what might have happened. The sword's blade was stained with dried blood, which cheered him. As for Hugh's armour... It seemed to be complete. Even his spurs were there, his sword belt and scabbard, too.

But of Hugh himself, there was no trace.

"There's no corpse," John called. "But there's still a chance, however slight, that he escaped with his life. He'll try to reach Skelmorlie, but I doubt he'll get very far. These are my lands, I know them well enough. I'll search for him here. I suggest you retrace your steps and leave no stone unturned until you find him."

"I'll recover his arms," one of the retainers offered.

"Make sure you speak to his lady," John said. "Tell her I'll send word once I have news."

They'd been searching along the narrow valley for a long while, seeking any trace of a corpse. The hounds, at least, were enjoying themselves, exploring the rocks by the stream with interest.

"Would he follow the burn?" William asked.

"Perhaps..." John broke off, watching carefully as one of the hounds rummaged by a low stunted hawthorn.

It lifted its head, barked loud. And at that moment John spotted it. A tiny shred of cloth, caught upon a branch.

"Saints be praised!" He scrambled down the hill and delved amongst the branches, ignoring the thorns which snagged his hands. Hauling the cloth free, he inspected it closely: a scrap of pale silk, flecked with blood...

Glancing down he saw that the ground was softer here by the water. There were some indistinct marks, nothing clearly distinguishable.

"Over here!" William called.

John sprang across the water. Sure enough, there was a footprint, the left foot of a man, unshod.

John straightened, filled with a renewed sense of hope. "Let's fetch the horses." He beckoned to the hounds. "Caesar! Pompey!"

They ran up, tails wagging.

"Here." He thrust the rag of silk beneath their noses. "Find him. Go on."

"They're not sleuth hounds," William protested.

"They can try, at least." John looked up, frowning. He could've sworn he heard a horse, whinnying nearby. "Listen!" he said. "There's someone coming,"

He headed briskly up the hill, William and the dogs in close pursuit. The horses hadn't stirred: they were staring into the distance, ears pricked.

John climbed quickly into the saddle. Just in time, for they were no longer alone. Three horsemen were loitering near the scene of the melee. Scowling, John gathered up his reins in readiness.

"John," William warned.

"These are my lands. There's been enough treachery here already."

Andrew Cunninghame, the Master of Craigends. Riding out with two younger boys. They came to meet him, horses striding along at a walk, calm and unhurried.

John swallowed, trying to keep his agitation buried deep. "I thought better than this of Craigends' boy," he muttered to William.

William gave a hollow laugh. "So did I."

The hounds bayed as the horsemen drew closer. "Would you be quiet!" John called to them, acting as if this were an ordinary meeting, on an ordinary day. "Master Cunninghame!" He raised a hand in casual greeting. "Forgive the hounds. They weren't expecting to meet another soul out here. Nor was I. What the Devil are you doing in these parts? We're a long way from Craigends."

Andrew Cunninghame offered him a wan smile, eyes fixed on his horse's mane. "I'm sorry, Sir John. I didn't know we'd wandered so far." He gestured to the boys who rode with him. "My cousin Cuthbert, Master of Kilmaurs. And his brother Guido."

"Good day, sirs." John doffed his bonnet. "I'm pleased to meet you, Master Cuthbert. I knew your grandsire. He was a very worthy man."

"Thank you," Cuthbert Cunninghame replied. "My kinsmen always speak highly of your father. He was a much-valued ally." He shifted in the saddle. "Forgive us, Sir John, for crossing your lands. We were in pursuit of a stag. The quarry was wounded: we wanted to end his suffering." He caught John's gaze. "Have you seen such a beast?"

"Was it an uncommonly fine stag?" John asked. "Tall in stature, of noble lordly bearing?"

"Indeed it was." Cuthbert's tone was guarded.

"I can't say I have," John said. "I'll look out for such a beast. And when I find him, I'll take his carcass to my place." He smiled. "I'm afraid the law is quite clear on this matter. These are my lands. By rights his meat belongs to me."

The faintest of scowls crossed Cuthbert's face. "As you wish, Sir John. Once more, forgive us for trespassing. It won't happen again. Guido, Andrew, let's be gone."

The three youths turned their horses around, and rode off at that same leisurely pace.

John stared after them. "They're hunting him down."

"Perhaps they expected to find a corpse."

"Whatever the case, we haven't a moment to lose." John uttered a sour laugh. "God, what a mockery that was..."

"Let's hope they don't attack us in the night."

"I'd like to believe the Cunninghames are more honourable than that," John said. "I helped Sir William a while back. I stood my ground, and convinced Hugh to grant him his Coroner's office, though God knows it was a close-run thing. Surely that counts for something?"

"In these circumstances," William replied, "I wouldn't be too hopeful."

Chapter 20

Sunlight pierced the rocky hollow that afternoon, bringing some respite from the damp and cold. Water dripped from the vegetation, onto his hands and face: Hugh gathered it up on his fingers and licked the moisture off them.

It helped clear his head a little.

When darkness fell, he pushed himself upright, gripping roots and rocks to steady himself. He took a deep breath and thought of Helen, and that somehow gave him the strength to stir.

He took three steps then fell flat upon his face, his muscles rigid with cold. He struggled to rise, but there was no strength left in his arms to push himself upright. He snarled and wept and clawed at the grass, but this time his legs wouldn't respond.

I'm sorry, my love. I tried so hard to return to you. You'll never know what efforts I made. I failed you.

Despair engulfed him, draining his strength and self-will like an incubus. The soft earth pressed against him, the chill leaching right through him.

It could be days, or even hours. Either way, his fate was sealed.

*　　　*　　　*

Staring through the open window of the laird's chamber, Helen sat in silent vigil, still harbouring the vain hope that Hugh would return. She wasn't alone there: Bessie was curled up beside her, wrapped in one of Hugh's gowns for warmth.

Earlier that night, the girl had crept from her bed, eyes red from weeping. *I couldn't sleep,* she'd said.

Helen did what she could to console the child, though deep inside she felt just as bleak. But her words had provided some comfort, and eventually Bessie nodded off, head resting in Helen's lap.

Helen stroked Bessie's hair, absently. Outside it was a clear night, the stars glowing bright as they steered their stately course through the heavens.

She should've closed the shutters, but she couldn't find the strength to move. She kept thinking of him. Of the joys they'd known together.

Throughout their marriage, she couldn't think of a single moment she regretted. She'd been blessed, to be granted a husband like Hugh. He wasn't perfect, not by any means.

But then, she asked herself, what man was?

*　　　*　　　*

They settled for the night in an old ruined cottage. William set the fire in what remained of the hearth, while John sat upon the toppled gable-wall, the limp corpse of a hare in his hand.

Drawing his knife, he slit fur and flesh, ready to gut the creature before he roasted it. Though it was beyond the hounds to track down a missing man, at least they'd provided the rescuers with dinner.

The Gryphon at Bay

Throughout that long day they'd tramped the river valley, searching every crack and hollow. When night fell, they were exhausted, footsore and despondent: for Hugh to survive a second night alone in the wilds seemed impossible.

It's Hugh, John reminded himself. *If any man can weather this, he can.* He pulled out the entrails and cradled them in his palm, realising that he held the miraculous workings of a living creature, rendered useless now the vital spark was gone.

With a sigh, he tossed them to the dogs.

"Your wedding's ruined," he said to William.

William smiled. "So long as I'm there at the kirk to claim my bride, all will be well."

John didn't reply. He gazed into the fading embers of the fire, lost in thought. Perhaps it was foolish to think he had any bearing on Hugh's conduct. To think that perhaps his friendship and loyalty was a moderating influence.

He had good reason to hate Hugh, but reason to be grateful to him, too. No doubt Hugh had his own motives for being generous, but the truth remained. However hard he tried to dislike the man, he couldn't.

The Place of Eglintoun

The messengers from Skelmorlie awaited her in the hall. One was an older man, silver-haired and clean-shaven. His bonnet was clasped tight in his hands, his face dour and anxious. Accompanying him was a Montgomerie retainer, a young fresh-faced lad.

Helen took a deep breath, bracing herself for the worst. "Do you bring news?"

"My lady..." The older of the two studied his feet. "He left for Eglintoun, but when he rode the bounds a final time, there were difficulties. Davy here-" He gestured to the young man at his side, "-was the last man to see him."

"You left him?" Her voice shook.

"He sent me away." Davy's eyes shone bright with grief. "The third man in our party was killed. He instructed me to deliver the body to safety."

"When did you learn that he'd fallen into difficulties?"

"Sir John Sempill of Ellestoun recovered his horse by Southannan." The young man swallowed. "We were going to raise the alarm. But Sir John insisted our time would be better spent combing the hills." He caught her gaze, anxious. "I hope we did right?"

"Yes, you did. Thank you."

"We found his arms, and his sword. But his body wasn't there." He broke off, then added in a whisper, "We fear he was overwhelmed."

She couldn't quite absorb his words. They were too bleak, too shocking. "He was taken captive?"

"Sir John said we shouldn't give up hope. He bade us search our lands, and said he'd do likewise. He assures you he'll send word, if he finds any further trace of Lord Hugh."

Helen bowed her head. It wasn't much consolation, but it was better than nothing. At least in his hour of need, Hugh hadn't been abandoned.

Louise Turner

They laid everything out in Hugh's chamber. A dismantled suit of plate armour: the same set he'd worn when he left just a few days before, steel flecked with rust and streaked with dirt, helmet dinted at one side. A pair of silver-gilt spurs, the cherished possessions of a knight. And a sword, blade filthy, brown with blood.

Drawing a handkerchief from her sleeve, Helen dabbed her eyes. Hugh had always been full of life and vitality: she couldn't accept that all she had left of him was the hollow metal shell they'd brought down from the hills.

They haven't found a body, she reminded herself. *Perhaps he's still alive.* She almost hoped that wasn't the case, for then Hugh's situation might be infinitely worse. He might be imprisoned somewhere, in the hands of men who hated him. He might be tortured, abused...

And in the meantime she could do nothing. Except sit here and wait. Praying that God would have mercy on her husband, that his friends would find him before his enemies did.

Chapter 21

There were worse ways to die than this. The sun's warmth on his back brought solace, he heard birdsong, poignant and beautiful.

He remembered an old tale. About an abbot, who'd asked the Virgin to give him a glimpse of Paradise before he died. How she'd sent a bird to sing to him, and how he'd listened, entranced, for five hundred years.

He was content now. Ready to slip away to the life hereafter.

The birdsong ceased. There was a rattling alarm call and a flap of wings, so close he felt the breeze beat against his face.

A hound bayed nearby, his reverie was shattered.

Sleuth hounds. He hadn't bargained for that.

"We've found him. Thank God." It was a man's voice, strangely familiar. A hand grasped his shoulder, roughly shook him. "Hugh, are you still with us?"

He didn't answer. Feigning death seemed simpler somehow, than to beg for help...

"Come on, Hugh! Don't give up."

His arms were grasped, he was hauled onto his knees. Old instincts stirred: he snarled and struggled but his captor held firm, weathering the blows.

Without a sound, he slumped forward into a man's clutches.

"Hold still a moment." The voice spoke kindly. "We'll dress the wounds and get those wet things off you."

He heard the words. But they made no sense to him. His clothes were stripped from him, he was laid upon his back, just another indignity to be endured after so many others. He lay still, let them do what they wanted. His wounds were swabbed with a liquid that burned like vitriol. He moaned, despite himself.

A hand gripped his, and a doublet was slipped around his shoulders, still warm from the man who'd carried it. He was wrapped tightly in a blanket and lifted up onto the back of a horse. Someone sat behind him, holding him firm as they moved off at a walk.

The cold eased slightly, he felt himself shivering. He weathered the pain in silence, closing his eyes and resting his head against the shoulder of his rescuer.

"We'll take you to Southannan," the voice said. "It's only a couple of hours away. It'd take half-a-day or more to get you back to Skelmorlie."

Southannan. Skelmorlie. He knew these names, but couldn't place them. He mumbled his agreement, because there wasn't much else he could do, then dropped into a swoon, lulled by the slow pace of the horse and the engulfing warmth of the blanket.

Louise Turner

The Place of Southannan

John and William carried Lord Hugh between them. They laid him upon the board in the hall, and John unwrapped the blanket, revealing a wretched, filthy creature within.

Setting down the flask of *aqua vita*, Margaret wandered over to the fireplace. She rubbed her hands against her hips, awkward, uncomfortable. Lord Hugh was in such a miserable state that she couldn't tell where the dirt ended and the bruises began. He seemed devoid of life, limbs spilling loose across the board.

Katherine stepped close, ashen-faced.

"You needn't stay," Margaret said.

"What if I'm needed?"

She didn't answer. She had no desire to be involved herself. Married just five months, she'd already weathered such horrors, though this time she supposed she was grateful it wasn't John who was suffering.

"Margaret." John leaned against the board and stared straight at her. His shirt was daubed with blood, he looked like a butcher, or a barber-surgeon. He was smiling slightly, it was the kind of smile he bore when he was about to ask a favour. A great favour... "Could you help me, please?"

"Of course." She didn't mean to sound quite so reluctant.

"You're a seamstress. A magnificent seamstress."

She closed her eyes, brief denial.

"Oh go on, Margaret. It's not difficult," Jamie grinned. "Imagine you're stitching a cockatrice for the King's table."

She returned armed with a stout needle and thread and some shears. The preparations were already underway: John had hoisted Lord Hugh into a sitting position and was clutching him tightly, while Katherine poured a steady stream of *aqua vita* into his mouth.

Jamie and William grasped a leg each, and John restrained Lord Hugh's arms and shoulders within a blanket. A prudent move, for the warmth of the hall had revived him a little. Lord Hugh coughed and spluttered and struggled, glowering at them with his basilisk's stare.

Margaret hesitated, unwilling to approach.

John laid him down against the board, pressing on his shoulders to hold him steady. "Sooner it's done, the better. Katherine?"

She started, unnerved by his summons. "Sir John?"

"Fetch me a spoon from the kitchen. Something he can bite on."

Relieved, she nodded and scurried off.

"The herbs are stewing," Margaret said. "Ninian said he'd bring them."

"Good," John seemed very calm and unconcerned. When Lord Hugh twitched and moaned, he merely tightened his grip. "Steady," he said to Lord Hugh. "Won't be long now, I promise."

Katherine returned with a wooden spoon.

"Perfect. When he opens his mouth to snarl, slip it between his teeth."

"Are you ready?" Jamie asked Margaret.

She swallowed. Her palms felt moist. "Yes."

"Good." Jamie hauled Lord Hugh's leg aside. He cried out: a horrible sound, as if uttered by a beast, not a man.

Lifting the shears, Margaret sliced through the bandages. A thin wound snaked its way up the flesh, stretching almost to the groin.

She wanted to weep.

"Don't hesitate," John told her. "It'll only make things worse for him."

She swabbed the wound with *aqua vita*. Taking needle and thread in her hand, she leaned close. Her nostrils caught a foul waft from the wound and she swallowed, fingers shaking.

He drew a sharp hissing breath, but that was it. His flesh trembled beneath her fingertips, she could scarcely get a grip, the skin slippery with blood.

Margaret fumbled and gasped as the needle lodged deep.

"Steady, Margaret." John's voice was soothing. "Take your time. Leave some gaps so the wound can drain."

At last it was done.

They bundled him back in his blanket and carried him up the winding stair. They laid him on a bed and offered him a piss-pot, which came as a blessed relief, then left him alone.

The room was silent, still. Hugh wasn't sure if that boded ill or not. He supposed he was relieved that they'd seen fit to mend his wounds and that he'd been placed in a bedchamber rather than a prison.

His thoughts trailed. He was tired. So very tired. There was nothing more he could do to help himself.

So he dozed, grateful for the respite.

John stood by the doorway to the yard, pulling on his cloak.

"Where are you going?" Margaret asked.

"I must ride to Skelmorlie," he replied. "If you could clean him up and give him some sustenance. Warm milk, and some broth. Not too much, mind, and be careful in case he chokes."

Margaret blinked, unwilling to believe what he was saying. "Can't William go? Or Jamie?"

"I must talk to them myself."

"But I need you here!" She hopped from one foot to the other, unable to conceal her panic. "I don't want to be left alone with him." Her voice trailed away.

"Margaret." John paused at the threshold. He had that look about him, an air of pitying understanding which masked complete intransigence. "He's half-dead."

She glanced aside. "I don't like him. I've never liked him."

"Please, Margaret..." He dropped his voice to a whisper. "It's a woman's place to offer compassion to the sick." He paused. "When I was ill, you tended me..."

Margaret swallowed. "You're my husband."

"Hugh has a wife, who loves him dearly. What would the poor lady think, if she knew her husband was suffering alone, without anyone to offer him comfort and tenderness..." He squeezed her fingers. "Look after him. For my sake."

"Alright," she agreed. "But I wish you wouldn't go alone. Take William, at least..."

"-Don't forget: change the poultices as they get cold. You mustn't neglect it. The more diligent we are, the more chance he has of getting better."

"We need leaves of sweet camphor. And as much *aqua vita* as they can spare."

"I'll speak to the steward." He smiled gentle encouragement. "I'll be as quick as I can."

"Don't break your neck," she warned. "That'd be no good to any of us."

He nodded, and stepped outside.

Leaving her alone there.

She shivered, and turned to start the weary climb up the stair. The dread grew worse with every footfall, angry tears stung her eyes: she didn't want to confront the monster that lay in her chamber, violating their bed with his presence.

I hate you. I wish you'd never been brought here...

Katherine sat by the window in the laird's chamber, shoulders slumped, hands locked before her. "I brought water," she said. "And the rest of the *aqua vita.*"

"You shouldn't be here." Now the moment of reckoning was upon her, Margaret felt calmer. Pausing by the bed, she pulled aside the folds of the blanket. He'd been laid upon his back: she gazed upon his flesh and felt nothing. No hatred, no desire. Not even any sympathy.

"It's too late for that now, isn't it?" Katherine said.

"Perhaps..." She perched on the edge of the bed, wondering where to begin. His eyes were closed, he seemed barely aware of her presence.

Katherine stared in reluctant fascination. "He's not very pleasant to behold."

Margaret smiled. "No, I suppose not." She'd met Lord Hugh often enough to be on speaking terms, at least. Even at the best of times, he was intimidating, an overbearing man whose civilised facade did little to conceal the feral beast within. With his body encrusted with blood and dirt, he looked infinitely worse. Across his body, healed scars mapped out a lifetime of combat and feats of arms.

"Like Christ," said Katherine. "When He was taken down from the Cross."

"Then we should consider him beautiful," Margaret said. "Like the rest of us, he's made in God's image." She stretched out her hand, laid it palm-down against his chest. Beneath the wiry hairs, his skin felt cold, wax-smooth.

Like a corpse, she thought. And shuddered. "Is it our lot in life?" she asked Katherine. "To mend the evil things that men do to one another?"

Katherine shrugged, wordlessly.

"Last time it was John who suffered," Margaret said. "I blamed Lord Hugh for that. I hoped he'd suffer tenfold what his people meted out on John. Now he has, and I'm here to witness it..." She broke off, the words choking in her throat. *I shouldn't have said that*, she told herself. *I shouldn't even have thought it...*

Katherine laid a hand upon her shoulder. "It's not your fault," she said. "You didn't curse him, or conspire against him. From what I've heard about him, he's brought it on himself."

Chapter 22

Stifling a yawn, Margaret sat up and stretched her cramped arms, flexing her fingers to loosen them. She'd been scrubbing at Lord Hugh's grubby flesh for what felt like hours, trying to clean away the dirt and pick out the thorns.

She could've summoned help. But as time passed she'd become such an intimate witness to his suffering that she could never have entrusted his care to another. The fear and distaste had gone completely, she was engrossed instead in the challenge of making him better.

He smelled of earth more than male sweat, as if the mould had reached out its tendrils to pull him down into the land. Like the green man, who died each autumn so he might spring to life afresh the following year. She wondered how long he'd lain alone there, and she wondered about his injuries, too.

"You've witnessed such horrors," she whispered. "And you're keeping them a secret, aren't you?"

He didn't respond. He looked quite peaceful, laid out upon the bed like that. And perhaps, the more she sat with him the more she could glimpse the divine. Even here, in a man so far removed from a state of grace.

Lost in her thoughts, she started as the door creaked open.

She looked up, realised with relief that John had returned from Skelmorlie at last. But her heart sank when she saw the look on his face: hard, grim, with an ice-cold gleam in his eyes that she'd only ever encountered once before.

It had terrified her then, and it terrified her now. How convenient would it be for him to forget his own words, to see his wife attending to a stranger and assume the worst...

He settled against the bedpost, arms folded.

Margaret swallowed, trying to act like nothing was amiss. "Poor man. He's endured all this without complaint."

"Don't pity him." John sank down in the nearby chair and buried his head in his hands. "He'd hate that." He rubbed his eyes with a weary groan and said, "Oh, God. What a night."

She realised it now. That his anger wasn't meant for her. *I'm sorry*, she thought. *I shouldn't have doubted you.* "Who could do this?" she asked.

John looked up and shrugged. "Perhaps when you confront a man of such strength and power, you must resort to cowardice." He stood briefly, leaning over so he could tug the blanket across Lord Hugh's legs. "It's a cold night. Let's not make things worse for him." Slumping back down in his chair, he stretched his feet before him.

"He's been so quiet and still," Margaret said. "Do you think he can hear us?"

"I'm sure he can."

"Then why doesn't he speak?"

"Perhaps he finds it easier not to listen. Who's to say we're his friends?"

111

She shivered, chilled by his words. She'd never for a moment thought her care might be misunderstood. "What if he dies?" she whispered. "Will they hold us responsible?"

"Who knows?" John replied. "Reasonable men would agree that we did our best to help. But Hugh's kinsmen aren't reasonable. Let's just hope and pray that Hugh does the honourable thing and lives." Yawning, he pushed himself up onto his feet. "If I sit any longer, I'll fall asleep. I can't do that just yet. I must find a priest. Hugh should receive absolution, in case the fever takes him."

Blinking back his fatigue, John hurried down the stair, candle in hand. His limbs were leaden, but he couldn't rest yet. There was still too much to do. Too much uncertainty...

Margaret's face haunted him, the look of undisguised terror that had flitted briefly across her features. He'd tried so hard to make amends for past injustices - God knows, they both had - but all it took was something like this for the scars to reveal themselves again in fearful clarity.

He stepped out into the yard. The air was milder, flecks of rain blowing in from the sea. By morning, he reckoned, the weather would have broken.

The chapel wasn't far: he could see it when he left the barmkin, a small stone structure with narrow pointed windows and a tiny bell-cote at the west end.

It was long past vespers. The priest would be in his cottage by now, having supper. Bonnet in hand, John approached and knocked upon the door.

There was no reply.

He knocked again, louder. "Hello?" he called. "I'm sorry to intrude, but..." Silence swallowed his words, he opened the door and stepped inside. "Holy Father? A word, if you please. It's Sir John, from the place..."

Looking about him, he saw a fire burning warm in the hearth and the remains of a half-eaten meal on the table, enough bread and meat there to feed the poor folk of the fermtoun for a week.

But of the priest there was no sign.

John retreated with a sigh. *There'll be an explanation*, he told himself. *A death in the fermtoun, perhaps...*

A candle burned in the side chapel. Its eerie glow lit the chancel, making the shabby altar cloth gleam and the polished gilt cross shine bright as the evening star. But the tranquil beauty was soon ruined: metal vessels clattered on the stone flag floor, a woman moaned, an expression of ecstasy that had nothing to do with mystical revelation.

John halted, scowling. The darkness seemed to lean upon him, pressing his chest, stealing his breath. He knew there were problems with Mother Church. Everyone knew it.

Now the rot had reached as far as his lands, his chapel. A beneficiary paid for by the labour of his tenants and the generosity of his ancestors.

He took one deep breath after another, the rage building inside him. *Turn your back and pretend it never happened. For the sake of a quiet life...*

But it was no good. He'd fought so hard to keep Hugh from Death's clutches. Now when all they needed was a simple blessing to keep him safe from Damnation, it was denied him.

Heading for the source of the light, he found a girl lying flat along the bright tiled floor of the chapel. The priest pressed down upon her, robe pulled up over his buttocks, hose sagging around his knees. He heaved away, so consumed by lust that he didn't even notice John's arrival.

It was the girl who spotted John first. She shrieked and slid out from the priest's grasp, pushing her skirts down over her thighs. A thin-faced waif in a rough woollen gown, aged no more than fourteen or fifteen years.

The priest looked up. A young man of John's age, perhaps slightly younger, he opened his mouth to speak, but John had already grasped his shoulder and hauled him roughly aside.

"Is this why we support you?" John raised his fist, but somehow quelled the urge to strike. "So you can damn your own soul when you should be saving your flock?"

The priest cowered back, close to tears. "In the name of God, sir! Don't tell the Bishop..."

John released his grip. "There's a man in my care. He's wounded. He needs absolution. And a blessing..."

"I'll come now." Clambering to his feet, the priest straightened his robes, face flushed. "Where is he?"

"The Place of Southannan."

"Sir John Sempill?"

"Yes. That's right."

"I'm so sorry. That you should've witnessed this. Please accept my apologies. It won't happen again, I assure you."

The girl cast John a furtive look. He glared back and she scuttled away, head bowed.

The flurry of apologies continued. "For weeks now this girl's been laying temptation at my door. She caught my eye at mass one day, and like a fool I was bewitched..."

"She's young," John retorted. "Weak and prone to foolish acts. Surely it's your duty to keep her on a straight path, free from sin?"

"Are you so free from sin yourself, Sir John?" The priest's voice hardened.

John shrugged, exasperated. His head was hurting, a thumping ache behind one eye. "I've no desire to quarrel," he said. "I just want to help my friend."

    *   *   *

The Place of Eglintoun

One of Hugh's hounds was restless, scratching at the door and whining. The sound of its distress broke the silence, unsettling in the darkness.

He needs to pass water, poor thing, Helen told herself. *That's all it is. Go to him...*

But she couldn't bring herself to move. Lying flat along the bed, she stared unseeing at the canopy above, the sense of loss and isolation draining her of all strength and vigour. Alongside, Bessie murmured in her sleep and pressed closer.

Helen closed her eyes, numb with despair. Earlier that night she'd nodded off just briefly, and in that time she'd dreamed of Hugh. She remembered it all too clearly: a hasty embrace and a snatched kiss in the bower at *Caisteal Glowm*...

She'd woken with a gasp, his face fading in her thoughts. In her dream he'd seemed youthful, vital. Just as he'd been in the days of their courting...

If a man loves you, her nurse once said, *then when he leaves this life, he'll visit one last time to say goodbye.*

She wondered now if that was why she'd dreamed of him with such clarity. She choked back a sob, gripped with desolation. *No,* she told herself. *It can't be true. My one love, my true love. Your light can't be gone from this world...*

An urgent bark sounded, and Helen hauled herself up with a sigh. The reed-strewn floorboards were rough beneath her bare feet, the air cold, oppressive.

Hearing her approach, the hound whimpered, sweeping the floor with its tail. It whined and scrabbled at the door once more, making the knot of foreboding inside her tighten all the more.

She reached through the darkness and patted its shaggy head, then lifted the latch. It sprang off down the stairs, the rattle of its claws receding.

And the room was quiet and still once more.

    *   *   *

They offered him a trickle of warm milk and a few mouthfuls of broth. He couldn't stomach any more than that, but it was enough. It cleared his head a little.

He took a deep breath, marvelling because the taint of mould no longer clung like death to his flesh. He smelled herbs and clean linen, and he smelled *her*, rose-water and lavender mingling with the warm scent of a woman. He wondered where he was and who was tending him. He wondered, too, how best to thank her.

He stayed perfectly still as she wiped the blood from his eyes and nose and dabbed lightly at his swollen lip. He heard the rustle as she set cloth and bowl aside: once that was done, she took his hand.

"There now," she said, so close he could feel her warm breath against his cheek. "We've raised you from the realm of beasts and restored you to the world of men."

For the first time, he opened his eyes. It was dark, the room lit by an array of candles. Their flickering gold flames dazzled him. He could see the profile of her face, but the details of her features were lost. "I... thank you..." His speech was slurred, barely intelligible. "I... am not... very well..."

"I know that." She patted his chest. "With God's help, we'll make you better. You'll be left in peace now. Though we must keep changing the dressings, to help the wounds drain." She gripped his fingers, gently reassuring. "You're safe here with us. You can rest here until you're better. And John will be delighted to hear that you're awake. He'll be here soon. He's gone out to fetch a priest, so you can take Confession."

Propping himself against the door jamb, John watched as the priest sat with Hugh and took his confession. Vaguely coherent, Hugh mumbled something about slaying some men, and committing blasphemy.

John nodded, grim satisfaction. Hugh's soul was safe. That brought some consolation, at least. He straightened, reassured, content he could do nothing more.

Overwhelmed with exhaustion, he slumped down upon the window seat.

Margaret sat alongside. She smoothed her gown over her thighs, saying nothing.

He reached for her hand. "He looks much better now you've washed him. I daresay he feels better, too."

"That's more than can be said for you," she retorted. "Lie down. Get some sleep."

"I can't. Not yet. Not until I know he's on the mend."

She laid a hand against his cheek, concerned. "You've done what you can."

"I suppose so." Three months ago, he would never have thought Margaret capable of such tenderness towards any living soul. But once again, she'd surprised him, just as she'd surprised him in so many other ways.

"He spoke to me. When you were out fetching the priest. He opened his eyes and looked all forlorn. *I'm not very well*, he said, in the most unhappy croak I've ever heard."

John managed a smile.

"John…" Leaning close, she slipped her arm in his. "When I spoke with Marion… She said he killed your father."

John stared towards the bed, where the priest leaned over Hugh, murmuring words of absolution. "I saw them fighting. My father, and Hugh. That's all I remember. After that, I was knocked senseless. When I awoke, my father was dead." He hesitated. "We've never discussed the matter. I see no reason to open old wounds."

"Most men wouldn't show such kindness to the man who'd wronged them…" Margaret broke off, frowning. "Please don't misunderstand me. It's just… It would've been so much easier to stand by and let him rot."

He shrugged and stood in readiness, for the priest had left the bedside.

"Will that be all?" the priest asked.

John accompanied him to the door. "A mass for him on the morrow, if you please. Make sure it's done properly. I'll pay for your services once I'm reassured they've been completed to my satisfaction."

"Sir John." The priest bowed his head and departed.

"That was harsh," Margaret said.

"He was fornicating in the church." He felt the scowl creeping back. "At least his carnal pleasures were with a woman. But that doesn't help us much, does it? How can he intercede with God on Hugh's behalf when he's tainted by his own sins?"

She didn't reply. Her head and shoulders dropped, she tried in vain to conceal a yawn.

"You're tired, Margaret. You should sleep. Lie down on the bed beside him, there's plenty of room."

"What about you?" Her voice was accusing.

"Don't worry about me," he said. "Someone needs to look after him through the night."

Chapter 23

The Castle of Dumbarton

"For weeks we've perched upon our lofty spire, waiting." Matthew gestured across to the broad grey waters of the Clyde. "For what? A fleet of ships? An English army?"

Robert, Lord Lyle leaned against the parapet with a sigh. "Your father left instructions." His reply was dutiful, half-hearted.

Matthew paced back and forth along the wall-walk. "We can't wait for help that never comes, Robert. It's time to act."

Lyle shrugged. "Mattie, I can't tell you what you can or cannot do. Your father placed you in command of the garrison. Therefore I will support you, come what may."

Matthew halted with a sigh. "Thank you." He glanced about him, frowning. "Have you seen Alex?"

"He's in the stables, I think. Why?"

"No matter," Mattie said, briskly. "I wanted a word, that's all." He smiled. "You've been like a father to him, Robert. I appreciate that. We all do."

Lyle shook his head. "It's no trouble, Mattie. Breaks the tedium, I suppose."

"Time we put all that schooling to good use, don't you think?"

"Whatever do you mean?"

Matthew smiled, and walked away.

"-I know I shouldn't wish for war," the boy's voice drifted from the depths of the stables. "But it doesn't seem right, that I'm trapped here doing nothing, while Father fights our battles-"

Matthew sighed, sympathetic. Venturing closer, he found his brother engrossed in grooming Ajax. The black horse stood there with eyes half-closed, relishing the attention. "Alex, a word please."

Alex looked up, shamefaced. "Mattie, I'm sorry. I didn't know..."

Matthew shrugged. "He's always had the grace to hear me out when things are difficult. I'm sure he's pleased to do the same for you." He paused. "Alex, I have a task for you. A task worthy of a knight." He watched the boy carefully, gauging the reaction, then realised in grim delight that the boy was waiting eagerly for him to continue. "First of all, I want you to find one of the servants. Tell him you're going out into the town and that you need to borrow some clothes so you won't look out of place-"

His face fell. "You're sending me away?"

"-Once that's done, come back here. I'll be waiting. I'll tell you what's required. In the meantime-" He held out his hand for the brush. "-I can carry on where you left off."

* * *

"Mattie?" Alex called. "I've done what you asked."

116

The Gryphon at Bay

"Not so loud!" Matthew hissed. He clapped his horse's neck one last time, then sidled from the stall. Turning to confront his brother, he couldn't resist a smile: dressed in a scruffy pair of hose and a rough-looking tunic, Alex looked more like a cowherd than a kinsman of the king.

Just don't open your mouth to the wrong man, Matthew thought. "What I want from you is this: I need you to go into the town and find Elizabeth. Ask her what she knows about the King's forces. How many men there are, where they're camped. If you can't get back here safely, don't try. She'll look after you until the danger's past."

"A marvellous quest!" The boy's eyes glowed in expectation. "When will I be leaving?"

"Whenever you like."

"Then I'll go right now-"

"Alex..." Matthew gripped his brother's arm, firmly. He had the distinct impression that the boy would rather scale Castle Rock or die trying than abandon his kin to their fate.

"Don't fret, Mattie. I'm listening."

"I doubt that." He slipped an arm round his brother's shoulders, a last gesture of support. "I can't go with you to the gates. It'd rouse suspicion."

Alex nodded, and darted away.

Like a hound when the hare breaks cover, Matthew thought.

Nursing faint misgivings, he loitered a little longer to give the boy a head start. He left the stables at a brisk pace and climbed up onto the wall-walk: from there he could see the cobbled road that led from the main gateway to the town below.

He saw Alex at last, sauntering along as if he hadn't a care in the world.

A few soldiers leaned on their spears, just out of bowshot. They wore shabby brigandines and sallets – probably Argyll's men, Matthew thought – and they glanced up as Alex approached. When the lad nodded to them, they ignored him.

Alex went on his way unchallenged, and Matthew could breathe easy once more.

    *   *   *

Darkness enveloped him. Absolute. Overwhelming.

Hugh was on his knees. Naked. Hands bound with chains before him, head bowed with the weight of a heavy iron collar round his neck.

His fear was overpowering. It crippled him. Stole the breath from his body and the strength from his limbs. He shook uncontrollably, cowed by his blindness and the cold and the fearful stench of mould and death and filth.

Voices. Coarse and grating. He was relieved he couldn't see the creatures who spoke to him, for he had no doubt they'd be as foul to the eye as their words were to the ear. They stroked and prodded him, telling him how they'd enjoy his company throughout eternity. They spoke of what they'd do to him, if Judgement weighed against him. "The corporeal body has passed," they said. "And your misery will be all the more sublime, because you'll endure it endlessly, again and again. We'll make you lie upon red-hot coals, send serpents to attend you. They'll gnaw on your privy parts and chew on your belly, until the skin's shredded and they can slip inside to feast upon your entrails..."

    *   *   *

The Place of Southannan

Margaret stretched and yawned. She was curled on the bed, still fully dressed and pleasantly warm. Thick, heavy cloth enveloped her. It was John's gown, it carried his scent: she drowsed, savouring the memory of his presence. When she stirred, the fur trim tickled her nose and she fought the urge to sneeze.

"-We'll need to change the sheets," John was saying. "They'll be saturated in no time."

"Should we wake her?" Katherine asked.

"Let her sleep. God knows, she needs it. Oh, fetch some water for me, would you? I must wash."

The warmth subsided a little. She rolled over, her face striking the hard bone of Lord Hugh's shoulder. He thrashed alongside, she heard him moan loud, as if in pain or terror.

Suddenly awake, she sat up. "What's happening?"

"He took a turn for the worse last night." It was only when John turned to face her that she saw the gaunt look about his face, the hopelessness. "I didn't have the heart to wake you."

Standing by the edge of the bed, Margaret stared down at Lord Hugh. Last night he'd been calm and peaceful. Now he muttered and groaned under his breath, grey eyes staring out from a face that was deathly pale and rimed with sweat.

She waved her fingers before his nose, but he seemed to be looking right through her. Teasing back the covers, she took his hand. His fingers locked about hers, relentless and desperate. "He looks as if the angels and the devils are fighting for his soul."

John rummaged in the kist for a clean shirt. "Perhaps they are," he said.

Light chased away the darkness. Brilliant and glorious, it burned his eyes.

He glanced away, unable to confront it, while the creatures who'd tormented him shrieked and wailed and shrank away into the shadows. He could sense Their Presence, the Father and the Son. But he couldn't see them.

He realised then that it wasn't Their place to Judge him. Instead, he found himself confronting a venerable old man, Minos himself, who had in attendance four men, each clad in the brilliant white raiment of the righteous.

And he knew them. One was James, Lord Boyd, the youth he'd slain. The others were men he'd once called allies: Alexander Cunninghame, Earl of Glencairn; Sir Thomas Sempill, and King James himself. Men who shared a common grievance, for each had met his end challenging his ambition...

*   *   *

The Place of Kilmaurs

Christian heard the commotion from her chamber. Her boy's voice crying out from the yard below, wordless rage, frustration. She responded at once, leaping to her feet, throwing her prayer book aside. She was his mother. How could she ignore him?

She hurried down the stairs and paused at the door. Steeling herself, she took a deep breath and stepped outside.

It was Guido. He was hacking at the timber pell in the courtyard, sword biting deep, sending splinters flying. Hauling it out, he resumed the assault. He roared and howled, his blows growing ever more frenzied. Then he flung the blade aside and dropped to his knees, sobbing.

She grasped her skirts and broke into a run. "Guido!"

The Gryphon at Bay

His brown hair flopped over his brow, his face red from weeping. When he looked up and saw her standing over him, his slim young body shuddered all the more.

She crouched by his side and gripped his shoulders. "What's happened? For pity's sake, tell me!"

He raised clasped hands towards her. "Forgive me, Mother. I- I killed a man..." He gulped back a sob. "What am I to do?"

"Where's Cuthbert?"

"In his bed, asleep. I couldn't sleep. I don't think I'll ever sleep again..."

Pulling out her handkerchief, Christian wiped away his tears. "We'll fetch a priest. You must confess this sin, and then he'll decide what penance is required. Was it-" she swallowed. "Was it in cold blood?"

"I swear it was an accident. I was frightened. I didn't want to kill him. I thought I'd hit his horse. I should've wounded him, but I think the blow was mortal, and now I fear for my soul..."

"Hush, Guido. Hush..." She clasped him close. "What madness is this? What made you do such a thing?" She passed him the handkerchief.

He blew his nose, loudly. "I- I can't tell you."

"You can't tell your own mother? Guido, you must!"

"Please don't ask this of me."

Christian stroked his hair. "Very well." Her tone was firm, decisive. "But you must confess everything to your father when he returns."

"Is it always this way?" he asked. "Each time a man rides into battle? Is it always this hard?"

"I don't know," she said. "You'll have to ask your father. It's small consolation, I know, but I've heard it said that the first kill is always the worst."

"I thought that seeing the beasts die after the hunt would prepare me, but it's not the same..."

"It's not meant to be. To take a man's life is much more grave. No one expects the huntsman to confess his sins each day. Or the butcher." She straightened, and tugged his hands. "Come on, Guido. Come inside with me. Will you do this? Will you come with your mother?"

He nodded, and clambered to his feet. She put her arm about his shoulders, and for the first time in almost two years, he didn't shrug her away.

She spoke for him. She made an impassioned plea on his behalf. Citing the prayers of his wife and his children, who loved him dearly.

But not even Her intercession could move them. For how could the love of a woman ever weigh favourably against the death of four men?

"It grieves us all to see you cast into the Pit," Minos said. "But the Judgement is sound, you are condemned by your own wrongdoings."

He begged for them to reconsider, to grant him some means to mend his ways, but already clawed hands were closing about his shoulders, hauling him back.

Into the shadows, their domain.

The Light was fading. But as it failed, he saw her. Looming over him, standing ten foot tall, with skin like bristled hide and coal black eyes.

She smiled, revealing a row of blackened teeth. "My consort," she said. "My love. Let's retire to our bridal bower and celebrate our union."

He stared, stricken, for there was a serpent's mouth where her cunny should be, the hairs above a mass of writhing worms. He felt his bowels go and he pissed himself, as she took him by the heels and hauled him away. The chill was creeping up his skin, the stench of decay prickling his nostrils.

He howled himself hoarse, but couldn't even hear his own voice any more. For the clamour was growing louder, drowning out all else, the shrieks and groans of countless souls, all damned like himself to suffer for their sins for the rest of Time...

Dumbarton Castle

I

t wasn't much of a feast. A solitary goose graced the boards, along with a few loaves. With Alex absent, Matthew stepped in to carve the meat and pass the slices amongst the diners at the top table.

His mother stared at him, keenly appraising. "Where's Alex?" she asked.

"He slipped out this morning," Matthew replied.

Her face darkened. "He did *what?*"

"He spoke quite cordially to the guards at the gate, and they sent him on his way without question."

"I should break your neck for this," she muttered.

Lord Robert glanced towards Matthew. He looked faintly perplexed, nothing more. "And what, exactly, does your brother intend by this sortie?"

"I'm going to sack the town," Matthew said, in a pleasant, matter-of-fact voice. "Alex has gone to warn Elizabeth. And to see what news she's gleaned about the host."

Lord Robert bowed his head, shoulders shaking with laughter. "Ah, Matthew," he said. "What a delightful thing this is..."

The countess fixed Matthew with a piercing stare. "You shouldn't have placed such a burden upon your brother."

He'd learned long ago not to let that stern, bright-eyed look intimidate him. He stared back, unrepentant. "I have every faith in Alex. He wants to play his part. Surely you won't begrudge him that? Or would you have him rot here like the rest of us?"

She considered his words, saying nothing. Eventually, she offered up a weary smile. "You're right, Mattie. I forget, sometimes, that he's almost a man." She poured more wine into their goblet. "Tomorrow, when he returns, we'll have a feast in his honour. He'll deserve it."

The Place of Southannan

John drew up a chair and sat down there. He leaned forward and rubbed his eyes, exhausted, despondent. "How is he?"

"Very quiet and still," Margaret said. She'd been tending Hugh all afternoon, laying cool cloths against his brow, bathing his limbs and body. "It was like this when you were sick." She cast him a sideways look, faintly accusing. "I thought you'd die."

"I'm sorry," John said. "I didn't mean to cause such worry." He slumped back. "God, this is unbearable."

"Go to the chapel," she said. "Pray for him." She laid her hand on his. "He's in safe hands."

"I know that-" He broke off, for Jamie was hailing him from outside. He wandered to the window: peering out, he drew a sharp anxious breath, for a mass of horsemen were milling round the gates. "Oh, Hell..."

Margaret looked up. "Whatever's the matter?"

"It's the Montgomeries, I think. They've come seeking Hugh." Grabbing gown and bonnet, he headed for the door.

Jamie loitered on the wallwalk with William. "I'm right glad to see you," he told John. "I'm not much good at parley."

John sighed. Looking down beyond the wall, he counted at least thirty men, armed and mounted. Hugh's kinsman, John Montgomerie of Hessilhead, rode at the head of the party, thickset, bearded and irate.

"Open up!" he roared, and battered the hilt of his sword against the door.

"Strike out first, ask questions later," muttered William. "That should be their battle-cry."

John smiled grimly. "What's the meaning of this, Master Montgomerie?" he called.

"I'm told you're holding our kinsman captive within these walls," Hessilhead challenged. "And that you've purloined a certain horse..."

"What in God's name are you talking about?"

"My cousin." Hessilhead scowled at him. "Deliver him at once."

"He'll be granted my hospitality until he's fit to travel. So will the horse."

Hessilhead glanced around his men, face hard, determined. "I'll be the judge of that."

"I'd invite you inside to make that appraisal in person," John said. "*If* you addressed me in a more civilised manner. Forgive me if I'm reluctant to admit you. I won't put my wife and retainers in peril."

Undeterred, Hessilhead thumped the pommel of his sword against the gate a second time. "For Christ's sake! Open up!"

"You're not convincing me that you came here peacefully, Master Montgomerie," John retorted. "Will you assure me that you'll grant us all due courtesy?"

Hessilhead studied his horse's mane, rage fading to surly resignation. "For pity's sake, Sir John. Let me speak with my kinsman."

"We can't take your men tonight," John mentioned as he led Hessilhead across the yard. "We don't have the provisions to feed them."

Hessilhead cast him a sullen glance. "Damned notary," he muttered. "Always muddying the waters with argument and rhetoric. You think you can run rings round a soldier like me."

John paused outside the tower-house. "That's a fine tone to take with me, after what I've done for you."

"You should've brought him to Skelmorlie." Hessilhead's tone was emphatic.

"I was five hours from Skelmorlie, and two from Southannan." He started up the stair, Hessilhead following close behind.

"He's injured?"

"He's lost a lot of blood, and he spent two nights out in the cold with his wounds untended. He's very weak."

"Where did you find him?"

"On my own lands." John rubbed his forehead. The ache had resumed there: it wasn't helped by the fact that he desperately needed sleep.

"Did he say what happened?" Hessilhead persisted. "Did you see anything that might hint at how things unfolded?"

Three young men from the House of Kilmaurs, John thought. *But the least said about that, the better.* "He's been in no state to talk. And I saw no more than your own people did. I thought at first he'd been taken captive."

"But you kept looking for him?" The other man sounded baffled. "Whatever for?"

John didn't answer. Opening the door to his chamber, he gestured for Hessilhead to step inside. "Come in," he said. "Margaret's been tending him."

Margaret stood as they entered.

"Lady Margaret." Hessilhead nodded to her. "I'm here to claim what's mine."

"You can't move him," she said.

"Jesus Christ Almighty!"

"Please don't curse like that," Margaret said. "He needs peace and quiet."

"Stupid woman..." Hessilhead turned to John, scowling. "I won't be dictated to by *her*." Barging past, he hauled back the covers. "Stir yourself, Hugh. Time to go." He grasped Hugh's arm and pulled.

"You're wasting your time," Margaret said.

Oblivious, Hessilhead swatted his kinsman's cheek. "Come on, Hugh. Don't do this..." He shook him, roughly.

"Leave him alone!" Margaret pushed his hand away. "The last thing he needs is an ogre like you pawing at him."

Hessilhead batted her aside. "Keep your nose out of our business."

John leaned against the wall, watching carefully. Margaret caught his eye, a subtle look that told him she wasn't afraid. "It's my concern, too," she told Hessilhead. "I won't let you take him." Without another word, she replaced sheets and coverlet.

Hessilhead turned to John, making no attempt to conceal his derision. "You just stand there, and let her dictate the terms? What kind of a man are you?"

"I'm content to heed her advice. If I were you, Master Montgomerie, I'd do likewise. If you force him to travel, he won't survive the journey."

"Perhaps that's what you want," Margaret said. "He's given you the fruit of his loins. I don't suppose you have any further use for him."

"Of all the damned insolent-" Hessilhead raised his hand.

John straightened, fingers gripping the hilt of his dagger. "Lay a finger on my wife, and I'll gut you."

Hessilhead glared back, defiant.

It was Margaret who spoke first, breaking the impasse. "We're doing what we can for your kinsman, Master Montgomerie," she said. "I don't think we merit this discourtesy."

The Gryphon at Bay

Hessilhead studied the floor. Eventually, he shrugged. "Forgive me. I spoke out of turn." He nodded towards Hugh. "I won't disturb him." Sinking down into one of the empty chairs, he hunched forward, frowning. "He's my cousin. And my friend." He glanced up, pale with worry. "What happened to him? Do you know?"

"He was set upon," John said.

"He's very sick," Margaret added. "But we've plastered the wounds and we're doing what we can to help him."

"Leave him here," John finished. "I'll send word if there's any change."

"Uh, yes, I suppose so." Hessilhead pulled off his sallet. His limp black hair drifted forward, past his face. He rubbed his bearded chin, deep in thought. "Oh, Christ, Hugh. What possessed you to ride off alone..."

"You should go to Eglintoun," John said. "Tell Lady Helen that her husband's still alive."

Hessilhead gazed at him, blankly. "He was set upon, you say. Was he injured in the melee?"

"The wounds came later."

Hessilhead stared at his kinsman, deep in thought. He scratched his chin, and frowned. "If what you say is true, then it's unpardonable. He represents the King..."

"Speak to Lady Helen. Put her out of her misery."

"When there's more pressing matters to attend to?" Hessilhead pushed himself to his feet, scowling anew. "We'll have those base-born cowards squealing by the time we've finished with them."

"You could burn a dozen villages and still not find the guilty men," John countered. "Why strike out prematurely? Hugh knows the truth of what happened. Let him be the one to exact retribution. He deserves that much, surely?"

But Hessilhead had already turned his back and was thumping his way down the stairs.

John sat down by the window. He twisted his bonnet in his grip, realising then that his hands were shaking. "Would a word of thanks be too much to ask for?"

Margaret closed the door. "They're animals," she said. "A pack of wolves." She wandered over, standing before him with arms folded. "For Heaven's sake, John. You must rest."

"I'll lie down for a little while," he promised, and drew his legs up on the seat alongside.

She fussed around him. Placing a cushion beneath his head, pulling off his shoes and unfastening his belt. He closed his eyes, savouring her presence. Her gown rustled as she moved, her lips briefly touched his cheek. "Sleep now," she whispered. "God knows, you deserve it."

Chapter 24

The Place of Kilmaurs

"Lady Christian!" An armed retainer burst into the ladies' chamber, too agitated even to knock. "They're attacking the fermtoun. There must be two, three dozen of them!"

Christian sprang to her feet, heart pounding. "Are the gates closed?"

He nodded. "Barred and bolted, my lady."

"We'll keep watch from the wall-walk, and do what we can to defend the place."

As she swept down the spiral stair, her limbs were trembling, her throat dry. She remembered Guido's face, stricken, remorseful. *I killed a man...*

What manner of a man was it, she asked herself, *for them to take such retribution...*

Peering out over the parapet of the barmkin wall, Christian stifled a moan. It was like looking out on the Apocalypse: the fermtoun was ablaze, she counted five houses alive with fire. Men, women and children ran back and forth, aimless, screaming loud with fear.

A wagon burned. Five men dragged it closer, defended by a dozen armoured men on horseback. It struck the gates with a thump: the timbers creaked and groaned, the door-check jumped in its brackets.

Cutbert came running, crossbow in hand.

"Cuthbert, please!" she called. "Stay there!"

He ignored her, springing up the stairs two at a time. His face was pale and drawn.

When he drew level, she gripped his arm. "For pity's sake, Cuthbert. Do nothing. Not until we know what they want."

"They want us dead, Mother. That's what they want."

Flames crackled against the gate, reaching almost to the parapet. The scent of fire reached the stables, making the horses scream loud with fear. *It's like Kerrielaw,* she thought. *The time they burned it. It's happening all over again.*

An armoured horseman approached below, bearded, thickset. A brute of a man, face set in a grim scowl.

"What do you mean by this outrage?" Her voice rang out, clear, determined.

He pulled his horse into a half-rear. "Don't play the innocent with me!"

"John Montgomerie of Hessilhead," Cuthbert muttered, "I could bring him down..."

"You'll do no such thing!" She pushed him aside. "I won't sanction murder!" She leaned against the parapet. "Master Montgomerie, you seem aggrieved."

"For every precious drop of his blood that was spilled, the Cunninghames will shed a gallon." His horse fidgeted, agitated by the leaping sparks from the burning cart. "And if he dies, then by God the burns will run red when we come for retribution!"

The Gryphon at Bay

Her heart pounded so hard she could scarcely breathe. "I don't know what you're talking about."

Cuthbert lifted the crossbow, aimed it.

"No!" She seized his arm, jolted it aside.

"Witch!" Hessilhead spat. "Devil's whore." He spun his horse around and urged it away at a canter.

And they'd gone. Just as quickly as they'd come. Cottages and barns were burning, women wailing, the gates still blocked by the burning cart.

"Damn." Cuthbert studied the departing warband, a slight frown on his face. "I could've had him."

"What did he mean?" Grasping his arms, she pulled him close. "You must tell me." She emphasised each word with a rough shake. "Was it something you did?"

Cuthbert said nothing.

"For every precious drop of his blood... *Whose* blood? Cuthbert, talk to me!"

He prised her hands loose. "You're not my keeper," he said, and walked away.

The Place of Southannan

He was warm, comfortable. Linen sheets felt crisp against his skin, he could hear women's voices speaking nearby.

Lying still with eyes closed and mind half-aware, he realised then that he wasn't dead, and that he wasn't dreaming, either. He'd been delivered to a place of sanctuary. Beyond that, he couldn't imagine where he was. He knew only that he wasn't lying in his own bed at Eglintoun.

Hugh shifted slightly. Pain shot like lightning through his spine, into his head. He gasped and opened his eyes, but it felt as if the world was spinning, he was gazing down into an immeasurable void.

"Rest easy." A woman spoke nearby. Her fingers pressed light against his shoulders, holding him down. "All will be well, but you must give it time."

He blinked, and his surroundings settled. The woman who looked down on him was young, aged fifteen or sixteen years, with a cheerful smile and a delicate face. Her deep brown hair was braided down her back and she wore a neatly-worked gown of dark-green velvet.

And he knew her.

"Lady Margaret," he acknowledged. "I thought I might be dead. And amongst the angels." He sighed. "But I'm not dead. I'm at Ellestoun."

"Not Ellestoun, Lord Hugh. Southannan. We were visiting our place here. Which is as well for you. Else you'd be feeding the corbies..."

"Ah..." He closed his eyes. "God is merciful."

"You were very ill yesterday," she said. "You gave us all a bellyache with the worrying we had to do."

"I've caused such inconvenience. I should be gone, before I'm responsible for yet more." He tried to move, but pain erupted in his neck once more. "Holy Mary!"

"Be still!" Her grip tightened. "I'm under strict instructions to keep you in your bed. I'll sit on you if I must, or bind you to the bedposts. Anything, to keep you from wandering."

"Heaven forbid!" He managed a smile of sorts. "Very well. I'll submit to your authority. There's worse fates that could befall a man, than to find himself captive in the bower of Diana."

She laughed, a joyous, heartwarming sound. She reminded him of Bessie, impossibly young, still innocent of the world. An absurd comparison, for Margaret Colville was already married and running a busy household. "You're so much better now," she said. "But you mustn't expect miracles. You should rest with us at least another week."

"I feared you'd want rid of me sooner," he admitted. "I don't think I could sit upon a horse just yet."

"You don't think much of your fellow men," she retorted. "If you think we'd throw you out to fend for yourself, when you've not so much as a set of clothes to your name."

"I'm sorry." He swallowed, overwhelmed. "Where's John? He's been very gracious, granting me such care from his good lady."

The smile lit her face once more. "He's in the stables, tending your horse."

"Zephyr found himself in safe hands then." He sank against the pillow, eyes closed. "Thank God..."

"John shows much more tenderness towards a big mute beast of a horse than he does to his fellow men. But he'll be overjoyed when I tell him you're awake." She sprang to her feet. "Now, I have one last reason to trouble you. Are you hungry?"

When he thought about it, he *was* hungry. And thirsty, too. "I'm famished, Lady Margaret."

"Then Katherine will fetch some pottage, without delay. And I shall fetch John."

And without another word she was gone, a breathless whirlwind of joy and vitality.

Zephyr whickered expectantly, hooves threshing swathes through the straw. John threaded his way past, placed the bucket down, then stood back and watched as the horse devoured its breakfast.

He felt pleasantly refreshed. Margaret had left him undisturbed; he'd slept right through the night and on into the following morning.

"John!" Margaret hurried in, skirts lifted high to keep them from trailing in the dirt. "He's awake. He wants to speak to you."

"That's excellent news!" Ducking under the rope that closed off Zephyr's stall, he followed her outside. "For a while, he had me worried."

They stepped out into the yard, hurrying back towards the tower-house. "He's not himself," Margaret said.

"He's lost a lot of blood. That'll have cooled his temperament. Which may not be too bad a thing..."

"It's disconcerting."

"I'm sure his fiery humours will soon be restored. And then you'll get exasperated, and want to throttle him." Opening the door, he gestured for her to enter ahead.

She darted past him up the stair, feet thudding soft against the stone.

The Gryphon at Bay

Hugh was lying back against his pillow, vague and tired perhaps, but very much awake. He offered a half-hearted smile as John drew a chair alongside.

"I thought I knew the voice," he said. "But I was dazed, and fearful. I'm sorry, if I wasn't helpful." He swallowed. "I don't know what to say."

John reached out and squeezed his shoulder. "I couldn't have left you there."

Hugh said nothing. He was frowning slightly.

"What happened?" John asked. "Can you remember?"

"They were lying in wait. A score of them, maybe more. They baited me, like a bear. A wound here, a wound there, until they weakened me. They knew my strength would fail eventually." He broke off. "The rest I'd rather not recall."

John's grip tightened. "Would you know them?"

Hugh's eyes narrowed. Despite the bruises, the swelling about his face, he was fierce, determined, his old self. "Oh, yes."

"When I rode out to find you, there were strangers on my lands. The Masters of Craigends and Kilmaurs, and one of their kinsmen." John paused. "Did they do this?"

Hugh sagged against the pillow, visibly exhausted. "How much they witnessed, I don't know," he said at last. "But they weren't directly involved. In fact, Master Cuthbert stepped in and saved my bollocks. For that I'm grateful. But I doubt he did it out of kindness. He wanted to be the one who killed me. If I'd bled to death first, that little pleasure would have been denied him."

John couldn't hide his incredulity. "He said he'd kill you?"

"When the moment came, he couldn't." Hugh grimaced. "There I was, grovelling on my knees before him. Bound and bleeding like a dying hog and with my clothes ripped asunder so the world could witness my humiliation."

"Christ, Hugh..."

"And yet I wasn't afraid. They knew I wasn't afraid..." He closed his eyes. "You've heard my confession. I never thought I'd share those memories with any man."

"To have encouraged such violence against a gentleman. A King's officer..." John drew a sharp breath. "It's not acceptable."

"Don't look so horrified," Hugh said. "I'll have retribution. In good time. I presume Cuthbert returned to retrieve my corpse. At least we thwarted him on that count."

"I'll ride to Eglintoun."

"If it's not too much trouble," Hugh said. "I'd appreciate that."

"Any message?"

"Tell Helen that no action must be taken until I'm fit and well and ready to dictate its course. Whatever my kinsmen say, she must hold her ground."

"I'll do that. And gladly." John stood. "I'll be gone overnight. But Margaret's here. She'll look after you."

"You're very trusting. To leave me alone with her."

John smiled. "I hardly think you're in a fit state to seduce her. Besides... You're an honourable man. And she's an honourable lady. I have every faith in you both."

"I shall guard her virtue with my life, John," Hugh assured him, and grimaced. "For what that's worth."

Margaret watched from the wall-walk as John's horse dwindled from sight. Once he'd vanished, she shivered and wrapped her arms tight about her. She felt very small and insignificant, completely ill-suited to the task ahead.

Jamie bowed his head, mock-servitude. "We're in your care now."

"We should keep the place secure."

"Perhaps..." Jamie slouched against the parapet, lips pursed. "But just think, Meg, what an opportunity this presents. The most reviled tyrant in the Westland is entirely at our mercy." A slight smile crossed his lips. "He's slaughtered so many innocents already, and never accounted for his sins."

Margaret stiffened. "You'd murder him?"

"We could slip some hemlock in his wine. Though we needn't do the deed ourselves, when there's others more than eager to oblige. We could get a message to interested parties, and leave the gates open at night. Accidentally, of course..." He paused. "I'm sure his end would be carried out discreetly."

She glared at him. "Don't say such things, Jamie. Not even in jest."

Jamie gazed back, unbowed. "Who said I was jesting?"

Her heart pounded as she climbed up to the laird's chamber, her thoughts filled with fearful possibilities. If the Cunninghames knew where Hugh had been taken, perhaps they'd storm the place, burn it to the ground...

Katherine met her on the stair. "I couldn't stay in there alone."

"For Heaven's Sake, Katherine!"

"He makes me nervous. He's got eyes like a hawk, the way he looks at you..." Katherine cast a sidelong glance at Margaret. "What are you going to do? You're supposed to tend him."

"He's not a monster. He's just a man. Now, go downstairs and see if the pottage is ready."

"Will you be alright?"

"Of course." Margaret hurried on her way without a backwards glance.

But outside the door to the laird's chamber, she paused. Lord Hugh had been placed in her care, but the more she thought about it, the less she knew how to deal with him. It was different when he'd been senseless. He'd been infinitely more amenable...

She opened the door with a sigh.

"Lady Margaret," Lord Hugh acknowledged. He seemed painfully frail, for someone who was always robust and full of vigour. More wraith than man, weak and insubstantial.

She forced a smile. "Katherine won't be long. Shall I help you sit up?"

"Please."

Pulling back the covers, she grasped his shoulders and supported him as he struggled to sit. The effort pained him, for he grimaced, but he didn't cry out. Moving the pillows so he had something firm to lean against, she rearranged the coverlet in his lap.

"Thank you." He tried to smile, but didn't quite succeed. With his bony shoulders and the coarse black hairs upon his chest, he still looked vaguely bestial.

Perching on the bed beside him, she laid a hand upon his shoulder. "I heard what happened," she said. "I'm sorry."

"It's behind me now. Not worth worrying about."

"But to have been at their mercy, waiting for death..."

His gaze met hers. Despite his bruised and battered body, his eyes were just as she remembered them, bright and brilliant. She wasn't surprised that Katherine had fled, for at such close quarters his presence was unnerving. "They wanted me to fear them," he told her. "They wanted me to be ashamed. But it was as if a great light shone from the Heavens and pierced my heart. It gave me the strength and courage I needed. I wasn't alone there. I had stronger powers helping me that day."

"You've very brave, Lord Hugh."

"I learned a valuable lesson," he told her. "That a man's dignity can't be measured by arms or wealth. It comes from here." He seized her hand and laid it against his chest. "From his soul. If that remains strong and unbowed, then the fate of the flesh no longer matters."

She smiled, half-heartedly. "I wouldn't wish to face my death so willingly."

"You misunderstand me." He spoke with surprising earnestness. "I didn't want to die. I'd have done anything in my power to avoid it. But if death was necessary, then I was prepared." He seized her hand. "Tell me, Lady Margaret. Was it you who tended me that first night?"

Margaret glanced aside. "You were in a sorry state."

He gripped her fingers, tightly. "You were very kind and gentle. And very patient, too." He swallowed, close to tears. "It helped very much."

"I hope you'll forgive me, if you thought I was too familiar. But you were in such a mess, with all the blood and grime." She hesitated. "I didn't think you knew what was happening. Until you spoke."

"I was sick as a dog from the *aqua vita*, but all too aware of my circumstances. I wasn't sure where I was, or into whose hands I'd fallen. But you helped convince me that I was in the company of friends."

"I'm sorry. I didn't know you were frightened. You seemed so distant..." She bowed her head, remembering... "I stitched the wounds. John asked me to. I hope I didn't hurt you."

"It had to be done." He winced. "Ah, God. My neck. It hurts whenever I move. The rest I can live with."

"It'll mend in good time."

"You deserve a sainthood. You've lavished such care upon me. It can't be pleasant. I'm a mangled old beast, and not very fair to behold."

"I'm sure Lady Helen would say that even a mangled old beast like you has his merits."

"A diplomatic answer, Lady Margaret. And one which is appreciated." He sighed, weary, thoughtful. "It's a ridiculous thing," he said. "When my enemies exposed my flesh and mocked me, I felt nothing. But here, in the presence of my friends, I'm ashamed."

"We're as God made us, Lord Hugh. That's all that matters."

He studied her carefully. "We're on intimate terms now," he said. "You've cared for me as a man, not a lord or courtier. Let's not burden ourselves with formalities."

She fiddled with her hair, unsure how to respond. To deny him his rank was to deny all those attributes she'd once feared and adored in equal measure. "I'll try," she said. "But you're a mighty man, very noble and puissant."

Hugh smiled, but there was no humour there. "I've none of those qualities just now."

Margaret swallowed, suddenly overwhelmed. She patted his hand. "No more of this, please. You're not yourself. Rest quietly, and in a few days it will all be better."

Dumbarton Castle

The gates groaned open a sliver and Alex sidled through the crack. Following close behind came Elizabeth Sempill, dressed once again in sober grey.

Matthew stepped into the gloom of the gatehouse. "Hello, Elizabeth." He kissed her lightly on both cheeks then turned to Alex. Clutching him close, he slapped his back and said, "Well done, lad. You did us proud."

Alex grinned. "Told you it would be alright."

"I know it's late in the day," said Elizabeth. "But I thought we'd dine first to save your stores."

Matthew inclined his head. "A gracious gesture, Elizabeth. Thank you."

Elizabeth glanced towards the gates. "Where can we talk?"

He gestured grandly towards the rough-cut steps that wound around the rocky crag. "Come this way." He beckoned to his brother. "Fetch Lord Robert. This will be of interest to him, I'm sure."

Lord Robert hurried into Matthew's chamber with Alex at his heels. He nodded to Elizabeth in passing. "Another visit from the midwife?"

She'd settled on a stout wooden kist. "Let's hope we deliver a successful conclusion to your plot."

"And what an ungrateful child it is," Lord Robert remarked.

Matthew poured some wine. "Apologies for the quality. I suppose it's better than nothing."

Taking a mouthful, she winced. "God, you should hang the cellarer."

"He does his best," Lord Robert said. "In conditions we'd all describe as inhuman…"

"All the more reason for you to slip your bonds and escape." She smiled. "What do you need to know?"

"I can see for myself that the King's forces are trickling away," Matthew said. "But it's not clear whether the bombards have moved yet."

"They're still in Renfrew," she replied. "I presume His Grace the King won't want the expense of shipping them if it can possibly be avoided."

"That's good." Matthew paused, considering her words. "Have they any artillery?"

"I haven't heard talk of any. There's around four-score armed retainers, and a further two-score mounted men-at-arms. I think that's all Argyll's prepared to commit to this venture."

"The Islesmen will be moving, once the weather closes in. Stands to reason Earl Colin will want to send most of his men home."

"He'll be nearing the end of his forty days," Lord Robert mentioned. "The King'll have to summon men to replace him."

"Now's the time, then." Matthew smiled at Elizabeth. "Best leave in the next day or two. After that, I can't guarantee your safety."

Chapter 25

The Place of Southannan

She found William sitting at the board in the hall, shovelling down a bowl of broth.

He looked up, nodded in acknowledgement. "He's not happy." He glanced towards the yard, indicating Jamie.

"I don't care," Margaret said. "I want those gates barred and bolted, and I want a watch set until Sir John returns. If Jamie doesn't like sitting out in the cold all night, then he'd best hold his tongue in future." She paused, then added in a low voice, "You were there, William. You saw what happened. Do you think I'm being too cautious?"

He frowned, considering her words. "Once we'd have trusted the Cunninghames with our lives. Now there's no love lost between us."

"John thinks the boys came back to kill him."

William fiddled with his spoon, saying nothing.

"Speak with Jamie. Be courteous, but firm. If he argues, send him to me. And William..." She leaned across the board. "Give me your knife."

Casting her a doubtful glance, he slipped it from his belt and presented it to her. "Watch how you handle it. You could do yourself an injury."

Margeret carefully grasped the hilt. "Don't worry. I'll give it to someone who knows what he's doing."

Hugh struggled to sit. "A lady with a dagger," he said. "Have you come to plunge it into my heart?"

"Don't be daft," she retorted. "Hasn't it occurred to you that you might be in danger here?"

He frowned. "I assumed my enemies already had ample opportunity to finish me."

"Half the county will soon know you're here. If loose tongues wag in the wrong ears, we might find ourselves beleaguered."

"It's possible," he agreed. "But I think we're safe enough."

Halting by the bed, she offered him the dagger. "Take it. Please."

He glanced aside. "I lack the strength."

Margaret studied it, nervously. "Then I'd best do the deed if it's required... Though I have no idea what to do."

"Aim for the belly. Anywhere below the ribs. And slash, don't stab. You won't kill him quickly, but at least he'll be too busy scooping up his innards to press home an attack."

"That's horrible."

"Yes. It is." He fell silent a moment. "Put it under my pillow. Out of harm's way."

"Won't it comfort you? To know that it's there?"

He smiled. "Yes, it will. Thank you."

She slipped it into place there. "I'm sorry," she said. "Please don't take this wrong, but... I should change the dressings."

"Of course." He settled back down again.

"I won't be a moment." She bustled about the room, pouring hot water from the copper pot by the fire into a bowl, and retrieving cloth and crushed herbs for the poultice.

His eyes were half-closed, he was feigning inattention. But all the time she knew he was watching her keenly.

Once everything was ready, she flicked back the covers, arranging them carefully over his loins.

Grimacing, he pulled back his leg in readiness. "There," he said. "Do what you will."

She sat beside him and laid a tentative hand upon his thigh. She felt his warmth, silk-smooth skin over muscle and sinew, and she thought of John. Her heart sank as she remembered how he'd been when she'd tended him in his sickbed. Wary, hostile, like a stricken wild creature caught in a trap.

Margaret sighed and tugged at the bandages. It had been hard to care for him when he'd so obviously mistrusted her. And though it seemed so long ago now, it still hurt to think of those times.

Even now she couldn't bear to speak of it to him. It stung her all the more to think that a stranger could be more comfortable in her keeping: Hugh was relaxed now, no longer watching her but resting instead with eyes closed while she wiped the wound and set a fresh dressing in place.

But when she pulled the bandage from his belly, he flinched like a nervous horse. "I'm sorry!" He looked up, shamefaced. "I'm not used to such intimate care from a stranger."

She smiled slightly. "I find that hard to believe."

"It's God's truth," he retorted. "I love my wife."

"Then I've misjudged you," she replied. "And for that, I'm sorry." She eased away the dressing and swabbed his flesh with *aqua vita*. The wound still oozed slightly along its length. But altogether it seemed cleaner, more wholesome. "Does it hurt?" she asked.

His agitation ebbed, he gave a weary smile. "It itches, more than anything. But the heat soothes it. Thank you."

"I'm sure you're on the mend."

He didn't answer.

"Are you concerned for her?"

"Yes."

"Don't be," she told him. "John'll ride to Eglintoun with all due speed. At least he's bringing good news. It's not as if you're lacking any of your necessary parts, is it?" She smiled. "Though from what you were saying, you had a narrow escape in that respect."

He scowled. "Thank you, Margaret. For that indelicate reminder..."

"Not at all." She pressed a fresh dressing gently into place. "There. That wasn't so difficult, was it?"

* * *

The Place of Kilmaurs

Half-a-dozen men stood outside the blackened gates, hauling aside fragments of charred wood. The remains of the wagon were still jammed there, standing proud like the roasted carcass of a beast. The harled wall above was streaked black with soot, daubed as if by a devil's hand.

Studying the burned timbers from the back of his horse, Craigends scowled in silence.

"Arson," Rob muttered. "He tried it once with Kerrielaw. Now he's done it again. And while my family was here. Does he have no honour?"

"Rob! Will!" Christian waved from above. "Thank God you're here!"

"When did this happen?" Rob called up.

"Last night." She paced the wallwalk, brisk agitated steps back and forth. "We'll open the sally port," she decided.

"A sound suggestion, Chrissie." Rob steered his horse around. "We'll head that way now."

Christian awaited them in the yard. She smiled in greeting as they approached, but her face was pale and drawn, her eyes flicking nervously about them.

Rob dismounted and hugged her tight. "My poor Chrissie. What happened here?"

"I've never seen men so gripped with rage, and hatred." She shuddered at the recollection. "John Montgomerie of Hessilhead led the assault..." She glanced furtively over her shoulder, towards the solid square bulk of the tower-house. "He said the strangest things..." Lowering her voice, she added, "Something's happened. And Cuthbert, Guido..." They're at the heart of it, I'm sure."

Rob took her hands. "Steady. One step at a time..."

"The boys came home, two nights ago. They said nothing." Her voice rose, her bewilderment clear to behold. "They didn't even tell me they'd returned. I found Guido the following day. I've never seen him so distressed! He said he'd killed a man..."

"Oh, God..."

"Then last night Hessilhead rode up, roaring and shouting like the brute he is. *For every precious drop of his blood, your kin will shed a gallon,* he said. Guido knows what he meant. And Cuthbert, too. But they won't talk to me."

Craigends felt his scowl deepen. "Jesus Christ..."

"What if they've killed *him*?" Her voice choked into silence.

"We'll hold a feast to celebrate," Craigends retorted. "Just a pity we don't have his head. It'd look mighty fine up there on the parapet."

Christian shot him a disapproving glance.

Craigends laughed. "Don't take my words to heart, Chrissie. Whatever's got their tails up, it won't be the death of their kinsman. That man enjoys Satan's protection. If he's dead, then I'll take this bonnet of mine and I'll eat it for my supper."

"Your mother says you know more of this than you'll admit." Rob sprawled in his chair, a figure of comfortable authority.

Cuthbert glowered at the floor, with Andrew and Guido flanking him, slump-shouldered and sheepish.

Craigends studied Cuthbert, carefully. It wasn't defiance, he was sure of it. It was more profound than that.

Rob met Craigend's gaze briefly, then continued. "The attack last night was unprecedented. Were they justified, do you think?"

Guido choked back a sob, and Andrew, too looked close to tears. Taking a deep breath, Cuthbert lifted his head high. He was trying hard to appear unapologetic, but there were cracks there, the strain showing in the faint sheen of sweat that touched his brow.

"You weren't hunting, were you?" Rob's voice was misleadingly gentle.

"We went to Glengarnock." Cuthbert's voice shook. "We wanted to do something. To help our kin, our tenants. We spoke to some of the men who suffered last year. We encouraged them to take revenge-"

"We thought you'd be pleased," Guido interjected.

Craigends closed his eyes, briefly, a chill running through him. "It went wrong, didn't it?"

"A madness took hold," Guido said. "They slew a man and burned his place. There was a woman there. They tore the clothes from her back. And then they raped her. Five men in all, one after the other. There was a child at her feet. A girl. She kept crying so they hit her and threatened to throw her into the flames..."

"Jesus Christ..." Rob muttered.

"We were afraid," Cuthbert said. "We thought they'd turn on us, if we tried to stop them." His breath shuddered in his throat.

"*He* came in pursuit," Guido added. "He confronted us, and more or less accused us of the crime. I panicked, and shot one of his men. I think I killed him."

"Well, that's not too bad," Craigends said. "It's a hard lesson to learn, Guido, but Lord Hugh accepts that-"

"That's not the worst of it," said Cuthbert. "He came alone, and they were waiting. When we arrived, he was on his knees. Stripped of his arms, bound and beaten. God knows I hate the man, but it wasn't right that they should slay him like a dog. I intervened. I sent them away."

"And they heeded you?" Rob said. "Thank God for that."

"I was going to kill him myself. But... It was wrong to take his life in such circumstances." Cuthbert's eyes closed, tears trickled down his cheeks. "I'm sorry, Father. I failed you. I couldn't avenge our dead..."

"You did the right thing," Rob replied. "You were merciful."

"But what was his fate?" Craigends persisted. "Do you know?"

"He was wounded. I don't think he suffered any mortal blows, but he was bleeding heavily and he seemed incapable of walking very far. The following day, we came back to see what had happened to him." Cuthbert swallowed. "I'd have helped him, I think. But it was too late. He'd vanished."

"Not much later, we met Sir John Sempill," Andrew said. "He was looking for Lord Hugh, same as we were. He made it quite clear that our presence wasn't welcome."

"We agreed then that Lord Hugh's fate no longer lay in our hands," Cuthbert added. "So we left for home."

"It's a sorry tale," Craigends conceded. "And the part you played is scarcely a noble one. But the situation could be worse."

"From what Hessilhead said last night," Cuthbert spoke more strongly now. "I think we can assume he still lives."

"For once their grievances are justified," Rob said. "Like it or not, he's the King's man round these parts. We must find the guilty men and hand them over for justice. You'll help me in this, I hope? We'll call it atonement for the part you paid..." Rob sighed, and shook his head. "Ah, Cuthbert. You excelled yourself..."

"Don't punish the boy," Craigends said. "He's suffered enough from this. And he's learned from it, too." He leaned back, smiling. "Congratulations, Cuthbert. You can count yourself a man at last. Let's just pray we can smooth the Montgomeries' ruffled feathers before they roast us in our beds."

Chapter 26

The Place of Eglintoun

A sharp knock sounded on the door. "Lady Helen?" the steward called.

Helen stood, almost without thinking, as he entered, face sober. "Sir John Sempill of Ellestoun is here," he said. "He asks to speak with you in confidence. He says it's urgent."

She swallowed back her terror. "Is he in the hall?"

"Yes, my lady. What word shall-"

But she'd already pushed past him, out onto the dark stair.

Sir John rose to greet her, bonnet in hand. He'd always struck her as being calm and wise beyond his years, but this time when she looked upon his face she wished she could find something, anything, which might hint at the news he brought.

Helen halted before him. "Sir John." She didn't quite know how to begin. "Do you-" Her voice trembled, so she broke off and tried again. "Do you bring word?"

A smile touched his lips. "All's well, Lady Helen. He's in my care at Southannan. He was set upon and wounded, but he's mending quickly and should be back upon his horse before a fortnight's passed."

"Oh, thank God!" She'd have hugged him, had it been appropriate to do so. She gripped his hands instead, unable to conceal her relief. "I feared the worst. When they brought his arms, I thought I'd never see him again."

"He needs clothing. Enough to tide him over for a few days. And a cloak and boots for travelling. I'd provide what's required, but I'm away from home and running short myself."

"How's he faring?"

"He's weak and sore and out-of-sorts, but he'll soon recover, I'm sure. Rest assured he'll be granted every comfort."

Helen could scarcely contain her joy. "This is glorious news! Thank you!"

"You haven't heard from Hugh's kinsmen?"

"No," she replied. "Not at all."

A faint frown crossed his face. Disapproval, perhaps. Or disappointment. "Hugh asks that no retribution be taken as yet. His kinsmen may argue otherwise, but it's Hugh's wish that he should be present to decide how justice is meted out for the injuries and insults that he suffered."

Helen inclined her head. "If that's what my lord commands, then that's what will be done."

"Hessilhead will scoff and say I've invented this tale to try and protect the Cunninghames." Again that ghost of disapproval flitted across his face. "But that's not true. I swear, Lady Helen, by God, the Saints and Holy Mary, that your husband gave me those instructions. If his kinsmen dispute my words, then they should speak to Lord Hugh in person."

"Of course I'll accept your words as truth and act upon them. We're indebted to you, both myself, and Hugh. I hope he's made that clear to you?"

Sir John smiled, faintly. "Hugh has made his thoughts very clear."

"He would never have expected such kindness," she said. "If there were more men like you, Sir John, the world would be a better place." She nodded to him. "You'll dine with us this afternoon, of course. And rest under our roof tonight. The least we can do is offer you hospitality."

> *   *   *

The Place of Southannan

Crouching by the fireplace, Margaret lifted the curfew and slipped it over the glowing embers. With the remnants of the fire kept safe for the night, the chamber was almost in darkness.

Just one candle remained, flickering close by. Licking finger and thumb, Margaret snuffed it out.

"I can't stay here," Katherine said.

"Then go back to the hall. Put your trust in Jamie."

"I don't want to stay alone with Jamie."

"That's the first sensible thing you've said all day. Now come on, Katherine. There's no shame in this."

"Jamie says-"

"The Devil take Jamie! There were no complaints last night."

"Sir John was there."

"And I'll be here tonight. There's nothing to be afraid of." Margaret rose stiffly to her feet, aching from the countless times she'd climbed the stairs throughout the day. "If lying next to him is so abhorrent, then sleep on the floor."

Plodding over to the bed she found herself wondering why life was so very complicated. She had enough to think about seeing to Hugh's needs. The last thing she needed was Jamie stirring up trouble at the slightest opportunity.

Least William's sensible, she thought. Tucking her feet up beneath her skirts she settled comfortably, making sure she stayed a respectful distance from Hugh.

Muttering misgivings, Katherine lay down alongside.

There was silence. Stifling, ominous.

Margaret stared through the darkness, aware of Hugh lying there beside her. She wondered if it was shameful, to lie so close to a man who wasn't her husband. She wondered if John would be angry.

Then she remembered her half-brother's ominous words. *I don't trust you,* she told herself. *What's to stop you sticking a knife in him, if we leave him unattended. I hope the lure of Cunninghame gold wouldn't be enough to make you betray us both, but...*

I can't be sure, Jamie. I'm sorry...

Her mind was made up. She'd look after Hugh tonight and face the consequences later. It wasn't as if she was going to fall asleep here. She just wanted to find somewhere to rest her weary limbs.

"Lady Margaret," Hugh said.

Hearing his voice so close made the hairs stand up on the back of her neck. "I hoped we wouldn't wake you."

"To steal a lady's bed is unforgivable. If anyone's banished to the floor, it should be me."

"What a ridiculous notion!" She grimaced, instantly regretting her outburst. "Please don't say such things. We should be leaving you in peace, but... There's scarcely a bed to be found here. We never expected to stay very long, and we never ever thought we'd have someone lodging with us." She bit her lip, holding back the words that perched on the tip of her tongue. *And besides, I can't possibly leave you because I'm mortally afraid that someone might do their best to murder you.* "When you lay there alone in the wilds," she said, in a brave attempt to change the subject, "-did you ever hope to be found?"

"In truth, Margaret, I hoped *not* to be found."

"But didn't you realise that your friends would be looking for you?"

"I was more concerned that my enemies would find me first. Mercy isn't guaranteed. A sharp blow to the neck with a dagger is the kindest way to despatch a man, but sometimes even that's denied him. When I served Argyll we heard evil things about the women of the Isles. How they'd treat the men they captured as if they were dogs, chaining them up in squalor and filth, using them at their pleasure. With thoughts like that to console a man, death seems a better path to follow, believe me..."

"How terrible!" she gasped. "Is it true?"

"I never wanted to find out. Even the rumour was enough to make me sleep close to the fire at night, I can tell you..."

"Did you tarry long in the north?"

"About twelve months. Like Hercules I laboured hard. And while patrolling the northern wilds and serving Earl Colin wasn't quite as dreadful as tending the flesh-eating mares of King Diomedes, there were times when I thought I'd been set an impossible task."

"To win your lady." She glowed inside at the thought. "I hope she appreciated your efforts."

"I'm sure she's regretted her choice a thousand times."

"No," Margaret whispered. "I don't think so." She closed her eyes. "Tell me of the north."

"The winters are very harsh. The snow sweeps across the land for days on end and the cold eats through to your bones, no matter how many layers of fur or plaid you wrap yourself in. All through the dark nights the wolves sing their devilish songs. When you're safe inside a stone keep it's comforting to hear them. But when you're out on the hills with just a few friends and a sharp sword to protect you, it's a different matter."

"I can imagine..."

"And the people there are very strange. Fey, and prone to the old ways. They'll put their faith in the spirits of the hills and streams as much as the One True God. And woe betide the young man who wanders too far on his own in the wild country. If the bogs don't claim him, the faerie folk will. They come in the guise of maidens or magnificent horses, preying on the weak-minded, the unwary..."

"I hope I never have to tread these paths."

"But it's a beautiful thing, to see the moon hanging low over the mountains. To see the mist shroud the land..."

"Don't you ever want to go back there?"

"My dreams often take me there," he replied. "But I wouldn't wander there by choice. I belong here in the Westland. With my wife and children."

"That's very sweet," she said. "But perhaps Lady Helen's glad to see the back of you, if this is what she suffers each night."

"Whatever do you mean?"

"You chatter like a starling."

"You're telling me to hold my tongue?" His tone was injured.

"No, not exactly. But I'm very tired. Not that I'll be sleeping, of course. Because that wouldn't be right. I'm here to protect you."

"Of course you are," he said. "And a more loyal and valiant defender I've never known. Let's just hope and pray your services aren't required."

*　　　*　　　*

Slivers of light shone through the gaps in the shutters. Another day had dawned, and he was glad to witness it. Beyond this chamber, the household braced itself for the tasks ahead: out in the stables horses neighed for food, Zephyr's clarion whinny echoing loud amongst them.

Hugh closed his eyes, relieved that Zephyr like himself had found a safe harbour in which to weather out the storm.

He lay still, unwilling to move. He'd never paid much attention to the intricate workings of his body before now. Everything had been in order, limbs and organs working together as required, and that was the end of it. There'd been minor injuries to deal with, but never a time where it felt as if he'd had been torn apart then carelessly rearranged.

Other matters were becoming ever more pressing. He needed to visit the privy. The piss-pot was an easier option, but he'd lain in his bed long enough.

Propping himself up on his elbows, he paused, partly to muster his strength, partly to convince himself that he wasn't being over-ambitious.

He realised then that he wasn't alone. Beside him, the two girls were sleeping, curled up together on the bed. Fully dressed, huddled close for warmth.

Hugh smiled. For all her determined words, Margaret had succumbed to her fatigue at last.

He felt no inclination to disturb either of them: with John absent, he decided instead that he'd appoint himself their guardian. An absurd notion, for he couldn't even have lifted a hand to defend himself. But the thought cheered him, and gave him some purpose in life.

He threw back the covers and heaved himself to his feet. Taking steady even breaths, he tried to assess what worked, and what didn't. His legs were wobbling, everything was stiff and sore.

The entrance to the privy lay at the farthest corner of the chamber. There was no curtain there: Hugh frowned, puzzled because the entire room was like a hermit's cell, the walls bare, no curtains round the bed, either.

Gritting his teeth, he took one last deep breath and then he set off. It felt like he was treading on knives and his legs wouldn't bend properly: when at last he'd reached the doorway to the privy, he clutched the moulding with both hands to steady himself.

His chest was heaving and he poured with sweat, but he was giddy and elated nonetheless.

A small achievement, but in his present condition even that was worth celebrating.

When he emerged, he found young Margaret Colville confronting him, hands on hips, doing her very best to look fearsome. "What are you doing?" she demanded.

"I needed to make myself comfortable."

"And what if you'd fallen?"

His head was spinning. He screwed his eyes shut, fighting the ever-encroaching weakness. "I didn't fall, and all's well. Now let me go to my bed, and you can do what you like with me. Though if you could stay nearby, I'd appreciate it very much."

He made it halfway across, then had to lean on her shoulder the rest of the way.

"Come on!" she urged. "Just a little further."

"Ah, God Almighty..." Eventually, he was able to lay himself down.

Margaret grasped his hand. "Can you sit up? Here, let me help you." She manoeuvred the pillows into place behind his back.

He felt profoundly uncomfortable. Yesterday, he'd been too tired to care, but today he was all too aware of her presence. The touch of her fingers, the waft of her hair... When they'd talked together the previous night, she'd seemed youthful, innocent. A far cry from the composed figure who dealt with him so deftly.

She pulled away the dressing on his belly and inspected it carefully. "That's much better." Fetching a cloth, she wiped away the residue.

Now the wound was clean, he examined it himself. The surrounding flesh seemed paler, less angry to the eye. "It's quite a scar, isn't it? Helen will be most impressed."

"Surely not."

He sighed, crestfallen. "You're right. She'll detest it. At least you've made a neat job of mending it."

"There's been nothing seeping from it since yesterday."

"Then we'll leave it uncovered, shall we? And let it heal."

"Fingers crossed." Margaret turned her attention to his thigh. Gently teasing away the poultice, she studied the thin, snaking wound, carefully. "Much better,"

"Then it's a glorious day. I shall be back on my horse and wielding a sword in no time..." Feigning nonchalance, he folded his arms behind his head and stretched out with a sigh.

"I thought you'd hate to be confined like this."

"Weeping and wailing won't speed my recovery."

"I wish John was like you. He's sullen and unpleasant when he's sick."

"That's because he's young. One lost moment seems like an eternity."

She shrugged and gathered up the dressings, placing them in a basket by the bed. "You're through the worst of it now. Which is a good thing for all of us, for the less we have to do with you, the better."

"Your care has been exemplary," he said. "Thank you."

"I've had ample practice." She threw open the shutters with such vigour that they clattered back against the wall. "Have you forgotten how your men left my husband battered and bleeding after the wappenschaw?"

"I never wished any harm upon your husband."

"I wish you wouldn't make such efforts to be charming." She bustled about the chamber, briskly efficient. "John wouldn't approve, I'm sure."

"Your husband has little to fear. Why spare a thought for a battered old knight, when you share your bed with Adonis?"

Halting by the bed, arms folded. "I don't see why you're complaining. You're wed to the Lady of Troy. Fair Helen, whose face launched a thousand ships."

"Then my doom must surely be at hand. Paris has already departed, leaving poor Menelaus languishing in his bed."

"John isn't Paris. He's more like Ulysses. He'd battle mighty foes if it brought him back to Penelope's side..."

"Your wits have grown sharp. This is a very different lady to the one I teased with tales of Actaeon..." He broke off, then added, "I remember the day I first set eyes on you. You hated me, didn't you? The day you were summoned before me at Ochiltree. The day I told you that you were to be wed."

Her face showed nothing. "No. Of course not."

"I saw the look in your eyes. The absolute loathing." He laughed, softly. "There's precious few bold enough to make their hatred so obvious."

"He's a good husband, everything I could ever wish for."

"You didn't think so then."

"You say the most dangerous things, considering your situation."

"He loves you. I think his heart was lost the moment he first set eyes on you. And in return, you despised him."

"I wished him dead at first." She glanced aside, face flushed.

"He must have suspected as much. Yet he loved you all the same. And deep inside, I think you loved him, too. But you were too proud to admit it."

She flashed him an irritated look. "You're leading me a merry chase on matters that I might not wish to air with you. There are ulterior motives, I'm sure. I just wish I knew what they were."

"It's conversation, nothing more. A means of passing the time."

Margaret laughed. "You'll soon be home, and safe in your lady's arms."

"You're both so generous. It overwhelms me. John has very little to thank me for. I've committed grievous sins against him."

She settled in her chair, suddenly thoughtful. "He doesn't dwell upon the past. We never speak of it. When the anniversary of his father's death came, he was deeply troubled. But at that time, he didn't involve me much in his affairs."

"I've tried to make amends. I've helped him as much as I can. And I'll continue to do so, if that's what he desires."

"It concerns you, doesn't it? That he should do this for you, when he has absolutely no reason to..."

He smiled. "Now it's your turn. To lead me a merry chase..."

Margaret held his gaze, eyes narrowed. "The church has absolved your sins, surely?"

"Yes."

"But it's not enough, is it? You want to know he's forgiven you. If that's so, why don't you ask him?"

He drew a sharp anxious breath. "It's a difficult matter."

"You're afraid of what he'll say, aren't you?"

"Perhaps."

"John has great capacity for forgiveness. I'm quite sure he's forgiven you." She paused, head cocked in contemplation. "Whether he's forgiven himself is another matter entirely."

Chapter 27

The Place of Kilbirnie

They were shown into the hall, where Sir Malcom Crawfurd and his family awaited them. The Sempill woman served them with wine; Craigends studied her carefully as she poured a measure into his cup.

She was handsome, yes, but not particularly beautiful, face pale and solemn, too thin in the body for his tastes. Rumour had it young Robert Crawfurd married her for love, though marrying the girl would have been daft whatever the motive. In her early twenties, by most men's reckoning she was long in the tooth. Why, even after a year of marriage, she hadn't brought a child into the world...

"Thank you," Craigends said.

She smiled and bowed her head, distant acknowledgement.

Cuthbert was watching her. It wasn't the hungry look of a lusty youth, more a measured glance of appraisal. Despite his tender years, Cuthbert was subtle enough to understand that if there was a chink in the Crawfurds' armour, it was their gude-daughter, a Sempill born and bred.

"It's good of you to speak with us," Craigends said.

Sir Malcolm Crawfurd inclined his head, measured deference. "It's a pleasure to have you here, Sir William." He glanced towards Cuthbert. "And this is?"

"Cuthbert, Master of Kilmaurs," Cuthbert replied.

"Master of Kilmaurs *and* Glencairn," Sir Malcolm rebuked, gently.

Cuthbert brightened. "My thanks for your kind words, Sir Malcolm. And thank you, too, for the alms you gave through the winter. You saved many lives."

"I hope and pray that this year Glengarnock will be spared such tribulations," Sir Malcolm replied.

"A quiet and peaceful winter is what we all yearn for," Craigends agreed. "But, alas, it seems unlikely." He paused, wondering how best to proceed. He wasn't the most eloquent of men, and the subject he was broaching was delicate, to say the least... "I hope you won't think me impertinent, but certain matters are unfolding which may upset the balance."

The Sempill woman exchanged anxious glances with her husband, but Sir Malcolm's face showed nothing. "Oh?" he asked, non-commital.

"Have you heard word of the Lord Montgomerie?" Cuthbert asked, all-innocence. "Has he been seen in these parts?"

"No, we haven't set eyes on him," Sir Malcolm replied. "Nor would we expect to."

"What of your gude-son?"

It was Sir Malcolm's turn to catch his son's eye. A brief shadow of unease flitted across both men's features, then Sir Malcolm said, "Sir John called here just a few days ago. He was visiting his Southannan lands, but he only planned to stay a day or two. We thought he'd have returned by now." Faint worry coloured his voice.

"I'm sure there's a perfectly good reason for his delay," Cuthbert assured him, quickly.

Sir Malcolm didn't reply.

"Speak to Sir John," Cuthbert continued, his tone honey-smooth. "Find out if he has tidings of Lord Hugh."

Sir Malcolm's frown returned, more obvious this time. "We have no quarrel with Montgomerie."

"I appreciate that," Cuthbert replied.

"We'll be at Glengarnock for a week or so," Craigends added. "We'd be grateful for news."

"I sincerely hope that by passing on such information, I won't be compromising Sir John," Sir Malcolm said. "Or Lord Hugh, for that matter."

"Of course not," Cuthbert responded. "Relations may be strained between our households, but the Lord Montgomerie remains my kinsman. I hope and pray that all's well with him."

The Place of Southannan

A swathe of thick, dark-red brocade engulfed Margaret's skirts, spilling across the nearby floor. She'd found this treasure tucked away in one of the kists: a set of curtains and matching canopy for the bed in the laird's chamber. Much was faded, but in places it remained dark and brilliant.

Like fine wine. Or blood.

Margaret slumped against the wall with a sigh.

The silence and the loneliness was overwhelming. Setting her sewing aside, she rose to her feet, and ventured over to the bed. Just a quick look, to make sure everything was alright.

Exhausted by his earlier expedition to the privy, Hugh was asleep. He was curled beneath the covers, black hair tousled and unkempt against the pillow. For a man renowned for treachery and deceit, he looked peaceful, child-like...

Lost in her thoughts, she started at the sound of voices echoing in the yard.

It was Jamie. He was calling to someone.

Her heart skipped in anticipation. It was John. It *had* to be. Gathering her skirts, she headed for the door and scurried down the spiral stairs.

Footsteps approached, equally animated. She saw the glow of the candle ahead and stopped just in time as William appeared.

"We have a visitor." His tone was terse. "Master Crawfurd's ridden down from Kilbirnie."

Her elation faded. "I'll speak to him. But ask Katherine to attend me first."

Once her hood was fitted, she headed down to the yard. Master Crawfurd waited there, holding the reins of his bay horse. He nodded in greeting. "We expected you back two days ago."

Louise Turner

She bobbed into a curtsey. "We didn't mean to cause concern. Circumstances conspired against us and we couldn't spare anyone to send word." She offered her most brilliant smile. "We'd love to have you at the board. But our hospitality mightn't live up to expectations should you wish to stay here tonight. There's only one bed between us, and-" Grimacing, she put a hand to the small of her back. "-I'm in dire need of comfort just now."

His eyes narrowed. "Is anything amiss?"

"What makes you say that?"

Master Crawfurd's gaze didn't waver. "Is John here?"

"Not at this moment. But we expect his return imminently. He'd be delighted to see you."

"As long as all's well."

"Shouldn't it be?"

He glanced aside, his expression guarded. "The Laird of Craigends paid us a visit this morning. He was asking after the Lord Montgomerie. And asking after John, too."

"I can't think what John's business has to do with the Laird of Craigends. Or the Lord Montgomerie, for that matter..."

"That's what I thought," Master Crawfurd agreed. "But on my way here I was waylaid by Montgomerie's retainers. They would have slain me, if they hadn't paused long enough to let me explain that Sir John was my gude-brother." He paused. "Is there anything you wish to tell me?"

"I'm not at liberty to discuss John's affairs with anyone." She wasn't adept at pinning on a coy look, but she tried it now, hoping it would be sufficient to distract him. "Would you have me disobey my husband?"

He sighed and shrugged. "Of course not."

"Dine with us, please. He won't be long." She grasped the reins of his horse. "Leave him with me. Jamie can stable him for you."

He didn't relinquish his grip. "He's not well-disposed to strangers."

To her relief there was no sign of Zephyr. Just an empty space amongst the line of heavy heads that turned in her direction.

Storm whickered in greeting, and Robert Crawfurd paused in the aisle beyond. "He didn't take his horse?"

"He took Jamie's course-" Margaret began, then broke off as hooves scraped on cobbles.

In the farthest stall, Lord Hugh's grey heaved itself upright. Master Crawfurd studied it intently. "Does John know the Lord Montgomerie's horse is stabled here?"

"Zephyr's lame. Lord Hugh needed a place to keep him until he was sound."

He gave a dismissive wave. "I won't ask further," he said. "Perhaps John can explain, when he returns."

But as the hours crept past, there was still no sign of John. Margaret tried her very best to be a gracious host, but once the meal was over, Master Crawfurd took his leave.

"I won't impose," he said. "If I go now, I'll reach Kilbirnie by nightfall,"

"I'm sorry," she said, and meant it most sincerely.

"Shall I fetch your horse, Master Robert?" William asked.

146

He smiled. "If you could, William. Thank you."

She waited anxiously at the door until their footsteps faded. Master Crawfurd was pleasant enough company, but for once she was relieved to see the back of him. "I'm sorry I had to leave you," she told Katherine, then hesitated, seeing the stricken look on her maid's face. "You did think to look after him?"

Katherine glanced aside, blushing fiercely. "I'm sorry. It slipped my mind."

"You didn't want to, more like."

The other girl shrugged, unwilling to face her.

"You're hopeless!" she snapped. "The poor soul will be starving. Go to the kitchen, and fetch some food. Quickly!"

She found Hugh sitting up in bed. He was staring towards the window with shoulders slumped, a picture of melancholy. But as she pushed open the door, he brightened. "There you are."

"Is everything alright?"

"My company must weary you, but... When I'm abandoned here, the moments just trudge past."

"I'm sorry. Do you need to use the privy? I can fetch William to help you..."

"I found the piss-pot."

"Well, that's better than nothing, I suppose."

He studied her, frowning. "You've had a visitor."

"How-"

"You're wearing your hood." His gaze didn't waver. "Who was it?"

Margaret shivered. There was something about his voice, a quiet intensity that unnerved her. "Robert Crawfurd of Kilbirnie."

His eyes flickered closed, quiet relief. "Ah."

"He saw Zephyr,"

"It doesn't matter." He looked up, hopeful. "Is there anything to eat?"

And the tension was gone. She felt reassured somehow, that Hugh had judged Master Crawfurd's motives and found them acceptable. "Katherine's bringing some broth. After that... I'll fetch Katherine, and we can play cards together."

"I'd appreciate that, thank you," he said, with a look of such pathetic gratitude that her conscience pricked her all the more.

"I won't be a moment," she promised.

Ducking back out onto the stair-tower, she leaned against the rough cool stone, face flushed. She missed John more than ever. She wanted to hold him, to bury herself in his embrace. To know that he was there in case the worst should happen and Hugh's enemies should move against them.

You're not a child, she told herself, sternly. *Compose yourself...* Continuing on to the hall, she found Katherine spooning the last of the pottage from the cauldron that hung over the fire.

"Hurry up," Margaret said. "We're summoned."

"Fasten your chastity belt, Kate," Jamie added. "His Lordship wants some entertainment."

"Don't be so vulgar," snapped Margaret.

"If I crawl home from a fight," Jamie retorted, "I get banished to the corner and told not to bother anyone. Lord Hugh gets more ladies-in-waiting than the Queen of England."

William looked up. "He's a more worthy investment."

"Oh, don't you start, Master Haislet. You know more about cuckolded lovers than the rest of us put together. If it wasn't for the misery of love, then you'd be shovelling horse-shit to earn a crust each night. Anyway, where's your husband, Margaret? Do you think he'll come home tonight? Or will the wiles of Lady Helen prove too much for him?"

"I'm not listening." She shepherded Katherine out before her.

"She'll be grateful for a strong shoulder to cry upon!" His voice rang out after them. "And what's sauce for the goose is sauce for the gander!"

Chapter 28

The Place of Southannan

They sat together on the bed with Hugh propped between them, one of John's gowns draped over his shoulders to keep the cold at bay. Katherine dealt the cards: she was shy at first, speaking only when spoken too, but as the evening wore on, she grew more confident. Soon she was laughing and flirting with Hugh as if she'd known him for years.

Margaret tried to keep her thoughts on the game, for Hugh was a formidable opponent. But with each passing hour her concentration waned. Thinking she heard a horse approach, she'd strain her ears to listen, but every time she was mistaken.

Jamie's words gnawed at her, she wondered if John would seize the excuse to stay at Eglintoun, preferring Lady Helen's company to her own. *No,* she told herself. *He wouldn't betray you. And he wouldn't betray Hugh, either...*

"It just as well we're not playing for a forfeit," Katherine said, smirking. "Margaret would be in compromising circumstances."

"Leave her be." Hugh glanced at Margaret, concerned. "What's troubling you?"

"I know what it is," Katherine cut in. "Jamie was saying horrible things. About Sir John and your wife, Lord Hugh."

Margaret drew a sharp anxious breath, wondering how he'd respond.

But Hugh just laughed, and laid his hand against Margaret's cheek. "You should wait by the window and watch your knight's return?"

"What if he doesn't come?"

"He will," Hugh replied. "I'm sure of it."

It had been a frustrating journey: Jamie's courser had served him well when he'd travelled out alone, but now its speed was compromised by the massive sumpter horse plodding alongside.

With a weary sigh, John turned his horse into the barmkin at Southannan. Though it was almost dark Margaret was waiting, a lonely figure amongst the gloomy shadows.

"I thought I'd come and meet you," she said.

"A whole day in the saddle." Taking his feet out of his stirrups, John dropped the reins with a sigh. "Keeping an eye open for brigands all the way..." He slipped down from the horse's back. "William was right. He should've ridden with me."

Margaret grasped the bridle and stroked the horse's nose. "How is Lady Helen?"

"As I suspected, they didn't inform her."

"You did another good deed, then."

"I suppose so." He waved to William. "Unload the baggage, will you? I'll deal with the horses."

He led his mount to the stables. Its hooves echoed against the cobbles, the other horses stirring and whinnying in welcome.

Margaret followed. Grasping a bucket, she turned it over and sat down there, hugging her knees close. As he flung his cloak over the hurdle partition, he was aware of her watching him, a silent presence at his back.

Removing his gown, he folded it and placed it carefully in her lap. "Aren't you going indoors?"

"I'm happy here."

John shrugged, and found a pitchfork. Soon he'd laid a deep bed of straw, manoeuvring his way confidently around the restless legs of the horse. He'd scarcely finished before the beast balanced up on its toes and emptied its bladder. He stood back until it was done, then moved in quickly, taking off its harness then currying its coat, rubbing away sweat marks and mud. The horse appreciated his efforts, laying its muzzle against his shoulder and chewing at his hair. "Is everything alright?" he asked Margaret.

"Robert Crawfurd was here. He saw Zephyr."

"That can't be helped."

"I didn't say anything."

"Good."

"Do you really think it matters?"

He paused, one arm flung across the horse's quarters. "I don't know," he said. "We were good friends once." Ducking under the horse's neck, he started on the other flank. "He'd judge me harshly, I'm sure."

"For saving a man's life?" Margaret asked. "Then he's not much of a friend, is he?"

John sighed, unwilling to answer. "How's Hugh?"

"He walked today. But he's very weak and unsteady."

"Is he eating?"

"Like a hog."

"That's good." John paused. "Now, if you want to make yourself useful, give them some oats. Three handfuls each, generous ones. Moistened with a little water."

      *   *   *

She did as she was bid. And emerged intact, though she had to bellow at Storm, who snaked his neck and launched a nip at Zephyr. But if she thought she'd have John to herself after that, she was mistaken. Once he'd finished with the horses, he went upstairs to speak with Hugh.

She met him later on the stair. It was dark there, with just a flickering light from a candle placed in the niche beyond. "John..."

He hesitated. "What's the matter?"

"I did what was asked of me." She paused. "John, there's something I must tell you. I- I stayed with him last night. I didn't want to leave him alone there. I was afraid that someone might steal in and try to kill him-"

"Whatever made you think such a thing?"

"You said to lock the gates, and..." She swallowed, then added in a whisper, "- Jamie said we'd be doing everyone a favour if we sent word to the Cunninghames so they could put a discreet end to him. I gave him a dagger when you left, but he said he didn't have the strength to hold it, and I thought I ought to be there, just in case."

John gripped her hands, tight reassurance. "I'm sorry, Margaret. I shouldn't have frightened you. The situation probably wasn't so dire as that. And Jamie..." He grimaced faintly. "Surely you, more than anyone, knows better than to believe everything he says. It was a jest, that's all. A cruel one, at Hugh's expense. And yours, by the looks of it."

She sagged, overwhelmed with relief. "It's hard, to be on such familiar terms with a man. We've both been chaste, and honourable. But what if people think otherwise?"

He was silent a moment.

"Please don't think ill of me. The truth is... I missed you. I wanted you back here, and the hours and the minutes just kept crawling past and there was no sign of you."

"Well I'm back now, and everything's as it should be. What's more, we can restore Hugh back to his kin safe and sound and that'll make everyone's lives more bearable." He broke off with a sigh. "I haven't eaten since this morning. After that... Wait up for me." He leaned close and kissed her lips.

Margaret sat alone by the window, staring out across a black silent world.

Katherine paused alongside, candle in hand. "Can't you close the shutters now?" she asked. "It's late." She paused, then added, "Will Sir John be joining us?"

"In good time."

"What about you?"

She glanced up. "I'll wait for him."

Katherine stifled a yawn. "I'm exhausted."

"Then lie down. Try not to disturb him. He's sleeping."

"Shall I put out the candle?"

"Please." Margaret shivered and rubbed her arms.

Long minutes drifted past. She should have felt sleepy, but instead she felt profoundly alive, gripped with eager expectation.

The door creaked, faintly.

She heard John at last, his feet padding soft across the floor. She patted the cushion beside her and he settled there, cautious in case he misjudged the distance. She could feel his knee against her own, smell his scent...

As she reached out and unlaced his doublet, John put his arm about her shoulders and pressed close, swivelling around and pulling his legs up onto the cushion alongside. His lips met hers, eager, urgent. She giggled, and tugged at the laces that fastened his hose, while he grabbed handfuls of her skirts and hauled them up around her hips. He caressed her legs, nibbled at her neck, her ear, his breath soft and warm against her cheek...

Once their lovemaking was done, they huddled close, arms entwined around one another, quietly content. He'd uttered a faint gasp when he'd come inside her, nothing more, and she'd been just as restrained. The silence and darkness made it all the more satisfying, because there were no words, no glances to disturb their time together.

He sighed softly, and she smiled, relishing his return.

She understood now. That lust was just a very small impure part of it. That to love him was to enjoy bestowing pleasure upon him, and to celebrate the time they shared. Burying her face in his shoulder, she revelled in his presence, and wished the night would never end.

The Burgh of Dumbarton

Darkness had settled over the town and now only the pigs roamed the streets, snuffling through the middens for scraps of food. All respectable folk had taken refuge indoors for the night: a few unlucky burgesses still manned the gates, maintaining the duties of watch and ward.

Within the castle, men stirred in readiness. Horses mustered in the courtyard, but scarcely a sound could be heard, their hooves muffled by a mat of dirty straw laid across the cobbles.

Matthew led Ajax out from the stables. The horse glanced restlessly around, eyes gleaming in the orange glow from braziers and bracket-mounted torches. It pawed the ground and snorted as he sprang into the saddle. "Steady." Matthew stroked the jet-black neck. "We'll soon be on our way."

He'd amassed eighteen horsemen altogether: a small force, by any man's reckoning, but at least he had the advantage of surprise.

"We attack the houses and the granaries," Matthew told his men. "Hit those buildings from where the blaze will spread."

He manoeuvred his horse towards a nearby brazier. Lowering his torch into the flames, he waited until the fire took hold, then raised the burning brand aloft. Glancing towards the wallwalk, he saw his mother watching, Lord and Lady Lyle alongside.

He raised his hand in salute. "We've cowered in the shadows long enough!" he called. "Let's strike a blow for righteousness."

"Godspeed, Mattie!" his mother's voice rang out.

Smiling grimly, he pressed his spurs against his horse's flanks. Ajax sprang away, heading for the gate at a determined trot. The portcullis was still grinding upwards as they passed; Matthew had to duck to avoid striking his head.

Beyond the open gates, the cobbled road sloped gently before them. Throughout the town, the shuttered houses were in darkness, the heavens alive with stars. Matthew breathed deep, relishing the fresh chill air, the peace of the night.

Dogs barked, heralding their approach, and Matthew urged Ajax onwards, keeping the pace brisk but steady for fear of slipping. Time was his ally: it would take a while for Argyll's men to rally themselves. By then the sally would be complete, the castle gates secured once more.

Alex rode alongside, torch gripped tight in his hand, young face shining with joy and excitement. He was ill-equipped for his first foray into battle, arrayed in a makeshift suit of plate armour made up of spare pieces gleaned from the armoury.

When this is over, Matthew thought, *we'll give you the arms you merit. A fine suit of mail, worthy of an Earl's son, and a knight...*

Spilt grain and flour, dust and dry timber, a combination of ingredients guaranteed to produce a roaring conflagration.

Doors were heaved open, firebrands lobbed inside.

"Fire!" The scream rang out. "Fire!"

Too late. Already, people spilled out of first floor windows, leaping out onto the backlands where the roofs of sheds and outbuildings or the soft mounds of midden could break their fall.

Isolated buildings burned at first. Soon, though, the fire spread, leaping up timber stairs, heading inexorably into attics then consuming the thatched roofs.

The good people of Dumbarton were too concerned with saving their lives and rescuing their property to notice what was happening close to the harbour. The wharves and stores were pillaged, barrels of herrings and sacks of flour stolen to help augment the garrison's dwindling stores. Then once everything useful was plundered, the arson continued, bales of wool and hides burning with a stink that made men retch,

Matthew waited at the gates, counting the men back in. Some dragged booty – pots and pans, lengths of cloth. Others brought fowl or herded the pigs that had been foraging through the streets when the raid began.

Alex halted beside him, face aglow. "Was it a good night?"

"Oh, yes," Matthew replied. "It was a very good night."

Chapter 29

The Place of Southannan

Lying alone, Margaret revelled in the luxury of space. She stretched out along the bed with a sigh, basking in the warmth of the sunlight which spilled through the open shutters.

She lay still, gathering her senses. When she'd drifted off to sleep the previous night, she'd been wrapped in John's embrace. He must have picked her up and carried her here as she slept, for she remembered nothing more.

She sat up, skirts spilling out around her. "John?"

"He's not here," Hugh said. He was standing by the window, resplendent now in garments of rich satin and velvet. "He's fetching my breakfast."

"Have the heavens always revolved with you at their centre?" she asked.

He frowned. "Whatever do you mean?"

"Expecting John to fetch and carry for you. Hasn't he done enough already?" Seeing his crestfallen expression, she smiled. "I'll wager he's much more capable of performing such a task than you are just now. Are you sure you're well enough to leave your bed?"

"I won't wander far." He limped towards her, clutching the bedpost to steady himself. "I'll dine downstairs with the household. Apart from that, I'll remain here. John has promised a game of merelles to while away the time." He smiled, gently. "Thank you, Margaret, for being such a loyal and unflinching guardian. But you're free of your labours now. It's John's wish – and mine – that you rest this morning. He told me of the treasure you carry. We should all be looking after you."

She yawned. "I'm sorry," she said. "I'm very tired."

"No wonder," he retorted. "You had a midnight tryst. With your glorious Adonis..."

She glowered, despite herself. "Your humours must be restored."

He stared ahead, mouth faintly downcast, a look of melancholy sufferance, of martyrdom. "Don't fret for me. Abstinence is good for the soul. And the heart..." He made his painful, halting way back to the window. "I shall retreat, and watch the wildfowl. Tomorrow, I hope I'll be sound enough to hunt them."

Margaret frowned. *I doubt it,* she thought, and was about to tell him so when the door opened, and there was John, armed with a flagon and a basket of bread while Katherine followed on behind carrying an array of meats and cheeses.

"Time for breakfast, I think," John said with a smile. "Though I'm not entirely sure there are enough chairs to go round. If you'd only walked the other way, Hugh, we'd have found ourselves at Ellestoun, and life would be much easier for everyone."

"Most men travel with their beds, John. And their servants."

"And most guests are polite enough to give ample warning of their coming," John retorted. "Now let's eat, shall we? The bread's fresh out of the oven, it'd be a shame to let it grow cold. Hugh, would you care to bless the board?"

The Gryphon at Bay

The Place of Glengarnock

With the shutters thrown back, the views from this remote Cunninghame stronghold were breathtaking; perched as it was on the edge of a steep rocky chasm, with the nearby hills bathed in late summer sunlight.

But these days Craigends had precious little inclination to admire the scenery. "Come in, Master Crawfurd," he said, holding open the door and gesturing to a nearby chair.

"Thank you." Robert Crawfurd settled there, bonnet in hand. Cuthbert followed him inside, perching against the board with arms folded.

"Have you spoken with your gude-brother?" Craigends asked.

Master Crawfurd shot him a wary glance. "When I arrived at my gude-brother's house, I thought I was approaching a place under siege." He paused, frowning, then added, "Might I ask, Sir William, what all this is about?"

"There was a dispute a few days back." Cuthbert shifted slightly. "Between the Lord Montgomerie and myself."

"He survived, I presume."

"As far as I'm aware," Cuthbert said. "Montgomerie was vanquished," he added. "I wounded him, and he slipped away. Perhaps he sought refuge at Skelmorlie, or tried to press south for Eglintoun."

Craigends caught his breath. It was a plausible lie, elegantly delivered.

Master Crawfurd smoothed his bonnet with his fingers, making no attempt to conceal his unease.

"He made it as far as Southannan, didn't he?" Cuthbert said. "He's staying with your kinsman."

"His horse is there," Master Crawfurd conceded. "But I saw nothing of Lord Hugh. The bounds were crawling with Montgomeries. I thought they'd have my head when I said I had business with Sir John."

"He's there then." Craigends rose to his feet and poured some wine for himself and his guest. "And he's poorly, by the sounds of it."

"I don't care whether Montgomerie lives or dies," Master Crawfurd said. "But I'm concerned for my gude-brother. And his wife."

"Rest assured that we mean no harm to your gude-brother," Craigends replied. "Nor to Lord Hugh. There's no honour to be had in slaughtering a sick man in his bed."

"There's a certain balance to the world." Craigends frowned, setting the last card in place. The pyramid teetered before them, fragile and delicate. "In the lowest levels, we have the base-born, the landless. They look to the strength and wisdom of the barons to keep them safe." He gestured to the uppermost tiers. "Each man must know his place. Respect those above him, and safeguard the needs of his inferiors." He snatched a card from the middle, and the tower collapsed. "When the balance is disturbed, there's Chaos. Montgomerie knows and respects this. Just as we do."

"They're our kin," Cuthbert said, softly. "They rely on us for protection."

"They betrayed us first. By attacking him, they made our position untenable."

Cuthbert sighed, and slumped against the table. "Conceding ground to Montgomerie sickens me."

"I know that," Craigends agreed. "But your father believes in keeping the moral high place. His wishes must be upheld."

Cuthbert was silent.

"Rape and arson alone are serious crimes," Craigends persisted. "If we don't deliver these men, then Montgomerie will take revenge his own way. Innocent people will pay a heavy price."

"Very well," Cuthbert agreed. "I'll do what's required of me."

"One question," said Craigends. "When we talked to Master Crawfurd... Why the lie?"

Cuthbert shrugged. "You said yourself that the attack on Lord Hugh was dishonourable."

"When word gets out, there will be no better way for Montgomerie to win men's sympathy."

"All the more reason to conceal the truth," Cuthbert said. "Who will they believe? A youth like myself, or a man who's proved himself an inveterate liar time and time again?"

Chapter 30

The Place of Southannan

It seemed like an unending trek to the shore. John was walking ahead with Hugh, keeping him steady as he hobbled along, cursing with every misplaced stride.

Margaret followed along behind with Storm and Zephyr in tow. "You could've let him take your horse," she pointed out.

"The walk'll do him good," came John's curt retort.

Not for the first time, she wondered why Hugh had ever agreed to this venture in the first place. *Because he couldn't bear to be cooped up indoors a moment longer,* she told herself. *And on a day like this, who can blame him?*

She paused, taking a moment to savour the fresh scent of the ocean. A light breeze flicked against her hood, out in the bay the islands basked in sunlight, painted in the subdued russet and gold tones of autumn. The sea was flat and blue as lapis, the air pleasantly warm.

Sensing her inattention, Zephyr seized the opportunity to pull a sly mouthful of grass. But just one sharp word from her was enough to move the stallion on. The horse wasn't faring much better than its master: it was still lame, and missing a shoe.

She smiled. Her brothers would have been amazed to witness this: just a year ago, even the thought of handling a horse would have filled her with dread.

"Here, Margaret." John halted beside a rocky outcrop near the shore, large and level enough to provide them with a makeshift seat.

Taking the folded blanket from across Storm's saddle. Margaret placed it carefully down over the rock. It was the same one they'd wrapped round Hugh just days before. Washed now, it smelled fresh and clean. But the bloodstains were still there, faintly visible in the sunlight.

She shivered, disturbed by the memories. Of that dreadful night they'd brought Hugh back to Southannan, more corpse than man.

"There now." John helped Hugh sit down. "You've earned your rest."

Hugh grimaced, settling comfortably down and stretching out his legs. Like John, he didn't seem to care much about the horrors of the past few days. It was as if he'd shrugged aside the bad memories already.

"Your horse?" Margaret passed him Zephyr's reins.

Hugh smiled. "That's very kind of you. I'm sure the poor brute's delighted to escape his stall." He turned his relentless gaze on John, who'd taken Storm's reins and was climbing into the saddle. "Come on then," he encouraged. "Show us what that nag of yours can do."

Sitting down beside Hugh, Margaret drew her cloak tight and watched intently as John pressed Storm forwards at a brisk walk. The stallion flexed its neck and chewed its bit, white foam gathering at its mouth.

"He looks very elegant," Margaret said.

"Your husband? Or the horse?"

Margaret said nothing. Lifting her head, she sensed a chill edge to the air. Clouds were looming grey in the west, a portent of bad weather to come.

She hugged her knees tight, watching the way John sat very tall and proud upon his horse. The wind caught his hair, there was a look of absolute concentration on his face.

"The day the fever threatened me," Hugh said. "I had a vision. That I was Judged, and sent to Hell." He stared out at the ocean, brow faintly furrowed. "I think all this happened for a reason. The suffering I endured, the long hours I spent awaiting death. I asked the Virgin for help, and She saved me. I've been fortunate. I've been granted an opportunity to turn my back on the past, to make up for previous transgressions."

Margaret swallowed, unsure how to respond.

"That's why I was spared." He glowered at his feet. "How can I change what I am? A wretched creature, consumed by fiery humours? Sometimes I wonder if my soul's already lost, when men call me a devil and declare that I'm the Antichrist."

"If John believed such things, then he'd never have helped you. You're a man, that's all. Flawed and imperfect, like the rest of us."

He didn't answer.

She shifted, suddenly uncomfortable. He'd been a different man over the last couple of days. But the old Hugh was coming back, restless and irascible.

"It must have given you enormous satisfaction," he muttered.

"What do you mean?"

"To have me entirely at your mercy."

"You were distressed and in pain," she replied, in as level a tone as she could muster. "I only wanted to make things better."

"And what did John think of this? When he learned that you'd lavished such attention on another man's flesh."

"He thought nothing of it," Margaret replied. "He knows I find his flesh far more appealing than yours."

Hugh laughed, deep in his throat. Then he stirred, suddenly agitated. "For God's Sake, John!" he called, voice booming out as if he were addressing a whole host of men. "Give the poor beast some freedom. You're hauling him around as if he's a common sumpter nag."

"Must you always be so critical?" Margaret asked.

"When a man abuses a horse of that quality, yes."

Putting a hand across her brow, she watched intently. She saw the change, the moment when John's hand lightened on the reins and the stallion's mood lifted. The beast carried itself proudly, an eager instrument of its rider's will. And from the enrapt look on John's face, she knew that he'd experienced something wondrous.

"There!" Hugh slapped his hands against his knees. "Sheer poetry."

Dumbarton Castle

"It's a miracle!" Alex called, darting along the wallwalk ahead. "Look at them!"

The Gryphon at Bay

Matthew leaned against the parapet, scarcely able to believe his eyes, so overwhelmed with relief that he could scarcely even speak.

A small host of men approached; most on foot, with a respectable number mounted. The chequered *azure*-and-*argent* fosse on *or* of the Lennox Stewarts flew at the vanguard, with more Lennox barons following on behind. They progressed slowly through the town, where smoke still seeped from windows and ruined roofs.

Now Dumbarton was burned, there was no way to feed the King's host. Bereft of supplies, Argyll had retreated east to Dunglass. Where no doubt he'd be rethinking his strategy and praying that King James would relinquish him of the responsibility of subduing his kinsman.

"Open the gates!" Matthew called. He gripped his brother's shoulder, a broad grin on his face. "We'll be feasting tonight!"

Matthew threaded his way through a yard packed with men and horses, eyes fixed on one man in particular, his half-brother, Sir William Stewart of Glanderstoun.

Glanderstoun nodded in greeting as he approached. He was like his father the Earl, broad and strong and dour, with a thick thatch of greying black hair and a rough beard. "God, it's good to be back," he said, stretching in the saddle.

Matthew took the reins, smiling. "I'd give my eye teeth to be away."

Glanderstoun dismounted and embraced him. "Your time will come, Mattie. And Alex-" He cuffed the youth's head. "Have they been keeping you busy?"

Alex grinned.

"Where's Father?" Matthew asked.

"Off courting more allies," Glanderstoun said. "Things are moving on apace. We must bring the King's men to bay before winter's upon us."

"Ah..." Matthew tried not to sound too wistful.

"Don't be so disheartened. You're buying us valuable time."

Matthew shrugged and nodded to Alex. "Take him to the stables," he said, relinquishing the horse into his brother's care.

Glanderstoun watched as the youth departed. "It's been months since we last spoke," he said. "Alex has grown a few inches."

"He rode out in anger when we razed the town," Matthew said. "He did us all proud."

"Takes after his father then."

Matthew clapped the horse's neck, ran his fingers through its coarse black mane. "Elizabeth was here."

Glanderstoun hissed through his teeth, face clouded with concern. "All's well with her?"

"Yes."

"I feared she'd suffer for our audacity."

Matthew slapped his half-brother's back. "Your lady's hard as nails," he said. "God help that good-for-nothing kinsman of yours if he ever dares take her on. She'd flay him."

Glanderstoun laughed. "That's a comforting thought." He draped a comradely arm about Matthew's shoulders, gripped him tight. "There's a keg of fine claret amongst my baggage. We can share it tonight."

"I'm sure there's much to tell," Matthew said. "My news is limited, I fear. Not much happens when you're confined within your castle walls. You must speak with the Countess. She'll be eager for news of Father."

Chapter 31

The Place of Southannan

"The worst kind of guest is one who outstays his welcome." Hugh slouched against the stable wall, arms folded. "No doubt you're desperate to see the back of me."

John smiled. "Not at all."

Hugh's glance was faintly disparaging. "No need to be polite. Twelve days is a long time to endure any man's presence."

"You were never a burden," John said.

And he meant it, too. Away from his kin, Hugh was agreeable company. If he chafed for revenge, he never spoke of it. He cared more for the cry of the hounds as they scented a hare, or the sudden plummet of a duck shot from the sky.

Today, though, their wardship was at an end.

A dozen Montgomerie retainers had arrived that morning, ready to escort their lord back home. Southannan was alive with the clatter of hooves and the restless chatter of their visitors, once the baggage was readied, Hugh would be gone. Zephyr was newly shod and trotting sound, Hugh sufficiently recovered to wield his sword and take to the saddle once more.

"I envy you," Hugh said.

John frowned. "Whatever for?"

"You lead a simple, straightforward life."

"It can't continue."

"Cherish these days, John," Hugh said, softly. "Success carries a heavy price. Men still want to knock you down. They just have more difficulty in doing so." He stared out to where Zephyr awaited him, harnessed and ready. "Ah, well," he said. "I must be gone."

"You seem reluctant."

"I'll have a brace of kinsmen at my back by nightfall. They'll be nipping at my heels and baying loud for vengeance." He grimaced. "All I desire is some time spent in Helen's company. Where I can remember all that's good about the world."

"You deserve some respite."

"I'm indebted to you both," Hugh added. "You welcomed me into your home, and offered me the tender care a man might offer his own brother..." He looked John in the eye, suddenly anxious. "This kindness isn't lost upon me, you know. If there's anything I can do to repay you..."

John gripped his shoulder. "There's no need, Hugh."

"At the very least... When William's nuptials are concluded, I'd like you both to ride south and enjoy my hospitality for a week or two. That way, Helen and I can thank you properly."

"We'd be delighted," John replied. "I want Margaret to see the world while she still can. In a few months, I doubt she'll have the inclination."

161

Louise Turner

* * *

Tantallon Castle, Lothian

Tantallon Castle had been the traditional stronghold of the Red Douglases for generations. Lying just a few days' ride from Edinburgh, it was isolated nonetheless, perched on its tall clifftop overlooking the German Sea.

Angus loved its craggy majesty. He relished, too, its comfortable distance from courtly intrigue and routine.

It was rare to be granted any visitors, save the odd herald bringing letters from the King. So when Angus received news of the unexpected arrival he was quick to respond, grasping gown and bonnet and heading off down the stair.

He crossed the yard at a saunter, a half-smile on his face. "Well, well!" he said. "What a delight this is! To meet with such a celebrated fugitive."

"I'm pleased to be granted such a cordial reception." John Stewart, Earl of Lennox, swung himself down from the saddle. He was big, broad-shouldered, with a dense head of silvered black hair and a neatly-trimmed beard. He had the look of a man used to living his life in the saddle, his fine leather boots splashed with mud, his cloak, too.

Angus' smile broadened. "What else did you expect?" he retorted. "I'm most impressed that you risked life and limb to come here. We're just a stone's throw from Patrick Hepburn's lands."

"When the cat's crouched over the mousehole, the mouse may frolic where he likes."

Angus cast a glance over the trio of retainers that accompanied him. "You're a brave man. Entrusting your precious self to this meagre escort..."

Lennox shrugged.

"Might I assume that you've come here courting my support in your little, ahem, *enterprise?*"

There was a snort from Lennox. "You sound like you're the one doing me the favour."

Angus raised his brows. "No doubt you'll do your best to convince me that your position is unassailable."

"Not exactly," Lennox conceded. "But dissent is growing. And Earl Patrick has scarcely been going out of his way to win allies." He nodded towards Angus. "As you yourself will be aware."

"True," Angus agreed, tight-lipped.

"Time we wiped that complacent smile off his face." Lennox gazed straight at him. "Don't you agree?"

Angus gestured towards the door of the keep. "Come inside."

Lennox accepted his wine with a grateful nod. "Don't be offended if I haven't approached before now," he said. "If the truth be told, I wasn't convinced you'd move against James unless you saw a significant chance of success."

Angus stroked the polished silver bowl of his goblet. "You can offer me such assurances?"

"Five hundred men have pledged to fight in the old king's name. More will follow, I'm sure. Many more. From Moray, and the north."

"Rebellions come and go. Sometimes they succeed, sometimes they fail..."

Lennox laughed. "You think mine's doomed to failure."

Angus made a show of studying his nails. "Not necessarily."

"My allies will meet at Dumbarton within the next few weeks. From there, we'll be riding on to Doune. We're already raising merry hell in Angus and Forfar..."

"Doune, you say?" Angus considered his words, carefully. "I may attend."

"I'm sure that when the spoils are divided, there will be a role for you. A significant role. One worthy of the man who's the sole heir to the Douglas name and reputation..."

"Flattery doesn't become you, John."

Lennox chuckled. "Oh, don't consider it flattery. I'm stating the facts, nothing more. You're a Douglas, you lead one of Scotia's most formidable families. As a Stewart, I acknowledge this. I appreciate the sacrifices your ancestors made in their efforts to serve my royal kinsmen." He half-closed his eyes. "We must stand together, you and I. Co-operation is essential, if we're to hold our ground against the advance of the lesser families. The likes of the Hepburns should learn their place. And stay there, too." He paused. "We need you, Angus. James is very fond of you. You weren't appointed his tutor for nothing."

"I was offered similar rewards before," Angus replied. "They weren't honoured then. Why should you be any different?"

A slow smile crossed Lennox's face. "You'll just have to trust me, won't you?" he said. "Ride to Doune, Archie. Lend us your full support. And then you'll see just how generous the Stewarts can be to those who merit it."

The Place of Eglintoun

Hugh's staghounds raced to greet him, two grey streaks surging across the yard at full gallop.

And close behind them, Bessie. Lifting her skirts in both hands she ran across the cobbles, a broad grin spreading across her face. She threw her arms wide and launched herself towards him with a wordless cry of joy.

Hugh caught her and swung her from the ground while she wrapped her arms around his neck.

Stifling a sob, she burrowed close. "We were so frightened. We thought-"

He held her tight, a witty retort poised upon his lips. *Come now, child. It's as if you're sad to see me home...* But the words died in him. He just buried his face in her hair, and breathed her deep, savouring the reunion.

It was short-lived. Within moments, a mass of kinsmen closed in, brothers, cousins, all eager to greet him.

"Come now, lassie." James Montgomerie tugged Bessie loose. "There's no need for that." He grasped Hugh's shoulder, smiling. "You were sorely missed."

"You didn't look so hearty when I last set eyes on you," Hessilhead cut in. "Thought you were on your way to the angels."

"Or the devils!" James added, and they all laughed.

"You'll soon be your old self!" Hessilhead wrapped a comradely arm about Hugh's shoulders. "And then we'll put wrongs to rights, and the world'll be a better place."

Helen waited beyond the melee, hands clasped before her. Her gaze spoke eloquently, her dark eyes filled with questions and concerns.

He caught her eye and nodded.

She waited a little longer, then shouldered her way through. "Come inside," she said, seizing his arm and pushing Hessilhead aside. "We dine in an hour," she told everyone. "Give His Lordship some peace while he changes for dinner."

Without further ado, she shepherded him away.

Hugh limped at her side, conscious of everyone's collective scrutiny. Beyond the good-humoured crowd of kinsmen, servants and household staff looked on from doorways and windows. They whispered amongst themselves, curious, unsettled.

He was grateful to escape onto the dark and silent stair. Helen was a steady presence at his back: as he hobbled into his chamber, she put a gentle hand upon his arm.

But the peace was soon broken by the mob following close behind.

"You had us worried," James Montgomerie said.

Hugh sank into the nearest chair. He tried not to wince, but the long journey had taken its toll. "In future, I'll try not to be so inconsiderate."

"What in God's name went wrong?" Hessilhead demanded. "How could you let this happen?"

"I'm tired, John."

"Tired? You've been sitting on your arse for a fortnight!"

Helen touched his shoulder. "You should make yourself more comfortable. I'll fetch Ringan, if you like."

He grasped her fingers, briefly. "I'll manage. Please, help me undress." He shrugged cloak and gown aside.

"-That's the last time we let you wander abroad on your own-" Hessilhead was saying. "It's far too dangerous."

Helen's hands moved deftly at his back. "Do you want to wash?"

"Later." Hugh glanced about him, frowning. A fire had been set to welcome him, the chamber exactly how he'd left it. He ran his gaze over the vast bed with its heavy curtains, the elegantly carved kists and chairs. The tapestries upon the walls showed the same battling knights and charging horses, stitched by the industrious fingers of his ancestors.

But now he was back he felt nothing. He seemed detached from it somehow, an outsider peering into a world where he didn't quite belong any more. His glance settled reluctantly on Hessilhead, who was prattling away regardless, oblivious to the fact that his cousin wasn't listening to a word.

Helen leaned close. "Hugo, my love, I must feed the little one. I'll see you at dinner." Kissing his head, she swept away.

He followed her with his gaze. "Helen?"

She paused at the door.

"I'm sorry."

The Gryphon at Bay

She smiled, a smile far older than the face that bore it. It was as if she harboured the divine wisdom of a goddess: Minerva perhaps, who'd offered strength and counsel to the Ancients. "You're home now," she said. "That's all that matters."

"Oy!" Hessilhead glared at him, irritated. "Were you listening? Did you hear a single thing I said?"

     *   *   *

The mood was buoyant at dinner. The wine flowed, the table was piled high with food. There was much bold talk about burnings and retribution.

But not from Hugh. He weathered his kinsmen's enthusiasm with quiet humour but said very little.

Helen studied him, wondering if she was the only one to perceive a change. It wasn't just that he bore the evidence of injuries: a healing gash over one eye, the ghosts of old bruises around his face. It was something more profound than that. She thought he looked strangely frail, his skin pale, almost translucent; he gazed upon the board with a vexed expression, as if he'd grown weary of the world and everything within it.

She wasn't invited to his chamber that night. It was clear indication that something was wrong, so once Marion was safely swaddled in her crib, Helen headed down regardless.

She knocked lightly upon the door. "Hugh?"

There was no reply.

Lifting the latch, she stepped inside.

He was slumped in his chair, hounds slouched at his feet. Holding a goblet of wine in one hand, he gazed into the fire, disconsolate.

She approached carefully. He gave no sign he'd even heard her. But when she perched on the arm of his chair, he reached for her hand.

"I've glimpsed mortality," he said. "It's not a pretty thing."

She said nothing.

"What did they tell you?" he asked.

"Sir John considered it your own private business." She squeezed his fingers, gently. "You're tired. You should rest."

He glanced aside. "In good time."

"Now, Hugh." She tugged his arm. "Come to your bed."

He grimaced, visibly reluctant, but didn't try and argue. She helped him out of his gown, then unlaced his doublet. He let her ease it from his shoulders, then stiffened. "No more."

"Hugh…"

He cast her a pleading look. "I'm disfigured."

"I don't care," she retorted. "I just want to hold you in my arms, to know you're safe. Is that too much to ask?"

     *   *   *

He hoped the shadows and the darkness would hide the scars. If Helen noticed them, she had the grace to say nothing, helping him to his feet, deftly loosening the laces of his hose and steadying him as he struggled to free himself.

For once she left them lying. "You should rest tomorrow."

"I'm perfectly alright."

"That's not what I mean." She tossed back the bedclothes and patted the bed. He sank down there with a sigh.

Rearranging the covers, she perched beside him. "I'll stay with you tonight," she said. "At times like this you need a wife's comfort." She met his gaze, face sober, unsmiling. "Don't be afraid to ask." She turned, presenting her back to him and pushing her hood aside.

Leaning close, he untied the laces of her gown and picked them loose. "It's the first time I've had to."

"The shame isn't yours, Hugh." She shrugged him aside and wandered over to the fire. "It lies with the men who did this." Unpinning her hood, she freed her hair and shook it loose so it slid in dark waves down her shoulders and back.

"You don't know what happened."

"But I know you." She slipped out of her gown, laying it over a nearby chair. Her kirtle hung loose, firelight outlining every curve.

Hugh watched, unable to draw his eyes from her. She pulled off her kirtle, revealing strong sturdy limbs and rounded hips, breasts still swollen with milk. When he saw her like that, lit by the glow of the flames, he felt he was confronting something unfamiliar, primeval. A creature possessed by some deep dark power that passed on through the generations, from one daughter to the next. Inspiring love and fear in equal measure, like the enchantresses of old, Circe, Calypso.

She caught his eye and smiled, and the sense of awe was gone. It was only Helen, who'd been his treasured confidante for years now, who'd borne and raised his children. He loved and desired her all the more, knowing how close he'd come to losing her. But when she climbed in beside him, his body was too weary to respond; he lay there limp and tired as she pressed against him, her skin warm, soft, sweetly scented.

He sighed and closed his eyes. The agitation trickled away, little by little. She kissed and caressed him, exploring his broken flesh with careful reverence.

"Hush now." She spoke to him in the *gaelic*, the tongue of her forefathers. *"My bright one. My fierce one. Rest in your lady's arms while you find your strength. She loves you more than anything else on this earth. She will keep you warm at night, and safe from harm..."*

He laid his cheek against her breast. She held him close, bringing heat and consolation. And then she sang to him. An old song, from the islands that lay across the sea to the west. The words, the melody, sounded strange and wondrous, full of barbaric pride and sadness.

He listened, entranced, as she sang of a maid's heartache and loss at a lover's desertion, her voice rich, achingly beautiful.

The song faded. Silence settled.

The hairs still prickled on the nape of his neck, and his loins at last were showing an interest. She touched him there, gentle but insistent, while she kissed his face and whispered kind words in his ear.

Then she loved him. Quietly, and with great care.

Afterwards they lay together, limbs meshed close, savouring the reunion. "You were my comfort and my curse," he said. "I'd have lain down and died, if it hadn't been for you."

She gripped him closer still, but didn't speak.

The Gryphon at Bay

"When my strength was gone, I pictured your face and wept. I thought you'd never know what happened. I thought you'd think I betrayed you by not coming home."

"I dreamed of you," she said. "I thought then that you had come home, that I'd lost you. But you're here now. With me. That's where you'll stay, I hope. For a little while, at least."

Chapter 32

It was just a short walk from the ladies' apartments to the lord's chamber below, but the air in the stair-tower was chill. Barefoot and clad in just her kirtle, Helen felt it keenly.

She shivered and drew her cloak closer.

Despite the joy of Hugh's return, her heart was heavy. Last night, he'd recounted everything. It had been hard for him. He'd wept, while she held him tightly.

I'm sorry, he'd said afterwards. *I know it hurts you to hear all this. But... You're the only one I can confide in.*

She hadn't said a word. There wasn't really much she could say in the circumstances. She was honoured that he valued her counsel so highly, but it was a difficult burden to carry.

It stung her deep to think that young Cuthbert Cunninghame had taken such pleasure in taunting him before leaving him to die. The thought kept gnawing at her. At least as she'd held Marion in her arms and suckled her that morning, she'd been able to forget, to lose herself in the selfish demands of their child.

Helen opened the door and slipped quietly inside.

He'd been sleeping when she left. Now, though, life was returning to the chamber. Of Hugh there was still no sign, the curtains drawn around the bed. But his venerable manservant Ringan was crouching by the fire, coaxing the flames to life.

He glanced up as she approached, face troubled. "How fares the master?"

She laid a hand upon his shoulder. "I'm sure his strength will soon be restored."

"God bless you, Lady Helen," Ringan replied. "You've always taken such good care of him." He nodded to the kist at the far wall. Dishes had been set there, neatly covered by a clean cloth. "I brought victuals."

"That's very kind." Shedding her cloak, she headed for the bed. The hounds lay sprawled on an old plaid nearby, fast asleep: one twitched and whined, dreaming of the chase.

Stepping briskly over them, Helen pulled the curtain aside and slid into bed. "Hugo?"

He rolled onto his back, and stretched, yawning. "How's little Marion?"

"Her appetite is lusty. As ever."

"Good." He closed his eyes.

Helen nudged him, sharply. "You've slept long enough."

He smiled. "Perhaps you should encourage me to stay awake."

Helen giggled and sat up. Lifting her kirtle, she straddled his thigh, resting her knee lightly against his groin. She ran her fingers over his face, down his neck and body; he twitched and laughed.

Seizing his wrists, she held him fast. "I should lock the door, and never let you stray."

"It would be the sweetest confinement of all."

"You'd tire of it eventually," she said. "You'd want to slip your bonds."

"Perhaps," he agreed. "But that would go against your wishes." He snuggled down against the mattress. "So how would you punish me, if I disobeyed?"

Nestling close, she whispered in his ear, "I'd bind you with the finest silken cords, my love..." Her hand strayed to his loins. "And then I'd inflict the most exquisite torments upon your flesh... You'd beg me for release. But I wouldn't relent. Not until I was satisfied that you'd learned the error of your ways."

"Ah..." He fixed his gaze on her, a glance fixed with eager devotion. Though the years had left their mark, when he looked at her like that, he was still the same man who'd courted her.

How easy it was to take him for granted, to forget how fragile he was, mere flesh and bone...

She swallowed, suddenly overwhelmed.

He laid his hand against his cheek. "Helen?"

"You have the most glorious eyes," she said. "They shine so bright, like the howlet's. They pierce the shadows, and chase away the darkness..."

His smile was gentle, child-like. "My treasure. I was blessed the day I first set eyes on you."

"Hush..." She laid a finger on his lips. "Let's waste no more time in pity or reproach. There are better ways to spend the day."

The Place of Kilbirnie

The mood at dinner had been cordial, but as the afternoon progressed, the atmosphere within the hall grew steadily colder. It was – Margaret thought - as if a shadow had been cast across the board, a shadow with a face, a name, which for a long while no-one had the courage or desire to mention.

"Why in God's Name can't you be honest with us?" Sir Malcolm snapped at last. "We're your kin. Your friends."

John studied the contents of his cup, frowning. "Because it's nothing to do with me," he said. "Everything that happened is Lord Hugh's concern, and his alone. Why should it be of any interest to you?"

"What if Glengarnock burns?"

"Why should it?"

Malcolm was silent. He clasped his hands and leaned his forehead on folded knuckles. "The world's on the brink of madness. And you just shrug it aside..."

"I've weathered enough strife and turmoil already," John retorted. "I'm just grateful that for once I can step back and look on from the lists. I strongly advise you to do the same. As I said, Malcolm, it's not your business. And it's not my business, either."

* * *

She escaped when she could. Though even then there was no respite, for it was only polite that she sat with Marion in the ladies' chamber while the men remained ensconced downstairs, discussing their business in private.

She spoke as required, but most of the time, she kept silent. She didn't really know what to say: a ball of dread had settled in her stomach, growing tighter whenever she heard the men's conversation grow more heated below.

Marion picked up her sewing with a sigh. "I can't understand why John should be so hostile," she complained. "Sir Malcolm meant no harm. He was worried when you didn't return. We were all worried."

"I know that," Margaret agreed, in as mild a tone as she could muster.

Marion regarded her carefully. "All's well, I hope?"

"Of course," came Margaret's bright reply.

"Sir William Cunninghame of Craigends called here. He was asking after John."

Margaret's heart sank. "I can't think why he'd take such an interest in John's affairs."

"Sir William seemed agitated. If something's happened to fuel the feud, then we'll all suffer the consequences."

"I can see why you're concerned."

"Did you speak with Lord Hugh?"

Margaret gnawed a nail, unwilling to reply. "Yes," she said at last. "We spoke with him."

"And he was well?"

"Yes."

"Oh." Marion almost sounded disappointed.

Margaret glowered at the floor, nursing a quick surge of indignation on Hugh's behalf. "I'm sorry to bring such bad tidings," she said, "but rumours of the Lord Montgomerie's demise are greatly exaggerated. Pay no heed to them."

"John helped him, didn't he?"

"This is exactly what John feared," she snapped, surprised by the strength of her indignation. "Condemnation, from his kin and so-called friends. Because he did the honourable thing and helped a man."

Marion opened her mouth to protest, but Margaret wasn't finished yet. "Hugh suffered greatly," she said, "and I for one think it was God's intervention that saved him. Not the Devil's..." She broke off, face flushed, realising now the extent of her betrayal. *I'm sorry, John,* she thought. *I betrayed your trust...*

John retired late to the guest range. When she heard him climb the stairs, she was still awake and dressed herself. She couldn't have found rest. Not when her failure weighed so heavily upon her.

She knocked on his door and peered into his chamber. "Am I disturbing you?"

He was resting on his bed. Hearing her voice, he pushed himself onto his elbows and smiled in weary greeting. "No. Of course not."

"I'm so sorry. I didn't mean to say anything, but Marion kept hounding me. Then it just slipped out, about Hugh and how we helped him."

He gestured alongside. "Sit down."

Margaret settled on the edge of the bed. "Are you angry with me?"

"Not at all." John lay back down with a sigh, hands clasped before him. "God, I'm as stuffed as a Yuletide goose. How's a man to keep lean and supple when his kinfolk pour sweetmeats down his throat all afternoon?"

"You didn't have to eat so much."

"It was impolite to refuse."

"John-"

He opened his eyes. "If they'd wanted a direct answer, they should've asked a direct question."

"You enjoyed it, didn't you? Tormenting them like that."

He smiled slightly. "Perhaps."

"I think they wish Hugh was dead."

"Yes," he agreed. "I'm sure they do."

"Because of your father?"

"I don't think so," he said. "They consider him a source of chaos." He paused, considering his words. "On reflection, perhaps they're right." He drifted into silence, eyes closed. "Did you find him attractive?"

She swallowed, caught off-guard. His expression hadn't changed. It was as if the question was asked through mild curiosity, nothing more. But she'd seen him weave a similar web that afternoon, and she knew better.

"No," she said. "He's like a gnarled old tree."

"Some day, I'll be like a gnarled old tree. You mightn't love me then."

"*She* does..." Margaret said. "Lady Helen, I mean. I hope that when ten years pass, we can be like them. Devoted, and content."

"My heart won't waver." He looked her in the eye, and for a moment, the mask was gone, he was vulnerable and afraid. "Will yours?"

"No." She leaned close, and kissed his lips, gentle reassurance. "Of course not."

Chapter 33

Tantallon Castle

"You have a grandson." George Douglas paused at the threshold, scarcely able to contain his grin. "Both mother and child are well. And the Countess is delighted."

"That's quick work, George!" Angus gripped his son close. "You were against the match at first, I know, but the woman's proved herself. As have you..."

George laughed at that. He was a robust young man, just twenty years old, but mature for his age, graced with a thick head of brown hair and a warm, endearing smile. Pleasant in character, and instantly likeable – just like his sire, Angus thought, with an inward smile.

"Have you thought of a name?" he asked.

George bowed his head. "I shall continue the old tradition. And name the boy Archibald. In honour of his grandsire, and a dozen worthy Douglases besides."

"I can't argue with that," Angus said. "Now come upstairs, if you will. We have much to discuss."

"Is your mother keeping well?" Angus settled comfortably into his chair.

Stretching his legs towards the fire, George sipped some wine before replying. "Oh yes," he said at last. "She runs her household with an iron fist, and woe betide anyone who puts a foot wrong." He gave a mischievous smile. "But you know that already."

"Why do you think I avoid her at all costs?" Angus retorted.

George glanced heavenwards. "I wasn't exactly reluctant to leave her company, either," he replied. "I pity poor Marion. She has no choice in the matter just now. Now... You summoned me. How can I be of service?"

"Ride south to Lanark, and muster our men," Angus said. "I need no less than a hundred retainers. Bring them north, and await my word."

George frowned, suddenly serious. "You're not thinking of joining Lennox?"

Steepling his fingers, Angus said nothing.

"I thought you'd finished with the old king's cause."

"I've no reason to love his successor."

His son's gaze didn't waver. "You'd tell me if you were plotting with Montgrennan..."

"This has nothing to do with Montgrennan. Though I'm sure he'd be most interested to hear of my intentions."

George waved his hand in airy dismissal. "I don't know why you have dealings with him."

"It pays to be flexible. That's why my men will be held safely in reserve..."

His son's smile crept back. "So you haven't decided?"

"No," Angus said. "Not yet."

The Gryphon at Bay

The Place of Eglintoun

Relieved to step out from the heat and clamour of the kitchens, Helen paused to wipe her brow. "When did he arrive?"

"Just a few moments ago," the steward replied. "We thought this news might be better received from you."

Folding her handkerchief, she pushed it discreetly into her sleeve. "Yes, I think you're right," she said, then led the way across the yard, steward and tacksman in close pursuit.

The Lord Kilmaurs stood by his horse at the gatehouse, a handful of disgruntled men-at-arms in attendance nearby. He was older than she'd expected, Hugh's senior by perhaps a dozen years.

"Lady Helen." He bowed and doffed his bonnet. He seemed forlorn, slightly wistful, a man eaten up by uncertainties and regrets. "I'm delighted to meet you. Men speak in hushed tones of your beauty: for once the truth exceeds the rumour."

Helen curtsied, briefly. "You're very kind, my lord. Welcome to Eglintoun."

"I often dined here when I was a boy," Kilmaurs said. "Back in Lord Alexander's day..." His gaze swept around the barmkin, taking in the ranges and stables, the busy bustling servants. "Hugh keeps the place well, I see."

A tremor of hostility coursed through her, she frowned, despite herself. She could almost read his thoughts. *Yes, Hugh's doing very nicely, thank you. Profiting at my expense...* "How may we be of service, Lord Robert?"

"I seek an audience with Lord Hugh."

"I'll inform him of your arrival," came her curt reply. "In the meantime, come this way."

She left him in the hall, with the steward and three Montgomerie retainers in attendance. She wasn't sure how Hugh would react: she was flustered and a little angry herself.

When she swept into Hugh's chamber, she confronted the same domestic idyll that she'd left not long before. Bessie sat by the window mending one of her father's shirts, while Hugh confronted his heir across a chessboard. Young John was perched upon a cushion for added height; a miniature version of Hugh, dark and pale, but graced with a child's cherubic features.

Hugh glanced up, concerned. "What's the matter?"

She closed her fists in her skirts, unsure even now how to begin. "Kilmaurs. He's downstairs. He wants to speak with you."

"Good God..." For once, Hugh was lost for words. "I'll see him here," he decided. "Bessie, John, let's make things tidy for our guest."

Bessie sprang to assist, while young John loitered. "But he's just a Cunninghame..."

"He's a Lord of Parliament-" Hugh snapped back, sharply, "-and worthy of respect. Help your sister. And be quick about it."

With the children's departure, order was restored. Hugh retrieved his gown, pausing briefly to tug a comb through his hair. "Shoes..." he muttered.

Helen grabbed them, and hurried to his side. "Here." As he crouched to put them on, she retrieved his sword belt. "Do you need this?"

He straightened. "That won't be necessary."

"Hugh..." She seized his arm.

He shrugged her loose. "There's nothing to fear," he said. "Rob's the gem amongst the Cunninghames' midden. He's come in good faith, I'm sure."

Hugh sank in his chair with a sigh, goblet of wine in hand. His levity was all for show: deep inside, he nursed a chill sense of foreboding. It was nothing, he supposed, just the rekindling of bad memories best buried and left forgotten.

He'd been just nine years old when his parents died. He didn't come into his inheritance immediately; his great-grandsire clung to life a little longer. But the old Lord Montgomerie couldn't cheat Death indefinitely and he'd passed away before the year was out.

At his great-grandsire's funeral, Hugh had tried very hard to act like the proud inheritor of the Montgomerie legacy, smiling graciously at the endless queue of nobles and barons who lined up to offer their condolences.

But it wasn't easy to take on the role of seasoned statesman when there were snivelling siblings lined up on either side and he felt sick with uncertainty himself.

It was only years later that he'd learned his childish apprehension had been justified. Despite his great-grandsire's efforts to secure Hugh's future before his death, the inevitable had happened. The young Lord Montgomerie, along with all his lands and titles, became a ward of the King, who'd bestowed guardianship of the boy as he saw fit.

It had seemed an appropriate choice to send the boy away to live with his Cunninghame kinsmen at Kilmaurs. Alexander, Lord Kilmaurs had given assurances that all the Montgomerie children would receive an education befitting their rank. Being a nobleman himself, he would personally help young Hugh progress at court.

He'd done what was required in that respect. It was only later, when Hugh came of age, that he'd realised how the rents and monies that should have been his had been placed instead in Cunninghame coffers. And that his right to the Bailie's title was being disputed by his Cunninghame relatives, who'd grown too used to the profits that it brought them.

Hugh sipped his wine, quietly thoughtful. The recollection of these unhappy days wearied him. In the six or seven years he'd lived at Kilmaurs, he'd made only a passing acquaintance with Rob. The Master of Kilmaurs had been too engrossed in learning the knightly arts to concern himself with his young Montgomerie kinsman. It was Will Cunninghame who'd made Hugh's life a misery, the younger brother who knew he'd never amount to anything...

He looked up as footsteps echoed on the stair.

Helen appeared at the door, with Rob Cunninghame following on behind, bonnet in hand. "The Lord Kilmaurs, my lord," said Helen. Her gaze flitted briefly in his direction, subtle indication of her unease.

The Gryphon at Bay

"Hello, Rob." Hugh rose to greet him. Thirteen years it had been since they'd last spoken like this, man to man, in strictest confidence. "You're keeping well, I hope?" He extended his hand.

Rob accepted it, his grasp careful and cautious. "I am, Hugh. Thank you."

Hugh slouched back in his chair. "Please be seated." He raised his hands. "I'm unarmed. You're perfectly safe here." He nodded towards the sword and dagger at Rob's side. "Whether the same can be said for me is another matter."

Helen poured Rob some wine, then retreated. She sat on the edge of the bed, head bowed, hands folded before her, a picture of meek subservience. A misleading impression, for despite her placid appearance, she was poised and vigilant.

Rob nodded, curt acknowledgement. "You're recovered, I hope?"

Hugh took a measured draught of his wine. "I still can't take to my horse."

"Your presence is sorely missed," Rob said. "We feared an escalation, when your kinsmen tried to burn Kilmaurs."

"I never sanctioned their actions."

Rob sat tall in his chair. "And I certainly never wished to injure you. I want to make amends, in the hope that we can pull ourselves back from the brink. I think our situation has become intolerable."

"Yes," Hugh agreed. "I suppose it has." He paused. "I want the guilty men."

"For what purpose?"

"I'll hang them."

Rob considered his words in silence. "That's entirely reasonable," he conceded at last. "Cuthbert has agreed to help. He's ridden out with Will to find the men responsible." He swallowed, painfully self-conscious. "My heir played but a small part in this affair, but the result of his meddling was disgraceful."

"He's only young. Let's pray he learns from this."

"He went back to look for you the following day. He meant to help you."

Hugh glanced towards Helen, who caught his eye, thoughtful, concerned. He smiled, stared at his wine, swilled it around and around. "I'm grateful that young Master Cuthbert was so concerned for my welfare," he said at last. "It sounds like he takes after his sire and not his grandsire. That, I think, is good news for all of us."

Rob's expression didn't waver. "We'll deliver the guilty men into your hands two weeks from today. I suggest we meet at the bounds between our Auchenharvie lands and your own. I'll bring an escort of two-score lightly armed retainers. Is that acceptable?"

"Oh, yes," Hugh said. "I'll have men to match your own, of course. And I'd like to bring a witness. A man impartial to our feud, who can judge our conduct if anything goes wrong."

"I may do likewise." Rob took another mouthful of wine, then set the goblet down, half-full. "Thank you, Hugh. I expected a less cordial welcome."

Hugh laughed. "We're civilised men, Rob, though some would argue otherwise. We surround ourselves with fools and ruffians: they offer us false counsel and force our hands, sometimes against our better judgement."

"Amen to that." Rob stood and replaced his bonnet. "Lord Hugh, Lady Helen. Good day to you both. I hope someday we'll set aside this conflict and renew the old friendship between our houses."

"Good day, Rob. And thank you."

And Rob was gone, with Helen escorting him, just in case. He heard the footsteps recede, shifted in his seat and idly tapped the arm of his chair. *The boy lied. He lied to his own father.*

What a monster you've begotten, Rob...

Helen returned alone. Sitting down nearby, she shook her sleeve. Out slid a small knife, a fragile weapon, meant for no more than peeling fruit.

Hugh chuckled, softly. "Such courage didn't help the first King James. Even together the Queen and her ladies couldn't save him."

"Not through want of trying." Helen looked up, held his gaze. "Perhaps it's a trap."

"I doubt it."

She glanced aside, face flushed with concern. "I know you're bold, Hugh. But perhaps this time you should be circumspect."

He smiled. "When you first came here, you were so sweet and trusting. You loved your fellow men and thought the world a kindly place. It's a sorry state of affairs, when you - of all people - think that everyone plots and schemes against me."

"I wish you wouldn't speak of this so lightly!"

"I'll be prudent," he assured her. "I'll make sure I can defend myself. Let's pray I don't have to."

Chapter 34

The Place of Ellestoun

"Where have you been?" Mariota heaved Margaret's sodden cloak off her shoulders, wincing as water dripped from the hem and pooled on the timber floor. "*Expect us back in a week,* Sir John said. But there was no sign of you. And no word, either. We thought something terrible had happened."

Margaret gritted her teeth to keep from shivering. She was soaked through, hair and hood hanging in a heavy mass down her back. Rain had swept in during the night: the Crawfurds had offered to accommodate them until the weather cleared, but with William's wedding just three days away, John was anxious to press on.

"Alison, will you run downstairs and ask the servants to pour us a bath?" Margaret asked. "Be quick about it, or Sir John will get there first."

Alison giggled and darted away.

"He'll moan at you," Katherine warned.

"He can moan all he likes. My needs are greater."

"How was Southannan?" Mariota asked.

"Very sparse and dull," Margaret replied. "But John says we can get whatever's required to cheer the place up. Now help me out of these wet clothes, Mariota. And hurry, or Katherine will catch cold."

"Of course!" Mariota turned her attention to Margaret's gown, fiddling with the laces.

Margaret frowned. Her maid seemed flustered, on edge. "What's the matter with you?"

"Master Haislet has a son!" Mariota gasped. "He's like his father, but much younger, of course. And taller, a little lighter in build. With such a courteous manner..."

"Where is this marvellous creature to be found? And why haven't I been introduced?"

"He was given a space in the hall last night, but today he visited his sister in the fermtoun. It was sheer good fortune he passed this way: he says he travels far and wide. He's a minstrel: he says his father's skills are nothing compared to his own..."

Margaret pursed her lips. "So this paragon of manhood is modest, as well as handsome? What of the wedding? Is all going well?" She stepped out of her gown and peeled off her damp kirtle. "Oh, heavens! The chill's gone right through me."

Mariota wrapped a sheet around her. "Alan's seeing to everything. Sir John ordered a bed to be made, and that was delivered two days ago, along with a feather mattress. Preparations for the feast are proceeding apace, and young Master Haislet's agreed to assist with the music." Mariota clapped her hands, face shining. "It's very exciting!"

"I'm pleased to hear it," Margaret replied. "What of William's intended? Have you met her?"

177

The elation faded. Mariota studied the floor, stubbornly silent.

Margaret shook her head. "There's no need to pity me. Or gossip behind my back. I know what happened."

"Alan has dealings with her," Mariota said. "She's found lodgings in Kenmure, with William's daughter. But she hasn't set foot in Ellestoun. If the truth be told, I don't think she wants to."

The Place of Glengarnock

The baronial court was held in the hall, with Craigends presiding over the board. His senior kinsmen sat in attendance: he had old Sir Humphry Cuningham at one shoulder while Adam Cuninghame of Caprington sat at the other.

As for Cuthbert... He observed the proceedings from a distance, sitting at the window with arms folded, his disapproval clear to behold.

"You know why you've been brought here," Craigends said.

The prisoner sat opposite, hands folded in his lap. Face worn with hardship, it was hard to tell if he'd lived through thirty or forty summers.

"Rape, arson, theft and murder," Craigends continued. "A guilty verdict on any one of these counts would be enough to hang you."

The man gazed at the board, eyes lowered.

"With regards to arson and theft," Craigends said. "These things happen. Even murder... We could have conjured up some kind of viable defence. But rape? That's unacceptable." He shook his head. "If that wasn't bad enough, you made matters a hundred times worse by assaulting the Bailie."

His prisoner said nothing.

"Well?" Craigends demanded.

The response was little more than a whisper. "I should've slit his throat."

"You didn't, did you? And now he's baying for your blood." Craigends paused a moment, then added, "We'll hand you into his custody, so he can deal with you. Least he won't keep you waiting long for judgement."

"If I'm to hang, sir, I'd rather meet my end at your hands."

"I won't have your death on my conscience," Craigends countered, swiftly. "You had genuine reason to hate him, I know."

The prisoner swallowed, face moist. "For pity's sake, don't give me to that butcher..."

"Beggars can't be choosers." He waved to the men-at-arms who waited by the door. "Take him away and put him in the pit. Give him enough victuals to fill his belly."

The stream of entreaties continued as the prisoner was dragged away. But at last the door closed, and there was silence.

Craigends rubbed his temples, weary resignation. He'd be lucky if he found any sleep that night. In their hunt for the guilty men, he'd been witness to the aftermath of Montgomerie's predations. He'd visited house after house full of half-starved, mangy children and hollow-eyed, desolate women. He'd wondered, many times, why Justice was meted out so unfairly, why God and Dame Fortune helped Montgomerie prosper, when he'd committed such despicable crimes against his fellow men.

The Gryphon at Bay

Cuthbert wandered across the hall and slumped down on the bench, sullen and downcast. "It's not right," he muttered. "That he should get his own way so easily."

"It's not your place to question your father's decisions," Craigends snapped. "Just do what you're told. D'you hear me?"

The Place of Ellestoun

"Good morning," Robert Crawfurd sidled up close to John's shoulder. "Fine day for a wedding, isn't it?"

John glanced up. The sun had broken through the clouds and the rain had stopped at last. The throng that mustered in the kirkyard was growing ever larger, the little church of Saint Bryde's scarcely big enough to take them all. He shifted his weight, frowning. "I detest weddings."

Robert smirked. "Can't think why."

John didn't answer. He should've been enjoying William's nuptials: instead, all the unpleasant memories were flooding back with uncomfortable clarity.

Margaret approached with her maids, a vibrant blaze of colour against the faded greens and greys of the kirkyard.

Robert doffed his bonnet. "Good day, ladies. Margaret, you're looking well."

Margaret inclined her head. "Thank you, Master Crawfurd. Could Marion not join us?"

Robert grimaced slightly. "Sir Malcolm thought it unwise for her to travel."

"That's a pity." Margaret settled into place beside John. She seemed subdued, so he slipped his arm in hers, subtle reassurance.

Together they headed to the church. The tiny building glowed like a beacon on the shores of the lochside, walls freshly harled, its slate roof gleaming, still moist from the morning's mists. The stunted trees that clung to the steep sides of Kenmure Hill were turning already, green leaves painted with russet browns and orange.

"Have you spoken with Mother?" John asked Robert. "She'd love to hear your news."

"We talked briefly," Robert said. "But I could scarcely get a word in, what with the impending birth."

John shook his head. "Heaven help us, when the day draws closer." He checked his pace, scanning the crowd. "Adam said he'd be here. He's bringing the family."

"Then it'll be just like old times." Robert tugged John's arm, gesturing towards the gate in the boundary wall. "Speak of the Devil. He's just arrived. With his brood in tow."

Theree, sure enough, was Sir Adam Mure, his hefty figure heading straight for John's mother, with his wife – John's older sister, Margaret – in close attendance.

"John Haislet's home," John mentioned. "Haven't seen him for five years or more."

"He came back especially?"

"It was sheer good fortune. He's been travelling abroad, earning his keep at rich men's hearths."

"I'm told he's very handsome," Margaret said. "Mariota and Alison are pining for him."

"Then William had better look out," John retorted. "Mary may abandon him at the altar and run off with his son."

"Hush now," Margaret said. "They're here."

William approached the kirkyard, dressed in smart, sober clothes. His son and daughters were in close attendance: John Haislet was acting as his father's groomsman, resplendent in bright silks and walking with a young man's swagger.

John looked skywards. "From the looks of it, he's wealthier than me."

Margaret elbowed him. "Be quiet, John!"

Robert laughed, softly.

And there was Mary. She wore a gown of fair day blue, her tawny hair concealed beneath a starched white hood. She nodded to John, gazed impassively at Margaret, then turned to greet William with a warm, contented smile.

The couple took their vows before the kirk door, then the priest led them inside, relatives and close friends following on behind.

Margaret clung tight to John's arm as they threaded their way into the dark depths of the kirk. "I never thought William would be granted such support."

"He's been with us twenty years or more," John replied. "And he's much loved by everyone. Besides-" John nodded as Sir Adam Mure approached. "-Adam never needs much excuse to feast at someone else's table."

After mass, they paused at the kirk door to pass on their good wishes.

Mistress White was a stately woman who must have been older than John by ten years or more. She had broad hips and strong shoulders, and an austere face that made her seem lost in melancholy thought. She had a sister in attendance, and half-a-dozen children trailing in her wake.

It was the first time Margaret had been granted any opportunity to study the one she'd once considered her rival for John's affections. She didn't feel hurt, or insulted. Just relieved that it was all behind them. And a little bewildered, too, that John could have sought solace in the company of this solemn, mirthless woman.

John spoke just briefly to the new bride, taking her hand and kissing her discreetly on the cheek. Mistress White smiled at that, but it wasn't the forced good humour of a spurned lover. It was more the kind of glance that might be bestowed by a kindly aunt or cousin.

The echoes of that encounter stayed with her all afternoon. But she managed to weather the feast with good humour and listen intently as John rose to lead the toasts and say a few words on behalf of the happy couple.

There was, she supposed, something wholesome and satisfying about the whole affair. Though both man and wife had left the bloom of youth behind them, their faces glowed with joy nonetheless.

And that, she felt, offered hope and comfort to the rest of them.

Once the feast was behind them, the tables were removed and benches set out around the walls.

Margaret rubbed her arms and shivered, feeling rather out-of-place as the bustling activity unfolded all around her. John had assured her that she wouldn't need to lift a finger: indeed, the servants were perfectly capable of readying the place without her. As for John; he'd taken on his customary role of authority with ease, giving directions, moving in to help as and when required.

Margaret wished he hadn't been so protective: she would have much preferred to have something to occupy her thoughts. She'd noticed William's new wife glancing at her from time to time. She'd even offered her a smile, albeit a hesitant one.

Margaret supposed she should go and speak to her, just to show there was no animosity, but she didn't feel inclined to just yet.

She was trying very hard to enjoy herself. But her heart was heavy: her own wedding day should have been a joyous occasion, but instead she'd hated every moment.

She regretted it now. But it was too late. That one precious day, when she should have been relishing the future, was lost forever.

"Congratulations, my dear!"

Margaret looked up to see a brightly-garbed cluster of women approaching, solid as a siege engine and just as menacing. They were led by John's mother, Lady Elizabeth Ross, who strode along with his sister Margaret and his nieces in attendance.

Lady Elizabeth seized Margaret's arms and kissed her cheeks, briskly dismissive. She was like Marion, only older, more portly. "John told me the good news." She cast stern glances around her entourage. "Doesn't she look well?"

The other women nodded and murmured their agreement.

"Thank you." Margaret wasn't much convinced by this demonstration of goodwill.

"You're taking enough rest? And eating properly?"

"Whatever I'm doing, Lady Elizabeth, it seems to be having no ill-effects." She searched the crowd for John, hoping for a show of solidarity, but he was at the far side of the hall, helping to shift the furniture.

The two older women were scarcely listening. "Of course it'll be a great weight off his shoulders," Lady Elizabeth said, turning away. "Once he's been granted an heir."

"It'll be a great weight off all our shoulders," Margaret Sempill agreed.

Cast aside and forgotten, Margaret curbed the urge to glower. She sighed, and glanced over to where the two nieces stood. They were wholesome girls, fresh-faced, full-breasted.

She smiled and beckoned to them.

They hurried across and curtsied. "Lady Margaret."

They couldn't have been much younger than her, but when she looked at them it was as if a yawning gulf of wisdom and experience lay between them. "Which of you is Lizzie?" she asked. "And which is Janet?"

The girls looked at one another. "I'm Lizzie," said the older of the two.

"Let's find a quiet place and sit down. We should get to know each other better, since we're kin." She herded them over to where her maids were sitting. "John's nieces," she explained, and the girls eagerly greeted the new arrivals.

Janet gazed at her, curious. "Is it really so horrible?" she asked. "Being married to Uncle John?"

"Whatever makes you ask that?"

"Father said you didn't want him."

She swallowed, feeling her face colour. "It was different then."

"He's very handsome," Lizzie spoke out, a little defensively.

"Yes, he is. And I wouldn't want to be wed to anyone else, not for all the Queen of England's jewels."

"I'm to be married next year," Lizzie added.

Margaret smiled, and took her hand. "Don't be frightened," she said. "Men may seem like ogres, but they're not, really. Most are very well-meaning, though they can be thoughtless at times." Her eyes followed John: he was talking with young Master Haislet, they were laughing together like old friends.

Glancing up, John caught her eye. He nodded to Master Haislet and ambled over towards her.

"Would you mind very much if Sir John danced with me?" Janet Mure asked.

"I'm not his keeper," Margaret replied, stiffly.

The musicians were taking up their instruments, making final adjustments to pipes, lutes and fiddles.

"Move over." John squeezed himself into the tiny gap between Margaret and Lizzie.

"We were here first," Lizzie complained.

"I'm bigger than you. And stronger, too. So don't argue." He parted his legs slightly, pushing their knees aside. "Well, isn't this a momentous occasion? The son is gracing his father's nuptials. If he doesn't grant us an outstanding performance, he'll never live it down."

"You're eager to acquire him, aren't you?"

"If only it were that easy," he said. "But he hasn't shaken off the wanderlust just yet. He wants to travel north, and cross the sea to Ireland. So he can learn more about the harp from those he believes to be its real masters." He paused. "I've agreed to give him funds."

"Then I hope he'll remember your generosity when the time comes for him to settle."

"So do I." John seized Margaret's cup, and downed the rest of her wine. "Thank you."

"John!"

"I'll fetch some more." He heaved himself to his feet.

The music started, a merry tune. William took to the floor with his new wife, who seemed hesitant at first. Soon others joined them: Robert Crawfurd danced with John's sisters, Sir Adam Mure with Lady Elizabeth Ross.

John pressed a brimming cup into Margaret's hand. "Here you are."

Ask me, she thought. *Please ask me."*

Instead, he sat back down and studied his feet.

Lizzie nudged him. "Is this a pleasure, Uncle John? Having all these ladies in close attendance?"

"It's like being a magnificent Sultan." John stared ahead. "Surrounded by his harem."

"Lady Margaret said she'd permit you to dance with me."

"That's very gracious of her." He caught Margaret's eye. "Well?" he asked. "Will you let me slip the leash?"

She forced a smile. "Go on."

The Gryphon at Bay

John took to the floor with Lizzie hanging upon his arm. They joined the rest of the dancers for a *ballade*: he steered the girl through each move with grace and care.

"Excuse me." Janet gathered up her skirts and sprang to her feet.

There was no hope of him returning. His mother, sister and nieces surrounded him, admiring, adoring. And John, of course, was charm personified. Gracing each and every one of them with as much time and attention as they desired.

Time ground onwards, and she was left there. Alone, beleaguered.

Katherine slid close. "What's wrong?"

"In all this time, he hasn't asked his wife to dance."

Katherine frowned, slightly. "Perhaps he thinks you don't like to."

"I can't exactly say anything," Margaret complained. "It would look ridiculous. It looks ridiculous anyway..."

The music faded. John bowed low towards Margaret Sempill, who'd been his partner for the rondeau. Almost immediately, Janet Mure stepped up to take her mother's place.

"He means no harm, I'm sure. It's just slipped his mind." Katherine squeezed Margaret's hand. "Wait here."

"Kathinere, no! I don't want—"

But Katherine had already gone. She threaded her way through the laughing couples, paused at John's side and tapped him sharply on the shoulder. When he turned, Katherine clutched his arm and pulled him close, standing on tiptoe so she could whisper into his ear.

He glanced at Margaret, concerned, then patted Katherine on the back.

Katherine returned triumphant. "There," she said. "All he needed was a little reminder."

Sure enough, John was taking leave of his kin. He strode across the hall, eyes fixed on Margaret. He offered his hand. "Well, my lady," he said. "Would you grace me with your company?"

She rose and placed her fingers in his.

His grip tightened, careful, secure. "I'm sorry," he said. "I never meant to offend you."

"It doesn't matter," Margaret said.

He looked at her and smiled, and for just a moment, his measured restraint was gone. "Let's imagine the bad times never happened," he said. "I'm yours now, for as long as you want me. We have music, and hearty company. Let's enjoy it while we can."

The stranger trudged into the hall at Alan Semple's side, grim-faced and weary from travel. Mud splattered him from head to foot, but beneath this layer of dirt, his herald's tabard could just be seen.

Spotting their unexpected guest, John knew that his festivities were at an end. He'd been dancing with Alison; drawing her aside, he grasped her shoulders. "I'm so sorry. We have a visitor."

Alison bobbed into a curtsey, blushing fiercely. "It was a pleasure, Sir John."

Crossing the hall, John tried to catch the herald's eye. But Bute Pursuivant's attention was elsewhere: Alan was already deep in conversation.

Bute Pursuivant inclined his head as John approached. "Forgive me, Sir John," he said. "I know you won't want to be disturbed on such a merry occasion."

"The King's business comes first. Do you have quarters?"

"A bite to eat and a bed to rest my bones wouldn't go amiss." The herald paused. "Could we talk together? Somewhere quieter..."

"Of course." John gestured to the door.

Stepping outside brought relief after the stifling heat of the hall. John's thoughts had been fogged with wine, but now his head was clear. "How may I assist His Grace the King?"

"Two matters, Sir John." The herald presented him with a rolled-up parchment, bound with ribbon and sealed with wax. "Firstly, the letter you asked His Grace to provide."

John grasped it. "Let's hope it's never needed."

"Secondly, the King asks that you bring your men to the butts at the city of Glasgow on the Twenty-Eighth of October. Along with the other households throughout the shire of Renfrew, you're required to enforce the siege at Dumbarton. Since you're the Sheriff, it falls to you to pass the word along, and ensure a respectable turnout."

John listened in silence, scarcely able to contain his anger. It was hard to believe, that even now the Stewarts and Lord Lyle couldn't accept defeat and yield themselves to the King's mercy.

"His Grace regrets the inconvenience," Bute Pursuivant continued. "He knows it's already approaching the end of your forty days. But these are extraordinary circumstances."

"He shares my sentiments, I'm sure."

"No wappenschaw is required. Not so soon after the last one."

Margaret appeared at the door. "John?" She saw the herald and blanched. "What's happened?" She halted alongside, arms folded close as if a fearful chill was already seeping into her bones.

"I've been called to war."

"The King's situation is very grave, Lady Margaret," the herald added. "He needs the help of all good men if he's to keep his crown."

Margaret held her head high, keeping a bold front. "I understand. Do you need food? And lodgings?"

"I'll attend to it," John said. "Go back inside."

She loitered. "Poor Mistress White," she whispered. "For these tidings to come on her wedding day... Hasn't she already lost one husband in battle?"

"Then I'll make sure she doesn't lose another." John handed her the parchment. "Take this. Place it upstairs in the charter kist, and keep it safe."

She frowned. "What is it?"

"Our means of defence, if the tide should turn. Letters of fire and sword, giving full authority for what happened at Duchal."

She clutched the parchment tight. "Do you think the King will fall?"

"Let's hope not," John replied. "But we must prepare ourselves for the worst."

Chapter 35

For the first time in weeks the great hall resounded with laughter and song. Wine flowed, and the cooks surpassed themselves, making up for months of restraint and frugal living.

Matthew spoke very little, savouring his father's return. The Earl of Lennox had ridden into Dumbarton that afternoon with a hundred men marching at his banner. Tonight would be spent in feasting and merriment, and on the morrow the leagues would be signed.

In addition to the mass of minor barons who were gathered at the lower tables, some more distinguished figures dined with the household on the dais. Keith was there –the Earl Marischal, no less – alongside the Earl of Atholl, the Master of Huntly and Lord Forbes.

They'd even found themselves a herald...

Matthew caught his mother's eye and smiled, quietly reassuring. The Countess's relief was plain to see: throughout the last month, she'd hidden her thoughts beneath a fearless facade, leading the household by example. Now, though, she made no attempt to hide her delight at her husband's safe return.

"-I wouldn't say it was a warm reception," John Stewart was saying. "But the Earl of Angus wasn't exactly lacking in interest."

"I've heard he's in league with the English," Margaret Montgomerie remarked.

"Aye, well, they accused poor James of being in league with the English. That's why they slew him." Stewart paused. "Angus would be a very useful ally," he conceded. "I hope he'll support us when the time comes."

"What do you intend to do?" the Countess asked.

"We'll plot our course on the morrow," Stewart replied. "I won't sit here and wait for Hepburn to bring me to bay. I'll choose my own battleground. We'll press north, to Perth or Angus, where the ground's less suited to the men of the south and west. If we can capture Stirling, so much the better."

"And Argyll?" she persisted.

"By the time he's called back into service, it'll be too late."

"Well, that's some consolation," she said. For a moment she seemed wistful, laden with regrets, but then the levity was back. "At least you'll be well-fortified with meat and drink before you set out."

"Can't understand your mother," John Stewart heaved himself down into his chair with a groan. "I thought she'd thrown herself wholeheartedly into all this. But today she seemed reticent."

Matthew drew up another chair and sat down there. Even here in the lord's chamber he could hear the ongoing clamour from the hall. "She's worried about Hugh," he said. "She wants him in our lists."

"Hugh's a lost cause."

"And Kilmaurs?"

"Hugh's not *that* much of a lost cause. He'll see sense in time."

"So his Privy Council seat means nothing?"

"Fate has him marked. Sooner or later, he'll offend someone in high office, and then he'll be kicked back into obscurity."

Matthew had to smile at that.

"You've taken all this very well," Stewart continued. "But I can tell your spirits are flagging." He studied Matthew's face, carefully. "It's not that I think you incapable. You proved yourself long ago."

"Come now!" Matthew laughed, too quickly. "It's not like you to speak so gently to your first-born!"

"Perhaps before I was too sparse in my praise," Stewart replied. "You're a man of courage and purpose. That's why your place is here. Your presence inspires the garrison. And it does much to encourage your mother. God knows, she's determined enough, but... She needs you."

"I wouldn't think to question your decisions."

"You may assume you've been singled out for neglect. Or even punishment. But that's not the case." Stewart stroked the arm of his chair, suddenly thoughtful. "I'll remain here three days. After that, I'll be gone."

"You're taking Alex?"

"Lord Robert's coming, too. You'll be on your own, Mattie. I'm relying on you to hold this place till the bitter end." He sighed, and swilled his wine around in his goblet. "Whenever that may be..."

The Parish of Dunlop

They stayed one night with Sir Adam Mure at Caldwell, then pressed south towards Dunlop. It was a cold day, bringing a foretaste of winter: the girls were wrapped in fur-lined cloaks and hoods to keep out the biting wind.

Despite the unpleasant weather, they remained cheerful, treating their journey as a grand adventure. John was pleased with the girls' progress; Margaret and Katherine in particular were becoming quite proficient in the saddle.

Mariota was less confident. She tried hard to conceal her nervousness, but it revealed itself nonetheless, in the way she talked, loudly and incessantly.

"So that's what kept you at Southannan!" she gasped. "Why didn't you say?"

"Because you can't keep your mouth shut," came John's sour retort. "Do you think Lord Hugh wants his troubles discussed throughout the Westland?"

"Don't be cruel, John," Margaret said.

"I can scarcely hear myself think for all this chatter..."

Mariota giggled and studied her horse's mane.

"At least you're safely away from Ellestoun," John said. "I noticed the sly smiles you sent in young Master Haislet's direction during the wedding feast."

"Whatever do you mean, Sir John?" Mariota was all innocence.

"I thought at first they were meant for me-"

"-And you were disappointed!" Katherine broke in.

John shot a disapproving glance in her direction. "I already have a wife, thank you."

"Don't pick on Mariota," Margaret chided him. "Alison was just as guilty. Perhaps we should've brought her with us."

John glanced heavenwards. "God, no. Alison would've been complaining every step of the way. Besides, at least we can rely on Alison to possess a shred of common sense." He nodded towards Mariota. "Unlike some."

Mariota sniffed, feigning injury.

"You should all be more circumspect," John warned them. "Baiting a man's much like baiting a bear. It's all very well running to me or Lady Margaret: if it's too late, there's not much we could do to help you."

"Surely Master Haislet would welcome a wife?"

"At his tender age, not likely," said John. "He'll promise you the world, and forget what he said a week later. You'd be left with a child in your belly and a broken heart."

Katherine smirked. "Do you speak from experience, Sir John?"

John didn't deign to reply.

"What of Lord Hugh?" Mariota interjected. "Has he a son?"

"The Master of Montgomerie's just turned eight," John told her. "His brother's only two. They're probably betrothed already."

The girls made disappointed noises.

"Will Hugh be annoyed if we arrive unannounced?" Margaret asked.

"That's what he said," John replied. "*Come and visit once William's nuptials are behind you.* Best get it over with, I say."

"You make it seem like a chore," Katherine said.

"I don't remember much about Eglintoun," Margaret remarked. "It was dark when we visited it last. And raining, too. But it seemed very big, and quite a stern place, too."

"I'm sure we'll be given a detailed tour of every nook and cranny," John said. "We'll be fed and entertained like royalty, and treated like treasured kinsmen."

Mariota shivered. "I'm not relishing it. Lord Hugh frightens me."

"Oh, you shouldn't fear him," Margaret said. "I always thought him cruel and selfish. But he's not like that at all."

John smiled. "Don't misjudge him," he said. "Like the wyrm, he shed his skin and lay quiet and docile while he recovered his strength. Before long, his scales will harden. He'll soon be wreaking havoc throughout the land, breathing fire and tearing all asunder. When that day comes, we'll wonder why we fought so hard to nurture such a monster."

Louise Turner

Lifting the knife, Helen watched the light play along the steel. The smallest blade she could find, it still seemed too clumsy for the task. Picking up the whetstone, she honed the edge some more.

"Helen?" Hugh called from within the curtained isolation of his bed. "It's cold. Am I to lie here all day?"

"I'll be with you now."

She'd had him completely to herself for a week now. For once he'd been sensible, keeping well away from his horse so his wounds could heal. He'd been an exemplary father, spending most of his time in the company of his children. He'd wrestled with young John, and tutored the boy in how to improve his skills with sword and crossbow. He'd even played with little Robert, though the child was still too young to fully appreciate his father's company.

He'd been an exemplary husband, too. They'd spent long nights and mornings in his bed, enjoying each other with the hungry love of newlyweds. Making the most of their privacy, for young John Montgomerie would soon be leaving the ladies' chamber and moving in with his father.

"There," Helen said. "I'm ready. This should do what's required." She sat down on the bed beside him. "Sit up," she said. "And for Heaven's sake, hold still!"

He cocked his head towards her and she leaned close, holding the knife in one hand, steadying his head and shielding his eyes with the other. Breathing deep in readiness, she slipped the tip of the knife beneath the thread that pierced the wound, and sliced through it. With a gentle tug, the stitch was gone, leaving just a neat blemish behind.

She could breathe again. "There," she said. "That's the worst one."

"There are other parts more precious than my eyes."

"Don't be ridiculous," she said. "This is marvellous work. I couldn't have done much better myself."

"I'm sure young Margaret took great pleasure in the task. It's not often that anyone's granted licence to inflict such agony upon me. Though I think her hostility may have thawed now she's learned to pity me."

"Your attempts at finding sympathy might work with her, Hugh, but I am impervious. Come on now."

He laughed, and stretched out on his back.

"Now then," Helen said. "Let's see what we can do to make this chore more pleasurable." She lifted her skirts and settled over his hips. "Just be careful not to twitch too much."

Helen frowned, concentrating on the task, deftly slicing through one stitch after another. Hugh was surprisingly patient, letting her do whatever was needed. Though when she drew close to his groin, he scooped his parts aside, just in case.

He fidgeted. "Ah, Helen. You inflict such beautiful cruelty."

"Be still now. I'm nearly done." There were just a half-dozen stitches to go, but they were in the most awkward place of all. And even Hugh was squirming. "Please keep still!"

The Gryphon at Bay

There was a knock upon the door. "My lord?"

Helen sighed. "I'll attend to it. Wait here." She slid from the bed and threw the covers over him. Heading for the door, she straightened her hood.

The steward stood on the stair beyond. "Sir John Sempill and Lady Margaret Colville are here," he said. "Sir John says you were expecting them."

Helen shrugged, acknowledging his confusion. "It must have slipped my lord's mind to tell us," she replied. "I'll come and speak with them. In the meantime, show them to the hall and offer them refreshment. Some mulled wine, if there's some to hand. They'll be chilled to the marrow."

The steward bowed and disappeared down the stairs.

Helen closed the door. "Did you hear that?"

"Wasn't listening," Hugh said. "I can't think past my immediate needs..."

"Sir John Sempill and Lady Margaret Colville are here."

Hugh uttered a desolate moan, and battered his head against the pillow. "God! Is the whole world conspiring to torment me?"

"I'll escort them to the range and settle them in there. And then we'll finish this business." She smiled. "Don't look at me like that!" she said. "Perhaps next time you'll think to warn me that our friends are coming to visit. That way we won't find ourselves in such awkward circumstances."

"I'm sorry I couldn't greet you in person." Hugh grasped Margaret's hands and kissed her swiftly on both cheeks. She didn't quite know how to respond: it was as if his trials had never happened, he was boisterous, exuberant. "I had urgent matters to attend to." He caught Lady Helen's eye.

Lady Helen smiled slightly. "Are your quarters adequate?" she asked.

"More than adequate." John shifted, uncomfortable. "Thank you."

"We'll dine together tonight," Hugh continued. "Just the four of us. Tomorrow I'll arrange something more elaborate."

"Hugh, there's no need-"

Hugh slapped John on the back, briskly dismissive. "I appreciate your modesty."

"Was your journey uneventful?" Lady Helen asked Margaret.

"It was cold." Margaret studied the floor, embarrassed in Lady Helen's presence. The Lady of Eglintoun struck her as being very gracious and composed, her lavish dark-red gown embellished by an elaborate array of jewels and pearls. "But riding a horse is so much better than being jolted about in a wagon."

"How long are you planning to stay?" Hugh was asking.

"As you said yourself," John replied. "The worst kind of guest is the one who outstays his welcome."

"A week?" Hugh persisted. "Ten days?"

"The host should be mustered. Word's already been sent out, but I shouldn't loiter too long. A week's quite enough, I think..."

"Can I persuade you both to dally a few days more?"

"I hadn't really thought-"

"I've a tryst arranged for eight days' time. With Robert, Lord Kilmaurs."

John shrugged. "What does this have to do with me?"

"I'll be delivering justice on certain individuals who committed injuries against me. I'd be grateful for a witness. A competent man who's not attached to my own household, or to Kilmaurs'. A man I can trust..."

John regarded him with eyes narrowed. "That's all this is? A tryst between gentlemen?"

"We've made an agreement. I intend to honour it."

John didn't answer. His frown deepened.

"John..." Hugh ventured, quickly. "In view of what happened, I thought-"

"It's alright," came John's brusque reply. "I'll be your witness."

Hugh sighed, visibly relieved. "Thank you."

Lady Helen grasped Margaret's arm and steered her aside. "They've much to discuss," she said. "All's well with you now?"

"Yes, indeed."

"I guessed that marriage brought you little joy at first."

"He frightened me to begin with," Margaret told her. "But since those days he's tried hard to make amends. I wouldn't change him for the world."

A warm smile touched Lady Helen's lips. "I'm very pleased to hear that."

"Lady Helen," Margaret ventured, nervously. "If I was too familiar with your husband, then I'm very sorry. But he needed help, and there was no one else who could tend him. He told me that his heart was yours, and that he missed you."

Lady Helen took her hand. "You offered him comfort and kindness when he needed it most. What wife could resent that? Hugh is very grateful to you both. I am too. I hope you understand that."

Margaret smiled. "Yes," she said. "We do."

Margaret couldn't sleep. To be resting in an unfamiliar bed in an unfamiliar room... Everything unsettled her, from the mattress to the bed linen to the sounds from the yard.

At least John was an enduring constant, his warmth alongside a comforting reminder of home.

The girls had a chamber to themselves, just next door. They were supposed to be sleeping, but once or twice she'd heard them giggling. At least her maids had a bed to call their own: the men-at-arms had to content themselves with a space in Hugh's hall.

As she lay there, she wondered how William was faring. They'd left him behind so he could spend some time with his new wife, which meant that John was reliant on her to help him dress, but she didn't mind that. It was a good excuse to spend more time in his company.

He was lying on his back, very quiet and still. She thought he was asleep, but suddenly he stirred.

"It's a peculiar thing," he said. "How circumstances change..."

"What do you mean?"

"It's been seven or eight months since I first stayed here. That night William slept by the door with his dagger drawn. We were both convinced that Hugh lured me here to murder me."

The breath caught in her throat. "What made you think that?"

"I made things very difficult for the Earl of Lennox, and Hugh's his nephew."

"But if you feared for your life, why did you come here?"

He thought about it a while. "There was no other way," he said. "Others were in command of my destiny. I thought it best to make the most of any opportunity that arose."

"No harm came of it."

"Quite the opposite," he agreed. "If it hadn't been for Hugh, I would never have won your hand. Though your kinsmen didn't exactly welcome his interfering."

"Nor did I."

He was silent. "What did they say?" he said eventually. "About me?"

"That you were a traitor. And a coward." She screwed her eyes closed, wishing with all her heart that he hadn't aired the subject.

"I wrote you a letter," he said. "Trying to explain my circumstances."

"I burnt it."

His laughter echoed soft in the darkness.

"How can you find this amusing?" she demanded.

"Because the whole situation was ridiculous," he said. "We had no choice. We should just have made the best of it."

She wrapped her arms about him, burying her face in his shoulder. "I still regret what happened."

He returned her embrace. "Regret's like a canker," he said. "It eats away inside you. You should shrug those memories aside, and smile at how foolish we were. In that respect, Hugh should be an example to us all. He storms through life, regretting nothing."

"I think he regrets what happened to your father."

"Don't you believe it," said John. "He's incapable of regret."

"If you think so little of him," she said. "Then why are you here?"

"It'll do him good, to think he's no longer in my debt."

"And that's all it is?"

"Yes."

"So it doesn't concern you at all? That you're here in his house, drinking his wine and enjoying his hospitality? Accepting his praise and gratitude when all the time it means nothing?"

"He understands well enough."

She didn't attempt to argue. She supposed that being a man, he had more insights into Hugh's thoughts than she did. But she still couldn't understand why he should be so scathing, when Hugh was going out of his way to be generous. "John-" she began.

"I'm tired." His tone was sullen. "It's an early start."

And that was it. The conversation was ended. Her words had needled him, as she'd hoped they would.

"Goodnight, then," she said.

"Goodnight," he muttered, and rolled over.

Chapter 36

Iron-shod hooves clattered loud against the cobbles as Angus and his party passed the sturdy yett into the vaulted passageway beyond.

Seizing Doune had been a stroke of good fortune for Lennox and his allies: furnished with a solid stone curtain wall two storeys high, the castle was virtually impregnable, a stronghold that even bombards would have difficulty overwhelming.

The air in the courtyard was raw with the sound of hammering and grinding as spears and swords were sharpened. A long line of horses and oxen awaited the farrier, the stink of burnt hooves drifting rank on the wind.

Angus felt the skin at the nape of his neck prickle with expectation, old battle instincts stirring. He wearily dismissed them, reminding himself that officially at least, he remained loyal to the King.

Reining in his mount, he spotted a familiar figure: the Earl of Lennox himself, a big square man with grizzled hair and beard. He was taking a personal interest in the proceedings, inspecting weapons, checking the horses for galls and sores.

But he wasn't too absorbed to spot a visitor. Raising his hand in greeting, he approached with a cordial smile upon his face.

Angus dismounted. "Things are progressing well, I see."

"Indeed they are." Lennox was a man in his natural element, an island of calm amidst the frenzy. "I'm delighted that you came, Angus. How many do you bring? One hundred men? Two?"

"I've mustered one hundred and thirty armed retainers."

"We can assist with supplies," Lennox told him. "We've seized enough provisions to keep us two months or more."

"Let me be blunt," replied Angus. "I've received a summons from His Grace the King..." He paused, frowning. "I've decided to ride with him."

Lennox's gaze did not waver. "Ah..." He laughed, softly. "That's not quite the answer I'd anticipated."

"What I can offer is some manner of assurance, at least. You have my word that my men will not take up arms against you. They'll ride to the field, and after that... We'll see. I don't anticipate success coming easily to James. If the battle turns in your favour, we'll fight on your behalf. If it doesn't..." Angus smiled, slightly. "Then we won't be fighting at all."

"James'll love you for this."

"He must learn that he can't take men's loyalty for granted," Angus said. "I hope the coming months'll teach him a lesson he'll remember the rest of his days."

"And what's that?" Lennox retorted. "That it's unwise to trust a Douglas? Whether he's Black or Red. You're treading on dangerous ground, Angus. I hope and pray you've read the portents right."

The Gryphon at Bay

The Place of Eglintoun

With a dozen hawks in the mews, there were plenty to go round. Hugh furnished John with an elegant goshawk, but Margaret declined to take a bird. The reason soon became clear: she didn't know the first thing about hawking.

To Hugh's relief, Helen quickly took the matter in hand, providing Margaret with a sturdy dogskin gauntlet and as much advice as was needed. "Don't be afraid," she said. "His talons won't pierce the leather."

Margaret flinched as the hawk settled on her wrist. "He's not very heavy."

Hugh opened his mouth to deliver a biting retort, but one sharp look from Helen silenced him. He hissed through his teeth in faint frustration, and cast a relieved glance towards Bessie and young John. The two children stood nearby, each sporting their own small falcon, too polite to look askance.

Margaret glowered. "My mother always said that if I wished to serve my husband properly, I should improve my needlework and learn to manage the kitchen staff."

"Then she did you a disservice," Hugh retorted. "Helen's a match for any man in the hunting field. Give her a crossbow, and she'll bring down a goose at fifty paces." He nodded towards Bessie. "Bessie's no mean hand with a crossbow, either. Your mother expected you to mingle amongst mere barons. She never taught you how to hold your own amongst lords and earls."

John flashed Hugh an irritated look. "She'll learn soon enough."

"It's about time you started teaching her," Hugh countered. "Someone will have to show your children what's required. Because when you're at court, John, you won't be granted much opportunity." Flapping its wings, the tiercel on his wrist fluttered impatiently: Hugh stroked its breast to soothe it. "Now shall we begin?" he asked. "The ducks'll be wondering what's keeping us."

They worked up a healthy appetite that morning, wandering through the parkland and nearby marshes in pursuit of their quarry. At around noon they returned to Eglintoun: after changing their clothes, they made their way to the great hall for dinner.

"I promised you a feast," Hugh whispered in John's ear. "By God, that's what you'll be given." He gestured for him to take his seat at the top table.

John sighed, visibly uncomfortable. "Hugh, this wasn't necessary."

Hugh sent him on his way with a subtle push. "You're far too modest." He paused to glare at the stragglers, who hurried to their places below the dais.

Once everyone was seated, Hugh ran his gaze around the gathered kinsmen and servants, indication that he wanted silence. When the chatter subsided, he rose to his feet and battered his spoon against the nearest flagon. "Friends and kinsmen," he called. "As you know, I was ailing and absent from this household for almost a fortnight. I might never have returned, had it not been for the kindness and diligence of this man." He clapped a hand on John's shoulder. "Today we've gathered so I may extend my thanks in the proper fashion. And I hope you'll join me in extending the hand of friendship to both Sir John Sempill himself, and his kin.

"It's my sincere wish that from henceforth, the Montgomeries and the Sempills will consider themselves friends and allies, and that our friendship will grow ever stronger as the years pass. Gentlemen, ladies, I ask you to drink a toast to our honoured guests, Sir John Sempill and Lady Margaret Colville."

"Thank you very much," John muttered through gritted teeth, as three-score voices hailed him from the floor.

"You could at least try and muster some enthusiasm." Hugh settled comfortably in his chair, surveying the scene with satisfaction. He beckoned to the servants, who stepped forward with laver bowls and napkins.

Before long, the first dishes appeared. A dressed swan had been prepared, and a cockatrice, and some exquisite marchpane pastries, along with a dozen other dishes. And to crown it all, once five courses had made their way down to the lower tables, there appeared the most marvellous subtlety: a stag with gilded antlers, coursed by two fleet rachehounds. Hugh was immensely proud of it: he'd dreamed that one up himself, making careful reference to his guest's coat-of-arms, and somehow his cooks had conjured meat paste, pastry and marchpane into something elegant and beautiful.

Margaret was quite overwhelmed. She clapped her hands and gasped in amazement as it was set before them.

But John merely smiled and nodded, unmoved by all the accolades.

The early morning mist writhed and twisted like a living thing. One moment it'd come in so thick that Eglintoun's walls vanished completely, the next it dwindled and the sun could be seen, a pale sickly disc in the east.

Margaret's mouth was dry, her heart beating fast. She gripped the reins tight, scarcely daring to breathe as Zepyhr cavorted nearby, circling around and leaping up on hind legs. Hugh sat unperturbed, laughing at the grey stallion's antics, while John and Helen discussed the coming hunt as if nothing was amiss.

Margaret couldn't bear to look at Zephyr. She studied her horse's neck, trying not to recollect the last time she'd hunted as a child. The beat of the hooves, the loud sharp breaths of the pony, the break in its stride as a log loomed up. At the last moment, her mount had swerved, she'd known a few seemingly endless moments of sheer, silent terror as she tumbled through the air.

Faces had loomed over her, full of concern. Father, mother, brothers. There'd been a fierce pain in her shoulder, she'd moaned and cried as they picked her up. She'd been lucky. The bone hadn't broken. But it had hurt for weeks...

"Margaret." John's voice pierced her thoughts. He was studying her intently, his concern clear.

She'd never told him why she'd avoided horses for so many years. And she couldn't exactly confess now, not with Hugh and Helen watching. "All's well, John. Please don't worry."

"She's a good horse," John reminded her. "She'll do what you ask."

"Don't worry, John." Helen steered her horse alongside: she rode a brown courser, a big brute that looked as if it would require a man's hand. "I'll ride with Margaret. Go with Hugh. Enjoy the gallop."

"I'm happy with that," Margaret agreed. "Don't fret, John. I'm in safe hands."

The horn rang out, the hounds sang, and the chase was on. Hugh and Zephyr sped off, with John and Storm in close pursuit.

They followed at a sedate canter.

The Gryphon at Bay

"Keep a steady pace," Helen advised. Her bay horse stayed close, head pulled in tight against its chest. "Bessie, John!" she called to the children. "Keep behind me!"

Margaret sat tall, remembering all John had told her, gripping the reins, but not holding on too tight...

Her fears faded at last, a smile crept across her face. She knew she wouldn't fall, or lose control of her mount. Then the mists blew thicker. Trees loomed alongside, they were alone. The men had vanished, they could see nothing. The muffled cries of the hounds echoed ahead, lost and eerie in the gloom. The horn called, far away.

Margaret felt her throat close. She took a deep shuddering breath,

"Don't be frightened, Margaret," Helen spoke out nearby. "I know this country. If the worst happens and we lose our bearings, the horses will bring us home safely."

They gathered around the beleaguered stag, watching in silence while Hugh and John helped the huntsmen dispatch the beast. It lay slumped on its knees, tongue hanging out and flanks heaving, while Hugh stepped in to deliver the killing stroke.

Margaret looked away as the blood poured out. Now the pace had dropped, the chill was creeping into her clothes. She was damp and breathless from the chase but euphoric, too, because she'd conquered her fears and ridden to hounds for the first time in eight years. Even so, she was desperate to sit close to a roaring fire in a fresh set of dry, warm clothes.

"We'll leave them to it, I think." Helen turned her horse around. "My husband has a talent for butchery."

Bessie rode ahead, with young John Montgomerie at her side. The two children bickered about who'd ridden faster, who'd shown most courage.

"They're fine children," Margaret said, "But..."

"-I look too young to have dropped a maid of Bessie's years?" Helen smiled. "She's Hugh's child. But that doesn't matter. She's very precious to me."

"My mother hated my half-brother."

"He didn't ask to be brought into the world."

"My mother was like that."

"Do you miss her?"

"Not at all."

"I'm sorry to hear that," Helen said. "I miss my kinfolk still. My brother Archie calls sometimes, but I haven't seen my mother and sisters in years."

"Don't you see them at court?"

"My place is here, defending my husband's lands and property."

Margaret's gaze lingered on Bessie. "What became of her mother?"

"She married a burgess in Irvine. She was a maid in Kilmaurs' service, a Cunninghame."

"Does the girl know? About her lineage?"

"Of course. But it doesn't concern her. Her father loves her. That's all that matters."

Chapter 37

The Abbey of Lindores, Perthshire

The room he sought was pitifully small, but lavishly furnished nonetheless. There was a narrow bed, canopied to keep out the cold, a scattering of chairs near a stout table, and a carved wooden kist.

A crucifix hung upon the wall, a hefty Bible rested on the table. Alongside the Bible, Angus glimpsed a flagon - filled no doubt with the finest wine from Burgundy - and a platter piled high with cakes. In the far corner, a curtained doorway led to the privy.

Confined within this prison was the last of the Black Douglases: James, erstwhile 9th Earl, sitting hunched by the window with his corpulent body wrapped in a thick, fur-lined gown.

He lifted his head. "Who is it?" he asked, his voice weak, tremulous.

Angus approached with bonnet before him. "It's your nephew, Earl James." He spoke slowly, with deliberate clarity.

The old man glanced about him, blinking. "Come close, Archie. Over the last few months, my eyes have dimmed."

With some reluctance Angus stepped alongside. His nostrils caught the stench of slow decay, and he suppressed a grimace.

He wondered if this was the reflection of God's plan. Only the truly evil seemed to live on into their dotage, as if old age itself was a punishment from God. He saw no benefit in lingering like this, endlessly pondering old fears and regrets while the body rotted and withered from within.

"Is your pension adequate?" he asked. "I could petition the King for more."

Earl James laughed, deep and guttural. "What would I do with gold?" Breaking off, he coughed some more. "Why am I entombed here? It's been five years. The man I fought is dead and buried." He turned anguished eyes upon his kinsman. "It's all a lie. A damned lie. Those who sit at the heart of the King's council are just as guilty. They were never punished. They were feted."

"Perhaps if you'd courted men's favour instead of lopping off their heads, you wouldn't have found yourself cut adrift."

"The world has changed..." Earl James murmured, oblivious. "It's the time of the younger houses. The old names have gone. They've been usurped..."

Angus bit his lip, saying nothing.

"Anyway," Earl James said. "What brings you to my side, nephew? We've scarcely passed the time of day since your little jape at Lauder..."

"I put that incident behind me long ago." Angus paused to inspect the Bible. The cover was embossed leather, marked in gold with the Douglas arms: the heart of Bruce, with three stars above. "I'd have come sooner, but the mood at court has been... Difficult..."

The earl laughed. "It's a plausible excuse. But there are other motives, aren't there? Like the corbie, you scent death. You've come to scavenge the corpse."

"Now that's uncharitable," Angus replied. "Though I must confess I have concerns. We come from a noble line, you and I. This legacy must be secured for future generations." He smiled, slightly. "In that respect, I think this visit wholly justified, don't you?"

The Place of Eglintoun

It was no place for a woman: the yard bristled with armed men, all laughing loud and cursing as they awaited their departure. Even Helen had scorned the place, remaining in her chamber while the last preparations were made.

But Margaret stayed regardless, a forlorn figure amidst the clamour and the chaos.

She cast the assembled Montgomerie retainers a furtive glance. "They're staring," she whispered.

"They can stare all they like," John retorted. Gripping her hands, he kissed her lightly on the lips. "Please don't worry. I'll return as soon as I can." Retrieving his horse from a waiting groom, he climbed into the saddle.

He'd pinned that cheerful facade on for Margaret's sake, but he knew she was aware the turmoil he was enduring. He'd barely eaten that morning. His belly was unsettled, he felt sick with apprehension. For a week he'd been made welcome by Hugh's kin and household staff. But the mood had changed now, the men who'd once greeted him with cheerful good humour regarding him instead with suspicion and hostility.

Storm stood tall, ears pricked, head held high. John ran his hand down the beast's neck, comforted by its solid, reliable strength.

He'd barely spoken with his host that morning: Hugh had been busy mustering the men-at-arms, making final preparations. Seated on Zephyr at the other side of the yard, he was flanked by a detachment of grim-looking kinsmen. He certainly didn't look like a man who anticipated a fight: he'd refused to wear armour, favouring practical garb better suited to the cold weather: long boots, and a thick heavy cloak that covered his clothing. Though he'd talked of donning a leather jerkin in case things went awry, he carried neither helmet nor shield.

Hessilhead caught John's eye, scowled briefly in his direction and muttered something under his breath.

John sighed and averted his gaze. He smiled one last time at Margaret, then tightened his reins, ready to move off. He wondered if he'd been wise to refuse Hugh's offer of a brigandine. If indeed he'd been wise to involve himself at all...

Lifting his hand, Hugh signalled for silence. The chatter ceased, each man listening intently as Hugh circled Zephyr around to face them. "The time's upon us!" His voice rang out around the yard, clarion clear. "Let's settle our grievances in a just and dignified manner."

A chill ran through John's flesh. It disturbed him, to witness this facet of Hugh's soul that was dark, undisciplined. He hoped to God that the Montgomerie retainers hadn't been privy to the details of Hugh's ordeal.

If they had, then all the good intentions in the world wouldn't make a difference. There'd be bloodshed: carnage and grief meted out on both sides.

And himself. Caught awkwardly in the midst of it.

Their trysting place lay at the bounds between the Montgomerie lands of Eglintoun and the neighbouring Cunninghame estate of Auchenharvie. The road to Kilmarnock passed that way, but today there wasn't a traveller to be seen. It was as if even the rumour of this meeting had sent men scuttling back to their hearths.

A stout old tree grew by one of the marchstones, bent and gnarled by winter winds. Hugh glanced at it, satisfied: its lower boughs would easily hold two men apiece.

He leaned upon his pommel, watching carefully. Twenty-five Cunninghame retainers approached, a dozen mounted, the rest on foot. Rob rode in the vanguard, along with Cunninghame of Craigends.

And those boys: Cuthbert, Andrew, Guido.

Hugh flicked his gaze across the faces, but didn't linger on any of them. He focussed instead on the cart that followed. Drawn by two shaggy black oxen, five men sat within, hooded and cloaked in rough peasant's garb, heads bowed, faces hidden.

Rob Cunninghame raised his hand, signalling peaceful intent. "I've brought witnesses, as per our agreement. The Laird of Hunthall, and Sir Adam Mure of Caldwell."

"Sir John Sempill of Ellestoun." Hugh gestured towards John.

"If you'll excuse me, Lord Hugh," John muttered, steering his horse over to where Constantine Dunlop and Adam Mure were waiting.

Hessilhead shook his head. "Coward!" he sneered, half under his breath.

"Enough!" Hugh snapped. Sensing his impatience, Zephyr snatched at the bit and stamped.

Hugh spurred the stallion forwards, halting beyond his retainers. "I seek three men." His voice rang out, bold, forceful. "Together, they conspired to assault and wound the King's officer. By the powers invested in me by His Grace the King, I'll judge them and deliver an appropriate sentence with all due speed."

Rob gestured to the cart. "We've brought the men in question."

Two Cunninghame retainers dismounted and ushered the offenders out. The five captives shuffled awkwardly, wrists and ankles loosely shackled. Eventually they all stood in a ragged line.

"David Cunningham, George Cunningham and Patrick Hamiltoun," Rob said.

Hugh beckoned to Hessilhead. "Let me see them."

Hessilhead slid from his horse. Approaching the first prisoner, he grasped a handful of hair and hauled the head up.

Hugh steered Zephyr alongside. He'd pushed the events of that night to the furthest recesses of his thoughts. The light had been fading, the man he confronted now even more gaunt and filthy then he remembered. But when Hugh looked into his eyes, there could be no doubt about it.

He'd met that stare before.

Hugh breathed deep, comforted. "Yes," he said, and Hessilhead moved on to the next.

The Gryphon at Bay

The prisoners were frightened, without a doubt. Understandably so, for no man wanted to die. But like sheep or oxen penned up in a shambles, they seemed resigned to their fate.

Three men whose faces had haunted him since he'd suffered at their hands. Three men, who before long would no longer be alive to trouble him.

Of the others he had no enduring memories, good or bad. He nodded towards them. "What of these two?"

"Rape," Rob said. "Cuthbert attested to their guilt."

"Very good," Hugh said. "Well, we needn't loiter. I said I'd mete out justice swiftly. I'll be true to my word."

There was no quick, merciful end. The first man was still suffering his death throes as the last was hauled into the air. Everything was quiet: there was just the sound of men gasping and choking as their strength ebbed from them. Bodies jerked and twitched, urine pooled beneath the massive boughs of the tree.

John watched in silence, a reluctant bystander. It was a just decision. There was no denying it. All the same, it turned his stomach. Such a miserable way to die. Lingering, undignified. For men to have risked this, their lives must have been worth nothing.

Hugh sat upon his horse, unmoved.

"It's done," Kilmaurs muttered, sourly. "Are you content?"

"Just one matter remains."

Kilmaurs flashed him a wary glance. "Which is?"

"The death of one of my men-at-arms. A worthy soul, whom I trusted greatly. He leaves two children, who should be provided for."

Cuthbert Cunninghame fidgeted, visibly dissatisfied.

Kilmaurs shot his heir an angry glance. "How does that concern me?"

"The guilty man's there." Hugh pointed at Guido Cunninghame. "Shouldn't he be made to account for his sins?"

The boy blanched. "It was an accident. I didn't mean to-"

"Out of the question," Kilmaurs cut in, his face hard, determined.

"He killed a man. In cold blood."

"What proof is there?" Kilmaurs snapped back. "Save a child's babbling?"

"I witnessed it at first hand."

Cuthbert drew his sword. "You won't have my brother!"

"Cuthbert-" Kilmaurs began.

"Arrogant devil!" Cuthbert spat. "How dare you dictate the terms, when we've already granted so much!"

Hugh was silent.

John swallowed. He knew when Hugh was fired by battle, eager to prove his prowess. What he saw now was different. A misleading calm, the dark peace before the storm...

It was a change Cuthbert Cunninghame was blind to. "You weren't so cocky when we came upon you in the hills-"

"Be silent!" Rob snapped.

"He begged me to slay him, because he couldn't face the shame-"

"I asked for silence!"

Hugh smiled. "So you're a liar, Master Cuthbert. As well as a fool."

"Father, let's be gone," Cuthbert said. "I won't have my brother's fate decided by him."

"It's not your place to demand anything," Hugh retorted. "Hold your tongue. Learn some respect."

"How can I respect you, after what I witnessed? Have you forgotten already? How you grovelled there, a pitiful creature, bound and bleeding-"

Hugh roared and unsheathed his sword. Spurring Zephyr forwards, he shrugged aside his cloak, revealing a thick brigandine beneath. He launched himself at Cuthbert, blade slicing down.

Cuthbert blocked him. But Hugh was undeterred. He jostled his horse close, hacking again and again at Cuthbert.

"Hugh, for God's Sake!" Kilmaurs rode alongside. "Enough!"

Hugh was oblivious, face set in a fierce mask of hatred. His onslaught was relentless: Cuthbert countered every blow, but already the fatigue was showing. His face ran with sweat, his eyes wide with fear.

"Hugh!" Kilmaurs drew his own sword. "Stop this madness!"

A sideways sweep of Hugh's blade silenced him. Kilmaurs sat there, mouth open. Blood spurted out from his shoulder, seeped through his clothing further down his chest.

He slumped over his horse, then fell.

There was silence, shocked, disbelieving.

A cry went up throughout the Cunninghames, and suddenly the place erupted. Men launched themselves into the fray: Cunninghames, Montgomeries, setting upon their foes with vigour. And in the midst of the melee, Hugh and Cuthbert, locked in combat.

Hessilhead lifted a horn to his lips and blew two sharp blasts upon it. From a hollow near the roadside another score of Montgomeries emerged.

"Christ Almighty!" Constantine Dunlop fought to control his panicking horse.

"We should be gone!" Adam called. "They'll kill us!"

"Wise words, Adam!" Constantine snapped as two combatants swung close, sending his horse scrambling back. "Come on, John! We can't do anything more."

John didn't speak, his attention fixed on the spot where one man lay amidst the carnage, alone and unheeded. Blood still gushed from the wound: Robert Cunninghame hadn't quite breathed his last.

He dismounted. "Hold my horse."

"What in God's name-" Constantine began. "John, don't be a fool..."

Oblivious, John darted between the armed horsemen, ducking low to dodge men's swords. Horses trampled the ground, dangerously close. He threw himself between their hooves, crawling the last few feet to where Kilmaurs lay. "Lord Robert." He pulled at the torn clothing. "Let me help you."

Kilmaurs' eyes focussed vaguely upon him. "I'm dying..." Blood sprayed from the gaping wound at his neck. "God... Help me..."

John pressed the wound, staunching the flow as best he could.

"I tried... to keep... the peace."

The Gryphon at Bay

"Save your strength." Glancing down, John saw blood welling through his fingers.

He stirred. "I-"

John leaned close.

"What'll... become of us?" The breath sighed in Kilmaurs' throat. He'd gone.

Chapter 38

Rob was down. Dead or wounded, it didn't matter. Not now, in the heat of the fray.

"Andy!" Craigends bellowed loud to make himself heard. "Stay with Guido!" But he couldn't see Guido, or Andy, either.

He urged his horse forwards, bludgeoning a path through the melee towards Cuthbert. The boy was fighting well, confronting Lord Hugh with skill and determination. He'd cut flesh: the sleeves of Montgomerie's brigandine were ripped and bloodstained.

But it wasn't enough, and now Cuthbert's inexperience was showing. The youth was exhausted, blinking back sweat and gasping for breath, his features tight with terror and despair. While Montgomerie continued his attack unchecked, hard grey gaze locked unerringly on Cuthbert.

When a horse swung its quarters round a gap was revealed. Craigends forged through, and grasped Cuthbert's bridle. "Hold that beast at bay!" he called to his men. "For God's sake, don't give way!"

He dragged the horse away.

"What're you doing?" Cuthbert howled.

Oblivious, Craigends drove his spurs against his horse's flanks. He heard Lord Hugh's roar of frustration and smiled, grimly. For the moment, they were safe: while the Cunninghames stood firm, Montgomerie would have quite enough to keep him occupied.

"Your father's gone," he told Cuthbert. "Get all thoughts of glory out of your head. Your blood's too precious to be spilled this way." He pushed his horse into a trot, Cuthbert's reins still gripped in his hand.

"Release me. I'm not a child."

"I know," Craigends retorted. "And you're not a coward, either. Now let's be gone from here."

Cuthbert said nothing. Glancing round, Craigends saw that the young man's fury was fading. He was pale and shaking, his shoulder soaked with blood, his thigh, too.

"Well done, lad," Craigends said. "You did your father proud tonight. You took on the finest swordsmen in the Westland and lived to tell the tale. You left your mark on him, too."

"I could've killed him..."

"Put that from your thoughts," Craigends said. "The price of losing was too great."

John leaned close against the corpse, one arm thrown over his head, hardly daring to breathe as hooves churned and tore the earth to either side. He prayed for deliverance, promised a substantial sum to Holy Church if his life was spared...

The clamour faded slightly, the skirmish moved on.

He straightened, cautiously.

The Gryphon at Bay

Adam and Constantine were hailing him, but they might have been a league or more away, the path blocked by a mass of angry men-at-arms. In their midst Hugh fought alone, slashing and stabbing wildly, sword in one hand, dagger in the other.

John stared transfixed. Hugh had transcended all doubts and fears, gripped by brutal, all-consuming fury. It gave him an edge unmatched by other men. One momentary lapse of concentration by his opponent, and Hugh would strike the killing blow.

A Cunninghame retainer moved in, raising his sword to strike. Hugh slammed a fist in his face. The man reeled in the saddle and Hugh wrapped an arm about his neck, hauling him close as Zephyr spun round.

There was a sickening crack as the bone snapped, and another of Hugh's foes dropped to the ground, lifeless.

One Cunninghame turned tail and fled. Then another. The rout set in: men threw aside helmets and shields, running for their lives.

Zephyr reared high. The grey stallion was daubed with blood, apocalyptic amongst the carnage. "After them!" Hugh called. He was bleeding from a nick on his forehead and a dozen wounds besides, but the light in his eyes was undimmed. "Let's run these foxes to earth!"

His men cheered loud. They rode at his heels, horses springing away at a gallop. Hessilhead paused a moment longer, rallying the stragglers.

There was silence, broken only by the groaning of the injured. Half-a-dozen Montgomeries lay slumped upon the ground, along with another dozen or more dead and wounded Cunninghames. The carter sat perched in his wagon, too terrified to move. Five corpses swung gently from the tree. One still twitched, faintly.

John braced his hands against his knees and briefly closed his eyes. His limbs were trembling.

"Damned idiot!" Constantine wove a careful path through the chaos. "I thought you'd be crushed to death."

Adam followed close behind. "Of all the stupid, arrogant-" Breaking off, he waved to the carter. "You there! Bring that over here." He took off his bonnet, a mark of respect. "Might as well let poor Lord Robert travel home in comfort."

A cry rang out. Guido Cunninghame approached at a canter, Andrew Cunninghame close behind. The boy leapt from his horse and crouched beside his father. "He murdered him...."

John stepped back. "I'm sorry." The boy's distress stung him: he remembered how just over a year before, he'd found himself in similar circumstances. Staring down at a corpse slain by Montgomerie's hand, wondering what the future held.

He waited for the sobs to subside, then grasped the stricken youth's shoulder. "It's no time for grieving. You must get your father home safely."

Guido stood, slowly. The lad was dazed, uncomprehending. "What about Cuthbert? Lord Hugh wants my brother dead."

"Pray to God he doesn't catch him," John replied. "Come on. You must try and get home before darkness falls."

"Sir John," Andrew Cunninghame spoke out. "Thank you. We didn't expect such kindness."

Louise Turner

"You're not the first to suffer this way," John said. "And I doubt you'll be the last. Let's lift his corpse, and grant your father some dignity."

Chapter 39

They followed the road for several miles, then Craigends changed course, heading off across the fields. By the time they slowed their pace, the horses were blowing and lathered in sweat.

Craigends cocked his head. He could've sworn he'd heard the bray of a horn. "Alright." He halted near a small stand of trees. "Let's leave the horses. They'll find their own way home."

"What?" Cuthbert demanded, disbelieving.

"Montgomerie's after us."

"Surely we can outrun him?"

"He has the instincts of a sleuth-hound. And the persistence." Craigends was already dismounting. "Don't give him the satisfaction of hunting you down. This way, we'll leave him a false trail." He cast the boy an anxious glance. "Can you walk?"

Cuthbert winced as he lowered himself to the ground. "I'll have to."

"Good lad. Now get on with you!" He lunged and hissed at the horses, waving his arms to drive them away.

"I don't even know where we are," Cuthbert whispered.

"Ah, but I do. If God wills it, we'll get home in one piece, and in reasonable health, too. We owe it to your mother."

"We could seek shelter until he calls off the pursuit?"

"He'll search every byre and cottage. If he found us, he'd slay us. As it is, he'll burn the poor souls out of their homes and kill their beasts."

Mist hung like a shroud over the land. A reassuring sight, Craigends thought, for it meant that even Montgomerie might call off the chase sooner rather than later.

Sounds travelled far in the still evening air, so they heard the hue and cry in plenty of time. The thunder of hooves, the blood-chilling calls of their pursuers.

"We'll find cover over there." Grasping Cuthbert's arm, Craigends tugged him over to a dense thicket of whin and brambles that overlooked the river. They ducked deep into its depths, oblivious to the thorns that snagged their clothes and tore their flesh.

Cuthbert was trembling. Craigends held him close, an attempt at reassurance. "Not a word, for God's Sake..." Staring into the gloom, he saw two Cunninghame retainers approach, unhorsed and stumbling with weariness. They skirted the river, wading through reeds and sliding over rocks.

Cuthbert stirred. "We must help them."

"Hold still!" Craigends growled.

The enemy soon appeared: a dozen Montgomerie men-at-arms, fanning out across the valley.

Craigends swallowed. Sweat settled chill across his shoulders and back.

The beleaguered Cunninghames were spotted. One of Montgomerie's retainers shouted out to his companions, and spurred his horse in pursuit. Splashing through the river, he headed up the sloping ground at a lumbering trot. He drew his sword and swept past, bringing one man down. The other fled, back towards the jeering pack of men that waited below.

Craigends glanced aside, unwilling to witness the slaughter. As he did so, he glimpsed something from the corner of his eye, a flash of white.

A horse approached, walking shin-deep through the river. A grey spectral beast, bloodstained and terrible.

And on its back, Montgomerie himself.

Lord Hugh halted, just twenty feet away. He was bloodied and unkempt, his unsheathed sword resting against his shoulder. He lifted his head, a wild beast scenting the air for quarry, nostrils flared, a feral light in his eyes. His steel gaze fixed on the thicket and he stared into its depths.

Craigends screwed his eyes shut, briefly, praying for a miracle. Alongside, Cuthbert bowed his head and stifled a moan.

A twig snapped, a figure moved nearby. It was the Cunninghame retainer they'd dismissed as dead: he scrambled to his feet, staggered a few steps.

Montgomerie's head jerked round. He sat quite still, watching keenly as the wounded man tried to flee. Then he stirred. Lifting his sword, he closed in at a canter. With one lazy sweep, he hacked the man down as he passed. He didn't look back, riding onwards through the river with spray flying from his horse's hooves. He called to his men, and soon they were gone.

The silence returned.

They stayed quiet, too fearful to move or speak.

Craigends shifted at last. "We're safe now." He winced as he stood, limbs aching from crouching in the damp mould so long. Hauling Cuthbert upright, he glanced anxiously down at the young man's leg. "Are you bleeding?"

Cuthbert shook his head. "It's nothing."

"We'd best staunch the flow. Then we'll head for home. If we keep a steady head, we should outflank them."

Afternoon drifted into evening, the shadows lengthened. Hugh's chamber, normally so bright and cheerful, became shrouded in gloom.

Helen retrieved a taper and lit the candles. With darkness banished, and the room suffused with soft golden light, the mood lifted, but only a little.

"You should go to your bed." Helen resumed her place by the window. She'd been sitting there all afternoon, bent over her sewing and saying nothing.

Margaret briskly rubbed her arms, trying to banish the cold. The shutters were still open, the air frigid. "I can't sleep," she said.

"You've a babe to think of." Helen's tone was curt.

"But I need to know that John's safe," Margaret argued.

She nodded. "Yes, I suppose so... Forgive me. I'm poor company today."

Margaret reached for her hand. "I'm sure all will be well."

"Hugh lives by the sword," Helen said. "Some day he'll come home in a casket." She pulled her fingers free and rose to her feet. "I must attend my children."

The Gryphon at Bay

Once the boys had been put to bed, they returned to Hugh's chamber. The fire roared high to welcome him, his shaggy-coated hounds slumped alongside the hearth. Flagons of ale and claret waited on a nearby kist, along with an ample supply of bread and meat.

Helen sat down in Hugh's chair. She clasped the arms tight, saying nothing.

For an hour they must have waited there. Maybe more. Then one of the hounds jerked up, tail thumping.

Horses. Moving slowly through the yard. But only a handful, compared with the small host that had left earlier that day.

Helen stared into the fire. There was no relief, no excitement in her face, just bleak resignation.

A rout... Margaret's heart lurched. *They were set upon and scattered...* She closed her eyes in brief denial.

Hushed voices spoke on the stair, but she heard no hint of anger, or panic. Footsteps approached. A man's tread, weary, exhausted, but familiar.

The door opened, and there was John. His face was smeared with blood, his hair matted with yet more, his clothes stained crimson. Relief gave way to horror, she sprang to her feet, tried to speak, but her throat tightened. Her eyes blurred, her head swam and darkness closed in.

She swayed and toppled.

...She felt she was floating, detached from the world.

"-Margaret!" John was hailing her from far away. His voice seemed urgent somehow, even fearful. "Can you hear me?"

Fingers lightly patted her cheek.

Opening her eyes, she found John leaning over her, staring anxiously down. He'd wiped the worst of the gore from his face but some still clung to his brow.

"I thought you were hurt." She struggled to sit.

He gripped her shoulders tight, steadying her. "I'm fine, Margaret," he said. "Not a scratch on me."

Helen stood. "I'll ask the servants to pour a bath," she said. "Then I'd best see to the wounded."

"I'd appreciate that, thank you." John laid his hand against Margaret's belly and caressed her, gently. "I am so sorry. I didn't expect this..."

"Please tell me what happened. Where's Hugh?"

"Kilmaurs is dead. Hugh killed him."

"But how? Why?"

John stared ahead, eyes unseeing. "He tried to help his son."

Margaret frowned. She couldn't quite grasp John's words: they seemed at odds with Hugh, who'd been so generous, so eager to accommodate their every need. "Poor Helen," she whispered. "What'll she do, if something happens to him?"

*   *   *

The Place of Kilmaurs

"Lady Christian." The steward touched her hand.

Christian started. She'd nodded off while she waited for news of Rob's safe return; it was dark now, shutters closed, candles lit. "What hour is it?"

"Close to nine of the clock, I reckon. Sir Adam Mure of Caldwell is here. Along with the Laird of Hunthall."

So they'd returned alone. Two men who'd ridden out with Rob just hours before...

A void of fear opened inside her. She rushed for the stairs, hurried down to the hall, where her guests awaited her. They held their bonnets, lowered their gaze in respect as she approached. Guido was with them, eyes red from weeping.

The Dowager was there, too. Christian nodded to her and caught her eye, but the older woman's face showed nothing.

Dunlop swallowed. "Lady Christian. Lady Katherine... I'm sorry..."

"He's dead!" Guido could no longer contain himself.

"How?" The Dowager approached, tall, unmoved.

"Slain by the Lord Montgomerie's hand," Dunlop said.

Christian couldn't speak. Tears welled up, blinding her. She wanted to deny this nightmare was happening, to wake in her bed, preoccupied with nothing more than all those little things that had once seemed so important: Rob's melancholy, Rob's indifference, his preoccupation with restoring his fortunes.

A low moan sounded, building in pitch and volume until the hall echoed with an unearthly howl that seemed more animal than human.

It was the Dowager.

Bile rose in Christian's throat. Her skin crawled, she longed to scream and batter the Dowager with her fists for daring to show such grief, when she'd never shown Rob any compassion or encouragement throughout the rest of his life.

"And Cuthbert?" Her lips moved of their own accord, her voice steady.

"I don't know," Guido whispered. "He left with Uncle Will. Montgomerie went in pursuit. I came back with Andy, to try and help Father."

"Sir John Sempill tried to save your husband," Sir Adam Mure told her. "But the wound was mortal. Lord Robert's body lies below. He died bravely, trying to protect the Master of Kilmaurs."

"Montgomerie attacked Cuthbert?"

"To be fair, Lady Christian," Dunlop said. "Cuthbert provoked him."

"What madness is this, that a man of his years takes pleasure in slaying a youth?" She stood tall, regaining her composure. "Thank you for your kindness, Master Dunlop, Sir Adam-" She nodded to each in turn. "We'll give you lodgings in the guest range. It's foolish to travel when Lord Hugh's wolf pack ravages the land. In these dire circumstances, we can't offer you much hospitality, but..." She drew a deep, shuddering breath, "-we'll do what we can."

Chapter 40

The Place of Kilmaurs

They cut away Rob's clothes and laid him out on the board in the great hall to be washed and stitched into his shroud.

Looking down on her dead husband, Christian was too numb to speak. He'd been felled by a sword blow that ripped down his neck and across his chest: the artery had been severed near the throat so at least his end was mercifully quick.

It was hard, to reconcile her memories of Rob with this corpse that lay cold and still before her, flesh touched all over with a grim grey pallor. He'd been a source of great pleasure to her once. Now, though, she found herself reluctant to touch him at all.

But she was his wife. It was her duty.

Soaking the cloth in perfumed water she wrung it out, then dabbed gently at his face. He seemed calm, at peace, eyes closed and mouth gently parted, far happier in death than he'd ever been in life.

Rest now, Rob. You're free of your labours. Leaning close, she kissed his lips, gently. *God bless you, my love...*

Her strength failed her. She sagged to her knees. Laying her head against the board, she gripped his hand tight and sobbed so hard she could no longer hear, or see, or even think. She howled and wailed and beat the timbers with her fist. They could question her courage and her fortitude all they liked: he was gone, and that was all that mattered.

Thin hands seized her shoulders. "Christian," the Dowager said. "I know this is hard for you." Her voice shook. "Let me do this. I'm his mother. A mother always loves her son, no matter what..."

Lifting her head, Christian drew a harsh rasping breath. "How many times must we weep for our dead?"

"Hush my dear..." The Dowager gently stroked her hair.

"-I want that Northern bitch to know my pain. I want her to suffer, just as I'm suffering. I want *him* dead."

"I know that." The Dowager prised the cloth from Christian's fingers and wiped Rob's legs, careful, efficient. "That beast has gone too far," she said. "Once poor Rob's asleep in his tomb, we'll do what we can to put wrongs to rights. You and I, Chrissie, will travel to Edinburgh. We'll seek out my brother, and tell him of our plight. He *must* do something. He's the man who inflicted Montgomerie upon us in the first place."

     *   *   *

The Place of Eglintoun

Helen rejoined them later. She resumed her place by the open window, oblivious to the cold, saying nothing...

John settled opposite, and Margaret curled up next to him, tucking her legs onto the cushioned seat alongside. She was weary, but even now she refused to retire to bed. *Helen needs us*, she'd said when pressed. *We can't abandon her.*

Perhaps she was right to think of Helen. While the Lady of Eglintoun hadn't spoken of her fears, her face was pale and anxious.

"He had the upper hand when I left him," John said, doing his best to reassure her. "I don't see anything ill befalling him."

Margaret shivered and pressed close, slipping her arm in his. He rubbed her shoulders gently, trying to warm her.

"You must be cold." Helen rose stiffly to her feet. "Wait a moment." She retrieved one of Hugh's fur-lined gowns from a kist, draped it carefully over Margaret's shoulders. Sitting back down again, she choked back a sob. "They say he's evil. They say he's possessed by the Devil." She pulled a handkerchief from her sleeve and dabbed her nose, her cheeks wet with tears. "They've harried him all his life. They plundered his inheritance and did what they could to impede him at court. They envy him, because they lack those qualities he's been blessed with in abundance."

"It wasn't murder," John assured her. "He wasn't first to draw his sword."

"They'll twist the truth. They always do."

John grasped her hand. "I'll vouch for him."

She glanced aside, face bleak. "Then you'll be alone in doing so."

They drifted into silence, lost in their own thoughts and fears. The lateness of the hour got the better of Margaret at last and she drowsed, head heavy against John's arm. Sometimes she'd twitch and moan, then jerk upright, blinking.

John shifted, cradling her against his side so she'd be more comfortable.

And Helen... She remained patient and attentive in her vigil, dark eyes glittering in the light of the candles.

A horse neighed nearby. Another answered, far away.

Helen sighed, but said nothing.

Time crawled: it might have been ten minutes that passed, or half an hour, but eventually hooves rang loud against the cobbled yard. Horses poured in at a canter, the clarion call of a stallion splintering the silence.

"Zephyr." Helen rose stiffly to her feet. "I'd know his cry anywhere."

*   *   *

Hugh flung open the door and swept across the room. "I'm parched!" Making straight for the flagons, he poured himself a hefty measure of ale. He downed it in three swift gulps, then quickly refilled his cup.

The liquid was cool, refreshing. It cleared his head, left him well-disposed towards the world.

He turned to face them. If he'd hoped for a joyful reunion, he'd been deluded. Instead, the mood in his chamber was chill and dismal, as if they'd all gathered here to mourn him.

Helen stood desolate by the fire with shoulders slumped and hands clasped loosely before her. While John watched him with that keen, all-seeing gaze of his, a glance more in keeping with a senior churchman than a young knight in his prime.

As for young Margaret Colville... She flinched at the sight of him, as if she'd just glimpsed something monstrous.

The Gryphon at Bay

He unbuckled his sword belt. Tossing it roughly aside, he sprawled in his chair. The hounds pressed close, tails wagging. He caressed their ears and faces, while they whined in pleasure. "Least my hounds are pleased to see me."

Helen looked up. "You're wounded."

He'd lived with the gnawing aches in his arms and shoulders so long he'd almost forgotten they were there. "Nothing to worry about," he said, and took another long draught.

John still studied him, face revealing nothing. "Did you find your quarry?"

"The little shit ran from me."

"He has a duty to his household."

"So did you," Hugh retorted. "If you'd died that day in Stirling, your line would've passed with you. But you faced me, just the same."

"With hindsight, I'd have acted differently."

"You'd have stood your ground, even if it killed you." He paused to swallow more ale, then wiped a torn and grubby sleeve across his lips.

"Kilmaurs is dead," John said.

Hugh frowned. He could recall nothing of Rob. All he remembered was Cuthbert's sneering complacent face, the moment of burning joy when the boy's confidence collapsed into terror.

John pressed away like his confessor. "You don't remember, do you?" he asked. "That's two of their line you've slaughtered. In little more than a year..."

"Go to my father," Helen urged. "He'll advise you. You should flee to France. At least until the hue and cry dies down..."

Hugh stared at them, uncomprehending. "Why should I flee? I've done nothing wrong."

"You've killed a Lord of Parliament!" John snapped back.

"I was acting in self-defence."

John shook his head. "You're impossible."

Helen dropped her head in her hands and wept. He'd never seen her like that before. He rounded on her, fiercely. "There's no need for that!"

"Don't you see?" she snapped back, face hard, eyes bright with desperation. "Your enemies will use this against you."

"If the worst should happen, you'll be well provided for."

"I don't *want* to be provided for!" she countered, fists clenched, cheeks flushed with rage. "I want you to be here. For me, and for our children. Do we mean nothing to you?"

He waved his hand in brisk dismissal. "Why the concern?" he asked. "Rob signed his death warrant the day he started negotiating with Lord Lyle. If pressed, I can say I was exercising the King's orders. I executed a traitor who was conspiring against the Crown's interests." Draining the dregs of his ale, he offered them his most encouraging smile. "That's if it comes to it," he said. "And I sincerely doubt it will."

I can't reason with him, John muttered, pausing before he retired with Margaret for the night. *I'm sorry.*

211

Helen didn't answer. It wasn't the time or the place to explain the intricacies of Hugh's nature. That once the heat of the skirmish faded, there'd be regret and recriminations enough.

Once they were alone, Helen took the time to mend Hugh's wounds. As he'd said, they were neither deep, nor serious. Just a few stitches here and there, which she administered swiftly. Hugh cursed and muttered, scolding her for being slow, and making him suffer unduly. But he tolerated her attentions nonetheless.

The discomfort didn't cool his ardour. When she'd done with him, he whisked her off to his bed and mounted her with all the brutal vigour of a youth. She weathered him in silence, consoling herself with the knowledge that at least he wouldn't keep her very long.

When he'd finished, he rolled over without a word.

She lay flat in the darkness, heart pounding. She didn't dare disturb him, not until the echoes of his rage had faded. It was hard to remain distant and aloof, when all she wanted to do was hold him tight, relish his warmth, his strength. Hugh had shrugged aside fears of mortality, but she felt them more keenly than ever.

She wept silently, tears burning hot trails down her cheeks. She felt gripped with an overwhelming sense of loneliness, as if a vast dark gulf had suddenly opened up between them both.

"Helen?" His voice was soft, concerned. The beast in him had fled, back to the dark place where most of the time it lurked unseen.

Her breath shuddered in her throat, she stifled a sob.

He reached for her hand, squeezed it tight. "Helen... What on earth's wrong with you?"

"I don't want to lose you." Her voice sounded small and pitiful in the darkness.

He took her in his arms. "Hush, my love. My sweet thing... You mustn't worry about me."

He stank of sweat and horse and leather, but she didn't care. He was alive, and that was all that mattered. Leaning her head against his chest, she breathed him in, reminding herself that the fears plaguing her had to be voiced, and that now was as good a time as any. Mustering all her courage, she said, "I *am* worried. And sometimes I wish you'd worry, too. There's higher courts than those sanctioned by Man. Some day, you'll be made to pay in full. War's looming. It would hurt enough to lose you in battle. But to think you were suffering endless torments in Hell because of what you did in life... Do you want to make my pain a thousand times worse?"

Silence settled around them, stretching out for what felt like an eternity. "I do think of such things," he said at last. "And yes, I have no desire to offend God."

"His poor lady, weeping for the husband she's lost. She did you no harm..."

"Rob was never my enemy," Hugh whispered. "It was a mistake." He battered his head against the pillow with a groan. "Ah, God, John's right," he said. "A terrible mistake. And one I'll come to regret, I'm sure."

It was an unfamiliar feeling. To lie awake after a raid, so stricken with remorse that he couldn't sleep.

He'd taken the lives of half-a-dozen men that night. He vaguely remembered each individual slaughter, but the details eluded him. Hugh supposed it was a mercy: if the men had voices and faces, families he knew, it would be much more difficult to live with the knowledge that he'd killed them.

Helen lay quiet alongside. He wondered if she'd found rest yet. Somehow, he doubted it.

He thought back to the vision he'd had. Of Judgment. Damnation. A warning that should not have gone unheeded. A warning that had perhaps come too late to save his soul...

"I think of him sometimes," he said.

"Who?" she whispered.

"Boyd."

She didn't speak.

"If my mood is black, I can picture him there, dying at my feet." He swallowed, unsettled by the recollection. "The dead are always there, waiting... When I'm away from home, alone with my thoughts and fears, they torment me. Boyd and Cunninghame... Sir Thomas Sempill, too..."

"I thought that was forgotten."

"Sometimes when I look on John, I see his father's ghost, lurking there behind his features. Perhaps steering him safely through his troubles was like a penance. I thought that once my debt was paid, we'd both move on and all would be forgotten. Instead, Fate has brought us closer." He paused. "Why should he show me such kindness? Most men would want me dead."

"You should speak of this to John. It would ease your worries, and it might comfort him."

"I've thought about raising these ghosts," he conceded, "but my courage always fails me." He sighed and gripped her hand tight. "I can face Death in battle. I can confront a man and take his life. But I can't look a so-called friend in the eye and tell him that I'm truly sorry for all the wrongs I committed against him."

"You owe him that much," she persisted. "And not just because of what he's done for you already. Even now, he hasn't turned his back on you. He says he'll speak out in your defence, even if the whole world turns against you. That's true friendship, Hugh. Don't put it aside lightly."

213

Chapter 41

The Place of Eglintoun

Katherine and Mariota attended Margaret that morning, washing and dressing her for the new day. John sat nearby, a silent brooding presence by the fireside. The girls hadn't asked for privacy while they worked: if anything, they were relieved to have him there.

"We knew something terrible had happened." Mariota briskly pinned Margaret's hood into place. "There was such a commotion! Men shouting, and horses..."

"And you still weren't in your beds," Katherine added. "We wondered if Sir John had returned safely."

"-I've never been so frightened-" Mariota scarcely paused to draw breath, "-we just clung to each other and prayed all would be well."

"What if the place had been stormed?" Katherine's voice shook. "We might all have been ravished, or put to the sword..."

Margaret glanced at John. She thought he'd scoff or scold the girls for being silly, but he didn't even look as if he'd heard them. He was staring into the fire, deep in thought.

Picking up the mirror, Margaret studied herself briefly, noting the dark shadows around her eyes, the pale skin of her face. She was exhausted: it felt as if she'd scarcely slept before she'd had to drag herself out of her bed.

"Are you alright?" Katherine asked.

She didn't answer. Looking at John now, she felt a sudden flood of relief because he was so unlike Hugh in every way. She shivered, remembering how she'd tended Hugh so closely, soothing his wounds, offering him comfort and counsel. She'd grown fond of him in the short time they'd spent together. Perhaps too fond...

Her face coloured at the thought. A girl's foolish fancies, nothing more. She could see that now. It wasn't as if she found him attractive. Just more approachable compared with John, who was always so opaque, so difficult to understand.

She'd confess her sins on her return. Confide in the priest, and never again let her thoughts stray unguarded, even for a moment.

"It was a fearsome thing," she whispered. "To see a man so consumed by anger and hatred, so proud of the carnage he'd committed." She swallowed, unsettled by the recollection. "It was as if some dark force had seized him..."

John glanced up. "Don't be too quick to judge him. He's born of sin, like the rest of us. Now a new day's dawned, he'll be perfectly contrite."

"He killed a man!" Margaret countered. "But you're willing to forgive him?"

"We all do things we bitterly regret," John replied. "And must live with the consequences, as best we can. Past transgressions nearly finished him: this time men won't be so forgiving."

* * *

214

The Gryphon at Bay

Beyond the bed, the floorboards creaked as old Ringan shuffled here and there, tending the fire, setting out Hugh's clothes.

A hound whined and clawed at the curtains, trying to rouse them. But Hugh was oblivious, a silent mound beneath the sheets and coverlets.

Helen lay still, savouring this brief moment of blissful normality. All seemed well with the world. But the events of the previous night soon raised themselves like spectres, the promise of the day quickly fading.

She wondered what should be done. She'd seek out their chaplain, ask his advice on how Hugh might atone for his sins. At least she had some small consolation in the knowledge that for once Hugh had been candid. He'd confessed his remorse, his fears of divine retribution.

Until now she'd considered him devoid of conscience, impervious to the destruction he inflicted on the world. Instead he was as prone to melancholy thoughts as any man. He'd kept that safely hidden: it troubled her a little, to think that all through their marriage, she'd misjudged him.

"I have it!" Hugh sat up, spilling the covers before him.

Helen propped herself up with a sigh.

"I shall embark on a pilgrimage!" Throwing open the curtain he sprang from the bed.

They'd grown accustomed to his ways through the years. Even so, they stared – herself, Ringan and the hounds – while Hugh stalked back and forth, face aglow, oblivious to his natural state. "I shall go to Jerusalem," he declared. "And if I can join a Crusade against the Turks, so much the better!" Still battered from the fray, he carried himself with grace and purpose, addressing them like an ancient hero performing an oration before his men. "I'll pledge my sword to them. And devote myself to God's service."

Grasping a shirt, Ringan helpfully presented it to his master.

Hugh seized the garment, pulled it over his head. "What more could a man do to cleanse his soul?"

Helen sat up, clasping the bed covers against her breast. "You'd abandon your poor wife and children for two years or more?" she asked. "How can you even consider such cruelty? What if you don't return at all? Would you condemn me to a nunnery?"

Hugh halted in mid-stride.

"And what of the King?" she persisted. "He asked for you by name..."

"I'd serve him better if my soul was cleansed," he argued. "God favours the righteous, they say..."

"You mustn't betray your King," she persisted. "Not now, when he needs you most."

Hugh gave a fitful sigh, and glowered at the floor. "Whithorn, then..."

"In a matter of days, the host will muster. You should ride with them."

"Are you trying to damn me?"

Helen glanced aside, deliberately demure. "How could I let my wishes and desires come between you and God? Or between you and the King, for that matter. You must follow your conscience, but I think it only right that you put the King's needs alongside your own." She paused to let him reflect on her suggestion, then added, "Ride to

Kilwinning. Speak to the abbot, and explain your situation. You're a loyal servant of his order. And a frequent benefactor."

"But Kilwinning, of all places!" Hugh complained. "I can almost shout to him from the sally port. What manner of a pilgrimage is that?" Then he brightened. "I'll walk," he decided. "Surely that's a worthy token of my humility..."

A light drizzle had blown in from the sea overnight. The road was ankle deep in mud, water pooling in ruts and hollows. John grimaced as he navigated round a vile-looking puddle: even with wooden patons strapped to a man's boots, it was proving impossible to walk without slipping.

"I should be plotting a course for Jerusalem," Hugh muttered. "Or the shrine of Saint James in Compostela."

"Pilgrimage is all about sacrifice," John said. "With the muster of the host imminent, every day is precious. For you to give of your time in such circumstances must count for something."

"That's just what Helen said." He shot John an accusing glance. "You must've plotted it together." He sighed. "I don't know why you've resorted to walking. Or why you even bothered to come at all."

"I was with him when he died," John said. "It's not an easy thing, to watch a man's life ebb from him."

"I know that."

John glanced aside, unwilling to reply. Catching his horse's eye, he found the beast regarding him askance, as if intrigued that two creatures so ill-suited to this expedition should even be attempting it. With every footfall, its hooves sent up a spray of filthy water, showering them both. "Why are you doing this?" he asked. "It's not as if your actions were pre-meditated. Even if they were... If you pay enough, they'll forgive anything these days."

"What comfort does that bring a man?" Hugh countered. "Knowing he's put his soul in the care of a debauched, pox-ridden friar, who spends half his time uttering *Ave Maria's* and the other half fondling whores... Would that bring you much consolation?"

"It wouldn't bring me any consolation at all."

"I've relied too much on the hollow promises of others. It's been a convenient way of shirking my responsibilities. Now I must take my soul's well-being into my own hands."

"Jesus Christ..."

"Enough of the blasphemy!"

John tried in vain to keep a straight face. "I never thought I'd witness such a transformation."

"Oh, but this is all your fault. You speak like a churchman, but unlike most of them, you actually mean what you say."

"What you're trying to tell me is that I'm no courtier."

Hugh pushed his rain-dank hair back from his brow. "If it's any consolation, I don't think I'm much of a courtier, either."

"That's quite an admission, coming from a Privy Councillor."

Hugh winced. "My Privy Council days are numbered. If I'd stayed at court, signing land charters and waging war on the corn marigold, then perhaps this mess might never have happened." He gasped as his foot sank deep: he'd have fallen to his knees if John hadn't seized his cloak and kept him upright. "-A man can't apply himself to conflicting causes. I could've been successful at court, I could've been successful here. Instead, I've failed on both counts."

"You can't be sure of that."

"News will reach Edinburgh soon enough," Hugh said. "At least then, I'll be in command of my destiny in a spiritual sense. Even if my flesh ends up thrown to the dogs. Not to mention my reputation..."

It was a long while before they finally arrived in the outskirts of Kilwinning. Thatched cottages huddled close along both sides of the street, while in the distance the abbey towers loomed high.

A short trudge brought them to the abbey gates. Despite the inclement weather, quite a crowd was gathered there. A band of pilgrims had just arrived to pay their respects at the tomb of Saint Winning, satchels slung over their shoulders, stout staffs in their hands. Their weary faces were shadowed by broad-brimmed hats, heavy cloaks drawn tight about them.

One of their number arranged lodgings while the rest waited nearby, weathering the company of some local women. One loudly berated her husband's abilities in the bedchamber while her companions laughed in raucous delight, oblivious to the statue of the Virgin that stared disapprovingly from above.

Hugh stared ahead, ignoring the curious glances. The women all fell strangely silent: as he passed, they nudged one another and whispered.

A beggar approached, shaking his bowl. His tattered clothes fluttered in the breeze, he moved with a carefully-crafted limp.

Hugh pinned on his fiercest look. "I know you," he said. "You were moved on before, last time you tried begging here without a licence."

"I can earn my keep," the beggar whined. "I got something." He fumbled in his clothing and pulled out a nail, six inches long and pocked with rust. "It's from the True Cross. An old man gave it to me as he lay dying on the road. Picked it up in the Holy Land. I'll sell it to you if you like, my lord. It'll guarantee your salvation."

"Heard that one a hundred times," Hugh said. "And it never gets any more convincing. Be off with you, before you're thrown in irons."

"See? I told you," one of the women whispered. "I knew it was him."

"But what's he doing here?"

"There's only one good reason to visit the Place of God," Hugh told them. "And it's not to idle away the day in fruitless gossip. Don't you have houses to keep? And children to tend?"

They skulked away, muttering.

Hugh watched them go. "There are some things in this world which never fail to satisfy."

"That's very true," John agreed. "But if I'm to attend mass and reach Eglintoun in time for supper, then I've no time to loiter." He prodded Hugh forward. "Go on then. Sooner you endure this moment of reckoning, sooner you can put it behind you."

The Place of Kilmaurs

Will's brown courser was tethered in the stables alongside Cuthbert's roan. Both beasts looked weary, heads drooping, coats matted with dried blood and sweat. The stable boy was currying the roan, whistling through his teeth as he worked.

"Who found them?" Christian asked the groom.

He gestured to the grubby farmer who stood nearby. "This man, my lady."

The farmer doffed his cap and bowed low. "I recognised young Master Cuthbert's horse."

"Where were they recovered?"

"Near the bounds of Clonbeith."

"And yourself?"

"My ricks were burned," he muttered. "And the kye slaughtered. God rot them all..." He swallowed. "I should be thankful, I suppose, that they left my wife and children unmolested."

"It's a bitter blow nonetheless," Christian said. "Rest assured my kinsmen will strike a blow on your behalf when the time's right." She turned to the steward. "Please reward him for his efforts. And send him alms, so he can keep his family through the winter."

"Consider it done, my lady."

"You're most gracious, Lady Christian," the farmer said. "God bless you."

"What about the horses?" Christian asked, running a concerned eye over them. "Are they unharmed?"

"They are," the groom replied. "But Master Cuthbert's saddle..." He broke off, and swallowed. "It was stained with blood."

"Let's just pray the wound wasn't mortal. And that my son still has sufficient strength to find his way home." With those stern words, she turned and swept out into the yard.

Tears stung her eyes, but somehow she stifled her grief. When she spoke with her household, she found herself gripped with a fortitude that she'd never known existed. They relied on her for guidance and support: she gave her best, because that's what Rob would have wanted.

She didn't want anyone to know the truth. That she'd hardly slept the previous night, that when at last she'd found rest, she'd been haunted with dreadful visions. She'd dreamed that Rob came home, a moving corpse upon his horse, mangled with wounds and dripping with gore. He'd rallied them all to vengeance, calling for retribution.

There'd be vengeance in good time. She was sure of it. It sickened her to think that others would suffer, that the feud would flourish unchecked. But her desire for peace was fading fast. She didn't really desire anything now, except to know that Cuthbert was alive and well.

At least there were other matters to occupy her thoughts. Rob had always been a prudent man: he'd already made a will, which made their lives much easier. The Dowager had asked Christian to make preparations for her son's funeral, a task Christian relished, throwing herself heart and soul into her duties.

She'd do it for Rob, and be a worthy wife to the very end.

Chapter 42

The Abbey of Kilwinning

Thronged with visiting townsfolk and pilgrims, the abbey church resounded to the sound of chattering voices. The chanting of prayers from the chancel and side chapels added to the cacophony, giving the place an air of busy excitement.

Stepping into the claustral range, Hugh felt he was entering a different world. The abbey precincts were tranquil: a few tonsured figures haunted the place, clad in habits of beige or brown. Some walked alone, others moved in small groups, conversing quietly. They glanced briefly in Hugh's direction, but didn't acknowledge him.

Hugh frowned. It irked him slightly, that here his presence scarcely registered in men's thoughts.

The door creaked open, a grey-haired monk peered out. "His Grace awaits you, Lord Hugh."

Twisting his bonnet tight in his hands, Hugh stepped inside.

Abbot William was a jovial man, red-faced and broad-shouldered. He wore the same nondescript habit as the rest of his order, his shining pink pate surrounded by thick brown hair, faintly touched with grey, that was cut short about his ears.

Hugh dropped to one knee, and kissed the ringed hand that was offered. "Thank you," he said. "For seeing me so promptly."

Abbot William sighed, suddenly sombre. "I rather think we've gone through this before, Hugh."

"I know that," Hugh agreed. "And no doubt you've given me up as lost already."

The abbot raised his brows. "No man is beyond redemption. If you wish to spend some time alone to contemplate your sins, then we'll make the necessary arrangements."

"I'm not here for spiritual succour alone, Your Grace. I'm here to do penance. But two weeks seems insufficient."

"Indeed," Abbot William agreed. "Of course, if you wanted to be sure of Salvation, you'd devote the rest of your life to God. Considering the gravity of your crimes..."

Hugh glanced aside. "Yes, I know, but..."

"You doubt your commitment." The abbot smiled, thinly. "That's no surprise."

"Surely there's some way of atoning..."

"A year of penance might be appropriate. A month, at the very least. But the King's situation is delicate, and if God put you on earth for any higher purpose, it was to serve your king." The aboot paused, frowning, then said, "I'll find you suitable accommodation, away from the temptation of your worldly goods and comforts, not to mention the distractions of the flesh. That way, you can reflect upon your transgressions and ponder the Word of God." He pressed his fingertips together,

219

considering his words. "I shall appoint you a confessor. He can discuss your sins in detail and decide how best to cleanse your soul." Abbot William broke off, smiling. "Of course, a token of your appreciation would be welcome..."

"Name your price," Hugh muttered.

His chamber measured just a few paces in length, large enough to hold a narrow bed and a table. The floor was covered by stone flags, cold and damp beneath his feet. A small window, open to the elements, was set high up in the white plastered wall. A finely-wrought crucifix looked down upon him: apart from that, the place was barren, austere.

Hugh sank down upon the bed. In this chill silent space, with the pale walls pressing in, the sense of desolation was almost overwhelming. The hair shirt they'd given him itched and chafed: it was too small, pulling tight about his shoulders. Apart from that, his only garment was a long linen shirt, which concealed his body and granted a little extra warmth.

He buried his head in his hands with a groan. He'd never meant to offend God. He'd always tried to impose justice fairly, to defend those incapable of defending themselves. But somewhere along the way he must have wandered from the path of righteousness, because his soul was troubled, more than it had ever been before.

*   *   *

When mass was over, John retreated to a side chapel. He lit a row of candles to the Virgin, dedicating one to Margaret, another to his unborn child and a third to himself. A fourth to his mother, a fifth to the soul of his dead father. A sixth to the soul of Robert, Lord Kilmaurs, a seventh to poor, long-suffering Helen.

And a final flame to Hugh.

Dropping to his knees before the altar, John closed his eyes and prayed. He prayed that reason would be restored, that the feud wouldn't blossom unchecked.

But deep inside he knew he was asking for a miracle...

The soft slap of a monk's sandaled feet echoed nearby, a hand touched his shoulder. "Sir John Sempill?"

John looked up to see a beige-robed figure standing over him. "The Lord Montgomerie asked to speak with you," the monk said.

"But I thought he'd retreated from the world. Surely it's not right-" He broke off, and stood. "Did he say why?"

"He says he's wronged you."

Hugh leapt to his feet, greeting John with a smile of undisguised joy and relief. Bereft of all his fine clothes, he seemed a forlorn figure. Even so, the cell scarcely seemed large enough to contain him.

"This hair shirt is appalling," said Hugh.

"That's not the right attitude."

"I'm too accustomed to my comforts. It'll do me good, to live without..." Hugh glanced away and swallowed. "I've something to say. It's been poised upon my lips a hundred times-"

John stiffened. "It's not necessary." So much had changed since his father's death: it was a hurt he'd confronted in another place, another time.

The Gryphon at Bay

"Please. Hear me out," Hugh urged him. "Your father... He was a great friend to me. He helped me at court, he gave advice freely, without condition..." His voice faltered, his eyes bright with grief. "I never meant to kill him."

"I saw the corpse, Hugh. There was no wound. How could you kill him, when you didn't even draw blood?"

"One moment he threw himself into the fight, the next he crumpled in the saddle." He swallowed, visibly shaken. "His heart stopped, I think. That doesn't absolve me."

"You gave him exactly what he wanted. A glorious, heroic death."

"I seized his corpse, and withheld it from his kin. I used his mortal remains for my own ends."

"You did what you thought necessary."

"I've sinned against you. I've sinned against your household." Hugh's voice faded.

"I forgave you long ago," John said. "What I said to you at Caldwell still stands, though God knows, things have changed between us. It's God's place to Judge, not mine. You've done more than enough to make amends with me; I only hope you'll learn to make your peace with God."

Hugh sank down on the edge of the bed, shoulders sagging. "I've always strived to do what's right, and just. But somehow I've been thwarted at every turn. Everything I do is tainted."

"That's not true." John sat alongside. "Helen would be deeply hurt, if she could hear you talk this way." He slipped a consoling arm about Hugh's shoulders and gripped him tight. "We'll pray for you. And when you next ride north, we'll be glad to receive you. You'll be in better spirits then, I hope."

Chapter 43

Perched high upon its rock above a bustling town, Stirling Castle was the treasured prize over which battles had been fought and won.

At Bannockburn and Stirling Bridge, the foe had been the Southern invader. Though the wars with England were fading rapidly into history and legend, memories of another altercation at the Bannock Burn were still raw. Fought just one year earlier, between the Scots themselves...

The way things were going, Angus reflected, they were rapidly heading for a repeat performance.

Steering a familiar course towards the castle gates, he rode along a cobbled street that wound ever upwards. Houses rose high on either side, blocking out the sunlight. Chickens picked their way through piles of refuse, laughing children darted from a pend ahead, narrowly avoiding his horse's hooves.

The town seemed peaceful, prosperous. But beneath its tranquil surface, there were ripples of unease. Already, a major portion of the host had mustered on the plains below. Their camp sprawled across the common grazing, brightly coloured silken banners fluttering amongst tents and horse-lines. They were men of the South and East mostly, from the Lothians and nearby Stirling.

Angus reined in his horse as two guards approached. They'd emerged from the brooding bulk of the gatehouse which loomed ahead, the points of the portcullis glimmering in the sunlight.

"Halt!" one called. "Who goes there?"

King and court were nervous, rightly so. "His Grace, Archibald Douglas, Earl of Angus," Angus replied, smoothly. "I'm here to see the King. If it pleases him to admit me."

"Let him in." A broad-shouldered young man in rich clothing stepped out from the shadows of the gatehouse, sword swinging at his side: Sir Adam Hepburn, a kinsman of Earl Patrick. He nodded to Angus, arms folded. "We were expecting you."

"You were?" Angus was all mock-levity. "I'd be grateful, Sir Adam, if you'd tell the King that I'm here to assist him." He paused. "Failing that, inform Earl Patrick."

"They're both in council," came Hepburn's stiff reply. "But I'll pass on word of your arrival."

To his surprise, an invitation to attend the King was quickly forthcoming. He'd barely seen his horse settled before the summons came, brought by a disgruntled-looking Adam Hepburn.

They found James in his privy chambers, cloistered there amongst his council. The furnishings were sumptuous: silks from the orient, finely-woven hangings from Flanders. But those gathered there were dressed in more sober fashion, as if already resigned to the austerity of war.

222

He noted quickly that the usual faces were in attendance: a brace of Hepburns, another brace of Homes, the Bishops of Glasgow and Aberdeen, and Earl Colin of Argyll.

Angus dropped to one knee. "Your Grace."

James waved a dismissive hand. "You mustn't grovel, Angus. Not when you've granted us your presence so promptly. We weren't expecting you before the end of the month."

Angus straightened. "I guessed your situation was dire."

"It is," James conceded. "But not so dire as to be beyond hope." He gestured to an empty chair beside Argyll. "Join us, please."

Argyll caught Angus' eye, face inscrutable. Patrick Hepburn's glance was equally opaque: he stared at Angus, frowning faintly.

Angus gazed back, unabashed. He was as welcome here as a leper at a busy fair day market. "Have you any word of Lennox?"

"They've left Dumbarton, of that we're certain," Hepburn said. "We think Stirling may be their prize. There have been raids in Moray and Angus, but it's still unclear where the main portion of their host is massing. We may be attacked from the north, or from the west."

James glowered at the board. "I won't be confined like this. If they want war, that's what they'll be granted. Surely we can engage them before their forces are at full strength?" He looked hopefully at Angus. "Do you bring men?"

"I have fifty mounted men-at-arms. Good swift horsemen from the Marches. And another four score from my Lanarkshire lands. I hope that will be helpful."

The King's relief was tangible. "That's most helpful, Angus. Thank you."

He dined in the King's presence that night, but was disappointed when he found himself languishing amongst the lower tables. Patrick Hepburn and his kinsmen had seen to that, a reminder that his presence was neither welcome nor wanted.

Angus was undeterred. He left the board early, positioning himself in just the right place to intercept King James as he headed off to the chapel for mass.

He fell into step alongside. "Your Grace."

James smiled. "You wish to speak with me?"

"A few moments of your time would be appreciated." He paused, then added in a low voice, "Your Grace, I know you want capitulation. You know you're capable of ruling wisely, and justly, and all you desire is the opportunity to put those plans into practice. But haven't you thought that some of their grievances must be addressed? God knows, I don't condone Lennox and his allies, but... There's fuel to their fire..."

The young king's smile waned. "Earl Patrick warned me that you'd be the voice of dissent."

"Consider me instead the voice of reason," Angus countered. "Your father suffered long years of his reign in exactly these circumstances. Men came to him with legitimate concerns, he'd respond with indifference or tyranny, depending on his mood. In the end, even his most loyal lieges turned against him."

"Your advice is noted, Angus," James retorted. "But it doesn't help me. It's early days yet. I can't afford to show weakness."

"Then make sure you find the foe. And beat them soundly. After that, you'll be in a position to impose your will. Until then you should be prudent."

*   *   *

The Place of Kilmaurs

She'd been working hard all morning, checking the stores with the head cook, ensuring that all necessary provisions were purchased ready for the feast. The task was completed by noon, so she sat with the household through dinner, keeping a brave face for the sake of the servants.

It was only now, in the quiet of late afternoon, that Christian found some time to rest. She was relieved to be removed from the world, if only for a little while, away from the demands of household and widowhood.

She lay on Rob's bed, brown hair flowing loose and unbound over the pillow. She'd found some solace the previous night, by following Rob's lead and taking a mug full of *aqua vita*. For a few blissful hours she'd been snatched away from her troubles. Now, though, she was weathering a fearful headache.

Hearing clamour downstairs, she stirred, suddenly uneasy. Women were calling to one another; from sorrow or delight, she couldn't be certain. She wasn't even sure she cared any more.

The door to her chamber creaked open. "Mother?"

Cuthbert's voice, hailing her...

She sat up with a gasp.

There he was. Walking with a limp, his clothes stained with dried blood and dirt, but alive and that was all that mattered.

Springing to her feet, she rushed to greet him, her fatigue forgotten. "Cuthbert!" She threw her arms about him, not caring that he reeked of earth and stale sweat. "My poor, sweet boy... Andy and Guido returned, but we didn't know..."

He returned her embrace, gripping her tight. "I'm well enough. A little battered, but it's nothing."

She placed her hand against his cheek. "I thought he'd kill you."

"He wanted to. But God preserved me, kept me safe." He seemed so strong, so self-assured. He'd changed, in just a few short days, become a man, worthy and responsible. Smiling gently, he wiped away her tears. "The fate of the household rests on my shoulders," he said. "I should take a bride without delay, so I can guarantee the succession. I'd be grateful for your help, Mother. My decisions may not be the right ones."

"If you were an earl, your prospects would be so much better."

"I know that." He sank down in Rob's chair. "My situation's delicate just now," he said, "but if we tread carefully, and work hard to restore my family's fortunes, then I can improve my lot. That's what Father would have wanted, isn't it?"

Stirling Castle

"Ah, Angus." James nodded in his direction. "Join us, please."

Angus scanned the faces. This time around Argyll was absent, and there was still no sign of his kinsman Montgomerie. Other than that, the balance of the Privy Council remained largely consistent.

Another man stood nearby, clad in battered, blood-stained plate armour. His greying black hair was tangled and damp with sweat, his face unshaven. Angus nodded to him, briefly. He knew the man well enough: John, First Lord Drummond. Gudefather to Angus' eldest son and heir, grandsire of the latest addition to the Douglas dynasty.

"Thank you, Lord John," James said. "You've served us well. You'll be rewarded in due course."

Drummond bowed his head and retreated.

"We've found the whereabouts of the rebel host," James explained, once Angus was seated. "We'll be riding out within an hour. If we head north, we should intercept them."

"What of their forces?" Angus asked.

"They're already in disarray. Lord Drummond sprang a surprise attack on Lennox's men last night. A number were slain or captured, the rest fled. I won't grant them any opportunity to regroup."

"And their leaders?" Angus asked.

"We captured Thomas Galbraith of Culcreuch. The rest have given us the slip."

Angus breathed deep, relishing the thud of his horse's hooves, the creak of his plate armour. He held the reins loose, letting his steed stride forward.

He'd taken his place at the head of his retainers, amongst a long snaking column of men marching north for Dunblane. It was easy terrain, the ground low-lying and fairly flat, a little soft underhoof. But the hills were already looming close. To the southwest lay the bleak heights of the Campsies, to the east the Ochils.

He heard the scuffle of hooves and the jingle of harness alongside, but didn't turn his head. "How very typical of James," he commented. "Rushing into the fray, without a moment's doubt or hesitation."

George Douglas grinned as he trotted his horse alongside. "No point in loitering, I suppose."

"He's left the town unguarded. What's to stop Lennox slipping through in the dead of night and locking the gates in our faces?"

"His Grace clearly isn't averse to taking the odd risk or two."

"Apparently not." He glanced curiously towards his son. "Did you speak with your gude-father?"

George grinned. "He bade me stay a while, but I took my leave."

"And what did he have to say for himself?"

"It's a sorry tale. Lennox was betrayed by one of his own men. It's said that Kenneth McAlpine found the lure of the King's gold more appealing than loyalty to his liege-lord."

"I daresay Lord John's well-pleased."

"Yes indeed," George agreed. "And the news of his grandson's birth only served to raise his spirits further. He says he'd love to drink a toast in our company, but reckons he deserves to sit by the fire and rest his bones a while."

Angus chuckled.

"Now James has given Lennox a thrashing," George said, "I suppose you'll be riding out with the King?"

"I'll make that decision in due course."

"I shouldn't toy with James. He's already in a foul mood. Rumour has it he'll have Culcreuch hanged for treason."

"Can't think why. The man's a pawn. Clinging to old-fashioned values, that's all. He pledged himself as a vassal to his liege-lord Lennox, so he'll fight for him, come what may. I'll speak with James, and see if he'll consider clemency. It seems unjust to mete out such harsh punishment against a man whose role in this affair is inconsequential."

"I never thought you'd speak out in favour of a condemned man," George remarked.

"I've been reflecting on the fate of the last Black Douglas. If he'd shown more mercy to his foes, then perhaps he wouldn't still be wallowing in the King's care."

"If he hadn't been so foolish as to lose his battles in the first place, then he'd never have found himself imprisoned."

"Ah, George," Angus laughed, softly. "You're your father's son and no mistake. It comforts me, to know my legacy will pass into safe hands."

Chapter 44

The Lands of Eglintoun

Glancing at the heavy skies above, Margaret snuggled deeper into her cloak. The day had started grey and dank, the bad weather not far away. It was John's intention to reach Dunlop by mid-afternoon; she just hoped they'd arrive before the rain started.

Riding slightly ahead, John was attentive to every little thing, the flutter of a bird in the bushes or the drifting shapes of kye grazing on a distant hillside.

He was anxious, without a doubt. She'd known that from the start. That morning when Helen insisted on providing them with Montgomerie protection, John hadn't argued. *You can't be too careful*, he'd explained, as he helped her up onto her horse. *You never know who you'll meet out there.* And then he'd smiled, too quickly for her liking.

At such close quarters, Margaret found the Montgomerie retainers far more terrifying than any perils they might face upon the road. They were big, uncouth men: they wore brigandines stained with blood and reeked of old sweat and horses. Some had fearsome scars across their faces, too.

John wasn't much enamoured by their presence either. In over an hour's travelling, he'd spoken just once, not long after they left Eglintoun.

The world has changed, he'd said.

She'd thought his words curious, because to her untutored eyes nothing seemed any different.

Not at first. It was only as they approached the bounds of Montgomerie lands that she realised what he'd meant, when she saw smoke curling up into the heavens, smelled the waft of burning.

She tightened the reins, suddenly apprehensive.

"What's that?" Katherine asked.

Following Katherine's gaze, Margaret saw the pale gleam of fresh timbers ahead.

John steered his horse alongside. "Don't look at it."

Too late, she realised she was looking at a gibbet. Hanging from its wooden platform was a fresh corpse bound by iron chains, creaking faintly as it swayed in the breeze. It had once been a man, but now the flesh of his face was scratched and pecked by birds, his eyes gone. She'd heard of such things, but until now she'd never seen one.

Most of the Montgomeries didn't so much as glance in its direction. Save one, a young man who spat at the corpse as he passed.

Katherine urged her horse close to John's. "Is he dead?" she whispered.

"Yes," he replied.

Margaret turned away, stomach heaving. The vision still haunted her. Of a pale bloodless face with voided eye-sockets, glimpses of livid flesh revealed beneath ragged clothing.

"A hundred years ago, there'd have been a corpse at every crossroads," John told them. "Thankfully, we live in more civilised times."

"Then what's that one doing there?" Mariota asked.

"Lord Hugh's an uncompromising man when it comes to justice."

The stench of death followed them, sickly sweet and cloying. Margaret didn't want to appear weak with so many of Hugh's men looking on, but soon her guts heaved so much that she had to dismount.

John steadied her while she retched by the side of the road. "Don't try and fight it," he said. "It'll be worse for you, what with the baby." He passed her a flask of ale. "Drink something. You'll feel better then."

Her hand trembled as she wiped it across her lips, but the bittersweet liquid helped settle her a little.

"Is your belly alright?" John asked. "There's no pain?"

Taking deep breaths of fresh air, she filled her lungs with the wholesome scents of earth and damp vegetation. "The baby," she whispered. "I'm not supposed to see such things..."

He patted her arm. "Don't fret about it, Margaret. You'll make yourself ill. Try and put it from your mind."

"Sir John." One of the Montgomerie retainers rode up close. "We're on Cunninghame lands. It's daft to loiter here."

John scowled. "My wife will move on when she's ready, thank you."

Margaret swallowed, frightened by the possibilities. "Is it true?" she whispered. "That they might be lying in wait for us?"

"Of course not." Taking her arm, he steered her back to her horse. "Can you continue? You mustn't spend any more time out in the cold than you have to."

When she was back in the saddle, John remained by her side, quietly supportive. There was silence, heavy and thoughtful, until Katherine spoke out. "Have you ever hanged a man, Sir John?"

"No, thank God. I've never had to."

"But you'd do it, if the need arose."

"Some crimes can't go unpunished. Like rape, and murder."

"If it's such a dreadful crime to kill a man," Mariota added, "then surely the King must hang Lord Hugh?"

"It's not that simple," he replied. "Learned men must decide, first of all, whether the act was intended, or pre-meditated. Whether indeed it could be described as murder at all." He glanced cautiously about him, making sure that Hugh's men were out of earshot. "Even if it was, Hugh's kin would consider his death to be an injustice, and rise against the King. There'd be rebellion, and dissent, and the King's influence in the Westland would weaken."

"But it's not justice, is it? If one man can commit such a crime, and escape the consequences, while another must pay with his life."

"You mustn't worry about such things," came his brisk reply. "Even the wisest of men can't decide amongst themselves what's right, and what's just."

"What a joy it is," Margaret said. "To be married to a man who's good, and kind, who does his best to do the right thing, whatever the circumstances..." She broke off. "Thank you, for being that way."

John didn't reply. But he smiled, with such warmth that she knew she'd said something precious, something he'd treasure in his heart for years to come.

*   *   *

Near Stirling

"He's been sighted." James circled his horse impatiently around. Clad in his armour, he no longer seemed like a slender youth. Instead, he'd gained stature and bulk more appropriate in a King. "Near Gartloaning. If we move fast, we can cut them off."

Hepburn levelled his gaze at Angus. "Can I assume you'll ride with us?"

"Why should I desert you now?" Angus asked.

Hepburn didn't reply. Turning his horse around, he urged it forwards into a trot.

"We'll take the eastern flank," Angus offered.

James nodded. "God Speed!" he called, then headed after Hepburn.

The horses were fresh, the men cheerful. There'd been news of skirmishes the previous day, clashes between portions of the King's host and the remaining fragments of the rebel army. But nothing decisive, nothing conclusive. And James himself had been cut adrift from the action. The lad was becoming increasingly frustrated, he was eager to prove himself, determined to show that last year's victory hadn't been down to good fortune alone.

Angus steered his horse back down the lines to where the Douglas contingent awaited him. George waited there: like rest of them, he was mounted on his warhorse and in full array.

They lined up away from the main body of the King's host, along a stretch of sloping ground where they could watch the proceedings from a distance.

Further down the hill, the King's men had gathered. Amongst the massed ranks of armed men, it was hard to tell one knight from another, but Angus knew who'd be amongst their number: Schaw of Sauchie, Lord Gray, Sir William Keir of Stirling. Men who'd stood with James the previous year and who'd ridden to victory against his father. John, Lord Drummond, was there, too: after resting his men he'd hurried north to join them.

Amongst them James was a conspicuous figure. He'd placed himself right at the front, near his Lion Rampant banner. Mounted on his big grey horse, his armour polished so it shone like silver, a gold circlet about his close-helmet.

Angus winced. "How unlike his father," he remarked to George. "In the vanguard, throwing himself into the fray. Let's hope he doesn't get himself killed."

"That might prove a blessing in disguise," George commented, wryly. "It would certainly resolve this current dispute."

"We'd be slicing off the head of the Hydra," Angus replied. "A hundred more would spring up in their place."

George laughed at that.

"Hello," Angus settled deeper into the saddle. "They're stirring. Sit tall and stay sharp now..."

Sure enough, the situation was progressing. Hepburn and Home left the King's host at a brisk trot, veering off to the west with two hundred men or more pressed close at their backs. The intention was to put the rebel forces to flight, to drive them here, where James would be waiting...

Like hunting. But this time the quarry were men, not deer.

The Angus contingent waited, enduring the inactivity as best they could. It seemed as if hours had passed, the sun sank lower, and lower, while the horses stamped and tossed their heads in boredom.

George stirred. "There!" He stood in his stirrups, peering at the low hills to the west.

Within moments, the situation changed. Where there'd once been tranquillity, there was chaos. Men running, mostly northern clansmen, poorly armed with dirk and small shield, clothed in little more than a long sark and plaid. Pitiful wretches, fighting for their lords because of ancient obligations of honour and kinship, they slithered across the mossy ground, wading knee-deep through the bog.

Mounted retainers loyal to Hepburn and Home followed, swords raised. They pounded forward at full gallop until the mud sucked at their horses' hooves, slowing their pace. As they closed in, another mass of men approached from the north. The banner of the Lennox Stewarts flew high in their midst, but at the forefront of their ranks they carried something else. A plain white shirt, flying from a spear. Their armoured knights swept in, bearing down on Hepburn's men.

James lifted his sword in readiness. He let it fall: the trumpets brayed and the charge began. The King's men surged forward in tight formation, a rippling wave of horseflesh and solid, impregnable steel.

To left and right, armed retainers glanced at Angus, eager, expectant.

Angus raised his hand. "Hold!"

They muttered and cursed, but did as they were asked.

Further down the field the melee unfolded. Men and horses were falling, the dead piling up. It was as if the battle they'd all endured the previous year was repeating itself. Lennox and his people made a brave stand, but they were outnumbered. Gravely outnumbered. After some brief fierce fighting, the lines snapped, and the rout began.

Angus glanced heavenwards. The light was fading. In less than an hour, the fleeing men would at least be granted the cover of darkness.

He stretched in his stirrups with a sigh. "I'll give the King this victory," he said. "But there wasn't much in it."

"Father..." George nodded to the floodplains below. Men streamed across it, some armed in plate mail and mounted on fine horses, others struggling to run on foot.

"Leave them," said Angus. "Let's return to camp."

The flaps of the tent were tossed aside and in stormed James. "Out of my way!" he snarled in passing, venting his ire on a hapless retainer who wilted visibly under the onslaught.

James didn't look quite so polished now. His gleaming suit of mail was smeared with blood and he was limping. "You treacherous dog!" He fixed his gaze unerringly on Angus, face red with fury. "To treat your king with such deceit. I should have your head for this!"

Angus stared back. He'd expected this confrontation, but not so soon, and not in these circumstances. He'd barely had time to shed his armour and settle in his tent. "Some wine, Your Grace?" He gestured to the flagon and goblets on the table before him.

James roared and heaved over the table. "Don't toy with me, Angus! You belled one cat, but this one's too young and potent for your wiles."

Angus didn't flinch, or stir from his chair. "Whatever do you mean?"

"I'll hang you. Along with Culcreuch."

"On what grounds? Treason, I suppose. Because I refused to fight for a cause I considered unjust." He gazed beyond James's shoulders, noted that his retainer had been joined by others, trusted Angus men-at-arms who were gripping their sword-hilts, unsure how to respond. He caught their eye. "Leave us."

Once they'd gone, he smiled. "Your Grace," he said. "If you wish to discuss this matter further, I'd be delighted, but only when the rage of battle's faded, and you're in a more civilised mood. To enter into such a debate just now would be fruitless, don't you think?"

"Do you mock me, sir?"

"Of course not."

James jabbed a finger in his chest. "Liar! You won't bewitch me with that quicksilver tongue of yours-"

Angus clasped his hands before him, unconcerned. "You can summon the host, time and time again. You can chase Lennox here and there, until the goodwill of your lieges is exhausted and there's none left to support you. You will not win. You cannot win."

James stared, mouth agape.

"That's precisely what happened to your father," Angus continued, smoothly. "By seeking the advice of a privileged few he neglected the needs of many and paid a heavy price. But he was fortunate in one respect: he died a martyr." Raising his head, Angus looked James straight in the eye. "Lennox has won widespread support because your father was murdered. Your father was murdered, and you cannot bring yourself to punish the men who killed him. You wear that chain about your waist as a symbol of your penitence, but you've let the culprits escape justice. That's why the government you trust is deemed rotten to its core. You must sue for peace, because that's the only way you'll bring the men of this land into accord, and make it prosper."

"I want you gone from here, without delay," James said, voice chill. "You, and every one of your stinking kinsmen."

"As you wish."

"There's many men who rank much higher in my favour than you, Angus. Men who are honourable, valiant and righteous. If you won't help your king, then I don't doubt they will. Together, we'll defeat Lennox, and when we do, you'll have to crawl to me, and beg my forgiveness, because that's the only way I'll have you back amongst my council."

"May God Bless you, Your Grace," Angus said. "And may He Grant you wisdom and prosperity. When you require me, I'll be at my place of Tantallon." He inclined his head. "I'll always be your humble servant. In time, you'll come to understand that, when the mists fall from your eyes and you see what folly you've been party to."

Chapter 45

The Abbey of Kilwinning

It was a simple philosophy. That to deprive a man of all physical pleasures meant he was forced to look inward, to confront those things that really mattered.

The Word of God, the fate of the soul...

For three days Hugh had survived on just a few chunks of bread washed down with some weak ale, plus a bowl of thin soup at dinner. To make matters worse, when the wind was right the most delicious aromas would waft from the kitchen and refectory. The men of God who lived here devoted their existence to spiritual contemplation, but curbing gluttony didn't loom large in their priorities.

He'd snatch isolated fragments of slumber, nothing more, his bed so small that he couldn't even stretch his limbs out fully. Most of the time, he'd lie awake shivering beneath a thin blanket which – like the bed – was too small, or fidget endlessly because the hair shirt made every waking moment a misery. His joints ached, the wounds he'd suffered in the skirmish still plagued him.

At least his wretched efforts to find sleep were restricted to just a few hours each night. He was expected to attend Nocturn in the early hours, then roused again just before six to attend Prime. He attended neither Matins nor Vespers, being allowed instead to pray in isolation or confess his sins with one of the senior monks in attendance.

Rumour of his arrival had stirred quite an interest in an abbey always busy with pilgrims. Now their numbers were swelled by curious locals, eager to glimpse the Lord Montgomerie humbled before God and his fellow men.

But Abbot William spared him the humiliation of parading before the masses. *What transpires here is between you and Almighty God,* he'd said. *It'll serve no useful purpose to diminish your standing within the community.*

He was grateful for that. He'd promised the Abbot another generous denotation for his pains.

Turning over in his bed, Hugh grunted as his kneecap struck the wall. He was no closer now to finding solace or enlightenment. He wondered if perhaps it was already too late. That he was so deeply snared in the corporeal world that he couldn't stretch his mind to the hereafter.

Have faith, his confessor had said. *It's early days yet. There's still hope. There's always hope.*

Gritting his teeth, Hugh murmured a prayer to Holy Mary, asking Her not to forsake him, asking Her for strength and guidance. But there was no divine light of inspiration, no angelic voice calling out to him.

Just cold black empty silence, that pressed like dread upon him.

* * *

Dumbarton Castle

The Gryphon at Bay

"Matthew. Wake up." A hand shook him, gently.

Opening his eyes, he saw his mother standing at his bedside, candle in hand. It was late in the night, but Margaret Montgomerie was dressed, her greying hair confined within a gabled hood.

"I was dreaming." He sat up, rubbing the sleep from his eyes. "I was a child again, and the sun was shining. I was in the garden at Darnley, wandering amongst the rose trees. My sister was there, she was about eight, or nine. Wearing a pale blue dress with her hair drifting loose and she was laughing..." He fixed his gaze upon his mother, realising with a jolt that she seemed older somehow, worn and weary. "What's wrong?"

"It's Alex," she whispered. "He's come home."

His heart lurched. "Did he bring news?"

"They were routed, Mattie. Their forces have been scattered through Perth and the Lennox. Your brother took it on himself to inform us." She swallowed. "He's scarcely had a bite to eat in three days."

"God..." He threw back the covers. "I'll be there as soon as I can."

She handed him a shirt. "Be gentle with him. He didn't want to see you, but I insisted." Setting the candle down, she retreated to a nearby chair where his clothes lay ready. Picking up his hose, she gripped the garment tight, her knuckles pale in the candlelight. "He's a brave young man, Mattie. A credit to both our lines."

Alex sat hunched by the fire. He was wrapped in a blanket, a cup of hot wine gripped in his hands. His clothes lay piled nearby, soaked through and blackened with mud.

As Matthew approached, he looked up and offered a half-hearted smile. His face was pale and filthy: he had a black bruise around one eye, and a cut on his temple.

Matthew crouched alongside. "Well, little brother. What tales of valour do you bring?"

"I lost my armour when we fled. And Ajax..." Alex gulped back tears. "He stumbled, I fell off, and then he ran away."

"He's just a horse."

"You put him in my care."

Margaret Montgomerie sighed. "The pottage should be warm by now. I'll fetch some."

"He was worth a king's ransom," Alex muttered. "You said so yourself."

Matthew ruffled his hair. "You're alive and in one piece. That's all that matters." He paused. "What happened?"

"We were camped one night, and they came from nowhere. We fled while we could, and the following day we regrouped. But the King came after us. His people harried us, again and again. We had no respite..."

Matthew laid his hand on the boy's arm. "It's war, Alex. That's what happens."

"I don't know where Father is. Or Lord Robert. I don't think they were captured. But Culcreuch was. There's rumour the King'll hang him." Alex shuddered, despite himself. "He'll hang Father, won't he? And us, too..."

"He'll do no such thing," Margaret Montgomerie spoke out from the door. "We still have friends, Alex. And kinsmen, too. They won't let any ill befall us."

Louise Turner

The Place of Kilbirnie

The Crawfurds didn't mention the business with Kilmaurs. Not at first. They welcomed John like a long lost kinsman; Malcolm sat him in the place of honour at the board, the atmosphere jovial, light-hearted.

On the face of it, at least. But underneath the mood was taut, brittle. John sensed it, keenly, but said nothing.

They were polishing off the final dishes when Malcolm spoke out at last. "To business, John. Because I assume that's why you're here?"

"I've received word from the King. The men of the Westland have been summoned to the host."

"So soon?" Marjorie made no attempt to hide her displeasure.

Malcolm smoothed out the boardcloth, visibly uneasy. "Hush, my dear. Don't vent your spleen on our poor Sheriff. We could have worse than him."

There was silence.

"Can I count on your support?" John asked.

Malcolm exchanged glances with Robert, who studied his trencher, grim-faced. They didn't need to voice their opinions. He knew their answer, plain as if they'd shouted it.

John slapped his palm against the board, scowling. "This call to arms has nothing to do with either the Montgomeries or the Cunninghames. It's about an act of treason against the King."

Malcolm winced. "I know that, but..."

"There should be no doubt, no hesitation. And no dissent, either."

"It's not as simple as that." Malcolm argued. "A man must make a stand against injustice. And the slaughter of Kilmaurs was more than that. It was an outrage."

"You have lands in Renfrew. As your sheriff, I'm obliged to remind you-"

"My course is already decided," came Malcolm's stiff reply.

"But you saw what happened last year, how they treated me. Your people suffered, too. At Lord Lyle's hands... How can you turn your back on what happened? All those injuries, those cruelties..."

"You're hardly in a position to lecture me on principles."

Further down the board, Robert cleared his throat, visibly embarrassed. While Marion sat with head bowed, her face desolate.

"When the King grants us a more even-handed man as Bailie, we'll support him," Malcolm said. "Until that day dawns, he can seek help elsewhere."

"Can I assume you won't be joining forces with the enemy?" John's tone was icy.

"We're not traitors," Malcolm's voice faded to a whisper. "Just decent men, with a legitimate grievance."

"What Craigends told you was flawed. Ask Constantine, or Adam. The Master of Kilmaurs was first to draw his sword. Lord Hugh took up arms in self-defence."

"Montgomerie had an armed party lying in wait. That he kept them concealed from view is proof enough of his treachery."

"He was nervous, that's all. And rightly so..."

"The man's cunning, I'll grant you that. You've fallen for his wiles completely."

234

John leaned his elbows on the board, resting his forehead against clenched fists. "You're my kinsmen. I thought you'd support me."

Malcolm toyed with his spoon. "When did you say the host would gather?"

"The Twenty Eighth of October. In Glasgow."

"It's a bad time of year," said Malcolm. "We'd lose horses, for sure. Perhaps even some men."

Silence fell across the board, awkward, uncomfortable.

Tearing his napkin from his shoulder, John flung it down before him. "Why am I the one who's being judged here? I didn't kill Kilmaurs."

"John..." Malcolm reached for his shoulder.

John shrugged him aside and rose to his feet. "I won't embarrass you with my company."

"John!" Marion looked up, grey eyes bright and anxious. "Please don't do this."

"Sit down, John." Malcolm seized his arm and tugged him back into his seat. "I'm sorry. It's not your fault. We know that. We're all on edge here. No-one knows what will happen, whether any of us will escape this turmoil unscathed."

"I'll ride with John," Robert spoke out. "At least then we'll have shown willing. I'll take a dozen men. That's better than nothing."

Chapter 46

Tantallon Castle

The isolation was enjoyable at first. Angus hunted most days, which helped keep the boredom at bay. It was the evenings he found wearisome. Tranquility soon gave way to tedium: the long cold dark nights sapped the soul, gradually bringing him close to despair.

He missed court. He missed the conversation, the cut and thrust and parry of his rivals' wit, the heightened senses that brought a man to life when every moment could bring about his downfall through a misplaced word or gesture.

He didn't squander his time. He practiced the lute, well aware that music disciplined the mind. But it wasn't something he enjoyed, too much hard work in pursuit of elusive perfection.

So he'd try instead to amuse himself with a game of chess or cards with his steward. But each and every time he'd win; before long the constant stream of victories galled beyond all measure.

He missed his wife, though he would never have admitted it. The spark of desire had died between them years ago - if indeed it had existed at all - but Elizabeth brought certain qualities to life: pleasant conversation, and spirited debate about politics, philosophy and the liberal arts.

She kept a separate household now, but wife or no wife, a man had his needs, and Angus prided himself on his adaptability. He always kept a careful watch when he toured his lands and every so often a shapely young maid would catch his eye.

For a few months he'd take an interest. He'd buy her new gowns and trinkets, bestow gifts of livestock and a few extra fields on her family. But when her belly started to swell his desire would fade. He'd find a husband amongst his retinue, give the young couple sufficient funds to keep the child fed and clothed for the first few years, then leave them to it.

Taking a leisurely draught of wine, his gaze lingered on his latest acquisition. A fresh-faced girl younger than himself by twenty years or more, she wasn't overwhelmingly pretty: she had a turned-up nose, a freckled complexion and a timid manner. But her flesh was soft with youth, her breasts enormous. She wasn't blessed with much wisdom, her accent so thick and broad that he could barely understand a word.

Setting down his goblet, he ambled over to the bed. She gazed up at him, her black hair streaming out across the coverlet, her naked flesh pale, enticing.

He pulled off his shirt. Pushing her legs apart, he mounted her, sliding comfortably into place. He heaved himself deeper, grunting with the effort.

She closed her eyes.

He didn't know what she was thinking, whether she was even capable of much thought at all. Not that it mattered. He gasped as the moment of climax approached.

The door banged open. "Have you heard the news?" Elizabeth's voice rang out, shrill with triumph and agitation.

"Ah, my love..." He drew a sharp breath, blinked as splendid ecstasy flowered and died in his loins. "Forgive me. I wasn't expecting-"

His wife sat at the foot of the bed, still wrapped in her riding cloak. Her face was flushed with excitement. "Montgomerie's murdered the Lord Kilmaurs."

Extricating himself, Angus sat up, weary and breathless. He set his consort on her way with a rough push. "Now, my dear," he said, addressing Elizabeth. "Be so kind as to repeat all that. Forgive me, if my mind was playing tricks. But what I heard seemed beyond belief."

Elizabeth looked the young woman up and down with glittering, merciless eyes. "Did you scrape her off the floor of the byre?"

"You were saying?" He glanced at the girl, harbouring a brief shred of remorse. She was gathering her clothing, blushing and close to tears.

Elizabeth watched her departure with lips pursed. "Little whore," she muttered. "What's her name?"

"Meg, Margaret, Mary. Something like that."

She shook her head. "You're despicable."

He headed for the kist at the far wall. "Do have some wine," he said, pouring a measure out in readiness.

She stared at him now, disapproval still etched hard on her face. "For God's Sake put some clothes on, Archie. I could do without the distraction."

He shrugged. "Your wish is my command, my dear. Just let me wash, will you?"

Once she was warmly ensconced by the fireside, with her cloak set aside and her hands wrapped tight around a cup of wine, Elizabeth launched eagerly into her tale. "Word has it he attacked the Master of Kilmaurs. When the Lord Kilmaurs tried to intervene, Montgomerie slew him. The Master was forced to flee, with Montgomerie in pursuit." She paused, took another sip of wine. "There's no doubt what Montgomerie had in mind. He wanted to eradicate their entire line." She shook her head. "He's an animal. He should be removed, before he can unleash yet more havoc on us all."

"He was acquitted the last time round. What makes you think the Lords'll reach a different conclusion when this case comes to court?"

"That's what makes it all the more outrageous. That he can commit the same atrocities, again and again. No-one has the courage to bring him to bay."

"It's not as simple as that. He's a powerful man. He commands a strong following, and the King, quite rightly, would rather have him as an ally. He's also extremely useful on the battlefield." Angus swilled his wine around and smiled. "Perhaps King James hopes that one day the Lord Montgomerie's valour will prove his undoing."

"The funeral takes place in the parish of Kilmaurs in ten days' time," Elizabeth said. "I will be attending. And I'd be grateful, my dear, if for once you'd show a little solidarity with my kin and ride there with me."

"I don't see why not," Angus said. "I'm sure James would want someone of stature to attend in his stead."

"I wonder how he'll take this news."

"Badly, I'm sure. He was hoping for peace in the Westland."

"He was misguided, if he thought Montgomerie could subdue the Cunninghames by force."

"Hindsight's a wonderful thing." He stretched comfortably in his seat. "It's an interesting turn of events. I'm curious to see how it all plays out."

The Place of Ellestoun

The Crawfurds arrived around noon, along with a small retinue. They weren't expected, but despite the growing ill-feeling between their households, John was quick to offer hospitality.

With Sir Malcolm and Robert Crawfurd seated alongside their hosts at the top table, the dishes were brought out and set before them.

Margaret watched in dismay as John rose to carve the meat. It embarrassed her to see him carry out such a menial task, but with no young kinsman there to assist, he had no choice.

With the meat sliced and handed round the top table, John blessed the board, then resumed his seat.

They could begin.

She was sharing her trencher with Robert Crawfurd. He spoke very little. He asked after her health, and briefly told her how Marion fared. After that, he fell silent. She didn't press him. She had the distinct impression that he was more interested in eavesdropping on John's conversation.

"So when did you say the funeral's taking place?" John asked.

"Day after tomorrow," Malcolm replied.

John considered Malcolm's words in silence. "I think I'll attend," he said, eventually.

Malcolm nearly choked on his wine. "What?"

"You heard me."

Margaret fought the urge to smile. It was so typical of John, to utter such startling things in that calm unflustered manner.

"Don't you think that's a little misguided?" Robert ventured cautiously. "You're not exactly well-loved by the Cunninghames."

"I want to pay my respects."

"God, you're stubborn," Malcolm muttered.

"It's what my father would have done."

"Aye, but..." Malcolm broke off, eyes fixed on the board. "You're not your father, are you?"

John flashed him a quick, irritated glance. "Let's speak no more of this matter," he said. "Have you chosen your course for tomorrow? If it were my decision, I'd head for Dunlop. Constantine will give us a roof for the night, and stuff our bellies besides, I'm sure."

* * *

The Gryphon at Bay

The Place of Neristoun, Kyle

They took supper in a crowded hall, where the diners were packed so tight that the smell of fresh rushes was insufficient to mask the scent of sweating men. It wasn't the most opulent of surroundings, but then, the Neristoun Boyds were hardly a prosperous family. The tapestries were worn, chewed by generations of moths, the timbers sun-bleached and faded.

But the food at least could not be faulted.

"An atrocity." Elizabeth Boyd tore into her bread with determined fingers. "No other word for it."

"They were riding under a flag of truce," Archibald Boyd of Neristoun said. "But Montgomerie had men-at-arms lying in wait. When the signal came, they sprang their trap."

Angus didn't comment. He should have guessed that the only topic of conversation would be the recent slaying of Kilmaurs. With the funeral just a day away, it was no surprise that tempers were running high.

He cast a sideways glance to the end of the table. His niece sat there, young Marion Boyd. She was fourteen now, a fruit swelling quickly to perfection and ripe for the plucking. She sat in silence, dutiful, compliant. Listening attentively to all that was said but offering no thoughts, no opinions...

Angus sighed. He had daughters of his own who needed husbands. Perhaps Elizabeth would have been better occupied attending to their needs, instead of filling her thoughts with old resentments. Not that he'd press the issue: daughters needed dowries, and he found it hard to part with property at the best of times.

After dinner, they retired to the laird's chamber. Like the hall, it was sparsely furnished, chairs and bed polished from use and held together by countless repairs. But Archibald Boyd wasn't a man to lament his family's waning fortune: if anything, he counted mediocrity as a blessing. For it meant he'd been spared the King's wrath when his kinsman Lord Boyd was forfeited almost thirty years earlier.

While they talked together, Neristoun's daughter Marion stepped forward to entertain them. While her father played the lute, she sang to them.

Angus watched and listened, entranced. The girl's breasts and hips were broad, enticing, she carried herself with elegance and restraint. Her hair was polished chestnut brown, faintly tinged with russet. She had bright grey-blue eyes and the clearest skin he'd ever seen in a maid, flushed pink around the cheeks.

And her voice... Sweet and true, like the laverock. To hear her sing this melancholy air of love and yearning made his flesh creep with desire. For one brief moment of madness, he'd have given anything to tear her gown from her and take her to his bed.

Elizabeth stared at him, accusing, reproachful.

He smiled back, gently reassuring.

As the strains of the lute faded, they were all quick to express their approval. Angus nodded in the maid's direction. "She's a lovely girl," he told Archie Boyd. "And most accomplished. Have you thought of marriage?"

Boyd studied the floor, uncomfortable. "We've considered the matter. But I fear my wife sets her aim too high."

"Cuthbert of Kilmaurs will be seeking a wife," Elizabeth said.

"We're a family of little means," Boyd replied. "I approached the Cunninghames last year, but they'll stoop no lower than a lord."

"If that's the case, then they'd best hurry along and find someone," Elizabeth commented. "Or King James will lose patience, and make them marry a Montgomerie."

Angus laughed. "Young Cuthbert would have to choose between a babe and a bastard," he said. "I wonder which would prove most appealing..."

"With regards to Marion..." Boyd cut in. "I was hoping, Your Grace, that a man of your influence might help us in our quest for a husband."

"A sound suggestion," Angus nodded. "In the meantime, perhaps we should ask the maid herself." He caught the young girl's eye. "Niece," he said. "Have you any thoughts on marriage?"

She gazed at her toes, hands folded neatly before her. "I shall do whatever is asked of me."

"An exemplary reply," Angus said, lifting his goblet in jaunty salute. "Fear not, young Marion. We'll find you a consort worthy of your grace and beauty. Meanwhile, I hope a new gown and a string of fine pearls will console you. Your aunt shall make arrangements, and I'll have them sent to you with all due speed."

She curtsied low. "You're most kind, my lord."

The Abbey of Kilwinning

A week into his penance, and Hugh had learned at last to ignore the distractions of the flesh, devoting his thoughts to prayer, and the lessons of the scripture.

That morning, he'd allowed the monks to bleed him. As he lay back along a bench in the infirmary, he watched as they opened a vein in his forearm. His life blood was a precious commodity, to be preserved at all costs and never squandered. But as the bowl slowly filled with the dark garnet-red liquid, he'd felt no anger, no fear, just quiet tranquility.

When evening came, he knelt in the solitude of his cell, rosary in hand. After what seemed like an eternity enclosed within this humble place, the waft of venison scarcely registered in his thoughts. The light from a single candle lit the room: his shadow loomed tall before him, black and ominous. Above it, free from the taint of his presence, hung the Crucifix, the figure of Christ gleaming as the flame guttered and flickered in the draught.

Hugh fixed his gaze upon it, skimming through the beads, murmuring the words over and over again. In the world beyond these walls, penance was a chore. But here, where life had no other purpose, it took on a new significance. The lack of food and sleep was taking its toll: he felt pleasantly light-headed, as if drunk on too much wine. He could scarcely concentrate, but in a way that made his task easier, for his mind was freed. He could ponder the mysteries of the Passion, contemplate the sorrow of the Virgin and marvel at Christ's Resurrection.

He prayed for guidance, for knowledge, hoping he'd be granted peace of mind, spiritual consolation. He'd been offered such comfort when he'd confronted his foes and looked Death in the eye. Now, though, the prize eluded him. Like the Grail it beckoned him onwards, a flickering light in the far distance.

But for the moment he remained in Darkness. A lost soul, blundering onwards in search of Truth and Revelation.

Whatever those might be...

Chapter 47

The Parish of Kilmaurs

The death knell rang, solemn and relentless, to mark the passing of Robert, Lord Kilmaurs. It was a bright October day. There'd been a frost that morning: even now, close to noon, the air was cold enough to make the breath mist.

A respectable contingent of lairds from Cunninghame and Renfrew were in attendance: forming a tight, close-knit group amongst their number were Sir Malcolm and Robert Crawfurd, Sir Adam Mure of Caldwell and Constantine Dunlop of Hunthall.

And then of course there was John.

Malcolm and Adam had begged him to skulk amongst their retinue, but he'd refused. Wearing his best clothes, carrying his Sheriff's chain of office about his shoulders, he was a conspicuous figure amidst the crowd who jostled for space about the kirkyard: tenants of the Lord Kilmaurs, mostly, clad in their brightest fairday clothes.

A good half-hour passed, and still they waited, rubbing their hands and stamping their feet to fend off the chill.

The longer they loitered, the more the numbers swelled. Scattered here and there amongst the common folk were groups of more worthy men, richly garbed and accompanied by liveried retainers.

"That's interesting." Adam leaned on John's shoulder, standing on tiptoe so he could get a better view. "Wallace of Craigie. And Wallace of Ellerslie."

"There are Kennedies here, too," Constantine commented.

"There's a change in the air," Malcolm observed. "You can almost smell it."

John pulled his gown close with a sigh. Then he stiffened, for the funeral procession had arrived at last.

Men chanted in the Romish tongue as the party drew close. The priest came first, accompanied by a group of mourners, dressed in black. Thirteen men in all, representing Christ and the disciples.

Behind them came the hearse, drawn by a sturdy black horse. Kilmaurs' destrier strode alongside, clad in an argent caparison, sable shake-fork embroidered boldly on shoulders and quarters.

They doffed their bonnets. No-one spoke. There was just the endless tolling of the bell, the constant murmurs of priest and mourners, uttering prayers for the dead man's soul.

"It's a bad state of affairs," Adam whispered in John's ear. "I always knew that Montgomerie was a man of dubious character. He has sinister tendencies, you know."

"He can wield a sword with both hands," John retorted. "But he signs with his right. That's hardly diabolical. Besides, you were the one who introduced us in the first place. If I remember right, I wanted nothing to do with him-"

The Gryphon at Bay

He broke off as the hearse drew level. The coffin was obscured beneath a costly cloth of red velvet, fringed with gold thread. A banner bearing the Cunninghame arms was draped across it.

It lurched laboriously on its way, the family following on behind. The dead man's close kinsmen formed the van: his three sons, followed by Sir William Cunninghame of Craigends and the Master of Craigends, with a gaggle of cousins following on behind.

Walking slightly ahead of the others, Cuthbert Cunninghame was the embodiment of injured dignity, a youth forced now to shoulder a man's responsibilities. His younger brothers were less composed, trudging along with eyes downcast.

John swallowed. He remembered it well, the yawning realisation that the fate of his line lay entirely in his hands. The sudden understanding that youthful innocence was gone forever.

Cuthbert's gaze met his, briefly. The young man frowned, but didn't acknowledge him.

And then he'd moved on.

Behind the menfolk came the women, two generations of Dowager, husbands slain by the same hand.

"To slay Kilmaurs was folly," Malcolm said, nodding towards the older woman. "His mother's a Hepburn. Lady Margaret Hepburn. Earl Patrick's sister."

Looking closely at the widow of Sir Alexander Cunninghame - the woman who should have been Countess of Glencairn – John could see the resemblance: the arrogant tilt of the brows, the tight line of the lips. She forged a determined path towards the kirk, her majestic figure defiant in adversity with skirts and hood billowing behind like the sails of a mighty ship. The younger lady at her side walked in a daze, face pale and drawn from weeping, dark eyes haunted with sadness.

John shifted, uncomfortably. *You have the gift of being able to reason with the unreasonable,* King James had told him. *It would serve me well if you used that gift to keep the peace between the Montgomeries and the Cunninghames. It would serve Lord Hugh well, too; if he continues on this present course unchecked, then sooner or later he'll stretch the law so far that not even I'll be able to protect him.*

Turning his bonnet over in his hands, John sighed, deeply. He'd failed the King. He'd failed Rob Cunninghame and he'd failed the poor woman Rob was married to. He supposed he'd failed Hugh, too, for like the rest of them, Hugh was at the mercy of his nature.

Was there anything else he could have done to alter Fate's course? Perhaps if he'd intervened, then Hugh would have listened. Perhaps if he'd stayed by Hugh's side instead of pretending it was none of his business...

He doubted it. To curb Hugh's instincts that night would have been like trying to tether a whirlwind.

Once the requiem mass was over, they loitered in the kirkyard.

"I should go," John whispered to Malcolm. "I won't be welcome at the feast." He broke off, glimpsing an unfamiliar figure amongst the crowd. A man of medium height, with a presence that set him apart from the rest. In his late thirties or thereabouts, he was graced with the strong shoulders and solid build of a knight. Clean-shaven, his brown hair lightly touched with grey, he carried himself with a courtier's swagger, sword swinging at his side. His doublet was embroidered with gold thread, his bonnet – which sported a dazzling jewelled pin – set at a careless angle, while his gown was adorned with a rich spotted fur trim.

At his side strode a lady. She was his senior by ten years or so, small and neat with a bright intimidating gaze.

They paused to talk with Lady Margaret Hepburn.

John nudged Malcolm. "Who's that?"

"Bell the Cat," Malcolm replied, in a hushed tone.

Gooseflesh stole up John's back. Archibald 'Bell the Cat' Douglas, Fifth Earl of Angus. An enigmatic man, he'd first risen to prominence years before, when he'd led an uprising against King James the Third. Despite his dubious past, he'd stayed loyal to James until the debacle at Blackness, when days before his death, the old King had reneged on a treaty made with his son.

"What's he doing here?" John asked.

"Married to a Boyd. The aunt of the lad your friend Montgomerie slaughtered six years ago."

"Ah..." John watched the Countess of Angus reach out and embrace the weeping widow, drawing her close, patting her back gently.

He wished he could have heard what was being said.

A hand roughly pushed him. "You!" Cuthbert Cunninghame confronted him, face flushed with fury. "How dare you show your face here!"

"I came to honour his life and mourn his passing," John retorted. "I see no disrespect in that."

Cuthbert seized John's gown and hauled him close. "You sealed my father's fate when you brought that beast into your house and nursed him back to health."

John scowled back, unbowed. "You had him at your mercy. You let him live."

The young man's grip loosened. "How did-"

"He told me." John tugged himself free and straightened his gown. "Don't let anger cloud your reason, my lord. I did what was right. So did you. There's not one man who can be singled out for blame. Not even Lord Hugh."

"Damn you," Cuthbert muttered.

"Now then," a friendly voice interjected. "Why all this ill-feeling?"

It was Angus. He laid a hand on Cuthbert's shoulder, and smiled at them both, concerned, interested.

"I was about to take my leave," John said. "The Lord Kilmaurs has heard me out."

"And you are?" Angus asked.

"Sempill of Ellestoun." Cuthbert spoke through gritted teeth.

"Ah, Sir John," Angus continued in that same pleasant voice. He extended his hand. "I'm delighted to meet you."

John reluctantly accepted it. "It's an honour, Your Grace."

"You've enjoyed a remarkable change of fortunes just recently," Angus said. "We all thought you'd be strung up as a traitor. Made friends in high places, I suppose?"

"I've been fortunate."

"Indeed you have," Angus replied. "Let's hope this rash of good fortune continues, eh?" he said, and turned away.

The Gryphon at Bay

*　　　*　　　*

The Place of Kilmaurs

"It's a great privilege to have you here," Lady Margaret Hepburn said.

"It's the least we could do," Angus replied. "In these unfortunate circumstances." He lifted his goblet and nodded to a nearby servant, who stepped forward and refilled it.

Setting down his drink, Angus tore himself a portion of bread and cast a subtle glance towards Cuthbert. The fledgling Lord Kilmaurs seemed an earnest young man, hot-headed, not much disposed to common sense. Angus had met men of his ilk so many times before; bold youths who'd earned themselves a fearsome reputation by the time they reached their perfect age.

Or a space in the kirkyard.

In his younger days Montgomerie had been just like that, quick to anger, all too eager to start a fight. In his case, age was doing nothing to curb his excesses. Sooner or later, most men of that temperament met a violent end. But somehow Montgomerie escaped that fate. Whatever the circumstances, however much the odds were against him, he slipped through unscathed. Small wonder, then, that superstitious men swore he enjoyed Satan's protection.

Angus wondered what had really happened, the night Rob Cunninghame died. The Montgomeries would say one thing, the Cunninghames something entirely different. Cuthbert Cunninghame didn't look like the kind of boy who'd shirk a fight, and Hugh Montgomerie's reputation spoke for itself.

Angus caught Cuthbert's eye. "You're lucky you escaped so lightly."

"He wanted to kill me," Cuthbert said.

"That doesn't bode well for the future."

"I won't run from him," Cuthbert muttered. "I won't give in."

"An admirable show of courage," Angus replied. "But it's not a question of giving in. You're still young, my lord. I daresay your father still had much to teach you. It's unfortunate your education was unfinished."

"No matter. I must struggle on regardless, I suppose."

"Now that's not necessarily true."

Elizabeth glanced up, suddenly interested. "His Grace the Earl is right," she said. "You should seek out a lord of good standing, and pledge yourself into his service. For a year, at least. That would allow this ill-feeling with Montgomerie to fade. And give you an opportunity to hone your skills."

"These are wise words, Countess Elizabeth," Cuthbert replied. "But I'm needed here. I can't abandon my mother at her time of grief."

Lady Christian studied her trencher. "A mother shouldn't cling to her son, whatever the circumstances. It would comfort me more to know he was safe, and far from Montgomerie's reach."

Elizabeth reached for her hand. "I can understand that. We'll discuss it further, once the funeral's behind you." She caught Angus' eye. "My husband will advise you. That is, if you'd be willing to hear his counsel."

Cuthbert Cunninghame smiled, every inch the accomplished statesman. "Of course we'd be grateful," he said. "And we greatly appreciate this offer of support."

Chapter 48

The Castle of Whiteinch, Renfrew

They stepped into a vaulted hall packed with guests, all richly garbed, bedecked with jewels. Heads turned, curious faces peered in their direction.

Pride was a sin, but as John walked through that room with Margaret's hand resting lightly on his arm, he was the proudest man alive. If she was anxious, it didn't show; she smiled sweetly and dipped her head in gracious acknowledgement at everyone who greeted her.

Soon they were besieged with well-wishers. Burgesses and guildsmen mostly, they congratulated him on how the siege at Duchal had progressed and asked if there'd been any news from Edinburgh on the King's situation.

He answered as best he could, wondering when he'd be invited to express his views on the situation in Cunninghame.

But no one even mentioned the death of Kilmaurs.

Talk turned to the inevitable subject of trade levies and taxes. He knew Margaret was struggling to stay attentive; eventually he caught her fighting the urge to yawn.

"If you'll excuse us," he said, bestowing a particularly gracious smile upon his audience, "we'd best attend our host."

"I could tell you were flagging." He steered her through the crowd to the other side of the hall. "If it's any consolation, hearing old men discuss the prices of wool and ox-hides makes me want to weep, too." He scanned the faces. "There's someone I'd like you to meet. A kinsman, and a very worthy knight." Hearing a deep throaty laugh echoing across the room, he changed course. "The very man," he said. "Sir John Ross of Hawkhead. You'll like him. He's a kindly soul. Very generous, too. In fact..." He paused. "I thought I'd ask him if he'd care to be godfather to our child."

Margaret made no attempt to conceal her surprise. "I thought you'd ask Hugh."

John laughed. "Hugh's conduct is hardly a good example for a child to follow."

She smiled. "I suppose you're right."

"There he is." John spotted his kinsman at last, a grizzled old knight aged fifty years or more. He was a massive big bear of a man, with broad shoulders and a tousled beard. Despite his advancing years, he was gifted with robust health and vigour. Though these days, it seemed his paunch was beginning to get the better of him...

Ross nodded as John approached. "Good evening, Sir John," he said. "It's a pleasure to see you. And with such a lovely companion, too." He beamed at Margaret.

"This is my wife, Margaret Colville." John presented her before him. "Margaret, my kinsman, Sir John Ross of Hawkhead."

"I'm delighted." Sir John Ross seized her hand in a crushing grip.

Margaret smiled and curtsied. "It's a pleasure, Sir John."

"Margaret's finding it tedious."

Sir John Ross erupted into laughter. "Aren't we all?"

"-I'm sure she'd find a lady's conversation much more appealing..."

"Then we'll find suitable companions, without delay." Ross offered his arm to Margaret. "If you'd care to step this way..." He steered them both towards a group of ladies who had congregated near the fireplace, followed a convoluted course which skirted the gathering. "You'll forgive me, I hope, if I remove your husband for a little while," he said to Margaret. "But I must speak with him in confidence." Casting a wary glance in John's direction, he leaned close. "Certain matters have arisen," he said in a low voice. "Regarding our mutual kinsman, who currently resides abroad."

John said nothing, but his nape prickled with anticipation.

Montgrennan. It had to be Montgrennan.

Though whether his kinsman's tidings would prove good or ill remained to be seen.

She'd never set foot in a Royal castle before: its carved stone corbels and vaulted ceiling reminded her of an abbey church. Everything was lavishly decorated, the stonework brightly painted. The plastered walls sported a dense array of flowers and leaves, liberally scattered with rearing red lions and silver unicorns.

She hadn't thought she'd find herself attending an occasion of such importance. It was quite by accident, too. John had sent word that the town-house in Renfrew should be made ready; taking these instructions to heart, she'd set off for Renfrew the following day with half-a-dozen servants in attendance.

She'd been anxious that John would scold her for showing such ingenuity. Instead, her gesture overwhelmed him. When he'd finally arrived back in Renfrew late the previous night, he'd confessed that the last thing he expected was to be granted all the comforts of home.

Now she was rewarded, taking her place at his side in a world which was still very new to her.

But the novelty was waning rapidly, and she found herself wondering why she'd ever craved it in the first place. She nodded wearily as another woman was presented before her, richly dressed and glittering with gold rings and jewelled brooches.

"-This is Bessie Ralston. Wife to Master William Ross, who leads the Webster's Guild-"

Mistress Ralston curtsied stiffly. "It's a pleasure, Lady Margaret."

The names. The faces. Floating into one another, an endless procession of Margarets, Marys and Catherines, with the occasional Agnes and Elizabeth thrown in for good measure. She hoped to God she'd remember which was which, and who was talking to her...

"His Grace Sir Archibald Campbell!" The steward called from across the hall. "Master of Argyll and Lord of Lorn."

Her heart lurched, she felt a sudden pang of unease. She'd heard the name before: Hugh's gude-brother, heir to the mighty Campbell earldom.

"-And this is Margarita Whiteford, wife to Master John Mossman, whose father sits upon the council-"

Suddenly anxious, she glanced about her, looking for John, but there was no sign of him. "Excuse me, please," she said with an apologetic smile. "I must find my husband."

Margaret heard Sir John Ross before she saw him, his laughter ringing out tantalisingly close. Guessing John would be with him, she changed her route, following the echo of his voice.

She found her path blocked. "Oh!" she said.

"Well, what's this?" The man who confronted her reminded her of Hugh, in the way he carried himself, full of confident authority. He was of a similar age, too, tall and elegant, with dark red-brown hair. The skin of his face was tanned and weather-beaten, his cheeks ruddy. Pearls glinted on his doublet, and he carried a sword. "For a lady like yourself, so fair of face -and so young, too - to be wandering alone..."

She drew herself tall, affronted. "I seek my husband, sir."

He grinned. "And who might that be?" He spoke like Lady Helen, with a faint northern lilt.

"Sir John Sempill of Ellestoun."

"Ah." He bowed low and seized her hand, pressing it to his lips. "The erstwhile Maid of Ochiltree. I've heard much about you."

"The Master of Argyll, I presume?"

He feigned surprise. "My reputation goes before me."

"Yes, sir. It does." She returned his gaze, unabashed.

"And how, might I ask, does such a delicate young woman know so much about my business?"

"I know your gude-brother, the Lord Montgomerie. And your sister, Lady Helen."

Campbell smiled, sagely. "You'll have spoken to them, I'm sure."

Margaret sniffed. "My husband may not be ennobled, but that doesn't mean he can't count nobility amongst his friends."

"And how is dear Hugo, since you count him as a friend?" His tone was guarded.

"Very well, sir. Or he was last time I saw him."

"And when was that?"

"Not more than a fortnight ago."

"I see."

"You think I'm lying."

He feigned injury. "I never said that."

"Margaret, I'm sorry." John appeared at her shoulder, slicing through the crowd like a hawk after a lure. "We were engrossed in other matters." He nodded to the Master of Argyll. "Lord Archibald."

Campbell smiled. "I was just getting acquainted with your wife."

"So I see." John's tone was cold.

For once, her restrained indifferent husband was jealous. Margaret wasn't sure whether to be anxious, or flattered. "The Master of Argyll was asking after Lord Hugh," she explained to John.

"He's well enough," John said. "We've not long returned from Eglintoun." He caught Margaret's eye, subtle warning. "We're expecting Lord Hugh to join us at

Ellestoun any day now. Once the bombards are on their way, we'll be pressing home to meet him."

Archibald Campbell smiled. "Then you must tell Hugh that I was asking for him. And that I sincerely hope he's been keeping out of mischief." He took a thoughtful sip of wine. "It's a curious thing," he remarked. "That you should get on so well with Hugo. He's not exactly well-loved at court. Why, he's scarcely even liked!"

"A man's choice in friends should be his own business."

"Perhaps. But you'd be wise to watch your step, Sir John. There's men praying for the day when Hugh falls from grace. While others work hard to ensure that day dawns sooner rather than later..." The faint smile played on his lips once more. "Rumour has it that your uncle Montgrennan has been pardoned. That his lands have already been restored. If that's the case, then Hugh's situation need never concern you."

John didn't reply.

Campbell caught his eye, suddenly serious. "I don't envy you, Sir John," he said. "In terms of patronage, you seem to be caught between a rock and a hard place."

Chapter 49

The Place of Whiteford

As he followed the Laird of Whiteford to his chamber, Sir William Cunninghame of Craigends breathed deep, catching the scent of dampness. The air in the hall had been wholesome enough, but beyond its warmth the building reeked of age and disrepair. The winding stone steps were worn and uneven, the walls of the stair tower sodden and crumbling.

The door creaked open ahead. "Come this way, Sir William," Whiteford invited.

Craigends followed him inside without a word. The laird's chamber was small, the painted plaster on the walls flaked and faded. John Whiteford of that ilk was one of the lesser lairds in Renfrew, clinging to an honourable past and struggling to maintain his presence in a land where success in politics or commerce meant as much as ancient accolades.

Whiteford heaved himself into his chair with a sigh. "How can I help you, Sir William?"

Craigends paused by the fireplace, grateful for the warmth. "It's a hard subject to broach, but a necessary one. No doubt you've heard what happened to my kinsman, the Lord Kilmaurs."

Whiteford gestured to an empty chair. "I've heard nothing."

"Slain by Montgomerie. Just a few weeks back." Craigends settled comfortably down.

Whiteford stared. He said nothing for a few long painful moments, absorbing the news. He was an amiable man, not much older than Craigends. His brown hair was faded and thinning, he had the stooped posture of a man who suffered the winter chills more than most. His shabby doublet of brown velvet had been darned a dozen times, the black gown about his shoulders was thread-bare and moth-eaten. A cautious man in all respects, he'd wisely stayed away from the conflict last year and had been keeping his head down ever since.

"I'm very sorry to hear this," he said at last. "In what circumstances, if you don't mind my asking?"

"A gentleman's tryst," Craigends said. "Where one of the parties broke faith."

"Oh, dear..."

"No doubt you've been summoned by the King?"

"Not yet. Though I'm reliably informed that Sir John Sempill is in these parts. He left Renfrew yesterday and is lodging with his kinsman Sir John Ross at Hawkhead."

"If he approaches you, what will you tell him? Will you ride out in the King's name?"

"I thought I would, yes."

"Sir John Sempill's a personable young man. But he's just a stripling, and prone to false counsel. He's a lackey of Lord Hugh's. To support him is to ride to war behind the banner of a murderer."

Whiteford grimaced faintly, avoiding his gaze. "I understand why you're taking this stance, Sir William, but I don't think Sir John can be blamed for Lord Hugh's shortcomings."

Craigends spread his hands wide. "I never said he should. But I think the King should learn the extent of our displeasure. Unless you want the King's law enforced by men like Montgomerie, who care nothing for justice and honour?"

Whiteford licked his lips. He was wavering, as Craigends hoped he would. "It could be said that your best way of winning the King's favour is to fight in his name. To prove yourself loyal."

"We'll take nothing to do with him. Not until he puts wrongs to rights."

Whiteford was silent.

"There." Craigends sat up tall, and slapped his palms against his knees. "I won't keep you any longer. But I thought you should know why we've decided not to obey our king's summons. It pains me to turn my back on His Grace, but I think in such circumstances, our decision is justified." He leaned closer. "It would mean so much more if we could win the support of others. I'm not pressing for armed rebellion. Far from it. I just want His Grace to know that the men of the Westland won't tolerate tyranny or oppression. What better way is there of expressing our displeasure, than to let our Sheriff's summons go unheeded?"

*   *   *

The Place of Stanely

"It's been a good harvest, for sure." Maxwell of Stanely poured out a measure of wine. "A peaceful winter, that's all anyone can ask for, eh?"

"Amen to that," John replied. It was the third place he'd visited that day: another laird's chamber, in another tower-house. Another local dignitary he could score off his list...

"Now then." Stanely made a pompous show of settling himself into his chair. He was a Maxwell: his family, though not well-represented in Renfrew, was powerful nonetheless. "I presume this isn't a social call?"

"The host will be mustered. At the end of the month."

Stanely smiled slightly. "Terse and direct, Sir John. Much like your father."

John leaned forward slightly, fixing Stanely with his gaze. "I assume His Grace the King will be granted your support?"

Stanely didn't quite meet his eye. "Forgive my discourtesy, but... I don't plan to attend."

"The King grants you land in good faith." John's tone hardened. "It is your duty to attend."

"When word of the King's summons first reached me, I fully intended to. But certain matters have arisen..."

"What matters?" John snapped back.

"To be blunt... I've heard talk of how the King's representative in the Westland overstepped his bounds." Stanely caught John's gaze at last, unapologetic, defiant. "Tell me, Sir John. Why should I support His Grace, when the men who impose justice on his behalf are no better than brigands?"

"I hope you don't count me amongst the brigands."

Stanely laughed, too loudly. "Of course not! But you, of all men, should know how poorly justice was dispensed in these parts. Before your good self resumed the Sheriff's office, of course..."

"There were problems, yes. But these never swayed my loyalty to the King."

"No," Stanely said. "They didn't." He smiled sagely into his goblet.

"Are you suggesting that I compromised my principles?"

"I'm sure that whatever you did was done with the best of intentions. And no doubt your judgement was based on what circumstances dictated at the time. But you must let other men act in a manner compatible with their own conscience. Many of us cannot and will not condone Montgomerie's slaughter of Kilmaurs. We wish to make our displeasure known to His Grace the King but we don't want to launch open rebellion. What better way is there than this?"

John didn't answer.

"If you want my own personal opinion, Sir John, then it's this. I hope John Stewart gives King James a bloody nose. The lad must realise that he can't pass through life without making some atonement for his father's death."

"Might I ask your source?" John asked, carefully.

"Regarding what?"

"Regarding the death of Kilmaurs."

Stanely shrugged. "I can't rightly remember."

"And do you speak for your kinsmen at Newark?"

"I can't say." The condescension was barely masked in Stanely's voice.

John fought the urge to scowl. It was an excuse, nothing more than that. An excuse for a man to sit safe in his tower-house all winter, sleeping in a warm bed at night, stuffing his guts with venison and wildfowl. While the rest of them – what precious few there were – camped out in the cold, braving the storms and the winter fevers just so they could do their duty to the King.

"I'm most terribly sorry, Sir John." At least Stanely made an effort to look sympathetic. "But what other way is there to respond given the circumstances? And might I remind you that just last year, you were yourself advocating a similar course when you suffered your own misfortunes at the hands of the King's men?"

*　　　*　　　*

The Abbey of Kilwinning

For two whole weeks Hugh had survived on precious little food, and even less sleep. He'd been bled again that day; right now he wasn't even sure he had the strength to stand unaided.

He was on his knees again, a rope halter hanging loosely round his neck as a symbol of his penitence. But despite all his efforts, he'd failed to find enlightenment. That afternoon he'd scourged himself, beating his flesh again and again while he wept and begged for salvation.

It was now past midnight, and even indoors the air was frigid. The rood screen loomed ahead, arrayed with glittering ranks of brightly-painted, gilded statues. Saints and apostles, with Christ Himself at the very pinnacle and the Virgin close at hand. Their features shifted in the dancing candlelight, making it seem as if they were alive.

He stared, entranced. The pain and despair faded, he felt strangely euphoric as the voices of the monks swelled around him, wandering trails of melody that combined to form a wondrous satisfying whole. He marvelled at the beauty of their song, at the sweet overwhelming waft of the incense.

All around him, candles shone like stars, the high vaulted roof sparkling as if the firmament had been recreated here on earth.

He swallowed, gripped with a sense of absolute insignificance. In God's plan he was no better than an ant. A fleeting worthless creature, beyond redemption. His vision blurred, he blinked then stared, amazed, for it seemed as if the statue of the Virgin on the rood changed before his eyes. Her features softened, gilded robes and painted face transforming into textile and flesh. She seemed to shrug Herself free, drifting down to stand amongst the oblivious monks.

He couldn't speak. Gripped by fear and devotion, he looked on in wonder as she approached, immeasurably tall. Her eyes gleamed like lapis, and he squirmed inside, for it felt as if She stared deep into the furthest corners of his soul, casting light upon the darkness, exposing every sordid action and questionable deed.

Forgive me, Holy Mary, for I have sinned. I have stolen men's lives. I've left widows and children weeping in the ruins of their homes. I've slain the meek, the innocent...

Stretching out Her arms, She enclosed his clasped hands in Her own. She glowed as if lit from within, as She held him, his flesh prickled and his heart beat faster. She didn't speak: he heard only the sinuous melody of the song as the monks raised their voices loud in a glorious cry of exultation. But from the smile on Her lips and the tears in Her eyes, he knew She understood.

I'm sorry. So sorry. For Rob. For all of them...

His sight blurred, the golden light that bathed him was gone.

She'd vanished.

He ached with despair, feeling a profound sense of loss, tempered with joy and relief because She'd seen fit to acknowledge him, to forgive him.

Throwing himself down on the place where She'd stood, he wept so hard he could scarcely breathe. His ribs ached, his head ached, too. Voices called his name and when he looked up he saw figures looming over him. He tried to tell the monks what he'd seen, but all he could do was stutter and babble.

Hands gripped his shoulders and helped him to his feet, but his strength was fading. The world swayed and shifted, and he swooned.

The Place of Ellestoun

Margaret buried her head deeper into the pillow, trying to blot out the sound of John shouting from the laird's chamber. Weathering his wrath was one of the Crawfurd boys: not Robert, but a younger brother. The lad had arrived before noon, bringing a message from his kinsmen.

Closing her eyes, Margaret willed the argument to stop. She'd retreated to her bed after dinner, nursing a niggling ache in the small of her back.

The long journey home from Renfrew had marked a turning point, the impending birth no longer beyond concern. The babe was growing, weighing her down; she'd toss and turn at night, trying to get comfortable. She hadn't felt the child stir yet: she wasn't sure if that was a good thing, or not.

A door slammed below, the conversation resuming on the stair. At least now John's tone was amicable. Whatever the subject of their disagreement, both men were still on speaking terms.

Their voices receded.

She rolled onto her back and lay still. She couldn't bear to think of John sitting alone in his chamber, nursing his worries. Heaving herself to her feet, she trudged her weary way downstairs.

John stood by the open window, staring out across the countryside.

"You were shouting," she said.

He tried to smile. "I'm sorry. I didn't mean to disturb you. Were you sleeping?"

"Just resting." She could tell he was doing his best to put on a cheerful face. She wondered how long it would be before the facade cracked, whether it was best to skirt the issue, or confront it head-on... "What's wrong?"

John bowed his head. "I hope Andrew makes it home before nightfall."

"Didn't you offer him a bed?"

"He declined."

"No wonder."

He turned away, frowning. "It's the strangest thing," he said. "The more time passes, the more I wonder if someone is deliberately trying to thwart me."

"To turn men's thoughts against their Sheriff? Who'd do such a thing?"

"My Coroner. The Laird of Craigends."

"Isn't that treason?"

He didn't answer.

Margaret swallowed, suddenly nervous. She sensed the change in him, the tightness in his jaw, the way he held himself, stiffly formal. "It's hardly your fault."

"I demanded his appointment."

"Don't scourge yourself over it," Margaret implored him. "You've done your best, in difficult circumstances." She headed for a nearby kist and poured him some wine. "That's all you could do, isn't it?" She pressed the cup into his hand.

He took a deep draught. "The barons all talk of Hugh. About how he killed Kilmaurs, how he isn't fit for office." Gulping down his wine, he roughly set the empty cup down. "They won't support the King, because it means supporting Hugh. When Hugh's conduct isn't even an issue!"

Margaret swallowed, unsure how to respond.

"The Crawfurds agreed to send men," John continued. "But now they've halved the size of their force. Robert won't even ride out with me because Hugh will be resting here on his way to Glasgow."

Her back twinged anew, she stifled a wince. Wandering over to the bed, she sat down there.

"The discontent's spreading," John continued. "Some even had the gall to voice their support for Lennox. 'Hope he gives the King a bloody nose,' one said..."

"Perhaps he didn't mean what he said."

John retreated to the fireplace. Leaning a hand against the lintel, he stared into the flames below. "Last year I suffered, because I stayed loyal to my King. But he's cold in his tomb now. It's time to move on. I *have* moved on. Now I'm beleaguered, because I've pledged my loyalty to the man who took his place." He grasped the poker, roughly jabbing the burning logs. Sparks glowed briefly, the wood crackled and spat. "Lennox is a rebel. He says he wants justice, but it's a lie. He's fighting for himself. He called me a traitor. He said I should hang. Now he takes up the cause that I paid for dearly so he can satisfy his own greed."

Leaning her cheek against the bedpost, Margaret studied him. She'd longed for this day, for the moment when at last he'd find it in himself to confide in her. But now the moment had come, she didn't know how to respond. "I'm sorry," she whispered.

He set the poker down and hurried to her side. Perching on the bed beside her, he took her hands, smiling in that melancholy way of his. "No. I'm the one who should be sorry. I shouldn't burden you with my troubles. You've got enough to concern you."

"I *want* to know what's happening. I just wish I could do something to help."

He stared ahead. For a moment she wasn't even sure he'd heard her. Then he turned to her, with such a desolate look on his face that she quailed inside.

"I detest war," he said. "One moment you're civilised, mindful of your duties to God and your fellow man. The next you're no better than a beast, lashing out at anything in your way. Moving forward, always forward, because once the line breaks and you're running, it's only a matter of time before they slay you..."

"John..."

"I don't want to go. My place is here. With you."

She brushed his hair back from his face. His shoulders were slumped, his eyes bright with tears. Her heart pounded, she was overwhelmed with terror. But somehow she found the strength to hide her fear. Putting her arms about him, she pulled him close, burying her face in his hair and stroking his shoulders while he clung to her. "Keep a brave heart, my love," she whispered. "We'll all pray for you. And before you know it, you'll be home again, and we'll be together."

Chapter 50

The Place of Eglintoun

It was a subdued homecoming: just half-a-dozen men riding into Eglintoun with Hugh and Zephyr at the fore.

Hessilhead reined in his horse. "Look at him!" he complained, gesturing in Hugh's direction. "He's wasted away. There's nothing to him."

Looking at Hugh now, Helen could see why Hessilhead was so concerned. Her heart skidded when she realised how pale he was, face drawn, eyes hollow.

But he grinned when he saw her, and that banished her fears completely.

"Wait there," Hessilhead said. "I'll help you down."

Hugh dismounted without hesitation. "I'm not made of glass." Seizing Helen close, he kissed her lips. "They think I'm about to expire," he told her. "But after seeing you, my strength is restored."

"Though not the colour in your cheeks, I fear. Are you quite well?"

"Never been better." Releasing her, he set off for the tower-house with a spring in his stride.

"His brains are addled." Hessilhead shook his head. "Next thing we know, he'll be taking the tonsure."

"Not if I can help it." Quickening her pace, Helen set off in pursuit.

Pausing ahead, Hugh offered his arm. "You should be proud of me," he said. "I have atoned for my sins, and my conscience is clear. I am forgiven. And what's more, I *know* I am forgiven."

"You must tell me everything."

"Oh, I will." He glowered at Hessilhead. "But not while I'm in the company of fools and rogues." Turning to Helen, his glance was beseeching. "I'm famished. I could eat a whole hog, and still have room for more. Perhaps you could rally the cooks..."

She leaned close and kissed his cheek. "Whatever you command, my love."

"Meat." Hugh thrust his spoon deep into the venison pie. "Joy of joys. Bliss beyond measure."

His hounds, *Molach* and *Grad,* flanked his chair, tails waving, mouths moist with drool. They stared at him with sad brown eyes, but for once Hugh was impervious.

"You're very thin," Helen said.

He looked up, face lit with weary relief. "My belt goes in two more notches."

"You were hardly fat before."

Hugh shrugged. He lost interest in the pie, gulped down some ale then turned his attention to the roast haunch of lamb that waited nearby. He tore a few strips loose with his fingers, then, casting a furtive look about him, picked up the joint in both hands and savaged it with his teeth.

Molach whined, pitifully.

"That's disgusting," Helen said. "I see your sojourn in the abbey taught you nothing."

"Aren't you relieved-" Hugh retorted through a mouthful of food, "-that I decided to break my fast here."

"I'm just sad that I'm forced to witness this debauchery."

"At least I appreciate God's bounty, instead of taking it entirely for granted. Which reminds me... I've promised lands to Abbot William. I'll leave instructions on what's required. You can summon the notary and make sure everything's in order. But don't let them talk you into signing away more than I've agreed to. You know what they're like, these churchmen. They'd take the sark off a man's back if they could..."

Hugh sprawled out across the bed with a groan. "My God, Helen, it's good to be home."

Helen combed out her hair, saying nothing. It pained her to think that tomorrow he'd be riding north with his men. When he didn't look like he had enough strength to wield his sword or wear his armour for hours on end.

Setting comb aside, she settled alongside and took him in her arms. "Rest now. So you're in good fettle for the morning."

He pressed close, eager for her touch, and she responded, running her hands gently over him. Hugh revelled in the attention, pushing against her like a cat. "I'm very tired," he conceded at last.

"Then sleep, my love. You need your rest."

"I don't regret it. Not for a moment," Hugh said. "It was the right thing to do."

"I'm sure you're right."

"I know I am." He paused, eyes shining. "I saw *Her.*"

"Her?"

"The Holy Virgin. She came to me. She forgave me."

"How incredible."

"It was a miracle." Hugh lazed back in her arms, smiling softly. "I swear to God, Helen, that I saw Her. Clear as I can see you here with me now."

He was so earnest, so vehement, that Helen didn't doubt his words. Hugh wasn't inclined to flights of fancy: whatever he'd witnessed had stirred him profoundly.

She stroked his chest, wincing when she felt his ribs jutting proud beneath his flesh. "You'll make sure you keep well fed?"

He burrowed deep into her embrace. "Don't worry," he said. "I'll be at Ellestoun tomorrow. Young Margaret'll take one look at me and heap my platter high."

"And once Ellestoun's behind you? What then?"

"I'm resourceful. I won't starve for want of victuals."

*   *   *

The Place of Ellestoun

Rain was blowing in from the west, dark clouds gathering. Taking a deep breath to brace herself, Margaret picked up her skirts and darted across the yard to the range.

She'd scarcely spoken with John since they broke their fast that morning. He was around somewhere: she'd spotted his white dogs sniffing around the barmkin not long before. She doubted she'd see him before they dined, for he still had much to do. There were weapons and armour to check one last time, a final batch of horses to recover from the farrier.

Over the last few days he'd been his usual self, cheerful and efficient. There'd been no sign of the desolation she'd witnessed at first hand, but no doubt the melancholy was there, hidden deep.

She was hardly overwhelmed with joy herself, but like John she had much to occupy her. They'd be feeding a hundred men or more that afternoon: the cooks had to be instructed, the hall made ready.

Margaret slipped through the heavy wooden door into the hall. A fire roared in the fireplace, the tables laid out ready. The floor was freshly spread with rushes, the girls just putting the final touches to the crisp white boardcloth that covered the top table.

Margaret nodded, satisfied. "That's very good."

"Why make such an effort?" Katherine complained. "They're only men. They wouldn't notice if you fed them off the floor."

"Our guest is a lord. Whatever the circumstances, he should be given the very best of hospitality."

"You wouldn't be so attentive if it wasn't Lord Hugh," Mariota giggled.

Her cheeks burned hot with indignation. "What a ridiculous thing to say!" she retorted. "If you want to be useful, go to the kitchens and tell the steward to make sure the wine's poured. Alison, go with her."

The two girls left without a word.

"Was that necessary?" Katherine asked.

"That's enough!" Margaret glowered at the board. "Look at this cup. It's filthy! Take it to the kitchens and tell them to do something. I'll check the rest."

Katherine shrugged and left.

The cloth draped over John's chair was awry; Margaret set it carefully back in place. She hadn't meant to talk so brusquely. But with Hugh's arrival imminent, she was nervous, on edge.

These days, she preferred not to concern herself with Hugh. It embarrassed her, to think how she'd grown close to him when he'd been in her care. John had warned her not to pity him, but despite his words of caution she'd been deceived by Hugh's weakness. In retrospect, she could see that even at his most vulnerable he'd been dangerous.

She could still recall the night of Kilmaurs' death, the look on Hugh's face. After witnessing that, she didn't think she'd ever be able to look him in the eye again.

But she'd have to. He was coming here, to Ellestoun. Before long she'd have to greet him with warmth and affection, because he was John's friend, and a welcome guest beneath her roof.

Margaret sank down on the chair arm with a sigh. She wished the evening were over, because then at least Hugh would be gone. But when Hugh rode away, John would leave with him, riding off to battle at his king's command. The worst might happen. She might never see him again.

Pulling out her handkerchief, she sobbed silently into its folds. It was the only show of grief she'd permit herself: she wanted everyone to think she was in full command of her situation, not a frightened young woman who feared for the future.

The Gryphon at Bay

But here in the hall where she was granted the luxury of privacy, she gave in to her despair, if only for a little while.

Chapter 51

The light was fading as they drew near their destination, Ellestoun's harled walls just visible in the twilight gloom. The horses' heads were turned against the wind, their coats sodden.

With the end at last in sight, Hugh gave the crisp order to trot: the three-score men at his command spurred their mounts onwards, eager to find a warm dry place for the night.

He raised his hand as they entered the yard, curbing the pace in readiness. The cobbles were sleek with water, Zephyr snorted and twitched as a back leg skidded. Wind howled round the outbuildings, banging the shutters on the tower-house.

Robert Montgomerie caught his eye and grinned. "Thank the Saints that's behind us."

Hugh regarded the heavy rain-clouds one last time. "Don't get complacent," he told his brother. "There's much worse to come." He lowered himself down with a sigh. "God help me. I'm sick of this campaign already-" He broke off as Zephyr shook from head to hoof, showering him with ice-cold droplets. "Damned horse," he muttered half-heartedly. But he could sympathise. Like Zephyr, he was soaked to the skin and very cold. Though the prospect of a warm fire and a hearty meal did much to lift his mood.

The door of the tower-house opened, and there was young Margaret Colville. She'd donned a warm cloak and hood to keep off the worst of the rain, but even so he could see the change in her, the swelling of the unborn child in her belly.

She ventured cautiously out to meet him. "Hello, Hugh."

"Lady Margaret." He took her hands and kissed her on both cheeks. "It's such a relief to be here."

Margaret nodded. "It must be." She fell silent a moment. "Are you keeping well?"

"Helen said this morning that I looked no better than a corpse. Which was very charitable of her, I must say."

Margaret glanced aside, biting her lip. "Hugh..."

"I did what was required to cleanse my soul. It was an arduous affair, and it took its toll. But now all's well, I'm pleased to say."

For the first time she looked up, meeting his gaze. "I'd sooner not kill a man."

"Wise words, Margaret." He pulled a leather satchel from beneath his cloak. "Helen asked me to give you this. She's packed two pounds of salt and a small bag of peppercorns. Along with some of the choicest spices from the east: a clove of nutmeg, some cinnamon and mace. And there's two barrels of herrings amongst my baggage. Irvine's finest, freshly salted. That'll eke things out through the winter."

She received the bag with a smile. "You're very kind."

The Sempills' old groom stepped forward. "Your horse, my lord. I've been asked to see it stabled with the master's."

"Of course." He relinquished the reins. "Where's John?"

"In the armoury," said Margaret.

"I'd best join him."

"You don't have to. The guest range is ready, if you want to settle your men. I'll take you there, if you like."

"Hear that?" Hugh said to Robert. "See to it, will you?"

"What about the horses?" his brother asked.

Margaret shifted from one foot to the other, agitated. "There are so many of them!" she complained. "How many in all?"

"Sixty-five," said Robert. "Plus twelve sumpter horses."

She looked at Hugh, panic-stricken.

"Don't you worry about them," Hugh said. "John and I will deal with it. Just go indoors and keep warm."

John glanced around the armoury one last time. The place looked forlorn and empty: the only things left in a room that had once bristled with weaponry were a dozen crossbows, half a dozen bills and another half-dozen swords. "It's not much," he told young John Alexson, "but it should be adequate."

The Alexson boy nodded. Just thirteen years old, he was slightly built and no match for a full-grown man. But his wits were quick, and he was an honest, dependable lad.

"Make sure everything's kept in order," John continued. "Master Colville won't want to concern himself with minor matters. And mind the horses are well looked after. Henry loves them like children but his wits aren't what they were."

"Ach, don't you worry about that," the boy said.

"I hope you don't think me cruel," John told him. "Putting so much responsibility on your shoulders."

John Alexson grinned. "I'm honoured, Sir John."

"There's one more thing," John said. "Lady Margaret may need a midwife."

The boy regarded him carefully, eyes bright as a bird's. "Ma will take good care of her."

"I'm sure she will. And I want you to take good care of your mother. God knows, she's a woman of courage, but... She lost your father a year ago. I don't want her suffering such heartache again." He looked about the room one last time, hoping he'd forgotten nothing. "That's everything, I think. I'd best find Lord Hugh-" He paused, spotting movement beyond the door. "Talk of the Devil..."

"Christ! What a foul night!" Hugh bludgeoned his way inside, leaving a trail of sodden footprints in his wake. Water streamed from his cloak and hair, a torrent forming at his feet.

John nodded to the Alexson boy. "Go to the stables. There's a fine Spanish horse which needs attention."

"Look after him well," said Hugh, "and I'll give you a groat."

The boy nodded and hurried away.

John watched him go. "A fine lad," he said. "He works hard, and learns quickly." He looked Hugh up and down, frowning.

"Don't say a word," Hugh said. "Yes, the last two weeks have been arduous, and no, I'm not about to die. In a day or so I'll be right as rain."

"How was it?"

"I've made my peace with God. And I feel better for it."

"I'm pleased to hear it." Unsheathing his sword, John studied the edge carefully. "I'm glad you sought me out. I wanted a word in private." He drew up a stool and settled there. "Please, be seated."

Hugh shook his head. "I won't loiter."

Unhooking the whetstone from his belt, John honed the blade, one leisurely stroke after another. "I attended Kilmaurs' funeral."

"Oh?" Hugh's brow creased faintly.

"The affair was graced by some worthy men. Amongst their number was 'Bell the Cat'. His wife was with him."

"The Boyd woman."

"The very same," said John.

"Thank you for telling me." Hugh's frown deepened.

"It's bad news, isn't it?"

"I don't know... Angus always makes mischief. It's in his blood. He'd sell his own mother if the price was right."

"I believe the Boyd woman has reason enough to hate you."

Hugh's breath hissed faintly through his teeth.

"On a more encouraging note... Archie Campbell asked after you."

"What did you tell him?" Hugh asked warily.

"It's not my place to comment on your business. But word of Kilmaurs' death still hadn't reached Renfrew before he departed for Dumbarton. I doubt he knows."

"Informing Archie is a priority. The support of my Campbell kinsmen may be the only thing that gets me through this mess intact." Hugh sighed and rattled his fingers against the jamb. "For two weeks I've been living the life of a monk, devoting my existence to God and the Scriptures. It's been easy to lose sight of the corporeal world, and all its tribulations."

"Perhaps you should have stayed in the cloisters."

Hugh smiled, thinly. "That would be the coward's way out."

Setting the whetstone aside, John lifted the sword and regarded his handiwork carefully. "We'll be dining in an hour. You should change your clothes without delay. Have you spoken to Margaret?"

"I had the distinct impression that she wasn't pleased to see me."

John laughed. "You made everyone's blood run cold when you stormed in that night."

Hugh hung his head. "I'm sorry for that. The last thing I wanted was to cause distress."

"She'll forgive you, I'm sure."

There was silence.

"Oh, and before it slips my attention," Hugh said. "Our horses need accommodation for the night."

"Then let's find them somewhere, shall we?" Setting his sword aside, John sprang to his feet. "I think I have the answer. Come with me."

The Gryphon at Bay

Tearing off a small piece of bread, Margaret glanced anxiously in John's direction. The cooks had made a marvellous meal, but he was picking at his trencher without enthusiasm. It was sure sign his thoughts were in turmoil, though one would never have guessed it to look at him, his expression calm and placid.

Where John lacked an appetite, Hugh more than made up for it. He devoured everything in sight, regarding each new dish with a predatory gleam in his eye. He'd pounce on every morsel almost before John had even finished transferring it to their trencher.

"I'm still famished after my fast," Hugh explained shame-faced, when she gave him an admonishing glance. "Bread, water and a thin stew in the evening. That's all they gave me."

"At least you'll be used to hardship by now," John muttered. "That's all any of us will be getting in a day or two."

"If we're lucky," Hugh added.

Margaret sighed, unsettled by the thought. "It's very crowded in here," she commented, in an effort to change the subject. It was, she thought, an understatement. She was amazed they'd managed to fit so many men into such a small place. She could scarcely make herself heard over the voices, the high table jammed back so far that even with the fire-screens, the heat was almost unbearable. "I can't imagine why you didn't use the hall in the guest range. We worked so hard to prepare it, too."

John sighed, and turned his spoon over in his hands.

"Whatever's the matter?" Margaret asked.

Both men exchanged furtive glances. "Please don't speak of it," said Hugh.

"Speak of what?" Margaret demanded. "What are you hiding from me?"

"It's a ferocious night," John said. "We couldn't let the horses stand outside."

"I'm really very sorry," said Hugh. "But we couldn't see any other way."

"There's five hundred pounds worth of horseflesh there," John added, unrepentant. "The floor can be washed down in the morning. So long as you air the place properly, the smell will be gone in a week or two."

She didn't know what to say. Her precious hall. Piled high with dung and stinking of wet horse.

"It can't be helped." John's tone was apologetic, at least.

"Would your mother have allowed this?" she asked.

Hugh snorted. "Would she, by God! She'd have crucified him..."

"I should fetch hammer and nails after dinner," she said. "And have both of you pinned up on the battlements by morning."

"And what of His Grace the King?" John countered. "He needs our help. The way things are going, we'll be the only ones there."

It was late in the night before John retired to his bed. The tempest still raged outside, rain lashing the western wall, gusts howling through the slit-windows.

Passing his own door, he continued on up the narrow curving stair towards the ladies' chamber. For him to be spending the night in the company of his wife and her maids was unprecedented, but there'd been no choice in the matter. Eighty men or more were bedded down in the hall and guest range, and he'd given up his own bed to Hugh and Robert Montgomeric.

Louise Turner

Margaret and the girls were graceful about the inconvenience, but he remained mindful that just a few months before, he'd have been as welcome as a fox in a hencoop.

Pausing outside Margaret's door, he pulled off his shoes so he'd make less noise. Then he lifted the latch and slipped inside. One small candle flickered on a kist to guide him; other than that the place was in darkness. Margaret's lapdog, curled on one of the chairs, twitched its ears and opened an eye as he approached, but didn't consider him worthy of further attention.

A last visit to the privy was required, but getting there was a challenge in itself. The floor was cluttered with truckle beds, Katherine, Alison and Mariota tucked warm beneath their blankets.

John sidled past, one hesitant step after another. He'd nearly made it across when he caught his toe against the kist by Margaret's bed. The blow made his eyes water, he grunted and bit back an oath.

Katherine sat up with a yawn. Her dark hair hung loose, breasts and shoulders concealed beneath her kirtle.

"I hoped I wouldn't wake you," John said.

"It's alright." Katherine settled once more.

Alison groaned. "Is it time to rise?"

"No it's not," Katherine told her. "Sir John's here."

His hopes of maintaining a subtle presence were dashed: they were chattering together as he ducked beneath the curtain that concealed the privy.

When he re-emerged the room was still. He peeled off his hose, leaving his shirt in place for the sake of decorum until he'd retreated behind the curtains that screened the bed. He tried not to disturb Margaret, slipping beneath the covers at a discreet distance, but before long she sidled close, wrapping her arms about him. Her heat enclosed him, piercing the damp and the chill that had settled in his limbs.

"I thought you'd be asleep," he said.

"I can't sleep," she replied. "It's a fearful night."

"Let's hope it blows itself out by morning." He settled against her, resting his head upon her breast and marvelling at how things had changed between them. Once he'd dreaded her company, but now he relied upon it more than anything else in the world. And tomorrow he'd be gone. Exiled from Ellestoun, and everything he cherished...

"Is everything ready?" she asked.

"Pretty much."

"You've packed lots of winter furs? And extra cloaks and blankets?" Her voice was tight with concern.

"Of course."

"It's absurd. To be having a campaign at this time of year."

"Yes," he said. "I know."

She tightened her grip, as if she feared he might slip from her grasp. "Is it any consolation?" she asked. "To know that I love you?"

"Not really," he said. "It just makes it all the harder to be apart."

Chapter 52

The Place of Ellestoun

Margeret yawned and shifted. The mattress felt chill alongside, she was alone.

Contentment turned to fear, dread opening up like a void inside her. Pushing back covers and curtain, she swung her legs out of the bed, suddenly afraid. *What if he's left already,* she asked herself. *What if he didn't want to make a fuss?*

Katherine was sitting by the window, bent over her sewing as if she'd been busy half the morning.

"Why didn't you wake me?"

She sprang to her feet, guilt-faced. "Sir John said not to disturb you."

"How long ago?"

"An hour. Maybe slightly more."

"Get me washed and dressed. Quickly!" Grabbing a comb, Margaret pulled it irritably through her hair. The teeth snagged; she tugged it all the harder, hating the delay, hating herself for sleeping so late. She wanted to rail and snarl at the girls, but held her tongue, reminding herself that anger would achieve nothing.

"He wouldn't leave without saying goodbye," Katherine reassured her.

Tears stung her eyes. "It would be easier that way."

"He wouldn't do such a thing." Katherine's voice was tight with reproach.

A door opened and closed below, she heard men's voices. She gasped with relief: if Hugh was still in his chamber, then John would be close by. But Hugh wouldn't dally. He'd be on his way as soon as possible, and the Devil take anyone else's needs or priorities.

Margaret screwed her eyes shut, sharp denial. To blame Hugh for her misfortunes was unfair, but she had to blame someone. Better him than the hapless Katherine...

Katherine shook out a clean kirtle. "Alison will have the water here before you know it. It won't be long now, I promise."

Dressed in a fresh gown and hood, Margaret felt ready to face a new day. She left her room, quickening her pace as she approached the laird's chamber. Part of her dreaded the possibility that the door might open, another secretly hoped it would. There was so much she wanted to ask Hugh: why he'd betrayed them all by killing Kilmaurs, whether he'd known or even cared how much Helen suffered as she'd waited fearfully for news.

She paused at the door, heart pounding. Raising her fist, she swallowed back her fear and knocked.

"Yes?" Hugh's voice rang out, stern, commanding.

She opened the door a sliver and peered inside. Her heart nearly stopped: Hugh was confronting her with such a fearsome expression that her flesh turned to ice.

Margaret swallowed, lost for words. She'd thought of him in familiar terms once. She'd considered him a friend. But now he was a stranger. "I hope you don't mind my intruding," she whispered at last.

His expression softened, he smiled. "Come in."

To her relief, he wasn't alone. His brother was there, packing clothes for their departure. "I'm sorry I spoke sharply," he said. "I've suffered a constant stream of fools all morning."

She fiddled with her hood, unsure how to begin. "Was the room adequate?"

"Very comfortable. Thank you."

"Good." She closed her fists, opened them again. "Please don't tell John I came here. He'd never forgive me. It's just-"

He studied her carefully, saying nothing.

"-I'm frightened for him. He doesn't want to ride to war. I know you're a man of great courage and prowess. I know you've earned a peerless reputation as a knight..." She glanced aside, suddenly embarrassed. "Please take care of him."

"He can take care of himself," Hugh said, softly. "Have faith in him. You do him an injustice." He smiled. "But you mustn't worry. I'll do whatever I can to keep him safe from harm."

"Thank you," she said.

"Now you'd best be gone, hadn't you? Before people put two and two together. And most likely make six..."

She nodded. As she retreated down the stairs, she felt strangely reassured. For all his faults, Hugh was honourable to those he cared for. He'd do as she asked. He'd look after John and steer him safely through the perils of war.

Mid-morning on a dank grey day, and the men were mounted and ready. From the look of him, Hugh was anxious to be off, sitting sullen in the saddle, flashing quick disgruntled glances around the barmkin.

Pausing at the threshold, John waited for Margaret and the girls to file out from the tower-house. He cast Hugh an apologetic glance, half-expecting a curt admonishment. But for once Hugh sat patiently upon his horse, saying nothing.

Margaret wore a brave face, but her maids were inconsolable. Alison was by far the worst, close to tears and snuffling into her handkerchief.

"With luck," John said, briskly, "this business will be over by Yuletide."

Margaret held her head high. "We'll all pray that there's a speedy resolution to the crisis."

"If I'm not back by midwinter, then Alan will help you with the rents. Listen to his counsel, and all will be well." He smiled at the girls, touched by their melancholy. "Come along now," he said. "I'm not dead yet."

Alison stifled a sob. "I wish you weren't leaving us," she said. "What'll we do?"

"You'll help Lady Margaret," he told them. "You'll be strong for her sake. You'll conduct yourselves wisely, and pay no attention to the lies of ardent young men." He grasped Margaret's hands, gentle reassurance. "I hope I've done the right thing, leaving Jamie to command the men-at-arms. He can be difficult sometimes, but you're well capable of handling him. Remember that in all matters relating to this household, you represent me."

The Gryphon at Bay

"I shall manage, John, thank you." She fumbled in her sleeve for a handkerchief. "John, the last time you rode out like this, you carried my favour. I like to think it helped bring you luck."

Taking the scrap of lace-trimmed fabric, he slipped it into the folds of his jerkin. "I'll treasure it," he said. "Goodbye, Margaret. Look after my place. And take care of yourself and the babe. I have every faith in you, remember."

She sniffed miserably. "Goodbye..."

He shook his head, exasperated. "Margaret, please... There's no need for this." Hugging her tight one last time, he kissed her lightly on the lips.

Once they were clear of the gateway, Hugh brought Zephyr alongside. "Women!" he scoffed. "They fuss so. And you encourage them. Clucking away like a mother hen..."

"She'd be hurt, if I didn't say goodbye. And her girls like to be acknowledged."

"They dream of the day when you grow tired of your poor wife and seek out pastures new. You can see it in their faces. The glow of a young girl's lust..."

"That's ridiculous." John reined in his horse, swinging its quarters around so he could savour their departure.

It was an impressive sight: a snaking column of men clad in sallets and worn brigandines, some mounted, most striding along on foot. The faces seemed cheerful enough, Sempill retainer marching alongside Montgomerie man-at-arms without complaint or resentment.

The spectacle hadn't gone unnoticed. A crowd was gathering in the fermtoun below. Women called to their menfolk, children shrieked with excitement. Some of the coursers tossed their heads and sidled sideways down the track, eager to be off, while the sumpter horses plodded onwards, patient and uncomplaining.

Hugh reined in beside him. "Ah, what a joy it is," he said. "To be out on the road once more..."

"I wish I shared your enthusiasm."

Hugh's shoulders sagged. "I confess," he muttered. "It's all for show. I wish I was back at my place, slumped before a warm fire with a hound at my feet and a goblet of fine claret in my hand."

"I thought you said you liked war. That it was the only time you felt truly alive..."

"That was in the summer. When the sun was shining." Hugh shifted in the saddle with a grimace. "I'm getting old, I suppose."

"I just hope and pray that life under siege is as miserable for them as it for the rest of us. If that's the case, then I'll cheerfully tolerate any hardship put before me."

Hugh laughed. "Woe betide the man who wrongs you," he remarked. "There's a brutal streak in there. Buried deep perhaps, but once it stirs..."

John kept his eyes forward, saying nothing.

"You'll do well at court," Hugh added. "Once you shrug aside the desire for justice and truth, and learn to weave a web of flattery and deceit."

"That won't happen."

"I said that myself once. And I believed it, too. Now look at me..."

"You chose that path, Hugh."

"I didn't. It chose me."

"I've no sympathy. We're each in command of our own destiny."

"You like to think so," Hugh persisted. "But a year from now, I'll remind you of this day, and then we'll see how your circumstances have changed. And you know? I'll warrant I'm proved right. You'll sell your soul if needs be, once the opportunities present themselves..."

"Perhaps..." John glanced back one last time, to where Margaret stood on the wall-walk. He raised his hand, and she waved back, a forlorn, distant figure. "I hope she'll be alright," he muttered.

Chapter 53

The City of Glasgow

The spire of the cathedral church reached high into the heavens, a slender finger stretching up to God. Smaller towers flanked the western doorway, each bristling with scaffolding: across a broad cobbled yard stood the Bishop's Palace. Its solid curtain wall and hefty tower-house expressed the church's earthly power as eloquently as the cathedral itself embodied God's glory.

Hugh spared tower-house and cathedral no more than a cursory glance. He was studying the terrain with a practised eye: already, he was confronting a swathe of mud, grass crushed by the passing of men and horses. "Move slightly to the left!" he called to his men. "There's a hollow over here. Ground's too soggy."

His retainers responded, picking up a folded length of canvas and shifting it as instructed. It took six men to carry it, while another six stood by with poles and heavy hammers.

John trudged up alongside. He looked thoroughly disconsolate, smothered in a thick woollen cloak, hood pulled low over his face.

Hugh nodded towards the cathedral. "That place changes every time I look at it."

"At least the Bishop works hard to glorify God's house," John conceded, tone slightly grudging.

"Not to mention his own," Hugh reminded him. "Rumour has it that Bishop Blacader's got more gold in his coffers than the rest of us put together. Including the King..."

"Hugh..." John warned.

Following his gaze, Hugh spotted a lone rider, threading his way through busy ranks of men and horses. He recognised the horse at once: a bright bay destrier, striding out with pride and confidence. It carried Patrick Hepburn, Earl of Bothwell, Master of the King's Household and trusted advisor to King James.

Hugh's heart sank. He swallowed, apprehensive, yet strangely resigned. He'd hoped to hear Archie Campbell's counsel before he confronted Earl Patrick, but Fate had, unfortunately, conspired against him. "My doom approaches..." he muttered, flashing a warning glance in John's direction. "Not a word about Kilmaurs."

John scowled. "I'm no fool."

"I know that..." He fell silent as Earl Patrick halted his horse before them.

"Lord Hugh, Sir John," Hepburn spoke, brisk acknowledgement. He seemed oblivious to the foul weather, smiling his crooked, half-hearted smile as though he were out for a casual jaunt in the springtime. But the plumed feather in his bonnet drooped and his breath misted before him, indication that he, too, was finding his circumstances unpleasant. "Good of you to join us."

Hugh bowed his head. "We await His Grace's instructions."

269

"Don't make yourselves too comfortable," Hepburn warned. "We'll be moving off tonight."

"If you like."

"James wants to talk with you, Lord Hugh. As a matter of urgency."

John glanced in his direction, concerned, but it was such a subtle look that not even Hepburn would have noticed it. Hugh smiled, as much to reassure John as to bolster his own confidence. "Lead the way, Earl Patrick. I'm sure Sir John'll take care of everything in my absence."

The King's tent was spacious and imposing. Lit by candles and braziers, its canvas walls appeared luminous against the darkness. An awning shielded its entrance from the elements; beyond, the heavy curtains hung to keep out the draught had been pulled aside to let the smoke disperse.

Inside the furnishings were basic, almost spartan. Just one item of opulence was evident: a vibrant cloth-of-state that adorned the King's chair, lion-rampant device and silver unicorn supporters touched with gold and silver threads.

As for James himself... He looked unusually subdued, sporting clothing that scarcely set him apart from his courtiers: a sober gown, an understated doublet of dark brown velvet. His brown hair was unkempt, his chin lightly furred with a young man's beard.

He sprang to his feet, smiling. "It's good to see you, Lord Hugh!" He wrapped a comradely arm round Hugh's shoulders. "What host would be complete, without the strongest and most valiant of my generals?"

Hugh suppressed a grimace, for the lad had caught the bruises on his back. "You're very kind, Your Grace."

"What ails you, my friend?" James asked. "You're pale and gaunt. Has all been well?"

"A slight affliction of the soul."

James patted the iron chain that encircled his own waist, suddenly rueful. "I can sympathise. Has everything been dealt with?"

Earl Patrick was watching keenly, with that narrow-eyed, suspicious look of his. Hugh stared back, undaunted. "Yes, Your Grace. It has."

"I'm delighted to hear it," said James. "And how fares the Westland?"

"The same as ever," Hugh replied. "Racked with rebels and traitors, who care nothing for the King's laws."

"There's nothing that His Grace should be told about?" Hepburn asked, a little too pointedly for Hugh's liking.

"Nothing that concerns him at present."

James gestured to an empty chair nearby. "Sit with me a while, Lord Hugh," he said. "Let's discuss what must be done."

* * *

"-Dumbarton was razed a month ago." James himself refilled Hugh's goblet. "Earl Colin's forces were dislodged; he set up camp beyond sallying distance, at Dunglass."

"That's unfortunate," Hugh commented.

"Most of the rebel forces left Dumbarton a few weeks later," James continued, resuming his seat by the table. "We've been harrying them as best we can. We engaged them near Touch and put them to flight. But their leaders are still abroad. Worse still, they've had ample opportunity to regroup."

"So Dumbarton's merely a distraction?"

"I want Lennox to think that taking his citadel is all that concerns me. I hope that way I'll draw him out."

"What of yourself?" Hugh asked.

James stared. "Whatever do you mean?"

"It might be safer if you withdrew. To the relative safety of Edinburgh, say."

The young man's face coloured with indignation. "Absolutely not!"

"Let me assure you, Lord Hugh," Hepburn said, "that all eventualities have been considered. A safe conduct has been applied for, so our King can flee to England if necessary."

Hugh winced. "Let's pray it never comes to that. The English are usually more than willing to accept our kings. But they're remarkably reluctant to let them leave again." He paused. "What of your brother?"

"What about him?" James glowered at Hugh, sullen and petulant, as if he were a youth chastised by an irate tutor.

"The Duke of Ross could be a valuable asset to those disaffected by your rule. If they seized him, they'd have the rightful heir in their power."

"We've considered that," Hepburn replied. "And yes, it is a matter of concern."

"He's my brother," James muttered. "I can scarcely imprison him."

"Be wary, that's all I'm saying." Hugh sipped his wine. "And the English? Has there been any word?"

"Sir John Ross of Montgrennan is sailing north as we speak. We expect him to dock at Leith before the week's out. I'm hoping he'll bring tidings from King Henry."

"Ah," Hugh said.

"Did Sir John Sempill ride with you?" James asked.

"He did."

"Good. If you can instruct him to attend me without delay..."

Hugh rose to his feet. "At once, Your Grace."

*   *   *

They strode along the horse-lines one last time, making sure the beasts were settled.

"Least it's not raining," Robert Crawfurd said.

"Not yet." John glanced towards the heavens. Wisps of cloud scudded across the stars, the air was damp, cold. Further down the lines, a sumpter nag coughed, harsh and unsettling. John shivered and rubbed his hands. "God, we'll all have the ague before this week's out."

"How's Margaret?"

John paused alongside Storm and Zephyr. The two horses stood with ears drooping and eyes half-closed: they'd been tethered next to one another, forelegs hobbled, blankets thrown over their backs to keep in the warmth.

"You can see the swelling in her belly now," he said. "But she's very brave. She's still trying to act as if nothing untoward is happening." Storm whickered hopefully and nudged him gently; he fumbled in the pouch at his belt, where a stale bannock still lurked, left over from the journey. Pulling it out he tore it in two, handing one piece to Storm, the other to Zephyr. "You said once that it was hard for a man to be parted from his wife at a time like this..." He sighed, remembering the lonely figure who'd watched him depart from the wall-walk that morning. "You're right. I'd ride home now if I could." He scratched Storm's ear, thoughtful. "Damn Lennox."

"I'm sure he'd be overjoyed to know what inconvenience he's causing."

"At least the turnout's not as bad as I'd feared." John cast his gaze over the rows of tents and horse-lines. "I should have learned by now that a man will say one thing then do the complete opposite."

"They daren't oppose the King."

"Ignoring the King's summons hardly counts as open rebellion." John pulled his cloak tighter. Though he wore a quilted arming doublet over his shirt and thick woollen tunic, the chill air still settled deep into his marrow. "The horses will stay outside tonight," he said. "Tomorrow, when we reach the Lennox, we can put them under cover."

Robert shook his head. "That'll take an acre or more of canvas."

"Hugh's taking care of that."

"He takes care of everything, doesn't he?"

"Sir John!" Robert Montgomerie approached. He nodded to Robert Crawfurd, distant acknowledgement, then turned to John. "Hugh's looking for you," he said.

"Well?" John asked Robert Crawfurd. "Will you join us?"

Robert shrugged and followed.

Hugh wasn't alone in his tent. Earl Patrick was with him, indication enough that the matter was of some importance. Both men sat on lightweight chairs that had been unpacked for the occasion, a flagon of wine between them.

John nodded to Earl Patrick. "Your Grace."

Hugh smiled slightly. He had that distant courtier's look about him: he always did, when he was in Earl Patrick's company. "The King wants to speak with you. His Grace the Earl of Bothwell will take you into his presence."

"Forgive me, sirs... But what does it concern?"

"Your uncle," said Hugh. "Seems he's coming home at last."

"You'll be there to welcome him," Hepburn added.

"But I'm needed for the host," John protested. "I've thirty men in my command."

"I'll take care of them," Hugh said.

John nodded, reassured.

Robert Crawfurd wasn't so easily appeased. "And what about my men?" he demanded. "I wouldn't entrust Lord Hugh with my own life, let along the lives of my retainers. I ride with Sir John Sempill, or I don't ride at all."

"It's just for a little while," John urged.

"I won't be pressed on this matter!" Robert countered, red-faced and agitated. "I won't rely on the decisions of a liar and a murderer!"

Hugh grasped the hilt of his dagger. "Those are strong words, Master Crawfurd," he said, voice ominously soft. "Be thankful I'm in a mellow mood. As it is, they might come back to haunt you."

"Master Crawfurd doesn't mean to cause offence," John cut in. "He knows he spoke rashly."

"You could've fooled me," Hugh snapped. "You'd have thought I'd killed his mother, from the fuss he's making..."

Hepburn scowled. "Obviously you killed someone."

"Lord Hugh slew Robert Cunninghame of Kilmaurs," Robert told him. "Just a few weeks back."

There was silence. Hepburn studied Robert Crawfurd, unmoved. "Christ, Hugh," he said. "Not again..."

"The men of Cunninghame have had enough of your justiciar, Earl Patrick!" Robert added. "That's why just a handful of us have turned up here to fight for their king. And there'll be even less tomorrow."

He turned and strode away.

"Excuse me, sirs..." John muttered, and moved to follow.

"Stay where you are, Sir John!" Hugh's voice rang out, emphatic enough to make him stop in his tracks. "If Master Crawfurd won't put his petty differences before the safety of his king, then that's his decision." He smiled wearily at Hepburn. "I'd have told you soon enough."

Hepburn's glance was scathing. "Would you?"

Hugh shrugged. "Best the tidings came from me than from another."

"If you value your neck, Lord Hugh, then say nothing to James. He has enough to concern him just now."

"I'd already decided that was the best course-"

"What you've decided is irrelevant," Hepburn countered swiftly.

"Your Grace," John said. "Master Crawfurd's words weren't wholly accurate. Kilmaurs' death wasn't murder. Manslaughter, perhaps..." He caught Hugh's eye: for once, Hugh had the grace to look grateful.

Hepburn's scowl grew more entrenched. "I'm sure Lord Hugh appreciates your support, Sir John," he said, "but it's not your place to pronounce judgement." He stretched in his chair, then stood. "Come along," he added. "His Grace'll be wondering where you've got to."

Patrick Hepburn escorted John deep into the king's tent, where even now James was attending to court business. Just one small table stood there, littered with parchments, a flagon of wine standing close by. James wasn't working alone: he was attended by one of his close advisers, the Director of Chancery, Robert Colville.

"Ah, Sir John!" James looked up with a smile. "Good of you to join us!"

"Your Grace." John dropped to one knee.

"Get up, for Heaven's Sake." James reached for his goblet and took a hasty mouthful. "Master Colville needs your assistance."

Catching Colville's eye, John straightened, quickly. One of Margaret's distant kinsmen, Colville was a notary who'd achieved considerable success over the last year or so. In his early thirties, he was elegant, impeccably groomed, his chestnut-brown hair neatly combed and his face freshly-shaven.

John ruefully rubbed his own stubble-covered chin. The prospect of venturing out in Colville's company didn't bring much comfort: on the few occasions he'd spoken with Colville informally, he'd found him much like Patrick Hepburn. Distant. Unapproachable. More than a little secretive...

"We leave tomorrow," Colville said. "We're expecting Ross of Montgrennan to dock at Leith before a week's out. His Grace the King thought it fitting that his kinsman attend him."

"Of course." John spoke boldly, determined not to let his misgivings show.

"You're a lucky man, Sir John," James added. "You'll be enjoying one last night of luxury as a guest of His Grace the Bishop. The rest of us will be leaving shortly."

It was all happening so fast. He'd come here expecting to wage war: instead he'd found himself embroiled in court business. "What about my men?" he asked.

James waved a dismissive hand. "Speak with Lord Hugh," he said. "He'll arrange something, I'm sure."

As he splashed and slithered his way back through the mud, John couldn't help harbouring a brief pang of regret. He'd dreaded the hardships of a winter campaign, but at least in the field he had a measure of his enemy, and a clear idea of what he was expected to achieve.

It took a while to track Hugh down amongst the chaos. The tents had been lowered already in preparation for the night's march. But John found him eventually. He'd set up his chair in the shadow of the sumpter horses: with Robert Montgomerie and a few of his trusted retainers in attendance, he was wolfing down bread and mutton and sipping some ale.

"The knight errant returns." Hugh offered John the remains of a loaf. "Here. Plenty to go round."

"I won't deprive you. Supposedly, I'm dining with the Bishop..."

"Better say your prayers then. If he doesn't like the look of you, you won't make it past the subtleties-" Hugh smiled, registering John's consternation. "No need to look so nervous. It's your uncle who has an appetite for pretty young men, not the unfortunate Bishop."

"That's not what concerns me."

"It's your retainers, isn't it?"

"Most were loyal to my father. They fought with him last year..."

"Against my people. I know." Hugh thrust his platter into his brother's grasp and heaved himself to his feet. "Shall we see if we can charm them into accepting my authority?"

They waited in silence as the Sempill retainers were mustered. Ten men-at-arms and a dozen spearmen weren't a major contribution to the host, but in the circumstances even this small force couldn't be set aside lightly.

"I've been summoned by the King," John told them. "I must leave you for a week or two." Looking around the faces, he saw no enthusiasm whatsoever, just weary resignation. "Since you're pledged to serve me, you're entitled to return home in my absence. But the King's in dire need of your help. On account of this, I entreat you all to stay and do what you can to assist." He nodded towards Hugh. "Lord Hugh has kindly agreed to take care of you until my return. Grant him the loyal service you'd give me, so we can help our King remain safely on his throne."

They whispered amongst themselves, one or two disgruntled, all visibly anxious.

John said nothing, unwilling to press them. What he wanted was more than most men would ever demand of their lieges. "I know we had our differences with the Montgomeries last year," he added eventually. "But circumstances have changed. I'd trust Lord Hugh with my life: I'm asking you to do the same."

Hugh stepped forward. "Don't listen to idle gossip," he said. "I make a relentless enemy, it's true. But speak to any man who serves me, and they'll tell you why I merit such loyalty. No man in my care will want for meat or ale, and I'll strive to find you all a dry place to lay your bones each night. Plus a share of the spoils, should we be called to battle. That is my promise to you, if you agree to fight in my name."

They conferred, their voices hushed, urgent. Then someone spoke out. "If that's what's required, Sir John, then so be it."

"Good," said Hugh. "I like men of wisdom. But your love for me may soon fade, for I have bad tidings. We'll be setting out tonight, and travelling for six hours or more. It's the King's decision, not my own," he added, catching the reproachful looks. "If you want to remonstrate with him, then by all means do so. Though I doubt he'll pay much heed to your entreaties..."

Chapter 54

While a brisk night-time march was the last thing any of them wanted, Hugh knew that forcing another man's retainers into such a miserable journey was courting disaster. So before they set off, he sought out every single man amongst the Sempill contingent, learning their names and speaking with them at length. He reassured them, too, that once they'd reached their destination, they'd have as much rest as they needed, and a silver penny for their pains.

It wasn't a good night for travelling. The pace was slow, the moonlight patchy at best. Once they were on their way, Hugh let out his reins to the buckle, letting Zephyr pick a careful path through the darkness.

They followed the narrow rutted track that led west along the coast, heading into the heart of the Lennox. And as he rode onwards, Hugh found himself thinking back to the last time he'd embarked on an urgent nocturnal march at the King's request.

It felt so long ago now, that night they'd ridden in haste from Linlithgow to Stirling in the twilight balm of a June evening. Hoping to meet with King James the Third's army before it was too late to fight...

God knows how they'd found victory that day, when they'd all been weary from lack of sleep and anxious for the future. It was young James who'd inspired them, their vigorous boy-King who feared nothing.

And his kinsmen, the Darnley Stewarts, who'd kept their own counsel in the weeks, the months, preceding that last battle. Until at last they'd made their choice, throwing in their lot with the new King, who had now himself abandoned them...

Hugh sighed, wondering how Matthew was faring. Had he fought in that ill-fated clash of arms between the King's men and the rebel host? Or was he still locked away in Dumbarton? Surely he couldn't still be enduring the siege, for Matthew could never have tolerated confinement for so long...

"Ho there, Lord Hugh!" He was hailed from the darkness, the muffled thud of hoofbeats heralding a horseman's approach.

He knew the voice. It belonged to James himself.

"Your Grace!" He pressed his spur lightly against Zephyr's flank so the beast stepped aside.

The men-at-arms passed like shadows, black against the gloom. There was little to mark their presence, just the tramp of weary feet, the creak of leather or the faint rattle of steel.

Then the cloud broke and the moon slid out, bathing them in a pale eerie light.

James reined in alongside, horse jostling close, as lively now with the witching hour upon him as he'd been on their departure. He seemed impervious to fatigue or defeat, possessed of almost supernatural qualities.

"It's a fine night to travel." James took a deep satisfied breath. "The air is fresh and wholesome so far from the town. And the company's more wholesome, too." He nodded in Hugh's direction. "I'm right glad to have you here, Lord Hugh. I need your insights, your observations. When the opportunity arises we'll inspect the castle, and you can advise me on how best to capture it. We have bombards, we have two hundred men. Surely that will be enough?"

"Let's hope so."

"I have faith in you, Lord Hugh," James said. "You've never failed me yet."

The Bishop's Palace, Glasgow

The Bishop of Glasgow was a small quick man, with eyes sharp as flints and a cool precise manner. His robes were worth a king's ransom: purple silk from the orient which he wore with a swagger, comfortably assured of his own self-worth.

He spoke to John just once through supper. *So you're Montgrennan's nephew,* he said, tightening his brows in measured appraisal. *You'll go far. You have all the right attributes...*

With that, he turned his attention back to his platter, while the younger clerics smirked amongst themselves.

John suffered their derision in silence. That he was being judged on his kinship with James the Third's favoured counsellor irked him. Small wonder, when even those who'd ridden to war with Montgrennan had mistrusted him, blaming the former Lord Advocate for the betrayal at Blackness, when four men handed over to the rebels as surety were abandoned by the King.

John still remembered with unease how at Montgrennan's urging King James had reneged upon a treaty forged with his son. The hostages had suffered, two men hanged, the others struggling even now to regain their fortunes.

Montgrennan was ruthless, undoubtedly. But he'd fought hard to defend James the Third, even when the tides were changing. And for a long time after, he'd remained faithful to the dead King's memory. In that respect, his loyalty could not be questioned. Nor could his intellect: Montgrennan's reponse to an accusation of treason had been to fuel the dissent that poisoned the realm even now. With young James suffering the same troubles his father had endured before him, perhaps he'd grown to understand at last the importance of winning Montgrennan's favour.

William waited in their lodgings. "No poisoned larks at dinner?" he asked.

"Not exactly." Pulling off his shoes, John sank with a sigh into the chair by the fire. At least his surroundings were pleasant. The room, though small, was richly furnished: walls decked with boldly-patterned hangings, the canopied bed amply provided with blankets and coverlets.

"Least we'll have dry clothes for the morning," William reminded him.

"Let's be thankful for small mercies," John said. "It's the last comfort we'll be granted all year." Wandering over to the bed, he stretched out along it. "God forgive me, William, but I'm dreading this."

"Because of your uncle?"

"In part." He'd served as a page in his uncle's retinue half a lifetime ago, a boy of ten learning to be a gentleman. His uncle had always slept alone, sitting up late in the night while he read his books. A private man, who kept his thoughts and motives entirely to himself... "He considered me an idiot. Beneath his notice."

William laughed, softly. "Then he'll have to think again, won't he?"

"Not if I can help it. If he thinks me a fool, so much the better." He sat up with a sigh. "How's Mary?"

"Well enough." William's tone was guarded.

"Is everything alright?"

William stared into the fire, avoiding his gaze. "She's with child."

A chill slid across John's shoulders. "When's the babe due?"

"Early in the spring, she reckons."

It didn't take much to work it out. To realise that when the child had been conceived, it wasn't William who'd been sharing Mary's bed...

If he'd been a youth not yet wed, he'd have shrugged it aside as a minor inconvenience. But he was married now, with a young wife who'd take the birth of his bastard as proof of her own failings.

For once William misread his silence. He swallowed, ashen-faced. "I'm sorry," he said. "She didn't want to birth it, but it wasn't right to sanction the murder of an innocent. She didn't want to tell you, and I'd hoped to keep it secret, but..." He breathed deep, summoning his courage. "I'd rather speak the truth and face the consequences."

"I'm concerned for Margaret, William. Not for me. It'd break her heart."

"Then don't tell her," William urged him. "It's not as if the child will suffer. Better for them to live in blissful ignorance, than to wish that Fate had been kinder..." He met John's eye, earnest and anxious. "I'd hoped you'd be willing for us to raise the babe as our own."

"If that's what you wish, William. Then yes, of course," John replied. "But I'll provide for them. They must never want for anything."

William smiled. "I know that," he said. "And the child will be loved, believe me."

Chapter 55

The Lands of Dunglass

"You misunderstand me," Hugh said. "I wish to rent your barn and purchase your cattle. The fate of your kye should not concern you: if you accept my offer – which is, I think, rather generous – then you needn't worry about sheltering them."

The woman leaned against the door-jamb of her cottage, arms folded, face dour. Beneath a shapeless hood, she had the face of someone accustomed to working the fields in all weathers: ruddy skin like tanned leather, gnarled calloused hands to match. "We wanted the hog for Yuletide."

"Then the hog can stay, Mistress Stewart. And the pony, too. But I require the kye and the sheep for my own use."

"How much are ye willing to pay?" Mistress Stewart asked.

"A fair price," Hugh replied. "But bear in mind that if I find your demands unreasonable, I can seize your property and take what I like for whatever sum I see fit."

She shrugged and rubbed her hands against her hips. Her skirts were patched and worn, her apron grubby and discoloured. "Well, my lord, if that's the way it is, then I'd best agree," she said. "But what I've got's mine, and I don't want none of yer people taking it for himself. I expect that all my goods and chattels'll be well looked after. It's hard for a poor woman to make ends meet, when she's left on her own, husband dragged off to fight another man's war-"

"Yes, yes..." Hugh muttered.

Her eyes narrowed. "For all yer lordly ways, yer no very civil."

Hugh briskly rubbed his hands. "Mistress Stewart, my feet are blocks of ice and I'm numb with cold. When I've had some rest and I've enjoyed some hearty food, I shall be the very flower of chivalry, I promise."

"Thank God for a dry place and a blazing fire!" Hugh unbuckled his spurs, then pulled off his boots. Handing them to one of his servants, he sank down with a groan onto the packed earth floor by the fire. He pulled his legs close, and tugged off the thick woollen socks that had kept the worst of the chill off his feet. His clothing clung to him, his flesh clammy. He stank of dirt and sweat already.

At least he was indoors, protected from the elements. That was enough to lift his spirits and make the deprivations tolerable. Wriggling his toes, he savoured the warmth.

Robert settled alongside, saying nothing.

The cottage had just one room. A fire burned in the stone-lined hearth at its centre, filling the whole place with peat smoke, which drifted up towards the roof and lingered there, before dispersing through a hole in the thatch. There was a rough ramshackle table and a doddery-looking bench near the fire, while assorted stools and a low bed lurked in the corners.

279

Louise Turner

A cauldron hung over the fire, its contents bubbling furiously. The waft from it made his mouth water.

Mistress Stewart ladled a respectable helping into a wooden bowl. "Some pottage for His Lordship?"

"That's most gracious of you," Hugh said. He ambled to the table and sat down at the bench, gesturing for Robert to join him. Bread had been placed there, a coarse black loaf scarcely fit for the pigs, but at least it filled a man's stomach.

Mistress Stewart thrust the bowl down before him, a beaming smile on her face.

Hugh retrieved his spoon and took a small box of salt from the pouch at his belt. He added a pinch to the stew, stirred, then pushed the bowl closer to Robert so his brother could take his share. "Tomorrow, we'll have meat."

Robert's face glowed at the prospect. "Amen to that."

They'd spent hours sluicing out the cobbled floor of the byre so the men could rest there, though it would be days yet before the place had dried out enough to grant them a comfortable night's sleep. They'd kept one stall aside as a stable for Zephyr: the rest of the horses had to brave the damp and cold of the horse-lines.

Things could be much worse, Hugh reminded himself. *We might have a muddy ditch as a bed, and the lashing rain as our bedfellow...* With that thought as consolation, even the pottage seemed appetising, despite its watery flavour and the skim of grease that formed droplets on the surface. "Thanks be to God," said Hugh, "for granting us this fare. And may He bless us with a timely end to this conflict, so we can leave this good woman in peace and return to our families."

The Place of Ellestoun

Taking her place in an empty hall, Margaret felt a twinge of loss as she viewed John's vacant chair alongside. It was the silence that upset her most of all. There was scarcely any chatter from the lower tables: if anyone so much as whispered, their voices echoed so loud they might as well have been shouting. There'd be awkward glances, some clearing of throats, and then the deathly hush resumed.

Below the dais, old Henry sat at one long table, with three young boys nearby, while lined up along the opposing board were half-a-dozen women. Old Annie Semple was amongst them, approaching seventy years now, an indomitable and irascible woman feared by all the younger maids and laundry women.

Footsteps echoed against the flags as Alan Semple the tacksman took his place with Margaret and her maids on the dais, sitting on the men's side at a respectful distance.

Once he was seated, Margaret glanced about the room one last time. The serving staff were poised and ready, but there was still no sign of her half-brother Jamie.

She sighed, overwhelmed by the dismal atmosphere. She wanted John back there amongst them, presiding over the household with his usual confidence and good humour. She wanted William to be playing his lute, chasing away the silence as they dined.

She wanted normality.

Bowing her head, she studied her trencher, trying not to let anyone see the tears welling.

280

"Lady Margaret?" Alan Semple ventured, cautiously. He eyed her with real concern, as if she were his own daughter, left alone and abandoned.

She forced a smile, unwilling to appear like a weak snivelling child in front of John's trusted servants. Breathing deep to fortify herself, she was about to rise and bless the board when the door to the hall swung open.

Jamie stamped his way to the top table, still wearing his sword. He offered her an unapologetic nod then barged past Alan. Halting at her side, he hauled back John's chair and heaved himself down there.

There was a shocked silence.

Her despair gave way to burning resentment. "How dare you!"

Jamie shrugged. "He's not here."

"It doesn't matter," she retorted. "Learn your place."

"I'm your brother. If your husband's absent, then-"

"My husband left clear instructions." Her glare was relentless. "Besides, you're *not* my brother. Don't you ever forget that."

With a sigh, Jamie relinquished the chair and retreated to the adjacent bench, just as the first dishes were set before them.

Margaret stood, and smiled serenely at her household staff. "We thank God for His Goodness, and accept His Gifts with humble hearts."

"Amen," came the feeble chorus.

She took her napkin, and placed it with a flourish upon her shoulder. The servants were staring, but the looks they sent in her direction were respectful. If Jamie's intransigence had been a test, then she'd survived it comfortably.

But it was early days yet. It would be weeks, even months, before John returned. Suddenly the future seemed something dark and fearful, the thought of struggling on alone, unaided, almost too much to bear.

Katherine nudged her, hopeful. "Eat up," she said, eying their trencher with expectant eyes. "Your dinner will get cold."

Chapter 56

The Lands of Dunglass

"On your feet, sluggard!" A toe roughly prodded his back.

Hugh groaned and rolled over, cursing as he crushed his face against Robert's back. It seemed like no time had passed since he'd wrapped himself up in a blanket and dropped off to sleep.

"Get up, Hugh. You should be paying homage to the God who made you, not snoring like a pig!" The voice, with its lilting northern tones, was unmistakable.

Hugh sat up. Opening his eyes, he saw Archie Campbell crouching alongside, grinning broadly. "Ah, Hugo," he said, batting Hugh's head with his bonnet. "You look no better than a beggar."

"Not all of us have been granted the luxury of a laird's residence."

His gude-brother shrugged and straightened. "You can lodge with me if you like."

Casting his glance around the sleeping men who littered the floor, Hugh grimaced. "Don't torment me."

"You won't be anything like as self-righteous when you're crawling with lice."

Hugh pushed himself to his feet, flicking straw off cloak and jerkin. He grasped his boots, still damp from the previous day, and pulled them on. "What hour is it?"

"Well past dawn, but nowhere near noon. Now come with me, kinsman, and let me escort you to my lodgings." Putting an arm round Hugh's shoulders, Archie steered him to the doorway, where Mistress Stewart was vigorously sweeping the floor.

Doffing his bonnet, Archie smiled in her direction, faintly patronising. "You'll break fast in my company," he told Hugh. "I've fine wheaten loaves. None of this coarse shit."

"Mistress Stewart is a very fine cook." Hugh nodded graciously in the guidwife's direction. "I'm proud to eat at her table. But perhaps this once I'll make an exception. Important matters must be aired," he explained, as she glared at him. "It wouldn't be right to discuss them before strangers."

A short walk along a muddy hoof-pocked track brought them to Colquhoun's place at Dunglass. The residence itself was unremarkable: a four-storey tower overlooking an obligatory cobbled barmkin surrounded by ranges and outbuildings.

What interested Hugh more was the distant form of Dumbarton Castle. From here its walls and ramparts seemed insignificant. But the same could not be said for the vast, steep-sided rock on which it sat. Set against the hills of Kintyre and the Lennox, it seemed like a miniature mountain, impervious to all but the most determined assault. With the tide at its ebb, the castle seemed to float in a sea of mud.

"Ah," said Hugh. "And I'd hoped to be home by Yuletide."

Archie's laugh was hollow and desolate. "Little chance of that, I fear."

"What of the bombards?"

"They arrived here safely. Though how we'll use them this far from our target remains to be seen."

"True," Hugh agreed. "Last thing we want is for Mattie to snatch them from under our noses."

"God forbid." Archie looked heavenwards. "If that happens, Hugh, then I swear I'll cut my losses and pledge my loyalty to Lennox."

He dined with Archie that day. Just the two of them, lodged in the guests' chamber at Dunglass. And afterwards he confessed it all, the whole sorry tale. The confrontation with Cuthbert, what had happened with Kilmaurs.

Archie listened quietly, not at all judgemental. "Does the King know?"

"Not yet. But Patrick Hepburn does."

"From what you told me, it wasn't murder. Unless of course you're not telling me the truth."

"Why should I lie to you?"

Archie's gaze didn't waver. "Why indeed?"

Hugh stretched with a sigh. "I thought perhaps your father might help me. For Helen's sake, at least."

Archie smiled. "You're our kinsman, Hugo. You're very dear to us. And you've always served Father well. We'll deal with it." He tossed back the rest of his wine. "I'll send word to the earl. He'll know what to do."

The Castle of Blackness

The high curtain walls of the Royal gaol reminded John of a vast pale ship, narrowing at the prow, swept high on the shore and stranded there. Blackness was a place of fearful rumour and reputation: many of those brought here at the King's displeasure never left alive.

Entering the yard, he stared in awe at the tall forbidding walls. Guards idled on the battlements high above and not one but two tower-houses stood within the barmkin. In the larger of the two, lights burned behind shuttered windows. The other was more austere, masonry pierced by small black voids that passed for windows.

John shivered. He'd never seen a building so unfriendly. "Is anyone confined here?"

"Just a few lost souls who were caught in the rout when we defeated Lennox's men. Galbraith of Culcreuch was imprisoned here a while. Before we hanged him." Colville's tone was almost gleeful.

Here but for the Grace of God, thought John, and crossed himself.

"Here you are." Colville poured some wine into John's cup.

John accepted it with a quiet word of thanks. They'd dined well, on fish and fowl and half-a-dozen other dishes besides. Then, with supper behind them, they'd retired to the guest chambers for the rest of the evening.

Colville slouched back in his chair. "This is far better than languishing in the mires of the Lennox." He paused, fixing John with a searching glance. "You seem preoccupied."

John shrugged. "I'm contemplating the whims of Fate..."

Colville chuckled. "It's been a curious year, I must say. At our first meeting, I considered you dangerous, not to be trusted. Now?" He sighed and settled comfortably in his chair. "Lord Hugh speaks very highly of you. Which intrigues me, given the circumstances..." He broke off, then added, cautiously, "The Church encourages us to forgive our enemies, but it's not always easy."

"We can't stay locked in the past."

"That's very true," Colville agreed. "And if I seemed hostile when we first met, I hope you'll forgive me. That day last year, which seems to long ago now... Well, I lost my father that day, too."

"I'm sorry," John said. "It's difficult to endure such a wound, I know." He studied his cup. "This land is tired of war," he said, softly. "It yearns for respite, I think."

Colville chuckled. "An attitude which seems at odds with Lord Hugh's, Sir John. How you reconcile your principles with his, I can't imagine."

"I'm grateful to him. If I escaped a hanging last year, he had much to do with securing my reprieve."

Colville stared, unapologetic. "Do you think, hand on heart, that you could maintain your success without his help?"

John frowned. "Whatever do you mean?"

"Your uncle's return may transform your fortunes. With the right opportunities you could put the troubles in the Westland behind you. If you pursue a careful path at court, then the advantages could be tremendous."

"My uncle isn't exactly renowned for winning allies," John responded.

"What alternative is there?" The other man's tone was deceptively casual.

John paused, on his guard. Like a hound sniffing out game, Colville was searching out his loyalties. As for Colville himself... John had no idea whether he spoke for the King, or merely for himself. "If I desire anything from this world," he said, "it's to leave a secure and prosperous legacy for my children. I serve my king and I offer my loyalty to those who prove their worth." He paused. "As for Lord Hugh... He's done more to make amends than I'd ever expected. I'd strike a blow in his defence, undoubtedly, but unless there was a damned good reason, I would never take up arms on his behalf."

The Place of Kilmaurs

Craigends sighed and tapped his fingers against the board, unable to conceal his unease. All the key members of his family were with him in the hall: Cuthbert, Christian, the Dowager.

They seemed comfortable enough with him shouldering the roles that had once been Rob's: tutor to Rob's sons, and administrator of Rob's lands, now held in trust for the day when Cuthbert came of age.

Only he was uncertain. He didn't want to control, to manage. He wanted to wage war, to have revenge for the death of his father and brother.

He'd have shrugged his responsibilities aside and carried on the feud regardless, had Cuthbert not argued for forebearance. *The time's not right,* the boy had said. *Let them think we're broken. Let them drop their guard.*

He'd listened out of politeness at first. Though still in his minority, Cuthbert was Rob's son, the rightful head of the family.

To begin with, Craigends feared that Cuthbert's first taste of battle had turned him craven. But the more he listened, the more he realised that Rob's first-born surpassed them all.

In his time, Rob had been skilled at plotting and negotiation. But Rob had been a peacemaker. He'd wanted justice to be served, for the Montgomeries and the Cunninghames to live together amicably, as they had in the days of their forefathers.

Cuthbert desired something else. Not Montgomerie slain, because that was too easy, too straightforward. He wanted Montgomerie crushed, vanquished. And to succeed in this meant a battle that couldn't be won through force of arms alone.

In such a battle, Craigends felt powerless to help. He understood the might of the sword, the honour of armed conflict. He was a simple man: treachery and subterfuge were alien to him.

But there were others in the household who had honed such skills aplenty.

His mother the Dowager stared at him, hands folded carefully in her lap, eyes cold as steel. "I don't expect your blessing," she said. "Or even your agreement."

"It's absurd!" Craigends scoffed, before he could stop himself. "What can two women hope to achieve, without a man's strength of arms behind them?" He glanced at Christian, trying to catch her eye, to coax forth some admission of defeat.

Christian hung her head and looked away.

Craigends swallowed. Christian's grief touched him most keenly of all. Throughout these hard times she'd weathered her trials bravely, never complaining, never arguing.

"Listen to me, Will," the Dowager persisted. "What more is there for me to live for? My husband's dead. My first-born is dead. And it's a miracle my second-born wasn't cut down to join him. Let alone my grandson."

"Cuthbert needs a wife." His reply was sullen, half-hearted.

"Well he won't get one, unless we change his fortunes."

Craigends shifted, unwilling to admit that she was right. "If you must plead your case with Earl Patrick, then at least let me speak out on your behalf."

Her eyes flickered shut briefly. "A woman's distress is more potent than a man's."

Cuthbert stirred. He'd held his tongue until now, biding his time. "Let them go," he said. "They feel my father's loss more than any of us. Let them strike this blow on his behalf. If they succeed, so much the better."

Beleaguered on all sides now, Craigends fought the urge to scowl. "I see no worth in it," he said. "But... Very well. You have my permission to travel to Edinburgh. And you have my blessing, too."

For all the good that'll do you, he thought.

The Port of Leith

The wind howled, the rain lashing down upon them. The horses were beyond resentment: they stood in a shivering line along the quayside, tails clamped tight against their rumps, heads turned against the tempest. In the distance the glow of lanterns marked where the ship was anchored, rising and falling in the swell.

Another light approached, defying the elements. It was held aloft in the prow of a small rowing boat, which ploughed its way towards the shore, sometimes vanishing in the trough of a wave, sometimes teetering high.

"Why did he come ashore tonight, of all nights?" John wondered aloud.

"Perhaps he couldn't bear to spend another night at sea?" suggested William. "It won't be a very dignified homecoming. His first enduring memory of setting foot on Scots soil will be of emptying his guts all over it."

Men shouted from the quay; the voice that answered from the boat spoke a tongue like his own, but strangely alien.

Englishmen, John realised with a jolt. Montgrennan's crew was full of them.

Ropes were thrown to shore, the boat secured.

And out stepped a figure. Tall, imperious, wrapped in a thick cloak to keep out the weather.

Robert Colville stepped forward. "Sir John Ross of Montgrennan?"

Lit by the glow of the lantern, Montgrennan smiled, gracious and composed. He might have stepped ashore from a voyage where the seas were smooth as glass. "That's correct. And you are?" His voice was light with airy dismissal.

Colville bowed his head. "Sir Robert Colville, my lord. I'm privileged to hold the office of the King's Director of Chancery. I believe you knew my father, who was Secretary to the late Queen for many years..."

"Ah, yes."

"Might I introduce your escort?" Colville continued. "Sir Adam Hepburn, Lord Hailes, and your kinsman, Sir John Sempill of Ellestoun."

Montgrennan gazed at them a moment, mildly interested.

"We've brought a horse for your convenience. A princely steed, which you may consider a gift from His Grace the King. His Grace asks that you come with me to Edinburgh, where you'll be given quarters for the night."

A frown crossed Montgrennan's impeccably smooth brow. He cast a secretive glance to the Englishmen who stood in silence on the quay, their faces impassive. "What surety do I have of the King's good intent?"

"His Grace the King hopes that peace will soon be restored throughout this realm. He hopes that you will help him in this task, and as further token of his gratitude and generosity, he bade me give you this." Colville presented Montgrennan with a rolled-up parchment, then doffed his bonnet and bowed low. "Your lands are restored in full, Sir John," he said, raising his voice so he could be heard above the storm. "Welcome home."

Chapter 57

Dumbarton Castle

Matthew stood on the wall-walk with eyes half-closed. A light wind whipped his hair, he breathed deep on air that was fresh and wholesome.

He was witness to a grey damp dawn, with just a pale tinge of pink in the east. He felt pleasantly refreshed, invigorated. Savouring that precious time of day when he'd just broken his fast and taken comfort in the words of his chaplain.

The world seemed peaceful, content with its lot. With Red Rab singing heartily on the plain below, he could believe that life was progressing according to God's plan, that all might still be well...

"My lord!" One of the men-at-arms waved from the eastern wall. "Come quickly!"

He stirred with a sigh, climbing swiftly up the steps to join his retainer. Following the other man's gaze, he peered down the sheer cliffs to the reedbeds below. Where two figures wandered without concern amongst the marshes, beyond the range of the garrison's crossbows, perhaps, but even so... To venture there was foolhardy.

His flesh crept with anticipation. Though difficult to see through the thick vegetation, there was something familiar about them both. One moved quickly, a lithe young man. The other, though less nimble, was lean and tall. Their cloaks were the garb of peasants, thick wool, dark brown in colour. But once or twice Matthew thought he spotted the flash of richer fabrics. And both men carried heavy broadswords on their backs.

"I could try and pick them off," his retainer suggested.

"And sign our death warrants?" Matthew countered. "It's the King."

"Saints alive!" The soldier crossed himself. "What's he doing here?"

"I suspect he's sallied forth to assess our weaknesses," Matthew replied. "What's there to fear? He's brought a peerless knight to protect him. And he's right, too. I won't sanction an assault against either of my kinsmen." Breaking into a smile, he slapped his companion roughly on the shoulder. "Fetch the Countess. Ask her to join me here, and quickly. Tell her that our circumstances may just have taken a turn for the better."

*   *   *

The reeds reached chest height, obscuring ground which was soft and waterlogged. Pools and trickling rivulets lurked beneath piles of rotting vegetation, waiting to trap the unwary.

Hugh winced as his foot sank to mid-calf in the silt. Ice-cold water filled his boots: his socks and hose were soaked through, the straw packed around his feet for extra warmth squelched with every step.

James moved swiftly ahead. He'd been absent a week, attending court business in Stirling, but as he'd set out with Hugh before sunrise that morning it was as if he'd never been away.

Hugh wished he shared his liege-lord's enthusiasm. Even with the bombards, an attack on John Stewart's citadel seemed fruitless. He cast a withering glance up at the massive height of *Alt Cluit*, at the sheer whinstone cliffs that veered straight and unforgiving alongside. Only a few stunted bushes and some sorry-looking grass clung precariously to the barren rock, while high above their heads the castle perched at its summit, distant and unattainable.

James paused. "Come along!" he urged. "What's keeping you?"

Hugh sighed. His youthful companion seemed to skim through the reeds with the light-footed ease of a fox or cat. "The years are creeping up on me, Your Grace."

"Away with you!" scoffed James. "You're in your prime." Springing onto solid ground, he waited for Hugh to catch up. He offered his hand as Hugh waded the last few yards, then helped him alongside.

Hugh glanced up, wary. They were close enough now to glimpse figures patrolling the wall-walk.

"Now..." James gripped Hugh's arm and drew him close. "It's a difficult venture, I know. But surely, if some long ladders were tied together, it would be possible to scale the rock in the dead of night. The defences are much weaker on the north-east face."

"Forgive me for saying this, Your Grace, but..." Hugh paused, wondering how best to couch it. "What you're suggesting is virtually impossible."

James blinked, disappointed. "I considered you impervious to fear or doubt, Lord Hugh. I thought if any man were willing to take on such a task, you'd be the one..."

"I'll do so if asked, Your Grace, but... I consider it madness."

"Oh..." James considered his reply a while. "But you once helped my father escape confinement in Edinburgh..."

"There was one important difference, Your Grace. I marched up to the gatehouse and I demanded entry. John Stewart was the castle's keeper at the time. His men were not entirely unsympathetic."

A grin spread across young James' face. "Then since it worked so well in Edinburgh, I suggest we do the same again. You're going in there, Lord Hugh. You'll speak with your kinsmen in person, and you'll settle this dispute without delay."

*   *   *

The Place of Ellestoun

Pushing aside her platter, Margaret pulled an unenthusiastic face. "I'm not hungry."

Katherine set down the flagon of ale with an emphatic flourish. "You're eating for two."

Margaret rolled her eyes, exasperated, then ate some bread and cheese without enthusiasm, forcing herself to chew and swallow each mouthful.

She'd noticed it the past week or so. A faint sickness in her stomach each morning. It grew worse when she ate, but usually wore off in time. She didn't know much about carrying a child, but she knew it was a hardship endured by many women. Her gude-sister Elizabeth Kennedy had suffered greatly, retching for hours each morning and taking to her bed throughout much of the day.

Margaret stood with a sigh. The bulk of her belly strained against the stiff confines of her stomacher; she hated the discomfort, even now, with three months or so to go. "I want to go to mass," she said. "Where's Jamie?"

Most of the servants were gathered around the long tables in the hall. Jamie was with them, playing cards with one of the grooms, a flagon of wine to hand.

"I'm going to mass," Margaret said. "I want a horse made ready."

Jamie grunted in acknowledgement, then glowered at his companions. "So who'll attend the lady?"

"I'll see to it, Master Colville," a boy offered.

"You do that." Jamie turned back to his cards.

Gobbling down the rest of his bread, the boy sprang to his feet. He was a slight fair-haired lad aged thirteen or fourteen years, fresh-faced and pleasant.

"And you are?" Margaret asked, as they headed for the door.

He bowed his head. "John Alexson, my lady."

"Oh..." Margaret frowned. She knew the name somehow, but couldn't quite place it.

"I'll fetch your horse, Lady Margaret. She'll be ready in a little while."

Young Master Alexson waited at the mounting-block, reins in his hand. "It was very kind of you to help," Margaret said, settling herself comfortably into the saddle.

"It's what Sir John would want," he said.

"Have you served here long?"

The boy stroked the horse's muzzle, his touch firm, confident. "I came here in the summer, not long after Sir John returned from Duchal. I help out with Old Henry, mostly. Seeing to the hounds and the horses."

"So your family lives in these parts?"

"Mary White of Bar's my mother," he said, then added, "I'm sorry, Lady Margaret. I didn't mean to cause offence."

"It's alright." She tightened up the reins in readiness.

He was a steady presence at the mare's head as she set off with her maids. Margaret was glad to have him there: her swollen belly made her feel just as ungainly in the saddle as she did out of it. Every step of the way she worried. About what might happen if she fell, about how John would cope if something happened to her or the babe. She remembered the fate of Marjory Bruce, who'd tumbled from her horse and had her child torn from her womb as she lay dying...

Her stomach heaved anew at the thought.

* * *

Edinburgh Castle

Watching from his vantage point at the doorway, John shifted uncomfortably. A page stood nearby; the boy caught his eye, wondering if he was needed. John shook his head and flicked his hand, subtle dismissal.

He was a world away from Ellestoun, and the comfortable informality of the baronial courts. Montgrennan and Colville were confronting each other across a solid-looking table, a flagon of wine to hand. They'd been there for hours, tucked away in a small chamber high in the Middle Ward, quibbling over fields and feus and proportions of income.

Louise Turner

John remained a distant bystander. He poured the wine when asked, arranged for the delivery of food as and when required, as if he were a humble servant, not a baron and knight in his own right.

It was the way of court. A man started off like this, doing others' bidding, seeking favour from the great and the worthy, while all the time he watched and learned, seeing how the mechanisms of state operated.

He smothered a yawn. He could see why Hugh avoided his courtly duties whenever possible: loitering like this numbed a man's mind.

But at least the food was good, and his quarters excellent.

Montgrennan shuffled through the parchments. He was cautious, no doubt about it. Making sure that every detail was correct, every legal point meticulously set out.

"Very well," he said. "I'm satisfied with the arrangements for my Kinclevan lands. So if we might turn now to Cunninghame..."

Colville smiled, unusually subservient. "Certainly." Leafing through the piles of sasines, he retrieved the relevant document.

John studied his uncle carefully. Searching the smooth, flawless face for any sign of nervousness or misgiving, he found none. More than ever, his uncle was a mystery. It was as if he'd never fallen from favour in the first place. The charges of treason were forgotten: he'd been granted lodgings with the rest of the court and he'd certainly made himself at home.

Immaculately dressed in the finest of garments, his nails spotlessly clean and without so much as a hair out of place, he seemed superior to those around him in every way, gifted with the finely-sculpted features of an Achean hero and the intellectual vigour of an ancient philosopher. It wasn't hard to read men's thoughts when it came to Montgrennan: they resented him, they feared him, and yet they longed to win his favour.

As for Montgrennan... He remained oblivious to the hopes and ambitions of lesser mortals. He had his own concerns, and they were all that mattered.

St Bride's Chapel, Near Ellestoun

The priest was at prayer when Margaret entered. She stepped as quietly as she could, lifting her skirts to avoid sweeping aside the sweet herbs and rushes that covered the tiled floor.

St Bride's was a humble place, simply furnished with a single gold cross on the altar. Plastered walls were covered with roughly painted figures: Christ in the Firmament took pride of place over the arch that separated nave from chancel, welcoming the Blest into His company while the Devil and his minions lurked below to snatch the Damned. On the side walls of the nave were scenes from the Passion, along with images of the Virgin Mary and the Four Evangelists.

If the silent presence of God and the saints wasn't intimidating enough, then she had the illustrious Sempill dead to contend with, too. An arched niche in the north wall held a knight and his lady, lying side by side with lapdogs at their feet. John's grandsire Sir William Sempill was entombed there, along with his second wife, Lady Margaret Montgomerie. The floor bore yet more monuments to the departed, their resting-places marked by crudely-carved stones bearing a cross or a sword and a short inscription.

The Gryphon at Bay

Margaret shivered, her gaze drawn to the Doom painting above. To the cowering naked figures who awaited Judgement, to the face of Christ with his huge languid eyes and the sneering demons that cavorted below. Her mood, already grim, grew blacker still. She cradled her bulging abdomen, suddenly fearful. For herself, as well as the baby.

After mass, she remained in the chapel a little longer. She lit a candle to Saint Bryde and asked the saint to grant her a straightforward birth. Then she prayed to the Virgin, but this time her prayers were for John. She asked Holy Mary to look after him, to keep him safe from injury and hardship and to speed him home. *I want him back with me*, she lamented. *I know it's wrong, but I want his warmth at night. I want to know he's there...*

Once that was done, she spent a little while with the priest in Confession.

"I've been free of the pains until now," she told him.

"Then you've been fortunate," he told her. "You must expect some discomfort. You've committed carnal sin and for that there's always a price to be paid."

"I try my best to do what's right and good," she said. "I eat moderately and I pray to God each day, morning and night."

"That's all very well," the priest replied. "But you must work hard to earn God's favour. You might help the poor, the disadvantaged. Your presence would do wonders to lift the spirits of those in need. And I'm sure that a woman of your standing might be able to help them in more material ways..."

That evening, she sat upon the bed while Katherine carefully combed out her hair. "I wonder what should be done," she said.

Mariota looked up from her needlework. "You mustn't visit the sick," she said. "If the air's foul, you might become ill. And with the baby..."

"But it's only right that the laird's wife shoulders her responsibilities," Margaret argued. "Sir John is always riding out with Alan to see how his tenants are faring. I know I don't know one end of a cow from another, but..." She slipped into thoughtful silence. "Perhaps I should visit those women who are near to labour," she decided. "Or those who've just given birth. I'll give them alms, and see what I can do to make their circumstances better."

Edinburgh Castle

The steward stepped back to admit him. "Sir John Sempill of Ellestoun is here, my lord."

"Ah, yes," Montgrennan's voice answered. "Bid him enter."

John ventured inside. "You asked to see me, Sir John."

Montgrennan looked up from his books, a distant smile on his face. "Come in, John. And don't look so discomforted. It's a social call, nothing more. You're keeping well?"

"I am, my lord, yes."

"Good..." The older man paused a moment. "By all accounts, you managed your hardships with admirable courage and tenacity."

John studied the floor. "I did what was required."

"And you've prospered as a result. Well done." Montgrennan slouched back, hands behind his head. "And your mother?"

"She's in good health. Though my father's loss grieved her greatly. And she was anxious about your good self, not to mention your changing fortunes."

"She had a wise son to console her, at least. And you're wed now, I believe. To Robert Colville's kinswoman."

"I am."

His kinsman nodded. "Very good..." He tapped his finger idly against the table, thoughtful, preoccupied. "As you're no doubt aware, my lands have been restored."

"Yes, my lord."

"Lands require administration, but if the truth be told, my duties look set to keep me in the King's company..." Montgrennan closed his book, a weary vexed expression flickering across his face. "Regarding my lands in Cunninghame... I'd be grateful if you keep them in my absence. There's rental payments to be collected, baronial courts to be established and the like."

"I'm sure I could assist."

"Good. You can collect sufficient monies, over and above what's due, to cover your own expenses. That goes without saying. You'll need to make arrangements with the Bailie of Cunninghame, so he's aware of your role, but I don't think that'll prove too hard." He looked John squarely in the eye. "You're said to be on excellent terms with the Lord Montgomerie."

John shrugged, noncommittal. "Thank you, my lord. You're very generous."

"If you could ride out to my Perthshire lands in the meantime. Speak with my steward, inform him of my return and ask him to tell me of any difficulties. And when the opportunity arises, you can visit Montgrennan, to make sure everything's in order there, but only when you're released from the King's service. Take these, and distribute them as required." He passed John a bundle of rolled-up parchments. "My thanks, Sir John. That'll be all."

Chapter 58

Montgrennan's Kinclevan lands lay a day's ride north of Saint John's Town. A wearisome journey at the best of times, but with light rain blowing in from the west most days, and winter's hold growing ever stronger, the task was beyond thankless. John pressed on regardless, more grateful than ever for William's company. With everything in order, they returned to Stirling. For two nights running they'd been content with tiny inns and hostelries; now, with the Abbey of Cambuskenneth lying just outwith the town, John decided instead to seek lodgings there.

As they approached the abbey precincts the sun broke through at last. John made the necessary arrangements for accommodation and enquired after supper: to his relief, he still had time to wash, change his clothes and attend mass before they were required to take their places for dinner in the guest range.

Mass was already underway when John entered the abbey church, the refrains of the *Gloria* reverberating around the elaborate vaulted ceiling. Brilliant shafts of sunlight shone through the western windows, flooding the nave with warmth and making the glazed floor tiles come alive with colour - golds and reds, vivid blues and greens.

John revelled in the air of peace, tranquility. He would never have admitted it to Hugh, but his soul was troubled, too. This was his own personal pilgrimage, seeking the remains not of a saint, but of a mortal man.

Making his way past scattered groups of worshippers, he headed for the choir. He halted at the rood screen, peering past painted statues of saints and apostles into the sacred space beyond.

The monks were lined up in their stalls, tonsured heads bowed as they sang the mass. Towering tall at the eastern end was the high altar, draped with rich embroidered cloths and surmounted by a carved retable. And, lying close by, a tomb: wrought of finely carved stone and obscured beneath a magnificent cloth-of-gold emblazoned with the Lion Rampant. He knew at once who lay there: the king he'd once served, scorned in life by his lieges and betrayed at the end by his nobles. A king murdered by a coward's hand as he lay wounded and defenceless...

A year had passed now. In a land still torn by treachery and rebellion, where James's former allies still clung to his name and cried out for justice.

Perhaps, like them, he should have remained loyal. But looking at the tomb, he harboured no shame, no regret. Instead he felt strangely comforted. Here at last the troubled king had been granted the respect and the devotion he'd lacked in life.

He lit a candle for the soul of James, and another for his queen, Margaret of Denmark. He paid for a mass to be sung in their name. And once that was done, he turned his back and went upon his way. He'd paid his dues, and laid the ghosts to rest.

"So where have you come from?" The lay-brother asked, sliding onto the bench alongside.

John had to raise his voice to be heard over the chatter in the busy refectory. "The parish of Kinclevan, just north of Saint John's Town." Taking a leisurely sip of ale, he nodded his thanks as a measure of mutton stew was ladled into his trencher. More lay-brethren arrived at his back bearing laver bowl and aquamanile: he carefully washed his hands then took up his napkin and placed it over his shoulder.

"Was all well in those parts?" his companion asked. "Rumours have been rife, about unrest in Moray and Forfar…"

"I saw nothing untoward," John said. "But men seemed wary, I suppose."

"I've heard it said that the Earl of Lennox was determined to capture Stirling, but since his people were routed, he's gone to ground." The lay-brother stared anxiously at John from pale, heavy-lidded eyes, his glance accusing.

"He's not a man to relish subterfuge." Tearing a piece from his bread, John dipped it into his stew and ate it with relish. With the warmth of the fire and the security of the abbey precinct all around him, it was hard to remember that just a few hours before, he'd been a fearful traveller on a lonely road, flinching at every unexpected sound.

"You speak as if you know him," the other man commented.

"My sister's married to his bastard."

"Well, that's a curious thing!" He cast John a cautious glance. "You're not trying to find him, are you?"

"Absolutely not," John retorted. "In fact, now I know he's abroad, I'll be doing my best to avoid him. He'd gralloch me, without a doubt, if ever I had the misfortune to run into him."

The Fermtoun of Kenmure

The cottage was no more than a grubby hovel. Bulging daub-and-wattle walls squatted beneath a heavy thatched roof. Its windows were shuttered slits, the doorway closed off by a stout sheet of ox-hide. There was no chimney: the smoke merely seeped through a rough gap in the thatch.

Alan Semple the tacksman had warned the family of Margaret's arrival. Master Henry Semple waited ouside his door, a solemn fellow dressed in his best clothes who gripped his bonnet tightly. Four grimy children were lined up alongside, the oldest a brown-haired girl of ten, the youngest a mere infant.

Seeing them standing there, Margaret felt a twinge of guilt inside because God had granted her wealth and comfort, while leaving others to moulder in squalor.

She slid from her horse as gracefully as she could, grateful for John Alexson's steady grasp as she landed.

"This is Master Semple, Lady Margaret," Alan said.

The man bowed. "My lady."

"How is your wife, Master Semple? I understand the babe was due."

"It slipped out last night. A little boy."

"I'm very pleased for you. Might I speak with your wife?"

Master Semple nodded and led her to the doorway. He held aside the curtain, and she stepped cautiously into the smoke-filled interior. Katherine and Mariota followed, each clutching an armful of provisions.

The Gryphon at Bay

It took a while for Margaret's eyes to become accustomed to the gloom: besides a fire in the hearth a couple of rushlights burned, without a candle to be seen.

A thin-looking dog lay by the fire. Raising its head, it regarded her with disdain as she brushed past, setting her course for the bed at the far wall. A woman was confined there, sitting up with a swaddled babe in her arms, her back supported by a makeshift pillow stuffed with straw. Her kirtle was dingy and dishevelled, the thin linen cap upon her head equally worn.

Another woman lingered close by, dressed in a plain grey gown with a stiff white hood. She moved carefully, her belly heavy with child. It was only when she turned and smiled in greeting that Margaret recognised her: Mary White of Bar.

"Good day, my lady," Mistress White said. "Are you keeping well?"

A wave of hostility washed through her. She swallowed, trying not to let her surprise show. "Yes, thank you." She was annoyed at getting caught out like this: she should've known that where a child had been delivered just hours before, the midwife would be present.

"You should sit down." Mistress White gestured to a stool beside the bed. "A woman in your condition needs rest. I'm sure Mistress Atkin will agree. She was delivered of a son last night: a fine child, who will do his parents proud."

Margaret settled as demurely as she could. She smiled at the exhausted-looking woman who lay within the bed. "I'm very pleased to see that you both made it safely through the birth."

Mistress Atkin smiled, weakly. "I'm right glad to be rid of him."

"You'll be lying-in for a month?"

She glanced aside. "I doubt that. There's work to be done."

"You should rest as long as you can. There must be others who can help you."

"We'll do what we can," said Mistress White. "The little ones will have as much food as they need, until their mother can cook for herself."

"If you run short then come to Ellestoun. I've brought a few loaves in the meantime. And a keg of ale, too. There's other things: some herbs, and ointments, and binding for the babe."

Mistress Atkin managed a smile. "That's very kind of you."

"Would you like to hold the baby?" Mistress White plucked the child from his mother's grasp.

"No, I couldn't. I might drop him." Margaret recoiled, but the babe was thrust into her arms regardless. The infant's eyes were closed, his face wrinkled, not very pleasant to behold. But the perfection of the tiny nose and lips touched her deep inside.

She swallowed back tears, moved by the knowledge that she'd witnessed the miracle of a new life brought into the world, and that in a few months she'd play her own part in a similar miracle. She was terrified beyond measure, but hopeful, too, that all would be well. That in a few months, she and John would have a precious child to call their own... "He's beautiful," she said. "You must be very proud of him."

Chapter 59

The Kippen Muir

Crouched over the kindling, William coaxed the sparks to life. "Perhaps we should have pressed on."

John hugged his knees. "The horses need rest." He cast a searching glance at William. "So do you."

"You don't look so good yourself," William retorted.

"It's just a pity we couldn't find a hostelry in these Godforsaken parts. At least, not one we could trust." He glanced warily about him, remembering the time he'd sought refuge in these hills. Fleeing from a battle lost, a bewildered young man who'd feared for the future...

"What I'd give for some men-at-arms," William muttered. "We're too close to Doune Castle for comfort."

A horse whinnied, far away, and Storm whickered, softly.

John hunched deep into his cloak. "We'll keep watch tonight. It's just one more day."

The horse called again.

Storm stood taut, nostrils flared, then neighed, an ear-splitting blast that could have woken the dead.

John lobbed a clod of earth in the stallion's direction. "Damn you! Are you trying to tell the whole world we're here?"

"Let's cook our porridge, then quench the fire," William said. "That way no one'll find us. To seek a man out in wild country like this would take sorcery."

"I'll take no chances." Rising to his feet, John kicked dirt into the flames. "We dine on bread tonight, and nothing more. Let's snatch some rest. At first light we'll move off."

William devoured his meagre dinner with enthusiasm, but John couldn't bring himself to eat. The surrounding darkness pressed closer with every passing moment; when a howlet screamed he jerked around with his hand on the hilt of his dagger.

He'd have given the order to move off, if he hadn't been so fearful of losing his course in the darkness. Unsheathing the blade, he turned it over in his hands, relishing its comfortable weight. Reassured, he replaced it.

A twig snapped, further downslope.

"I thought-" William broke off as John raised his hand, signalling for silence.

Drawing his knife, John ventured cautiously down towards the valley, alert to every sound. He could've sworn he'd seen something pale drift through the trees, though whether bogle, ghost or man he couldn't be sure.

Seeing no further signs of movement, he shrugged and started back up the hill.

The Gryphon at Bay

Then, catching the pungent scent of a man's sweat, he faltered. Even as he readied himself, a shadow loomed ahead.

A fist struck his chin, sending him toppling. His knife was knocked from his grasp, he lashed out with hands and feet, but there were two men on top of him, maybe more, kicking and battering him. He struggled to rise but a knee drove into his groin. His legs buckled, white-hot pain flowering in his loins.

Voices hissed to one another, their tongue foreign, unfamiliar.

John coughed up bile. He opened his eyes, fought to focus.

The darkness revealed little. But he could see enough. A knife levelled at his throat, the man who held it crouching over him, staring down from a cruel hard face. A long beard grew on his chin, matted hair cascaded down his shoulders and he stank of old sweat. He wore a padded linen *aketon*, stretching from chin to knees, sword belt buckled over it. His helmet looked as if it were a hundred years old or more, a simple steel cap with a bar protecting his nose.

He barked at John in that same impregnable tongue.

An Islesman, John thought with a jolt. *Then what's he doing so far from the coast?*

Unless Lennox had made a pact with the Lord of the Isles... If that was the case, then not even the Westland would escape unscathed...

He realised then that they'd dealt with William as efficiently as they'd dealt with him. Two of them were ushering him down the hill, he limped with every step, wrists bound before him.

William's gaze met his, eyes fearful.

"Keep calm," John said, softly. "Do as they say, and pray there's a shred of mercy lurking in there somewhere."

His scabbard was unbuckled, swift fingers searched the purse at his belt. The letter from Montgrennan was removed and studied closely, but left otherwise untouched.

There were half-a-dozen in all, all fierce Northern men. They found the horses, loosed their hobbles and led them away. John bit his lip, smarting at the knowledge that his fine black horse, a gift from the king himself, should end up in the keeping of a savage from the north.

Just a sliver of a moon and a few stars lit their way. But the Islesmen moved across the inclement terrain without hesitation, passing with the ease and determination of sleuth-hounds.

For an hour or more they walked, heading westwards, deeper into the Lennox. It was a hard journey after such ill-treatment. But they persevered, mindful that their captors wouldn't tolerate either weakness or disobedience.

They were stumbling with weariness by the time they reached their destination, a small camp nestling in the foothills of the Kippen Muir. John looked about him, carefully, though it was hard to take in much with one eye swollen and half-closed. He saw a handful of tents and a dozen horses tethered to a line, eyes gleaming in the light of three or four braziers. Most were hairy-heeled garrons, but he noted one or two quality beasts present.

Men squatted here and there, throwing dice, playing cards. They laughed together, amicable words exchanged in *gaelic*. A banner hung listless from a pole next to the horse-line: John strained his eyes, but couldn't make out its device.

Instructions were barked out nearby and John's wrists were tugged, indication that they wanted him on his knees. He did as they bid, grovelling with William in the shadow of the horse-lines. Three men were left to guard them, while the others disappeared into the tent.

John cocked his head. He could hear the strains of a harp, sweetly played. A man sang, again in *gaelic*. There was laughter, cordial and civilised.

A soldier emerged. He called out to his companions and soon John found himself grasped by the arms and hoisted to his feet. His bonds were severed, his arms freed. He was prodded to the tent, but the voices were less hostile now, the demeanours of his captors courteous, even apologetic.

Mystified, he limped inside.

"Sir John Sempill of Ellestoun!" Earl Colin of Argyll rose to greet him, smiling ruefully. He looked John up and down, visibly concerned. "You must forgive my kinsmen. They can be ruthless, when they think the safety of their lord is compromised."

"I think we've escaped lightly," His lower lip felt thick and awkward, his words slurred.

"You have," Argyll agreed. "They found the letter and thought it prudent to keep you alive." He gestured to the nearby bench. "Please be seated. Let me offer you hospitality, as a means of atoning for previous injuries. I've not yet dined, Sir John. I'd be grateful if you'd join me."

John sat without a word. His head was hurting, his ribs and shoulders too. The pain in his privy parts still nagged him, but under the circumstances, he was profoundly grateful he still lived.

A trencher was set before him, a horn cup filled with ale pressed into his hand. He took a hesitant sip, its sweet honeyed taste tinged with the salt tang of blood.

"You're a foolhardy man," Argyll remarked. "Travelling through the wilds of the Lennox with just one retainer to defend you. The remnants of John Stewart's forces are still roaming these lands. If they found you, your life wouldn't be worth living."

"I know that."

"Then what brings you this way?" Argyll raised his hand. "No, I don't expect an answer." He brandished Montgrennan's letter. "That's all I need to know. He's back, isn't he?" He slid the folded parchment towards John.

The seal was still intact. Relieved, John plucked it from the board and replaced it in his purse.

"And the message?"

"It's not important. It's to the steward of his lands in Cunninghame. I'll deliver it when the opportunity arises."

"What of yourself?"

"I was heading to Dunglass to rejoin the host."

"Then our paths have converged, Sir John. Perhaps you'd best ride with me?" Argyll's lips lifted into that same, half-smile. "That way, we'll be sure you survive the rest of the journey intact."

"Thank you, Your Grace. I'd be grateful for your company."

"Of all the men I should meet upon this road, it's remarkable it should be you. I'd hoped we might talk with one another. Sooner, rather than later." There was a coldness behind the cheerful expression. Despite his pleasantries, Argyll had ulterior motives.

John returned the earl's gaze, undaunted. "How can I be of service, Your Grace?"

"It seems my gude-son has found himself in a tight spot," Argyll said. "I understand you witnessed the whole affair."

Chapter 60

The Place of Ellestoun

Hiding behind its dense blanket of cloud, the sun hadn't shown its face all day. By mid-afternoon a dozen candles were lit to cheer the place, but it did nothing to lift Margaret's spirits.

She retreated to her chamber after dinner, where her maids dutifully joined her there. The girls amused themselves with a game of tables, but for once Margaret took no interest.

She retired to bed, claiming exhaustion. But the weariness wasn't just in her body. It had seeped into her very soul.

Lying alone, Margaret nursed her bulging abdomen, fearful of the future and filled with resentment because unlike her the girls were lithe and full of vigour.

She wished she'd been barren, that she'd never taken a husband. At least in a nunnery she'd have been spared the perils and indignities of childbirth.

She swallowed a sob. Perhaps these black thoughts would seal her fate, provoking God's wrath at the time she was most vulnerable. But it was hard to stay cheerful when the doubts were gnawing away inside her, the growing fear that John would come home, see her swollen stomach and despise her.

Meeting Mary White had done nothing to ease her despair. The woman was with child, closer to birth by a month or two. Which meant her babe was conceived at the very time when John had spent his days and nights away from home, in Mistress White's company.

Margaret closed her eyes, tears burning her lids. It was fitting punishment that Mistress White was bringing her husband's bastard into the world. Would she have to love the child as her own, just as her own mother had been expected to love Jamie?

She thought of Helen, whose love for Hugh's daughter was genuine enough. But Hugh had never been unfaithful: he'd dallied with a mistress before he took his marriage vows and after that he'd remained loyal. Even with temptation at his door, confined to his bed with Margaret as his keeper, he'd refused to betray his wife.

Unlike John...

She stifled a moan. If she'd been a good wife, meek and unprotesting, John would never have strayed. *I could have lain with Hugh*, she reminded herself. *I could have betrayed my husband, just as he betrayed me. Perhaps I was wrong to be chaste. Perhaps I should have dealt him the same bitter draught he gave me...*

What would it be like, she wondered, to have Hugh for a lover? Would he'd treat love as a tourney, determined to flaunt his prowess? Perhaps not - when he'd been in her care, he'd shown a more gentle side, something unexpected, even endearing...

Margaret dug her fingers deep into the coverlet. To desire Hugh, who slew men without remorse, who carved his brutal path through the world, felling those who stood in his way...

The Gryphon at Bay

She swallowed back the grief, determined to hide her fears. She didn't want their pity. She just wanted John. She wanted him back by her side, his calm steadying presence in all their lives.

The Place of Dunglass

A band of men-at-arms filed through the gates of the barmkin, led by Earl Colin of Argyll. The first score or more were mounted on solid-looking garrons, while the rest travelled on foot. Earl Colin himself sat upon a bay Spanish destrier, oblivious to the chill wind that whipped in from the west.

He reined in his horse, pausing to inspect the Campbell and Montgomerie retainers who'd gathered there to welcome him. He swept his accomplished gaze over each man in turn, taking in every patched brigandine and tarnished belt buckle.

Archie Campbell stepped forward. "Welcome back, Your Grace."

Argyll dismounted. "I'll be staying a day or two." His gaze lingered on Hugh.

Hugh approached, head bowed. "Your Grace."

"Hello, Hugh." Argyll kissed him swiftly on both cheeks. "I understand my fine gude-son needs assistance." Slapping a firm hand upon his shoulder, the earl gripped him tight. "The situation could be worse, Hugh. At least this time you're not without an ally." He turned, flicking a faint nod towards his men.

Hugh followed his gaze. There amongst the earl's retinue he saw John and William. Sporting a black eye and a thick lip, John looked like he'd been wrestling a Cyclops. And William Haislet looked no better.

"Fell foul of my men," Argyll explained.

Hugh stifled the urge to smile. "Then they're lucky they're still with us."

Argyll laughed, softly. "Yes," he said. "And they know it, too." Wrapping an arm around Hugh, he steered him towards the tower-house. "Let's dine together, shall we? We'll discuss this matter fully, and decide how to make the best of these- ahem - *difficult* circumstances."

They dined alone, just the three of them, in the quiet privacy of the laird's chamber. A roast fowl was set before them, along with some freshly baked bread and a few platters of vegetables.

"Hugh." Argyll beckoned to him.

Hugh rose to his feet. Grasping the serving knife, he carved the meat, slicing it small in the proper fashion.

Argyll watched in silence, long fingers clasped before him.

When the food was blessed, Argyll offered Hugh his cup. "I understand a babe was due."

Hugh accepted it, took a long leisurely sip of wine. "Helen birthed a daughter in July. A beautiful child, who's growing well."

"And what of Helen?"

"Hale and hearty, Your Grace. But understandably anxious about my circumstances."

"You've wandered into a mire this time," Argyll agreed. "But the situation isn't impossible to resolve. Though you'll have to concede some ground, with our help you should emerge with life and limb intact." He smiled faintly. "Though it may take a while to scour your tarnished reputation into something resembling its former brilliance."

Hugh studied the board, suitably subservient. "Thank you, Your Grace."

"That I met with Sir John Sempill was a stroke of luck," Argyll said. "He's already running errands for Montgrennan. I'm sure that with the right encouragement, Sir John would agree to courier a message to his kinsman."

Hugh looked up, caught off-guard. "Montgrennan?"

"Best he's employed in your defence," said Archie.

"Besides," Argyll continued, "it occurs to me there could be added benefits in harnessing him to our yoke. Not just for ourselves, but for Matthew."

Archie's smile was triumphant. "Of course..."

"If there's anything amiss with the degree of forfeiture, Montgrennan will find it."

"He'll expect rich rewards," Hugh warned.

"I'm sure I'll find something to tempt him," Argyll replied.

"On a related matter," Hugh said. "The King asked me to negotiate with Matthew. I thought it best to wait, until you'd joined us."

"Good," said Argyll. "If Mattie evades capture until we've sought Montgrennan's advice, then we can help him. But if we could win custody of Dumbarton then we'd go some way to appeasing James's wrath." Argyll swilled his wine around and around, suddenly thoughtful. "I'll summon Sir John Sempill. He can take a message to his kinsman without delay."

"A word of advice, Your Grace," said Hugh. "Say nothing to Sir John about Mattie."

"Yes," Argyll agreed, "I can see that perhaps he wouldn't welcome our involvement." He sat back with a sigh. "Well then, my lips are sealed. Let Sir John remain in ignorance. He'll be doing this for you, Hugh. At least we can rely on Montgrennan to leave all the details unspoken."

The summons came as no surprise. Hobbling up the spiral stairs to the laird's chamber, John gritted his teeth and concentrated on keeping Hugh's retreating back in sight. He'd stiffened up after the journey, making even the short walk from Mistress Stewart's cottage arduous.

Hugh had offered to help him, but he'd refused. Last thing he wanted was for Argyll and his people to dismiss him as a weakling.

Hugh paused ahead, knocking smartly on the door to announce their arrival. "Sir John Sempill, Your Grace."

They entered.

Argyll looked up. "Thank you, Hugh. That'll be all." He gestured to a chair. "Please be seated, Sir John. How are you faring?"

John settled carefully, trying not to wince. "It'll be a day or two before the stiffness goes."

"My men tell me that you acquitted yourself well."

"I beg to differ."

"They're taught to fight like wolves from the cradle. Stealth and surprise are their strength. As fighting goes, it's hardly chivalrous. But the foe they often face doesn't care much for chivalry."

"I can imagine that might be so."

Rising to his feet, Argyll poured some wine. He left his place behind the table and handed the goblet to John, then sat back down again. "Men scoff," he said. "They say I'm too lenient towards Hugh. They call him a tyrant. They say he doesn't possess qualities suitable in a King's officer."

"The only judgements I've witnessed were sound enough."

Argyll stared towards the window, fingers steepled, a half-smile on his face. "Perhaps I'm too sentimental. A man should never admit to favouring one child over another, but of all my daughters, Helen is closest to my heart. She has wisdom and courage you'd more often find in a son. She chose him, you know. She loves the man. I'd be inclined to defend him on those grounds alone, but there's more to it than that.

"The men who demand my gude-son's head on a platter don't understand his place in the wider scheme of things. Hugh learned his skills in the north, where men are cruel and hard. In the wild country, a man can't afford to show mercy. To spare a life without good reason is a sign of weakness. Men like you, Sir John, live your lives in blissful ignorance of the threats you face. Not from your own ilk, but from the Sea-wolves of the Isles."

"Everyone fears the Islesmen," John said. "Mothers speak their name to disobedient children, old men remember their predations and weep. Even now, if a strong man sees a mast on the western seas, he'll cross himself and pray for deliverance."

"When the winters are hard they'll be back. They'll take to their ships and ravage the west once more. They plunder and burn, they slaughter without remorse. They have no regard for the King's laws, and precious love for their own kind, either." He held John's gaze, that soft regretful smile playing across his lips once more. "Is that what you want in the Westland, Sir John? A land blackened and ruined, where the burns run red with the blood of innocents."

"Of course not."

"Then Montgomerie must be allowed to dispense justice as he sees fit. The Islesmen know what he's capable of. They fear him. His presence is enough to keep them at bay. Men like you would defend hearth and home to the death if need be. But men like Hugh have different qualities. If he suffered any injury to himself or those he swore to protect, he'd follow a raider across the seas and repay him tenfold."

"I understand that," John said.

"You'll be well-paid, if you speak out in his defence."

John shook his head. "There's no need for this, Your Grace. I'd stand by the truth, whatever the circumstances. And the truth is this: Hugh did not murder Kilmaurs in cold blood."

Argyll nodded, visibly reassured. "I'm grateful for your support, as no doubt Hugh is grateful." He stretched in his chair with a sigh, suddenly thoughtful. "We must all work together to ensure he escapes this business unscathed."

Dawn was breaking when John set out for Dunglass the following morning, the sky burning red in the east.

"Are you sure it's wise to ride alone?" William asked as they approached the gates.

"Don't worry," John told him, all false confidence. It was an honour to assist in Argyll's business, but it unsettled him nonetheless. To be bearing letters on behalf of a senior member of the Privy Council, with no idea of what exactly they contained... In such circumstances, ignorance was poor defence when dealing with matters that might be interpreted as treason.

Hugh led a slim brown courser out from the stables. "Here's your horse," he said. "Archie says he'll serve you well."

John climbed into the saddle without a word. His mount danced and twitched and pawed the cobbles, eager to depart.

"I still don't think you should be travelling alone," William persisted.

"It's best this business is undertaken with subtlety," Hugh assured him. "Besides, I doubt any peril on the road could be worse than Argyll's wolfpack."

"Sir John!" Argyll's voice boomed in greeting. He emerged from the tower-house and strode briskly across the yard, a satchel clutched in one hand. "Here you are." He passed it to John. "I've enclosed a letter for Montgrennan, for his eyes alone. There's money, too. It'll help pay your expenses, plus a little extra besides. Consider it a token of my gratitude. And Hugh's of course."

John grimaced. "Your Grace, I don't need-"

Argyll's face crinkled into a smile. "Never refuse a gift granted in good faith. Just remember that Campbell of Argyll looks after his own. Serve me well, grant me the loyalty you've given my gude-son and you'll be amply rewarded."

"Many thanks, Your Grace." John took up the reins in readiness.

"Keep south of the Clyde and avoid the Lennox," Argyll advised him. "You'll find a fresh horse at Glasgow, and you can change again at Edinburgh if needs be. Just find Montgrennan, without delay. We must have him in our lists as soon as possible."

Chapter 61

The Place of Ellestoun

Margaret awoke with a gasp, skin misted with sweat. She'd been dreaming. That John returned. That she'd been lying in her bed, bathed in the soft gloom of twilight. Hearing his footsteps echo light across the floor, she drew the coverlet close. Calling his name, she cajoled him to join her.

He settled alongside, flesh hot against hers. Taking him in her arms, she kissed his face, his chest, running her hands all over him. He seized her shoulders, pressed her down.

Closing her eyes, she moaned as he mounted her. He seemed different somehow. Quicker, more careless in his manner. She weathered his vigour with good humour, then when the deed was done, she opened her eyes.

And couldn't breathe for the horror, because it wasn't John who'd lain with her, it was Hugh.

She recoiled with a cry, but he grasped her wrists and held her firm. He was smiling at her, fearless and beguiling. *Don't be afraid,* he said. *It's what you wanted all along...*

Bile rose in her throat. She scrambled from her bed and made it to the fireplace before she doubled over and retched, again and again.

The girls came running. "Margaret!" Katherine confronted her, whey-faced with panic. "What's wrong?"

"I- I can't say-" She broke off. Deep in her belly, something stirred. She felt a kick, brief but fierce. Her heart soared, she felt terror and elation all at once. "He moved, Katherine."

"He?"

"I'm bearing a son. I *know* I am." She leaned on Katherine's arm, faint with apprehension. "I must speak with the priest. Now."

Margaret clung tight to the saddle, the mare's gentle sway making her stomach churn. Screwing her eyes shut, she willed the horse onwards.

A shudder passed through her. It was all her fault. She'd thought about lying with Hugh to punish John for his infidelity, an idle fancy, nothing more. Now the image had lodged in her soul, eating away like a canker. Poisoning her. Poisoning her child...

She dismounted and hurried into the kirk, just in time for the start of the mass. The relief was overwhelming, until she turned and spotted *her*, attending mass with her household.

John's mother, Elizabeth Ross.

Margaret did her very best to avoid her, clasping her rosary and rattling single-mindedly through the beads. But the older woman's gaze was strong enough to flay her, it was the most she could do to keep from weeping.

Eventually, it was over. Her gude-mother came bustling towards her, but Margaret was in no mood for conversation. She flicked the older woman the slightest of nods then cornered the priest. "I must take Confession."

The priest nodded politely to Lady Elizabeth, who glared at Margaret, visibly annoyed. "We'll walk outside, shall we?" he said.

Margaret made a valiant attempt at a curtsey. "Thank you, Holy Father."

"Whatever's the matter?" The priest demanded, his face flushed with concern. "Has something happened?"

Margaret cast a forlorn gaze across the tombstones. Dread knotted in her stomach, she wished she'd been speaking to her familiar old chaplain at Ochiltree instead of baring her soul to the priest who shared her husband's secrets. Perhaps months before John had confessed his sins, justifying his adultery with the fact that his new bride was harsh and cruel, a twisted heartless shrew...

"I've been thinking impure thoughts..." She could barely manage a whisper. "About a man who's not my husband. Last night I dreamed of him. And now I'm frightened. Because of the child..."

The words poured out. He didn't interrupt: he just listened, neither angry nor judgemental while she explained everything. About Hugh, how she'd tended him and kept him from death. "I did it to be charitable," she said. "My husband placed him in my care, because he trusted no-one else to look after him."

"And where was Sir John at this time?"

"He had to go to Eglintoun, and tell the Lady Montgomerie that her husband was safe."

"He left you alone with Lord Hugh?"

"Yes."

The priest regarded her carefully. "You remained chaste?" His voice hardened. "You must speak the truth. If you lie to me, you lie to God Himself."

"He was very ill. But even if he'd been capable, I would never have committed carnal sin with him. I wouldn't betray John. He's my husband, and I love him. I don't love Lord Hugh. I don't even like him much. He's disagreeable, and sometimes he frightens me. But there have been moments when my thoughts of him were less than pure." She shivered. "Saints preserve me. I didn't want to put my child in jeopardy."

"You should have mentioned this before."

"They were idle thoughts, that's all."

"Conjured by the Devil, so he could tempt you to sin. It's a good thing you confessed it, before you were moved to act."

"And the babe?"

"If you fast, and pray, then God will look kindly upon you both, and all will be well."

Her knees wobbled with sudden, overwhelming relief. "I'm so sorry."

"Lady Margaret." The old priest smiled at her, faintly pitying. "The error was your husband's. To leave you alone with temptation so close... Such a cruel thing to do. It's in a woman's nature to be fickle and inconstant. She craves a man's heat to warm her humours. Your husband knows this. He knows, too, that without the wisdom of a husband or father to guide her, his wife will seek comfort elsewhere. That's why the Devil's quick to act in such circumstances."

Margaret blinked, taking in his words. "I did nothing wrong?"

"It's sinful to desire a man's flesh, even if nothing comes of it. But in the circumstances your restraint was admirable. To have curbed your cravings was more than most women could aspire to. It pains me to say this, as Sir John is very dear to me, but... He acted foolishly. You're young, inexperienced in the ways of the world. He should be steering you along the right path, not leaving you to forge your way through life unassisted." He caught her eye, concerned. "Shall I speak with him on his return?"

"Please, no..." Margaret whispered. Her anxiety was gone, she felt guilty instead, because John was the one who'd suffered most condemnation, and he wasn't even here to defend himself.

"Have you spoken with a midwife?"

"No, I should, I know, but..."

"The midwife should be visiting every day to check that all's well. You've made a valiant effort to maintain your spiritual health, and for that God will smile upon you, but..." He laid a concerned hand upon her shoulder. "You can't battle on alone indefinitely, can you?"

Dumbarton Castle

Pushing his hair irritably back from his face, Hugh took a deep breath then set off at a saunter. Heading up the cobbled track his careless attitude was all for show; already, his mouth was dry with apprehension, his chest and oxsters damp with sweat.

The barbican loomed ahead, a solid wall of neatly worked stone, aloof and impregnable. The heavy wooden gates that pierced its masonry were closed fast.

With a rattle and a squeal the portcullis mechanism moved unseen; Hugh looked back one last time to where Archie stood with Zephyr's reins clutched in his hand. His gude-brother smiled, sympathetic: Hugh nodded in farewell then continued on his way, braving the shadows and gloom of the gatehouse.

The door creaked open a sliver: an arm snaked out, hauled him inside.

"Hugo," Matthew said.

And there he was. A little pale and thin, perhaps, but still himself, broad-shouldered and cocksure. Closing the door, he shot home the check, then gripped Hugh in a warm embrace. "It's good to see you!"

The spikes of the portcullis glinted above and Hugh grimaced, picturing the heavy mass of iron-tipped timber thundering down... "We shouldn't loiter here, Mattie. It just takes one counterweight to fail."

Matthew laughed. "It's not like you to be so cautious." He held out his hands. "May I?"

Hugh relinquished sword and dagger without a word.

Placing a comradely arm about Hugh's shoulders, Matthew steered him through the cobbled expanse of the lower ward. "Welcome to my humble – and somewhat under-provisioned – abode." He led Hugh to the stair that climbed up towards the keep. "You're our guest, Hugh. You must stay with us."

Hugh smiled, thinly. "That's very kind."

"You seem reticent."

"These circumstances are – *awkward*."

"Only if you make them so." Pausing on the stair, Matthew caught his eye. "I saw you last week. In the marshes. With the king."

"I'm surprised you didn't try and slay us."

Matthew's gaze didn't waver. "And what would that have achieved?"

Hugh shrugged. "It might have relieved the monotony."

"And made us guilty of regicide?" Matthew countered. "Regicide being - may I remind you - the very issue we're contesting at the moment..." He quickened his pace and Hugh followed, striding up the worn steps two at a time.

"Hugo!" A woman's voice hailed him.

Looking up, Hugh saw faces peering down from the parapet: Margaret Montgomerie, Countess of Lennox, waiting there with her ladies. So too was young Alex Stewart. Hugh raised a hand in acknowledgement: Alex waved back, grinning in delight, while the countess conferred with her companions, her relief tangible.

But of Lady Lyle, there was no sign.

"Where's Lady Margaret Houston?" Hugh asked.

Matthew paused. His chest heaved from the climb, a sure sign that confinement was taking its toll on him, too. "She sends her apologies. She finds her circumstances - *wearisome*. But she'll join us for dinner."

"I daresay she wants to go home."

"To what's left of it, yes."

"Duchal's fate shouldn't concern her. Her place is being rebuilt, at the King's command."

"And I'll wager all her fine furnishings are adorning John Sempill's hall."

"They're being stowed safely at Ellestoun. Awaiting recovery by their rightful owners."

"He'll demand a heavy price for that." Matthew's tone was bitter.

"And you wouldn't, were the situations reversed?" When Matthew didn't answer, he added, "Duchal's in Archie Campbell's keeping. He doesn't take much of an interest, but at least he's not bleeding it dry."

"Unlike Earl Patrick. He'll be pressing hard on Cruikston."

"I can't say what's happening there, Mattie, I'm sorry."

They'd reached the entrance to the keep at last. They paused briefly to compose themselves, then Matthew ushered him through one last set of gates.

Where the household awaited him...

Matthew gestured grandly toward Hugh. "Our prayers are answered."

Margaret Montgomerie stepped forward, face glowing with delight. "What a joy this is, Hugh!"

Hugh took her hands and kissed her dutifully on both cheeks. "Aunt Margaret."

"You'll dine with us this afternoon, I hope?" she said. "There'll be time for negotiations on the morrow."

"Archie has promised to send two wagons loaded with victuals. We both agreed that men are more amenable to reason when they've been granted the luxury of a full stomach."

The Gryphon at Bay

After dinner, he sat with Matthew in the deserted hall. Night had fallen long before, the shutters closed against a chill damp ink-black sky. The fire had burned low and just one solitary servant remained, sweeping the floor with leisurely strokes.

Scratching his knife against the timbers of the board, Matthew crudely carved a tiny image of a ship. It was a *birlinn*, like the boats that plied the western sea; with long thin hull, tall mast and a single sail. "I'm twenty-six years old," he muttered. "I've reached my perfect age. I should wed by now. Or at the very least, settled with a mistress in a town-house somewhere." He stabbed the blade irritably down into the wood. "I used to think that a woman's love meant nothing, that fucking a whore was all a man needed in his life."

"Mattie..."

"Least you've got a wife that loves you. A beautiful wife who just so happens to be an Earl's daughter."

Hugh laughed and shook his head. "I'm the last man alive who merits envy. I've been acquitted for murder once. I'll be damned lucky if I don't get dragged before the Privy Council a second time."

"That's not Fate's doing. That's your own stupidity."

"Thanks." Hugh refilled his cousin's goblet, then his own.

"Christ, Hugh." Matthew slouched across the board, head propped against his hand, face sullen. "What happened? One moment there was everything to play for. The next we were caged here like foxes. At what point did Dame Fortune abandon me?"

"I told you James would never betray Earl Patrick. I knew this would happen."

Matthew scowled. "Self-righteous whore's son..."

"No sense in languishing over what's done," Hugh said, briskly. "We need to find a way out of this mess."

"We'll end up in exile. Like Albany..."

"You're not in direct line to the throne. You're not a threat."

"Not to James. But he's not the man who rules this land. Patrick Hepburn has that privilege. The Earl of fucking Bothwell."

Hugh stretched comfortably in his seat. "Hepburn can't defeat you. God knows, he's tried these past four months or so. The blunt truth is you're as strong as ever. It's the second time this year the men of the Westland have been summoned. We're tired, we're resentful. We don't want to spend the winter rotting in some Godforsaken hole while your people skulk like shadows in the hills."

"What do you suggest?"

"Relinquish the castle."

Matthew was silent. "He'll kill us," he said at last.

"Only if he catches you. But he would never lay a finger on your mother. Leave the castle in her care, and flee. We'll sort out this mess somehow, without further bloodshed."

Matthew didn't so much as look at him. "How, pray, are you to do that?"

"Montgrennan's back."

Matthew turned to Hugh at last, his dark gaze intense and disbelieving. He started to laugh, a twisted bitter sound. "That lying serpent..."

"You needed his support, didn't you?"

Matthew didn't reply.

"Don't rely on him," Hugh said. "He's playing the game by his own rules. But while you're trapped here you can do nothing to help either yourself, or your father." He leaned close, then added, "Take Alex, and go. I'll help you. When the time's right, your mother can hand Dumbarton over to the King's men. I'll take her to Eglintoun; she can stay there until your lands are restored. God knows, you can send Alex there with her if you like. It's not as if anyone will care."

Matthew pulled a miserable face. "I want to trust you."

Hugh reached out and gripped his hand, tightly. "You *have* to trust me, Mattie. There's no other way."

Chapter 62

Christian gritted her teeth and clutched the bench tightly as the wagon lurched and juddered, almost throwing her from her seat. It seemed forever she'd been weathering this journey. Her hips ached from travelling, her body weary to the core.

Twelve days they'd been on the road, making their tortuous way from one abbey or baronial residence to the next. From Kilmaurs to Dunlop, Dunlop to Paisley, Paisley to Govan, Govan to Glasgow. They'd plodded across the entire country, moving from the uncouth lands of the west to the civilised realms of the east. Where the King lived. Where his courtiers lived. Chivalrous men. Courteous men. Men who wouldn't let the grievances of a loyal widow go unheard.

She sighed, suddenly doubtful. They had no reason to help her. No reason at all. They'd listen to her tale of woe, murmur their sympathy and that would be it. Life would go on, same as before. Montgomerie would make their lives a misery, same as before,

They jolted to a halt, the wagon listing so badly that Christian was surprised it didn't topple. The carter cursed his oxen with an uncouth string of obscenities, urging them onwards.

Wincing with distaste, Christian peered out, curious to see how the journey was progressing. Goaded into action, the oxen heaved against their yokes with one last gargantuan effort and soon they were on their way again.

There was Edinburgh, at last. She could see its tangled skein of tall houses stretching out beneath an ominous blanket of smoke. Towering high above the stink of the city was the castle: seen from afar, it looked so beautiful that a lump came to her throat. It shone like a jewel amongst the filth, a beacon of hope amidst her sorrows.

Her heart beat quicker. Even in these dire circumstances she could appreciate why men held this place in high regard. Now, for the first time, she was here, at no man's beck and call.

Her eyes smarted. Drawing her handkerchief, she dabbed at tears.

The Dowager took her hand. "Courage," she said. "We'll find a sympathetic ear, I'm sure."

"And if not? What then?"

The Dowager slumped back with a sigh. "Then we consider other measures."

*   *   *

Edinburgh Castle

There was an air of vaguely organised chaos about the castle of Edinburgh. As John wandered through the Middle Ward he passed a horde of visitors, as varied in their backgrounds as they were in their business. From burgesses to goodwives, minor barons to religious dignitaries, each hoped for a promise of assistance, perhaps even patronage. Two minutes of a Privy Councillor's time, a few feverish moments' audience before the King.

Unlike the rest of them, John prayed for anonymity. Heads turned in his direction nonetheless. Some studiously ignored him, others nodded in curt acknowledgement.

He did his best to remain inconspicuous. He *had* to speak with Montgrennan, but he couldn't let other men know his business. He certainly didn't want anyone to know that Argyll had sent him. For once, he found himself having to lie and mislead, all the time keeping a cordial smile on his face, muttering pleasantries to all who encountered him.

"Hello, John." Robert Colville passed him in the yard, a flock of young clerks and notaries at his heels. "I thought you'd be back at Dunglass by now."

"My kinsman asked me to bring word from his Perthshire lands," John explained. "As you can well imagine, he hasn't the time to visit them in person."

Colville frowned. "He's expecting you?"

"He is," John replied. "Though I'm not entirely sure where I might find him. I hoped you might have word of his whereabouts."

"I'm sure I can find out," Colville said.

John kept a straight face, masking his relief. "That's very kind, sir. Oh, and hospitality would be appreciated, at least until I can establish what's required of me."

Colville waved his hand. "I'm sure I can arrange that."

John allowed himself a slight smile. He hadn't expected it to be so easy. But there was a glint in Colville's eye, a hint of unspoken understanding. It was indication enough that Montgrennan's star was waxing, and that Robert Colville wanted to be counted amongst his friends.

Later that evening the King took mass in St Margaret's Chapel. He was attended by his favoured courtiers: Patrick Hepburn, Robert Colville and Montgrennan, too, amongst a dozen others.

John skulked in the shadows, fervently hoping that he wouldn't be spotted by either Patrick Hepburn, or James himself. He slipped out first, watching carefully as Montgrennan paused to speak with the king. Colville fell into step alongside; a perfect ruse, for Colville distracted Montgrennan just long enough to allow Hepburn and King James to move away.

John hurried over. "My lord?"

Montgrennan's serene expression didn't even waver. "You know my nephew?" he asked Robert Colville, then laughed, feigning surprise. "Of course you do! He's a kinsman of yours, too." He smiled at John "Do you bring news?"

"I've spoken with the steward. He says that everything's in place as you've instructed. He also asked me to give you this." Without hesitation, he thrust Argyll's letter into Montgrennan's grasp.

Montgrennan studied it briefly. "Walk with me, Sir John." He grasped John's arm, steering him away. "And my good wishes to *you*, Master Colville," he called over his shoulder. "We'll talk on the morrow."

"It's not quite the Royal apartments, but it's adequate." Montgrennan pushed open the door and gestured for John to step inside. "Wine?" Pausing by the buffet, he lifted the waiting flagon in readiness. "Do sit down."

Taking the cup that was offered, John sat without a word on a nearby stool.

Montgrennan sank comfortably down into a chair by the fireside. He drew his dagger, sliced the seal, then studied John a moment, frowning. "You ran into trouble?"

"Some ruffians on the road, that's all. It's perilous to travel near St John's Town these days." John smiled, wearily. "I'd hoped the bruises would have faded by now."

"When the light falls a certain way, they're still quite obvious. Now if you'll excuse me..." Montgrennan read carefully, frowning. "This is curious." Sitting back, he fixed John with his searching gaze. "My own nephew, running errands for Earl Colin of Argyll..."

John shrugged, vague dismissal.

Montgrennan sighed, and shook his head. "Oh, John, what foolishness is this?"

"My lord?"

"Friendship should never steer a man's course."

"It guided yours."

"A king's friendship should never be set aside lightly."

"The principle's the same," said John. "Will you help him?"

Montgrennan's gaze didn't waver. "Alright," he said at last. "I'll do what Argyll asks. But in return I'd like to ask one more favour from you, John, before you can consider yourself free from obligation. I shall write a letter to Argyll tonight, and in the morning you'll leave, and bear it to him. Is that acceptable?"

"Yes, my lord," said John. "It is."

"I admire your courage," Patrick Hepburn said. "But to wander abroad like this was foolhardy. Of course, Lord Robert's death has been a shock to us all."

Christian bowed her head, weighed down with despair. Her gude-brother had spared them just one glance throughout. The rest of the time he'd been staring out through the open window, down towards the distant city and the port of Leith beyond.

"Don't patronise me, Patrick." The Dowager spoke through gritted teeth. "Something must be done. I want this man punished."

Hepburn turned with a sigh, face etched with regret. "Dearest sister," he said. "Affairs of state are delicate matters. Much as I'd like to help, taking punitive action against Montgomerie would be counterproductive. Why discard a perfectly capable officer when he commits just one indiscretion?"

"How can you say such a thing?" The Dowager snapped back, red-faced with rage. "He's been abusing our family for years! He robs, he burns, he slaughters without remorse. He's a monster. If you won't punish him, then at least let us govern our own affairs. Let us answer directly to the King..."

Earl Patrick's expression didn't waver. "That's not possible."

"Your own nephew died at Montgomerie's hand. What more must he do before you bring him to heel? How many more will die?"

He spread his hands wide. "Of course I sympathise."

"Don't lie to me!" The Dowager's voice was shrill with venom. "It's clear to me that you won't lift a finger to assist. If that's so, we'll find someone who will."

He regarded her carefully, eyes narrowed. "Whatever do you mean by that?"

The Dowager smiled, lips tight with triumph. "That's my own business, Patrick." She nodded to Christian. "Come with me, Christian. We'll achieve nothing here." Turning briskly on her heel, she marched out.

Christian trudged along, legs moving of their own accord. The long corridors had impressed her at first, with their rich geometric hangings and the candles burning brightly in their brackets. Now, though, she scarcely heeded them.

She felt ashen inside. Empty. For a brief moment there'd been hope. Now even that shred of comfort was denied them.

The Dowager strode alongside, fierce as an Amazon. Her lips formed a thin line, her eyes glittering like cold hard steel in a face that was deathly pale. "Betrayed by my own brother," she muttered. "God rot him..." She stopped in her tracks and turned to Christian. "Why should he help us? We can't help him progress at court. We can't take up arms when he commands it."

"Cuthbert can."

"He's just a boy. A lamb wandering alone amongst a sea of wolves..." The Dowager took a deep shuddering breath. "Patrick knows what Rob meant to me. He knows that Montgomerie's taken everything in my life that ever mattered-" She hissed and flinched, suddenly watchful, and seized Christian's arm.

Following her gaze, Christian drew a sharp anxious breath. A group of courtiers loitered ahead: they laughed together as if they hadn't a single care in the world.

"I forget myself," the Dowager whispered. "We're treading on dangerous ground."

It was only when they'd drawn level that Christian realised why her gude-mother was so agitated. Her heart nearly stopped, for she found herself confronting a slender, fair-haired young man whose angelic features seemed oddly familiar.

He met her gaze, and offered her a smile, faint, almost apologetic.

She clutched the Dowager's sleeve once they'd left him behind them. "Who is he?"

"Sempill of Ellestoun. He's a friend of Montgomerie. Cuthbert had words with him at the funeral."

She remembered him then. Remembered Cuthbert's reaction, the anger... Panic stirred inside her. "What's he doing here?"

The Dowager pursed her lips. "Paving a way for himself at court."

"Who was he talking to?"

"I don't know," she said. "But I'm determined to find out."

"John Ross of Montgrennan!" Slamming the door behind her, the Dowager stamped across the room. The candles twitched as she passed, wilting before her fury. "My husband's ally from the old King's last days."

"He was in London."

"He's obviously returned." Slumping into a chair, the Dowager buried her face in her hands. "How could I be so blind? Montgomerie's persuaded Sempill to help him. He's used Ellestoun's kinship with Montgrennan to good advantage, buying his loyalty." She snapped back in her chair, eyes staring into nothingness, tears trickling down her cheeks. "Curse this fragile flesh of mine! A man can move at court unquestioned, while a woman must rely on her kin. And Will... He fights like a lion, but in a war of such subtlety, he's helpless. We're all helpless..." Her voice drifted off, she closed her eyes.

Christian took her hand and gripped it tight. "But there's always hope," she whispered. "We can pray to God at least, and ask for His Deliverance."

The Dowager shook her head. "Poor Christian," she said, laying her thin hand against the younger woman's cheek. "Even now, you dare to hope. When King and court and the whole world stand against us."

Chapter 63

The Lands of Dunglass

By the time John reached his destination, the sun was sinking low behind the grim bulk of the castle rock. The weather had stayed fair, at least, though it was cold. Bitterly cold.

A banner flying high from the place of Dunglass bore the Campbell gyronny, alternating panels of *or* and sable; seeing it, John smiled, tightly. As he'd hoped, Earl Colin was still in residence.

He urged his horse onwards. Racked with fatigue, still stiff and sore from his encounter with Argyll's retainers, he couldn't rest. Not until he'd seen Montgrennan's letter delivered safely into the hands of a senior Campbell, preferably Earl Colin himself.

His bay courser fared little better. The beast had maintained its steady amble for hours, but now its head was drooping, coat curdled with sweat round neck and shoulders.

Eventually, he slowed to a walk, letting the horse find its own pace. Men watched carefully from the barmkin as he came closer, but no-one challenged him.

Until he steered his horse into the yard, when a dozen burly men swathed in filthy *aketons* came swaggering up, faces hard and hostile.

John lowered himself down with a sigh. "I request an audience with Earl Colin. I've a message. And I'm returning his horse..." Their faces were blank, uncomprehending, he broke off, wondering how best to explain himself. Whether French was required, or even Latin...

A curt instruction was barked in *gaelic*, and John soon found himself escorted into the tower-house by a grim-faced retainer. Once he'd trudged into the hall, his guide abandoned him to the mercies of another half-dozen Campbell men-at-arms. Some played merelles by the window, while others sat around the board, engrossed in a card game. He hoped they'd ignore him, but instead they looked up and studied him with interest.

"*Ioin!*" one bayed in joyous greeting. "*Ioin Semphaill!*" He beckoned for John to join him.

John shrugged and smiled and did as he was bid. No sooner had he settled on the bench than he was wrapped in a brotherly embrace which nearly crushed him. A long conversation in *gaelic* followed: it was, he suspected, a blow-by-blow account of the night he'd been accosted by Earl Colin's men.

He clasped his hands and bowed his head, trying not to attract too much attention. He had the distinct impression they were all enjoying a joke at his expense.

A mazer, half-filled with honeyed ale, was thrust into his grasp and he was slapped on the back with cheerful good humour.

Reassured, he drank deep, grateful for the refreshment. And relieved, too, that he'd at last found a respite from his travels.

"John Sempill is here," the man-at-arms announced. *"He asks to speak with you, my lord."*

Earl Colin caught Archie's eye then looked to Hugh. "Go and fetch him, Hugh," he said. "And then we'll see what Mongrennan has to say for himself." He rubbed his chin, thoughtful reflection.

Hugh rose to his feet without a word. As the door closed behind him, Earl Colin and Archie resumed their conversation: terse exchanges, barely audible.

Hugh sighed: he'd have given his eye teeth to know what exactly they were saying.

Banishing the doubts from his mind, he followed the Campbell retainer down the winding turnpike stair. Apprehension gnawed away inside him, a dull, persistent ache in his soul.

It was hard to place his fate in the hands of a man he mistrusted. It riled him. So much so that he didn't know how he maintained that air of levity as he breezed into the hall where John was waiting, beleaguered amongst a crowd of Campbell soldiers.

"The errant knight returns," he remarked. "Earl Colin's eager to hear your news."

John set down the mazer and climbed wearily to his feet. He clapped a hand on the Campbell retainer's shoulder, a gesture of wordless camaraderie.

Hugh steered him over to the stair.

"I think he is surprised we did not eat him!" one of the Campbells called after him. *"These Southern lordlings are all the same."*

Hugh laughed, and prodded John onwards. "Come on," he said. "Let's not keep His Grace waiting."

Earl Colin smiled in vague welcome and extended his hand as John was brought before him.

John handed him the letter; it was accepted with a nod. Slicing the seal with his knife, Argyll unrolled the parchment. He scanned its contents in silence, while the rest of them looked on.

The earl sat back with a sigh, saying nothing. Then at last he looked up, a satisfied smile on his lips. "Excellent," he said. "Things are indeed progressing." He nodded to John. "Thank you, Sir John. You've served me well. Consider yourself free from any further obligation."

John bowed, and retreated from their presence. The door closed behind him, and still they didn't speak, just exchanging cautious glances while the tread of his feet dwindled.

It was only when the door to the hall banged shut below that Archie slipped over to the stair, one final check that all was clear.

Hugh shifted uncomfortably, wondering why he was finding all this duplicity distasteful. It wasn't as if there was any other way. And in the long run, a successful outcome to this problem will benefit everyone, John Sempill included...

Archie re-appeared, and closed the door. "He's gone."

"Good," said Earl Colin. "Very well. The situation is this: Montgrennan has agreed to help us. On all fronts. I suggest we progress the matter tonight, while the weather holds."

"And Sir John Sempill?" Hugh asked.

Earl Colin sighed. "What he doesn't know need not concern him. Let everything seem normal, Hugh. He must not suspect that anything's amiss."

They ate together that night, Montgomeries and Sempills. Hugh studied John closely throughout, gauging his mood. His friend seemed numb with fatigue, too exhausted to show much interest in anything. He listened politely while Hugh told him how things were progressing at Dumbarton, then muttered his apologies and said he'd share his news upon the morrow. After a mumbled goodnight, he found himself a quiet corner, wrapping himself up in his cloak and a couple of blankets.

Hugh joined him there later, making sure that he settled close enough to gauge John's breathing, alert for the moment when the younger man fell fast asleep.

The night air was frigid, and for once, Hugh was glad of the cold; it helped him stay awake.

For what felt like hours, he lay there, waiting...

Then at last he stirred. Throwing his blankets aside, he sat up. His eyes, accustomed to darkness, took in the mounded forms of sleeping men, scattered around the floor of the cottage.

No response from John: satisfied that all was safe, Hugh shoved Robert's shoulder, roughly. By the time his brother had gathered his wits, he was already on his feet, boots in one hand, sword-belt in the other. Despite his efforts, the hilt of his sword scraped along the cobbled floor, he hissed, quiet frustration.

John rolled over. "What's the matter..." he murmured. "I thought-"

"Some drunken brawling in the horse lines," came Hugh's terse reply. "I'll deal with it. Go back to sleep."

John grunted an inaudible acknowledgement, and retreated back into his blanket.

Hugh glanced heavenwards, murmuring a silent prayer to Holy Mary. Asking her to ensure that by morning, the Laird of Ellestoun would have forgotten this disturbance ever took place.

Inching his careful way past the sleeping men-at-arms, Hugh paused at the threshold to pull on his boots. Robert joined him there, together they stepped out into the cold black night.

The air was sharp with frost, stars and planets glittering in a velvet black sky. The half-moon hung high overhead, veiled in a faint misty halo.

Hugh breathed deep, relishing the excruciating cold and the darkness. "That was too close for comfort," he whispered.

"We're not done yet," Robert replied.

Together they made their cautious way through the camp, past lines of dozing horses pressed close for warmth. Once they reached the track, they followed its curve round through the marshes until they found the path which led out to the jetty. A chill mist hung over the reedbeds: too late Hugh saw the shadows of men looming ahead; a single horseman, half—a-dozen soldiers armed with spears.

Someone barked a terse query in *gaelic*.

"*We are here,*" Hugh replied.

"*The boat is ready.*" Archie Campbell spoke from the horse's back, hood pulled low. "*Go with them, Hugh. I will wait here.*"

The Gryphon at Bay

One of the foot soldiers passed him a lantern: Hugh accepted it with a weary sigh. The flame shone dim through horn panels, scarcely visible.

"*God be with you,*" Archie said, tersely.

Eight of Argyll's men manned the oars. Born and raised in the sea lochs of the West, the darkness didn't daunt them. Knowing the need for silence, they didn't utter so much as a sound.

Hugh stood tall in the prow, nursing the lantern close against his chest so the flame wouldn't fail. All around him, the waters of the Clyde were flecked with shifting shards of silver, moonlight fracturing and dancing in the boat's wake.

He breathed deep, catching the scent of the sharp sea air, alert to every rustle from the reed beds. Every sinew was taut with expectation: it was as if he'd drunk of a fine exotic wine, which warmed the flesh and fired the soul.

A duck quacked soft nearby and he flinched, half-expecting a crossbow-bolt to slam into him from the reeds. He gripped his dagger, just in case, but all he could hear was the faint splash of the fowl taking off from the water.

Sheer cliffs loomed close as they skirted the southern shore. Confident he could no longer be seen from the king's camp, Hugh removed the panels from the lantern, exposing the guttering flame within. He held it high, heart scudding in relief as he realised that a tiny sliver of light was glimmering in kind from high upon the rock.

The boat jolted as an oar struck the rough stone wall of the boat naust. A man cursed softly in *gaelic*, then - in one single well-drilled movement - the oars were lifted high, the keel grating against the rocks below.

Hugh sprang to shore, grimacing as his foot slipped. The ground was rimed with ice, the going treacherous. Squinting into the darkness, he could just make out the thin line of the stone stair that clung to the rock's unforgiving sides.

Two figures approached, vague shadows against the relentless black of the whinstone cliffs. They'd hooded the lantern, which meant progress was painfully slow. All he could do was wait, and pray.

Reeds rustled underfoot, two men loomed close in the murk.

"Mattie?" Hugh asked.

"Hugo!" Matthew stepped forward. "My bold and worthy cousin, you don't know how pleased I am to see you..." He took a deep, luxurious breath. "And to stretch my wings unfettered once more. Ah, God and the saints be praised!"

Hugh gripped his hand tightly. "Let's not loiter, cousin. Archie awaits us at Dunglass."

The boat sped to shore, renewed urgency in every oar stroke. Both fugitives sat hunched and furtive at the stern, and even Hugh was wary, searching the bank for anything amiss. The mist was rising, curling up around the shore: as they pulled in at the jetty, a horse snorted and stamped.

"Hugo?" Archie hissed.

"Our cargo's safe." Hugh climbed carefully onto the slippery timbers of the jetty.

Stretching out his hand to Matthew, he helped his kinsman alight. Alex followed, leaping onto dry land with all the vigour of a hound unleashed.

"Careful!" Hugh warned, but too late. There was a bang and a thump and the boy's legs went out from under him.

"Christ!" snapped Hugh. "Are you trying to hang us all?"

Alex sat up, blinking. He was cradling his arm. "I'm sorry."

"Can you move?" Archie asked worriedly. "We mustn't loiter."

"I'm alright. I slipped. I didn't think-"

"Obviously," Hugh replied, dryly. "Now, if you want my counsel, I suggest you travel separate ways. Robert will take Alex to Eglintoun, while you, Mattie... You're cunning and resourceful. You won't want for allies if you seek them in the right places."

"And the least said about that the better," Archie muttered.

"Cousins, I won't forget what you've risked for me this night..."

"I know that," Hugh said. "Now go, while you're granted the safety of darkness. Come to Eglintoun for Yuletide. We'll decide then what should be done."

"You'll take care of my mother?"

"She'll want for nothing," Hugh assured him. "Godspeed, Mattie. May He keep you both safe from harm." He nodded to Robert, who was helping young Alex Stewart up onto a waiting horse. "Ride upriver and cross the ford at Govan," he told his brother. "You should arrive there around daybreak. After that, ride south and in the name of God, don't stop until you reach Eglintoun!"

Chapter 64

The Place of Ellestoun

When Margaret looked out that morning, she saw a thin line of dark cloud hanging low in the west. It cast a malignant shadow over a chill, frost-shrouded landscape, nothing more. By mid-afternoon, the skies were grim; and by nightfall, the rain lashed wild against the shutters.

Margaret shivered, and drew her chair close to the fireside. She tried to concentrate on her psalter, but thought instead of John. She wondered how he was faring, whether there was any chance he'd make it back home by Yuletide...

She tilted her head, distracted. She'd heard a commonition in the yard, barely audible over the wind. "Katherine," she said, without looking up. "See what's amiss."

"It's Robert Montgomerie," Katherine said. "He apologises for the lateness of the hour, but requests an audience nonetheless."

A void of fear opened inside her, she wondered with a jolt if he'd come bearing bad news. "Fit my hood," she told Alison. "Katherine, tell him I'll join him when I can."

Robert Montgomerie was a disconsolate figure in the hall. He was soaked through and shivering: water pooled from his boots and cloak, his black hair was plastered against his scalp and his cheeks were red from the cold. He smiled in greeting nonetheless, though she thought he looked distant, a little furtive.

He wasn't travelling alone. A boy stood with him, a whey-faced youth who studied the floor, shame-faced.

And waiting in wary attendance on these travellers, almost every man who remained at Ellestoun. They loitered by the fire and near the doorway: Old Henry the groom, and young John Alexson, too, plus a couple of the kitchen boys.

Robert Montgomerie's glance flitted warily about the room. "Lady Margaret," he said, his tone soft, beseeching. "Forgive this intrusion. We were riding to Eglintoun on Lord Hugh's business when the storm swept in. I wondered if we might beg a space in the hall. We'll be gone by first light..."

Noticing again that furtive nervous look flicker across his face, she frowned, sure that something was amiss. She wished Alan Semple was there to advise her, but he'd ridden to Southannan a few days previously and hadn't yet returned.

She bowed her head and took a deep fortifying breath. John had entrusted her to make decisions on his behalf, so she had to act, with or without Alan's counsel. "The Montgomeries are always welcome in this house," she said. "The master's chamber is unoccupied. We'll prepare the bed if you like."

Robert Montgomerie bowed his head. "You're most gracious, Lady Margaret."

"How's my husband?" she asked. "Is he well?"

"I believe so, Lady Margaret. Though I haven't had much opportunity to speak with him. He was dispatched to Edinburgh on Argyll's business, and returned just yesterday."

She felt giddy with relief at the news. "Thank God," she said. "I'll ask the cooks to prepare some pottage. You must be hungry."

He smiled, too easily. "Please don't trouble yourself-"

"I insist. Let me show you to your chamber."

"Begging your pardon, Lady Margaret," John Alexson spoke out. "Shouldn't our guests give up their arms when they stay within these walls?" He marched up to Robert Montgomerie with a swagger that surpassed his years. "Your sword, sir," he said, and held out his hand. "Sir John left me strict orders to keep the ladies safe." He smiled, cold and distant. "We can't make exceptions. You don't know who'll come calling on a night like this."

Robert Montgomerie frowned and exchanged an opaque glance with his young companion, then unbuckled his sword belt. "As you wish."

As they left the hall, she followed. But as she drew level with the doorway, young Master Alexson stepped up close and tugged her sleeve. "Might I speak with you, Lady Margaret?" His eyes were wide with worry and agitation.

She shrugged him aside. "I must attend my guests."

The boy shook his head, imploring. "It's very important."

Already her guests were disappearing up the stair: for some absurd reason, she had no desire to let them wander unattended. "It's very late," she said. "And I'm bone weary. It can wait till morning, surely?"

The Place of Kilmaurs

"I heard you were in Edinburgh." Countess Elizabeth slipped off her fur-trimmed cloak and sat down by the fireside. "I arrived not long after you'd departed and was disappointed to hear I'd missed you." Leaning close to Christian, she laid a gentle hand upon her arm. "But Dame Fortune was not altogether against me. I was planning to visit my Boyd kinsmen before Yuletide. What better opportunity to see how you were faring, I thought, than to seek shelter under your roof on my journey south."

"I'm delighted to receive you," Christian said. And she meant it, too. For days on end, she'd sat in her chamber, thinking endless black thoughts about the cruelty of the world, the indifference of king and court. Now, though, it was as if the stars had shifted in her favour. She'd scarcely believed it, when she stood on the wall-walk and watched Elizabeth Boyd arrive in her horse-litter, accompanied by two dozen armed Douglas retainers.

"Of course, I have ulterior motives," Elizabeth Boyd said, lightly. "I'd hoped to speak with the Lord Kilmaurs himself."

"Lord Cuthbert isn't here at present," Christian replied. "He's staying with his kinsmen in the shire of Renfrew. We thought it prudent that he stayed well away from Montgomerie's reach until things settle."

"A wise decision," the countess agreed. "Rumour has it that you spoke with Earl Patrick."

Christian hesitated, wondering how best to respond. "He was not, how might one say it, *helpful...*"

"I'm sorry to hear this." Countess Elizabeth smoothed out her skirts, deliberately avoiding Christian's gaze. "I have my own reasons to be sympathetic. But I know my husband the Earl would agree that if the Hepburns won't help you, then assuredly the Douglases will." She caught Christian's gaze at last, her smile emphatic.

Choked with emotion, Christian couldn't bring herself to answer.

"I'm sure he's a worthy youth, at an age where he'll be eager to test his mettle. My husband would be delighted to welcome him into his retinue. In fact..." The countess paused, waiting for her words to sink in. "I thought that since I was heading back east in a week or two, Lord Cuthbert might ride with me. They say there's no time like the present."

Chapter 65

The Place of Eglintoun

Sitting young Alex Stewart down near the fire, Helen cast a concerned eye over him. He was trying his best to appear brave and manly, but the tell-tale signs were there. He was pale and sweating, his eyes bright with pain. And there was a slump to one shoulder that looked far from normal.

She crouched beside him. "How did this happen?" she asked.

Alex glanced at his feet, shame-faced. "We left our place at midnight, I was cold and tired. When I left the boat I stumbled."

"Did you know you'd hurt yourself?"

"I heard something snap, and everything went black a moment. But how could I complain in front of Hugh and Mattie?"

"We didn't have much opportunity to rest," Robert added. "Hugh told us to come here without delay."

"We'd best cut your sark off you," Helen said. "And then I'll see what should be done. We may need the bone-setter."

Grasping her knife, she gently sliced away his shirt and eased the cloth aside. When she pressed her fingers gently against the discoloured flesh above his chest, the collarbone shifted slightly. Alex stifled a moan, biting his lip so hard that a line of blood trickled down his chin.

"I'll bind it," Helen said. "And I'll bring a draught to ease the pain. I don't think the bone-setter could do much more for you."

"It's my sword arm," the boy muttered.

"You'll fight again," she assured him. "Just be thankful that you're here at Eglintoun, and not skulking in a muddy hole somewhere." She beckoned to the servant who approached, carrying a bowl of steaming, herb-infused water. "Set it down here, if you please." Dipping a cloth into the water, she asked, "Did my lord say when he'd return?"

"Before Yuletide," said Robert. "That's his intent, at any rate."

She closed her eyes, imagined Hugh sitting hunched over a fire in a draughty tent somewhere, complaining loudly about the inclement food and the even-more inclement weather. He'd be frustrated because it hadn't come to war, but she could live with that. She thanked God that he was safe, that the only hurt she'd have to mend was his bruised pride. "So it's over."

Robert Montgomerie shrugged. "Until the next time."

Helen sighed, and wrung the cloth out in readiness. "Now hold still, Alex," she said. "I'll be as gentle as I can."

* * *

324

The Gryphon at Bay

The Place of Ellestoun

Carts filled the yard, piled high with furnishings. It seemed to Margaret that every servant had been pressed into service, unloading baggage into the guest range.

Alan Semple was overseeing the proceedings, making sure that everything was carried out to his satisfaction.

Margaret set a determined course towards him. Seeing her approach, he flinched visibly and doffed his bonnet, red-faced with embarrassment.

"What's happening here?" Margaret demanded.

Alan studied the cobbles. "Lady Elizabeth arrived this morning and demanded lodgings. You were at mass, my lady. I couldn't disturb you."

Somehow her composure held. "Where is she now?"

"Inside. Making sure everything gets put in its proper place." He cast her an anxious look. "What was I to do?" he asked in a low voice.

Margaret bristled with indignation, but said nothing. All this time she'd dismissed the dowager as inconsequential. But she'd been wrong. Instead, Lady Elizabeth had been biding her time, awaiting the right moment to make her move.

She'd accomplished her task with admirable skill, too, for Margaret was in no mood for confrontation. But despite the queasy feeling in her guts and the ever-growing fatigue in her limbs, Margaret wasn't going to relinquish her authority without a fight.

Taking a deep breath, she marched into the range, determined even now to hold her ground.

Lady Elizabeth was in the hall, issuing strident instructions regarding the placing of wall-hangings.

Margaret approached without a word.

"Ah, good day, Margaret!" Her gude-mother spared her a humourless smile.

"I wasn't told of this."

"It's not your concern," came the brisk response.

The anger boiled inside her, she felt the babe twitch in her belly and laid her hand there. "Of course it is!"

"When my son placed Ellestoun in your care, he misjudged the situation, and he misjudged you, too. You're incapable of handling such responsibility. That's why I'm here, to rescue the household from further mishap."

"But this is nonsense! No one ever questions my decisions! And John said-"

The older woman's glance was withering. "You don't know what you've done, do you?"

"Whatever do you mean?"

"You let one of my son's sworn enemies seek shelter under his roof, not three days hence."

She felt suddenly faint. "I don't know what you're talking about."

"That boy. The one who came here with Hugh Montgomerie's brother."

She remembered him well enough. A pleasant lad, perhaps a little too anxious and ill-at-ease for her liking. "What of him?"

"He's the younger son of the Earl of Lennox." Lady Elizabeth's face shone with self-righteous indignation. "His brother Matthew laid waste to these lands last winter. He'd have killed my boy if he could. As it was, he nearly ruined him."

"I didn't know," she whispered.

"There's much you don't know. But that's hardly your fault." She bustled away, running her relentless gaze over the wall-hangings. "-I blame that boy of mine, for being too soft with you. But then, he's hardly the sharpest spear in the schiltron." She paused by the aumbry, opening the door and peering inside. "His poor father always said he'd be the ruin of this place."

"What right do you have, to pass judgement on my lord's decisions-"

"-I'm not here to argue. I'm here to put things right and I'll be starting with you. You're carrying my grandchild. How you've succeeded in keeping it so far I don't know. I daresay you've been lax in what you're eating-"

"I've suffered no harm this far-"

"And what about the midwife? Have you spoken to her yet?"

"I- I don't see-"

"Lady Margaret?" Alan's head poked round the door. "The midwife's here. She says you're expecting her."

Margaret half-closed her eyes, defeated. She could've wept.

"How did you know to come here?" Margaret asked. She'd delayed this meeting for weeks, but now the moment of reckoning was upon her, all she felt was overwhelming relief. Even though she was lying flat on her back on the bed, with her kirtle hauled up over her breast and her privy parts exposed to the world, the indignity no longer seemed to matter.

"I heard talk that Lady Elizabeth was on her way," Mary White told her. "I thought I'd call by and see how you were faring."

"I underestimated her," Margaret whispered.

"She ruled this place for twenty years or more. It must be hard, for a widow of her standing to yield to a younger woman."

Already, Margaret found herself warming to Mistress White, who went about her business quietly and without fuss. Her eyes were drawn to the older woman's swollen belly, stretched to accommodate the child within: they were linked in such an intimate way that she felt she was somehow in the presence of a kindred spirit. "What hurts most is how everyone jumped to her command. As if she'd never left... And Jamie... He was supposed to help me. But he's never here for me. He spends most of his time in Renfrew, playing dice and getting into fights..."

"Let it be," Mary said. "All that matters is your health, and the health of your child. Sir John will deal with this when he returns." Her fingers deftly kneaded Margaret's belly. "There's been no pain?"

She was only half-listening. "What if he doesn't return?"

"Your husband's well, Lady Margaret. I'm sure of it. What of yourself?"

"I've felt a little sick the past few weeks. Nothing more than that."

"That's to be expected," Mary said. "You're lucky it didn't strike you sooner. I'll leave instructions with the cooks to make you a draught. I know the priests say that it's the lot of womankind to suffer, but God granted us ways of easing the path."

The Gryphon at Bay

Margaret sat up. "Is everything alright?"

Mary smiled. "Of course it is. Once Yuletide's past, it'll be time to prepare in earnest. We'll find the birthing stool, and you can begin the lying-in, if you like."

"Must I be confined?"

"Only queens and countesses have the luxury of lying-in before the birth. Half of them never leave their chamber. I've never done it once, and it's done me no harm."

"Thank you," she said. "For coming to see me."

Mary shrugged. "It's no trouble."

"I'm sorry about William. That he's left you to go to war."

"From what I've heard, this isn't a real war." She crossed herself, briskly. "Saints be praised..."

"But when the birth's so close..."

"Like yourself, Lady Margaret, I shall endure."

Mary sounded so resigned, so sad, that Margaret felt her chest tighten. She drew a sharp breath, trying to contain the grief, but couldn't. Tears streamed from her eyes, she sobbed with sudden, uncontrollable anguish.

"Hush now." Mary perched on the bed alongside and put a careful arm about her shoulders. "What's all this?"

"What if I die? What if it hurts so much I don't want to live?"

"If you keep fretting like this, you probably will die. And what will your poor husband do then? You must be brave, and strong. You're a fine, healthy girl, and young, too. Your babe is well, your parts are in good fettle."

"But what if it's a daughter? He'll hate me. They'll all hate me."

"Sir John would never be that way. You know that."

She felt a little better then. Katherine passed her a handkerchief, which she dabbed against her nose.

Mary took her hand. "It's all very new and frightening, I know. But you're not alone. Women have faced these perils since Eve first walked upon this earth. Now let's get some clothes on you, so you don't catch cold. I'll speak with Lady Elizabeth and put her mind at rest, and all will be well."

Margaret nodded, too tired to argue. Katherine helped her stand upright, then Mariota slipped her gown into place and laced it up.

"Fetch your lady some spiced wine," Mary told Katherine. "To help warm her up."

"Go with her," Margaret told Mariota. "I want to speak with Mistress White alone."

Both girls curtsied and left.

"You're with child," Margaret said. "Does he know?"

"What he doesn't know won't concern him. And it mustn't concern you."

"But what about the child?"

"My husband will provide for us both."

"Do you love him?" Margaret barely managed a whisper.

"Sir John?" The older woman smiled. "For a time I was graced with his company. He was something to be cherished, like the bright colours of the leaves in autumn, and the light of the sun on the water. But it was never my place to love him. I knew that all along."

"I love him. But I don't think he understands..."

"Of course he does," she said. "I hope you'll forgive me, if I took him into my keeping for a little while. He was wounded inside, and wretched with despair. All I wanted was to make things better for him." She nodded. "Now if you'll excuse me, I must speak with Lady Elizabeth. Best I'm the one to reason with her. I'll call before the week's out, to make sure that all's well."

Chapter 66

The Place of Dunglass

James arrived amidst a frenzy of activity. Not a word was spared for his courtiers: instead, he made straight for the laird's chamber, closing himself away for the rest of the afternoon.

Eventually, Hugh was ushered into the king's presence. He found the room transformed into a mews: birds were lined up on perches along the far wall, docile beneath their hoods.

James was admiring a stately peregrine, studying the speckled breast and heavy yellow feet with a keen eye. Alone for once, lacking the company of councillors or pages.

Hugh dropped to one knee, but James flicked his hand in irritable dismissal.

He straightened.

There was a long, difficult silence. Hugh waited, trying in vain to gauge James's mood.

"I've had enough of court," James said at last. "All those audiences and supplications..." He fixed his piercing gaze on Hugh. "Strange how you're always the first to flee."

"That's unjust, Your Grace. I have much to occupy me in the Westland."

James rubbed a gentle finger over the peregrine's chest. "At least the hunting's good round these parts."

"I'm sure we could spare a few hours for the chase."

"I can," came James's swift riposte. "You, most certainly, cannot." He heaved himself down into a vacant chair with a sigh.

Hugh's gaze alighted on the flagon of wine that had been left in readiness. "Some refreshment, Your Grace?" When James waved in brisk acknowledgement, he quickly delivered a measure into the young man's grasp.

Gulping back a mouthful, James levelled his gaze upon him. "Did you negotiate?"

"I did. But if you hope to find the Master of Lennox within, then I fear you'll be disappointed. The birds have flown the nest already."

"Really?" The King's voice was chill. "How unfortunate." He paused a few moments, his stare relentless. "How do you suppose that happened?"

Hugh shrugged. "They must have slipped out at night. From the sally port, perhaps."

"Wasn't it watched?"

Hugh caught the young man's eye just briefly, long enough to show that he wasn't afraid, that he considered the unspoken accusation quite unjustified. "It's submerged at high tide."

"I want the Master of Lennox in my keeping." The king's tone was chill. "And I want that castle."

"I've explained this in no uncertain terms to the Countess of Lennox. She wasn't entirely unresponsive. But she's awaiting word from her husband on how to proceed. If we could offer safe conduct for her and her ladies. And for Lady Lyle..."

James was unmoved. "What if they flee north, to muster support for their menfolk?"

"You credit them with too much cunning," Hugh responded smoothly. "They're ladies, that's all. Ageing ones at that. They care only for the fates of sons and husbands."

"A pox upon their sons and husbands!" The young man's outburst provoked a flurry of cries and fluttering wings amongst the hawks. Springing to his feet, he strode briskly to the window; leaning against the rybat, he stared in futile frustration at the looming rocky mass which supported Dumbarton Castle. "What am I supposed to do with these accursed ladies? I can hardly slay them, or send them out into the world to beg for alms..."

"The Countess of Lennox is my aunt, Your Grace. I'll escort her to Eglintoun, and keep her under my protection until this storm is past. Lady Lyle, too, if that would be of help."

James slumped back against the wall with arms folded, considering. "They're agreeable to this?"

"They accept that they have little choice in the matter."

"As we passed through the camp this afternoon-" James moved, sinking quickly down upon the window-seat, glum-faced. "-everyone did their very best to be civil, and courteous. But men are tired, and losing patience. I've kept you far longer than your forty days..."

"If we take a lenient approach, Your Grace, we'll have the castle before Yuletide. That'll put us in a position of strength. If John Stewart wants to sue for peace, then he'll do so on our terms, and not his."

The Privy Council met at Dunglass the following morning. The hall was transformed: its walls were draped with rich hangings brought all the way from Edinburgh, the King furnished with a suitably ornate chair draped with a cloth-of-state bearing the Royal arms.

Accompanying James were his inevitable companions. Patrick Hepburn, Earl of Bothwell, sat haughty and self-righteous at the King's right shoulder. Argyll was present, too, and Robert Colville, with a few more Homes and lesser Hepburns in attendance.

James had the air of a disgruntled youth, restless and exasperated. "Lord Hugh informs me that he's spoken with the keepers of Dumbarton." He waved his hand, dismissive, as if the whole affair wearied him. "The Master of Lennox has fled already."

Earl Patrick looked at Hugh. "Where is he?"

"How should I know?" Hugh retorted. "I'm not privy to his secrets."

"Does anyone remain there?" Home asked. "Anyone of note, that is."

"The Countess of Lennox and Lady Lyle, along with a garrison of twenty men."

"Lord Hugh tells me they'll capitulate," said James.

"All they desire is an opportunity to escape with their lives and freedom. The ladies were anxious not to relinquish the fight too soon, for fear of bringing their husbands' reputations into question."

"How very noble of them," James remarked. "Perhaps their husbands should have considered these reputations more carefully. They've done much to drag the names of these poor ladies through the midden."

"I'll take the ladies into my keeping," said Hugh, "and lodge them at Eglintoun until this disagreement is behind us. The Countess of Lennox is my kinswoman, it's the very least I could do."

"Noble sentiments, Lord Hugh," James said, his expression grim. "Let's hope the lady demonstrates her gratitude by relinquishing the castle before this week's out."

The Place of Craigends

Craigends slumped back with a sigh, nursing a mug of warm spiced wine in both hands. It had been an inconsequential day, routine, uninteresting. The most excitement he'd had was a meeting with his tacksman before dinner, to discuss the harvest, and set the winter rents.

Then his mother and gude-sister arrived, armed with plans and good intentions. They told him that they wanted to send Cuthbert away, far from Cunninghame, far from the Westland. Where he'd be living in another man's house, earning his keep in another man's service.

Craigends took a deep draught of his wine. It stuck in his craw. That he couldn't guarantee his own nephew's safety, or ensure the young man's progress at court.

But deep inside, he knew that the women were right.

He'd retreated to his chamber an hour ago, to clear his head and ponder his decisions undisturbed. Since his wife had died two years back, he'd kept his quarters austere, free of excess comforts and distractions. The plain walls had just a single crucifix for adornment, and the furnishings, though comfortable, were plain and understated.

He shifted in his seat, suddenly uneasy. The Earl of Angus was a worthy man, no doubt about it, but... To seek help from strangers... It was almost too much to bear.

Hearing horses in the yard, he glanced up. He took a hefty draught of wine, heaved himself to his feet and wandered over to the window. Opening the shutter, he saw Cuthbert, Andy and Guido seated on their mounts there, three huntsmen in attendance. A dozen hounds milled about them, tails waving as they greeted the phalanx of servants who had come to take the fresh carcasses to the pantry. One dead roe deer was heaved down from the pack pony's back: two more were piled there, the slits in their bellies red with blood from the gralloching.

"Cuthbert!" Craigends called.

The young man glanced up.

"I want to speak with you."

Cuthbert held his glance, a look of measured appraisal. Then he dismounted, heading for the door with a determined stride.

Spattered with mud, Cuthbert still sported his long boots and spurs and his thick woollen cloak when he breezed into Craigends' chamber. He looked in good health, cheeks flushed pink with the cold and eyes bright with vigour. "You summoned me."

"Your mother's here."

"I know." Cuthbert sat near the fire and stretched out his legs.

"She wants to take you back to Kilmaurs."

Cuthbert chuckled. "I hardly need my mother's protection for *that*."

Craigends studied him, closely. The lad went about his daily business with careless disregard for his troubles, but Craigends knew it was all for show. In the depths of his soul, Cuthbert feared for his future.

"The Countess of Angus visited her a few days back. She's offered to place you amongst her husband's retinue."

"Angus?" Cuthbert remarked. "He has a dubious reputation." He caught Craigends' eye. "That's why you're reluctant to let me go."

Craigends sighed and chewed his nail.

Clasping his hands before him, Cuthbert perched forward in his chair, an eager conspirator. "Angus has a daughter, has he not?"

"Two. Both ripe for marriage."

"Isn't that convenient?" He smiled at his uncle: it was the look of a man, not a boy, measured and self-assured. "I'll be gone a year or two. No more than that. You can keep my inheritance safe in that time, Uncle Will. And Angus... He's a shrewd man, skilled in all the lordly arts." He sat back, visibly satisfied. "Yes, I could do far worse than that."

332

Chapter 67

The Place of Dunglass

"Least you smell better now." Archie Campbell led the way upstairs to Argyll's new lodgings on the first floor of the guest range. "When did you last think to wash?"

"A week ago." Hugh padded after him in shirt and hose, gown and doublet over one arm. His sword belt was draped over his shoulder, his hair dank and dripping. "For the Privy Council meeting."

"You're a disgrace."

"Some of us don't have the luxury-" he began.

"-You were offered accommodation," came Archie's brusque response. "You refused."

Hugh gave an irritable shrug, and said nothing.

The barber was waiting, a small portly man with a balding pate. Catching Hugh's disdainful glance, he swallowed nervously.

"This is Master Spreull." Archie steered Hugh over to a stool and sat him down there. "He comes highly recommended." Taking the garments from Hugh's grasp, he laid them on the bed then returned for the weapons. As he lifted Hugh's sword belt, he smiled. "So you don't do anything we all regret."

The barber set to work, comb in hand. Gritting his teeth, Hugh closed his fingers tight about the stool, curbing the urge to snarl and curse. The bone comb dug deep into his tangled hair; the barber paused and stepped back. "This might not be welcome news, my lord," he said, "but you've got nits."

Archie slouched against the bedpost, smirking. "You'd have an easier time combing a sheep!"

"And you'd know all about that, wouldn't you?" Hugh turned to the barber, scowling. "Be careful, damn you! I'd like some hair left once we're done!"

Eventually the comb was set aside. The shears came out, and Hugh's hair clipped to a more respectable length. Once that was done, Master Spreull produced his razor and whetted it, deftly. "If his lordship would keep still..."

A simple enough request, but Hugh wasn't sure he could oblige. Besides the nits, he'd gathered up a flea or two...

"My lord?" Master Spreull ventured.

"Oh, get on with it! But if you so much as shed a drop of blood, I'll gut you!"

"Come on now! Archie chided. "You look more like a gentleman already. Before, you'd have passed as one of Angus Og's bastards."

Hugh swatted the barber aside. "Is this really necessary? It'll be a year before we're finished here! The King will be wondering-"

"-The King requested this," Archie cut in. "Says he doesn't want you negotiating in his name when you look no better than a cattle-thief. Besides, you'll have to look your best in the presence of such illustrious company..."

Hugh studied him, frowning. "What do you mean?"

Archie straightened. "Montgrennan's here. He arrived just half-an-hour ago."

*   *   *

Whistling through his teeth, John curried his horse, pressing hard with every stroke so the dirt and grease slid away and the shine came through. Storm's black coat had thickened with the cold of winter, but the stallion was in good health, stabled indoors with Zephyr away from the the cold and damp of the horse lines.

These days, John found his desire for solitude growing ever greater. He'd been in close confinement with his fellow men far too long now: everyone stank to high heaven and the bickering was constant. To make matters worse, since Robert Montgomerie's departure he'd been dealing with all disputes and complaints amongst the Montgomerie contingent. He was an obvious choice for an arbitrator, for no-one dared pick a fight with Hugh. Small wonder he took solace in his horse's company: Storm never argued, or cursed, or questioned his intent.

John leaned his head against the horse's silken flank and breathed deep, filling his nostrils with the beast's warm scent. Sometimes he wondered if he'd make it back to Ellestoun before Margaret was banished to her chamber for the lying-in. Late at night he'd pray to God and Holy Mary that all would be resolved, that he'd soon be going home.

"I was told I'd find you here." A man's voice shook him from his thoughts. "But I hardly thought you'd be employed in such menial tasks."

Montgrennan was standing in the aisle beyond the stalls, a neat elegant figure, even in his travelling clothes.

Hiding his surprise, John nodded, curt acknowledgement. "He's a more amiable companion than most."

Montgrennan smiled slightly. "I've heard men speak that way about their whores rather than their horses." He pulled his cloak close with a sigh. "I understand your friend Montgomerie has left for Dunglass?"

"He was summoned to speak with the King. He didn't share the details."

"You chose not to ride with him?"

"I wasn't required."

"Clearly you have better things to do with your time." Montgrennan's glance flicked briefly over him. "You've made quite a cosy nest for yourself amongst Lord Hugh's retinue. He pays you well?"

John ignored him, turning back to the horse and smoothing the thick coat beneath his fingers. Despite his indifference, his curiosity was roused. He wondered why his kinsman had come here, what business he had with the King. And he wondered, too, what Hugh would have to say once he learned of Mongrennan's arrival.

Montgrennan walked away, his footsteps echoing across the cobbles. At the door he paused. "I'm reluctant to speak of such things," he said. "But has it occurred to you that perhaps your friend Montgomerie has not been entirely honest in his dealings with you?"

John looked up. "It has crossed my mind," he said. "But I can't see why you consider it your business."

That same smile crossed Montgrennan's face, all-knowing, faintly disconcerting. "You're my kinsman, John. It's my place to be concerned for you."

King James waited beyond the barmkin, in full array and mounted on his destrier. A thin gold crown was jammed over his brown hair, his horse smothered beneath a costly gold caparison. The epitome of kingly power and authority, he surveyed his surroundings with an air of haughty indifference.

He spared Hugh a brief nod then rode off. A score of courtiers followed, each in full array. Spotting Patrick Hepburn amongst them, Hugh curbed a scowl; then, to his relief, he spotted Earl Colin there, too.

Hugh caught his gude-father's eye – Argyll bowed his head, faint acknowledgement. His gude-father's neutral expression brought little reassurance: Hugh sighed, and stared beyond Zephyr's ears, towards the gatehouse. He didn't feel properly dressed without his harness, not in these circumstances: arrayed instead in costly garments of satin and velvet, today he was riding out as an emissary, not a soldier.

"Lord Hugh!" James barked.

Hugh spurred Zephyr forwards into a sprightly trot. The grey stallion's dappled coat had been scrubbed free of dung-stains, its long mane braided down its neck. Its harness had been polished until it shone, each brass buckle and strap-end gleaming.

James cast him a sideways glance as Zephyr fell into step alongside.

Hugh held his tongue, unwilling to provoke the king's ire. His caution was rewarded: as they trod the long mile to Dumbarton, James was silent all the way. And visibly resentful. Of what or whom, Hugh could not be sure.

They paused at last, on the cobbled road that led up to the castle. "I've been considering this situation," James said. "And I've decided not to place the burden of this task entirely upon your shoulders." He beckoned brusquely to the men who followed on behind. "Sir John?"

Another man broke formation, riding briskly forward to join his King: John Ross of Montgrennan, no less, settling back into court business as if he'd never been away.

He nodded to Hugh, who sighed and cast his eyes forward.

James chuckled, as if relishing his discomfort. "I thought that since Sir John Ross is adept with the arts of rhetoric and negotiation, he would be supremely suited to this task. You will assist as best you can, Lord Hugh."

"As you wish, Your Grace," Hugh muttered through gritted teeth.

"Good luck, gentlemen," James said. "Let us take no more of your time." Without another word, he wheeled his horse around and set off at a canter, his companions in close pursuit.

Mongrennan nodded towards Zephyr. "An elegant horse, Lord Hugh." Like Hugh, he'd declined to wear his armour: hooded and cloaked instead against the inclement weather.

"I could say the same of yours, Sir John," Hugh retorted.

Montgrennan stretched in his stirrups then settled comfortably back down into the saddle. "The King thinks you've not been entirely candid with us."

Hugh fixed his gaze firmly on Zephyr's ears. "If he seeks his quarry in Dumbarton, he'll be disappointed."

"Strange that the Master of Lennox should slip his bonds so easily..."

"These things happen."

"Yes," Montgrennan agreed, mildly. "They do." He stared at Hugh, careful, appraising. "I hear you've returned to your old ways..."

"I don't know what you mean."

"Come now. I thought you'd be more gracious in my presence. Considering your circumstances..." He spurred his horse forwards. "Well now, let's see what can be done. To restore the world to its rightful order, and allow the ladies some respite..."

Hugh loitered a little longer. Fighting the urge to scowl, he watched Montgrennan weave his complacent path towards the gate.

He couldn't exactly be discourteous, not in these circumstances. There was too much at stake.

But if there was any justice in the world, he told himself, as he urged Zephyr off in pursuit, he'd bequeath his impeccable companion a flea or two before their quest was behind them.

"It's far better to cut your losses." Montgrennan was at home already, sitting relaxed and confident in one of the castle's fine chairs, a goblet of wine held loose in his hand. "Relinquish the last of your husband's lands, and throw yourself upon the King's mercy. He'll be lenient. But the longer you loiter here, the more money is lost from his treasury." He paused for effect, taking a deep luxurious breath. "Lady Margaret, you know as well as I do that kings care more for the gold in their coffers than they do for anything else." He smiled, warm, beatific.

Rubbing her hands against her skirts, Margaret Montgomerie glanced towards Hugh. "My husband told me to defend this place."

"Indeed," Montgrennan acknowledged. "Don't forget, my lady, that I've been privy to your husband's secrets. I know what he intended. He failed in those objectives. Now the most he can hope for is to escape with his life and make a successful return to court..." He paused again, waiting for the words to sink in. "I can arrange that, but I need assistance from yourself."

"How can I trust you?" the countess countered.

Montgrennan replied in that honey-smooth voice, "Suffice it to say that I've been offered enough remuneration to negate any risk of treachery on my part."

Sitting tall and composed, Margaret Montgomerie fiddled with her hood. "Well then, how can you help my husband?"

Montgrennan lounged in his seat, arrogance oozing from every pore. "I've examined the degree of forfeiture in some detail. The King's advisers were in such haste to put your kinsmen to the horn that they quietly ignored one crucial fact: Parliament was never properly summoned to approve the forfeiture. The pronouncement was flawed, the King's actions illegal." Montgrennan smiled broadly, basking in his own superiority. "It's as well for all of us that His Grace the King was forced to rely on the work of others who were, in a legal sense, *incompetent*..."

The Gryphon at Bay

Hugh ground his teeth, irritated beyond measure. He'd been instrumental in drawing up the document: he'd known it might not stand up to close scrutiny, but all the same... To have Montgrennan poring scorn on his abilities was galling.

His aunt, however, responded quite differently. She breathed out, visibly relieved. "Oh, thank God and Holy Mary..."

"We'll have this whole matter resolved at the next meeting of Parliament," Montgrennan said. "All we need do till then is ensure your kinsmen maintain a subtle presence. I understand that your gracious nephew-" He nodded towards Hugh, "-is already making plans so this can be done safely."

With the negotiations complete, he joined his aunt on the draughty heights of the battlements. They tolerated the cold without complaint, for it was the only place where they were confident they couldn't be overheard.

"I don't trust him," Margaret Montgomerie muttered.

"I know that," Hugh conceded. "But there's no other way."

His aunt turned to him, fingers clamped tight about her rosary. "How do we know that you're not next in line for a hanging?" She glanced away. "God forbid, you've done enough already to be accused of treason..."

Hugh grasped her arm, reassuring. "Argyll's with us, and that must count for something. Once James has this Castle in his keeping, he'll be sated, at least until Yuletide is behind us."

"And you'll give me protection at Eglintoun?"

He inclined his head, gracious acknowledgement. "Of course."

"What of Lady Lyle?"

"She can remain with me, or travel back to her kinsmen at Houston."

"Very well," the countess agreed. "If you can assure me of the King's good intent, then I'll call an end to it." Her head sagged forward, her weariness clear to behold. "I've done my duty as a wife, haven't I, Hugh?" she whispered. "I've held this place as long as I could."

The Lands of Glanderstoun

Gripping his cloak tighter, Matthew Stewart clenched his teeth to keep from shivering. He'd been hiding in this thicket for what felt like hours; his boots were soaked through, his feet aching.

He'd pawned his horse at Ru'glen the previous day and travelled through the Westland on foot. That way, he'd been able to leave the road and avoid curious eyes when necessary. He hadn't eaten for the best part of a day – he'd have killed for a mouthful of bread and a measure of ale.

His destination lay tantalisingly close. Glanderstoun was the least of the Darnley Stewarts' residences: a simple place, nothing more than a draughty old tower with a ramshackle guest range. But at that moment, as he crouched in his cover praying that the wind would drop and the icy rain hold off, it seemed as welcome as the mightiest castle or palace.

At last the light was fading. Though he'd seen no-one for at least an hour, Matthew remained cautious. He was just a stone's throw from the Sempill lands at the

Fereneze: if anyone recognised him, then word would reach Ellestoun soon enough. Even if Sempill himself wasn't home to raise the hue and cry, others might be eager to take up arms on his behalf.

Confident the coast was clear, he crossed the last half-mile of open ground to Glanderstoun. He limped into the yard and headed for the door, fearful even now of discovery.

He knocked urgently upon the timber door and a venerable old servant answered. "Heavens above!" he gasped, as Matthew shook the worst of the water from his rain-soaked hair. "Come inside, my lord. I'll summon my lady Elizabeth right away."

"Thank you." Setting down his spoon, Matthew smiled warmly at his gude-sister. "This is the tastiest pottage that's ever graced my table."

Elizabeth Sempill shrugged and curtsied. "It's no trouble, my lord."

She'd done her best to make him comfortable. She'd given him the opportunity to bathe and she'd looked out some clean clothes for him. The laird's bed was ready, a fire roaring in his chamber. *My husband's place is yours,* she'd said, as she took away his noisome travelling clothes to be washed.

"How long will you stay?" she asked.

"No longer than I have to," he said. "If your brother hears of this, he'll burn the place."

"Then we won't tell him," she replied, firmly. "You were right to come here. What could be safer, than to hide in the place you're least expected?"

"God bless you," Matthew said.

Pausing beside him, Elizabeth refilled his cup. She looked down at him with those clear steady eyes and smiled, faintly. "There's venison roasting in the kitchen. I'll bring it when it's ready."

He settled back in his seat. "That's most gracious," he said. "I'll remain here for a few weeks at least. Before I move on to Eglintoun, to see what cousin Hugh has arranged."

She frowned. "You're sure it's not a trap?"

Matthew smiled. "I think my choices are limited."

"I'll pray this plays out in your favour," she said, and swept away to the kitchens.

Matthew watched her go. She carried herself with poise and elegance; a year ago, in different circumstances, he'd have looked at her with a different eye. Coveting her grace and beauty, fighting the desires which fired every man, however civilised he claimed to be. She was his brother's wife: to desire her was to offend God.

But the lust he'd once harboured was long gone. For all her loyalty and angry words, she was a Sempill. She looked like a Sempill, she carried herself like a Sempill. Now every time he looked at her, he thought of her brother and the rage stirred within him anew.

She returned with a platter of sliced venison and placed it before him. "This year will pass," she said. "And your fortunes will be restored. I'm sure of it."

"Let's hope so," he said.

With his belly pleasantly full, and the warmth seeping back into his limbs, he was replete at last. He closed his eyes, letting himself doze.

The Gryphon at Bay

His fate was no longer his to command. He'd placed it in the hands of others: he hoped to God that they wouldn't let him down.

Chapter 68

Dumbarton Castle

Mid-afternoon, and already the light was fading. Yet another squall was blowing in from the west, the rain turning to snow.

Inauspicious weather for an otherwise auspicious day: after six months of siege, Dumbarton Castle was restored to the King.

James sat upon his horse with Unicorn Puirsuivant alongside, both men dwarfed by the massive curtain wall and barbican that loomed ahead. The herald's voice was drowned out by the howling wind as he made his pronouncement, the parchment twitching in his grasp.

James was attentive nonetheless: John wished he could've shared his monarch's enthusiasm, but his toes were numb with cold and he could scarcely feel his fingers. Sitting deeper in the saddle, he wrapped his cloak tight and turned his face from the wind in an effort to keep the stinging sleet from his eyes.

He was in distinguished company. Hepburn, Montgrennan and Argyll were all there, as were Archie Campbell and Hugh. He never thought he'd be invited to join them, but James was adamant, asking for him personally. Even wearing his best garments, he felt impoverished, his velvet doublet darned in places, hose worn about the knees.

And James... He was in a foul mood. He'd acknowledged John with no more than a grunt and a curt nod. With the moment of victory approaching, his temper only worsened. There was no fanfare. No celebration. The gates ground open and James rode forward, oblivious to the danger as he passed beneath portcullis and murder-hole.

The ladies waited in the cobbled yard, a disconsolate group. John recognised Lady Lyle, who'd held Duchal in her husband's name; she declined even to acknowledge him. The scruffy remnants of Dumbarton's garrison were gathered there, too, a crestfallen bunch of men-at-arms who scarcely dared hold their heads up in the king's presence.

"Your Grace." Margaret Montgomerie curtsied low. "I'm very grateful for your kindness."

James reined in his horse before her. "Where's your husband?"

"I don't know." Her voice trembled.

"Your sons?"

She didn't reply.

"Be thankful that I value your kinsman's counsel," James muttered. "Else I might not have been so lenient." He caught John's eye. "Sir John Sempill! Take ten of my men and search this place. Empty every barrel, and tear apart each mattress. Make sure they're not here."

* * *

The Gryphon at Bay

It took most of the afternoon to complete the task to his satisfaction. John sent men to the main gate and the sally port, posting others to stand guard over every door and vennel in the lower ward.

While these hardy souls weathered the cold thick rain, John took William and one or two others on a tour of the ranges and outbuildings. Checking each room in turn, from the kitchens to the chapel, he made sure the search was thorough, emptying every kist and peering into the garderobes.

Nothing. Not so much as a trace of them.

Surveying yet another desolate bedchamber, he gave a fitful sigh, the sound of his disappointment echoing around him.

He'd sensed all along that the search would be fruitless. He was sure, too, that until recently his quarry had been hiding there. Something niggled in his thoughts, a half-forgotten memory of a night when he'd stirred from sleep to see Hugh disappearing into the darkness.

He dismissed his men and trudged back to the hall. The more he thought about it, the more likely it seemed. That Hugh had played a crucial part in organising Matthew Stewart's escape.

Patrick Hepburn awaited him, grim-faced. "His Grace wants to speak with you. He's waiting in his chamber."

James had retired to a spacious suite of rooms deep in the heart of the keep. Furniture had been brought there for his use, the bed draped with costly hangings. A lutenist sat near the window, plucking out a melancholy air, while two young page-boys loitered in attendance.

While James sat alone at a small table, a flagon of wine and a single goblet placed before him.

John dropped to one knee. "Your Grace."

James nodded briskly in his direction. "Pray rise, Sir John." He glanced towards Earl Patrick. "That'll be all."

Hepburn retreated without a word.

John approached warily, bonnet in hand.

James looked up. "No sign of them?"

"Not so much as a hair, Your Grace."

"Ah, well." James gestured for him to sit. "Join me, please." Even as John drew up a stool, his king gestured to the pages. "A game of chess, I think." James watched carefully as the boys hurried forward and laid out the board. "Are you wed yet, Sir John?"

"I am, Your Grace."

"Tell me about her."

"Her name is Margaret, Margaret Colville. She's kinswoman to your advisor, Master Robert Colville. She was born and raised in Kyle, she came to live with me in Ellestoun eight months back."

"Is she pretty?"

The question caught him unawares. He paused, unsure how to respond. "I think so, yes... I find her very beautiful."

James smiled. "Then you're a lucky man. You're looking forward to seeing her again?"

"Very much so."

The king gestured at the board, indicating that John should make the first move. "I'll be wed myself soon enough. To some haughty princess who looks like a horse and sings like a corncrake. I'll be lucky if she even speaks the same tongue as me!" James scowled at the board. "How in God's name can a man woo a woman if he can't even pass the time of day with her!"

"In Latin, I suppose."

A smile touched the young man's lips. "An excellent suggestion! So, how would you advise me on this matter, Sir John? Should I marry an English lady? Or seek a bride in France?"

"Perhaps the deciding factor should be whooever brings the better dowry."

James grinned. "That's sound advice, Sir John. Well worth heeding..." He sat in silence a while, then moved another piece. When he next looked up, his face was stern and grim. "They were here, weren't they? I can almost smell them."

John studied the chessboard, unsure how to respond.

"Did they slip away in the dead of night? Or were they helped?"

"I don't know, Your Grace." A frown crossed his brow, he hoped James wouldn't sense the shred of doubt he nursed deep inside him.

James sighed and handed John the goblet, indicating that he should drink his fill. "What does it matter?" he said. "It's all over. You can go home, Sir John. We can all go home. Thank God for that, eh?"

*   *   *

They'd be dining late that evening. Though the Royal cooks were working hard to deliver a hearty meal, it would be an hour or two before the meat was roasted and the sauces ready.

Tired of exchanging pleasantries with the hordes that thronged the upper ward, Hugh retreated to the comparative calm of the guest range.

Ranks of candles had been lit in the hall and the fire was blazing, bathing the room in warmth. Finding a quiet space at the board, Hugh drew out a pack of cards and laid them in serried ranks across the timbers, a forlorn attempt to take his mind off his empty stomach.

"There you are." Archie Campbell slumped down opposite.

Hugh grunted in greeting, but didn't look up.

Archie shifted with a sigh. Taking a deep draught of wine, he tapped his fingers against the board.

"What's wrong with you?" Hugh asked.

"Your friend Sir John Sempill. He's been talking to the King. He's been there an hour or so."

Hugh deftly laid out another row of cards. "He won't say anything."

"How can you be sure?"

"I know him."

Archie snorted in sardonic denial. "Oh, he likes us to think he's purer than gilded lilies, but... Every man has his price. Perhaps you should find out exactly what he knows, so we can do whatever's necessary to keep him quiet..."

"That's the last thing I'm-" He broke off, spotting John himself entering the hall, trudging along with shoulders slumped, a picture of weariness.

Archie offered the new arrival a beaming smile. "What's all this then? In secret counsel with the King?"

John shrugged. "Nothing important."

Archie caught Hugh's eye, a quick anxious glance.

"Join us, please." Hugh gestured to the bench. Even as John skirted the table and sat down beside him, he was gathering up the cards and shuffling them. "This'll kill some time before dinner," he said.

Archie poured some wine. "So what are your plans for the morrow, Sir John?" He pushed it across the board in John's direction.

"I'll make haste to Ellestoun, and see how my wife's faring." He dropped his head in his hands with a groan and kneaded his brow.

"It's hardly a commodious place to see out the winter," Archie remarked. "You should seek lodgings with your uncle in Edinburgh. I'm sure he has access to every luxury."

"My place is with my family."

"God bless him," Archie said.

"John, listen to me." Hugh clasped his arm about John's shoulders. "Your wife will still be there tomorrow. And the next day. And the next. Why gallop to her door? At best, your cock'll be numb from a day in the saddle. At worst, ah... Remember how King Alexander-"

"–God rest his soul-" Archie interjected.

"–Plummeted to his doom because Love overpowered his Reason. He took to his horse on a night when most prudent souls stayed safe in their homes..." He finished with a flourish, using a wave of his hand to depict the hapless horse's unexpected descent.

"Perhaps you take your lady for granted." John's tone was icy.

Hugh nearly choked on his wine. "What do you mean by that?"

"-Before I forget, Sir John," Archie cut in. "Have you considered your plans for Yuletide? Are you visiting kinfolk, or hoping perhaps for an invitation to dine at a wealthy lord's table? My dear gude-brother here-" he nodded to Hugh, "-hosts Yuletide feasts that can scarcely be rivalled for their scale and grandeur. Perhaps he'd ask you to attend?"

Hugh aimed a kick under the table, catching Archie square on the ankle.

Archie's face showed nothing. "I'm tempted to ride south myself. Just to see who shows their face there..."

"Even if Lord Hugh were to extend such a gracious invitation I'd have to decline," John replied. "I've family and friends of my own: it's my duty to provide for them. Now goodnight, gentlemen. I have a long journey tomorrow." He rose to his feet and headed for the door.

Archie watched him go, lips pursed with faint disapproval.

"That was clever," Hugh said. "Baiting him like that."

"I don't trust him."

"I'm sure the feeling's mutual. Which is a great pity for us all." He gathered up the cards again, putting them away this time. "Perhaps he's right."

"Oh, God. Don't you start..."

"I'd planned to sail for Irvine tomorrow and remain a night in Seagate. What if I rode on to Eglintoun instead? She'd certainly be surprised..."

"You should see yourself!" Archie scoffed. "If my sister has any sense, she'll lock the door and tell you to sleep in the kennels."

Chapter 69

The Place of Eglintoun

With the watchman in place and everything secure, Helen retreated to her chamber. Yuletide was fast approaching and there was still much to be done. New deliveries of food and wine were arriving every day, adding to the mountain of supplies that filled cellars and stores.

Throughout the last few weeks the yard had been a shambles, filled with sheep and cattle brought from the farms for slaughter. The butchers had done their best to gather up the blood and offal, but the stench was unpleasant nonetheless.

The worst, thank God, was over now, carcasses hanging from meathooks in the cellars, hides sold on for tanning. But there were still enough demands on Helen's time to make her profoundly grateful when another day was over. There'd be a host of hungry mouths descending in the coming days, and it was her task to ensure that they found their stay fulfilling.

Stifling a yawn, she plodded up the last few stairs and opened the door.

Bessie was perched on the edge of the bed, combing out her long black hair. A thin kirtle concealed her body: with hips and breasts defined by the candlelight, it was clear Bessie was growing up at last. Just a fortnight ago she'd suffered her first monthly flux, entering the realms of womanhood.

Sitting alongside, Helen grasped the comb and took over the task, one deft stroke after another. "Your father will see quite a difference in you."

"Do you think he'll come home for Yuletide?"

"He'll be here."

"But it's little more than a week away."

"He'll be here," she repeated.

Bessie swallowed, eyes glistening. These days she often seemed preoccupied, sometimes taking herself off to a quiet corner and weeping for no reason.

Helen didn't press for explanations. Bessie would come to her in her own good time: hopefully sooner rather than later. Pausing in mid-stroke, Helen rested an encouraging hand on the girl's shoulder. "Bessie?"

Bessie grasped her fingers, clinging tight. "I'm a woman now. When he comes back, he'll want to see me wed."

"That's not true!" Helen responded, voice tight with reproach. "He'd be deeply hurt, to hear you talk that way. We're in no hurry to see you go. Your father will want to find you the right husband."

The girl studied her feet, forlorn. "I'm frightened, Mama."

"Don't be. Your father loves you dearly. And don't forget: if anything ill befalls you, he'll strike the first blow on your behalf. The man who marries you would be wise to remember that."

Bessie giggled, reassured.

"You'll have your own place and a regiment of servants at your command. Just remember that a wife should serve her husband as a wise counsellor serves his king. Advise when necessary, and be a sympathetic listener when times are bad. Steer his course as best you can, but never judge him harshly. That's the path I've followed with your father, and it's served me well. I wouldn't trade him for another. Not the greatest earl in the realm, not even the King."

"Will you find me a man that I can love, Mama?"

"I shall do my very best, I promise. He may even find you himself. One thing's for sure: we won't leave that responsibility to your father. The sensibilities of women are beyond his understanding." She kissed Bessie gently on the forehead. "Now get to your bed. Sleep sound, so there's enough colour in your cheeks to entice any young suitor."

"Thank you, Mama..." Bessie threw her arms round Helen and hugged her tight.

Returning the embrace, Helen felt a sudden pang of sadness in her heart. It seemed so long ago now that she'd said her last farewells to her family. She missed her mother and sisters still. She hoped they'd find a husband closer to home for Bessie. A burgess, wealthy and profligate, tipped for future success amongst the town council. Being a bastard, Bessie would never win the hand of a lord and would be lucky even to find herself a baron. *Better a rich burgess*, Helen told herself, *than a baron with peerless lineage but scarcely a groat to his name...*

A shout rang out from the yard. It was the watchman, challenging a new arrival.

Bessie's grip tightened. "What's wrong?"

"Hush now." Helen tilted her head, listening carefully. She heard the creak as the gates opened, the clatter of a horse entering the yard at a restless trot.

"It must be a message from Father. Do you think all's well?"

"I'm sure it's nothing to worry about." Helen prised her loose. "Go to bed, Bessie. I'll see what's afoot."

She was about to retire for the night herself when she heard someone moving in the laird's chamber below. Helen cocked her head, puzzled: it wasn't Ringan: with Hugh absent, he slept in the hall with the rest of the servants.

But who else would have dared loiter in Hugh's room? Unless of course it was Hugh himself...

Rousing one of the maids, she dressed quickly and hurried downstairs. Opening the door, she peered inside.

Hugh was there. Sitting sprawled in his chair next to an empty fireplace. He still wore his travelling clothes, and though clean-shaven, was unusually dishevelled.

Helen wrinkled her nose in distaste: she could smell him where she stood, rank and stale from his travels. His hounds fawned over him, oblivious to the reek.

He grunted an incomprehensible greeting.

"Whatever's wrong?" she demanded.

"I came back to see you."

Her relief gave way to irritation. "You could at least've changed your clothes."

He stared at her, faintly petulant. Then his grim expression softened and he laughed. "Ah, whatever made me think you'd come running to my arms, overwhelmed with desire?"

She took a backwards step. "If you come any closer, I'll run the other way."

"I should warn you," he said. "I've caught a flea or two."

"God forbid!" she snapped. "Don't so much as move from there! I'll fetch the fleabane!"

She set about her task with military precision. Half a dozen sleepy servants were marshalled: the bed was made up, the fire set, a makeshift bathtub delivered. While the servants filled the tub with endless buckets of hot water, Helen hung bunches of fleabane from the bed and strewed some more between the covers.

Hugh eyed the bath with suspicion. "That's not necessary."

Seizing his cloak, Helen tugged at the brooch that fastened it. "You'll bathe, Hugh. Or you'll sleep alone." He opened his mouth to protest, but she was undeterred. Tossing aside his cloak, she grappled with the laces of his jerkin. "These clothes are fit for the midden."

"You're over-reacting."

"I've the welfare of three children to think of. Four, including yourself. Now stand up, and get out of those foul clothes." She tried to tug him to his feet. "I might as well be wrestling an ox."

His scowl deepened. "I'll sleep on the floor."

"You will not! We've all worked hard for you, but you're so ungrateful you won't even stir your lazy arse." She shoved him roughly, provoking a look that would have made most men's blood run chill. It only made her grit her teeth and push him all the harder. "Move, damn you!"

He stood with a martyred sigh. Before he could think twice, she stripped off his hose and shirt, then tugged him over to the tub. "Get in."

Steam drifted out, the whole room filled with the sweet scent of rose water. It looked enticing: she almost felt inclined to jump in herself. But Hugh eyed it as if it brimmed with vitriol. He took one step forward, then balked. The fearsome glower was back. "Do you want to unman me?" The cold was taking its toll, his shoulders hunched, his limbs a mass of goose-flesh.

"Some hot water never hurt any man. Get in!" She slapped his buttocks so hard that the hounds sat up straight with surprise.

"Witch," muttered Hugh, but crossed that last stretch of floor regardless and climbed into the tub. He slid into the water and pulled his head beneath the surface. Where he stayed, one long moment after another...

"Hugh?"

A tiny trail of bubbles escaped his nostrils. Apart from that, there was nothing.

"Hugh!" She leaned over the water, anxious.

He struck like a viper, seizing her arms and hauling her into the tub. She shrieked as she fell, but at least had sufficient foresight to take a deep breath. Somehow Hugh righted her, hoisting her up amidst a violent wave of water that spilled out and sent the dogs yelping.

She was pressed up close, her legs crushed against her chest, her knees resting against the timber staves of the tub. Her clothes were soaked through, her hair a sodden mat before her face and her arms pinned uselessly at her sides.

Hugh was smiling. "Like Poseidon," he said. "Wooing a delectable sea nymph."

Wriggling a little, she managed to extricate her arms. "Or Andromeda. Trapped and ravaged by the terrible sea monster."

"What harsh words with which to greet your husband." Pushing aside her skirts, he grasped her thighs and manoeuvred her so he could settle himself inside her. He clutched her tight, kissing her lips and nibbling her neck while he heaved away so hard she feared the tub might give way and they'd both be sent tumbling out into the cold. The hounds weren't sure whether to be excited or alarmed: they circled round, barking madly.

When the moment came, Hugh cried out, exuberant. The simmering anger had gone; he was grinning broadly. "Two months I waited!" he told her. "In all that time, I didn't even think of any other woman except you. And now the treasure of your company is mine, and by God, I'll relish it a thousand times more..."

She sighed as the old familiar fire flowered inside her, then held him tight, resting her head against his chest. He wrapped his arms about her and they stayed that way for one long moment after another, saying nothing, savouring each other's company.

"All that fuss over nothing," she said.

"It brought some compensation."

"So now you've had your way with me, I hope you'll allow me to attend to more pressing matters?"

"If you like," he agreed.

Once she'd stripped off her wet gown and pulled on a fresh kirtle, Helen spread out a blanket by the fireside. Hugh lazed by her side, sprawled like a hound with eyes half-closed, while she searched his scalp with a fine-toothed bone comb.

He stretched and yawned, basking in the warmth of the fire. "Did Alex make it back?"

She peered close, seeking out the pale flecks of the nits' eggs, easy to see against the midnight black of his hair. "He did," she replied. "But his journey wasn't without mishap. He cracked a bone in his shoulder."

He pulled a face, incredulous. "How did he manage it?"

"He says he fell when he left the boat at Dumbarton."

"I remember," Hugh said. "What an idiot."

"I'm sure it wasn't intended."

"His mother's lodged at Seagate. Along with Lady Lyle. I shall ride out and fetch them on the morrow."

"With so much to occupy your thoughts, you came all the way back here to see me?"

"Sir John Sempill accused me of taking you for granted. He said it's the mark of a true knight to put his lady first."

"Then I hope his wife is as mindful of his needs as I am of yours." She placed a kiss on the crown of his head. "Welcome home, my love. God knows why, but I've missed you."

348

Chapter 70

The Place of Ellestoun

Lying beached upon her back in the darkness, Margaret ran her hands over her swollen belly. The fear was growing, almost by the day. Fear of the babe which grew within her, draining her strength, her vitality.

Feeling it stir, she wondered again if she was carrying a monster. Tainted by the times she'd left the path of righteousness, enjoying carnal pleasure with her husband, allowing his seed to poison the growing child in her womb.

Her mother had said that a pregnant woman should shield herself from the world, avoiding all that was evil and horrible. Instead, Margaret had wandered blithely out beyond her walls and by doing so, she'd witnessed terrible scenes. She could picture still the corpse hanging from its gibbet on the road back from Eglintoun, the torn skin of its face, the bloodied eye sockets...

And then there was Hugh... Perhaps by tending him so closely, she'd jeopardized her child. Perhaps his restless malevolent spirit had seeped through cloth and flesh into her womb. Sometimes when the child kicked extra hard, she wondered if she was carrying a changeling, Hugh's changeling.

She supposed it would be just punishment. Adultery by thought was still adultery, a mortal sin. She'd been chaste throughout her marriage, but her protestations would mean nothing if John decided that she'd betrayed his trust. At the very least he'd send her to a nunnery, like Arthur had banished Guinivere for her love of Lancelot.

Margaret wept with silent despair. What terrified her most was the thought that John would take one look at her bloated body and thin drawn face and his desire would wither. At best he'd seek his pleasures elsewhere. Or worse, he'd pretend to be loyal while all the time he loathed every moment spent in her company.

Perhaps it would be easier to leap from the window and dash herself to pieces on the cobbles. That way she wouldn't have to face the perils of the birth.

But she feared the consequences too much. By committing such a crime, she'd be condemned to Hell for all eternity, and that terrified her more than anything else...

"My lady?" Katherine called, her voice muffled by the thick curtains round the bed. "Sir John's here."

Margaret drew a sharp anxious breath. What would he say, when he heard that she'd welcomed one of his Stewart foes into his home. With so many reasons to find fault with her, it would be a miracle if he deigned to speak with her again. "I don't want to see him," she whispered.

"But he rode back in haste to be with you."

At the thought of John waiting patiently at the door, she smothered a sob. Part of her desperately wanted the consolation of his presence. She closed her eyes, drew a deep shuddering breath. "You heard me."

"What will I tell him?"

"Whatever you like. I don't care."

John poured himself a measure of wine then sank down with a groan. It must have been well past midnight and he was weary from the journey, but he was too unsettled to even think of retiring.

"Sir John?" Katherine spoke beyond his door.

He glanced up. "Come in."

She stepped inside. Her gown was neat and well-ordered, but her hair hung loose like a maenad's. Her wanton appearance was at odds with her manner: she approached warily with hands clasped before her, gaze fixed firmly on the ground. "I'm sorry, Sir John. I begged her to speak with you, but she refuses…"

John gripped the chair arms tight. "Is she alright? Is the child alright?"

"Mistress White visits every other day, and she's very happy with my lady's progress. But I don't think my lady's being candid with her. When she's alone, she's gripped with melancholy. Yesterday she didn't stir from her bed at all. She just lay there and wept."

John slumped back with a sigh. He'd been that way himself, not that long ago. So lost in his own troubles that he couldn't comprehend the worry he brought to those around him. Setting his cup aside, he stood, quickly. "I should go to her."

Katherine blocked his path. "You mustn't!"

"Katherine, I can't ignore this."

She wouldn't budge. "Please let me explain!"

He shrugged, and sat back down, listening intently as Katherine told him how Margaret had been faring well until his mother returned. "She thinks she's failed you," Katherine said. "She thinks you'll be angry."

John considered her words, frowning. "Katherine," he said at last. "Tell me truly. Am I a monster?"

"No, Sir John. Of course not." She paced the room, her agitation growing. "I think something's happened," she added in a whisper, "but Margaret won't talk about it."

"I don't understand." John retorted. "My place is still standing, we're not under siege. The fermtoun seems prosperous and from the size of the midden I'd say we're not exactly short of livestock. What does she think she's done wrong?" He studied her carefully. "Did she argue with my mother?"

"I don't know."

"I'll speak with Lady Elizabeth in the morning," he said. "But my immediate concern is Margaret. I want to look her in the face and know that all's well. Go upstairs. Tell her I'll be waiting outside her door until she's ready to admit me."

But when he went back upstairs and tried again, there was still no reply. He hesitated, wondered if he should barge in regardless…

And decided against it. Sitting down upon the stair, he hugged his knees and thought of Marion, how she'd lain in that room and screamed as she fought to bring a stillborn child into the world. Before long Margaret would face the same trials, and he could do nothing to ease her path. Except pray to God, and hope He would have Mercy…

The door creaked open, and Katherine peered out. "You should get to your bed," she said, and when he didn't answer, she hurried to his side. Crouching beside him, she laid a careful hand upon his shoulder. "Please don't think ill of her."

He looked up, but couldn't bring himself to speak of his fears. "I should be there for her."

Katherine settled alongside. "If you sit here all night in these damp clothes, you'll make yourself ill. This black mood will pass."

He dropped his head in his hands. "The thought of losing her… I don't know what I'd do…"

She took his hand, gripping it tightly. "Please be strong, Sir John. We all look to you for wisdom and guidance."

He looked up, saw her studying him with anxious eyes. The haughty girl he'd learned to loathe in the first few months of his marriage was just a memory; her gentle, reassuring presence comforted him more than he would ever have cared to admit. "You can't do anything tonight," she said. "Go down to your chamber, and I'll make sure your bath's prepared. Everything will seem better when you've had a good night's sleep."

  *   *   *

The Place of Eglintoun

"A man's life is never his own." Hugh grumbled, pulling his doublet into place over his shirt.

Setting the garment straight, Helen pulled the laces tight. "At least you've done the honourable thing by your kinsmen. Now sit down please. Let me see your head."

He muttered his annoyance, but sat by the window regardless.

Grasping a cloth and draping it round his shoulders, Helen set to work with the comb, while Hugh squirmed like a child, impatient.

"How much longer?"

"Stop wriggling." She smiled, satisfied: searching his scalp, there was scarcely a nit or an egg to be seen. "I hope your cousins are grateful for your help."

"I hope so, too." Hugh twitched again. "Christ, Helen." He looked up, stricken. "What have I done?"

"Whatever do you mean?"

"They're fugitives from the King's justice. I drafted the pronouncement of treason myself. I stated quite clearly that any man who aided or abetted their escape should be hanged."

"Perhaps you should have considered this before you helped them?"

"Act in haste, they say…"

"As long as you don't have to repent from the depths of Blackness…"

He scowled. "Thank you for that."

"There now." She teased out his hair, patting it into place about his shoulders. "You look very presentable. When you rose from your bed this morning, I thought we'd never comb that mane into submission." Carefully folding the cloth, she pulled it aside and set it down.

Hugh stood, brushing imaginary flecks from his clothes. "I told you the bath was a mistake."

"Nonsense." She helped him into his gown. "You smell delightful. Which makes a pleasant change." Ducking aside, she neatly avoided the hand he swatted in her direction. "I shall ask the servants to fetch you some wine," she said. "So you can entertain your young cousin in the manner he merits."

With Robert Montgomerie and Alexander Stewart safely delivered to their host's quarters, Helen paid a quick visit to the kitchens then returned to her chamber.

The prospect of some peace and quiet before dinner was a welcome one. She nodded to the wetnurse in passing: young Maggie smiled back, little more than a child herself. The girl had arrived here as a poor thin-faced wretch, grieving over the loss of her own babe. But two months spent in Helen's keeping had robbed her of her timid manner, giving her a healthy glow in her cheeks.

Pausing to inspect Marion, Helen found her child firmly attached to Maggie's exposed breast. Helen felt a brief pang of regret, but it soon faded: after the night she'd spent with Hugh, there'd soon be another child on its way.

"The sky looks leaden," Bessie commented. She was sitting by the window, working away at a beautifully stitched panel for her gown. "Will it snow?"

"I hope so. The world looks beautiful when it's cloaked in white." Helen sat down by Bessie and inspected her workmanship. "Lovely," she said. "But you'd best make the most of it. Once the laundry's done we'll be darning sarks for a month." She grasped the doublet she'd looked out for mending the previous night and set to work with a sigh.

"At least everything will be clean," Bessie said.

"Let's be thankful for small mercies-" Helen broke off, startled. Downstairs in the laird's chamber, Hugh was shouting loud enough to stir a corpse.

Maggie flinched, face pale with fear. She clutched Marion tight to her breast, the babe snuffled a few times, screwed up her face and started to howl.

"Merciful Heavens!" Helen flung down her sewing. "There's enough noise from your father, without you making more."

Bessie cast Helen an uneasy glance. "Mama…"

Helen patted her shoulder. "I'll see what's amiss, shall I?" then added, almost under her breath, "And put an end to the row, God willing…"

When she peered round the door, she found Hugh stalking back and forth by the fireplace, red-faced from his tirade, incandescent with wrath. "-I should flay you for this!" he raged. "I leave you to carry out this one simple task, and you can't even accomplish that-"

Running her gaze around the room, Helen noted Alex Stewart sitting hunched in his chair, an unwitting bystander. It was Hugh's unfortunate brother who suffered the full force of his fury: standing there with head bowed and shoulders sagging, like a wayward hound awaiting its beating.

"Whatever is the matter?" Helen demanded.

Hugh didn't even acknowledge her presence. "-You've embarrassed me! You've embarrassed our entire line." He flung himself down in his chair and batted his goblet aside with a clatter. "You little shit."

The Gryphon at Bay

Retrieving the goblet, Helen set it back on the table beside him. She spotted the dint in the bowl, made a careful note to have the metal beaten out next time it travelled back to the kitchen. "I hope his sins warrant this unholy row," she said. "You've upset the children."

Hugh studied her wearily, head propped on his hand. "He was told to make his way back to Eglintoun without delay. So what did he do?" He paused for theatrical effect, the scowl crept back. "I'll tell you what he did. He took the boy to Ellestoun and he stayed there overnight. Gorging himself on John Sempill's food, drinking his wine."

"Ah," Helen said.

"You see?" Hugh snapped, grimly triumphant. "Even my wife understands what you've done," He gestured grandly in Helen's direction.

Alex Stewart looked up. "Sempill's only a baron," he ventured.

"He's my friend," Hugh retorted. "And God knows, your kinfolk haven't done much to endear themselves to him just lately."

"The boy was injured," Robert cast Hugh a sullen glance. "We needed a place to rest."

"Don't take that sanctimonious attitude with me! Christ, if you talk like that to me again I'll pack you off to the nearest monastery quicker than you can fart."

"I'm sorry-"

"Sorry's not good enough. You're going to Ellestoun so you can grovel to Sir John in person. And I'm coming with you, so don't think you can wriggle out of your responsibilities." Springing to his feet, he reached for his gown.

It was not, Helen reflected, the best time to remind him that he had duties and obligations at home. That within a day or two his hall would be packed with noble guests. Nonetheless, she felt compelled to make the effort. "Hugh-" she began.

He regarded her with his customary mildness. "Don't fret, my love." He paused to kiss her cheek. "I won't loiter. There's still time to prepare for Yuletide. Though if you ask me-" He glowered at Robert once more, "-the Feast of Fools has started early this year." Seizing his brother's collar, Hugh hauled him to the door. "Come along, wretch. There's no time to lose."

Chapter 71

The Place of Ellestoun

Someone moved beyond the bed. John paid no heed, burrowing deep beneath the covers, unwilling to face the world just yet.

"What time do you call this?" William pulled back the curtain and light spilled in, the pale grey gleam of winter.

"Christ." John sat up, yawning. "I didn't mean to lie so late." He grasped the shirt that William offered and pulled it over his head.

William's glance was heavy with concern. "You look like you've been ridden by a night hag."

"I couldn't sleep."

"Ah," William said.

John swung his legs out with a sigh. He'd spent half the night tossing in his bed, fretting over Margaret and the child. His eyes were gritty with fatigue, his senses dull. He blundered over to the kist near the fireplace, pausing briefly to splash himself with water before pulling on his hose. "How's Mary?"

William smiled, slightly. "She looks like she's carrying Leviathan."

"When's the birth?"

"Next month, she reckons. Until then, she'll be waddling around with all the dignity of a goose."

"You're very calm about all this."

"If Mary thinks all's well," William said, "then I'm content."

"Did she say anything at all? About Margaret?"

William shook his head. "Not that I recall."

"Speak to her, would you?" John grasped a comb and pulled it irritably through his hair, wincing as it snagged. "I'll go to mass." He set the comb aside. "Is it true what they say? That all women must pay for Eve's transgression? It seems unjust-" He grimaced. "Though perhaps I've just condemned myself to Hell for even thinking such things..."

"If you ponder the mysteries of this world much longer, you'll miss mass," William warned. "And then you'll be scourging yourself all the harder. It's the priest's task to consider such things. So long as he says his prayers on your behalf, then why worry?"

"Your mother's here," William said. "She requests an audience."

"God help me!" John groaned and glanced heavenwards. "You'd best show her in, I suppose."

As William bowed and retreated, John gnawed irritably at a thumbnail, wincing as he caught the quick. He took a brief fortifying mouthful of wine, just in time, as Elizabeth Ross swept inside, skirts trailing in her wake, a beaming smile on her face.

"Welcome home, John. What a joy it is to see you!"

He rose to greet her, tolerating her affection as she grasped his shoulders and kissed him on both cheeks.

"You're looking well," she said. "I thought I'd see a half-starved wretch, after all that time you lived out in the field. It's a miracle you didn't catch your death." If she noticed his distant manner, she didn't show it. "But never mind that. You're home for Yuletide, and that's wonderful news-"

John fought the urge to offer a stinging retort. He sat back down, sweeping his gown aside with an irritable flourish.

"-I've made such plans." His mother hurried about the room, flicking dust motes from the wall-hangings, tidying away his shoes. "I sent word to the Crawfurds and the Mures. I'm hoping Sir Patrick Wallace will join us, too. It's only right he enjoys good company at Yuletide, now his poor wife has passed on-"

John sipped his wine, saying nothing.

"-Marion will be lying in by now. I do hope she fares better this time. It was a crying shame she lost her first…" She turned to confront him. "I thought you'd be pleased to see me."

He flicked his hand, non-commital. "Of course I am. But I've concerns of my own just now. Perhaps it's escaped your notice, but… My wife's suffering an affliction of the soul." His voice hardened. "I hope nothing happened to upset her in my absence."

His mother stiffened. "I should've known this would happen!" She shook her head, disdainful. "You've been listening to those wretched creatures of hers, haven't you?"

"'Those wretched creatures', as you so charitably call them, are deeply worried about Margaret." He looked her in the eye, scowling. "For that matter, so am I."

Her face darkened. "If she's ashamed to face you, there's good reason."

"Please explain." His gaze didn't waver.

"In all my years as lady of this house, I never insulted my husband in the manner she insulted you." She paused for good effect. "Letting John Stewart's youngest boy stay beneath this roof. Your sworn enemy, sleeping in your place, under your protection."

"When did this happen?" John asked, carefully.

"A week ago, or thereabouts. He came here with one of the Montgomeries."

John ground his teeth in silent frustration. He'd been betrayed. Margaret had been betrayed. At last Hugh's part in the plot to help the Stewarts was exposed with stark clarity.

He should have been angry. Instead, the gnawing unease was growing ever more intense. "How was she to know this?"

His mother clasped her hands before her, standing tall and restrained, every inch the long-suffering martyr. "If she'd sought the advice of her betters from the beginning, this would never have happened."

John picked a knothole in the chair arm, unwilling to meet her gaze. "Then you should be criticising me, not her."

"You always take her side, John."

"She's my wife."

"Merciful Heavens! I've never heard such complacent talk." She paced the room, restless and distraught. "Has it occurred to you that there may be other reasons why Margaret Colville is unwilling to look you in the eye?" Halting at last, she caught his gaze, unabashed. "I've heard rumours. That your wife has been unfaithful."

His scowl grew more entrenched. "Where did you hear this?"

"I can't say." She paused. "But I know that when you went to Southannan-"

"Idle talk," John said in a flat clipped tone. "Cruel rumours, aimed at a woman who can't defend herself."

"Open your eyes!" she countered. "That wretch from Eglintoun mocks you whichever way he can. He abused your charity when you cared for him at Southannan. Now he's abused it again."

"How can you say this?" At long last, he'd been goaded into fury, the accusations pricking ever deeper. "You don't know what happened. I placed Lord Hugh in my wife's care for just one night. He was weak and close to death. And Margaret's womb was already sated..."

"What if he used his black arts to seduce your wife and sow his own seed inside her?" Lady Elizabeth spoke with gleeful condescension. "It's not unheard of..."

"He's a liar and a rogue, but he's not a sorcerer!" It was no good. No matter how hard he tried to deny it, there was an ember of doubt glowing deep within. That perhaps the time Hugh had spent in Margaret's keeping had not been entirely innocent, that even if the child his wife bore was his own, her heart might not be devoted entirely to him.

Because Hugh, for all his faults, was a lord. Rich and powerful, infinitely more deserving of a lady's love and admiration. While he was just a humble baron, scrounging for favour like a half-starved hound scratching at a worthy noble's door.

"Sir John?" William peered cautiously inside. "You have a visitor."

William paused at the door to the hall. "Come this way, my lord."

Hugh glared at Robert, who trailed at his heels, disconsolate. "Hurry up!" he snapped. "We haven't got all day."

William grasped Hugh's arm as he drew level. "Tread carefully."

"Thank you, Master Haislet," Hugh said. "I'll bear that in mind."

Feigning nonchalance, he breezed up the stairs and barged into the laird's chamber. He found John slumped in his chair, head propped on one hand. His mother was there with him. From the looks of her, she'd just delivered the winning riposte in an argument, her face aglow with triumph.

Hugh stopped in his tracks, sensing the hostility. It rippled through the room like a miasma, poisoning the air.

John looked up, disinterested. "Talk of the devil."

"My brother has something to say." Hugh hauled Robert alongside. "Out with it, wretch."

"Don't listen to his lies!" Elizabeth Ross pleaded, planting herself directly before her son. "Whatever the excuse, whatever the explanation, it's just another strand in his web of deceit."

"Whatever are you talking about?" Hugh demanded.

She turned on him. "You've tried too long to hook your claws into my son. You want to ruin him, don't you? You and those accursed Stewarts…"

"Lady Elizabeth-" Hugh began.

"-You slew my Thomas, and ever since you've been working hard to destroy us." Her tone was shrill with victory, her face flushed with passion. "If your great-grandsire only knew what you'd become. A monstrous tyrant, the like of which hasn't been seen round here since Longshanks' days."

He flinched, despite himself. "How dare you!"

"Your reign in the Westland's over. My brother's home now, and by God he'll put you back in your place. And there'll be plenty round here grateful for that, I can tell you-"

"That's enough!" John scowled as if their collective presence disgusted him. "Get out!"

Hugh thought of arguing, but John's grim expression made him think again. Grasping his brother's gown, he steered him for the door.

"Not you, Hugh!" John's voice rang out at his back. "I want to speak with you."

"John, no!" Seizing her son's hand, Elizabeth Ross cast him an imploring look. "Don't heed his lies."

He swatted her away. "Leave me in peace."

Robert loitered by the stair, reluctant to depart. He held the door for John's mother: sweeping past, she paused briefly to glare in his direction.

Hugh caught his brother's eye and nodded. Reassured, Robert bowed to John and disappeared after Lady Elizabeth, quietly closing the door.

"The mood downstairs will be colder than a midwinter morn," Hugh said. "At least William will be amply entertained." He drew up a stool. "What in God's name has happened here?"

"Don't distract me," John said. "I want the truth."

Hugh sighed, and scratched his head. "Yes, I helped him." He fell silent, offered John his best beseeching look. "He's my cousin. What else could I do?"

John shrugged. There was no judgement there, no accusation, just the exhausted look of a man hounded by circumstances.

"I can't defend Robert's decision. But I can assure you that he didn't mean to cause offence. He saw no other course to follow. The boy was hurt: they couldn't press on to Hessilhead, and they could hardly take refuge in Paisley, could they?"

John said nothing.

"John, I'm sorry." He paused to let his words sink in. "What more do you want from me? I can apologise a thousand times, it won't change circumstances."

"It doesn't matter, I suppose." He slumped back with a sigh. "Affairs of state can snare a man, like brambles in a thicket. In his efforts to break free, he loses sight of what matters most."

"Ah…" Hugh said. "It's Margaret, isn't it?"

John waved a hand in vague dismissal. "She's taken this business with the Stewarts to heart." He sighed. "Words were exchanged. Between Margaret and my mother. I don't know what was said. She won't talk to me."

"Old women always make mischief. They have nothing better to do with their time."

"There are rumours that when we were at Southannan, yourself and Margaret were..." John stared ahead. "Unduly close."

Bowing his head, Hugh leaned his brow against clasped hands. "I thought you knew me well enough by now."

"I thought I knew Margaret."

"Don't you?"

"Not really." He shifted with a sigh, meeting his gaze at last. "Christ, Hugh, I've been married to her eight months or more, and she's still a stranger to me."

"I daresay she says much the same about you."

"Whatever do you mean?"

"When she cared for me, we talked." He broke off, unsure whether to continue, as John looked away, the mask of indifference gone, his pain all too apparent.

"There was nothing else to do, was there?" Hugh's voice trailed away.

"Do you think that by telling me this I'll be grateful?" John snapped back. "I see now that Margaret's melancholy is all my doing. I'm a cold, unfeeling brute: I must be, if my wife's too fearful to face me, and she admits as much to a guest I placed in her care..."

Hugh buried his face in his hands. "This isn't necessary."

"-Perhaps my wife would prefer a man whose passion always gets the better of him. Who rides to tryst under an agreement of truce, then nearly lops his kinsman's head off through a tragic act of misunderstanding."

"Stop this!" He reeled inside, stung by John's words. "I'll speak to her, shall I? It's the least I can do, since I suppose in a way this is all my fault-" He stood and strode briskly to the door.

"Wait!" John followed, but too late, for he was already hurrying up the winding stair towards the ladies' chamber. "I don't want you-"

"Have faith in me, John," Hugh called. "Have I ever failed you yet?"

Chapter 72

The argument had raged for an eternity, her gude-mother's shrill tones alternating with John's bitter ripostes.

Margaret closed her eyes, wishing she could drift away into oblivion. Her heart raced in her breast, her mouth was dry with panic: she didn't want to hear them fight like that, especially when it was all her doing...

The angry exchange subsided at last. But her fear remained, a nameless prowling shadow. She stifled a sob, so gripped with uncertainty that she didn't quite know what to do or say next.

Perching beside her, Katherine took her hand. "I'm sure they weren't talking about you."

"Who else would they be talking about?"

"Please don't get upset. Sir John will deal with everything." Katherine rose to her feet and moved briskly about the chamber, re-tying the curtains, smoothing out the coverlet. "All that matters is that you keep in good health. Rest, eat plenty of wholesome food, the way Mistress Mary told you. Why don't you sit up? Mariota's making a draught to help lift your spirits. And you should change your gown. It's very stale..." She turned, casting a critical eye over Margaret. "If you moved around more, you wouldn't find everything so unpleasant."

"Stop fussing." She'd have rolled over if she could, to ease her aching back, but she feared she'd crush the baby. Hearing footsteps on the stair, the tread of a man, she drew a hissing breath. "Tell him to go. I don't want-"

The door banged open. "Lady Margaret." Hugh's voice boomed loud as he swept like a gale into the room. "Tell me truly. Do you want your poor husband sent to an early grave?"

Katherine and Mariota flocked to confront him. "Have you no shame?" Katherine snapped.

He swatted them aside. "None whatsoever." He flung himself down into the chair by Margaret's bedside. "Greetings, Margaret." He studied her, frowning. "You don't look unwell to me."

She pushed herself up onto her elbows. "How dare you! Does he know you're here?"

He shrugged. "Of course." His manner changed, his features softened. He leaned close, like a kindly uncle or older brother. "Margaret, please. If you can't tell John for fear of upsetting him, then at least tell me. What's troubling you?"

She drew a deep shuddering breath. It was easy to fall for his wiles, to think he embodied all the qualities of knightly virtue and courtesy. But then the memory returned unbidden, of the night he'd stormed into his chamber at Eglintoun, blood-stained, consumed with fury.

"I'm cursed." The words tumbled out, unbidden. "I have such black thoughts. Sometimes I think the child wants me dead. That this first birth will be my last."

He sat back with a sigh. "You speak as if the poor thing's a demon," he said. "It may be born of sin, but it enters this world as an innocent, and seeks to harm no-one."

"They say a woman should keep apart from the world. That she should surround herself with things that are wholesome and beautiful…" She choked back a sob. "I saw so much that was monstrous…"

"None more dreadful than my own broken flesh, I'll warrant." Hugh paused. "Yes, I suppose that's true. But there's babes born in this world whose mothers witness far worse. They go on to live pure and virtuous lives. Some, I daresay, achieve sainthood!" He moved to rise. "Now let me fetch John, and he-"

She caught his arm. "How can I say such things to John? I've caused him so much hurt already."

"And so you bestow yet more upon him," he retorted. "Have courage, Margaret. Of course you're afraid, but you must face those fears, look them in the eye and challenge them, as if you were a knight lined up for battle."

"You're incapable of fear," she retorted, bitterly. "Everyone knows that."

He gave a hollow, half-hearted laugh. "I'm as frightened as the next man. But I put my faith in God, and He protects me."

"I wish I was a man. I'd rather fight in battle, and die a valiant death…"

"I've seen men die, many times. It isn't valiant, or noble. It's brutal and squallid, hideous to behold."

Margaret glanced away. The tears were welling up again, she tried to sniff them back, but couldn't.

Hugh grasped her hand. "When I was weak and close to death, you were there, willing me to live. It's your fate to confront the trials of the birth alone. But John will do what he can to help you weather that torment. It's small consolation, I know, but if he could, he'd take that suffering upon himself, and gladly, too."

"Stop saying such things. He'll take one look at me, and hate me, because I'm fat, and swollen, and ugly."

"You're carrying his child," Hugh replied. "He'll think it's the most beautiful thing in the world."

John sat disconsolate upon the stair, arms wrapped around his knees. He thought of Marion, how she'd screamed and cried on God for help as she fought to free herself of the dead child trapped in her womb.

But more insidious thoughts kept surfacing unbidden, however hard he tried to banish them. His pride was pricked: Hugh's absence meant his friend had succeeded where he'd failed, and that stung him to the quick.

Perhaps his mother was right. Perhaps he was a poor misguided fool, too blind to notice infidelity at close hand. But Hugh didn't seem like a man who'd take pleasure in cuckolding a so-called friend. If he was guilty of any crime, it was of trampling others underfoot in the spirit of good intentions.

Hearing the scuff of booted feet upon the stair, John stirred. Too late - Hugh skidded into his back, nearly sailing over the top of him.

"Christ Almighty!" He grasped John's shoulder in his effort to keep from falling. "Are you trying to kill me?"

"We laid my sister in that room. She lost the child, and nearly passed away herself."

"So you blame the room for one misfortune?" Hugh cuffed his head. "Why, I daresay a whole succession of Sempill heirs were delivered safe within its walls. Now for God's Sake, John, keep your fears firmly to yourself, and be the source of strength and comfort Margaret requires. She needs you."

"Hugh-"

"Go to her." Hugh waved his hand in dismissal, offering not so much as a backward glance. "I've done what I can. Now I'll be gone, to comfort my own wife and counsel my children. Goodbye, John. We'll speak again when the New Year's upon us."

This time John didn't bother to knock. He slipped inside, the heat hitting him like a wall after the dank cold of the stair. The room was stuffy, the shutters closed and the fire rising high.

He shivered, despite the warmth, remembering the day he'd ventured into Marion's chamber at Easter Greenock. The shock he'd felt when he confronted a pale ghostly reflection of the lively sister he remembered from his childhood.

Katherine, Mariota and Alison curtsied. He nodded, half-hearted acknowledgement, his thoughts on Margaret, who lay stranded on her bed, belly swelling against the confines of her gown. His breath caught in his throat: suddenly the birth seemed imminent, frighteningly so.

She struggled to sit. She'd been crying, her eyes red and slightly swollen, cheeks still stained with tears. She seemed little more than a child herself, her hair dishevelled. He caught the waft where he stood, stale flesh and clothing scarcely masked by the scent of perfume.

He hurried over and took her hand. He didn't trust himself to speak, he just gripped her tightly.

"You should bathe and put on fresh clothes," he said at last. "You'll feel better then." His voice shook, so he gave up all pretence of detachment. He sat close, and hugged her tight.

Wrapping her arms around his neck, she buried her face against him and sobbed. "I didn't know who he was, I swear. I thought that if the Montgomeries sent him, then all was well. I thought-"

"Hush, Margaret," he said, softly. "How were you to know?"

"I am so sorry…"

"Margaret, enough!" Taking her face in his hands, he brushed away her tears and smiled. "There's nothing more to be said." He straightened, meeting the anxious faces of the maids with an encouraging smile. "Now let's see what can be done to raise your spirits. Once you've bathed and changed your gown, the world'll seem a better place."

Chapter 73

Hermitage Castle

With torches burning fiercely in the sconces, not even the mouldering gloom of this border fortress could dampen the spirits. Women's laughter rang shrill amongst the hearty greetings of the menfolk: after months of slumber, Hermitage had awoken, a place of warmth and good cheer once more.

Amongst the guests Angus spotted his wife. He plotted his course towards her, smiling. "My dear." Grasping Elizabeth's hands, he kissed her smartly on both cheeks. Her face was cold and pale as marble; reflecting the soul within, he thought with wry amusement. "This is indeed a surprise."

His wife nodded, gracious acknowledgement. "George told me of your plans for Yuletide. I thought I'd join you."

George appeared alongside, rosy-cheeked after a long day spent in the saddle. He rubbed his hands and stamped his feet. "Ah, it's perishing out there." He grinned at his father. "I've another surprise in store." He ushered forward a young woman. Obscured beneath the heavy hood of her travelling cloak, Angus noted her delicate oval face with soft dark eyes and thin black brows. Her outer garments were lined with thick fur, the gown beneath a deep dark red. She cradled a babe in her arms, wrapped warm for the journey, and sleeping soundly.

"Lady Marion," Angus acknowledged. "You're looking well." He reached for the child. "And this is my grandson?"

Marion Drummond relinquished her burden without a word.

Angus gazed at the pink fragile face and smiled. "Your first-born, George. What an absolute treasure!" He nodded to the young woman. "Congratulations, Marion. We're all very proud of you."

She glanced aside. "Thank you, Your Grace."

"Come along, my love." George took his wife's arm and ushered her away. "It's a miserable place, I know. But it's not nearly so stark and unpleasant when you get inside."

"Head for the hall, George," Angus called after him. "There's mulled wine and spiced cakes to be enjoyed before supper." He nodded to Elizabeth. "You've brought an impressive entourage."

Elizabeth surveyed the steady stream of kinsfolk and servants, filing their way into an already-crowded space. "It was a long, savage road. I wanted adequate protection."

"I'm surprised to see you here at all."

"You're my husband, Archie. In case you'd forgotten."

"How could I ever forget, my dear?"

"I thought it best that a lord of your stature was seen in the company of his wife." She cast a cautious glance about her. "I presume men of note will be sitting at the board this Yuletide?"

"Indeed."

"Men who may not entirely meet with the King's approval?"

"He'll be grateful for these negotiations in due course."

"Let's hope so. And besides…" She cast him a bashful glance, as if she were a timid maid and he her suitor. "I hoped to catch you in good spirits. I have a favour to ask."

"And what is that, pray?"

"There's a young man in my retinue. A youth of outstanding qualities, who seeks guidance and patronage from a lord of distinguished reputation. I thought you might take him into your household, and give him the instruction he requires."

"And who is this paragon of manly virtue?"

"Cuthbert, Lord Kilmaurs."

Angus chuckled, softly. "God, you're cunning."

That secretive smile danced about her lips once more. "Speak with him, Archie. He won't disappoint."

"All in good time. Perhaps we should let the lad settle in, before we ask him to justify his presence here?"

Cuthbert Cunninghame stood alone amongst the crowd. He studied the floor, gripping his cup so tight his knuckles shone pale. He'd talked with George earlier, a brief cordial exchange, but now George had moved on and the young lord from the Westland was visibly at a loss.

He's roasted long enough, Angus told himself, steering a leisurely course towards the young man. "Lord Cuthbert?"

Cuthbert smiled, cautious and reserved. He inclined his head in gracious greeting. "Your Grace."

"You're a long way from home."

"I travelled with Countess Elizabeth."

"You did indeed. In most curious circumstances."

He flinched. "She said you were seeking new blood for your retinue."

"And what qualities can you offer a hoary old statesman like myself?"

"A bold heart and a steady head." Cuthbert met his gaze and held it. "Not to mention a strong sword arm."

"You think my support will prove useful?"

"You're renowned at court, with a worthy reputation as a knight." He paused and swallowed, subtle nervousness. "Besides, I think our households have much in common."

"You mean we share a common enemy." Angus paused, frowning. "You've made the mistake of assuming that when I married, I also took responsibility for my wife's family feuds."

Cuthbert blinked, visibly shaken. "I wouldn't presume-"

Angus gripped his shoulder, smiling. "Welcome to Hermitage, Lord Cuthbert. I look forward to witnessing your prowess for myself."

"I have a fine destrier, and my own arms."

"And a disagreement with Montgomerie." Angus paused. "Doesn't it anger you, that you'll be confined here with me, when you should be seeking revenge for your father's death?"

Cuthbert's stare was level, unflinching. "I respect my enemy, Your Grace. Outwitting him won't be easy. In the meantime, I'll dedicate myself to those who help me, and grant them whatever skills are mine to give."

"Your eloquence astounds me, Lord Cuthbert. I see you've met George?"

"I have, Your Grace."

"Well, there are others in my household who might also be of interest. As you may be aware, I have two daughters. Who knows, if I'm sufficiently impressed by your merits, then you may be considered a worthy suitor. Is that what you intend?"

Caught off-guard, Cuthbert blushed. "Your Grace-"

"An Earl's daughter," Angus cut in, smoothly. "It's not unthinkable, surely? Or do you think that once I have full measure of your abilities, I'll find something lacking?"

Cuthbert's face coloured all the more. "I should be an earl myself, Your Grace."

"Of course you should."

Cuthbert fell silent, glowering.

"The wound's raw, I see," Angus said. "That's to be expected. Perhaps I should make this a condition of my patronage, Lord Cuthbert. If you serve me well, for a year or eighteen months, say, then I shall make it my business to win you that earldom. The Earl of Glencairn, eh? I think he'd be a very worthy husband for a daughter of the Red Douglas, don't you?"

"I'm flattered, Your Grace."

"As indeed you should be." He leaned close, pleasantly conspiratorial. "What a joy it would be, to force Montgomerie to swallow such a bitter pill-"

"He'd choke, I hope."

"-Why, you'd have won the very thing he's been fighting tooth and nail to keep from you." Angus chuckled. "It's a delightful thought. It warms me inside. Now come this way. I saw young Margery a little while back. I think you should meet her..."

Beith, Cunninghame

Shreds of snow were falling by the time they crested the hills above Beith. The air was frigid, the wind slicing across the barren ground and scouring their faces.

"We're a stone's throw from Hessilhead," Robert complained.

"John's cooks couldn't satisfy the palate of a corpse."

"If we lose our bearings, what then? We might stumble into Cunninghame's clutches."

"You've led such a sheltered life." Hugh had to shout to be heard above the whipping wind. "A winter in the wilds would do you the world of good. I should send you north, and place you in Earl Colin's care."

"I've apologised already. What more do you want from me?"

"An end to your whining, that's what."

"Look to the west, Hugh! The skies are black, and the snow's blowing thick there. We'll be buried alive, horses and all."

364

"You think I'll be parted from my good lady because you're too soft to endure a bit of snow?"

"They won't find us till spring, when our bones are bleaching in the sun." Robert broke off, scowling, then added, cautiously, "I'm sure Lady Helen would be grateful for that."

"Save your strength for keeping warm." He closed his legs tight as Zephyr frisked and sidled sideways. "Let's press on, shall we? It's not a day to linger on the road." Pulling his scarf up over his nose and mouth, he sat deep and urged his horse onwards, plunging into the teeth of the tempest.

Robert was right. To ride out in weather like this was foolhardy. But as the wind battered him and the elements conspired against him, Hugh felt the pleasures of life more keenly.

Taking a deep breath, he turned his head from the blinding bite of the snow, as even now misgivings stirred within him.

The Castle of Hermitage

A dressed peacock sat in pride of place upon the top table, imperious even in death. The metallic sheen of its feathers shimmered in the light of three-score candles, the crowning glory in a much larger feast. Servants bore dishes of beef and lamb and fowl and venison, all served with a delectable range of sauces, highly flavoured with spices from the orient.

"-I would very much like to visit the court of King Henry." George had to raise his voice to be heard, both over the chatter and laughter of their guests, and the lively music played by lutes and fiddles in the minstrels' gallery. "But the Scots, alas, can hardly be viewed as welcome visitors."

"Some Scots are always welcome." Lord Dacre of Westmoreland dabbed his napkin carefully against his lips. Dacre's solid frame and dark, swarthy features were well known throughout the Marchlands. A bold fierce knight approaching forty, he was a ruthless dispenser of justice, who'd hanged more reivers through the years than anyone cared to remember. "Let's not forget that your father has already been a great friend to the English."

Angus smiled. "That's most kind of you, my lord."

"I always give credit where it's due," said Dacre. "Whether it's a Scotsman or an Englishman is neither here nor there." He placed his hand discreetly over his cup as more wine was offered. "I hear Sir John Ross of Montgrennan has left King Henry's court?"

"I don't go out of my way to speak with him," Angus said.

"His opinions are hardly relevant," Dacre agreed. "To understand the Marches a man must live here all his life. As you're well aware, the needs of King and court don't necessarily go hand in glove with managing the borderlands." Wiping his fingers on his napkin, he selected another piece of meat and dipped it deftly in the sauce bowl. "Most of your retinue I know. Apart from the young man sitting yonder..."

"Ah, that's Cuthbert Cunninghame, the Lord Kilmaurs."

"He's a long way from home."

Angus half-closed his eyes. "He sought a patron."

"What manner of a man is he?"

"George has been putting him through his paces." Angus nodded to his son. "Well? How has my young squire been faring?"

"He's competent enough with sword and axe," said George. "And a skilled horseman, too."

"I told him he's welcome to try his hand in our little tournament," Angus added. "He was eager to accept the challenge, so I daresay we'll soon be seeing his skills at first-hand."

Dacre smirked. "He'll be hard-pressed to beat Percy's boy."

"Oh, I'd wager Lord Cuthbert has a fighting chance of victory," came George's brisk retort.

"Really?" Dacre snorted. "You think an unknown Scotsman can topple a proven champion of the joust?"

"He fought Montgomerie," said George. "And lived to tell the tale."

"Our friend Percy should remember," Angus added with a smile, "that history sometimes has a habit of repeating itself. It's been a hundred years since Sir Hugh Montgomerie built his place at Polnoon with Harry Percy's ransom, but the deed itself is not forgotten. Even now the Percy banner adorns Lord Hugh's wall at Eglintoun." He swallowed a mouthful of wine. "The English sneer at their lowly neighbours from the north. They forget that Scotia has herself nurtured some magnificent flowers of chivalry."

"And none more worthy than your own forefathers," Dacre replied. "God willing, the exploits of James the Good and Archibald the Grim will be recounted in the Marchlands a thousand years hence."

"Indeed." Settling back in his chair, Angus glanced to where young Cuthbert Cunninghame sat next to Marjorie. Studying his daughter with a critical eye, Angus would have been the first to concede that she was too lean and pale to be beautiful. But there was a fragile, ethereal quality about her that might bewitch a man. And while Cuthbert didn't yet appear bewitched, he was clearly attentive. It had been a deliberate move by Angus to place them together, a reminder to Cuthbert of what was on offer if he worked hard to win his new patron's approval.

Catching her father's eye Marjorie smiled, a look of quiet satisfaction. Angus nodded in response, almost imperceptible.

Dacre sat back and patted his belly. "May I commend your cooks, Earl Archibald. Until today, this jaded Englishman had thought the Scots incapable of creating a dinner worthy of the name."

"Your praise is much appreciated," Angus replied. "Now all that remains for Scotia's honour to be redeemed completely is for young Lord Cuthbert to triumph in the joust."

There was an amused snort from Dacre. "Then you'd best start praying, my friend."

Chapter 74

The Place of Ellestoun

Bedecked in her pearls and sporting her hood, Margaret was in better spirits at last. But when she ventured out onto the stair, she hesitated. "I might fall."

John took her arm. "I'll catch you."

He'd never seen her so nervous: she paused on every step, clutching his hand so tight he thought she'd crush his fingers.

It was a slow, tortuous journey, down the spiral stair past his chamber, but at last they reached the hall. He ushered her inside, then – when she was safely seated – he took his place.

The household was assembled, the air alive with chatter. John cast a baleful glance towards his mother, who studiously avoided his gaze. Before this day he'd never thought her capable of mischief: now, though, he wasn't so sure.

He beckoned to William. "Where's Lord Hugh?"

William leaned close. "He left us."

"But the weather's foul, William! It'll turn to snow before nightfall..."

"It's turned to snow already."

He felt a pang of concern. "He was welcome to stay. I thought I made that clear."

"He said he wanted to get back to his place. *A man should cherish his loved ones at Yuletide*, he said. *Sir John will understand.*"

John sighed. He understood only too well. If Hugh had wanted to convince them of his integrity, he'd gone about it the right way.

"My lord?" Two servants paused at his shoulder, one carrying the laver bowl, the other the aquamanile.

"He came all this way to apologise?" Margaret asked.

"Yes, he did." Placing his hands over the bowl, John scrubbed his fingers while a stream of fresh scented water was poured down from above. A clean dry cloth was presented: he dried his hands, briskly.

"Did he grovel?"

"He grovelled beautifully. It was a sight to behold."

"I heard you shouting."

John smiled. "The shouting was over before he even showed his face." He set his napkin neatly into place. "I'm sorry. I didn't mean to frighten you."

The serving staff trooped through the hall, carrying a respectable array of dishes and platters. An expectant hush fell: though the Yuletide feast wasn't quite upon them, the cooks were working hard regardless.

"Are you hungry?" John asked.

Margaret looked up. "Yes. I think I am."

"Good. I've asked them to be sparing with the spices." He nodded to Jamie Colville. "The meat, if you please."

Jamie stood, knife in one hand, flesh-hook in the other. As the meat was carved, John fiddled with his spoon, turning it over in his hands. *It's hardly her fault,* he told himself. *He's everything I'm not, a man of valour and renown. Perhaps, in a young woman's eyes, there can be no greater paragon of chivalry…*

"John?" She stared at him intently; he could see no guile there, no veiled secrecy. "Whatever's the matter?"

He smiled, half-heartedly. "Liveries, Margaret. It's something I've neglected before now…"

Her shoulders drooped. "That's a wife's task," she said. "I should have seen to it. But with the babe due…" She frowned. "Perhaps your mother…"

John smiled. "That's an excellent idea! I'll speak to her tomorrow."

And if that gave his mother something worthwhile with which to occupy her thoughts until the babe was delivered, so much the better.

The Place of Eglintoun

"Your poor husband, taking to the roads when the weather's closing in like this." Margaret Montgomerie cast her unforgiving glance around the hall, settling at last upon Hugh's empty chair. "Was it really necessary?"

"If Hugh thought so, then yes, it was." Helen nodded to the serving staff, who were bringing the last few dishes to the table.

"And all to visit the Sempill lad." Margaret Montgomerie set down her spoon and pressed her napkin against her lips.

"If I remember right," Helen retorted, "the Sempills took your aunt into their care throughout her twilight years, and laid her to rest amongst their own dead. I believe they take great pains to ensure a weekly mass is sung in her name. Hugh asked Sir John about the matter himself: he takes such kindnesses very seriously."

"He didn't show the Sempills much kindness when he slew Sir Thomas."

"That was war, Countess Margaret. Hugh has atoned for his sins and made amends with Sir John. It's in our best interests for the Sempills and the Montgomeries to work together as allies."

Margaret Montgomerie frowned. "In whose best interests?" she asked. "The Montgomeries? Or the Campbells?"

"Why both, of course." Helen gestured for a servant to pour their guest some more wine. "I hope you don't consider Hugh responsible for your husband's misfortunes?"

"His loyalty to the Sempill lad surprises me."

"If Hugh's Cunninghame lands are to remain secure, he'll need a loyal ally to uphold the law in Renfrew."

"He had a loyal ally in the Stewarts."

"But if John Sempill had been pronounced a rebel, he'd be fighting with the Cunninghames. Hugh thought it prudent to win his favour."

"At the expense of ruining his kin?"

Helen smiled, unperturbed. "He did what he thought best, under trying circumstances. And now he's doing what he can to restore your husband's fortunes. He has risked his life for your menfolk. Please don't forget that-" She broke off, startled, as the door banged open.

In came Hugh, hair encrusted with snow, nose glowing red from the cold. Water dripped from the hem of his cloak and his boots squelched with every step, while Robert trailed at his heels, cowed and disconsolate.

"Good day to you, Aunt Margaret!" Stepping onto the dais, Hugh confronted the Countess of Lennox across the board. Taking her hand, he bowed to kiss it, leaving a trail of melting ice in the shadow of his outstretched arm. "I'm sorry I couldn't greet you in person."

"You'll catch your death, Hugh," Margaret Montgomerie said.

"Let's hope not. It'd spoil the mood over Yuletide." He caught Helen's eye. "I'll eat in my chamber. Perhaps you'd join me there later."

Glancing aside, she placed a hand lightly against her chest, demure acknowledgement. "I shall do that, my lord. Once my guests are replete, I'll attend you."

Hugh grunted, and was gone.

"Such an abrupt fellow," Margaret Montgomerie complained. "He has too much choler."

"Better that than a surfeit of spleen…"

"The leech should attend him at least once a month, to bleed him and instruct him on his diet."

Helen smiled. "I doubt I'd find a leech brave enough to try."

"It would benefit you both. And it's your duty as a wife to keep him healthy."

Helen said nothing. It was the way of older women, to lecture the next generation. With her household dispersed and the fate of her husband and eldest son uncertain, it was little wonder that Margaret Montgomerie was trying hard to impose her presence on her nephew's household.

"Have you decided what to do with the boy?" Margaret Montgomerie asked.

"He'll stay here a few years more," Helen said. "When he's ten or eleven, I expect he'll be sent to serve in his uncle's retinue."

"And the bastard? She's old enough to be married."

"Bessie will be gone soon enough."

The Countess snorted, coldly dismissive. "If you're not careful, no one will want her."

Helen sighed, wearily. It was at times like this that she realised just how lucky she was to live her life free from the interference of older relatives. She helped herself to another chunk of bread, thankful that in a few weeks' time, her guest would be gone, her life her own once more.

The bed loomed tall in the dimly-lit chamber, but Hugh was reluctant to brave its chilly sheets just yet. He was comfortable where he was, shielded from the reed-strewn floorboards by a thick, fur-lined cloak, and from the frigid air by a warm blanket.

Helen stirred in his arms, running her hands delicately over his skin. He buried his face against her neck, too weary to respond, but grateful nonetheless.

Someone would disturb them eventually, creeping past with eyes averted. Until that time came, they were alone in the world. It was as if the years had slipped away, to that night years before in the guardroom at *Caisteal Glowm*, when he'd lain with Earl Colin's daughter clasped tight in his arms for the first time.

He wound his fingers deep into her soft dark tresses. "I should've spent Yuletide with the king," he said. "But as I lie here with you, I know I'd rather be nowhere else on earth."

She sighed and gripped him tighter.

"I'm the luckiest man alive, to have you as a wife."

"Am I perhaps being compared with another?"

"When I arrived at Ellestoun, John was beside himself with worry. Young Margaret isn't weathering her pregnancy at all well."

"When does the lying-in begin?"

"He said the babe was due in March."

"Perhaps I should call upon her when her time approaches."

"You have my blessing," said Hugh. "I did what I could to help, but I'm not sure it was appreciated."

"Sir John's a man like any other. Perhaps he thought you were casting doubt upon his prowess as a husband."

Hugh rolled onto his back with a sigh. "Do you think he took it that way?"

"I'm not privy to his thoughts."

"He said there'd been rumours. About myself and Margaret."

"I hope they're groundless?" The levity in her voice masked faint concern.

"It would be an offence against nature!"

Helen laughed, softly. "A profound misjudgement, perhaps. A sin, most definitely. But I can't see why Nature should take offence."

"He's like a brother to me. I would never betray his trust. Besides… Margaret's young enough to be my daughter."

"That hasn't stopped some men. Archie tells me that the Earl of Angus-"

"My love, I'm not the Earl of Angus."

She shook with laughter. "I've thanked God for that on many occasions…"

"John seemed irritated, that's true. But he was beset with fools, all demanding his attention. He was cordial enough when we were alone. Why should he mistrust me, or consider himself lacking in any way? He's young, graced with such fair features…"

"Sir John is like Apollo," Helen said. "A being of gold and brilliance. You, my love, are an entirely different beast. You have a fearsome aspect, like Mars, the warrior of the gods." She kissed his brow, gently. "You were just as fair, when the bloom of youth was on you. Cast in a very different mould, perhaps, but glorious nonetheless. Perhaps the years have blunted your grandeur, but what lies within could still ensnare a lady's heart."

"Normally I'd be relishing these compliments, but in the circumstances…"

"He's still a sapling. Long and slender, at the mercy of the fierce winter winds. As the years pass, he'll grow into a mighty oak. Ladies will weep into their pillows at the thought of him. They'll long for a kind word or the flicker of acknowledgement in his eyes. When that day comes, he'll understand his place in the world, and wonder why he ever doubted himself."

Chapter 75

The Place of Ellestoun

"You're looking well." Margaret Sempill kissed Margaret briskly on both cheeks. "It's not long now, is it?"

"No, it isn't." Margaret had to raise her voice to be heard as Adam Mure and his entourage spilled into the hall. The room resounded with laughter and cheerful greetings: William and John Alexson circulated amongst the crowd, bestowing mulled wine upon the new arrivals, while she stood near the door with John, poised to greet their visitors in person.

John nodded to Adam Mure. "You were sorely missed at the siege."

Adam winced. "My leg's been troubling me the last few months. Old age, you know."

John glowered, and declined to comment. Margaret flashed him an anxious glance: she knew that despite his courteous façade, he was tense, on edge. She'd noticed a change in him just recently; he often seemed agitated, a little preoccupied. But John, as usual, was keeping his misgivings to himself and saying nothing.

"John, about the boy…" Adam neatly changed the subject. "He's almost nine now. He's a good lad, and while he'll never be master of my lands, I'm sure he could do well for himself. If he were lodged with a gentleman, who could take him to court and show him how to conduct himself…"

"Have you considered Lord Hugh?" John asked.

Adam glanced aside. "I fear the Lord Montgomerie's influence in the Westland may be waning."

John studied his wine, frowning.

"It's what the boy wants," Adam persisted. "He thinks the world of you. Always has."

"What do you say, Margaret?" John squeezed her hand, gently. The turbulence had gone, he was his usual self. "Would it be too much trouble to have a young lad about the place? Not until the babe's delivered, of course."

"I'd like to meet him first."

"Go and find him, Adam," John said.

"Sir John?" Alan Semple cut in, unusually urgent. "Can you greet a guest, please?"

John frowned. "I thought everyone was accounted for."

"They are," Alan replied. "But in the circumstances I think your presence is required."

John offered his companions an apologetic smile. "Excuse me a moment," he said. "Margaret, can you take care of my kin? This won't take long, I'm sure…"

   *   *   *

Johnny Mure was an endearing boy. Tow-headed, gifted with a broad, heart-warming smile. Ushered forward by his father, he told Margaret with shy sincerity how he wanted to see the world, and how he'd always valued the wisdom of his Uncle John at Ellestoun. "I won't get in the way," he said. "I'll run errands, if that's what's needed."

"Running errands isn't what you aspire to, is it?" she asked.

Casting a guilty glance about him, he added in a low voice, "I want to be a knight. Like Father. And Uncle John."

Margaret smiled. "I'm sure we can help you." Though it was inconvenient to be burdened with the child, it would be a small price to pay: John's worth as a baron and a knight would be all the greater if he had a page amongst his retinue.

"I can fight with a sword and ride a pony," Johnny Mure confided. "But Father says I must dance and sing, and learn to carve the meat."

"There's none better qualified than a lady to comment on such things," Margaret agreed.

"You're very gracious," the boy whispered. "And very beautiful, too…"

She laughed. "You're learning quickly."

Distracted, Johnny Mure glanced to the door. "Who's that with Uncle John?" he asked with a child's brazen innocence.

She didn't answer, unwilling to betray her own ignorance. This latest visitor was unfamiliar: carrying himself with the poise of a knight and the quiet confidence of a courtier, he was clearly a man who measured his own worth very highly. And yet, he was listening carefully as to John as he conversed with him. As if he truly valed her husband's counsel.

Margaret frowned. It seemed as if the whole household had paused to take a collective breath. Men turned to greet the new arrival, but he shrugged them all aside as Elizabeth Ross approached. He acknowledged her with a brilliant smile, clasping her hands in his and delivering a careful kiss on both her cheeks.

"That, my boy, is Sir John Ross of Montgrennan," Adam told his son, in a hushed tone. "He was a mighty man in the old king's time. The Lord Advocate, no less. He's a kinsman of yours, so best be courteous."

A chill settled over Margaret's flesh. "What on earth's he doing here?"

"I'm sure we'll soon find out," Adam said. Clearing his throat in readiness, he bowed his head in greeting as John and Montgrennan approached.

Montgrennan nodded, amicable acknowledgement. "Good day, Sir Adam. You're keeping well?"

"Tolerably so, my lord."

"My wife, Margaret Colville," John said. "Margaret, this is my kinsman, Sir John Ross of Montgrennan."

"I'm delighted." He bowed low and kissed her hand. His face was flawless, finely featured, when he straightened and caught her gaze, she realized that his eyes were a bright, startling blue.

Offering him a valiant attempt at a curtsey, she blushed like a maid, unsettled.

"Sir John will be staying with us a day or two," John explained. "Before he travels south."

"You have business in these parts?" Adam asked, quickly.

Montgrennan shrugged. "I'll visit my lands in Cunninghame."

"Cunninghame's been in turmoil since you left, Sir John," Adam said. "No doubt you'll have heard all about this dire business with Lord Hugh?"

"Lord Hugh's conduct can be quite dire, when the mood takes him," Montgrennan replied, with the vaguest of smiles.

Adam leaned closer. "Can we assume this is the purpose of your journey?"

Montgrennan half-closed his eyes, noncommittal. "In part."

"Will he be tried for murder?" Adam persisted.

"The King will decide what action is required."

"He should be," Adam muttered. "I was there, my lord. I witnessed the whole affair."

"Really?" Montgrennan stared intently at the Laird of Caldwell. "And how, exactly, did events transpire? You may be candid with me, Sir Adam. I'm eager to hear as many accounts of the event as possible."

"I saw an impartial judge who allowed rage to overwhelm him. The murder of Kilmaurs was an act of savagery, committed by a man who cares nothing for the King's peace."

"I've heard it said that Lord Hugh was acting in self-defence." Montgrennan glanced towards John, who stood scowling nearby.

"Perhaps the gentleman who spoke out on Lord Hugh's behalf was mistaken?" Adam suggested.

"The situation was chaotic, was it not?" Montgrennan agreed. "Any man would be forgiven for misjudging his facts in such circumstances."

"Excuse us, please," John said, in a cold clipped tone. "We must visit the kitchens. Margaret, will you come with me?" He offered his arm.

She accepted it, quickly, providing what solidarity she could in a world which had suddenly shifted into something treacherous, uncertain.

*　　　*　　　*

The Place of Glanderstoun

Elizabeth Sempill lifted the copper pot from its hook over the fire. Bringing it to the table, she ladled another helping of pottage into Matthew's trencher.

Matthew gave a half-hearted smile and murmured his thanks. Though he'd stayed here a week, his gude-sister was still a mystery. Each afternoon she dined with him in the laird's chamber, out of courtesy more than anything else.

She was an austere woman, taciturn in her manner. He could see that Sempill look more than ever, her pale fine features coupled with a stern air that could almost be misread as indifference.

"The snow's a foot deep in places." She set the pot down at the fireside. "Are you sure you won't stay?"

"I've imposed long enough. If I pack enough grease in the hooves, travelling won't be a problem."

Elizabeth poured another measure of ale into his cup then resumed her seat, sweeping her skirts aside, brisk and forthright. "You're no burden."

He smiled. "I appreciate that. But cousin Hugh's expecting me."

She nodded. "I understand."

Setting his spoon aside, Matthew sipped some more ale. "Not long ago, the world seemed full of promise. Now it brings me one trial followed by another." He stretched back with a sigh. "Has it ever occurred to you that if Fate had been kinder, your first-born would be baron of Ellestoun?"

Elizabeth didn't answer.

He held thumb and forefinger an inch apart. "We were that close to having your brother declared a traitor."

She didn't meet his eye. "When the king died last year, he became a martyr. Thank God he wasn't joined by others less worthy."

"You don't like him, do you?"

"I was twelve years old when he entered the world, a tiny prince my parents doted on. When I was wed, he was a tottering infant, still in skirts. He cried when he fell over, and always needed someone to wipe his nose for him. Since the day I left my father's house, I've scarcely seen him."

"But if he'd died defending his birthright? What then? Would you have stood weeping by his grave? Or would you have toasted his passing?"

She swallowed, face flushed. "He's my brother. How could I find pleasure in his death?"

"I'm surprised he hasn't sought me here. Perhaps rumour of my presence has been enough to dissuade him?"

"I don't think so."

"Then what do you think it is?"

Elizabeth glanced aside, agitated. "I'd rather not say."

He slouched in his chair, smiling. "I'm curious. That's all."

"I think he's more honourable than that."

"But by his neglect, he's aiding a fugitive, a man charged with committing treason against the King. Do you think he considers that contradiction at all? Do you think it ever crosses his mind?"

She bowed her head and cleared her throat, her discomfort tangible.

"I think about it sometimes," he said. "I wonder if he lies awake at night, hating me, wishing me dead. If my fortunes are restored, then we must live together as neighbours, and maintain the pretence of civility, at least. I don't relish that: I'm sure he doesn't, either."

"It's what the King would want."

"Yes," he agreed. "I suppose it is."

*   *   *

John slammed the door of his chamber. "How dare you!" Flashing a scowl in Adam Mure's direction, he slumped down in his seat. "I invite you into my house, I agree to take your son into my keeping, and this is how you repay me!"

Adam studied the floor, apologetic. "An opportunity arose, I acted upon it."

"You called me a liar," John retorted. He gestured irritably towards a vacant stool. "Sit down." Looking Adam in the eye, he continued, "Who discussed this with you?"

Adam shrugged. "It's not your concern."

"You seek my support in a plot to throw a man out of an office that's his by birthright, and you tell me it's not my concern?"

"A man's right to impose justice depends on his suitability to judge," Adam said. "Lord Hugh's like a mad dog. To have a man like him representing the King is an offence against God."

John sipped his wine, carefully studying his gude-brother's face. Was Adam nervous, he wondered, or just plain embarrassed. It was hard to tell, from the downcast eyes, the hands tightly clasped before him. "You were eager enough to grovel to Lord Hugh last year."

"The world's moved on now." Adam pulled off his bonnet, turned it around and around in his hands. "If he's not dealt with, Cunninghame will never have peace."

"You want him charged with murder?"

"Isn't that appropriate, given the circumstances?"

"So you'd hang the man?"

His gude-brother glanced aside, unwilling to meet his gaze. "They won't hang him. He'll be acquitted. Banished from court for a few years, I suppose."

"You don't know that."

"Why are you so loyal to him?" Adam demanded. "He slew your father, and in the dark times, what did his friendship ever do for you? Like Pilate, he washed his hands of your suffering when the Stewarts pillaged your lands and hounded your tenants." He paused, searching John's face for a reaction. "Can you really call this man your friend?"

"You're asking me to sacrifice the truth. And condemn a man for a crime he wasn't even guilty of."

The older man shrugged. "He's committed crimes of equal gravity."

"And what if he's thrown out of office? Who replaces him?"

"That doesn't concern us," Adam muttered.

"-I suppose we'll be blessed with the judgements of Cuthbert Cunninghame, once he comes of age. From what I've seen of the boy, he's as bad as Hugh. As for Montgrennan... He scarcely even deigns to visit the Westland. If he hadn't let things slip so far to the Cunninghames' advantage back in the old king's time, then perhaps Hugh wouldn't have become what he is today."

Adam spread his hands wide, angry denial. "We're not talking about Montgrennan. We're talking about Montgomerie. If we all speak as one, and declare that Montgomerie attacked Rob Cunninghame unprovoked, then we'll be rid of him. The world'll be a better place."

"I've marked your words, Adam," John replied. "But I'll follow my own conscience."

Adam leaned close. "Please consider this carefully, John," he said. "Look beyond your loyalties, do what's best for the Westland." Rising to his feet, he gestured to the door. "It's Yuletide. A time for peace and goodwill to all men, whether they be Cunninghames or Montgomeries. Let's find the ladies, shall we? They'll be wondering where we are."

Chapter 76

The Place of Eglintoun

It was rare for snow to lie at Eglintoun. The land was too low, the air warmed by moist sea breezes. But yesterday the snow had fallen thick again and today the tree boughs were bent beneath its weight, the parkland cloaked in white.

Helen walked with her arm in Hugh's. Behind them a chaotic trail crossed a pristine wilderness, their steps marking a steady course while children's smaller footprints danced off to left and right.

Young John Montgomerie swooped past squealing, with Bessie in close pursuit. She held a lump of snow in both hands: laughing, she brought it down upon her half-brother's head. Shaking the residue from bonnet and hair, the boy spluttered in disgust while Bessie stood back and giggled.

Helen smiled. How innocent they seemed, how free from care. A pang of sorrow touched her heart: in a year's time, Bessie might be gone, no longer a maid, but a married woman.

Hugh bent down and moulded a lump of snow. He hurled it, catching his heir square in the back. The boy turned, startled, but before he could retaliate, Hugh had jumped on him and thrown him to the ground. They rolled like fighting dogs, kicking and pushing: John tried hard to best his father, but it was like watching a cat trying to bring down a bear.

Helen laughed so much her sides hurt and her eyes watered. Then Hugh seized her skirt and down she came. His lips found hers: she lay there, oblivious to the cold which seeped through skirts and plaid mantle and woollen stockings, while the children galloped in screaming circles through the trees.

With his arms wrapped about her and his long frame pressed so close, it made her think of the times they'd lain in the shadow of *Caisteal Glowm* during the long months of their betrothal. Chaste in their flesh, so overwhelmed with love that no words could express the thoughts and desires within.

Frost sparkled all around them, the sky fading to pale pink in the west. The land seemed magical, ethereal: though the light of day still suffused the sky, she could see the moon shining above, a pale disc glowing through a fringe of slender twigs and branches.

Savouring Hugh's embrace, Helen wished that time and duty could fade away and leave them there. Her limbs grew weak, her body filled from toe to crown with a tender warmth that chased away the fear and the chill completely.

"Father!" John's wail shook her to her senses. The boy stood over them, he tugged Hugh's sleeve, eyes wide.

Hugh sat up. Brushing away the dusting of snowflakes, he clambered to his feet. "Whatever's the matter?" Offering his hand to Helen, he helped her stand.

"There's someone on a horse. Over there, through the trees." The child looked close to tears. "Look!"

Hugh caught Helen's eye, mildly concerned. "Shall we go and see him?"

"What if he's a brigand?"

"He's beyond the pale. We're perfectly safe. Look after your mother." Hugh set off at a saunter.

"But he may have a bow!" John called after him.

"Hush now." Helen ruffled the boy's hair. "Your father says there's nothing amiss." She sounded bold, at least. "Come on. Let's go and see what's happening." Taking his hand, she tugged him onwards.

Hugh stood near the pale, talking to an isolated figure on a chestnut horse. Seeing no hint of a confrontation, she ushered the children closer.

"Hello, Helen." When the horseman pushed back his hood, his dark brows and haughty features were unmistakable.

"Mattie!" she gasped. "Thank God you're safe."

Her son stepped out from behind her skirts. "I thought the king wanted your head."

"My head's still in its rightful place," Matthew replied, smiling. "And there it will stay, God willing."

"Make your way to the place," Hugh invited. "We'll join you there."

Matthew nodded. "Those are welcome words, cousin. It's not good weather to be venturing abroad." He steered his horse away.

Hugh watched him go, brow creased in a faint frown.

His son pummelled his hip with clenched fists. "Why's he here?"

"Because we're his kin, and he needs our help," said Hugh.

The boy considered this a while. "But if the king finds out, then won't he want your head too?"

"Perhaps."

"Then I'll be the Lord Montgomerie, and have to ride to war against the Cunninghames!" young John announced, face aglow. "I'll have a big horse like Zephyr, and lots of men-at-arms-"

"No, you won't," Helen cut in. "You'll be locked up safe in the keep until you come of age. And you'll be married, too. All those carefree years you had before you as master of this house will be lost. So let's just hope and pray that nothing happens to your father, or it'll prove ill for all of us."

"Eloquently spoken, Helen." Hugh slipped his arm in hers. "And let's hear no such talk from you again, John. Or I'll lock you away for my own safety. I've never willingly betrayed my king: nor would I ever seek to do so. He rules by God's Grace, and that's all that matters."

"But a king died last year," his son countered. "And you fought against him. You told me so yourself…"

"That was different. The old king forfeited his right to rule. It was a complicated matter," he added, seeing the confusion on the boy's face. "Some day, when you're older, I shall explain it to you. Until then, hold your tongue and trust your father's judgment. Now let's find your Uncle Matthew, shall we? And see what tales he has to tell us."

Young John grinned. "I'd like to be a fugitive."

"Your Uncle Matthew will tell you that it's not very nice at all."

"But if it was good enough for Wallace. And the Bruce…"

"I'm sure they would have much preferred to sit safe in their halls, eating hearty food and drinking their fine wines. Sadly Fate conspired against them. As did our Southron foes." Hugh placed an arm about his son's shoulders and steered him gently onwards. "Now come along. We must be courteous, and greet our guest without delay."

Taking his place at the top table, Hugh swept his gown aside and settled imperiously down into his chair. He flicked his gaze about the hall, noting the closely-packed diners, the ever-growing number of guests. Helen had hurriedly changed the seating arrangements to accommodate Matthew, who sat at Hugh's right shoulder, sharing his goblet and trencher.

All these extra mouths to feed, and at a lean time of year, too. And there'd be more to join them in the days and weeks to come.

Hugh tapped Helen's arm. She leaned close, quietly attentive.

"I've been neglecting my duties," he murmured. "I didn't warn you that we'd be entertaining such a mighty horde."

She placed her hand on his. "I could accommodate the King's household for a fortnight if necessary. To keep your kinsmen in meat and victuals for the next month shouldn't be difficult."

Reassured, Hugh set his spoon down. "Have some more of the goose, Mattie."

"Please."

Helen glanced up. "It's been a month or more since you left Dumbarton, Matthew. How did you fare?"

"Fortune smiled on me," he said. "I hid in plain sight. I travelled to my kinsman's place at Glanderstoun." Wiping his fingers against his napkin he reached for the wine. "My gude-sister cared for me as if I were her own kin. Which amuses me, considering her lineage."

"Sir William Stewart of Glanderstoun is married to a Sempill," Hugh helpfully explained.

"Yes, I'm aware of that," she replied, then asked Matthew, "Did Sir John Sempill never suspect you were there?"

"I'm sure he suspected," said Hugh. "He had sufficient forbearance to do nothing."

"He lacks the stomach for a fight." Matthew's tone was dismissive.

"Don't flatter yourself," Hugh countered, swiftly. "He'd have your head if he could."

"Ellestoun may be a knight," Matthew countered, "but as a man he lacks substance."

"Underestimate him at your peril." Hugh sat back with a sigh, pleasantly replete. "I hope that when a year has passed, I'll host a feast where the two of you sit side by side at my board, conversing with some civility at least."

"They'll have found the secret of the Philosopher's Stone before that happens."

"I'm sure my father would prefer to have solidarity amongst the Lords of the Westland," Helen remarked.

"If Argyll wants peace and goodwill between the Darnley Stewarts and the Sempills, then I daresay he'll seek the same friendship between the Montgomeries and the Cunninghames." Matthew punched Hugh's arm, lightly. "Do you know what this means? Your gude-father will insist that you take Kilmaurs to your breast, and hug him close like a brother."

"Oh he did just that," Helen said. "And then he killed him."

Matthew stared, incredulous. "What?"

"Helen exaggerates." Hugh stared ahead. "It was an accident, Mattie. That's all."

"I hadn't expected such news! When did this happen?"

"Three months back."

"My God," said Matthew. "I hide my face from the world, and madness overwhelms it. What did the King say?"

"He doesn't know," said Hugh. "Patrick Hepburn said he'd broach the matter in due course."

"At least the crowd will be suitably entertained before we're strung up for treason," Matthew commented. "Their appetites will have been whetted already."

"That won't happen," Helen said, firmly. "Sir John Ross of Montgrennan has agreed to help us."

"So he's defending you as well as assisting us?" Matthew said. "Christ, we'll all be grovelling to Montgrennan come the springtime."

"My lord." The steward halted before them. "His Grace the Master of Argyll has arrived."

"Show him in without delay." Hugh turned to Helen with a smile. "What a marvellous day this has been! We're harbouring a veritable nest of serpents!"

Helen looked aside and swallowed.

"Why the sober face, my love?" Hugh gripped her hand, briefly. "They can't hang us all."

*   *   *

The Place of Ellestoun

Montgrennan was leaving them, heading south for Cunninghame. John tried his best to dissuade his kinsman from travelling when the weather was so inclement. So did his mother, who pleaded with her brother to stay with them a few days more. But Montgrennan was determined, brushing aside John's vague attempts at cajoling, and his sister's fearful entreaties.

At his mother's request, John accompanied his uncle to the bounds of his lands. The hills were a white wilderness, the track to Hessilhead and Beith barely visible.

"I'll travel with you if you like," John offered.

"That's not necessary." Montgrennan nodded to his retinue. "Proceed without me a moment." He waited until they'd moved away before he continued. "I wanted a word, before I left," he said. "In a place where we couldn't be overheard." He studied John with his clear blue gaze. "Adam's words offended you, I know. That's understandable. He's never been much good at expressing himself. But his sentiments were laudable."

John gripped his reins tighter, fighting the urge to scowl. "I can't betray the truth."

"Truth depends very much upon the intentions of those involved. It can be transmuted as required. I'm sure that as the months pass, you'll find your account at odds with the accepted version of events."

John didn't answer. He studied his horse's mane, unwilling to speak.

"For God's sake, John!" Montgrennan's tone was tense, urgent. "Don't let your friendship with Montgomerie cloud your judgement. Friendship's like love, an admirable thing. But it can cripple a man, make him fall from grace." He looked briefly troubled, then the jaunty smile was back. "Parliament will be meeting in February. It would be in your best interests to attend."

"But my wife-"

"Affairs of state must take priority. I know for a fact that certain matters will be resolved there and arrangements made which have implications for your good self. If you need lodgings, I can provide them. And perhaps you should keep your future success in mind when you're considering what we discussed today." He studied John carefully. "We'll meet in Edinburgh, then? Five days prior to the first session."

"I'll be there, my lord."

"Good." Montgrennan spurred his horse away and it sprang off at a swift trot, hooves kicking up clouds of powdered snow.

William stirred alongside. "What will you do?"

"What can one man ever do, when the whole world acts against him?" John retorted. "My choice is clear. When Hugh falls, I can fall with him. Or I can save myself by stepping back and letting Fate take her course."

"I thought it was Sir John's task to defend Lord Hugh."

"My kinsman will serve himself first, and the King second. I fear Hugh's fate depends very much on Argyll. If Sir John thinks that the Earl's influence is waning, he'll be the first to plunge the knife into Hugh's back."

"Shouldn't you warn him?"

"That the wolves are waiting to tear him limb from limb?" John smiled, grimly. "I'm sure he's well aware of that already."

"So you've turned your back on him." William's tone was heavy with accusation.

John shifted in the saddle, saying nothing.

"I hope there aren't other issues preying on your mind?" William ventured cautiously.

"Whatever do you mean?"

"I know what your mother said, about Lord Hugh and Lady Margaret. But... I was with them at Southannan. He never dishonoured her, or did anything to betray your trust."

"Well," said John. "I never expected this."

"It's my duty to speak out in his defence," William persisted. "There's too much at stake here. Not just for him, but for his wife and children. If his own poor father hadn't been stolen away so young, then perhaps Lord Hugh wouldn't have strayed from the path of righteousness. His nature's flawed. We all know that."

John turned his horse around. "Poor Hugh. If only he'd learned to curb his temper. My priority now should be how to get myself out of this mess unscathed, and the Devil take Hugh. He's only got himself to blame."

"It's not in your nature, to turn your back upon a friend."

John gave a weary smile. "Then perhaps my nature's just as flawed as Hugh's." He sighed and stretched uncomfortably in his stirrups, wriggling his toes to try and banish the cold. "Let's go home. You should visit your wife, and see how she's faring. It won't be long before the child arrives."

Chapter 77

Hermitage Castle

A makeshift stand had been set up in the courtyard: it was packed with onlookers, all eagerly discussing the forthcoming tournament. Despite the light-hearted mood, there was an air of tension and excitement about the place.

Jousting was a sport for the young, a chance for bold youths to hone their skills with lance and horse. The prizes didn't amount to much: Angus had donated a silver-gilt plate for the winner, and Dacre a horse of fairly respectable breeding. The rest of the field would have to be content with no more than adulation. That the contest would be hotly disputed was beyond doubt: for Scots and English alike, a realm's pride was at stake.

George was riding. So too were a handful of Englishmen: Earl Percy's boy, and Dacre's, too. Angus was familiar with their qualities. But there was one whose prowess was unknown: the young lord from the Westland, Cuthbert Cunninghame.

Marjorie had declared earlier that Cuthbert would conquer the field. Elizabeth scoffed, while Angus smiled, faintly pitying. Marjorie was fanciful, prone to wishful thinking. The day would no doubt leave her disappointed, but she'd bounce back soon enough.

A collective sigh rippled through the crowd as the flag came down for the next contenders. The horses sank back on their hocks, then jolted off at a canter, hoofbeats muffled by a thick bed of straw laid to help them keep their footing.

There was an almighty crack. Lance splintered against plate armour and one lad was thrown back in the saddle. His horse, already unbalanced, slid and went down so hard they felt the impact where they sat.

Thrown aside, the rider lay still.

They perched upon their seats, anxiously watching. The horse thrashed its legs, struggling to right itself, while attendants came running, some to aid the horse, others the rider.

The young man moved at last, sitting up with helmeted head hanging. His arms and legs flailed, with some assistance he righted himself. Everyone applauded, acknowledging his courage even in defeat. His horse was hauled up and led away with one hind leg dragging.

Dacre nudged him. "That's one Scots nag that'll feed the hounds tonight."

Angus slouched and sipped his wine. He'd already resigned himself to the possibility that his fine silver-gilt plate would soon be heading south in an Englishman's hands.

"I wish I could joust," Marjorie complained.

"Don't be ridiculous!" Elizabeth snapped.

"My lords, ladies and gentlemen!" The steward's voice boomed out. "May we proudly present Sir George Douglas, Master of Angus?"

"Oh, here he is!" Elizabeth remarked, while Marion Drummond remained sedately unmoved. "Look, Marjorie."

Marjorie wriggled in her seat, peering out. "I can see well enough."

Angus smiled as George appeared on a high-stepping, richly-caparisoned destrier, an imposing presence in his jousting armour. He bore a shield with the Red Douglas arms; the plumes of his panache trailed down his back, streams of *azure, gules* and *argent*. His brother Gavin was leading him: sporting a helm designed for tilting, George couldn't see more than a few feet to either side.

Approaching the dais, George lowered his lance before his wife. "For Love." His voice could scarcely be heard through the thick steel of the bascinet. "And Virtue."

Marion Drummond stepped forward. "God be with you, George." She tied her handkerchief to the point of his lance, then sat back down.

Elizabeth put a hand to her lips, concealing her smirk. "Since when has George been a staunch disciple of either Love or Virtue?" she whispered in her husband's ear.

Angus nodded to his son. "Ride well."

George bowed his head, and his horse was steered away.

Settling back in his seat, Angus hooked a gloved finger between his teeth. He knew better than to expect too much from George. He'd put on a creditable show, but he'd never been much good at the tilt.

He noted with some disappointment that George hadn't quite mastered the approach; his horse was running on, making it difficult to control the lance. George clipped the shield nonetheless. But Dacre's boy won the point, his lance broken.

They circled for the next round, pausing to replace their lances.

The horses sprang off at a canter. With a snap and a thud, George was hurled from the saddle, crashing to the ground in an ungainly steel-clad heap.

His sisters gasped and clutched each other tightly, while Marion Drummond looked away.

Angus sighed, exasperated by their concern. It would take more than this to finish George. He peered at his son's prone figure, unsympathetic. "He's alright," he said. "I saw him twitch."

Gavin hurried to his brother's side. He helped George sit up: the Master of Angus sat for a while, recovering his senses. His arms hung loose, his head flopped forward. His horse meanwhile ambled off of its own accord, two servants in pursuit.

Angus nodded to Dacre. "A worthy show of prowess."

Dacre folded his hands across his belly and smiled.

With Gavin's assistance, George picked himself up and staggered back to the lists. Encumbered in all that armour, and graced with a fine limp, George waddled as much as walked. The girls cheered and clapped, he raised his hand in weary acknowledgement.

Marjorie giggled. "Doesn't he look silly?"

"Alas, poor Scotia's pride is wounded," Elizabeth muttered. "Who will redeem her honour?"

Angus sighed and shifted in his seat.

"Cuthbert Cunninghame, Lord of Kilmaurs," the steward called.

Cuthbert trotted into the tiltyard, mounted on his stout roan warhorse. Compared with George, he seemed a man of little consequence, graced not with purpose-built jousting armour, but a set intended for the battlefield. At some time it had weathered the abuse of war, dinted and battered about shoulders and breastplate.

"He doesn't exactly look resplendent," one of the girls muttered.

Marjorie gave a little whimper under her breath.

"Compose yourself!" her mother snapped.

Angus sat up, suddenly interested. The way Cuthbert sat with lance resting comfortably beneath his arm showed that he knew his skills, that he'd practiced his arts long and hard. Leaning across Elizabeth, he tugged Marjorie's sleeve. "Remember Percival," he said. "Arthur's court dismissed him. But in the end, he was victorious."

Cuthbert stared at his opponent, neither arrogant nor defiant, just cautiously confident. He steered his horse for the dais, halting before Angus. "Your Grace," he said. "Might I ask Lady Marjorie for her favour?"

Angus paused, unwilling to indulge his daughter too soon. At last he flicked his hand. "As you wish, Lord Cuthbert."

Cuthbert laid his lance upon the rail, waiting patiently while Marjorie sprang forward. Unused to being the centre of attention, she blushed as she knotted her handkerchief into place.

There was some muted applause as Cuthbert raised his lance with a flourish. "For the fairest lady in the realm."

Marjorie blushed even brighter. "God bless you, my lord."

He spun his horse around on its hocks and it cantered off.

"Fate is cruel," their younger daughter Katherine grumbled. "No one speaks that way to me."

"Be patient," her mother replied. "Your time will come."

And then it began. Determined to prove their prowess, the jousters thundered down the track with lances couched. At the first meeting, Cuthbert's lance met Percy's shield and broke. In that same moment, Percy's splintered against Cuthbert's breastplate, nearly knocking his opponent from the saddle. But Cuthbert clung on, righted himself.

They rode back to renew their lances. This time, when the armoured horsemen met, Cuthbert's lance glanced aside.

Percy's broke against Cuthbert's shield; the young Northumbrian was one point ahead. Marjorie clung to the bench, eyes wide, as even now the two young men turned for the last bout. Percy's steed wavered slightly in the approach, but Cuthbert's aim was steady. He caught his opponent square in the chest, hitting him so hard that when he fell he almost dragged the horse down with him.

The Scots cheered, and even the Englishmen clapped in grudging appreciation. Shrugging aside the accolades, Cuthbert sent his horse striding back to the lists.

As if it had been just another ordinary moment in an ordinary day...

Gavin, meanwhile, rushed to the beleaguered Percy's aid. The lad was back on his feet, bruised and shaken, but with his bones, if not his dignity, intact.

Angus sighed, self-satisfied. "England's victory isn't yet assured, my lord," he said. "The Lion of the Westland may yet prove worthy of the champion's crown."

The Place of Ellestoun

The Gryphon at Bay

Sitting by the fireside, Margaret revelled in how warm it was, how comfortable, away from the draughts that whistled through the shuttered windows and up the stair. The logs in the hearth spat sparks and crackled: her lapdog, curled at her feet, shifted at the sound. Satisfied that nothing was amiss, it sneezed and settled once again.

Margaret stretched in her chair, yawning. The babe stirred, she paused from her sewing to soothe it, laying a gentle hand upon her belly. It had been restless all day, as eager to escape the womb as she was to be free of it.

Once she'd feared the prospect of confinement. Now she longed for the day when she could finally retreat from the world. She'd transformed the room in readiness. The stark walls were clothed by fine hangings of dark red brocade, picked out with bold geometric patterns in gold. They gave her humble chamber an air of grandeur and opulence. John said they'd come from Arras and that they must've cost a small fortune. They wouldn't be here long: part of the haul John had ransacked from Duchal, sooner or later they'd be going back to their original owners.

Katherine looked up from her handiwork. "Will you dine with the household?"

Margaret carefully considered her reply. After a week of feasting and carousing, she was finding the festivities tedious. "I'm comfortable where I am."

"Do you think Sir John will call?"

"He'll visit later, I'm sure." Picking up her sewing once more, she shifted her hips to make herself more comfortable.

"I wish William was here," Alison said. "He could entertain us."

"He rode out with Sir John," Mariota added. "At least, that's what Master Alexson told me."

"I'll ask Sir John to play to us later," Margaret told them. "I'm sure he'll agree if we ask him nicely-" She broke off as the dog sprang to its feet. It raced to the door, yapping fiercely, plumed tail wagging madly.

In came John, cheeks burning pink with the cold. He tossed his cloak over a nearby kist and headed straight for the fire, holding his hands out to warm them.

"I thought you'd be dining," Margaret said.

"They don't know I'm home." His tone was terse.

"John, whatever's wrong?"

He didn't answer. Leaning against the jamb of the fireplace, he stared into the flames.

Margaret caught Katherine's eye. "Go downstairs and see if you can fetch us some food," she said, then added, "Mariota, Alison, if you're quick you can dine in the hall."

"What do we tell Lady Elizabeth?"

John glanced up. "Anything you like," he said. "With luck she'll dismiss you as fools and want nothing more to do with you."

Exchanging anxious glances, they bobbed quick curtsies in his direction then hurried away.

Margaret discarded her sewing a second time. "I found your kinsman quite unfathomable. Is it true he was a friend of the old king?"

"What the nature of that friendship was, I can't be sure. Men have wicked tongues. They were quick to spread vile rumours when they saw the king's grip was failing. Montgrennan knew Cochrane, and the others Bell the Cat murdered at Lauder.

They were his friends. How he escaped their fate is hard to comprehend. He was always a worthy knight and a formidable foe. Perhaps that saved him."

"He's back in favour?"

John studied the hearth, brow furrowed. "Apparently so."

Taking a deep breath, she summoned all her courage. "This black mood of yours," she said. "I've glimpsed it more and more the last few days." She swallowed, determined to speak out. "Is it my fault?""

"No, of course not." Leaving his place at the fireside, he sat down on the floor at her feet. Flinging his arm across her lap, he leaned against her. The dog, unwilling to be ignored, trotted up and placed its paws against his knee.

He swatted it roughly aside.

She could feel the chill from him, smell the fresh cold of the winter world beyond the castle walls. She said nothing, just waited patiently for him to speak.

"Parliament will be summoned in the spring," he said at last. "My worthy uncle instructed me to attend." His voice was blunt with resentment.

"Then you must do what's asked of you."

"What about you?"

She breathed deep, steeling herself to reply. "It's not my place to demand otherwise."

"I'll return just as soon as I can." He paused. "I want to be here," he added. "I don't want you to think I've abandoned you."

"I know." She rubbed his shoulders, his back, and gradually he relaxed. His fingers closed about the heavy fabric of her skirt, his head sagged, as if he were about to fall asleep.

"Margaret," he said. "Do you consider me a worthy husband?"

She drew her hand away, unsure how to respond. "Why do you ask such a thing?"

"I have precious little valour, and even less prowess as a knight. I'm not much more than a notary, and I don't suppose I can even rightly call myself that."

"How can you talk that way! Look what you've achieved, in just a few short months…"

He raised his head and studied her, his gaze desolate. "I'm not as great as some. Nor as terrible, or as brilliant. Perhaps if you'd been granted the opportunity, you'd give your heart, if not your flesh, to them."

She flinched as if she'd been struck. "Are you talking about Hugh?"

He glanced aside, with such unhappiness that she'd have leaned down and hugged him, if she could. "It must have been hard, to have such a man in your keeping. To know he could have been yours, if only for a few hours, or a day, and that I would never have suspected…"

"But if I'd done such a thing, how could I forgive myself? How could I even look you in the eye?" She broke off, not trusting herself to speak. "To win your trust is a task worthy of Hercules," she said, softly. "But it's a prize well worth winning. And Hugh would agree. D'you think we'd toss it aside lightly?"

He didn't answer. He sat slumped at her feet, lost in his troubles. Running her fingers through his hair, she teased out the tangled deep gold strands, realising with despair that even now, she had no idea how best to console him.

The Gryphon at Bay

Chapter 78

The Place of Eglintoun

Hugh hurried down the spiral stair, candle in hand, with young John Montgomerie following close behind. "So Uncle Archie's here, and Uncle Matthew, too." The boy's thin treble voice echoed loud off the masonry. "Who else is coming?"

Hugh gritted his teeth, wearied by the onslaught. Helen always insisted that he encouraged their son's interest in men's affairs, but he often wished it could be someone else's task. Much as he loved the boy, John's presence was wearing; he chirped incessantly, like a nestling.

"Is it the King?"

"God, I hope not."

"Then *who*?"

"The Earl of Lennox."

"Oh." There was a brief silence. "I don't like him."

"He's alright. Just make sure you don't cross him."

"Did you ever cross him? When you stayed at his place?"

"I knew better than to try."

The wind whined through the narrow window ahead, an icy blast which made the candle flicker.

Hugh shivered and drew his gown closer.

Young John paused to peer out. "The snow's almost gone."

"I told you it wouldn't linger."

"Why did Mama look anxious?"

"It's a woman's place to look anxious." Hugh seized the boy's arm, herding him onwards. "Come on. Let's not keep our kinsman waiting."

       *   *   *

Horsemen filed into the barmkin, three-score lightly-armed retainers. Their weary faces spoke eloquently of the trials they'd faced since they'd been routed by the king months earlier.

John Stewart, Earl of Lennox rode in the front rank, gaunt and grim from his life as a fugitive. He'd set aside his plate armour, favouring instead a simple sallet and brigandine. His grey-streaked beard was unkempt, his hair sleek with months of grease and sweat. His bay horse barely looked strong enough to carry him, its ribs sticking out through a harsh, mud-encrusted coat.

And at his side, Ross of Montgrennan. Neatly groomed even in his travelling clothes, and mounted on that same spirited grey horse he'd ridden the day they'd entered Dumbarton.

Hugh hissed quietly through his teeth. An unlikely alliance. One which didn't bode well for the future...

The Gryphon at Bay

Sensing his unease, his son pressed close, all pretence of maturity fading. Catching his father's hand, young John dragged his feet as they approached their visitors.

John Stewart nodded. "Hello, Hugh."

"I'm delighted you made it here safely." Hugh nodded towards the west. "Wind's picking up again."

"It's the season for storms," Lennox agreed. "I've had a bellyful of them the last three months of so." He sighed and sagged in the saddle, face grey and haggard. "I said I'd be here by Yuletide, and Yuletide's been and gone." He exchanged a secretive glance with Montgrennan. "Certain arrangements had to be concluded."

"It's a joy to have you here, Uncle John. And I mean that most sincerely." Hugh caught Montgrennan's gaze, just briefly. "Greetings, Sir John, and welcome to Eglintoun. It's been a few years since you last graced these walls."

Lennox nodded towards the boy. "He's grown a few inches since I last saw him."

"He's like his father," Montgrennan added. "I hope that proves a blessing, not a curse."

Hugh smiled, thinly. "It's a chill evening. Please come inside."

"An excellent suggestion." Lennox dismounted. "A bath if you please, Hugh. I stink like a beggar."

Hugh bowed his head. "I'll attend to it, Your Grace."

Montgrennan loitered in the saddle a little longer. "All the necessary persons have gathered?"

"His Grace the Master of Argyll arrived three days ago," Hugh said. "Your rooms are ready: why don't you rest, and eat your fill tonight? We can begin our business on the morrow." He beckoned to his steward, who lurked anxiously nearby. "Andrew will take you to your chambers. If there's anything else you require, then we'll do what we can to assist."

"That's most gracious of you, Hugh," said Montgrennan. He nodded to Lennox. "Then I'll bid you goodnight, John. We'll meet tomorrow, and discuss these matters further."

*   *   *

Hermitage Castle

With Cuthbert Cunninghame victorious in the tiltyard, the Scots had good reason to celebrate. Angus granted the young man ample opportunity to savour his success, giving him the place of honour as they dined, encouraging him to share his goblet and platter.

Cuthbert coped well enough with the accolades. He was mature for his age, remarkably level-headed. *Another mark in his favour*, Angus reminded himself.

*   *   *

Later that evening they returned to the hall for dancing and merriment. Minstrels played in the gallery: somehow Angus found a brief respite from the endless niceties with an escape to the privy. But it was short-lived, for no sooner had he rejoined his guests than George sidled alongside.

"I see my sister is still besotted with the Lord Kilmaurs."

Searching the hall for Marjorie, Angus spotted her, moving amongst the dancers with Cuthbert Cunninghame at her side. "Indeed."

"You've been studying Lord Cuthbert most carefully." There was a mischievous lilt to his son's voice, a glint in his eye. "Might you perhaps be considering his qualities as a future gudeson?"

"Your perception astounds me."

"He's an excellent choice. To see our English friends discomforted was marvellous. Dacre's face is still a picture."

"At least he was gracious in defeat. As was Earl Percy."

"To sell a quality horse to a Scotsman is tantamount to treason. To give one away in a tourney must be a more grievous offence still."

Even Angus could barely conceal his smile at that. "Least said about that the better. Attend your wife, George. She's looking forlorn." He nodded to Marion Drummond, who sat with her maids nearby. She seemed bored, more than a little weary.

He could sympathise. Without another word, he brushed George aside and headed for his chair on the dais. Sitting down with a sigh, he beckoned for some wine then sipped it quietly.

His gaze fixed on Marjorie. She was a maid transformed; face glowing with pleasure, she carried herself with a dignity and elegance that seemed quite unprecedented. Cuthbert Cunninghame was a worthy consort, guiding her through one dance after another with confidence and care. Every so often he'd pause to whisper sweet words in her ear. She'd blush and glance aside, smiling in her sister's direction, making no attempt to hide her triumph.

Satin skirts rustled alongside and there was Elizabeth, settling down on an adjacent chair. "The Lord Kilmaurs is extremely attentive," she said. "Perhaps we should be taking better care of our treasure."

"Don't fret," said Angus. "Marjorie takes after her mother. The joys of love will never overcome her wits." He studied his wife carefully. "She knows all that's necessary?"

Elizabeth sat tall, haughty and peevish. "Of course!"

"Don't underestimate him." He nodded towards Cuthbert. "Sullying the maid and enraging her father would do nothing to aid his cause."

"The match seems perfect," Elizabeth said. "But I don't want my daughter to be widowed before she's twenty."

"Then we'll bide our time, wait a year or two. If he lives that long, he'll be our gudeson a good long while." He offered her a reassuring smile. "Besides, delaying the marriage gives us ample time to fashion him to our liking."

Elizabeth laid her hand on his. "There are times, Archie, when I thank God for granting me a husband of such quality."

"Don't flatter me, my dear. I know why you favour him. I'm not exactly unsympathetic to your cause, either. If I can be sure my house can prosper from this union, then I'll support it wholeheartedly."

"The Boyds' Kilmarnock lands. They're still held by the King..."

"Don't get your hopes up," he retorted. "I daren't show my face at court just yet. If Parliament is summoned in the spring, I won't attend unless invited. George, however, is a different matter..."

"Perhaps Cuthbert should go with him," Elizabeth suggested. "He's too young to take his seat in Parliament, but it'd serve him well to mingle with king and courtiers."

"Can we trust him to steer clear of Montgomerie?" Angus broke off as Marjorie approached, smiling broadly. Cuthbert strode alongside, his hand cupped gently about her elbow.

"-I still think it marvellous," Marjorie's tone was shrill with excitement, "that you confronted all those knights and squires, and never quailed."

"The weapons were blunted," Cuthbert replied. "There was nothing to fear."

"But you might have been hurt, or even killed!"

"This afternoon's capers meant nothing," he said. "I've endured far worse and lived to tell the tale."

"You mean your skirmish with Montgomerie. I've heard such evil things about the man. He slaughtered my poor cousin. Is it true, that he's the Devil Incarnate?"

"He's more Devil than man to be sure. He slaughters without honour and remorse, and he's the worst kind of rogue, for on the surface he seems civilized enough. But like the Roman generals of old, he is a tyrant."

"And you faced him in combat?" Her face glowed at the thought. "Incredible!"

"He killed my sire, and my grandsire. Compared to him, the foes today were men of little consequence. That night, he'd have killed me, too." He nodded to Angus, and gestured for Marjorie to sit. "Your Grace, Countess Elizabeth."

Angus stirred, mildly irritated. "Montgomerie's a man like any other. In the right circumstances, he can be defeated."

"Over the past five years, he seems to have led a charmed life," Cuthbert said.

"Fortune's wheel will turn soon enough."

"When that time comes we must all be ready," Elizabeth said.

Cuthbert bowed his head, courteous acknowledgement. "My sword is honed."

"It's the quill that must be sharpened," Angus said. "And the inkhorn filled. Montgomerie will be defeated by law, not by any feat of arms. Whether we play any part in his downfall remains to be seen. So far, he seems quite eager to destroy himself without any help from the rest of us." He passed his goblet to Cuthbert. "Let's just sit back, shall we, and see what the next few months bring. God willing, we may be pleasantly surprised." He nodded to Dacre, who was loitering nearby, frowning. "I'll be with you in a moment, my lord."

The Place of Eglintoun

Helen wandered through the hall, keeping a careful eye on the proceedings. Hugh's voice rang out nearby, strident and imperious: glancing up, she spotted him standing near the fireplace, addressing his kinsmen Hessilhead and Bowhouse. He was a man in his element, a magnanimous host who gave freely of his time, talking with eminent courtiers one minute, reassuring lowly cousins the next.

He certainly didn't seem like someone who feared for his future.

Helen wished she shared his confidence. But the hairs were tight on the nape of her neck, she nursed a solid ball of dread in her stomach, a growing feeling that everything boded ill for the future.

For whom, she couldn't tell.

Someone caught her arm, jolting her to her senses.

Archie leaned close. "You look as if you're attending a requiem."

She shook him loose, unwilling to share her fears.

"Courage, little sister," Archie whispered. "Have faith in your father."

She turned away, unable to look him in the eye. "Only God is omnipotent."

"In His Own realm, yes. But here, in Scotia… There are few men who possess the influence of Earl Colin of Argyll."

"Courtly power ebbs and flows. Like the tide, though more capricious."

"Such ingratitude!" Archie gave a tight smile. "Don't forget: everything you value in this world is down to Father's goodwill. Without his consent, you would never have married him in the first place."

Her stomach churned, she felt faintly sick. She loathed all their guests with equal vigour and she loathed her duties, too. She wanted desperately to get away from there, to seek refuge in the quiet solace of the chapel. "Excuse me," she whispered, and hurried away.

*   *   *

The Place of Hermitage

It was to be a private meeting, held far from interested ears and curious eyes. Angus led the way, following a winding course up the stair to his chambers high in the kitchen tower. "Come in." He gestured for Dacre and Percy to step inside. "At least here we're guaranteed some peace and quiet."

A fire roared in the hearth, the walls bedecked with thick hangings to hold in the warmth. Dacre and Percy settled gladly into the empty chairs, accepting the wine he offered, helping themselves to sweets from a platter the servants had laid out ready.

Angus sprawled in the last vacant chair. He lifted his cup high. "And now to business."

Dacre leaned close to Percy. "Earl Archibald has been absent from court," he said. "His news is limited, I fear."

Percy shrugged. A big broad man, his muscular frame was drifting slowly to fat now he'd put the rigours of youth behind him. "No matter," he said. "We seek guidance, that's all," he told Angus. "Insights will serve just as well as detailed reports."

"Lennox's rebellion," Dacre added. "Last thing we heard, it was proving quite a thorn in King James's side."

"That's true," Angus agreed. "I'd say that the king is no closer to resolving the problem than he was six months ago."

A smile lit Percy's face. He sat back and slapped his hands against his thighs, making no attempt to conceal his delight. "Excellent news! If your king is otherwise occupied, he won't take it into his head to ride south and burn our barns and byres. He's a young man, of bold disposition. We don't relish the day he first flaunts his kingly prowess by riding to war across our lands."

"In short, Angus," Dacre said. "We welcome war and rebellion amongst the Scots. The longer it continues the better. At present, Lennox serves our needs. But if he ever makes peace with His Grace the King, then we'd be grateful if another might draw James's attention away from his southern borders."

"King Henry would value any man who helped him in this aim," Percy added. "He'd reward him most handsomely…"

Angus smiled, grimly. "I'll bear that in mind."

"We've known each other a long time now," said Dacre. "We have – what might one say – an excellent working relationship…"

Angus said nothing. He watched them carefully, waiting…

"You know that the fates of our two realms are closely woven," Percy added. "Peace between the Scots and the English is what we seek, but I have my doubts that your king is willing or able to deliver such a thing. We want him to look to England for his allies, instead of casting his gaze to France."

"Patrick Hepburn is pressing for him to take a French bride."

"This would benefit no-one," Percy said.

"Except perhaps the French," Dacre added, dryly.

"Indeed," said Percy. He raised his goblet high. "To old friendships," he said. "May our alliance be a long and fruitful one."

Chapter 79

The Place of Ellestoun

Bute Pursuivant paid a visit, not long after Twelfth Night. Weary from his journey and caked in mud, he was in good spirits nonetheless.

Once he'd bathed and changed his clothing, the herald joined them at the board for dinner, grateful for the hearty meal and comfortable lodgings.

The talk, naturally enough, was all about Parliament. "You'll be attending, of course?" he asked John.

John slid an apologetic glance towards Margaret. "Do you know what issues will be raised there?"

"The crisis with Lennox, undoubtedly."

John toyed with his bread, frowning. "No sign of it being resolved?"

"None whatsoever. There's been no word of John Stewart's whereabouts. We think he may be skulking in the north." Catching John's eye, he added, hopeful, "There's been no news of him in the Westland?"

"I've heard nothing," John said, quietly.

Bute Pursuivant bowed his head, grim-faced. "Let's pray this matter can be laid to rest, for the sake of our realm."

"Amen to that," agreed John.

*　　*　　*

The Place of Eglintoun

"You're very quiet," Hugh said. He lay stretched out along the bed, hands folded over his chest. "I've noticed it the last few weeks or so."

Opening the kist, Helen crouched alongside with a sigh. Folded neatly away inside were Hugh's ceremonial robes: the brilliant red gown of a Lord of Parliament, the sober grey of a Privy Councillor. She sat back on her heels, frowning. To err on the side of caution, she'd pack both.

"It's something I've regretted," she lied. "To be so far from King and Court. And the splendour of Parliament."

"It's overrated," Hugh said.

"I suppose." Folding the garments, she placed them carefully down in the travelling kist, then returned to retrieve his coronet.

Hugh stirred at last. Kneeling alongside, he hugged her close. "You mustn't be afraid," he spoke softly in her ear.

She stiffened. "I am afraid," she whispered. "What if they turn against you? What if they make you pay for other men's crimes, as well as your own?"

Hugh caught her eye, puzzled. "Why should they do that?"

"Because you lack friends, and you lack an army at your back." She swallowed, biting back tears. "You've always courted danger."

"I've always survived."

The Gryphon at Bay

"Do you think John Stewart cares what happens to you now? Do you think Mattie would lift a hand to save you, if it meant hobbling his own success?"

His frown deepened. "But I helped them."

"Oh, my love." She laid her hand against his cheek. "You're too loyal. You like to think you're strong, invulnerable, but if the winds change, they'll pick you up and dash you against the rocks."

He held her close in his arms, his breath warm against her neck. "Hush now, Helen. Don't speak of such things."

Feeling his strength so close only served to make her realise how frail he was, how vulnerable. "I'm not fey. I can't see the future. But ever since they came here - John Stewart, and Matthew, and that fiend Montgrennan - I've had this cold feeling deep inside me. Sometimes I wake in the night and I know that soon my bed will be empty, and you'll be gone. I don't know what this means, Hugh, but I fear the worst..." Her voice faded into silence, tears pricked her eyes.

"This is nonsense," he said, but his voice was heavy with concern, his face bewildered.

"A king died last year. They found no one guilty of his murder. All it takes is for your name to be breathed in the right ear, and they'll have found his killer. You can protest your innocence all you like, but that will mean nothing if enough of them want you dead."

He drew back as if she'd struck him, the breath catching in his throat. She could see him confronting her fears, turning them around in his thoughts, examining them closely. And he relaxed. "It won't happen," he said at last, with airy confidence.

"I pray to God it won't," she said. "But I don't trust the snakes at court. They plot, they scheme, they trample others underfoot, all for the sake of winning favour with the King. They'll know you're weak, and make their move, I'm sure." She rubbed her sleeve against her eyes, fiercely wiping away the tears.

Hugh slid his arm around her shoulders. "Courage, Helen. Your father will help me. You know that."

"He doesn't lack enemies, Hugh. You're his hound in the Westland. To have you muzzled and hamstrung would weaken him. There are men who would attack you to punish him. That's what I fear. That you're just a pawn in a greater game that none of us properly understand."

"John will stand by me. Men know him to be honest. They'll heed his words."

"What if they've been poisoning his thoughts, too? You said he'd heard rumours about yourself and Margaret. What if such lies are being spread with the aim of turning him against you, so there's not one man out there willing to defend you?"

He shook his head, vehement denial. "No," he said. "I don't believe that at all."

She said nothing. But secretly, deep inside, she wished she shared his confidence.

Chapter 80

The Place of Ellestoun

It was an impressive sight to behold. Lord Hugh approached with a score of armed retainers at his back: each man sported his red and blue livery, with the banner of the Montgomeries flying proudly overhead.

Margaret stepped out to greet him, braving the chill and the fearful climb down the stairs so she could welcome her guest in the proper fashion.

Springing from Zephyr's back, Hugh strode across the cobbles. "Hello, Margaret!" he exclaimed, smiling. "That's more like it! There's colour in your face and a glint in your eye." Seizing her arms, he kissed her cheeks in the proper fashion. "When does the lying-in begin?"

Margaret shivered and rubbed her arms, acutely aware of the open shutters above, and her gude-mother staring down. "A week or so."

"It'll soon be behind you." He glanced up towards the tower-house, his gaze lingering there a moment. "And when the babe's delivered and you've been churched, you can venture back into the world." He glanced around the yard, brow creased in a faint frown. "Where's John?"

She glanced aside, awkward. "He left for Edinburgh two days ago."

"Ah." His shoulders sagged. "I hoped we might ride out together."

"He was summoned by Montgrennan."

Hugh's eyes narrowed. "That's unfortunate," he said. "Well, perhaps you can help me. I seek lodgings for the night."

"You'll be granted them, of course," said Margaret. "I'll speak to Lady Elizabeth, and instruct her to set places at the board."

She turned around and headed back into the tower-house without so much as a backwards glance.

Leaving Hugh beleaguered there, alone, unheeded.

She could feel his stare, piercing her back like cold hard steel. Closing the door with a sigh, she leaned her head against the timbers. *Poor Helen,* she thought. *When she said farewell, did she ask herself if she'd ever see him again?*

Hugh tried not to scowl as he took his place next to John's empty chair. "I see my presence is unwelcome," he commented. Grasping his napkin, he set it neatly into place over his shoulder.

Margaret shifted in her chair. "Don't talk that way, Hugh."

Hugh stared past her, levelling his gaze upon Elizabeth Ross, who glared back with equal venom. "Lady Elizabeth has good reason to detest me," he snapped. "But I'm damned if I'll have your name dragged through the mire for a deed of which we're both innocent."

"Hugh…" Margaret warned.

The Gryphon at Bay

"-I would never cuckold my friend. If anyone hints otherwise, then they should at least accuse me to my face so I can defend myself in the proper fashion." He scowled towards Elizabeth Ross. "Name your champion, and I'll confront them now. Because unlike Lancelot, I am blameless in flesh, heart and soul."

Margaret swallowed, and fixed her gaze upon the trencher.

Elizabeth Ross smiled, thinly. "But you would say that, Hugh. Your skill at arms has helped to conceal all manner of injustices through the years." She gave a little hollow laugh. "They say the Devil helps his own."

Hugh's gaze didn't waver. "I daresay you've done your best to poison John against me. And yes, I'd agree that you have good reason to. But Margaret..." He gestured in her direction. "What has she done to merit such cruelty?"

Elizabeth Ross stared ahead, lips tight with disdain. "Ask her yourself. She nearly buried him last year."

Margaret bowed her head, close to tears.

Gripping the board with both hands, he forced himself to breathe deep and calm, outraged on her behalf. And on John's, too. "I see." Somehow, he maintained a civil tone. "So we're in this together, Margaret. I understand everything now." He turned to the young woman, his face burning hot with triumph and indignation. "Do you?"

She shook her head, mute denial.

"We want him dead. Whether he kills himself or wastes away is immaterial; the fate of his immortal soul is no concern of ours. When he's cold in his tomb, you'll be free to marry again, Lady Margaret."

"Hugh," Margaret whispered. "Don't say such terrible things..."

"You see, I know just the man. My brother Robert. He's young, and pleasant, an excellent choice. Imagine that! A Montgomerie as Laird of Ellestoun and guardian to the future heir. Who could be smothered in his cradle, late at night, and we'd all be none the wiser-"

Shaken from her thoughts, Margaret was staring, wide-eyed with horror. "What are you saying?"

"-It was such a subtle plot, but alas, the noble lady of this house saw right through it and saved the day." He smiled at Elizabeth Ross, faintly mocking. "So how have you thwarted the plot? Did you poison the ale? Or are you content just to slit my throat when I sleep tonight?"

"I have no need to lift a finger, Hugh. You've accomplished your own downfall without any help from the rest of us."

"And you'll be dancing on my grave before my flesh is cold, I'm sure," Hugh said. "It's my fault your husband died, Lady Elizabeth, and for that I'm truly sorry. I can't bring him back. Do you think that doesn't weigh upon my soul? Do you think I never stop to ponder all the ills I've brought upon this world? I've tried so hard to make amends, and all you offer me in return is suspicion. You'd hang me with my own bad name if you had the chance." He tore off his napkin, flung it down before him. "Forgive me, but I'm poor company tonight. Ladies..." He nodded to them both, then stood. "I won't tarry in the morning. With luck, I'll be on the road before you've even stirred from your beds."

397

Margaret didn't have much of an appetite. She ate a little, for the child's sake. But every mouthful was an effort: the meat seemed tough, the spices insipid.

She didn't know why Hugh's distress should haunt her. He'd brought his misfortunes on himself, just reward for the havoc he'd wrought a few months earlier.

She wondered what John would have made of it all. She wondered, too, how he'd expect her to behave in his absence.

And the more she thought about it, the clearer it became. She could almost hear his voice. *You represent me, Margaret. Do what you think is right.*

Time crawled past. Her gude-mother talked to her ladies about the most trifling things. About the draughts coming in through the shuttering. Why the cats hadn't managed to chase all the mice from the guest range.

Margaret sighed and set her napkin down. "I'm going to the kitchens," she said. "Our guest must eat. Katherine, Mariota, attend me."

The girls helped her, carrying wine, bread and cold meats. "What if he shouts?" Mariota asked, as they made their way up the stairs.

"Oh, hush, Mariota. Don't be daft. We'll take the victuals to his room and leave them there. Whether he cares to enjoy them is a different matter." Pausing before the door of the laird's chamber, she knocked briskly. "Might I speak with you, my lord?"

There was a pause. "Enter."

He sounded calm, at least. Taking a deep breath, she stepped inside.

Hugh sat slumped by the fire, staring lost into the flames. "When you next see John, you'll tell him what I said, won't you? You'll tell him I was slandered, that I would never wish to supplant him in your thoughts?"

Margaret sighed, and studied her feet. That air of wild distraction had gone, he just seemed beaten, exhausted. "Can't you tell him yourself?"

Hugh shrugged. "He may not speak to me."

She beckoned for the maids to leave. "Why must you go?" she demanded, once the door closed. "If you're so certain that all this has been arranged to bring about your downfall, then why play into their hands?"

"I was put on this earth to do my duty to my king. If that requires the sacrifice of blood and flesh, then so be it. Whether it's on the battlefield or in the bearpit that passes for a court is neither here nor there." He looked up, caught her eye. "I'm not a coward, Lady Margaret. I won't turn and flee from Fate, even if Fate has turned against me."

She smiled, thinly. "I'll pray for you, Hugh. And I'll pray for Helen, too."

He shook his head. "You shouldn't have come here."

"John would expect me to receive a guest with courtesy. Particularly when he calls that guest his friend." She gestured to the food. "You haven't eaten a thing. You say you have no appetite, but… It's my hospitality that's questioned."

Hugh shifted with a sigh. "Then I shall eat for your sake, Margaret." He made a half-hearted attempt at a smile.

She paused at the door. "A hundred other men might step back and watch as you were thrown to the wolves, but John's made of finer stuff than that." She made a valiant attempt at a curtsey. "Goodbye, Hugh. And I hope that when we meet again, it'll be in happier times."

The Gryphon at Bay

"Margaret," he said, softly. "May God and Saint Margaret protect you. Whatever ills befall me, you'll be in my thoughts. Both of you."

Chapter 81

The City of Edinburgh

It had been a busy day. He'd visited the tailor that morning; arrangements were made for the purchase of four doublets of satin and damask, all at Montgrennan's expense. *I can't have you seen at court like this*, he'd said. *You're far too shabby.*

With business concluded, John dined with his kinsman in the castle. He'd been given lodgings for the duration of his stay: a small room in the outer ward, close to his uncle's chambers.

Montgrennan gestured towards the board. "If you'd care to carve."

Rising to his feet, John set to work with knife and flesh hook.

"I'm in celebratory mood," Montgrennan said. "I'm appointed to the Privy Council."

The comment was tossed aside, as if the news itself were nothing. Straight-faced, John slipped some meat onto the older man's platter. "Congratulations."

"Please be seated." Montgrennan passed him his cup. "I'll have plenty to occupy my time in the weeks ahead. There's the crisis with the Stewarts, for a start. Some manner of peace must be brokered, if this land is going to prosper."

"Do you think that's possible?" John asked.

Montgrennan paused, considering. "Yes," he said. "I do."

"And what about Lord Hugh?"

"The king was told about the business with Kilmaurs this afternoon. Naturally, he's very concerned. He fears that his efforts to find peace in the Westland have been thwarted. He has declared that Lord Hugh present himself on his arrival in Edinburgh. He will account for his actions and justify the killing. After that, the Privy Council will decide what's to be done with him."

"I thought Lord Hugh *was* a member of the Privy Council..."

The faintest smile crossed Montgrennan's lips. "Not any more."

So they'd moved behind Argyll's back, outflanking him. And outflanking Hugh, too. John stared at his platter, his appetite gone. Not even the rich food that graced their table, finely spiced and cooked to perfection, could entice him to eat.

"Argyll's an old man," Montgrennan said. "He won't last forever. Once he's gone, your friend Montgomerie is finished." He studied John with that keen blue gaze. "Have you considered my advice?"

"Yes."

"You can't be sentimental, not with so much at stake."

"But what advantage will it bring me to see him fall?" John countered, fiercely.

"What advantage does it bring you to stand by him? There are important people, powerful people, who will move heaven and earth to bring him down. Boyd's death still casts its shadow. And while Argyll thinks he can protect his wayward cub, he underestimates just how much ill-feeling Montgomerie's gathered through the years."

400

The Gryphon at Bay

Montgrennan smiled, melancholy reflection. "You're my kinsman. I abandoned you last year out of necessity and now I want to make amends. Thomas would want me to steer you on the right course; he'd want me to grant you an opportunity to succeed at court. That's why you're here, so I can carry on where my gude-brother left off." His smile widened, just a little. "Come now, John. It's what your mother would want, isn't it?"

      *   *   *

It was dark by the time they reached Edinburgh. Men were guarding the barasse, townsmen clad in padded jacks and sallets. Seeing the Montgomeries approach, they signalled for the new arrivals to halt.

Hugh rode up to the gate. "The clock's not struck nine yet, surely?"

"A man can never be too careful," his challenger replied, apologetic.

"The Lord Montgomerie is here to attend Parliament," Hugh said. "Along with his retinue."

The townsman bowed, suitably obsequious. "Please proceed, my lord."

The barasse was moved aside.

As his men filed through, Hugh loitered. "Has there been word from Earl Colin of Argyll?" he asked the townsman.

"Not yet, my lord," came the reply.

"Ah," Hugh said, heavily, and spurred his horse after his men.

Shutters opened in nearby houses. Their inhabitants peered out at the new arrivals, more curious than afraid.

Hugh paid them no heed, pausing outside Argyll's townhouse with his retainers milling at his back. Lights were burning behind the shuttered windows: a comforting sight and evidence that nothing was amiss. As expected, Earl Colin had a small household maintained here for his convenience.

Hugh had scarcely dismounted when the door opened, a mountain of a woman eclipsing the lamp's warm glow within. "Ah," she said. "It's yourself, Lord Hugh. I thought it might be His Grace the Earl."

"Unfortunately not," Hugh said. "Is he expected tonight?"

She shrugged. "He'll be here in a day or two, I'm sure. Come inside, my lord. Make yourself comfortable. I'll prepare some victuals for yourself and your men."

"Many thanks, Mistress Borthwick. It's much appreciated."

Mistress Borthwick waddled up the stairs, lamp in hand. She talked incessantly of aches and pains and dire winter weather. But within this torrent of trivia, occasional nuggets of interest dropped out. "Ross of Montgrennan is back on the Privy Council," she said. "So my Alex was saying."

"What do the good people of Edinburgh say of his return?"

"That it's no bad thing. It hit us hard, to hear the old King was dead. Maybe now the differences can be resolved, and old wounds plastered." She paused outside a doorway on the second floor. "My apologies, Lord Hugh. It's just a wee room. But young Master Archibald's retinue's getting larger all the time."

"So long as there's a roof over my head, I'm a happy man."

"Easy pleased, that's what I like about you…" She opened the door, revealing a small but well-appointed room within: plain plastered walls, a down-to-earth fireplace

401

free from ornament. The bed was a decent size, and canopied: two waif-like maids scuttled quietly about it, setting sheets, blankets and pillows out in readiness.

"Alex heard word from the castle this afternoon," Mistress Borthwick said. "He was asked to tell you, if he saw you, that you're to present yourself before the King." She looked troubled. "Rumour has it the Privy Council will discuss a matter which concerns your own good self."

He had to sit down. *It's the price for three days' brisk ride on horseback,* he told himself, *and you're not getting any younger...* But he was denying the truth. The fear was growing stronger, sapping his strength and courage like an incubus. "Thank you for that, Mistress Borthwick."

"The Earl will look after you." Her tone was emphatic.

"Mistress Borthwick," Hugh said. "Has there been mention of a companion to Montgrennan? A young man, very fair to look upon..."

She raised her brows. "Such a thing would soon be the talk of this town, I tell you."

"The young man I speak of is his nephew, a knight named Sir John Sempill. Any interest is entirely familial."

She frowned. "If I hear word of Sir John Sempill, I'll be sure to let you know. He's a friend of yours?"

"Yes," Hugh said, without conviction. "I think so."

    *   *   *

Edinburgh Castle

John browsed through his uncle's books, enthralled by the diversity of his library. The works were philosophy, mostly: writings by the likes of Aristotle and Duns Scottus. But other volumes caught his eye, manuals of warfare and strategy, historical accounts of ancient emperors and generals.

Montgrennan's delight at finding a kindred spirit in his nephew was obvious. He loitered with John, searching his books with a practiced eye as if he were seeking out rare spices in warehouse. "The gift of Reason is the greatest gift God ever thought to bestow upon Mankind," he said. "For knowledge alone brings real joy and fulfillment in this world. To bow down to the needs of the body is to submit to the basest of instincts. Take Lust, for example. It's a fickle failing of the flesh, which drags us down to the realm of beasts." Drawing forth another volume, he caressed it, looking fondly down upon it as if it were a cherished child. "As for love... No more than a symptom of that lust, clouding a man's faculties so Reason is compromised." He passed the book to John. "*The Aenid*," he explained. "Scribed by Virgil, one of the great Roman poets."

Leafing through its pages, John noted with interest that the tome was printed. "If Love's such an unwelcome thing," he argued, "then why do so many of the ancient poets write of it?"

"In how many of these tales is Love a source for ill?" Montgrennan retorted, rising to the challenge with relish. "Lancelot and Guinivere. Tristram and Isolte. A man's love for God is the only love that matters here on earth. All this devotion to the Virgin: no wonder the men of the Low Countries question its relevance." He turned back to his books with a deep, self-satisfied sigh. "Clarity of thought brings a man closer to God. The old king understood that. But the barbarians in his court couldn't see his true worth. The night James was slain was a blow to the very heart of this realm."

"His son has a mighty intellect," John pointed out. "He doesn't fear knowledge, he welcomes it."

Montgrennan smiled. "Yes, he does." Sitting down nearby, he gestured for John to join him. "Thank God, John. This time we're graced with a man who champions Wisdom and Intellect. And yet at the same time he glories in the blood and mire of battle. God willing, he'll be the man we hoped his father would be, strong and brilliant, capable and enquiring. For many years, I've prayed for such a king. Now I think my prayers have been answered."

"His books mean more to him than anything else on earth," John admitted to William, once they were alone that evening. "No wonder my aunt could never find any common ground with him."

"And yet he was on good terms with your father," William remarked. "I can't imagine two men more different."

"My father respected him as a courtier, and a counsellor of the king," John agreed. "But I concede, there's much that puzzles me about my father. I can't think why he took you under his wing, and offered you patronage."

William smiled. "Perhaps because I've worked hard through the years to convince my betters that I'm indispensible..."

"There's no doubt about that," John agreed. "Though I don't care to tell my guests that the household's prized musician usually spends his time otherwise employed." Settling back along his bed with a sigh, John lay with eyes closed and hands behind his head. "Now Montgrennan's appointed to the Privy Council, it might be wise to remain within his circle. If all that's required is the odd debate on ancient philosophy and the splendours of literature, then where's the harm in it?"

"And what about Lord Hugh?"

John drew a sharp uncomfortable breath. "I fear Hugh's doomed, no matter what I say," he replied. "If Argyll's time is really waning..."

"Your head is swelling," William warned. "It's the air of this place. It makes a man drunk with possibilities. This whole city's like a courtesan, all surface sparkle and glittering jewels, with a cold dead heart beneath."

"Then tell me what I should do, William," John urged. "Do I leave him to the mercies of Fate, or offer myself up alongside?"

William sighed. "It's your decision. I can't make it for you. And in God's Truth, I don't envy you."

John didn't reply. His thoughts were troubled, he kept thinking of Hugh; whether he'd arrived in Edinburgh, whether he'd been told of the King's displeasure. "It's been a difficult day," he said. "I think I'll retire now, so I'm fresh for the morning."

"A sound idea," William agreed. "If you're agreeable, I thought I'd slip out to the kitchens, try and scrounge a crust or two from the cooks. I haven't eaten since noon."

"I'm sorry," John said. "I didn't think to send word."

William shook his head. "It was my own fault. While you were beleaguered with the tailor, I found my way to the chapel. I listened to the choir rehearsing, and then I started talking. With men who breathe air wreathed with antiphon and organum, and who like nothing better than to share their love of music with their fellows." William drifted into silence, his eyes bright with joy. "For the pleasure of such moments," he added, "I'll forgive this place its many faults and relish the time I spend here."

He dreamed of Margaret. She was sitting in the bower at Ellestoun, rose petals drifting down around her. She smiled at him, running her fingers through long brown tresses. *Of course there's more to Love than lust,* she said. *It brings such joy, bathing the soul with light and warmth. But how can there be pleasure without anguish? How can you know one without the other?*

Picking up her skirts, she laughed and sprang to her feet, flitting like a shadow amongst the crowding boughs of the apple trees.

Do you love him? he called after her.

She paused in her dancing flight, bathed in dappled sunlight. *Of course,* she replied. *He's your shadow. He is darkness to your light. Chaos, to your order. You are his salvation, and he is a warning of what might happen, if you stray from the path of righteousness.*

Do you love me?

That smile again. Broader this time, filled with secret knowledge. *More than you can possibly imagine.*

She ducked away and was gone.

John woke with a gasp.

The silence was stifling. He listened for any indication that William had returned, but he could hear nothing. He was alone.

He started, realising then that there were hushed voices conversing outside his door. A man, talking in low gruff tones, and a woman...

Mystified, he seized the covers and threw them back. Flinging open the curtains, he slid out of his bed just as the door creaked open a sliver and a figure crept inside.

He could see her by the candlelight. A thin slip of a lass, her slight body outlined beneath her kirtle. She had long loose hair and pert tight breasts.

"What do you think you're doing?" he demanded.

Looking him up and down, she smiled. "I've fallen on my feet this time."

He snatched his shirt, pulled it roughly over his head. "William?" he called.

"If you're talking to your servant then don't expect an answer. The wine was too much for him." She settled on the bed, unapologetic. "Thought you might like some company tonight. Seeing as you're so far from home." She slid a coy smile in his direction. And when he didn't answer, she added, quickly, "I can find you a boy, if that's what you'd prefer..."

"Get out!" John snapped.

She placed an arm across her breasts, feigning modesty. "But I've nowhere to go, my lord!" she argued. "I've no bed for the night, and if I come home with no money, then my man'll beat me senseless. If you were truly a gentleman..."

John stared at her, his concern for William growing. "Stay here if you must," he said through gritted teeth as he rummaged for his clothes. Dressing quickly, he checked his purse, realising with relief that all his meagre funds were still accounted for. "Here." He tossed some pennies in her direction, felt some grim satisfaction when she sprang to retrieve them. "If this helps you escape a beating, then you're welcome to it. Once morning comes, you can tell the steward that Sir John Sempill has had a bellyful of his hospitality, and that he'll be finding lodgings elsewhere."

William lay slumped in the corridor beyond his door, snoring loud enough to wake the dead. A platter lay nearby, bearing the meagre remains of his meal. And - still grasped loose in William's hand - an empty cup, the remnants of its contents staining the flags nearby.

Crouching alongside, John shook him gently. "William!" he hissed.

There was no response.

He shoved, cajoled. He shook William's shoulders and slapped his face until his fingers stung. And when that provoked no more than a groan, the sense of isolation was suddenly overwhelming. "William, speak to me," he urged, heart hammering so hard he could scarcely breathe. "Please God. Would you wake up!"

William stirred at last. "Oh Christ," He sagged forward, head bowed. "My innards." He stared at John, eyes glazed. "What happened?"

"I think your wine was adulterated." John glanced anxiously about him. "This is too much. I want out of here. Right now. Can you stand?"

"I'll try."

Hauling William to his feet, John steadied him. "You were right about this place," he said. "There's something dead and rotten at its core." He made a valiant attempt at a smile. "Let's take our chances in the town, shall we? God knows, it can't be any worse than this."

* * *

The city slept: beyond the castle walls, pigs prowled the street, dark shapes flitting in and out of wynds and vennels. They squealed and grunted as they grubbed amongst the filth and trickles of stinking slime that drained down the hill.

William was a dead weight against his shoulders. "I can scarcely move my legs," he muttered. "I need to piss."

John fixed his gaze ahead, steeling himself to William's complaints. "It's not far, I promise."

"Where are we going?"

"Argyll's place." Glancing about him, John searched for some indication of their whereabouts. In the overwhelming gloom, one house looked much the same as another. Somewhere in the backlands, two cats were fighting. Their hissing screams provoked a flurry of abuse from an annoyed resident, behind them there was a splash as a piss-pot was emptied out into the street.

They passed the Cathedral of St Giles and headed down towards the Cowgate. John's heart jolted with relief: there at last was the house he sought, Campbell gyronny carved above the door. Hanging onto William with one hand, he hammered on the timbers. "Hello! Is there anyone there?"

There was no reply. Putting his ear to the door, he heard movement inside. Someone was stirring, at least. So he battered again, harder this time. "Can you let me in, please? It's very important."

He heard the grind of a lock and the door opened. A vast woman blocked the doorway, face grim, sleeves rolled up to her elbow. Her gown was dusted with flour, she brandished a skillet in one hand. "What a sorry sight this is!" she sneered. "Be off, or I'll put the dogs on you!"

"Please! I must see the earl. Or at the very least, someone in his household…"

"The Earl won't speak to anyone without prior appointment. Anyway, he's no here."

"Mistress Borthwick!" A familiar voice called from above. "It's alright. He's here to see me. Let him in."

John looked up, shaky with relief, for there was Hugh, peering down from an opened window in the upper storey.

Chapter 82

Hugh pulled on shirt and hose, then padded down the stairs, yawning. He shook his head, fighting fatigue; he'd scarcely slept a wink the previous night.

Which was lucky for John: if he'd been asleep in his bed and dead to the world, the young baron of Ellestoun would never have been allowed past the threshold.

He found John in the kitchen, crouched at William Haislet's side.

As for William... He was in a wretched state: on his knees, pale and sweating, and emptying his guts into a bowl.

John looked up, eyes bright with panic, while Mistress Borthwick loitered anxiously in the background.

Hugh smiled his most accommodating smile in an effort to placate her. "I'll deal with this," he said. Kneeling beside John, he laid a hand on William's shoulder. "What in God's name happened?"

"Bad wine," came John's terse reply. "It's been a difficult night."

"So I see." Hugh straightened. He fixed his gaze on Mistress Borthwick once more, hangdog this time. "Is the bread baked yet? And could we scrounge some ale?"

She shrugged, offered a half-hearted curtsey then bustled away.

Hugh helped William sit up. "Better out than in."

"My bowels aren't much better."

"Garderobe's up the stairs. Small corridor to the left." He helped William to his feet and steadied him. "Can you make it on your own?"

"I think so, Lord Hugh. Thank you."

Hugh exchanged anxious glances with John. "We'd best come with you, just in case. I'll break fast in my chamber, Mistress Borthwick."

"As you wish, my lord," came her reply.

"Sit down." Hugh gestured to a nearby stool. "You look like Death, John. Was your uncle's hospitality too much to stomach?"

"For William, yes." John grimaced at the recollection. "Some accursed whore tried to poison him."

"Or her keeper did, at least." Drawing up his chair, Hugh sank down there with legs outstretched. "That's why you take a retinue to court, John. So you can keep at arm's length all those enterprising souls who'd do anything to steal from a hapless courtier." He fought the urge to laugh. "You should just have opened her legs and got on with it."

John stared, making no attempt to conceal his disgust. "Would you?"

"No, I don't suppose so. I wouldn't know where she's been." He paused as a knock sounded on his door. One of the maidservants hurried in, carrying a tray laden with bread and cold meats, a flagon of ale and some horn beakers. She laid it before them, then hurried away. "If that's the most you had to endure, be thankful," Hugh continued, once she'd gone. "Those wretched squires and pages usually have to suffer much worse. And William? He's a tough old soul. If he rests here today, I daresay he'll be his old self by morning." Leaning close, he added in a low voice, "The less Mistress Borthwick hears about this, the better. She's a notorious purveyor of gossip."

John groaned, and buried his head in his hands. "That's the last thing I need."

"Ah well, look on the bright side. At least your uncle didn't make any unreasonable demands upon your person." He poured some ale for them both, then lazed back with a sigh. "Well, here we are then. Cast adrift together in a sea of depravity."

"I want nothing more to do with it."

"You may not have much choice," Taking a consoling mouthful of ale, Hugh wiped his sleeve across his lips. "And let's be honest. You're in much better circumstances than I. I face the Privy Council tomorrow. The King has commanded it."

"I know," John fell silent. "I thought Argyll would be here," he added in a low voice.

"Yes," Hugh conceded. "So did I."

"I'll come with you," John said. "I can't let you walk into the lion's den alone."

Hugh smiled. "I appreciate that, very much." He paused, wondering how best to voice his thoughts. "I called at Ellestoun as I rode east," he said, carefully. "I spoke with your mother, and aired some home truths." He shifted with a sigh. "I'll be less popular than ever, I suppose. But if the worst should happen, and they throw me to the dogs, at least the air will have been cleansed."

John frowned. "Whatever do you mean?"

"A king died last year. They still haven't found his killer. It would be convenient, to blame me for his murder."

John shivered. "Where in God's Name's Argyll?"

"I wish I knew." Hugh broke the loaf apart, handed half to John. "I feel like the condemned man. As last meals go, it's wholesome fare, though if the truth be told, I don't much care for eating it."

Approaching the castle, their pace was brisk. Hugh seemed cheerful enough, but John knew that his friend's brittle facade of bluster and arrogance was just for show. He stayed close, offering what moral support he could.

As they passed beneath the barbican, Hugh faltered. Taking his arm, John steered him onwards, along the cobbled vennel towards the Upper Ward.

Already, they were running the gauntlet through a sea of gloating faces: it seemed that almost every courtier from Caithness to the Marches had gathered there in readiness. They greeted Hugh's passing with barely-concealed derision, basking in his discomfort.

Adam Hepburn awaited them outside the King's chambers. "I'm pleased you could join us, Lord Hugh," he said. "I'll inform His Grace of your arrival." He nodded to John. "Good day, Sir John. I'd heard you were at court."

John shrugged. "I thought my testimony might prove useful."

"Thank you, Sir John. I shall inform the king." Hepburn smiled tightly in John's direction, then disappeared into the king's chamber, closing the door firmly behind him.

The Gryphon at Bay

Sinking onto a nearby bench, Hugh dropped his head in his hands and rubbed his eyes. "Ah, they stick the knife in deep, and twist it…"

John punched Hugh lightly in the arm. "That's enough!"

"Argyll's not here," Hugh whispered. "Without him, I may as well throw myself down before the axeman."

"Sit tall, damn you. For Helen's sake, if not your own. It would break her heart, to witness this…"

Hugh straightened with a sigh. But his face was flushed, his gaze restless.

The door opened, and he flinched, just slightly, as Adam Hepburn re-emerged, straight-faced. "Come this way, Lord Hugh. His Grace the King awaits you."

*   *   *

Of all the humiliations he'd endured just recently, this was by far the worst. He was groveling on his knees, weathering the tirade in silence while all the men who mattered looked on: Patrick Hepburn, Lord Home, Robert Colville, Lord Gray, and John Ross of Montgrennan.

But no Argyll. Still no Argyll…

"-I placed my trust in you!" James stalked close, red-faced and furious. "I gave you full powers in the west. There was a purpose to this gift, Lord Hugh. I wanted peace!" Halting in mid-stride, he turned upon his heel, gown swinging as he moved. "I trusted you to win the hearts of my lieges, to show them that my rule was just, and fair. But you just can't see beyond the tip of your sword, can you-"

Hugh swallowed. He fixed his eyes ahead, focusing on nothing, fighting the urge to wilt beneath the onslaught. But James's wrath burned like vitriol, stripping away all his pride and self-worth.

"You're a tyrant, Lord Hugh. A petty, miserable tyrant." James paused briefly to draw breath. "You failed in every task I placed upon you. Where I desired peace, you created more disorder, more hatred. There's no place for a man like you amongst my council-"

He breathed deep, and the fear was gone. His head was clear, it was as if the words which rained down like blows were coming from far away and petering out before they even touched him.

"-And you can no longer consider yourself the Justiciar. There's men in this realm much better suited to the task than you ever were-"

Raising his head, he studied James intently. *Ungrateful wretch. I risked my life for you, I risked the honour of my family. You throw it back at me now, because you listen to the counsel of flatterers. I was never disloyal to you. I found it hard enough to be disloyal to your father…*

"-As for the Bailie's title, I'll be reconsidering that, too. That is if I decide to let you leave here with your neck intact. Some think I should make an example of you. *He's murdered one lord too many,* they say, and you know, perhaps they're right."

Seizing Hugh's jaw, James jerked his head high. The youth's fierce eyes bored down into his own, there was a cold hard brilliance he'd never seen before. "I won't be pressed into making rash decisions," James said. "I'll ponder your situation at leisure, and then I will decide your fate." He released his grip. "Must I detain you forcibly, Lord Hugh? Or will you give me your word as a gentleman that you'll remain in Edinburgh, amongst my court, and accept my decision regarding your fate?"

"I remain your humble servant," Hugh said, softly.

"Wretch." James pushed him roughly aside. "Get out of my sight."

John sat alone, bonnet screwed tight in both hands. He could hear James shouting, an endless onslaught of abuse. It was as if the king were pouring out all his hatred and frustration onto one man's slender insubstantial shoulders.

There was silence at last.

John looked up. The door opened, and Hugh emerged, a shade of his ebullient self. Adam Hepburn followed, smiling grimly.

John stood. "I'd like to see the King."

Hepburn's glance was one of barely disguised contempt. "It's not convenient."

"Then I'll wait here until he's ready."

"You'll be there all day then." The door slammed shut.

"There's no point," Hugh said. "The decision's made, I think."

"A judgement made through gossip and slander. I won't tolerate that." He cast a critical eye at Hugh. "His Grace soars ever higher in my estimation. If he can crush a mighty man like you with such finesse, then he's a king in every sense of the word."

Hugh pushed an agitated hand back through his hair. "I'm nothing, John. A tiny lordling from the west, who squeaks no louder than a mouse." He flinched, remembering... "He called me a tyrant." Turning to John, he stared at him; dazed, like an ox felled in mid-charge by a poleaxe. "Is that really how men will remember me?"

"Get back to Argyll's place," John urged him. "And quickly, before word gets out. I'll join you there later."

Cocking his head, John strained to hear what was being said within, but all he could make out was the quiet murmur of voices.

Time passed, a steady stream of supplicants joined him: plump-faced goodwives attended by rich burgess husbands, a few minor clergymen. They nodded to him, exchanged polite greetings.

As the morning drifted onwards, still John remained there, a patient figure seated near the door. Food was brought in by a phalanx of servants, the platters removed, one hour turned gradually into three, the passing of time marked by a bell in the distance chapel.

And then it was over. One by one, the Privy Councillors emerged. Lord Home and Lord Gray formed the vanguard, with Robert Colville following. Colville caught John's eye and nodded, nothing more.

Then by some wondrous miracle James himself emerged. John opened his mouth to speak, but his throat was dry and the moment was lost. He cursed, inwardly, then started as James himself headed over in his direction, a cordial smile upon his boyish face.

"Sir John," the king said, pleasantly. "You wish to speak with me?"

"Your Grace, I-"

James grasped his arm, steered him towards the door. "Come this way please."

The King's chamber was in a state of chaos. Earl Patrick and Montgrennan were gathering up parchments and rolls, while a brace of keen-eyed pages scoured the room for discarded platters and utensils.

"Be seated," James gestured to a chair.

John obeyed. "Your Grace, if I might speak a word in Lord Hugh's defence." He was wary at first, unsure how James would respond. But James merely slouched against the table with arms folded, expressing mild interest, nothing more.

With renewed confidence, John continued, "I was there that night. I saw what happened. Lord Hugh killed a man. I can't deny that. But his action was not premeditated. The Master of Kilmaurs questioned his honour, his courage, and Hugh defended himself as best he could. And Lord Robert, God rest his soul..." John broke off, remembering the horror of that night, the moment Kilmaurs passed away before him. "He stepped in to protect his son. And paid a heavy price."

James was watching him intently. "I'm told Lord Hugh struck the first blow."

"They were mistaken. There was a great deal of confusion."

"Are you sure, Sir John, that it's not you who is mistaken?"

John met the young man's bright clear gaze and held it. "If Lord Hugh is guilty of any crime, Your Grace, it's of being reckless and over-eager to respond to another's challenge."

"Perhaps," James countered. "But Lord Hugh was acting as an officer of the law. He should have moderated his actions accordingly,"

"Perhaps too much was expected of him," Montgrennan interjected, gently.

James nodded in weary agreement. "I know that now," he conceded. "Alas, for the benefit of hindsight..."

"By your good grace I was made Sheriff of Renfrew," John persisted. "The lands under my jurisdiction are settled and law-abiding: the Montgomeries and Cunninghames dwell there peaceably, and show each other some degree of civility, at least. If Lord Hugh is slain to satisfy the appetites of his enemies at court, then there's nothing I can do to keep these two great houses from tearing each other apart."

James sank down in his chair with a sigh, and dropped his head in his hands. "I acknowledge your concerns, Sir John."

"You asked me once to try and maintain a steadying influence upon Lord Hugh," John added. "I failed in this and I'm sorry. Not just for Lord Hugh, but for the sake of his family, and for this realm, too."

"No." Glancing aside, James traced a spiral on the tabletop. "I should be the one to apologise. I placed an impossible task upon you. I know that now. I understand it. I hear your words, Sir John, and I applaud you for speaking out in Lord Hugh's defence. But..." Rattling his fingers against the board, the young man was visibly on edge. "Personal loyalties can't sway my decisions. I must look beyond the Westland, and do what's best for the realm." He rubbed his forehead with a sigh, betraying his weariness. "Thank you for your time, Sir John. Now let's let justice take its course, shall we?"

Chapter 83

They sat by the window, sharing a measure of claret and looking down into the Cowgate with its bustling daytime hordes. And there they stayed, as the hours drifted past, sunlight giving way to dusk.

"Why don't you leave?" John asked. "You could sail to France, at least until the hue and cry's died down."

Hugh's glance was bleak, long-suffering. "I gave him my word." Slumping back against the wall, he stared out at the leaden skies, where the gulls still soared like silver wisps on the wind. "Ah, I ache for Helen. She's lost to me now. The Westland might as well lie on the other side of the world."

"I'm sorry."

"I'm no poet, John. God, I wish I was." Letting his head fall back, Hugh closed his eyes. "Her hair, dark as the wild wood. When we first met, it burned to brown in summer, before she donned that accursed hood." He shifted suddenly, slumping forward with a groan. "Ah, I might never see her again…" He gazed at John, eyes bright with desperation. "You won't abandon her when I'm gone, will you? You'll cast your gaze to Cunninghame, and make sure my foes don't bleed me dry?"

"How can I ever have a say in your affairs when you've got the likes of Hessilhead and Bowhouse making decisions on your behalf?"

Hugh screwed his eyes shut, painful acknowledgement. "They're dolts, the pair of them. And Robert, he's spineless. The runt of the damned litter-" Hearing footsteps creak upon the stair, he broke off, wary.

There was a knock upon the door. "I've a message for Sir John Sempill," Mistress Borthwick called.

"Come in," Hugh replied.

She heaved her way into the room. She carried a sword-belt over her shoulder, the blade still lodged there, and held a pair of spurs in her hand. "Your uncle's man is here. The rest of your baggage is downstairs. I'm to tell you that no offence was taken, that you're welcome in his company at any time."

John sprang to his feet and recovered the items from her custody. "Thank you, Mistress Borthwick."

She shuffled off without a word and closed the door.

"God, what mighty breasts that woman has," Hugh whispered. "A man could suffocate there. Have you ever thought-"

"No," said John.

"Well," said Hugh with a sigh. "It's getting late, I suppose. You can have my bed, if you like. It's more comfortable than lying on the floor with the men-at-arms. And-" he added, with a wicked smile, "-at least here you know your arse is safe." He stifled a chuckle. "'No offence was taken,'" he said. "By whom, I wonder? By the noble Montgrennan? By his profiteering steward? Or by your good self…"

"Enough," came John's weary reply. "It's been an arduous day. Let's not dwell upon its consequences."

John was asleep almost as soon as his head hit the pillow. *The sleep of the righteous -* Hugh thought, with a pang of envy, as he settled alongside - *the sleep of the just.*

He wasn't granted such comfort. He tossed and turned, then finally he dozed a while. After that he grew restless.

Slipping out of bed, he pulled a fur-lined gown over shirt and hose and sat down by the window. He opened the shutters, breathing in the cold night air and watching the stars track their majestic paths across the firmament, until eventually the pale glow of dawn lifted the dark skies in the east.

Hugh tilted his head, listening. Horses were approaching at an idle walk. Coming from the Cowgate, a whole company of them. They paused below, a door slammed. Stairs creaked, men's voices conversed in hushed tones from the lower floors.

Argyll had arrived at last.

He settled back with a sigh, vaguely reassured. He hoped his gude-father would come and speak with him, but there was nothing. No knock upon his door, no words of comfort from the only man of influence who might speak out in his defence.

Hugh sighed. It was hard not to let this niggling disappointment blossom into full-grown resentment. His soul was troubled, the solace he'd found at the abbey a distant memory.

Gripping his rosary, he dropped to his knees before the *prie-dieu* in the corner and prayed, asking earnestly for God's help, asking that now, in his hour of need, he would not be abandoned.

John stirred at last, bedraggled and weary. He grovelled beneath the bed in search of the pisspot, muttering choice words about the cold.

Hugh looked up, only half-listening. "John," he said, quietly. "I hope you'll understand that what happens today isn't meant as a slight against you, or your line."

John glanced up, concerned. "What're you talking about?"

"Events are unfolding here, events in which I played my part."

"Whatever do you mean?" John demanded. "Why should it involve me?"

"I don't yet know what's going to happen, and I don't know how any of us'll be affected. I say this to you now because you're a friend, and I value your friendship more than you can possibly imagine. We're all tied through blood to kin and family, and while that's well and good, it's a rare and wondrous thing in these accursed times to find someone who will give his strength and support freely, without condition." The words were spilling out thick and fast, he couldn't stop them, aware all the while of John looking on, stunned and silent. Slowly but surely, the weight inside him lifted, as if he'd been confessing to his priest. He raised his head, offered his friend a vague, apologetic smile. "I never meant you any ill. Please don't forget that."

*   *   *

Matthew Stewart cast one last disparaging glance around the draughty barn, taking in its packed earth floors and slit windows and the foul drain running down its length. Gripped by a strange uneasy combination of excitement and apprehension, he'd had virtually no sleep the previous night. But he found consolation at least in the hope that it would be his last night as a fugitive.

Gritting his teeth, he waited impatiently while Alex fastened his gauntlets and set his helm carefully into place. For the first time in months he wore his family colours with pride, his velvet jupon marked with the chequered fosse of *azure* and *argent* over a ground of *or*.

Matthew took a deep breath, satisfied. At last he was confronting the world as a knight should. Challenging the enemy, instead of skulking in the shadows, furtive and wary.

Archie Campbell came striding in. 'I've acquired a horse, Mattie. One a little more worthy than the nag that carried you here.'

Matthew laughed. "Ah, don't mock the poor brute. He served me well, over long miles with precious little food."

Alex paused alongside. "Your spurs."

Matthew waved in brisk acknowledgement, pausing while Alex buckled them into place.

Once he was ready, he walked with Archie to where his men were mustering in the chill grey of the morning. A grey stallion waited nearby, swathed from poll to hoof beneath a yellow cloth caparison. It stamped a rear hoof, impatient.

Matthew laughed. "Ah, the noble Zephyr! Does cousin Hugh know that you took his horse?"

Archie shrugged. "He won't object."

Climbing into the saddle, Matthew grimaced as the horse tossed its head and side-stepped, unsettled by his unfamiliar hand.

He clapped its neck. "Well then, Zephyr! Let's be on our way." He raised a clenched fist as he moved off, and the men at his back all cheered, a hundred armed retainers, Stewarts and Lyles from Renfrew and the Lennox. With Argyll's men moving ahead to hold the barasse open and dissuade any opposition, he knew his way was clear. "May God grant us safe passage!" he called. "And bend the King's ear to reason…" he added in a low voice. Touching his spurs to Zephyr's flanks, he sat deep as the horse sprang off at a lively trot, tail switching.

Chapter 84

Edinburgh Castle

The Outer Ward bristled with dignitaries. At least two hundred men had gathered there: high-ranking churchmen, Lords of Parliament and Earls.

Amongst this sea of red-gowned lords, Hugh was just another anonymous figure. Once men would have been eager to offer him greetings and salutations, but now he was shunned by those he'd called allies. They slid aside as he approached, muttering excuses. Or worse still, they pointedly ignored him.

Somewhere in the city, John would be joining the crowd that thronged the streets and filled the public gallery in the tolbooth. Watching and learning, a fledgling courtier preparing for the day when he in turn would take his place here.

It was strangely comforting, to know he wasn't altogether friendless. In this godforsaken place where thieves and brigands paraded under banners of knightly virtue…

A hand gripped his shoulder. "Courage, Hugh. All will be well."

A whisper in his ear, nothing more. But his heart leapt nonetheless, for the voice was Argyll's. Turning, Hugh saw the earl's grey gown disappear amongst the restless sea of vermillion.

The trumpets sang out their triumphant summons. Hugh straightened his coronet one last time and stood tall, waiting for the signal to take his place in the procession. Soon they'd be winding their way from the grounds of the castle to the cathedral of Saint Giles. Then, after mass, they'd move on to the tolbooth, where the business of the day would begin in earnest.

The golden walls of the tolbooth lay ahead, a tantalising vision which beckoned him ever closer. Matthew levelled his gaze there, sitting deep in the saddle as if confronting a line of enemy lances. Sensing his excitement, Zephyr swept forward briskly, neck arched, throwing out each hoof with such panache that his heart sang for joy.

In Edinburgh's streets the crowd still lingered. At his passing, everyone stared. There'd be a moment in each face as the realisation dawned, and then the mood changed. Celebration tumbled into fear, as they realised that two hundred men-at-arms or more were gathering in the mercat place, seasoned rebels from the Lennox, and Argyll's people, too.

Matthew halted outside the tolbooth. Touched his sword hilt one last time, then dismounted.

Taking a deep steadying breath, he strode through the open door. He'd trod this path so many times before, but not in such circumstances, not with the stakes so high. The sun was shining down upon him, giving his plate armour an Arthurian glow that strengthened his resolve all the more.

On he walked, past the ranks of red-gowned figures. They were staring at him, incredulous. They were gasping and muttering amongst themselves, their agitation palpable.

"By the Grace of God I declare that the charges of treason made against me were false!" His challenge rang out through the silent hall. "I demand that my name be cleared. That the name of my kinsman John Stewart, Earl of Lennox be cleared. And that the name of my noble ally, Robert, Lord Lyle be cleared, also. I demand justice. I demand forgiveness. I demand to serve my King, as my family and kin have served their liege lord for generations."

A dog barked, far away. Closer to hand, one of his retainers coughed from beyond the door. But here in the tolbooth no one spoke a word or even moved.

Patrick Hepburn stood at last. He glared at Matthew with unveiled venom, and Matthew stared back.

While James gripped the arms of his throne and gazed in consternation at the drama unfolding there, right before his eyes.

Montgrennan stepped forward. Leaning close to James, he whispered in his ear while the young man listened, attentive.

One man dared to applaud. Then another joined in, and another. Soon dozens of lords and magnates rose to their feet, cheering and shouting their support. Men weary of war and rebellion, men eager to put the past behind them and move on.

James remained in urgent conversation with Montgrennan and Patrick Hepburn. Hepburn was red-faced and angry, while Montgrennan... He acted as if it were just another ordinary episode in an ordinary day.

The king raised his hand for silence. "My learned friend-" he nodded towards Montgrennan "- tells me that you have a valid grievance. He says that the charges made against you were indeed illegal." Smiling faintly, he cast a sideways glance towards Hepburn. It was a look of youthful rebellion, furtive and self-satisfied. "You are forgiven, my Lord Darnley. You are accepted back into the fold." Rising to his feet he approached Matthew, arms stretched wide. "Cousin," he said, and folded him in his embrace. "Welcome back."

"Parliament is adjourned!" Patrick Hepburn's voice thundered out. "We'll reconvene on the morrow, once this matter has been discussed amongst the Privy Council."

John pushed roughly through the crowd, heedless of the recriminations, blind to everything but Matthew Stewart's contaminating presence. Reaching for his dagger, he felt the smooth familiar shape of its hilt beneath his fingers.

He'd watched in disbelief as Matthew Stewart swaggered his way through the assembled lords and proclaimed that he'd been unjustly treated all along. He'd held his breath, thinking that it was only a matter of time, that soon the royal men-at-arms would seize him. Then he saw that little smile cross James's lips and understood at last.

He'd been betrayed. By King and court. By those he'd dared call friends.

Just one course was left. He'd pay with his life, of course. He accepted it. But in the face of such an insult he no longer cared.

The lords were making their dignified retreat back up the hill past St Giles, heading for the comfortable security of the castle. John quickened his pace, searching the sea of red gowns for the flash of yellow that would mark out his quarry. It didn't matter that Matthew Stewart was in full array, armed with a sword besides. He'd put his faith in God, for if his cause was righteous, then surely he'd triumph, whatever the odds.

Hugh paused on the cobbled causeway, heart thudding. Scanning the masses that loitered near the cathedral, he hissed through his teeth as he spotted John, bludgeoning a route towards the castle. Hugh scarcely recognised him: his friend seemed possessed by malice, fierce burning hatred etched deep into his face.

Taking a deep breath, Hugh braced himself for the confrontation. "John!" he called.

There was no sign he'd even heard him.

Hugh gestured quickly to some nearby men-at-arms: Argyll's men, in quilted *aketons* and battered steel bonnets. *"Quickly now!"* he called in *gaelic*. *"Stop that man. But gently!"*

They shouldered their way through the crowd and moved in briskly, seizing an arm each.

Hugh breathed a sigh of relief as John submitted to Argyll's people without so much as a struggle. "I'll look after him now." Stepping alongside, he grasped John's arm. "Thank you."

John looked away. "You knew." His tone was dull, defeated.

"I didn't know," Hugh said. "But I suspected."

"After all he did to me." John met his gaze at last, eyes bright with betrayal. "To my people. And you... You stood there and applauded."

"For God's Sake, John, stop this!" Hugh forced himself to look John in the eye, acknowledging the pain there, the confusion. "It doesn't matter now," he added, more gently. "You've secured your place in this world. He can't harm you."

"He made a mockery of me."

"And you made a mockery of him in return." He steered John swiftly over to the wall of the cathedral, where they could find a little privacy, at least. "All insults have been repaid in full. Now come on. Enough of this daft talk."

John sighed. He seemed dazed, all trace of his anger fading fast. He leaned back against the cool stone of the cathedral, blinking back tears. "What manner of a man am I?" he whispered. "If I can't win redress for what he did."

Hugh relinquished his grip. He took his place alongside John, his back buttressed by the nave's sturdy walls. "Is that really what you want?"

John said nothing.

"In the name of God, John, listen to me. Don't follow this path. Don't follow my example. Everything I care for, everything I love... It might all be lost, because of Rob's death. Because I killed him." Hugh paused, then added, in a low voice. "Don't throw everything away like this. It would break Margaret's heart-" Drawing a sharp apprehensive breath, he gripped John's sleeve tight, for Montgrennan was approaching.

John's kinsman halted beside them, his concern plain to see. He caught Hugh's eye, a glance filled with unspoken questions.

"It's alright, my lord," Hugh said. "He needs a moment to compose himself, that's all."

Montgrennan's gaze flicked restlessly over them both. It lingered on John a moment more, than he smiled, reassured. "Then I'll leave him in your care, Lord Hugh. Can I count on you to make sure that all's well with him?"

"You can, my lord. Thank you." Hugh paused, carefully watching Montgrennan's departure. Then, when they were alone, he punched John lightly in the arm. "Well then. For good or ill, it's done. Let me shed this gaudy plumage, and then we'll take ourselves off to an alehouse. Some day, we'll look back on all this and laugh when we remember what fools we were. Does that sound like an excellent plan to you?"

John shrugged in dismissal, but managed a wan smile, at least.

And that, Hugh thought, was better than nothing.

Chapter 85

"So you're still here, Lord Hugh?" Sitting tall in his chair, James's mood was unfathomable. He looked Hugh up and down as he approached, aloof, faintly condescending. "Most thought you wouldn't wait to hear your fate."

Hugh dropped to one knee. "It was your will, Your Grace."

"Yes," James said, absently. Rising to his feet, he wandered to the window where he lingered, staring out across the city. "To take the life of a Lord of Parliament," he said. "To leave his poor wife bereft of her husband, his children without a father…" He turned to Hugh, arms folded. "This was a grave misjudgement."

Hugh swallowed, throat dry. He didn't answer, didn't dare even to meet James's eye, for fear of seeming insolent.

"I have spoken at length with my Privy Council," James continued. "And I've consulted a committee of lords and learned men. You gave a fair account of your actions, and we've received the word of witnesses who were present on the day. In the light of this evidence, we have decided the best course. You'll understand that I can't be too lenient. That I must do something which acknowledges the gravity of your sin." He paused, letting his words sink in. "Just be thankful that you have friends at court," he continued. "Friends who spoke out eloquently on your behalf. *An error of judgement*, they said. *A rash act, which has been regretted ever since*. You should be grateful to these men, Lord Hugh, for their intervention did much to quench my wrath."

"Your Grace…"

"But your ability to dispense justice is questioned. I think, perhaps we should channel your vigour in other ways, until you've learned to be more moderate in your decisions and restrained in your actions." James settled back down in his chair with a sigh. "Your blood's too hot, Lord Hugh. It should be cooled, I think." The young man's gaze didn't waver, not for a moment. "You'll remove yourself to the north, where you will be appointed my Commissioner. There you'll make a full assessment of the land holdings and income of my brother the Duke of Ross. You'll be gone from the Westland for at least a year. Perhaps in that time men's memories will mellow."

Hugh swallowed, trying not to betray his relief. "Your Grace is merciful."

James sprang from his chair. "Pray rise, Lord Hugh." Grasping Hugh's arms, he helped him to his feet. "I hope and pray with all sincerity that on your return, you'll be committed to upholding the peace in Cunninghame." The young man embraced him warmly. "You are the most erratic and difficult of men, my friend, and yet… You are *uncomplicated*." James smiled, regretful. "You will be missed. Let that be your consolation, as you weather your disgrace."

The baggage was packed, half-a-dozen sumpter horses lined up ready in the yard for an early departure. Running a practiced eye over his companions, Hugh noted in satisfaction that all his party were accounted for: half a dozen clerks, bleary-eyed from the early start, and two-score retainers, there to ensure their safety throughout the long journey north.

Before long, another bleak late winter day would dawn across the city. But for the moment the sky was still dark, the sun concealed behind a leaden shroud of cloud. A grim reminder that venturing abroad at this time of year was little short of folly...

Hugh shivered, and pulled his thick fur-lined cloak closer. His horse awaited him, a shaggy hairy-heeled garron that he'd chosen from Argyll's stable. It didn't look up to much, but it was his mount of choice, a sturdy beast which would carry him safely through the snow-bound wastes of the north.

He checked the harness one last time, then lifted each broad hoof in turn to make sure the shoes were sound.

Someone tapped his shoulder, he straightened with a sigh.

Archie Campbell stood beside him, rubbing his hands with the cold and breathing mist before him. "Did you think you'd slip away unnoticed?"

"I didn't want to make a fuss."

Archie teased his fingers through the garron's coarse mane. "You were missed last night. The celebrations weren't complete without you."

Hugh shook his head. "I was indisposed."

"Playing wetnurse to a lowly baron, I suppose."

"I owe that lowly baron a great deal."

"Please don't think his words had any bearing on the matter," Archie countered, stiff rebuke. He swatted Hugh's head, an attempt at humour. "We were pondering your absence, while we caroused in James's chambers. And Mattie concluded that the reason why you prefer Sir John Sempill's company to our own is that you use him as a hair shirt. You keep him close as a constant reminder of your sins." Archie smirked, faintly mocking. "For shame, Hugh. He could at least have stirred from his bed to see you off."

"It was a late night. I saw no need to wake him." Taking the reins, Hugh sprang onto the garron's back, grimacing at its uncomfortable breadth.

"You're still on speaking terms, I hope?" Archie's tone hardened, his blue-grey gaze boring into him.

"I've done my best to heal the rift," Hugh replied. "But... His pride is dinted."

"Can't be helped," Archie said, briskly. "We've more important things to concern us. The earl will expect regular news from the north. If you hear anything that might concern him..."

"I'll keep him informed." Hugh raised his hand, signaling their imminent departure. "Let's be gone, shall we?" he called. "I want to be lodged at the Queen's Ferry by nightfall."

He spurred the garron onwards, ducking low to avoid the roof of the vennel, fixing his gaze on the sliver of grey light that marked the entrance to the street ahead. *I'd be better dead*, he thought, *than stranded in the northern wastes...* He checked himself, stern reproach. *If you're so despondent now, what will you be like when a month, six months, have passed?*

He'd weather the hardship, as he'd weathered it before. And Helen would weather it, too. She always did. No, what troubled him most - he realised with a jolt - was the knowledge of wounds left unplastered, festering grievances unresolved.

The Gryphon at Bay

He'd stayed by John's side the last few nights, looking after him, steering him clear of trouble. John had tolerated his presence, nothing more, making it quite obvious that he found greater solace in the wine jug.

Time after time he'd tried to apologise. Citing all the usual reasons for duplicity: kinship, politics, practicalities. But his entreaties, though meant sincerely, had gone unheeded.

Perhaps in a year those wounds will heal, too, he thought. But he wasn't convinced. Not at all.

Chapter 86

John rolled onto his back, nursing a grinding headache. As he lay still, collecting his thoughts, the resentments came trickling back, the reasons why he'd got so blindly drunk in the first place...

He sat up with a sigh. When they'd stumbled back from the alehouse, he'd been so tired and insensible that he'd toppled down onto Hugh's bed without even bothering to undress.

Now a new day was upon them. The curtains were open, and he was alone.

Except for William, who sat hunched in the gloom beside the shuttered window. A trail of thin grey light slid through the gaps, cold, unfriendly.

"Where's Hugh?"

William glanced around. "He left hours ago. He said I wasn't to disturb you."

John swung his legs over the side of the bed, trying to banish his misgivings. "We'll be leaving, too. Just as soon as we've broken our fast. Can you root out the rest of the Montgomeries? I told Hugh I'd ride with them to the Westland."

"That was before."

"I gave him my word. The promise still stands."

William shrugged, and rose to his feet.

He saw to the horses himself. To keep his mind occupied, as much as anything else.

Setting to work with brush and comb, John curried Zephyr's coat as if his life depended upon it. He heard booted footsteps echoing against the cobbles behind him, but he didn't turn around.

"I'm told you're leaving us," Archie Campbell said.

John turned with a sigh, to see the Master of Argyll settling nonchalantly against the wall.

"Why should I stay?" he retorted. "The business that concerns me is concluded."

Campbell shrugged. "It's your decision," he said. "And I'm sure Hugh would be delighted that you're taking the horse back with you. But before you go," he said. "The earl would like a word. In his chamber."

He couldn't exactly refuse Argyll's summons. Or pretend he hadn't received the message. But Earl Colin was at prayers with his chaplain, which meant there was nothing John could do but wait.

Sitting alone in a sparsely furnished antechamber, he bore the inactivity as best he could, though it galled him. He longed to be away from Edinburgh, and away from James's courtiers, with all their mocking smiles and false pleasantries.

The chaplain left, offering John a brief nod as he passed by. A servant followed, and he was shown inside.

The Gryphon at Bay

It was a homely chamber, elegantly furnished and well-appointed. With Arras hangings on every wall, and a roaring fire in the hearth. And at its heart sat Earl Colin, his strong jovial presence filling the place.

"Ah, Sir John!" Earl Colin greeted him with a smile. "I'm told I nearly missed you. I gather you're returning to the Westland?"

John bowed his head. "I'm most grateful for your hospitality, Your Grace."

Earl Colin laughed. "My gude-son's friends are always welcome beneath my roof." He paused, suddenly serious. "We all thought Hugh would attend his cousin last night."

"I hope the Master of Lennox wasn't too inconvenienced by his absence," John replied, sourly.

Earl Colin steepled his hands. "This hostility is quite unnecessary, Sir John. It's in all our interests to work together, to move forward." His smile returned, he leaned close, pleasantly conspiratorial. "We want you to prosper, Sir John. We *need* you to prosper. And prosper you will, if you look beyond your grievances, and put this unhappy episode behind you."

John bit his lip. The doubts he'd been trying hard to bury deep all morning were stirring afresh, a gnawing sense of guilt that was growing all the time. "Do you know what route he meant to take?"

Argyll stared at him, his jovial expression wiped clean, replaced by sober understanding. "He's heading for the Queen's Ferry. He's staying there tonight, I believe, and sailing in the morning."

Horses approached at a canter, hooves rattling against the stony track. A stallion called, a familiar cry which made his soul leap for joy: even as the men-at-arms stirred to draw their swords, Hugh raised his hand. "Hold!"

Looking over his shoulder, he could scarcely believe what he was seeing. For one of the horsemen who bore down upon them was sitting upon a lively grey, while alongside galloped a strong black horse from Flanders...

One of the horsemen waved, wildly, then urged his grey on faster. "Hugh, wait!" he called, his voice just audible over the sigh of the sea.

Hugh reined in his garron. The smile spread across his face and he made no effort to contain it, not even for the sake of the clerks and the soldiers who looked on and witnessed it. For there was John, mounted not on Storm but on Zephyr, who frisked like a colt, happy to escape the confinement of his stall.

Hugh nodded. "You're making good use of him already."

"He needed to stretch his legs." John brought Zephyr into step alongside. The grey horse towered over the garron, chafing at the idle pace.

Hugh nodded to William. "You're going up in the world, Master Haislet. Once Sir John lets you loose on his destrier, a knighthood surely can't be far behind."

"Over my dead body, Lord Hugh," William replied, straight-faced.

Hugh laughed. "Mind what I said," he told John. "If you can't find much reason to ride out with him, then buy some fine mares and run them. When the time comes to sell the foals, we can split the profit." He sighed, his breath misting before him. "Well then. To what do I owe this pleasure?"

"I'm heading west today. I thought I'd ride with you as far as the Queen's Ferry." John stared straight ahead, a faint frown touching his brow.

"You're leaving so soon?"

"There's nothing more to keep me here. And Margaret…" He winced, slightly. "Her lying-in will have begun. Who knows? She may…" His voice faded.

"She'll be alright, John. I can feel it in my bones. And you mustn't fret, because she's in good hands. Helen asked if she might ride to Ellestoun so she can help with the birth, and I agreed, of course. It seemed the right thing to do, considering that she's so well-versed with such things."

"Thank you. I appreciate that." Looking Hugh up and down, John smiled and shook his head. "You look like an Islesman already."

Hugh shrugged and laughed. Idly casting his gaze to the coast, he saw the waters of the Forth lying broad and grey as sheet pewter to the north. Beyond them stretched the flat drab grey-green lands of Fife. And lying further still, he could see the mountains, rising high in the distance. They called to him like sirens, echoing with the eerie cries of wolf and blackcock. A world haunted by the ghosts of heroes and fey folk, the echoes of their songs still drifting through the caves and the bogs and the glens.

"And so my banishment begins," he muttered. "A whole year, calculating wool yields and taxes."

"Your life is spared," John reminded him. "Be thankful of that." He nodded towards Blackness, its ominous black bulk growing ever larger in the west. "You might be in there. Languishing over the cruelty of Fate…"

"I might as well be dead. A man could rot in the north. And Helen…" The thought stung him deep. "Noble, long-suffering Helen… To be cursed with a reckless fool like me…"

"She'll thank God you're safe," John rebuked him, sharply.

"But now I'm gone she's beleaguered, surrounded by oafs and hotheads." He slid into a morose silence. "Much can happen in a year. If I'm not there, God knows what the Cunninghames will do. They'll know I'm weak, and act accordingly."

"Think how much worse it would have been," John pointed out, "if you'd been forfeited. Or even executed. How would your heir have survived, not to mention Helen?"

"You'll help her, I hope. Offer her measured counsel as and when she needs it."

"I would, if that were possible. But your kinsmen will never let me interfere in your business."

"They will if I demand it," Hugh replied. "I'll write a letter, if ever we find an opportunity."

John shrugged. "That shouldn't be a problem. I'll remain with your party tonight, and press on to Linlithgow on the morrow."

"Thank you, John. I appreciate this. And I mean that most sincerely."

"Sincerity is hardly a quality you're renowned for," John retorted. "But just this once, I'll take your words in good faith."

"You pierce me to the quick." Hugh glanced up, smiling slightly. "I'm told that Mattie mocked me in my absence. He said that you are to me as the hair shirt was to St Thomas the Martyr of Canterbury."

"Then I'll take that as a compliment."

The Gryphon at Bay

"Next time we meet, you'll be a father. When that day dawns, you'll wonder why you ever concerned yourself with the treacherous business of court." Hugh sank deeper into the saddle, lulled by the leisurely plod of his horse. "I wish I'd escaped it. I wish I could slink back to the Westland, and be done with court business forever."

"You don't mean that," John said. "As the months pass, you'll remember what it all means to you. You'll endure all manner of privations to help this realm stand firm. That's why James spared you. That's why he's forgiven you already."

"And you, John?" Hugh asked, quietly. "Have you forgiven me?"

"After all the insults and injuries you've committed against my house during the past two years? How could I live with myself?" Seeing his crestfallen look, a smile crept across John's lips. "Oh, I think so, Hugh. Though God alone knows why."

Notes

The journey which brought me through the writing of *Fire & Sword* and onwards into the creation of this, its follow-up, has been long and arduous. Make no mistake: the writing of a historical novel is not a task to be undertaken lightly, and it's certainly not recommended for the faint-hearted.

Even when lines are drawn beneath a specific project, the research goes on. This is especially true of someone for whom the local history of Renfrewshire and Ayrshire forms a major part of the day job, more often than not paying the bills and helping put food on the table. It stands to reason that I keep on reading around the subject, trying to learn more, to reach an ever deeper grasp of the complexities.

It was mainly due to personal circumstances that *Fire & Sword* had to be written through recourse to secondary sources. I was a freelance archaeologist in intermittent employment at the time, so gallivanting off to archives in Edinburgh and beyond just wasn't an option financially. The same has been true, to a lesser extent, for *The Gryphon at Bay*, which was written in rough draft between the years of 2005 and 2009.

This is the last of the series that will rely upon secondary sources, for over the last five years the researcher's life has been transformed. The collections of the National Archives of Scotland are now available to search online, which makes the exploration of primary data much, much easier.

But since secondary sources were the backbone of this book, once again I shall list my main ports of call. Up at the top of the list was Norman MacDougall's masterful book *James IV* (Tuckwell Press,1997), with Stephen Boardman's work *The Campbells: 1250-1513* (John Donald, 2006) providing much-appreciated insights (and inspiration) into the relationship between the Campbell clan and their wayward relation-by-marriage, Hugh, 2nd Lord Montgomerie. Stephen Boardman's Ph.D. thesis, *The Politics of The Feud in Late Medieval Scotland* also shed valuable light upon the whole Cunningham/Montgomerie disagreement, with a few Sempill-related issues highlighted for good measure. David Hume of Godscroft's *The History of the House of Angus* (Scottish Text Society, 2005) helped provide me with background information on the Red Douglases, with Michael Brown's *The Black Douglases* (Tuckwell Press, 1998) doing the same for the other notorious branch of the Douglas family.

I've also had the benefit of insights gleaned from conversations with archaeological colleagues. The names are pretty much the same as those acknowledged previously in *Fire & Sword*, but some additional names should be mentioned: I'd like to highlight, in particular, Tom Addyman and Tam McFadyen (for wisdom relating to tower-houses and late medieval architecture), Douglas Speirs (medieval burghs and ecclesiastical life) and – last, but by no means least - Thomas Rees, who has granted me the opportunity to go play (in a professional sense) on projects relating to various west of Scotland tower-houses, including Aiket Castle (Cunninghames), Ardrossan Castle (Montgomeries), Lainshaw (Montgomeries), and Caldwell Tower (Mures). As ever, the interpretations portrayed within this novel are entirely my own – my professional colleagues cannot be held accountable for what goes on in a novelist's head!

The events leading up to the death of Robert, 2nd Lord Kilmaurs are murky. We hear about the killing in retrospect, in part through a letter issued to Sir John Sempill, Sheriff of Renfrew, in November 1489, and in part through a much later document in which Cuthbert Cunninghame (then Earl of Glencairn) asks exemption from the justice of Hugh Montgomerie (then Earl of Eglinton) because the Lord Montgomerie slew his father. It's unknown why the fatal confrontation between the two feuding rivals took place: was this the second 'extra-judicial' killing undertaken by Montgomerie in a decade, an assassination carried out by a man who considered himself above the law? Or was it (as depicted here) the tragic consequence of an escalating cycle of confrontation and violence? There's no way of knowing – which is bad news for the historian, but great for the historical novelist!

And now, I think, it's down to business. For those who are interested, I have – as ever – included the facts, just so you know where reality ends and invention begins. If there's some overlap with *Fire & Sword*, I apologise, but in some cases, the factual basis remains consistent.

?, ?, 1458. Hugh, 2nd Lord Montgomerie is born.

19th May, 1468. Archibald, Earl of Angus married to Elizabeth Boyd, daughter of Robert, 1st Lord Boyd (and aunt to James, 2nd Lord Boyd).

?, ?, 1470. Alexander, Lord Montgomerie, dies. His great-grandson Hugh inherits the title, still a minor (aged 12).

21st April, 1478. Hugh, 2nd Lord Montgomerie, marries Helen Campbell, third daughter of Earl Colin of Argyll, in Dollar Church.

8th June, 1481. Colin Campbell, Earl of Argyll, visits Kilmun Castle where he meets with John, Lord of the Isles. He takes with him in this meeting his son and heir Archibald, and his son-in-law, Hugh, 2nd Lord Montgomery.

?, ?, 1481. John Ross of Montgrennan is Bailie of Cunninghame & James III's Lord Advocate.

28th September, 1482. Hugh, Lord Montgomerie, attempts to recover the title of Bailie of Cunninghame.

?, ?, 1484. James, 2nd Lord Boyd killed by Hugh, 2nd Lord Montgomerie

11th June, 1488. King James III killed at the Battle of Sauchieburn. Sir Thomas Sempill also dies here, fighting for his king.

8th October, 1488. John Ross of Montgrennan and John Ramsay, Lord Bothwell are amongst a group of men summoned for treason before Parliament. In their absence, their lands and titles are forfeited.

?, ?, 1488-9. Archibald, Earl of Angus loses the titles of Warden of the Western & Middle Marches and Sheriff of Lanark. The Wardenships are given to Patrick Hepburn, Earl of Bothwell.

12th February, 1489. A safe-conduct is granted to Archibald Douglas, Earl of Angus, by King Henry VII of England, allowing him to pass through England with 80 attendants on a pilgrimage to Amiens. Angus was ordered (by James himself) to report to the English king on his return.

1489-1499. The Bailiary court of Cunningham is suspended due to unrest between the Montgomerie & Cunninghame factions.

September, 1489. Letters of fire and sword are issued to Sir John Sempill of Ellestoun, Sheriff of Renfrew. These justify an earlier attack on the Place of Duchal carried out in 'times bygone.'

22nd October, 1489. King James IV writes to Arbuthnott of that Ilk from Stirling, warning him that the Earl Marischal, the Master of Huntly, Lord Forbes and others were making certain leagues and bands at Dumbarton Castle.

11th October, 1489. The 'Battle of The Moss' is fought between forces loyal to James IV, and those loyal to the rebels led by John Stewart, Earl of Lennox.

12th-17th October, 1489. Thomas Galbraith of Culcreuch is hanged for his role in the recent battle and his lands granted to Adam Hepburn.

24th October, 1489. Sir John Ross of Montgrennan is restored to his Perthshire lands of Kinclevan.

? October 1489. The gun 'Duchal' is floated across the Clyde on three boats and brought to the siege of Dumbarton.

6th November, 1489. Sir John Sempill, Sheriff of Renfrew, is issued with King's letters referring to the wardship of lands pertaining to the deceased Robert, Lord Kilmaurs.

23rd November, 1489. King James IV rode out from Linlithgow to return to the siege.

13th December, 1489. The siege of Dumbarton Castle was finally concluded.

5th February, 1490. King James IV, in the presence of the three estates, declared the forfeiture of the Earl of Lennox, his son Matthew Stewart, Master of Lennox and Robert, Lord Lyle null and void, for the original process of forfeiture was 'nocht launchfully led nor deducit be Just and gudely ordour'.

About the Author

Photo credit: James Dunlop

Born in Glasgow, Louise Turner spent her early years in the west of Scotland where she attended the University of Glasgow. After graduating with an MA in Archaeology, she went on to complete a PhD on the Bronze Age metalwork hoards of Essex and Kent. She has since enjoyed a varied career in archaeology and cultural resource management. Writing has always been a major aspect of her life and at a young age, she won the *Glasgow Herald/Albacon New Writing in SF* competition with her short story 'Busman's Holiday'. Louise lives with her husband in west Renfrewshire

Lightning Source UK Ltd.
Milton Keynes UK
UKOW02f1950130317

296541UK00001B/3/P